The Fatal Revenge; Or, The Family of Montorio

The Fatal Revenge; Or, The Family of Montorio

Charles Maturin

MINT EDITIONS

The Fatal Revenge; Or, The Family of Montorio was first published in 1807.

This edition published by Mint Editions 2021.

ISBN 9781513282831 | E-ISBN 9781513287850

Published by Mint Editions®

**MINT
EDITIONS**
minteditionbooks.com

Publishing Director: Jennifer Newens
Design & Production: Rachel Lopez Metzger
Project Manager: Micaela Clark
Typesetting: Westchester Publishing Services

Contents

Preface

The present style of novels is most piteously bewailed by those who are, or say they are, well affected to the cause of literature. *Diavolerie, tales fit to frighten the nursery,* German horrors, are the best language they give us. Whatever literary articles have been imported in the *plague ship* of German letters, I heartily wish were pronounced contraband by competent inspectors. But I really conceive that the present subjects of novels and romances, are calculate I to unlock every store of fancy and of feeling. I question whether there be a source of emotion in the whole mental frame, so powerful or universal as *the fear arising from objects of invisible terror.* Perhaps there is no other that has been at some period or other of life, the predominant and indelible sensation of every mind, of every class, and under every circumstance. Love, supposed to be the most general of passions, has certainly been felt in its purity by very few, and by some not at all, even in its most indefinite and simple state.

The same might be said, *à fortiori,* of other passions. But who is there that has never feared? Who is there that has not involuntarily remembered the gossip's tale in solitude or in darkness? Who is there that has not sometimes shivered under an influence he would scarce acknowledge to himself. I might trace this passion to a high and obvious source.

It is enough for my purpose to assert its existence and prevalency, which will scarcely be disputed by those who remember it. It is absurd to depreciate this passion, and deride its influence. It is *not* the weak and trivial impulse of the nursery, to be forgotten and scorned by manhood. It is the aspiration of a spirit; "it is the passion of immortals," that dread and desire of their final habitation.

The abuse of the influence of this passion by vulgar and unhallowed hands, is no argument against its use. The magic book has indeed often been borne by a rude ignorant, like William of Deloraine, journeying from the abbey of Melrose with his wizard treasure. The wand and robe of Prospero have often been snatched by Caliban; but, in a master's hand, gracious Heaven! what wonders might it work!

I have read novels, ghost-stories, where the spirit has become so intimate with flesh and blood, and so affable, that I protest I have almost expected it, and some of its human interlocutors, like the conspirators in Mr. Bayes's play, to "take out their snuff-boxes and feague it away." Such writers have certainly made ridiculous what Shakespeare has considered and treated as awful.

Such have occasioned the outcry against converting the theatre of literature into a phantasmagoria, and substituting the figures of a German magic lanthorn, for those forms which are visible to *"the eye in a fine frenzy rolling."* But *pace tantorum virorum,* I have presumed to found, the interest of a Romance on the passion of supernatural fear, and on *that* almost alone. It is pitiful to deprecate deserved and inevitable censure; every work must have faults, and the Reviewers are heartily welcome to mine. I am not insensible of praise, nor inaccessible, I hope, to animadversion. If youth, in acquaintance with literary habits, and the "original sin" of national dulness, be any mitigation of severity, *critical,* or *eclectic,* or of *the cold and bitter blasts of the north,* let this serve to inform my Readers, that I am four and twenty, that I never had literary friend or counsellor, and that I am an *Irishman* of the name of

DENNIS JASPER MURPHY
DUBLIN,
December 15, 1806

INTRODUCTION

At the siege of Barcelona by the French, in the year 1697, two young officers entered into the service at its most hot and critical period. Their appearance excited some surprise and perplexity. Their melancholy was Spanish, their accent Italian, their names and habits French.

They distinguished themselves in the service, by a kind of careless and desperate courage, that appeared equally insensible of praise or of danger. They forced themselves into a all the *coup de mains,* the wild and perilous sallies that abound in a spirited siege, and mark it with a greater variety and vivacity of character, than a regular campaign. *Here* they were in their element. But among their brother officers, so cold, so distant, so repulsive, that even *they* who loved their courage, or were interested by their melancholy, stood aloof in awkward and hesitating sympathy. Still, though they would not accept the offices of the benevolence their appearance inspired, they were involuntarily, always conciliating. Their figures and motions were so eminently noble and striking, their affection for each other so conspicuous, and their youthful melancholy so deep and hopeless, that every one inquired, and sought intelligence of them from an impulse stronger than curiosity. Nothing could be learnt; nothing was known, or even conjectured of them.

During the siege, an Italian officer, of middle age, arrived to assume the command of a post of distinction. His first meeting with these young men was remarkable. They stood speechless and staring at each other for some time. In the mixture of emotions that passed over their countenances, no one predominant or decisive could be traced by the many and anxious witnesses that surrounded them.

As soon as they separated, the Italian officer was persecuted with inquiries about the strangers. He answered none of them; yet he admitted that he knew circumstances sufficiently extraordinary relating to the young men, who, be said, were natives of Italy.

A few days after, Barcelona was taken by the French forces. The assault was terrible; the young officers were in the very rage of the fight; they coveted and courted danger; they stood amid showers of grape and ball; they rushed into the heart and crater of explosions; they literally "wrought in the fire." The effects of their dreadful courage were foreseen by all, and cries of recal and expostulation sounded around them on every side, in vain.

On the French taking possession of the town, there was a general demand for the *brothers*. With difficulty the bodies were discovered, and brought with melancholy pomp into the commander's presence. The Italian officer was there; every eye was turned on him.

There was an appeal in the general silence. The Italian felt and answered it. "No circumstances but these," said he, "in which I see those brave, unhappy men, would justify me in the disclosure I am about to make. I am acquainted with their name, and their country, and their misfortunes. The discovery cannot affect *them* now. *They* are for ever beyond the reach of shame or pain; but for the living, who are not beyond instruction, the tale is intended, and to them may it prove useful." At intervals which its length required, he related the following story.

I

Sæva Pelopis domus.

—Horace

"Pelops' cruel offspring."

About the year 1690, the family of Montorio, one of the most distinguished in Italy, occupied their hereditary seat, in the vicinity of Naples. To the tale of the strange fortunes of this family, it may be necessary to prefix a sketch of its character.

It was marked by wild and uncommon features, such as rarely occur in those of more temperate climates. But in a country, like the seat of these adventures, where climate and scenery have almost as much effect on the human mind, as habit and education, the wonder dissolves, and the most striking exhibition of *moral* phenomena present only the reflected consequences of the *natural*.

The general idea of the Italian character was fully realized in that of the Montorio family; weak, yet obstinate; credulous, but mistrustful; inflamed with wild wishes to attain the secrets and communion of another world, yet sunk in the depth of both national and local superstition. Their palaces were haunted by groups of monks, and magicians, and alchymists, and astrologers; and amid the most superstitious state of the country of superstition, the House of Montorio was distinguished by weak and gloomy credulity. The character and habits of the present Count were, like those of his predecessors, singular. In the early part of his life, he had unexpectedly succeeded to his ancestorial wealth and honours, by the sudden death of their possessor and all his family. Shocked by such a concurrence of domestic calamity, the Count had precipitately quitted his castle, nor could he, till after a considerable time, prevail on himself to quit Apulia, and revisit it. When at length he returned, it was visible that the blow, which his spirits had sustained, was irrecoverable. He returned, accompanied by his Countess, his children, and a numerous retinue of attendants, and from that moment, the sight or sound of cheerfulness was banished from the walls of Muralto. The aged domestics, who had resided there in their lord's absence, and to whom that absence had felt like their own exile, now saw with sorrow, that the change his return had produced was almost for the worse. The habits of the castle and its present possessor, recalled to their memory the former master, and the festivity of happier days, threw a deeper shade over the stately gloom of the present. Of their former lord, they were lavish in commendation; and as it is the nature of enthusiasm to remember only the virtues of the object it delights to praise, while they celebrated the excellences and graces of his character, they forgot that he had been jealous, violent, and vindictive, even beyond Italian irritability; that his credulity was without bounds, his rage without restraint, and his vengeance without remorse. The many graces however of his person and mind, and the melancholy fate of a man who had suddenly died amid the most exquisite sensibility and enjoyment of domestic delights, drew a shade over the memory of his failings, and those who remembered him, remembered him only as the master whose eye poured forth benignity, and whose hand was lavish of bounty.

To the remembrance of such days and characters, the present afforded a striking contrast. The Count, dark, silent, solitary, repelled all approach, retreated from all attachment; and when his attendants raised their eyes to his, it was said they saw an expression there which made them withdraw them, under an impulse of terror, intuitive and inexpressible. The temper of a master, however ungenial, soon pervades his household. The servants glided through the apartments with steps that seemed to dread their own echo; orders were communicated in whispers, and executed in silence; and the bells that summoned its inmates to rest or to religion, were almost the only sounds heard within its walls. Sometimes this calm was suddenly and strangely broken, and the Count, attended by his confessor, would often summon the family to attend him at midnight to the chapel, where they remained engaged in solemn and severe acts of religion till morning; and often, under still more terrible agitations of mind, he would hurry the Countess and his family from their rest, and compel them to accompany him by night to Naples, from whence, after a short residence, he would return to his castle, to silence and to solitude. A conduct so extraordinary excited many comments; but the recent misfortunes, and known character of the family, were a sufficient answer to these, and curiosity soon grew weary of a subject that furnished nothing to gratify inquiry. Besides, the Count had now arrived at that period of life when a man is chiefly represented by his children; when the stronger features of a character are dimmed by the distance of retirement and rest—when declining ambition reposes itself amongst those for whom it has toiled, and the hopes and views of society are transferred to its young successors.

Of the Count's numerous family, four sons, and four daughters, still survived. All of them partook of the peculiarities which marked their house, the two elder sons eminently. Amid the family group, the bold and original figure of the Countess stood alone. Her beauty still untouched by time, her mind unimpaired by the weakness of her sex or country, she yet seemed to share the dark despondency of her husband. But while the source and degree of their secret suffering appeared the same, their modes of sustaining it were strikingly different. His, was the gloom of a mind bowed by affliction;—hers, of a mind resolved to make affliction bow to it. He, was wild, dejected, and unequal;—she, calm, collected, and silent. But her calmness was evidently that of subdued pain; it was the calmness of one, who, stretched upon the rack, suffers not a groan to escape him. In the lower circles of domestic duty, she moved with a careless absence, which was neither the absence of indolence nor of affectation; it was the abstraction of a mind obviously capable of higher occupations, and from which the discharge of common duties neither required an effort, nor a suspension of its inward and peculiar operations. She performed the severest offices of religion, which her superstitious husband exacted from her, with the steady patience of one who submits to a remedy, but who expects not relief—with her children she took no comfort; from her husband she sought no counsel: whatever were her secret trials, she seemed bent to bear them, unaided, unallied, and alone. She presented the image of a great mind sinking under calamity, but sinking without complaint or weakness, like Cæsar falling at the base of Pompey's statue, but covering his face as he fell.

Of her children, her daughters appeared the most beloved, and of her sons, the two younger, though the elder were confessedly more the favourites of nature as well as of society. At Naples, the elder, the beautiful and dissipated Ippolito, was the delight of every assembly, the soul of every pleasure. Driven from retirement, from the gloom of the castle and its inmates, entitled by his rank to mingle in the first assemblies, and indulged by his father with a splendid establishment, Ippolito, plunging into all the voluptuous madness of Naples, seemed resolved to indemnify himself for the short restraint of his early years. All the rich assemblage of imagery that youth, talents, and sensibility can present, and flattery magnify and embellish, Ippolito sought to realize in his brilliant and tumultuous career. Thus the flame of genius, which should have been fed by close and inward cultivation, was wasted in wild and eccentric blazes, and society, with heedless selfishness, exhausted the powers in whose display it delighted. Had this young man been instructed, either by nature or by habit, in the conduct of his imagination, or the conquest of his passions, his being would have answered some better purpose than the delight of dissipation, or the example of a moral tale. Ippolito resembled his mother in the graces of a person which revived the finished forms of classic antiquity:—a face, warm with the rich tints of Italian beauty, a dark-brown complexion, over which the glow of conversation or of sentiment, the hurry of motion or of accident, spread a speaking crimson; eyes, whose lustre, sometimes softened, sometimes deepened, as his dark locks were parted, or permitted to cluster over them, spoke sensibility in every change—features, over which the very soul of expression hovered, in a thousand charms, mingled and mutable. Such was the form, that enclosed a mind bold, ardent, credulous, and volatile;—of which the reason was as little under regulation as the passions. He possessed talents, but he rather delighted in their *display*, than their *exercise*— and that display was of the most fantastic kind. He loved to soar into the untravelled regions of thought, to raise the airy fabrics of fancy on vacancy, to enter on the very confines of intellect, and bend over the world of shadows and unreal forms. This mental malady was aggravated by indulgence till no proposition struck him, but under the form of a paradox, no event interested him, unless darkened by a shade of mystery or adventure;—but this intellectual obliquity was only partial, it was confined to his mode of *apprehending*, not of pursuing objects; for, when the direction of his mind was once discovered, by an artful application to its assailable part, its future progress might be ascertained without the least allowance for delay or deviation. Under this heated and irregular state of mind he had embraced the study of astrology; a study of which none but those who have travelled know the influence, which is as general as it is violent, and under which foreign nobility are often known to maintain a professional astrologer in their palaces, rather as an assistant of habitual knowledge, than a hidden agent of superstition. On a mind like that of Ippolito, this pursuit operated with peculiar danger; by pointing out, as the subjects of its study, some of the most striking objects of sense, it tempted a mind but too susceptible of impressions from such subjects. Few can resist the emotions inspired by the night-view of an Italian sky; a view, unfolding the Host of Heaven in lustre, magnitude, and number, never witnessed and never imagined in our cloudy and contracted hemisphere;—and few can calculate the awful solicitude to which those emotions swell, when the gazer thinks he beholds in those solemn objects the arbiters of his destiny, traces in their progress the mysterious movements of fate, and seeks from their position, a knowledge of those events, which all are alike solicitous to know, though conscious that their knowledge can neither hasten nor retard their approach, neither diminish their certainty, nor mitigate their inflictions. At first, this study was confined to the more serious events of life; but in a short time, its influence became so extensive, that it mingled in the most trivial, even in those lighter moments of which solemn thought is deemed an interruption. If this topic was alluded to, the laugh was hushed, the frolic suspended, and the giddy Ippolito became intensely thoughtful, or laboriously inquisitive. Of this a proof occurred shortly after his arrival in Naples, attended by circumstances somewhat peculiar. At the gay season of the carnival, when superstition indulges her votaries with a remission of austerity, Ippolito was present at a masked ball given by a Neapolitan of rank. On this gay evening, every hour saw him a new character, and every character was marked by some frolic of levity, or some sally of wit. Through the gardens, which the softened lights, the foliage, the fountains, the invisible minstrelsy, and mingled moon-light, made to resemble the bowers of enchantment, he glided, sometimes as the shepherd of Guarini, and sometimes as the hero of Ariosto; he now attracted the multitude by a spontaneous burst of eloquence and song, and now entertained a female mask with the most animating gallantry—at length, weary of frolic, he assumed the habit of a domino, and mixing among the groups, endeavoured to receive the amusements he had so lavishly afforded. In a short time his attention was arrested by a mask who had hovered around the whole evening, apparently unconnected with any party. The dress and figure were fantastic, even beyond the licence of a mask; it had united the characters of a gipsy and an astrologer, under an emblematic habit; its mask depicted a countenance wild and haggard, and its language, unlike the quaint jargon of the place, was sombrous, solemn, and unusual. This mask had frequently approached Ippolito during the evening, yet when he attempted to address it, abruptly turned away. But its language and gesture were inviting, for it sometimes sung, and sometimes scattered among the groups, the following lines:—

I

Agents of this earthy sphere,
Now on joy's bright billow swelling,
Now pent in misery's murky dwelling,
The sport of hope, the prey of care—
But wildly anxious, still, to know
The mystic current's ebb and flow,
Attend my song, my skill revere,
List to believe, and pause to hear—

II

'Tis mine to bid life's colours glow,
To swell its bliss, or sooth its woe;
From doubt's dim sphere, bid shadows fly,
And people void futurity;—
To sooth pale passion's feverous dream,
To feed ambition's lurking flame,
Chastise proud joy with menaced ill,
Fierce pain, with promised pleasure, still,
Till hope wears, 'mid the mimic strife,
The tints of truth, the forms of life.

III

Nor wants me source the skill to gain
That mocks at nature's bounded reign—
Where ocean beats against the sky,
Beyond their mingling bounds I fly,
And all amid the wheeling spheres
I read their viewless characters—
Those waning forms, so wan and pale,
That thwart the moon, all dimly sail,
To the wrapt eye that reads, unfold
More than to mortal may be told—
Anon I wing the waste of night,
Arrest the comet in his flight,
And shoot upon his burning wing,

CHARLES MATURIN

And round my spells of wonder fling.
Agents of this lower sphere
List to believe, and pause to hear.—

The festivity was now closing, and the masks dispersing, and amid the last murmurs of departing gaiety, this mask again approached Ippolito;—he turned, it paused, and when it spoke, its voice was tremulous and hesitating.—"Youth," it said, "thy favourable star presides tonight."—"I have as yet experienced but little of its influence," said Ippolito, with careless gaiety: "I have sought amusement, and found only weariness and disappointment. I have sought nectar on the lip of a Hebe, and been almost stifled with the scent of diavolone. I was on the point of conducting the goddess of chastity to a cassino, when, intreating her to remain no longer under an *eclipse,* I removed her mask, and discovered *Diana* converted into *Hecate.* I encountered a vestal virgin, whose shrine"—Here he was interrupted by the mask, who, mingling moral strictures with a characteristic speech, informed him, he was commissioned by the stars to announce the approach of an aerial monitor, a little, benign, officious sylph; "Just now," said he, "darting from the planet Mercury, on an invisible line of light—invisible to all eyes but mine. His task is to be your moral improvement, your happiness his delight and reward. He will assume a form, he will speak a language like your own, He will attend, he will watch, he will warn you. Beware you repel him not, for if you do, he spreads his fairy pennons, and happiness flies you for ever."

On Ippolito's peculiarly constructed mind, this address had its full effect; similar language, on any other subject, he had heard with derision, but this, because mingled with the terms of astrology, arrested his attention and his curiosity. The circumstances, too, of time and place, gave an unsuspected force to the impression. Solitude succeeding to the concourse of crowds, and silence to their clamours, which still left a mixt murmur on the ear—the dim and partial light which fell on the wild features of the mask, and the tones of its voice, which every moment assumed a more plaintive and natural earnestness. "When and where shall I see this messenger of the stars," said Ippolito, almost seriously, "if you have power to announce his approach, you have also power to expedite it—shew me his form, let me hear his voice."—If "I do," interrupted the mask, "will you believe my prediction—will you admit the object of it to your service, your confidence?" Ippolito assented. The mask hesitated incredulously. His curiosity was now inflamed, and he promised solemnly. "Look here," said the mask, drawing from beneath its garment a glass, figured with strange characters, "look here, you are obeyed."—Ippolito eagerly gazed on the glass, and beheld a face, which looking over his shoulder, disappeared in a moment; the view was instantaneous, but the impression indelible; for the features bore a peculiar and interesting expression, which once seen, could scarce be forgotten. The mask glided away, and, while Ippolito yet paused in wonder, was lost among the groups and the shadows.

Of his wonder, he felt the effect to be both pleasing and painful; pleasing, because it soothed his love of the marvellous, and painful, because the curiosity it excited was ungratified. As he slowly returned homewards, he almost expected his promised visitor to appear behind the shade of a pillar as he passed, or cross his path with some strange greeting. He had arrived, however, without interruption at the Palazzo di Montorio, and was preparing to ascend the steps, when a light figure, which had been leaning half unseen against the balustrade, approached, and solicited reception in the language of the mask: as it spoke, it withdrew a large hat which shaded its face, and discovered the very features which Ippolito had seen flit over the glass of the wizard. Disarmed at this moment of every power, but the power to gaze, he viewed the figure, and for an instant suffered himself to doubt if it belonged to earth or not; then endeavouring to recal his spirits, addressed it in a style of appropriate gaiety:—inquired from what sphere it had fallen—and asked whether it had travelled on a meteor or a moonbeam? His raillery was only answered by more earnest petitions for admission, with which Ippolito, on whom the circumstances of the night had made more impression than he would either acknowledge or resist, at length complied.—Such was the conduct of this light-minded young man, whose judgment and imagination were at perpetual though unequal war, and who ridiculed at one moment the feelings, whose impulse, at the next, was suffered to decide the events of life.—He knew not, if the person he had admitted was not an assassin or a heretic, but he knew, that to admit him flattered his favourite propensity—the love of the marvellous.

CHARLES MATURIN

II

Ah, wretch! believed the spouse of God in vain.

—POPE

On the succeeding day, Ippolito found a recent extraordinary circumstance the theme of every assembly he visited. In narratives of wonders, we are never contented with facts, without inquiring into motives, though the subtler springs of human actions often elude the discovery of the agents themselves.—But here was ample room for conjecture:—On Rosolia di Valozzi, the daughter of a noble family, resident at Naples, were bestowed the most dangerous gifts of nature, an interesting form, and a mind susceptible "even to madness."

All the softer, and all the stronger, modes of this dangerous quality were assembled in her mind:—there is a domestic sensibility which expends itself on the common vicissitudes, and petty disasters of life; and there is a lofty frame of feeling which, overlooking the lower modes of human suffering, creates for itself a system of heroic dignity, and unaffecting distress.

The more subtle spirit of both these was hers, but both purified, blended, and reconciled; the former, without its hacknied parade of daily exhibition; the latter, without its proud and pedantic inutility.—Thus she was prevented from knowing that relief which vulgar and romantic sensibility *individually* enjoy, (the one from the natural diminution of divided feeling, the other from the necessary remission of superhuman loftiness) and her feelings were tempered to that exquisite mixture of softness and firmness, which, whilst it sought its object and its exercise among the things of this world, would employ in their attainment a reach and energy of power, only commensurate to the great objects of another.

These uncommon faculties were first developed amid objects and scenery eminently calculated to elicit the latent, and stimulate the awakening sensibility of a young mind;—amid woods, whose depth of shade soothed and solemnized—seas, whose vastness and serenity poured stillness on the soul—mountains, whose wilder features mixed fear with wonder—masses of Gothic and Grecian ruins, whose very stones breathed round them that nameless spirit of antiquity, which makes us tremble with a delicious dread on the ground marked by its remains:—amid such scenes, Rosolia, yet an infant, wandered—amid such her mind imbibed a tincture of enthusiasm, full, rich and deep:—amid such scenes, stood the convent where Rosolia, with other female nobility, was educated. Here she wandered, without a guide, or a companion; for melancholy is unsocial, and enthusiasm impatient of restraint or interruption, and the feelings which she delighted to indulge, sought no participation, and disdained all control. Here life was expended in stimulating a sensibility already too exquisite for reason, or almost for life, and instead of subduing her mind to the pursuit of rational utility and practicable happiness, in elevating herself into the agent of another system, surrounded by forms and objects of her own creation, whose brilliancy proclaimed their want of reality, and whose exquisite and fallacious delights *untuned* her mind for the simplicity of substantial enjoyment. Nature and solitude gradually lead the mind to abstraction, and of abstract imagery, the most powerful and splendid are the presence and perfections of the Deity. To these, therefore, her mind was naturally elevated; and no impressions from external or temporal objects could pervert the homage of her feelings.

At the age of fourteen, therefore, never concluding that her feelings could have any other object or occasion of exercise than the present—that any subject of interest could exist beyond the bounds of a cloister, or the sphere of monasticism; she announced her intention of taking the veil within the walls of the convent where she had been educated. Her family, too wealthy for the needy policy which devotes the younger daughters of Italian families to the veil, heard her resolution with regret, and endeavoured to dissuade her from her purpose. She remained inflexible, and her parents were compelled to content themselves with obtaining the respite of one year, which it was proposed she should pass with them at Naples. To this invitation she acceded, with that disdain of temptation, from which it borrows its greatest danger; and, rather to gratify her religious feelings by a solemn exercise, than to bind them by inviolable security, alone, at midnight, at the foot of the altar, she engaged herself by a solemn vow, when the importunity of the world had ceased, to return to the convent, and assume the veil. Thus fortified, she entered the world, to bestow on it a passing glance of disdain, and then quit it for ever,—and on her first appearance, was received with wonder and delight. Her pensive and nun-like beauty, the simplicity of her manner, and her mind over which the glow of enthusiasm, and the shade of melancholy chased each other alternately, like the varying shades of a beautiful complexion; the careless overflow of her sentiments, at once reaching by happy excellence all that the refinements of practice, and the labours of art profess slowly and painfully to teach; all this made her, even to the sophisticated sense of fashion, a new and exquisite feast. Rosolia at first retreated; for, though not unconscious of excellence, she was too timid for notoriety, and too delicate for flattery. But we are easily reconciled to our own praises, and she soon appeared content to stay a little longer in the world, to irradiate and delight it.

Amid this blaze of admiration, while a soft consciousness of pleasure seemed to be stealing over her mind and senses, she became on a sudden more lonely and pensive than ever; her cheek grew pale, and her eye wandered. Her family, who observed the change, and enquired the cause, received evasive answers; and when their solicitude, increasing with her increasing malady, became importunate, it was answered by her declaring, that her resolution to take the veil had been delayed too long, and she was resolved to put it in immediate execution.

The scruples of conscience, though all lamented, none could oppose, and about a year after her entrance into the world, she quitted it for ever. But from the moment that the grate was closed on her, her silence became gloom, and her melancholy, misery; and after lingering a few months in hopeless dejection, she disappeared one evening after vespers, and was seen no more. Of an event so strange, none could assign either the motive or the means; and after the usual forms of inquiry and lamentation were observed, a wild conjecture, or an exclamation of wonder, were all that commemorated the fate of Rosolia.

When Ippolito returned to the palace, he found a letter from his brother Annibal, who resided with the family at the Castle, and with whom he maintained a regular correspondence. The attachment which produced this was rendered remarkable by the total dissimilarity of their characters. Annibal was as timid, gloomy, and mistrustful, as Ippolito was bold, open, and credulous; but both partook equally of that attachment to dark pursuits which characterized the family, and of that inflexibility of sombrous resolution, with which they adhered to a visionary pursuit, however irregularly conceived.—The substance of the letter was nearly as follows.—

III

Præterea fuit in tectis de marmore templum—
Hine exaudiri voces, et verba vocantis.—

—Virgil

A marble temple stood within the grove—
Oft, when she visited this lonely dome,
Strange voices issued from her husband's tomb.

—Dryden

My mind has been so occupied by strange events, and the reflections they have suggested, that I have forborn, for some time past, to write to you. When about to relate them, I again revolve those circumstances, so simple in their commencement, yet gradually unfolding something that arrests incredulity itself, and still pointing onward to things dark and unknown—I revolve all this, I seem in a dream, and try in vain to give form and reality to the shadows that are hovering round me.—

I have slept and awoke again—I have stood at my casement—this is the arbutus and the laurel that wave beneath it—this is the sea-breeze that breathes freshness on me—I see the glorious sun standing in the heaven,—these all are the objects of the senses, and they make their due and wonted impression on mine. Yet the objects I have lately witnessed are not less palpable than these. You have often laughed at my visionary gloom, prepare now to share the ridicule, or to resign the evidence of your senses.

The old chapel, without the walls of the castle, has long been dilapidated, and is at present filled with workmen. You know my fondness for ruins. I strolled there after my *sieste*. I found the great doors closed, and that the workmen had entered through a chasm under one of the shattered windows. As I looked through the cavity, the various features of the view, the fragments of ruin, the rustic groups, some labouring, some gazing vacantly around, and the figure of a boy, who placed in a recess half-hid among the clustering shrubs, breathed a few wild notes on his pipe, touched me with that pleasant melancholy, which is suggested by the view of ancient decay and modern apathy, of desolated majesty, and ignorance gazing amongst its ruins. As I continued to lean on a projection of the chasm, unseen, I overheard a conversation, suggested by the place, and such as I would live to listen to on a wintry night, by a low, flitting, ember-fire. It told of spirit and shadow, and self-lighted tapers, and bells that rung untouched within those deserted walls. I listened with curiosity pleasantly stirred, till I was roused by some dark allusions. I listened, but could not understand; they spake "of the Count's not resting better in his bed, than his ancestors in their graves, if *those things were known;*" and observed that "old, white-headed Michelo, in spite of his guarded silence, was too well acquainted with them." Though my first impulse, on returning to the castle, was to send for the old groom of the chambers, and satiate my appetite for the marvellous with his legendary wonders, I had no other object than to pass a vacant hour in listening to a tale that required little effort either of thought or credit. I had at least little apprehension of what awaited me, little fear of being in a state like that of one who is gradually impelled towards a precipice, the terrors of which he can neither measure nor avoid. Michelo came on my summons. Desirous of full information, and aware of his cautious and timid temper, I endeavoured to frame my request skilfully. "Michelo," said I, "I have often listened with delight to the family legends your memory is so well stored with;—but I am informed you are in possession of some still more marvellous and terrible, something you will not communicate to a common ear, and which I hope you have reserved for mine." This address, so far from an accusation, and only implying a knowledge compatible with the purest innocence, produced the most terrible effect on the old man. His lips quivered, and his countenance changed, and with the most earnest solemnity he besought me, not to importune him for the disclosure I referred to. The impression I received from his agitation was indescribable. The vague curiosity with which I had begun the conversation was at once exchanged for the pursuit of something I could not well define, but whose importance was increased by its obscurity.

I told him I was now convinced he was acquainted with something—"something which it is perhaps necessary for me, as a son of this house, to know—something into which more than curiosity ought to inquire." I assured him of my favour if he complied, and if not, menaced him with my father's displeasure. His answer, though confused and broken, I shall not soon forget. "Oh, Signor, for the Virgin's sake, let not my lord your father know of this conference; do not draw his vengeance on us, his vengeance is terrible. Little do you know, little alas, do I know myself, if I knew all, or even believed what I have heard, how could I pass the chapel, as I do at night, how could I traverse these lone apartments, or venture to sleep in that little turret, over the *very room*— where the wind sings so doleful that if I suffered myself to think I might fancy it was—I might run mad listening to it." I bade him be composed, but the composure I recommended, I was far from enjoying myself. My anxious love of the marvellous was mixed with other feelings; nor could I, (though I affected to do so) believe the agitation of the old man was occasioned by the nugatory tales of menial superstition. He rose from his knees, condemning himself for having "foolishly and wickedly betrayed himself, overcome by my sudden question and piercing eye."—I will not harass you with the repetition of menace and intreaty, of expostulation and evasion. He at length consented to admit me to his lone, remote turret that night, for he still dreaded our being discovered or even observed by the family. The night, like every other period to which solicitude adds an imaginary length, was slow in arrival.

When I ascended the turret, I thought I observed in the old man's face an expression of artificial composure, the effort of recollected and resolute craftiness. He seated himself, trimmed his lamp, and then abruptly demanded what it was I required him to relate. In the tumult of expectation, in that state of suspense which expects the disclosure of something unknown, *this* had entirely escaped me; and apprehending that my curiosity would be mocked by some temporary and trivial invention, hastily and almost unintentionally, I desired him to relate the circumstances by which my father, who I understood was distantly related to the late possessor, had succeeded to the family honours. He appeared confounded, but unable to retreat; and it occurred to me, if I could engage him to commence the narrative, I might trust to his habitual prolixity to disclose what he might at first intend to conceal. After some delay, he informed me, *that* possessor had been my uncle, my father's own brother. Of this man he gave a character that seemed to warm him into eloquence; he described it as a mixture of the most shining qualities, and the fiercest passions. His love was madness, his courage, rashness, his hatred deadly, and his vengeance, though honourable, as the cavaliers in Naples call it, there was no escaping from with life.—"All your house," continued he, "were much attached to secret studies; your uncle was in particular much versed in strange books and arts, and in a way of going up to ask the stars whether he was to be happy or miserable.—Alas, it would have been better to have asked his own heart.—Many a night would my lord pass on the high turrets of his castle, and on his descent, he would walk about his apartment for hours, talking to himself about trines, and sextiles, and quadrants, and horoscopes, and ascendants, hard words, which I learnt, from hearing them repeated so often, without knowing their meaning."

"I would not, to be lord of this castle, know it. For a holy benedictine once assured me, it was all heresy, and that these were only different names for Lucifer." I will endeavour to abridge Michelo's narrative: he mentioned my uncle's marriage with the loveliest, the gentlest, the most heavenly of women. He mentioned that he had children; the picture of the Countess, he said, was yet in a deserted part of the castle, with most of the furniture of those gay days; *there* he had removed them on my father's return to the castle. The story was sad and intricate; he told of my uncle's domestic happiness being suddenly and strangely suspended by a habit of fierceness and gloom, which he *emphatically* dated from the arrival of my father, and a confidential servant of his, whom he called Ascanio, at the castle.—"Even amid all the revelry and mirth on my lord's arrival," said he, "it was whispered by the domestics, who accompanied them from Naples, that the lady was likely to lead a life of lone, uncomfortable splendour; for owing either to my lord's jealousy, or some secret cause of disquiet, that even then spread a shade of melancholy over her beautiful face; they both seemed resolved on total retirement.—Matters grew more dark and strange; my lady wept in her chamber alone; my lord stalked silently through *his*; your father appeared distracted with the distress he witnessed, and alternately conferred with each alone, I suppose, endeavouring to conciliate and sooth them. At length it was announced that my lord was to make an excursion to the Grecian Isles; this excursion the Countess, now near her confinement, was not to accompany; he was to be attended only by Ascanio. Ascanio, at this time, appeared to enjoy the confidence of both brothers exclusively. I envied him not; *my* love and fidelity to my lord were, what a domestic's should be, humble, and distant, though dear; I lamented my master's sorrows, without presuming to inquire into them, but Ascanio was bold, forward, and subtle."—"Is this Ascanio yet alive," said I, "he might eke out your narrative with some strange particulars." "He *might indeed*," said the old man—"no, Signor, he is dead, and his end was strange and fearful." I would not tempt him to digression by inquiring. "When my lord had now been some months gone, we could perceive that a greater consternation than ever reigned in the castle; packets were hourly arriving from abroad, the Countess never quitted her apartment, and my lord your father appeared overborne with agitation. At length, it was about the close of autumn, it had been a sickly, sultry season, and the mountain had been turbulent, and the people while they listened to its murmurs, said, that they presaged sad and strange events would soon happen. We were assembled in the hall of the castle for vespers, for the chapel was then repairing; a hot intermitting blast breathed through the casement, and some of the domestics who had been in Naples that day, told us that the mountain had sent forth strange sounds in the night, and that the city awaited the approach of that evening in terror; one of them said, that as they came along, there was a heavy murmuring through the woods, and that their tops waved without a breath of wind"—"Yes," said another, "but that was not the strangest object I saw in the woods today." We desired him to explain, and the domestic then affirmed with solemn asseverations, that the Count his master had appeared to him that day in the wood at a little distance from—at this fantastic account of one whom we knew to be absent in the Grecian Islands, all laughed, when the man suddenly rising from his seat, and rushing into the passage that communicates with the great stairs, called us loudly to "see *him*, ascending them, and beckoning to him from the balustrade."—In a moment every individual was in the passage, the echo of a step was distinctly heard, and some averred they saw a shadow pass on the stairs—but our attention was quickly withdrawn. Ascanio arrived, breathless and spent, and pushing away the eager inquirers with both his hands, hastened to your father's apartment. Meanwhile evening was aggravated by a gathering darkness; a mass of vapour issued from the mountain, and the sun appeared as a dim and bloody globe in the midst of an immense vault of black cloud— every one breathed an inward prayer, and none told their fears to the other—when, as in a moment, a column of fire, brighter than noon, rose from the mountain, flashing a horrible glare of yellow light on the woods, and shore, its edgings lanced with lightnings, and its centre white with intense heat; it was suspended a moment at its greatest height, or appeared so to our eyes, and the next came rushing down the sides of the mountain in floods of fire—a strong concussion of the earth followed, the air and elements were in wondrous motion, and the lightnings, or meteors rather, broad and flaky, hissed and wreathed in fearful play on the turret points and casements. When the first burst of

CHARLES MATURIN

terror was over, I thought of the Countess and her children; she used to sit with them in a high and lonely tower, of which I scarcely believed but it was crumbled to ashes. I hastened up the great stairs, when—the terrors of my tale are coming on, they are too strong for me, let me have air, let me have breath, Signor."—

Solicitous, both for the old domestic and his story, I assisted him to rise, and supported him to his narrow casement. In a few moments he respired; I watched the progress of his recovery; my eye was fixed on his; it became suddenly fixed and hollow; he extended his arm from the casement; but the breath which he had but just recovered, utterly forsook him—he could not speak—my eye followed the pointing of his finger. The night was still and dark, the ruined chapel was beneath the casement—as I gazed, a light, pale but distinct, fell on the walls, and on the shrubs that have mantled round them; I watched it, it wandered, borne by no hand, accompanied by no step, along the chancel, (I saw it gleaming past our windows), and expired at the tomb of our uncle. Michelo and I remained aghast—we remained near an hour, silent, scarcely breathing—we saw it return. Then I tried to swallow down the thick and stifling sensation with which my throat was filled. "Michelo," said I, "has this been seen before?" "Often," said the old man, "by me." "Has no visible form, no distinct sound attended it?" "Often," said he again. "And have you ever witnessed?"—"Listen, Signor,—to you alone would I tell what I *have* witnessed: other strange appearances have long been talked of within these walls; this is but recent. A few nights ago, when I first observed that light, I was tempted to follow it. I thought it might be some one whom curiosity or ignorance had led there, and I entered without apprehension. The light that glided before me, disappeared at the tomb of Count Orazio; I heard a sound issuing from it, that could scarce be called a groan, or any thing that signifies a human accent. I approached it, I know not how; I shudder now to tell it; yet I remember I did not shudder then. The massive grating of the vault was wrenched open—I descended—yes, I *did* descend: a flash of light burst forth again, and as it hissed on the damp arching, the palls waved with a visible motion—the coffins rattled on the biers— something, I could neither distinguish nor describe, hovered before my eyes—a pressure (not of a fleshly hand) came over my face; it was bony, and cold, and damp. I lost all further power or feeling, and when I recovered, I was laid without the walls of the chapel, on the damp grass, my lamp burning beside me; could I have travelled there in trance? I hasted to my turret-room, I stood to collect my breath, my eyes fell on that mirror you are looking at now, my face reeked with livid streaks of blood!!!—To none but you have I mentioned this."

No one could hear the old man's earnest voice, and look on his pale face, and disbelieve him. You know my habit, to reason on every thing: but what could I do, with what I had just seen and heard; they were too palpable for fancy, yet too wild for conjecture, and I endeavoured, alike in vain, to treat them as a fume of mental vapour, or try them by any rule of sober solution. My thoughts wandered from Michelo and his narrative to myself; insensibly I began to conceive myself in his situation, possessed, it should seem, of dark secrets, and tempted to supernatural intercourse. I examined, involuntarily, how such an emergency would find me prepared. I calculated the chances of deception. I inquired into the constitution of my mind, and the probable power of such impressions over it, were it exposed to them. The result gave me a strange satisfaction. I felt as if I were called to such a trial, and would approve myself in it. I am strong of frame, steady of nerve, slow in perception; possessing but little of the light or fantastic powers of mind; seldom indulging them in their airy play; and when I do, surveying it as the traveller surveys the fallacious dance of the fairy lights, only to shun their illusions. Such a character presents only one assailable part, in that attachment to visionary subjects by which, I have heard, our family are distinguished.

But even this has attained no habitual or positive influence over my mind. It diffuses rather a shade than a gloom; its effect has been like that of twilight, whose shadows inspire a dubious and grateful awe, not midnight that peoples its dark recesses with shapes of fear. The result of my deliberations has been what perhaps it would have been, if I had not deliberated at all,—to gratify the simple and original impulse of curiosity, by a pursuit of which I vainly flatter myself the object is higher. I determined to make Michelo conclude his narrative; I determined to visit the tomb of Count Orazio at night. I need not tell you I accepted Michelo's offer to accompany me, without reluctance. He has a knowledge of private passages in the castle which may be useful in eluding observation. "Signor," "said he, "the passages we must traverse, lead near those apartments so long shut up, the apartments of your late uncle and his Countess. You must permit me, as we pass them, to shut my eyes; do you, Signor, lead me, and as we draw near them speak cheerfully, and let me feel your hand on mine."

CHARLES MATURIN

I consented to his conditions. The *watch-night* has arrived; the family are at rest, and I am in the turret, awaiting the arrival of Michelo. Ippolito! what is there in that nature and state, to which our better part aspires, that the belief of its agency is thus awful, that the thought of its visible approach or presence is scarce supportable. I have no definite apprehension of what I may meet or see, but there is a busy and alarmed motion within me, as if something of evil impended, whose magnitude was too extensive, or whose features were too terrible even for expectation. I feel, at least, that its contemplation leaves room for no other object, though it is thus indefinite and vague itself. I have brought books; I cannot read them. I have commenced several trains of thought; I have *started from them all, imagining I was in the vault.* In spite of my resolution, I feel my respiration grow short, and a sensation like swelling, oppressing my throat. I will walk up and down my narrow apartment. It will not do. . . my steps seemed limited to a certain track, beyond which I almost feared to extend them, and their echo was too loud. The hour is approaching; a few moments more, and the castle bell will toll. The hour that I have longed for, I almost begin now to wish more distant. I almost dread to hear the steps of Michelo. . . Hark!—the bell tolls— the old turret seems to rock to its echo; and the silence that succeeds, how deep, how stilly—would I could hear an owl scream.—Ha! 'twas the lightning that gleamed across me. I will go to the casement; the roar of the elements will be welcome at such a moment as this. . . The night is dark and unruly—the wind bursts in strong and fitful blasts against the casement. The clouds are hurried along in scattering masses. There is a murmur from the forests below, that in a lighter hour I could trust fancy to listen to; but in my present mood, I dare not follow her wanderings. Would my old guide were come! I feel that any state of fear is supportable, accompanied by the sight or sound of a human being. . . Was that shriek fancy?—again, again—impossible! Hark! there is a tumult in the castle—lights and voices beneath the turret. . . What is this they tell me?

IV

——Nec mens mihi, nec color
Certâ sede manet, humor et in genas
Furtim labitur, arguens
Quam lentis penitus macerer ignibus.

—HORACE

My reason in confusion flies,
And on my cheek th' uncertain colour dies;
While the down-stealing tear betrays
The lingering flame that on my vitals preys.

—DRYDEN

From the messenger who brought this letter, no further intelligence could be obtained. While Ippolito read it, the visionary spirit kindled within him, and he wished himself at the castle, to feast his fancy with the dark imagery of spectred terrors; while Annibal's mind, differently constructed, was employed in resisting suspected imposition, and submitting with stubborn reluctance to the influence that thus inscrutably overcame him. But Ippolito's curiosity was now as much occupied by his young domestic, as his brother's was by his old one. Amused by the strange circumstances of his introduction, Ippolito had assigned him an apartment near his own, and exempted him from every office of servitude. This was indeed a gratuitous indulgence, for had Cyprian, as he called himself, actually dropt from the sphere of another planet, he could scarce have been more ignorant of every thing relative to this. Ippolito perceived it, and resigned him to his own pursuits.

The form of Cyprian was slight and delicate, a profusion of chesnut hair shaded his cheeks, and deepened the dark tint of melancholy thought, that sat for ever on his face. His head was seldom raised from a declining posture; his features seldom varied their pensive expression; but when they did, their sudden and eager brightness of intelligence, bespoke a mind of suppressed energies, and habitual dejection. Though voluntarily assuming a station of servitude, he possessed all the refinements of manner and acquirement that mark the higher ranks of society. Seated at the harp, or organ, Cyprian poured through his delicate, half-open lips a stream of sound, more resembling respiration than tones modulated by art and practice; they were the very sighs of music; while his fingers, sinking into the strings, seemed almost to partake living sensibility, and forget the power of motion at the cadence. As a painter, his merit was distinguished; but in all he did, nothing appeared laboured, nothing even finished; he seemed to possess the genius of art, apparently without its rules or its labours, and over all was spread a species of fragility, a certain delicacy of imperfection, that characterized the desultory efforts of a mind which only required stability to arrive at perfection. But it was soon discovered, that neither as a painter, nor a musician, did he remit that influence which he claimed for higher offices. He entered on his office of monitor to Ippolito with a spirit and power that actually seemed given him from above. Ippolito listened with surprise, but it was surprise which the gentleness of the pleader disarmed of anger, and into which his eloquence infused admiration.

Turning into jest, however, a conflict with a boy, he collected the powers of sophistry and declamation he was too well accustomed to wield, and imagined that a few sentences of rapid brilliancy, would overwhelm the poor little pleader at once. But this meretricious array was displayed before Cyprian in vain; simple, earnest, sincere, he pursued his florid opponent with the eloquence of a man, and the fervency of an angel. He was neither dazzled by verbiage, nor disconcerted by subtlety, and Ippolito's pride summoned him in vain to the cause which his conscience deserted. The conclusion of the debate proved that it was not for victory the young disputant had engaged; he proceeded with tenfold earnestness to press the *practical* consequences of his concessions on Ippolito. Such was *his* ingenuous pride, that what he could not defend he dared not practice; and a *boy* caught the promise of reformation from a blushing libertine. But a more difficult task yet remained—to direct the choice of life while it was yet suspended, and to effect a transition from one mode and habitude to another; yet to conceal the interruption, and prevent the intermediate wanderings of vacancy. At this moment, therefore, Cyprian displayed all his resources; painting, and harmony, and poetry; and over all his taste spread a charm, chaste and mellow, like that of moon-light on a landscape—till Ippolito was delighted by the conscious expansion of latent powers, which he mistook for the acquisition of new ones; and Cyprian succeeded in recalling to the forgotten pleasures of nature and of taste, a mind, fevered by the noxious stimulants of artificial voluptuousness. But minds thus habituated are not easily weaned from periodical indulgence, and when the night arrived, not all the taste or talents of Cyprian could prevent the chronic fit of vacancy. When *they* failed, even the pensiveness of the little monitor would yield to his solicitude for his pupil; in the graceful petulance of airy command, he would wind his slender arms around Ippolito, and with *female blandishments,* declare he should not quit the palace, blandishments, to which *he* bowed with the pouting smile of yielding reluctance.

They loved to wander amid the scenery of the shore, to gaze on the last rich day-streak of purple, on the landscape melting into shade, and flattering the eye with a thousand mixt and visionary forms. The sea pouring forth an expanse of infinite brightness, dotted with dark skiffs and gallies, the moles and promontories stretching their narrow lines into the sea, and terminating in watch-towers, whose summits still retained the sun-light; and to the North-East, Vesuvius, filling the view with masses of bold, tumultuous darkness. They lingered and listened to the stilly sounds of evening, the flow of the sea-breeze, the ripple of the tide, the hoarse voices of the seamen, and the lighter tones of peasants, who were dancing in groups on the shore, and mingled with, though distinct from, all that hum of ceaseless sound, which a populous city sends forth at night, forming together a kind of *animal music,* which soothed, if it did not elevate. They lingered till Ippolito's mind, "not touched but rapt," suggested to Cyprian an opportunity for the object of his never-ending solicitude.

He spoke of earthly things in all their excellency and beauty, being but as a veil spread before the fulness of impassible perfection, *to* which we are not to look, but *through* them; he spake of the dissolution of earthly things, as but the withdrawing of a veil, when that which it concealed shall break upon us in all its glorious beauty, filling our renewed faculties with a fulness of joy, "such as eye hath not seen, nor ear heard."

Ippolito listened, and was "almost *persuaded to be a Christian.*"

CHARLES MATURIN

V

Cum subito e sylvis, macie confecta supremâ
Ignoti nova forma viri, miserandaque cultû
Procedit.

—VIRGIL

When from the woods there bolts before our sight,
Somewhat betwixt a mortal and a spright,
So thin, so ghastly, meagre, and so wan,
So bare of flesh, he scarce resembled man.

—DRYDEN

Second Letter from Annibal

MY LAST CONCLUSION WAS ABRUPT; I broke off in expectation of something important—I was disappointed—the cries I heard were uttered by a servant, who passing near the chapel saw, or imagined he saw, something that terrified him almost to death. I listened to his story—I will listen to such no more; they unhinge and dissipate the powers which I would wish to concentrate and to fortify. I have a dark, inward intimation that I shall be called to something which will require no common energies of thought and action. The only circumstance of this man's fear worth relating, was, that when he recovered his senses, he demanded to be led to my father, and requested *his* confessor to attend. My father with a facility that astonished me, consented—but the monk was no where to be found. My father then seemed to recollect something that disturbed him, and was dismissing the man when, from the small door of his oratory, the monk issued, and stood among us. His appearance just at this juncture, his gaunt and sallow visage, the knots of his *discipline* stained with blood, the loose dark drapery of his habit, which as he stood in the shade, gave a kind of floating obscurity to his form, combined to make an impression on *me*, I do not like to recal. On *the man*, who had desired to see him, it was terrible; he again became insensible, and was conveyed from the apartment. I found Michelo had taken advantage of the confusion this incident had produced to defeat my intention of visiting the chapel that night, an intention of which it would be difficult to tell, whether the late circumstances had increased or diminished the force:—Have I mentioned the confessor to you before, Ippolito?—If I have not, let me do it now; he is a strange being. He was originally an ecclesiastic of the Greek communion, the errors of which he renounced, and shortly after entered into a convent in the neighbourhood of Naples, the superior of which recommended him as a person of uncommon sanctity and unction. To this was added the reputation of his strict and almost supernatural austerity; qualifications still more welcome to our gloomy father.

I never saw a form and air more unearthly, a whole appearance more remote from the beings or business of this world, than this man's, whose name is Father Raffaello Schemoli. In his large fixed eye, all human fire appears to be dead; his face is marked with the traces of past, rather than the expression of present, passions or events; it seems like the bed of a torrent that has flowed away, but whose violence may yet be traced in its deep, dry, unlevelled furrows. The very few who have seen or known this man, speak of him with a kind of obscure fear. He is indeed an object for superstition or fancy to scare themselves with. Even to my mind, he often has borne the aspect of those beings who are said to hold communion with both worlds, who are permitted to mock us with a semblance of human shape and intercourse, while they are doing their dark offices in other elements than ours. I am ashamed to write thus superstitiously of him, but I would you could see him. For three following days Michelo shrunk from me; at length I met him in the west corridor, and without waiting for a reply which I was determined to disregard, I told him I would visit his turret that night, and quitted him. But on my repairing to his chamber at night, what was my astonishment when he tenaciously refused to conclude the narrative of my uncle's disappearance. I entreated and expostulated; he was silent; I again threatened him with my father's interference. He shook his head emphatically: "Interference in this business," said he, "my lord is not likely to use; he already knows all that can be told, and perhaps is not solicitous that all should be known to you."—Incensed, I intimated violent means.—"Violence can do nothing but destroy," said he, "and what pleasure can there be in sending with pain an old man to the grave but a few days before he would sink into it tranquilly." To this pathetic obstinacy of the old man what could be replied? Yet still I continued to importune him, till casting a searching glance round the chamber, and rising, he grasped my hands for a moment, and whispered, "Signor, I

CHARLES MATURIN

am *forbid*."—I believe he meant to convey the impression which I at once received from these words, that the influence which constrained him was more than human; still my solicitude was resistless, more resistless for this dark intimation.—And I pursued the subject in the hope of leading him by vague and indirect questions to unfold it. "Have my uncle and his Countess been long dead,"—"their tombs have stood in the old chapel now eighteen years."—"This is evasive, Michelo, your knowledge must be positive." "Is it then possible to know the living from the dead," said he, wildly. "There are some who go in and out, and walk amongst us as living things, over whom has long been laid many a good weight of earth and stone, but" (checking himself) "for the Count Orazio, peace to his bones, they never rested in the chapel of his ancestors."—"Explain, Michelo." "Yes, Signor, for that I *can* tell. Shortly after the report of the late Countess's death,"—"The Countess then *is* dead." "Pardon me, Signor, I only mentioned the report of her death—I was returning from a journey, (on which I had been sent by your father,) and on approaching the castle by night I saw the chapel illuminated, and heard the chaunt of many voices, chaunting the requiem. I hastened forward and learnt from some of the attendants, that my lord had died abroad, and that they were now interring the remains, which had been brought over by Ascanio. I was at first stupified at the shock of such a desolation. The Countess, the children, my lord, within a few months!!!—I recovered a little—I wandered into the chapel—the service was over; the monks and attendants were dispersing; most of the torches were extinguished; nothing was heard but the low, faint beat of the last bell—I approached the bier, they had descended into the vault to prepare for its reception. I was alone, and longed for a last look of my master's face. As I bowed over the bier I thought the pall moved.—I retreated, but returned, and with a quivering hand, withdrew it.—There was neither shroud, nor cear cloth. I examined it with astonishment; there was no corse, nor any thing belonging to a corse within; the bier was overspread with pall and vestment only. I replaced them, I heard the steps of attendants ascending from the vault—I retired."—In vain I pressed Michelo for conjectures on this extraordinary circumstance—at length he said, "sometimes I think Signor, that if he be indeed dead, they have laid him in some remote and unhallowed place, and the poor wanderer comes here to seek rest among his ancestors, but cannot obtain it." A long pause followed this melancholy and unsatisfying solution. I recollected, that these circumstances must when they occurred, have caused some amazement, and I asked, had no doubts been suggested, no inquiries been made, had society slept over these marvels?

Michelo appeared to enter on his narrative with fear. "Shortly after these circumstances," said he, "my lord, your father, retired to his estates in Apulia, where you, and most of your family were born. *I* still resided in this castle, from which I brought my accounts to your father in his Apulian residence. About ten years ago, I set out on such a journey, in the close of autumn. As I was obliged to cross the Apulian mountains, I took care to provide me a host in that wild country, who, as is the custom there, shifted his hut and flocks, according to the vicissitude of the seasons. I expected to find him among the woody recesses of the mountains, but after wasting the evening in search of him, I at length directed my mule to the foot of the mountains, in hopes of meeting some other hut in which to pass the night. In the first I saw, a large company of peasants were assembled round a blazing wood-fire; I joined them, and perceived my old host among them; he was relating a marvellous tale, to which I listened among the rest. It was wild and strange; it told of something that had been lately seen on the mountains, the terror of which had driven them together into the valley; *what* it was, I could not comprehend; some described it as a good, some as an evil spirit; some said it was a human creature like themselves, and some affirmed, that it pursued and scared travellers out of their senses, to drag them to its den, and prey on their bodies. In this discourse the night passed on, and when the flaggons were dry, and the embers low, we stretched ourselves on skins and leaves around it, to sleep.

The strange tales I had heard, kept me for some time awake, and as the dying fire threw its red gleams around the hut, I almost fancied I saw shapes quivering in its light. At length, however, I commended my soul to the patron-saint of the mountain, and tried to rest. I heard a gentle noise at the door of the hut, as if the latch were raised and let down again; I immediately roused, and just leaned up on one elbow; my head was full of what I had just heard, and I watched the door silently. In a few moments, it opened, and something appeared at it which, after a pause, entered the hut. When I beheld it, I conjectured at once it was the shape that was seen on the mountain. It was indeed ghastly and horrible, and as it moved, all by the dusky ember-light, surely it seemed like something that had strayed from its prison-house of pain: I know not whether it was from curiosity, or the very extremity of my fear, but *I* disturbed no one, and it seemed to disregard *me*. At length it drew near the fire, and began a low muttering sound, accompanied with strange gestures, and I, who began to fear it was busied in some witchery, dreaded that the hut and its inhabitants would in a moment be wafted into the air. However, after some time, it rose and tottered out again, but after that, all the long night, as the blast came strong and loud from the mountains, such dolorous sounds were scattered on it as I could scarce think were uttered by a human voice. The next morning I concluded my journey."—"And did no consequence or explanation follow all this?"—"Whenever after that I went into Apulia, Signor, I was sure to hear the same tales repeated. It was about two years after that, passing over the mountains, I reached about the close of evening, a woody defile, thick and dark, with ash, and elm, and chestnut. As I entered it, I thought I heard a voice call on me; the sound was like no sound ever heard or uttered before. I turned, and saw approaching from behind, the very figure I had beheld in the woodland hut; my mule stopped—it approached, and uttered a sound that I thought resembled my name. It was dismal; around me were the thick trees, and the light dimly appearing above their tops. I tried to rush into the wood, but my mule would not move. I stood trembling, and crossing myself, and now it came nearer, and now it was close to me. It spake; but the sounds were wilder than the howl of wolves. Its language was all mows and chatterings; yet still it held me, and still seemed anxious for conference; I spoke, I know not what, in a pacifying tone, and I perceived, as my fear diminished, it became articulate. It spake at length in a kind of strange rhyme, which, though I did not understand, I cannot forget: among other things it said—

> *There is another of us here,*
> *And we two dwell alone;*
> *The raven that meets us, back doth fly,*
> *And the she-wolf looketh ghastily*
> *When she sees us by the moon.*

I now acquired some courage, and spoke to it rationally—but it interrupted me—

> *And wilt thou on my errand go,*
> *Nor baffle me with mock and mow—*
> *Like the foul things, whose nightly nest*

> Is in the cranny of my breast.—
> A fiery gush is in my throat,
> And drowns confession's struggling note—
> They bind me strong with darkling spell,
> And what I wis—I may not tell—
> And oft I bid on errand go
> The leaf that falls, the gales that blow.
> 'Tis in the roar of dark-brown flood—
> 'Tis in the moan of wintry wood—
> And every form that nature wears
> Blairs it in burnish'd characters.
> And still no eye the tale can read,
> And still no tongue doth trump the deed—
> Still, till my ghastly tale is told,
> I scream a-night on wood and wold.—

When it had ceased, it released me, and I sprung onward. But in a moment afterwards it crossed me, and all the live long night it beset me. Sometimes it would catch my mule's bridle, and stare me in the face; anon it would be seen playing its goblin-gambols among the branches of the trees, from which it would drop down beneath my feet, and then, with a wild cry, bound away into the woods. I arrived, spent, and breathless at a hamlet in the wood, and"—"But how can this contribute to the explanation of any events that may have happened at the castle?" "Pardon the prolixity of an old man, Signor; if I do not tell events in the order they occurred to me, I shall be unable to relate them at all. It is not long now, since I sojourned for the last time, with my old host in the valley; I saw when I entered, he was bursting with strange intelligence, nor did I wait long for his information. 'Two nights ago,' said he, 'we heard a knocking at the wicket of the hut, we were too much afraid of *the vampire* to open it; however, when the door *was* opened in the morning, *it* was found extended before it, without sense or motion. When it was brought in, and revived, we began to mistrust that it was a human creature, and when it was recovered, it addressed us in christian accents, and just like a christian man, besought us for shelter and blessed charity, and talked like one that was recovering from a long trance, and beginning to feel human feelings about his heart again. All that day he was faint and feeble, but still spoke in christian accents; but towards night, we somehow

CHARLES MATURIN

began to feel uneasy again, not knowing what evil thing it might be, and fearful of some unknown mischief, we made a great fire, and sat round it all night, telling our beads, and watching as it lay; it started and groaned often, but made no other movements all night. Towards morning it was still weaker, and it besought them for the love of the virgin, to send for some pious man, and have the offices of christian charity and grace done by it. They sent with all speed for a holy monk to a monastery in the mountains, and when he came, he started at the sight of such an object, but on conversing with him, and receiving clear and pious answers, he prepared to receive his confession, and administer the last rites. The peasant and his family left the hut, and the monk and the dying man were left alone. They were shut up that day and evening, and when the old man returned, he was struck with terror at what he beheld. The penitent had scarce a moment to live, and the confessor appeared nearly in the same state. He held out the crucifix with a trembling hand to the dying man, and the moment the breath left the body, he fainted. While they were using means for his recovery, he uttered some extraordinary words, which they believed referred to some terrible secret the confession had disclosed. When he recovered, he immediately prepared to return to the monastery, but a storm arose, that rendered it impossible for him to proceed. The monk was in an agony of solicitude; he stalked about the hut, and peeped from the casement, and at length demanded if the old peasant could supply him with materials for writing; 'For if' said he, 'the smallest article of what I am to attest, should escape, the consequences might be visited on me hereafter.'—The materials were procured, the monk sat down, and wrote all night, often crossing himself, and dropping his pen, and then again compelling himself to proceed. At length when he had finished his writing, he set out to return to the monastery; 'And we,' said the old man, 'are preparing to follow him with the body for interment.' I inquired, was the body still under his roof, and hastened to the room where it was laid. I approached it in curiosity and fear, for I remembered our encounter in the forest, when no power could have persuaded me the being I saw was human. I bent over it; the distortion of filth, and famine, and madness, was on the countenance no longer. I viewed it; I could not credit my eyes; again I looked on it, and again; it was indeed the figure I had beheld in the wood, and that figure, Signor, was—Ascanio."—"How, Michelo, who?—the confidential servant whom you mentioned in your former narrative."—"The same,

Signor: in my late visits to Apulia, I had indeed observed Ascanio's absence, and heard the strange conjectures of the domestics."—"But then, Michelo, the monk and the secret subject of the confession—did nothing ever transpire? are these intricacies to be without solution, and without end?"—"Peace be with the souls of the departed," said Michelo, crossing himself. "Strange means, it is said, were employed to suppress that story. Shortly after my return to the castle, there was a kind of report, that the monk was in possession of some secret, dark and terrible, relating to the Family of Montorio: it became an affair of public consternation and solicitude. The whole territory of Naples had their eyes fixed on the supposed movements of the monastery; it was said, they were preparing to divulge something to high authority, and that the monk who confessed the dying wanderer was to have an audience of the Pope himself; others said, that he had never been himself since the confession, and that the subject of it had been communicated to the prior, who was to assume the conduct of the affair. At length it was certain, that the monk set out on a journey with numerous attendants; that he seemed greatly agitated; that he travelled with extraordinary expedition; that he was often heard to say, (though in perfect health) he never would live to conclude the journey, and that after arriving at an obscure inn on the road to Rome, he could be traced no further; there was much inquiry and commotion about it. The host and his family were lodged in the Inquisition; and several in the neighbouring village apprehended, and vast rewards offered for the smallest intelligence of the monk or of the documents that were supposed to be in his possession, when he disappeared. The prior of the convent, supported, it was said, by the enemies of the Family of Montorio, pursued the search with all the zeal and tenacity of an inquisitor; but the grave kept its secrets well.—Thus, Signor, the last remaining possibility of any intelligence relative to those events, was removed, and thus we remain, in ignorance and in fear."

What passed through my mind, a moment after he ceased to speak, I will not dare to breathe even to you, Ippolito; if you can discover it from the question I asked, you may.—"My father, was he much shocked at these events?"—"He *was* much shocked at these events," said the old man, as if fearful of using any words but mine.

"Perhaps," said I, "his present gloomy dejection is owing to their preying on him still;"—"I firmly believe," said Michelo, "they continue o prey on him still."—There was a dreary pause; the bell tolled three;—"'Tis late, Signor, we have wasted many hours in this melancholy conference; permit me to see you to your chamber."—I rose almost unconsciously; the sound of what I had heard was yet in my ears, nor did it quit them after I retired to rest.

VI

————Attonitusque legis
Terrai frugiferai.————

It was not extraordinary that on Ippolito these letters should produce an effect merely slight and partial. His mind was not constructed to receive the impressions Annibal wanted to convey. That some strange obscurity had gathered over the fate of the late Count and his Countess, was plain from every part of the narrative; yet Ippolito, innocent and noble of mind, perused the letters, not with suspicion, but with curiosity; and in the avidity with which he read a *narrative of wonders,* the observation (relative to his father's concern in those transactions) which had been suggested to the dark penetration of Annibal, was totally overlooked by his brother. His two predominant passions, love of the marvellous, and love of heroic adventure, inspired him with the thought, that some dark act of oppression or violence had been committed, the unfolding of which was reserved for him; and, as he thought, of relieving distress, or of vindicating virtue, his cheek glowed, and his frame mantled and dilated with generous enthusiasm. He was roused from his trance of heroism, by Cyprian, who invited him to their evening excursion. Ippolito, who was in that state of mind, which is pleased with itself and its purposes, complied; and the smile which, as he assented, lit up his beautiful countenance, gave to it almost an angel brightness and benignity. From such an expression in Ippolito's face, Cyprian was always observed to turn away abruptly and tremblingly. When that face was partially averted, he would view it, with such a fixedness, as if his very *mind* was *eye;* when it was turned towards him with no marked expression, he would venture, timidly to look up; but when Ippolito smiled, Cyprian shrunk from him, with a sick and miserable delight, which was equally difficult to describe or account for.

They set out. It was one of those evenings, of which it is difficult for one not conversant with Italian scenery and climate to imagine the beauty. There was a blaze of animated, but tranquil loveliness, diffused over earth, and sea, and sky; there was a splendour which did not dazzle, a richness which did not satiate; there was not a cloud in heaven, not a dark spot on earth; the eye wandered over an extent of view, which its

CHARLES MATURIN

brightness made seem immeasurable, and rested on it with a fulness of complacency. The West, that presented a broad sweep of golden light; the sea, that chequered the reflection by the heaving of its waters, and the gliding of its vessels; the wooded windings of the shore, and the promontories clothed in their most verdurous and lovely hues, endless variety of shape and shade, from the dark brown tufts, to the feathery spray, that quivered in the breeze, and admitted the blue sky through its fibres; the spires and palaces, whose glowing western fronts, shone like jasper and topaz in the setting sun—all these objects, seemed to produce a kind of visible harmony, as sensible to sight, as the mingled accordance of sounds to the ear.

They ascended a path they knew, which conducted them to a recess, where shadowed by the arbutus and the mangolia, they sat, and surveyed the prospect.

After a silent pause—"Tell me," said Cyprian, "What is necessary to form a poet, but to be conversant amid such scenery as this?" "Many things more are necessary," said Ippolito; "labour, and art, and study, and knowledge, which must be supplied by experience, by observation on the mixt forms of artificial life, and by those hereditary habits of association, both of sentiment and language, which must be acquired by an intimacy with the works of similar authors. He who exposes himself merely to the impressions of nature, will indeed acquire a sensibility of them, but it will be a savage and solitary feeling, which cannot be embellished from want of internal cultivation, and cannot be communicated, from want of the aids and colourings of appropriate language." "Pardon me," said Cyprian, "your own observation seems favourable to me: you mention habits of hereditary association derived from one poet to another—that this is true I admit, and if it be true, it must follow that the first representations were distinguished by their fidelity and excellence; now the early poets must have copied from nature solely, for society was in a crude and elementary state, and of *previous* models the *first* artists can have had none."

"When I mentioned the early poets," said Ippolito, "I did not mean the aborigines of Parnassus, the bards of savage tribes, as savage as they—whose effusions were oral and traditionary—I meant the poets of an age cultivated, but not so cultivated as our own. Nature must indeed be the object of poetical representation, but it must be nature modified and conformed to the existing habits and taste of society."

"Were I a poet," said Cyprian, "I should invert your rule, and admit the influence of prevailing manners into my strains, so far as they were conformable to nature. From that species called pastoral, for instance, I would banish that trim and fantastic garniture, which removes it from every thing with which the observation or fancy has ever held alliance. Shepherds laying aside all concern for the simple objects and pleasures of a pastoral life, to pursue their mistresses with *speeches,* which to them ought to be unaffecting and unintelligible, expending a portion of time which rural life can seldom spare, to talk of pains and pleasures, which even refinement feigns to feel, and which here, therefore, divest fiction of all imposing resemblance to truth. All this I would exchange for the true and visible imagery of rural life:—For the little peasant boy chasing the fire-fly, or feeding the silk-worm, slumbering in the shade at noon, or led, in pursuit of some wanderer of the flock, to a scene of unexplored wildness, treading with rude awe where his steps are not echoed by a human sound, and gazing on views, which no eye, save the eye of the lone genius of the place, had ever before beheld; or touched with local and rural superstition, trembling in moon-light or in storm, amid ruins, deemed the resort of beings not of this earth. Or, if shepherds must be in love, I would represent them loving like shepherds, with simple fidelity, with unfastidious jealousy, with services such as pastoral life may require and receive, and with hopes of rustic enjoyment, such as labour may acquire, and simplicity relish. I am sure an assemblage of such imagery would give pleasure to those who love nature, and those who do not, might find at operas and carnivals, shepherds and shepherdesses sufficiently courtly and unnatural."

"You should study the poesy of the heretic English, as a penance for your own poetical heterodoxy," said Ippolito, "though perhaps the task would have little of penance in it. I have been acquainted some time with the chaplain of the English Embassy; he is reckoned a man of literature in his own country, and were he not a heretic, I should think him a man of sense and probity. He tells me, that (from the surly independence of the national spirit, from the roughness of the climate, or from a taste derived from their ancestry) there is a spirit in their poesy, quite different from that of the continental. A simple appeal to the strong and common feelings of our nature, often made in such language as the speakers of common life clothe their conceptions in. Of this he describes the effect to be inconceivable by a reader accustomed to the poetry of Italy.

CHARLES MATURIN

From their dramas and poems, remote and heroic adventures are almost banished, and they turn with more emotion to the indigent peasant, weeping over her famishing babes—to the maniac, who shrieks on the nightly waste—to age, pining in lonely misery—to honest toil crushed in the sore and fruitless struggle with oppression and adversity—than to the raving princess, or the declaiming hero. They have also a species of poesy among them, (unknown I believe to any but the northern nations of Europe,) which contributes to maintain this taste—the traditionary tales of their ancestry, the rude chronicles of a bold and warlike people, of which the language is wild and peculiar even to the ears of its admirers, from a kind of quaint and antique rhythm, which irresistibly associated in the minds of the hearers, with the thoughts of times long past, with melancholy and awe-breathing remembrances. These are the *ballads* of the West and North of Europe; they are set to a simple and monotonous melody, and chaunted with enthusiasm.

"There is a nation of people wild and little known, in a Western island, whose national poetry is still richer, and whose harmony is said to be more melting than that of the English—I have forgot their name, but of a people so endowed, the name will not be always obscure. The little poem I am about to read to you, relates the actions of a rude chieftain of that country."

Bruno-Lin, the Irish Outlaw*
A.D. 1302

Bruno-lin awoke in the night,
He griped his mace, and lie roused his might,
He deemed it long till his followers all
With food and plunder filled his hall.—

His followers food and plunder sought
From warded tower to hurdled cot—

---

* The subject of the following lines was taken from a note on a Poem, from which it is an honour to borrow a hint however slight or remote. It is perhaps the only merit of this trifle that it was suggested on reading a passage in "The Lay of the Last Minstrel," It is lamented that the scenery of this Ballad is so *topical,* that whoever has not been in Ireland, can scarce read it with pleasure; whoever has, will not be sorry to think again of the ruins of Melik, and the waters of the Shannon.—Bruno-Lin, (or Bryan-o-Lin, as he is sometimes called), is a Chieftain still famous in the memory of Irish song.

A band of blood—They raised the spear,
And never a foeman stood anear.—
A band of blood—They laid them down
And there was not a meal for four miles round.
Where saintly peace at Melik* dwells,
They burst the convent's seared cells.;
And broke the pix at altar's base,
And flung the wine in the Sacristan's face.

He griped his mace with a grimly smile,
(Hard to lift, and heavy to feel,
Banded with brass, and studded with steel)
The moon shone thro' a rift the while.—
He griped it, and swore by Mary's might,
To go and meet the traveller-wight,—

Bruno-Lin he left his tower
All in the mirk and midnight hour,
Through mossy bog, and matted brier,
He sprung with the speed of fairy fire,
Nor rested till his firm step stood
Where folds† dispart the wandering flood.

O'er Shannon's broad and bridgeless stream,
Was passage else nor far nor near—
Through buttress'd arch, and shadowy pier,
In its dark blue wave, now frequent gleam.

He leaned with his mace on the red-moss stone,
And watched for the step of traveller lone.
—Was not a sound to stir the ear—
—Was not a form that thought could fear—
The owlet slept in tufted nest;
The river's ripplings whispered—rest.
The ear might list, till murmurs still

---

* Melik, an Abbey, whose beautiful ruins are yet extant on the banks of the Shannon,
where it flows between Galway and Leinster.
† Fords of Melik.

CHARLES MATURIN

Of unheard sound the sense did fill.—
The eye might gaze, till forms of night
Gan quiver in the misty sight.—

The breathless calm of the lone hour
Held o'er his soul unwonted power.—
Bruno cursed the stilly night,
And waved his mace, to wake his might—
He would rather hear the tempest rave,
And shout to the toss of the crested wave.—

A step—he lurks behind the stone;
A step—he comes—the traveller lone.—

It was a knight of moody mien,
His hand unglaised, his lance in rest;
His barded steed scarce felt the rein,
His footing stint the stirrup press'd.—

Thrice as his step the brink assay'd,
A voice of woe did sweep the stream;
And thrice beneath the moon's wan beam
A bloody stain the waves embayed.

Bruno rushed from his trysting place,
And dashed in the courser's front his mace—
In bone and brain the iron stood,
Reek'd to its base both spike and stud—
The mad steed bounding with the pain
Rose like a meteor in the air,
Left in sore plight his rider there,
And plunged into the flood amain.—

Bruno rushed on the struggling wight,
And bore him to the earth outright:
On ringing plate, and riven mail,
The massive mace did bound like hail.
He cannot rise, he cannot breathe—
His lance is locked, his sword in sheathe:

From gash and rent the life-blood flows,
And faint and short his struggling grows:
His quivering head, and stark-swoln breast
The chase of hunted life confest—
"Lay me on Melik's holy shore!"
His last prayer sped—he breathes no more.—

Three paces backward Bruno strode,
And on the corse did sometime gaze;
Then in his arms assayed to raise—
And felt it was a dead-man's load.—
He rent the mail from his bleeding breast,
He rent the gems from his plumed crest:
The shield from his left arm unwreathed,
And half the burnished brand unsheathed:
But he would not the visor's band unbrace,
For he cared not to look on the dead man's face;
He heaps the spoil on the red-moss stone,
And lists for the step of traveller lone.

He comes—a lone and lowly wight,
Scant was his speed—and vilde his plight:
He is y'douned in dusky weeds,
And loud, as he goes, he tells his beads.—
Bruno 'sdeigned, this enemy
With craft, or weaponed might assail,
Or mell in perilous battaile;
So forth he strode, and bad him "die."
"For Christ's bless'd mother spare my blood;
I do not plead for craven life;
'Tis for a soul's most precious strife;
By Him who died on holy rood.—

Warrior—I held a wide domain,
Iron portals fenced my keep,
Mailed warders watched my sleep:
Warrior—I led an hardy train.
This hand, that marshalled my bold crew

CHARLES MATURIN

In the fell foray of the Pale,
Armed with glaive of iron scale,
This hand an only brother slew!—

Oh, what shall give a murderer rest!
Still, still I feel the worm within,
Still burns the unquenched fire for sin—
And I have roamed from east to west.
Full fifty choirs their requiems raise;
On fifty shrines the tapers blaze,
Them fifty priests do watch by night
With missal chaunt, and taper'd rite;
O'er flourished cross, and trophied tomb,
His banner waves in warlike gloom,
And bells shall toll—till day of doom.—
Oh, what shall give the murderer rest!
I feel th' undying worm within,
Still burns th' unquenched fire for sin,
And I have roamed from east to west.

Aid from each sainted name I crave,
From cloistered tower to Eremite's cave;
To stone and well I ceaseless wend,
At cross and cairn my head I bend;
I've knelt and wept from morn to morn,
My knees are stone, mine eyes are horn—

All vain of penanced lore, the rede
Rite, and relic, and charmed bead,   }
And vigil pale, and pilgrim weed.

And now with faltering step I go—
These costly gifts shall Melik gain,
To the last rood of my domain—
(The dark fiend doth beset me so)
Peace to the parted soul to win
Or free the living soul from sin.
Warrior—for grace thy weapon sheathe,

So may thy last prayer gracious be,
So may thy soul part peacefully,
So may it triumph gloriously;
Nor plunge a soul unbless'd in death."—

Bruno scarce marked his woful tale:
Small was his wreck of penance—rede
Scant was his ruth of saintly weed:
"Pilgrim, a shorter shrift shall 'vail,
If without book thou knowest a prayer,
Address thee, for thy corse lies there."
Sore strove the man in agony!

But Bruno wrenched him without toil,
Like tufted weed from mossy soil,
And plunged him in the darksome waste—
And still his death-cry swell'd the blast;
"Might I but reach the shadowed spire,
Within its shadow but expire"—
Till the dark waters quench'd his cry.
Then Bruno from his scrip 'gan pour
Pix, and chalice, and taper high,
And rood, and altar's imagery,
And vase, and vest for sacristy,
Of monkish wealth, a goodly store:

He heaped them on the mossy stone—
'Vails not to tell, how many a wight
Bowed beneath his mace that night;
'Vails not to tell, how, rich foray
With dint of perilous assay
Was won that night from traveller lone.

Bruno homeward now doth wend,
His prey around him heavy hung;
Beneath a part his shoulders bend,
Part in his mantle broad he flung,
And some was tied to his mace's end.
Home he wends with footsteps wight,

The moss beneath his backward tread,
Scant bow'd his lithe and limber head:
When lo—a meteor flames his tower,
Bright as the beam from faery bower
When wanderers,—mark o'er wat'ry Strath,
How burns the Elfin's taper'd path—
So shone that bright and wonderous light.—
Swift he comes—his followers all
With feast and foray had filled his hall.
There was note of boasting loud,
Pointing to prey, and staunching of blood,
Till Bruno check'd the wassel rude.
His eye was lit with high disdain,
As he threw the prede upon the ground }
And leant on his mace with idlesse stound,
All-while his followers gazed it round:
Then sudden with a startled mien—

"Who lapped our keep in nightly fire?
On towery ridge of castled wall,
Bartizan and beacon-spire,
Casement arch, and arrow loop,
And grated cleft and chink withal;
A flood of sheeny flame did tower—
When, as I entered, all was mirk."
None the cause could rede, I trow,
Much they mus'd, and murmur'd low:
"The lonely taper that lights our hall,
Gleams in a crevice of the wall;
Not broader seen than Melik's spire,
O'er Shannon's far and moon-light wave."

But soon they started from moody stound,
And as they bask round ruddy fire,
Gibe, and jest, in gamesome sort,
With the wide wassel cup went round—
When hark!—when hark!—
A blow upon the barred door!
The band,—each drew his unwiped dirk,

Indrew with quivering lip his breath,
And starting, grasped the board unneath,
And glanced around the hollow eye.
When louder, as of iron stave,
On boss and bar, the smiting rung—
The boldest of the rever's train,
Pressed on his lip his wary hand,
Seized with shorten'd gripe his brand,
And went—but ne'er returned again.
Loud and more loud the smiting grew,
As bar and bolt in splinters flew:
Another goes—his mazed feere
With ear that faltered on the sound,
Listened as down the stair he wound;
But thence nor voice nor step could hear—

Loud and more loud the smiting grew—
Others still, and others went—
Bruno sat in his lonely selle—
He heard his band, as one by one
They trod the winding stair of stone;
Adown the footing, hard and dank,
He heard their sandals' iron clank;
He heard them reach the arched door,
But thence nor step, nor voice heard more.
Was nigh him now, nor friend nor feere—
Lonely thought his heart 'gan quell,
His proud eye 'vailed its hardiment:
As slow he rose, and now through mist
Of umber'd arch the door mote see,
He sign'd the cross, which he deemed a spell,
And faltered a broken Ave-Marie.—
Untouched—the door far backwards flew,
What shapes are they—through mist and fog
Now dimly seen, now sudden lost,
That lap in flame the fenny bog,
And distant now, and now anear,
Edge the dark lining of the cloud,
Sweep in dim march the heathy hill,

And now below in darkling dell,
Mantle the toothed and matted briar
With ridgy head, and spiky hand,
Talon and fang, of fringed fire—
All instantly and visibly?

Shapes, now sheeted in paley fire,
That shimmer like the moon-shine frost,
Now embound in flaky gyre
Of eddying flame, whose high career
Whirls them round with waftage loud—
While through its bickering volumes still,
Fitful gleam'd the shadowings blue,
In umbered skull, of flamy eyne,
Like steely studs in Morion dun,
Or tombed tapers sapphire sheen,
Or carbuncle in ebony.—

The sight was drear—but Bruno bold
Had deemed it but some pageant strange,
Play'd by the quaint and antic sprites
Through fog and fen that darkling range,
Till 'mid the ghostly rout he knew
The shadowed forms of those he slew.

Stern scowl'd the knight—his rifted mail
Disclosed his body gashed and bare:
Wan gleamed the penitent so pale,
And signed a shadowy cross in air:
And far, far off in cloudy sail
Other and sadder shapes were there.—
Forward—the gasted murderer fled,
Mid horror's pith to plunge his head.
Even in that dread and darkling hour,
His soul's first impulse urged its power.

Forward—his thoughts unbidden tend;
Forward—his steps unconscious bend.—
While as he turned his scared eye,

He sees athwart the reddening sky,
The spectre-cloud, in folding fires
Enwrap his castle's smouldering spires—
Giant-shapes of warlike sheen
Grasping what seemed dart and spear:
And sulphurous lightning's streamy lance,
O'er crested tower their wild forms rear,
And mouths of other than earthly mould
(Gleaming through the casements barr'd,
Or o'er the portal battle-scarred)
Through ebon horns rung war-notes bold—
And every hue and tint so pale
Shone out in that unearthly light;
Shadowy stole and form of mist,
Flar'd like the sunny chrysolite,
Ruby or opals argent mail,
And emerald, and amethyst.—

Onward the ghasted murderer rushed,
Till Shannon's dark wave checked his flight:
Onward the fiery fabric urged,
And as he turned with hurrying tread,
Still seemed to topple o'er his head,
Still vollying, on the sulphured gale
Came skriek, and gibber, and ghost-like wail
Like stripes, his flying steps that scourg'd.

The river's depths lay dark in night—
And his broad surface, still and clear,
Gave back no gleam of unbless'd light.
He paused a moment in breathless fear—
Then with a cry, (whose nightly yell
Oft sweeps its stream, as legends tell)
He plung'd beneath—the winds are whist—
The echoes sleep—and all is hush'd.—

"I confess," said Cyprian, "in these I find a pleasure, which I seek in vain amid the sententious and cold *concetti* of our poetry. Would I were one of the *Arcadi*, or of those whose eminence in the literary world

CHARLES MATURIN

enables them to extend their influence to the arts." "Why should you wish for that influence, and how would you employ it?" said Ippolito. "I should wish for it," replied Cyprian, "because the connexion between literature and the arts is intimate and inseparable; I would therefore make each the channel of reciprocal improvement to the other. How much more striking would the effect be, if instead of the stiff figures of our drama, coming forward in modern habiliments to warble modern music, contrasting instead of representing the classic or romantic characters whose names they usurp—the bard of those distant days and regions you have described, should appear with the rude and flowing drapery, the harp of bold, unmeasured song, the themes of old and wondrous story; and all amid scenes suited to his character; not among the glare of artificial lights and picturings, but amid rocks and ruins, the murmurs of waters, and the tremblings of moon-light. I have mentioned only one character, but might there not be a thousand others, and all with the appropriate melody of their age and nation, simple, or rude, and wild, as they might be, but all rendered more interesting by remembered and heart-touching association, than the most scientific strains uttered by modern harmonists?"

"And how would you contrive," said Ippolito, "to extend a similar improvement to the department of painting?"

"Oh!" said Cyprian, "that mute language whose powers I am convinced are yet unexplored, that language now only intelligible to the eye, I would teach to speak to the very soul. Instead of copying the colouring of one artist, the design of another, the trees, and the sun-light, and the ruins, that are handed down from age to age, with mechanical improvement and imitation that excludes originality—I would have the painter look around life, and within himself; I would have him copy from nature in a state of motion, from *existing* life; from those forms and shades of manner and feeling, which are in a perpetual state of animated fluctuation around us, more numerous, more varied, and more vivid than they could have been, from the unimproved state of society, in the time of the elder masters: I would make all my figures, *characters,* and all my groups circumstantial and narrative. But for sensible representation, it is better to furnish example than argument. I saw a painting by an obscure master; the subject was common; it was the interment of a corse; it was the moment after the vault was closed: from the devices I conjectured it was the burial of a young person, and from the countenance of an old man (who assumed no particular attitude)

I was convinced it was his only child. Over the face of the priest was spread a chaste and holy sadness, such as men may be supposed to feel, to whom the fixed hope of a better life, have made the inflictions of this of light and trivial avail. But the wretched parent was bowing to the priest, for having performed the last rites; was thanking him with the humility of courteous misery, for having for ever removed from him his last earthly stay and hope. There was something in the expression of the old man, thus trying to work features, convulsed with anguish, into a gentle smile, to blend the duties of the moment with the wrung feelings of the parent, and not forget the decencies of grief, amid its stings and bitterness—I cannot express myself, but I looked at the other contents of the gallery with sufficient tranquillity. Such are the subjects I would introduce or search for, in every effort of mind or of taste; and to every subject, mental or artificial, I would attach its appropriate features of scenery and character."

"And with the present scene, what group would you associate?" said Ippolito. Cyprian paused. "What if I were to take the pencil from you, and become an artist in your new school. I feel the inspiration coming: let me try—shall I sketch a little, friendly, monitory sylph, soliciting with gentle art, a giddy, graceless wanderer, from a vitiated sensibility of pleasure, and recalling him to those pure and innocent enjoyments which he blushes to have forsaken so long."

"Oh, my master, my beloved master!" said Cyprian, "look forth, and wonder that you ever forsook them. This dim light that veils from us the forms and colours of the earth, gives to the sky a dense and sombrous majesty, which I love better than the bright blue of noon, or even the amber-glow of sun-set. See the high arch of heaven, above our heads, how vast, how spacious, without a star, and without a cloud. There is something in its aspect of calm stability and immutable duration. It stands in its strength, and its silence tells of eternity."

"And see far off, just over Capri," said Ippolito, "where the sky is of a paler blue, one little twinkling star of silver fire; and above it, the moon, with her slant crescent, slowly coming up. Does she not seem like a bark of pearl, floating on the deep, dark blue ocean. And see, while we speak, ten thousand stars are bursting into brightness. There is my *natal* Saturn—just where I point; how wan he looks tonight; oh, for a mental telescope to read the characters inscribed on that dark speck!" He mused, and Cyprian observed with anguish the change on his countenance, "Observe," said he, recovering himself, "in this deep silence of the night, the distinctness of the most faint and distant sound. Listen to that bell from the city; I think I could tell the very convent from which it sounds: how solemn it swells on the air—it is a death-bell."

"Peace to the parting soul—oh, it gazes on this scene with other eyes," said Cyprian, crossing himself.

"Yes, in a moment, how changed its views, its capacities, its range of existence and motion," said Ippolito, "from the dark, narrow bed of suffering, where all of nature that was admitted, was the sickly light that struggled with the watch-taper—in a moment, to see with a spirit's bright and boundless view, all nature, with her worlds and her systems, her laws, her causes, and her motions; yea, and the mighty Mover himself! Oh, wonderful!"

"And thither shall we follow; though not now, we shall be there in a space, which to the duration of that world, is as a moment," said Cyprian, "and be assured, that these cool and healthful moments of reposing thought, snatched from the fevering turmoils of the world, will have an effect that shall not be unfelt or forgotten there. There the best hours of our lives are numbered and valued, and the best of our hours, I believe, are passed amid the stillness of nature, and the silence of thought."

They descended, and returned to Naples.

VII

The influence which in these conferences Cyprian had obtained over the mind of Ippolito, was singular and powerful. The obscurity of his introduction, the peculiarity of his manners, gave even a hovering shade of awe to impressions, of which the character had otherwise been faint and fugitive. Not of a sex to inspire love, and still too female-like for the solid feelings of manly friendship, Cyprian hovered round his master, like his guardian sylph, with the officiousness of unwearied zeal, and the delight of communicated purity.

On their return to Naples, Cyprian observed, that a length of time elapsed before Ippolito joined him, though they had quitted the carriage together, and when he *did* appear, that his aspect was strange and altered. It wore an expression of ghastly wonder. His lips were white, and his eye vacant. He addressed abrupt inquiries to the servants, with the air of a man who wishes to satisfy his curiosity, without betraying the object of it; but from them he learned nothing. They "had seen no shape," they "had heard no sound," and Ippolito's inquiries seemed suddenly checked by something more than the difficulty of satisfying them. Shortly after, Ippolito retired to dress for an assembly, and Cyprian to his closet, where, in his master's absence, he was constantly employed in writing, and where (some whom the prying habits of an Italian servant had induced to watch him, declared, that) he gave himself up to emotions so terrible, they wondered so delicate a frame could support them.

When Montorio returned, his valet was summoned to attend him alone. His cabinet was contiguous to Cyprian's, who obeying an impulse, which his concern for his master justified to himself, listened at a partition, in a state of solicitous feeling, which the low, broken sounds, that issued at intervals through it, irritated instead of appeasing.—At times, the words "strange"—"fearful"—"terrible"— and every expression of painful wonder met his ear. Some observation was then made by the servant, of a tendency apparently palliative or explanatory, to which Ippolito answered with solemnity: "Impossible; if I have life and sense I saw it—three times tonight, distinct and terrible."

A sentence followed from the servant, which, partly from the stretch of most painful attention, and partly from the answer, Cyprian conjectured to be an inquiry about some form or shape. It was followed by some imperfect answer from Ippolito, but of which Cyprian could not discover whether the imperfection arose from the form being too obscure or too horrible for description.

The conference ceased, and Cyprian had scarce time to sit down to his papers, which he turned over with shaking hands, and a vacant eye, when Montorio entered the room. He stalked about for some time gloomily, then like one who wakens slowly from an oppressive dream, he gazed around him, and sighed heavily. Cyprian, who wished to ascribe to himself the uneasiness that prevailed, lest he should irritate a disturbed spirit, said timidly, "I have been writing, since you told me of the English poetry, and this has been the *cause of all this foolish embarrassment;* I was anxious and ashamed to shew it to you." He held out a paper, which Ippolito took with a listless hand, and while he read it, Cyprian watched his countenance with an emotion, the fate of his poetry did not excite.

The Lady and her Page

I

It was a sweet and gentle hour,
'Twas the night of a Summer day,
When a lady bright, on her palfrey white,
Paced across the moorland grey.

II

And oft she checked her palfrey's rein,
As if she heard footsteps behind,
'Twas her heart of fear that deceived her ear,
And she heard but the passing wind.

III

There trips a page, that lady beside,
To guide the silken rein,
And he holds up there, with duteous care,
Her foot-cloths sweeping train.

IV

And that page was a knight—who in menial plight,
For love of that stately dame,
Long served at her board, though a high-born lord,
And a foe to her father's name.

V

Across the haze, there streamed a pale blaze,
And the page's cheek blanched with fear;
"Oh, see, lady, see!—at the foot of yon tree,
The blue fire that burns so clear."

VI

"'Tis the prince of the night, 'tis the elfin sprite,
With his ghostly revelry:
Sweet lady stand, with this cross in thine hand,
Or thou and I must die."

VII

"For as legends tell, an unseen spell
Doth screen him from mortal wound,
Unless the steel be dipped in a well
That holy wall doth bound."

VIII

Sad was her heart when she saw her page part,
And she feared she would see him no more,
For in secret long, her soul was wrung
With a love that ne'er trembled before.

IX

Oh! what is the sound seems to come from the ground,
And now sweeps along on the air—

She dared not to look, for with terror she shook,
And she tremblingly murmured a prayer.

X

And o'er the dun heath, a balmy breath
Stole like roses and violets sweet,
And the lavender blue, all dropping with dew,
Strewed the ground at that lady's feet.

XI

"Fair maiden come, to our twilight home,
Where we'll sport so merrily;
The glow-worm by night, shall lend us her light,
As we dance round the grey ash-tree."

XII

"Or with unwet wings, we'll sport in the springs
That roll far beneath the sea;
Or to the bright moon, we'll fly as soon
If my love thou wilt deign to be."

XIII

Askance she gazed—and her eye she raised—
A youth stood timidly nigh,
And of a truth, 'twas as lovely a youth
As ever met maiden's eye.

XIV

His tresses brown, that came mantling down,
Seemed his snowy neck to veil;
And with chrysolite eyes, his wings' crimson dyes
Were starred like the peacock-tail.

XV

His eye was bright, as the north-streamers' light,
But his cheek was sad and pale;
And the lines of care that were written there,
A spirit might read and wail.

XVI

But his sky-tinctured vest to his eye-lids was prest,
And his heart seemed bursting with woe,
And the white, white rose that wreathed his brows
Seemed pale and paler to grow.

XVII

"I've watched thee late and early,
I've watched thee night and day,
I've loved thee, lady, dearly,
With a love that can never decay."

XVIII

"I've heard thy sleeping sigh, lady,
I've heard thy waking prayer,
No mortal foot was nigh, lady,
But I was weeping there."

XIX

"With an eye that no thought can deceive, lady,
I've seen love sweetly stealing on thee;
I know that young bosom can heave, lady,
And shall it not heave for me."

XX

The lady stood—and her unchilled blood
Gave her lip its warmest hue;

But the cross to her breast, was fervidly prest
And still her heart was true.

XXI

"Yet rest thee here, oh! lady dear,
And my minstrel spirits gay,
With harp and lute, and fairy flute
Shall play thee a roundelay."

XXII

All was hushed and still, on the elfin hill,
All was hushed in the evening vale,
Not a whisper was heard, not a footstep stirred,
Not an aspen-leaf shook in the gale.

XXIII

Then soft and slow, a note of woe
Came far on the breathless air;
'Twas wild as the strain of the mermaid train,
When they're combing their yellow hair.

XXIV

'Twas wild as the dirge, that floats on the surge,
The mariner's lonely grave—
All-while mortals sleep, they sing and they weep,
And they glide on the moon-light wave.

XXV

Then it rose rich and high, like the chaunt of joy, ·
That breathes round the hermit-bower;
When cherubim bright leave their mansions of joy
To soothe his dying hour.

XXVI

Oh! how the heart beat of that lady sweet,
But her heart did not beat with fear,
The strain so wild, her senses had guiled,
And she loved though she trembled to hear.

XXVII

But who is he that flies, with his soul in his eyes,
Wide waving a faulchion of steel?—
By the flush on her cheek, ere a word she could speak,
A nursling babe might tell.

XXVIII

('Twas an urchin-sprite, in the guise of her knight,
'Twas a wile of the elfin king,
And the vision so quaint, in form and in teint,
Her soul to her cheek did bring).

XXIX

"Hushed, hushed, be your fear, for your true knight is here,
With the brand that his patron saint gave,
No elfin wight may dare its might,
For 'tis dipped in St. Angelo's wave."

XXX

"And the cowled friar, and convent quire,
Are waiting our nuptials to say;
Haste, lady, haste, for the night's fading fast,
And the eastern cloud is grey.

XXXI

"But give me the cross that's hid in thy breast,
And give me the rosary too,

And I'll lead thee o'er the perilous moor,
On the faith of a knight so true."

XXXII

Oh, she gave up the cross that was hid in her breast,
And she gave up the rosary too—
As he grasped them, he frowned, and he smote the ground,
And out rushed the elfin crew.

XXXIII

And the goblin rout gave a maddening shout,
And danced round them in many a wild ring,
And the slender waist of that lady chaste,
Was clasped by the elfin king.

XXXIV

All loose was her hair, and her bosom was bare,
And his eye it glared fierce and bold,
And her wan lip he pressed, and her shuddering breast,
And he grasped her locks of gold.

XXXV

But instant a blow made the caitiff forego
His gripe of that victim fair,
And deadly he groaned, as he shrunk from the wound,
And phantom crew vanished in air.

XXXVI

"I've saved thee, my love, by help from above,
I've saved thee from mortal harms,"
And no word she spoke, but she gave him a look,
And sunk in her true-knight's arms*.

---

* This poem was communicated by a friend.

Ippolito, though he perused these lines with the apathy of one occupied by other thoughts, still seemed anxious to escape from *them*, by tenaciously seeking employment. He snatched up the papers that lay before Cyprian, and vehemently began to peruse them. Cyprian, all agitation, rose, and besought him to restore them.—"They are not to be read."—"You increase my anxiety to examine a composition that is written—*not to be read*," said Ippolito, with a languid smile. "They must not be read by you—to you they can afford no pleasure; they are a simple tale of woman's love, and we men believe that women cannot love; it is a tale not to be told in an hour of levity, or when an intercourse with the light, cold characters of the world has hardened the heart, and made it slow to believe, that there *are* beings, who only live to feel, and who have died of feeling. Choose some other hour, and bring with you another heart. I shall make no demands of outrageous sympathy, for I know that the subject is removed too far from the world's line and topic of feeling, to expect it. Nor do I think that real suffering ever sought relief, but in the patience of unanswering belief. This is all I would ask, but this I fear I would ask in vain at such an hour from you."—"Cyprian," said Montorio, touched by his words, "the frivolity in which you see me immersed, is artificial and irksome; I have a heart capable of passion, but the object capable of inspiring it, I yet seek in vain. It is but a little while since I entered society, with feelings ardent in youth, and exalted by hope—those feelings are repelled, crushed, almost extinguished. I submit to a pitiful compromise with the depraved system of society; I trifle with the triflers of the day, and languish even for the refreshing hope of imaginary excellence. All who are beautiful, I can admire; her only, who can *love,* can *I* love."—He clasped his hands, and threw up his dark, ardent eye to heaven, and stood with the look and energy of inspiration.—"If such a being ever existed," said Cyprian, "there is her history."—"And is she yet alive," said Ippolito, "and is she to be found?"—"No; she lives no more, she has passed away, as few have perished, without note, and without remembrance. All that loves to cling round the image and memory of the dead, has forsaken her; she perished without a tear, without a memorial, without *a grave!*"

"*This* is a narrative of thoughts, not of circumstances—no ear heard, and no eye saw her sufferings; and never did the subject of her sole thought enter into the thought of another. It is necessary before I begin to read these fragments, to mention to you, that the writer was young in years and in sentiment; the very child of simplicity and enthusiasm; an union not impossible in young minds. She entered into the world, she was surrounded, dazzled, and confused. But her feelings expanded, as the eye becomes accustomed to the glare of recent light. In the tumult of new pleasures, she saw an object, on whom she gazed with the smile of new-born love; it was her last, last smile.—*He* was indifferent, because he was unconscious; she never told her love, till its posthumous disclosure was no longer a crime in a vestal."

Ippolito prepared to listen, though it was now late, for every object combined to soften him to attention; the chaste and mellowed light, the quiet apartment, whose floating perfumes just stirred the sense, the soothing pensiveness of Cyprian, who concealed his face with his hand, and who reads with the voice of one who fears to trust his own emotions, as he reads.—"The first fragment," said he, "describes her feelings on the sight of this object."—

April 1st

It is midnight—all is silent around me—not a breeze, not a murmur, above, below. And I, amid this stillness of nature, how and what am I?—What is this feverish tumult of mind and sense that contrasts and deepens the silence around me? Whom have I seen? I know not; let me not speak his name; I will not think who he is; I am most happy. My feelings dwell in silence on their inward treasure. The gladness within me is still and balmy, like the morning-sun of a vernal day. There is no being blest as I am this night, except him; he must be happy, he is so beautiful. . . How is a tumult so wild, a calm so deep, as I feel tonight, reconcileable?—My spirits are agitated but my mind is still. . .

April 7th

The costly dullness, the cold faces, the heavy feasts of supercilious grandeur—All are vanished—All that is tedious, has ceased to be felt. What matters it where I am, when he is with me every where? A single spell of thought, an unuttered wish, a *moving of the mental* lips, brings him to my mind. There is a precious store of pleasant thought which we love to dwell on in solitude without communication, and without suspicion. This with me, is the thought of him.—

There comes to me amid crowds a mental and inaudible whisper of his name. I think of him, and happiness steals over me like the silent perfume of evening; like music trembling over a length of moon-lit waters.—

April 9th

For hours today have I sat, without the consciousness of thought, yet without vacancy; his image fills up the mind as if by fascination. Many passed me; I heard their steps, without feeling their presence.—*Is not this like love?*—Impossible; a *vestal cannot love;*—no, my happiness is unmixed with a lover's misery; no restlessness, no jealousy, no torture of impossible hope, no anguish of disappointment.—No; I *may indulge these dreams without danger, and without fear; for I cannot love;*—It is not of his beauty I think, 'tis of himself; yet I remember well his heavenly form, his sunny cheek, and the ringlets of his *brown, brown* hair; yet I do not think of them; I need not; they are before me for ever.—

April 20th

Whence is this new wish to mingle in the world? Can it be a wish to see him again? Why should I see him?—Those who have watched the showery scintillation of the meteor, and gazed upon the glorious vision with uplift hands and eyes, do not wait for its return; why should I waste away life in gazing! I have no *other* hope. What am I doing? Where have I wandered? *hope* and *he*—It is sometimes dangerous to think of danger.—

April 30th

I think too much of him; what I once thought impossible, is certain; I think of him too much. And must I lose that cherished thought; that charm, whose silent agency opens a glimpse of mental fairy land? Who would rob the poor hermit of his only treasure, the lovely face of his Madonna, that only smiling face he is ever permitted to see, and to which he turns in the hour of solitude and vacancy, with devotion animated, not extinguished?

Such I had hoped his image had been to me in the vigils of the dark hour, in the loneliness of my cell—and must I resign it?—

AT THIS MOMENT, SEVERAL SERVANTS entered, with each of whom Ippolito successively whispered, and after listening with much perturbation to their answers, he rushed from the palace, to which he did not return till late the following evening.

CHARLES MATURIN

VIII

Gaudet imagine *rerum—*

Rejoices in the pictured forms of past events.

The Castle di Muralto, the residence of the Montorio family, was totally unlike the modern mansions of the Italian nobility. Very few vestiges of Gothic architecture yet remain on the Continent in a tenanted state.

The style of their palates is marked by elegance, lightness, and novelty. Their polished structures are composed of marble, mingled with materials which are reckoned precious in more northern climes; they are beautified with all the orders and ornaments of architecture, and present images the most remote from gloom and solemnity. The castle had been built in the time of the Norman kings of Sicily; it possessed all the rude and massive characters of that age, darkened by the injuries of time, and the gloom of antiquity. The ramparts, like piles of rock, the deep length of windowless wall, the turretted and embattled angles, the narrow-arched doors crested with the defaced arms of the house and its alliances, some bearing the pedestals, and some the remains of the gigantic statues that once frowned over them; and whose huge fragments obstructed the approach of those their hoary grandeur invited to examine them; all these seemed to realize the descriptions of Gothic romance, and fill the mind with melancholy awe, and wild solemnity. It stood on an eminence of the rich Campagna, near the foot of the mountain; and amid a country luxuriant with cultivation, and sparkling with palaces, the castle reared its scathed and warlike front; seeming to enjoy a sullen repose from the wounds of war and time, and to tell the grandeur of those ages that beheld it in its strength. Such was the castle, of which it was necessary to tell thus much, to give clearness to circumstances, which would appear obscure and strange if related to have passed within the walls of a modern palace.—A few days brought another letter from Annibal.—

———I HAD BEFORE APPRIZED MICHELO of my intention to visit the apartments so long shut up. He had again recourse to dissuasives; but contradictory dissuasives defeat themselves, and I was only confirmed in my pursuit, by his telling me at one time, it would lead to me discovery, and at another, that the discoveries I should make, would prove a source of lasting inquietude. I was vexed that the old man should thus treat me as a child, who was only seeking to gratify a childish propensity, and could be diverted from it by childish arguments.

I entered on a vindication of my motives, and as the sudden flash of zeal often discovers what was concealed from ourselves, I involuntarily detected an earnestness and solemnity in my purposes, of which I had not hitherto been conscious. I desired him to consider me not as gratifying a vague and puerile impulse, but as pursuing a definite object, of obscure but real importance, and if real, demanding all the zeal, the energy, and the capacity of the most powerful mind.

"If my presages are just, Michelo, I shall enjoy the highest honour allowed to man, that of confirming the evidence, and fulfilling the purposes of divine interposition, and if they are not, I shall at least relieve myself from doubts and fears that are becoming intolerable; I shall probably detect and punish fraud, and certainly possess a resource against future imposition." As I said this, I turned my eye on Michelo, but his countenance was unaltered. I have indeed no reason to suspect *him*. I now declared my intention to visit the apartments that evening, and inquired whether he would be able to procure their keys? "I have kept those keys for many years, Signor; I enjoyed in my youth extensive trust under your uncle, and *still* there are some employments which my lord your father would not willingly trust to others, and which I am therefore still permitted to discharge."

Michelo, I find, is one who tortures his hearers by perpetual allusions to secrets, of which nothing more than the hints are ever suffered to escape him; who awakens expectation to a painful state of suspended existence, and leaves it there gasping and unsatisfied; and this not so much from malevolence, or casual indiscretion detecting itself, as from a perpetual struggle between a mind pressed with a burthen too great for its powers, (and therefore anxious to relieve itself by communication,) and the monitions of conscience, which tell it is not right, or of fear, which whispers it is not safe to disclose it.

I have therefore become accustomed to his manner, and forborne to importune him. In the dusk of the evening he promised to attend me. But by the beauty of two succeeding evenings, my father was induced to order ices and refreshments to the pavillion of the fountain; we were obliged to attend him. There, amid the indulgence of every wish, and every sense; music and fragrance, flowers and feasting; perspectives, through the foliaged lattices, of luxuriant gardens, warm with the brilliant amber of sun-set, which played on the limits of the view, in a quivering flood of indefinite brightness: of waters and woods, among which distant melody floated, breathing a low and dying note, so sweet, it seemed caught and echoed by the shells of listening spirits. Amid such scenes we sat in sombrous state, the mute, sad libellers of nature and enjoyment, more like statues that decked the feast, than human beings, partaking its pleasantness.

The third evening I awaited Michelo, in my apartment, and he arrived at the appointed hour. It was the dusky stillness of twilight; all was tranquil in the castle, and the grey light that came paler through the casements, seemed to promise quiet and obscurity. We passed hastily through the vaulted cloisters that lead to the lower stories of the tower; and then opening a door, that led to a long passage, we seemed to enter on a new region of the castle. Here all signs of life and habitation seemed to cease; the walls appeared never to have enclosed a human habitant. The very echoes had a strange hollowness, as if they were for the first time awakened by the tread of a human foot. We reached another door, which seemed intended never to open; Michelo applied one of several keys which he now produced, and I was obliged to assist him with my utmost strength before it yielded. I now discovered the foot of a stair-case, which wound beyond the sight, and on the ballustrade of which Michelo paused to take breath. I ascended the stairs, they were dark and narrow, and conducted us to a door which required our united strength again, to open. Michelo, who had exhausted his in the effort, feebly staggered onward when it yielded, and sunk into a seat. I followed, gazing round me; it was a spacious apartment, apparently heaped with faded furniture, but of which nothing could be distinctly seen, for the light that broke through the dismantled casements, and torn tapestries of the windows, could only discover its size. Michelo falteringly withdrew the drapery that obscured one of the windows. I now looked around the apartment; the decay appeared to proceed more from neglect than from age; Every thing was covered, and almost consumed by dust: all the furniture of a sumptuous chamber was there. The bed stood under a canopy, dark and defaced, but still retaining its draperies, its pillars, and its plumage. "This was the bridal apartment of the Count Orazio," said Michelo; "here the

Countess passed most of her melancholy life; and here"—he turned away.

I inquired why these apartments had been shut up, and why the costly furniture, that might decorate the most modern apartments, was here suffered to decay in obscurity.—"They would perhaps have revived painful recollections," said Michelo, falteringly; "when my lord therefore returned to his castle, I received orders to remove hither the furniture of those gay apartments, and then to close these doors for *ever;* an order which I lament I have been tempted to infringe." Again filled with wonder, which the circumstances of the place, and these dark suggestions inspired, I renewed my importunities to Michelo, to finish the tale he had begun in the turret-chamber.

He heard me with increasing anguish of perplexity, but with unyielding resolution. His eye wandered round the apartment, as if he dreaded that even the broken and unmeaning words he uttered were overheard; "I cannot, I dare not, you know not how I am straitened;" (he wrung his hands, and whispered in the struggling tones of misery) "a strong arm is stretched out upon me; it deals with me darkly, but feelingly; no, I cannot, I dare not." An impulse of inquiry struck me that moment, which I indulged, though I could not account for.—"Michelo, is this mysterious silence, connected in its cause, or its object, with the confessor Schemoli." I shall never forget the look which he assumed at this question; his countenance expressed the most exquisite pain, as if for danger *I* had incurred by the question, while rising on his feeble feet, and pressing his whole hand on his lips, he conveyed in the strongest manner by his attitude the dread *of being overheard,* though where we were it was impossible for human listeners to penetrate.—I was so confounded by his aspect, that I forbore to renew my question, and a long pause followed.—"Do you wish to see the other apartments Signor," said he; I followed him with that sullen silence, with which we comply with the proposal of one who has recently disappointed us, and from whom we wish in our spleen, to conceal that the remainder of his information has interested us.—We entered the other apartment—when I write these words, I pause in thought; I recollect how important in the account of life, that moment will be: and I *wonder that even unconsciously* I approached it with so little emotion. This apartment was like the other, dark and decayed. The light that streamed through dim discoloured windows, the last faint ray of evening, accorded well with the objects it disclosed. The silent mouldering of decay, the dusky stillness of desolation, and the old pensioner of memory, pointing with withered hand, to the images that supplied her morbid and melancholy pleasures.

He proceeded to display the pictures: the first was that of the Count Orazio. I think the painter to whom he sat, must have trembled to raise his eye to him; he must have felt as the prophet did, when he beheld steadfastly the countenance of Hazael, and foretold the sufferings of his country. It was one of those faces which tells the character at a look; the bold, thoughtful front, the dark brows that almost met, the strong curve, and prominent lines of the nose, the proud curl of the upper lip, of which even the smile seemed to hold alliance with contempt, the rich, dark, sanguine complexion, which seems to be the shade the stronger passions love. From such a character I would expect the fiercest bursts of passion; the proudest sternness of heroism; soarings of super-human virtue, or sallies of outrageous depravity; the impassive brightness of an angel, or the potent and glaring malignity of a fiend.

Michelo supported this picture with an averted eye, and as he replaced it, shook in every limb—"And this," said he, displaying another, "is the portrait of the Countess Erminia; when I look on that picture, twenty years seem to pass away, and I feel as I did when I first saw her; such she was, with that gay air of careless loveliness; yet even then there were some who spoke of a melancholy, a dejection, that they said was discoverable through all her beauty and splendour. I could not see it, she was so lovely, that to me, she ever appeared to smile." He continued to speak, I believe; I heard him not; yet the murmur of his praise dwelt on my ear, as something that accorded with my own feelings, and that was pleasant, though not distinct to me. I remained in the mute trance of admiration; I knelt without a breath, without a sound, almost without a thought before that picture. It was the first time I had ever beheld beauty, ever knew what was love: I will not call beauty, that assemblage of colours, to which the cold eye of judgment gives the praise of harmony, and quits it;—no;—it is the communication of unknown pleasure; it is the discovery of that unexplored chord of mind, which is touched for the first time by the hand of harmony: it is the realizing those forms which float in the morning's dream, in the musings of twilight: it is the picture of Erminia. In a space which appears as a moment, I had experienced every emotion that accompanies the varied character of passion; the delicious anguish, the painful joy, the fear sweeter than hope, the hope sweeter than enjoyment; the visionary existence, the pictured dream of thought, the high and super-human tone which this passion alone gives to the feelings and the character; in a moment I had lived the whole life of a lover; it was no longer a picture before which I knelt, I was convinced the original yet existed. It seemed to me more probable that the sun should be blotted from heaven, than that such a being should be permitted to quit existence, without trace, and without resemblance. There was a reality in my feelings, a fixed persuasion of her certain existence, which I know not what to ascribe to, except the living loveliness of that form. Brows that thought; eyes that spoke; lips that smiled; smiled mutably with living and sensible change; hair, of which lest I should disturb the gauzy waving, I held my breath as I gazed. She stood as in her days of early happiness; the scene and attitude were sylvan; a fawn was flying from her, to whom she held out her hand; mine was extended too.—And her hair;—it is that dark brown, whose deepening waves, and tendril ringlets, have a sunny and burnished brightness, that resembles the foliage of a bower, tinged with the rich varieties of autumnal light:—but oh, to play with those ringlets, to look in those living eyes, to kiss that breathing neck—You think me mad—I may be so—was I so, when kneeling and attesting the lovely form itself, I vowed to pursue the original through the world;— to preserve my affections for her with vestal-sacredness; to make life a long pilgrimage of love; and never to know peace of mind or body, till I discovered and possessed her.

Whatever may be thought of such a resolution, I at least experienced from it, what I expected;—it composed my mind; it exalted and gratified my feelings; from its bold impracticability, I actually derived an inviting omen. It seemed worthy of the dignity of my passion; it seemed to promise that no difficulties should obstruct that pursuit, which had set out by daring all.

The light was now declining fast; an hour had elapsed since I entered the cabinet; my original purpose had been utterly forgotten; but another resource was suggested to me, as I was quitting it, and the thought made me bless my happy facility in designing. I took out my tablets, and before the beam that seemed to linger on her countenance, like my own gaze, had died away, I sketched a likeness with such fidelity as convinced me the original inventor of painting, was *love*. I continued to compare it with the original, by a light which none but the quickened eye of passion could have distinguished any thing by; and the sketch so perfect at first, seemed to want a million of touches, when held to the picture. I continued to add them, rather with the *pleasure*, than the *hope* of amendment.—But Michelo, terrified at my delay, supplicated me so earnestly, not to expose us to the danger of discovery, that reluctantly, at length, I quitted the apartment. It was late when I regained my own, which I did however in safety, and obscurity When I was seated at my lamp, I reflected (and you probably have anticipated me) on the views with which my pursuit had commenced, and the visionary indulgence by which I had suffered them to be suspended. The being who goes forth in the doubtful confidence of a supernal summons, and the shadowy dignity of an agent of heaven; armed with all the powers of his nature, and dreading a demand for more than all; and who, when arrived, employs the hour of his trial in kneeling before a picture, and pouring out passion to an insensible representative of the dead; certainly presents no very consistent image of human resolution. While occupied in these sage thoughts, my eyes glanced on the picture in my hand, and I *forgave myself.*—The remainder of the night was passed not in self-reproach, and resolutions of future fortitude, but in finishing and colouring it. I now mix with the family, with the picture of Erminia in my bosom, and feel, like one who has found a treasure, which he smiles to think those around him are ignorant of; like one who carries about him an invisible talisman against care and pain, against the apathy of unawakened feeling, and the vacancy of an unemployed life.

IX

Sed mihi vel tellus optem prius, ima dehiscat,
Vel pater omnipotens adigat me fulmine ad umbras,—
Ante pudor quam te violo, aut tua jura resolvo.

—Virgil

But oh! may earth her dreadful gulph display,
And, gaping, snatch me from the golden day;
May I be hurl'd by heaven's almighty sire,
Transfixed in thunder, and involved in fire,
Down to the shades of hell, from realms of light—
Ere, sacred honour! I betray thy cause
In word, or thought, or violate thy laws,

—Pitt

In this letter, romantic as it was, Ippolito discovered strong traces of real passion, such as exists under the most unexpected circumstances, and contends for its existence with difficulties which any other passion would decline as impracticable. But for light subjects of thought, he had now no leisure, and no wish. One object, dark and bewildering, filled all his thoughts. Since the night he had betrayed so much agitation on his return from an excurtion with Cyprian, he had never recovered his tranquillity. He appeared either in contemplation, or in strong mental debate; perplexity and fear were in all his movements, and these had become so irregular, as to suggest he was engaged in no ordinary pursuit. The day he usually passed alone; about midnight he quitted the palace, and passed the remainder of the night, *where* no one followed, and none could conjecture. At this change, his gayer acquaintance laughed, his friends wondered, and Cyprian wept. But silence and wonder were all the resources they had; his silence remained impenetrable. Sometimes he mingled in society, and laughed and fluttered with the eager gaiety of one who is resolved to snatch a respite from pain:—but however pleased, or pleasing others, the clock striking twelve, dissolved the spell. Beyond that hour neither pleasure nor importunity could procure his stay. He rose abruptly, dismissed his servants, nor was visible till the morning, when he returned alone and slowly through the Strada di Toledo.

Sometimes, he admitted Cyprian, and listened to a continuation of the *fragments,* because he was not interrupted by demands for comment or approbation; while Cyprian, ignorant of any thing that held alliance with art, read simply on, hoping that attention was included in silence, or even when he discovered negligence, compromising for the pleasure of being admitted into the presence of Ippolito.

May 7th

This perpetual struggle is worse than either alternative.—*To do all I dread to do:—to see him again,* were only *the guilt of a moment;* would it not be better than to waste life in this misery of uncertain debate, which neither possesses the resolution of innocence, nor the enjoyments of guilt:—what if I see him no more—But why not see him, ever present as he is to my thoughts;—is he not perhaps more seductive, more fatally lovely, to the eyes of imagination, than of sense? Yes, I *will* see him, I will gaze on him, I will discover *how unlike* the object of my thought, the image of this *dream he is;* and then I shall cease to think of him.

May 16th

I *have* again seen him;—I am yet breathless;—I cannot yet look into my mind; yet let me think—yes, I have thought enough now for life. I shall think my live-long convent hours away.—Oh, he is gloriously beautiful. What thoughts hover around his image; like music streaming before the approach of aerial visitant; like the clouds of amber and rose that invest and mingle with the form of some fine creature of the elements. In such a gay blaze of mental brightness he burst upon me.—When the tints of the evening gathered round the group on the Corso, I hoped, I dared to hope, he might pass—in the obscurity he might pass without seeing me—my sigh would be unheard, my burning cheek would only be felt by me—I might see him, I might even touch him as he passed. Among a group near me, I saw a plume that overtopped the rest—it advanced— oh the tremulous pant, the suffocating swell of expectation;—I could not believe it for very excess of joy—he approached; I saw him not, nor heard him; it was all mist and darkness with me then; *but I felt*—it was he; and I felt he was gone. His departing was like the dying away of a scented gale; rich, languid, overpowering; from that moment there was a delicious sickness in the air; there was a soft oppression at my heart; I could not speak, and had any one spoken to me, I feel I must have answered with my tears. All night have I sat, repeating to myself at long intervals, "I have seen him."—Morning is now dawning through my chamber, yet still is evening and the *Corso* with me.—

May 20th

Can I remain in this state of dotage? Yet dare I look into my heart, he is food and rest to me;—yet I say I do not love; he is thought, and dream, and vision to me;—yet I say I do not love; my prayers are offered to him;—yet I do not love. Oh, whither shall I turn? I am sore beset. Let me fall into the hands of him whom I have offended; rather than that heart which has betrayed and destroyed me. What shall I say "I have sinned?" Must it, must it then be a sin to love?—

May 27th

And this was love; darkly I floated on; I never felt the tide; but when the light breaks, I am on the ocean waste; alone, frozen, aghast.— Had I heard of a tale like this in my days of innocence, how had I condemned the self-deluding, self-betrayed wretch? Oh ye, who boast of virtue yet untried, who defy temptations that mercy yet has spared you! I was once pure like you; like you I was proud. But I have strayed from the fold, I have wandered in the wilderness. The servant of the Lord hath forsaken her first love, the guide of her youth, and gone after strangers. . .

June 3d

It is neither light nor darkness with me now; I am in a mixed and twilight state, would I could sleep. Oh, for a deep, still slumber such as I slept, when I dreamt I did not love; and oh for such dreams that lit that slumber—for those bright bursts of vision, that had drank the meteor's light, and were the forms of heaven.—They are gone—

THEY TALK OF GOING TO Rome: let them carry me where they will: whence is this passiveness?—He has quitted Naples—I smite my breast, but my heart continues to beat there still.—

July 7th

What have a few, a very few months made of me! Oh, heaven! I was so happy, it was a sin to make me miserable. I was absorbed in divine things, dead, though in the world, to the things of the world; alive only to the objects of *that* where I believed my heart and treasure were.

CHARLES MATURIN

Mine were the pure pleasures, the hallowed hopes, the calm, corrected mind; a light that flowed from heaven shed a glad and quiet brightness around me, and I rejoiced to walk in that light. The morning awoke me to prayer; at night I paused upon the blameless day, and sunk to sleep in prayer. I reckoned that every day should be like the last, as free from guilt, as far from pain; that I should float on their equal motion, as on the wings of a cherubim, to that place of which I believed my enjoyment certain and near. Is it so short a space? And am I so already lost? Am I already this feverish, distracted, *guilty* being, who ventures every day a more daring length in indulgence, a length she would have trembled at the preceding one, and while she measures with miserable and reverted eye, the distance she has strayed from the path of peace, feels also that it has brought no nearer the object for which she has wandered till she has lost herself?

July 15th

It came to me cherub-smiling; it rose on me like the morning with her hundred hues and shapes of brightness; joy, and beauty, and splendour, all that is gay and rich in life, all that can seduce the senses and the heart, danced around it in fairy-vision. I looked, and listened, and was destroyed; and this was love. In the smiles of its birth, in the cherub-dawn of young passion, who thought of groans and anguish?—Yet let me acquit heaven; from the first I trembled and I feared; I touched the cup with a faltering lip;—but oh the sweet, sweet draught.—

July 27th

And I took no warning from my distracted devotions; from my long voluptuous day-dreams; from my coldness to better thoughts. *Oh!* if these sufferings would make me hate their cause. If these anguished and consuming hours could make me impatient or resisting, there might be hope; but, oh! not tears flowing for ages, could wash away the characters his first and single sight wrote on my heart.

Day and night my mind seems to hang over that with silent and helpless contemplation. Nothing rouses me, except to an impatience of disturbance. Guilty I cling to it. Miserable I cling to it. Self-condemned I cling to it. I have sunk into a dull and lethargic passiveness, and the reproaches of conscience sound like the storm in the ear of sheltered dotage, vexing his deafness, but not disturbing his sluggish comforts.

I pray—while a lurking hope tells me my prayers will not avail; I vary their form; I seem to redouble my earnestness, while something dares to whisper me, I would recal them, did I fear they would be granted.

I determined on some occupation for the day, to hide from myself how it is always occupied; and while I think I am engaged, a consciousness that to think of *him* will be its only employment, seems to mock at my efforts, and I feel it without emotion—without a wish to resist, or a fear to yield. Resolutions formed with a consciousness they will not be kept—the purposes of life maintaining a faint war with its employments. Tears, stifled by indulgences, from which their feeble remonstrances take away pleasure, while they leave the guilt; and prayers contradicted at the moment they are offered up, by the whispers of a rebel heart.—

Such am I become!—object of fatal passion—come and see what you have made me?—No.—Come not to see me rejoice in my guilt—come not to cast away compassion on sufferings whose enumeration only gives me a strange and dreadful delight.

July 23

'Tis in vain—I resist no longer—I cannot live, and not be this being—or to cease to be guilty, I must cease to be—Nor dare I wish that; nor do I wish it—This misery is but too precious to me—all that I have ever tasted of pleasure should not purchase from me, love's lonely, bitter, midnight tear. And dare I call this suffering? Oh, no.—No, no. His smile; his wicked, witching smile, upbraids me when I do.

His eye is on me, it seems to ask me, Do I complain?—Strange and wondrous being, what hast thou done with me?—His image comes to my soul like the moon in the night of storms. Amid the dark masses—amid the billowy ridges—amid the mixed and angry streaks—she bursts in brief and rejoicing splendour, and gilding their thwarted and fighting forms with beauty, while the vexed traveller looks up and blesses the sight for a moment.

July 25

And is it a crime to love?—Have I changed the passion, or the name?—In my childhood, I *loved* the light of the setting sun—the gush of the twilight breeze—the pale and wandering moon—glossing with her light the fleecy fretwork of a summer sky. I said I loved them, can I not love him, as I loved them—with sinless, placid, untroubled love! Is he not the work of the same hand: were they not both formed to be loved? Is it my curse, that *I* must mingle guilt with the feelings which all others indulge in innocence? Can I not think of him as of them— bright, beautiful, distant, impassable? Can I not sit and gaze life away, without a wish to soar upwards?—No, no. These words fall from my pen, they come not from the heart.

The wild and lawless thought, the wish of the dream, I dare not tell myself of, teach me a vestal cannot love a human being, as she loved a moon-beam in her childhood.

July 26

There are a thousand ebbs and flows of feeling, known only to the mind that *loves;* but which make me tremble every moment, lest my perturbation should discover them to others. His name I hear without emotion, when any other member of his family is mentioned by it—but when applied to *him*, when *he* is talked of by the most careless speaker, my frame thrills, my eyes grow misty, ruined as I am, my mind smiles with a sad and guilty joy at that name—

His name I scarce ever dare pronounce. My throat swells when I would breathe it; but how I delight to hear it uttered, and how many wretched pretexts of subtlety I employ, to introduce a conversation that will involve the mention of him; and when it succeeds, and when his name *is* mentioned, do they not see how I pause, and how I tremble! Alas, what if they do? Am I not beheld by an eye, to shrink from which, the detection of a world would be well exchanged? . . .

. . . My sufferings are very great; who but me has known misery without relief; who but me has known despair without hope: we deceive ourselves with sounds: when we talk of despair, we mean not, that relief is impossible, but that relief is distant or doubtful. . . But whither shall I turn—is there one speck in my horizon? No, no, no. Dark and deserted, I wade through floods of desperation. I struggle without vigour. I rise without consolation. I sink without hope. In those hours of intolerable anguish, when the mind, wearied with suffering, and stung to frantic energy, is driven, like the importunate widow, to knock loud and eager at the door of hope. In those hours, I have said to myself—who or what shall aid me? Shew me difficulties to be overcome—shew me sufferings to be endured. Give me to contend with all earthly and possible things; and I will do it. What will I not do? But I am as dust in the whirlwind. I am as a leaf in the torrent, that has swept away the forest. The force and current of things bear me along. To please *me*, the order of nature must be inverted. The Deity must change. The woman must seek the man, and be accepted. The vestal must be perjured with impunity, therefore I turn to hope, I turn to time, I turn to space: I turn to self, (for to self, endless in resource, and exhaustless in consolation, we turn and cling last), and all *is despair*.—But shall I dare to say so? I have made my purchase—yes—I have sold my soul for a smile—I am betrayed with a kiss.—Oh! my love, my love—hast thou not asked too much. Oh! look not on me with that smile of innocent loveliness—Glance not on me that fatal, fatal eye—Move not before me, with that witching form. Do not, or I shall think all, all too little. But surely thou hast asked much, my love. . .

July 27

Of the moon—I sometimes think he gazes on it when I gaze, and then a gush of tearful pleasure fills my eye, and I wipe it away to catch the moment of simultaneous gazing. Of the breeze—I guess it is cooling him, and then I spread my parched and pallid cheek to it, to taste pleasure with him.

But my supreme delight is to breathe his name to the ear of midnight, with ideot stealth; in the deep and silent hour, when the night-vapour, fine as an infant's breath, stands in the air—when the leaf of the poplar and the aspen is unmoved—when there is a hissing in the ear for very stillness—then I love to lean from my casement, and utter his name—once and softly: then swift, and bright, and thronging myriads of images, float in glittering play around me.

Then the early morn, the tepid glow, the vernal birth of cherub-passion, rushes on me. The first meeting—the rapturous flutter of young alarm—the expansion of a new sense—the opening burst of a world of pleasure. These are with me—his name makes them present. I am absorbed in them, I rush on with their unconscious flow. Some image of new and daring indulgence arrests me—I start, I recoil—but I only recoil to see I have gone so far. 'Tis less impossible to go too far, than to return. I hesitate—I am lost. . . when I recover, I am weeping: thinking I ought to shed the tear of penitence, and feeling it is only the tear of passion. . .

And is it a crime to love?—I cannot unite the thoughts of guilt and him—when I bend over my mind—when his image smiles on me—when the gush of early pleasure fills my heart—I am no longer guilty—I am no more wretched—I am only the happy visionary, who has given up life for a dream of joy. . .

Yet, sometimes, I am sorely smitten with fear and perplexity. Sometimes I would give worlds to know if I am thus utterly lost—if there is no hope for one who has dared to love. I have leant from my window in the anguish of my solicitude—I have gazed on the stars walking in their brightness—I have asked them, Is there any hope? I determined to decide it by the first I should see fall to the right—and I dared to dream, that he who regulates the sparrow's flight, might direct the fall of the meteor for good to his waiting, trembling creature. I lingered, and there fell one to the right—and then—I felt it gave no ease to me.

Returning through the portico this evening, I met a dog, who looked wistfully at me—the mute, melancholy eye caught me—I attempted to go—he continued to gaze on me—In the importunity of my misery, I said—art thou a spirit—and hast thou a power to serve me?—I tore myself away in time to save my reason.

"And was there such sensibility," said Ippolito, bursting out; "and was it suffered to pine to death? Was there such a heart? And was it permitted to break? Oh thou lorn and lovely trembler! had I been the object of thy affections, strong and gentle as they were, how would I have sought, how I would have soothed thee, how would I have kissed away the precious, precious tears, and looked in thy timid eye for the first beam of restored hope?"—"These are but sounds of softness," said Cyprian; "alas, what could you have done for one whom nature and society condemned."—"Nature," said Ippolito, "is no enemy to love; and for society, I would have borne her in my arms through the world, while one remained for me; I would have resisted every person that opposed; I would have fought with every man who dared to asperse her; I would have borne her to some quiet retreat, hallowed by solitude and love; for her I would have despised and relinquished a world that could neither understand nor taste such enjoyments as ours; and in the breathing pause of quiet delight, smiling I would have asked her, had love no counterbalance for his pains?" "Dreadful, delicious, maddening sounds," murmured Cyprian; "they had undone her; blessed be the saints she heard them not; shame was not added to her sufferings; she died by draughts of slow and cruel poison; but not the maddening cup of feverish impurity: of love she died, but pure and penitent. Had she heard such sounds, even dying she would have felt the racking wish; the luxurious tumult; the groan of death had been mixed with the sigh of desire; you could not have kept the sinner on earth; and you would have rent a penitent from heaven. But no, no, no; she slumbers in the dark bed; she cannot hear those sounds, her ear is as dull as the dead."—"Boy," said Ippolito, "it would have saved us both; she had not died of disappointed passion, and I had been spared many a dark and feverish hour.—But I wander; I was not the object of the passion you describe."—"You, and you alone;" said Cyprian, with a burst of feeling—"You she loved; and by you was she destroyed. For you she tempted the dangers of guilty pleasure; for you she dared to wish, to hope, to madden; for you she trembled, she sorrowed, and she wept; will you believe, she loved, Montorio, she died for you." "For me—for me," exclaimed Ippolito, while his frame quivered, and a glow of lovely shame suffused his cheeks and forehead; "why then did she not live for me? Cyprian, you only mock my vanity."—"No," said Cyprian, who had risen, and whose whole form mantled, and was buoyed up with sudden animation,—"no, I deceive you not; her spirit hovers near us, to attest the truth, to witness the avowal. Hear me, Montorio, would you have loved her?"—"You but mock my credulity;" said Ippolito, smiling;—"No, by her presence, by her near presence, which I feel this moment, I mock not. Answer my question, could you have loved her, Montorio?"—"Could I?" replied Ippolito, darting his eye to heaven, "if her spirit be indeed present, it is satisfied with the homage of my heart." "It *is* present," said Cyprian, eagerly, "it *is* present, and it must hover near us, till it be absolved."—"Enthusiast, what would you mean, what would you ask?"—"Imagine me her for a moment," said Cyprian, sinking at Ippolito's feet, and hiding his face—"Imagine me her; give me one kiss." "Enthusiastic boy." "Give me but one, and her spirit shall depart, pleased and absolved." "Visionary, you do what you will with me; I never kissed one of my own sex before; but do what you will with me;" half blushing, half pouting, he offered his red lip, Cyprian touched it and fainted.

CHARLES MATURIN

X

Letter from Annibal di Montorio

I HAVE BEEN SO TOSSED with doubt and distraction, since I wrote to you, that, I have been unable to form one sane reflection, or to divide events from the feelings that accompanied them. I deferred the continuance of my letters, therefore, in hopes of writing them at length in calmness, and in ease. The hope has been fruitless. The *extraordinary circumstances* in which I have been engaged, have deprived me of all distinct powers of discrimination and reflection; *they* are so woven into my habits of thought, that I feel myself able to do little more than to describe them; and even that, not as a spectator would, and as a philosophic mind would wish to do, but with all the confused perceptions, the superstitious minuteness, and the weak amplifications of real and present fear. I know not whether you will prefer this to a more composed account or not; but if you do not, you must compound with necessity; for it is the only one my present state of mind enables me to furnish you with.

The night was approaching, on which I had determined to re-visit the apartments, and to suffer Michelo to tell his tale. I remembered how I had once been overpowered by fear, and once by pleasure; and I now determined to collect every power, and confirm every resolution that could preserve me from the influence of weakness or of deception.

I even perused some of the old legends of our library, that abound in adventures similar to mine; I endeavoured to act a personal part in the narrative, and to shun the weakness, or acquire the fortitude, which their various agents exhibited. I passed some time in this mental disciplining; but I find ineffectually, if its influence was to have preserved me from fear.

As the hour approached, my wish to view the spot I was to visit so soon became irrepressible. I ventured on the terrace that leads to the tower, and I found myself under the walls of the apartment; its appearance without resembled that within, dark, lonely, and deserted. I saw a range of windows, which from their direction, I conceived lit the long passage through which I had been conducted by Michelo. They were narrow, and dismantled, and at a distance from the ground, but many cavities in the walls, together with fragments of the battlements that had fallen on the terrace, assisted me to climb to their level; I now looked round me with security; I had taken a time at which the servants were engaged in a distant part of the castle; and I enjoyed the leisure of full gratification. I looked through the window, it lit the passage as I had imagined; the passage appeared, as on the night I had visited it, damp, and dusky, and solitary; but, as, by holding my face parallel to the window, I looked down its deep length, I imagined I saw a figure issuing from the wall at the other end, and approaching with a slow, unsteady motion. That it was a human figure, I could only conjecture from its loose garments; of which, the darkness still prevented me from distinguishing the shape or habit.

It advanced—nor was it with a pleasant emotion that I recollected it must pass by the window at which I hung. It advanced, its head was covered; one arm was extended, and the dark drapery which hung from it, shrouded the face. I was so absorbed in wonder and curiosity, that till it drew within a few paces of the window, I forgot my station would discover me; I relaxed my hold, and concealed my head under the large pediment of the window. It passed; and though I felt through the shattered casement-pannels, the air impelled by its approach, its step gave no sound; I raised my head, it had passed; and I saw it floating away in the distant obscurity of the passage. I lingered long under the casement; but there was neither sound nor object. Of what I had seen, I knew not what to think; that it was not Michelo, I was certain; and no other being had means to enter those walls, except by such means as I was almost impelled to believe that form was master of. I loitered in vague and unsatisfied conjecture, till the hour at which Michelo had promised to attend me; when that arrived, he joined me, and employing the same precautions, we reached the apartments unobserved. Michelo again paused, to recover himself from fear and from haste; and I examined the apartments, with more leisure, and a better light than the last evening had allowed.

"Signor," said Michelo, recalling me, "I have led you hither that I might mention without interruption, and without fear, what in any other part of the castle I might not safely mention, not even in my own remote turret, at midnight; I came hither to shun the suspicions which I fear are already excited; those observations which I dread our frequent conferences may suggest, and which it is impossible to exercise here." Of this position I felt not quite assured; but concealing what I had seen, desired him to proceed.—My attention was that moment excited by a strange appearance on the floor. "Can this, Michelo, be the effect of the shade which these closed windows throw on the floor?" Michelo was silent. "See where it spreads in long, and dusky streaks, and ends just beside that door."—"It is blood," said the old man, shivering.—"Blood!" I repeated; "this stain that overspreads half the room! impossible; to produce this there must have been a massacre, not a murder in this apartment." "It *is* blood," said the old man, rising, and feebly following me, as I examined the traces—"here it fell; and here, splashes of it are on this wall, as if it had been forced out by violence; and at this door, all appearances of it cease."—I paused; all those dispersed causes and appearances, that had hitherto floated vaguely in my mind, exciting only a partial and unproductive emotion of fear, or wonder, or anxiety, now rushed on it with collected force, and produced one appalling conviction. "Here has been murder, Michelo; and you who know in whose veins this blood has flowed; you who were perhaps present at that hour, a witless to that deed; you preserve an obdurate silence; though perhaps your strange sufferings are owing to the visits of the victim; though perhaps it lingers near this spot, where its blood was poured, unabsolved, and unrequired; though perhaps its shroudless form was seen tonight, wandering in the passages of this chamber"—"Pursue your path," said the old man, with solemnity, "whither a hand mightier than mine seems to conduct you; I can lead you but a little way; my time is brief, and my task restrained; I would willingly have followed on, but a power, I may not resist, with-holds me."—Pursuing the traces, we had reached the other apartment, here they had ceased; but in my impatience of discovery, I again adverted, to the jarring looseness of the floor, and the damp and death-like steam that floated through it.

I strode across the room, it shook under me; frantic with impatience, I resolved to rend the boards asunder; a task my strength would have been easily equal to, and which would probably give some relief or object to my mind, which now could scarce support its feelings, wrought up as they had been to a pitch, solemn, severe, and terrible.—"Forbear, forbear, Signor," said Michelo, "solitary as these apartments seem, there is one who visits them; the Count, your father, I have too sure proof, repairs, at the appointed time, to these chambers; oh, fear his vengeance, should he discover that other feet beside his own, had trod these bloody floors, his vengeance is terrible!"—"Twice," said I, eagerly grasping at his words, "twice, Michelo, have you uttered these words; that they have a meaning beyond common fear, is evident; and whatever that meaning may be, I will know it before I quit this spot: what have you known or felt of his vengeance?" "His vengeance is terrible," said a voice, deep and distinct, beside me. "Again you have repeated it," I said, for impatience had confused my perceptions. "I spoke not, I breathed not," said Michelo, aghast, and clinging to me; "a voice issued from the wall; quit this spot, for holy St. Gennaro's sake, quit this spot, if yet we may quit it alive."

I was not, like him, congealed and rendered helpless by fear; but I suffered perhaps more from the keenness and strength of my own perceptions. Resist it as we may, the presence, or the fear of the presence of the dead, is almost intolerable. We endure it in a tale, because it *is* a tale; and the consciousness of fiction produces a balance with the pain of credulity. But I was oppressed by evidence that appeared irresistible, and I felt the natural fear, which I have in common with the peasant, and the child, and which my improved perceptions perhaps magnified with many an unfelt and subtle circumstance of addition. I deliberated a moment; a gush of visionary heroism came to my mind, and I resolved to examine the flooring, when Michelo, unable to speak, grasped my arm, and pointed to the opposite wall. My eye followed his involuntarily; they rested on the figure of an armed man in the tapestry, whose bold and prominent outlines rendered it even strongly visible in that dim light. A weapon which it held, was pointed in the direction I was about to explore; the head was thrown back, and the features of a strong profile were fixed on the same direction. As I gazed on it, the large eye appeared to live; it moved; it looked at me; it turned to the spot, to which the arm pointed, and the arm vibrated with a slow and palpable motion; then all became lifeless and discoloured and dead, as an artificial form. What hat I had seen and heard, was enough for me. I became inflamed, impelled, exalted; a certain supernal dignity mingled with my feelings, I felt myself the summoned agent of destiny, yet not the less did I feel that I was surrounded by horrors; that I was treading where the living inhabited not; that I was called by voices nature shudders to hear. But they appeared to me the instruments by which I was appointed to work out some great purpose, and I grasped them with a convulsed but daring hand.

I began to examine the apartment. In every part of the wainscot under it, pannels had been detached and shattered by age and neglect. But they only betrayed the solid wall. One that appeared less impaired than the rest, I examined therefore more closely. It resisted; but

CHARLES MATURIN

strength, such as I felt at that moment, was not easily resisted; and I soon wrenched it from the wainscot. The cloud of dust that followed, was soon dispersed, and I discovered steps rugged and unequal, and feebly lit, winding within it. I addressed a few words of comfort and courage to Michelo, who leant exhausted against the wall, and prepared to descend them. He attempted feebly to dissuade me; I heard him not. The stairs, down which I attempted in vain to descend steadily, appeared from the roughness of their formation, to have been scooped out of the wall; a discoloured light seemed to stream on them from a grating which appeared at a vast height in the roof above me. The dust that rose under every step, scarce permitted me to distinguish them; and the heavy steams I had observed in the adjacent chamber, seemed to constitute the very atmosphere of this passage.

The steps, decending for some time, terminated in a door which no key could open, and no effort could force; and Michelo, who had now followed me, declared he knew not, nor could conjecture from his knowledge of the castle, where that door conducted. Here all progress seemed to be suspended; and I looked around me with a desponding eye. That some secret was within my reach, I was convinced; and to lose its knowledge, after so much expectation and toil, appeared insupportable. My very exertions reproached me with my want of success. The very dull and murky stillness of the place seemed to offer a mockery to my inquietude.

Reluctantly as I returned, still examining every object, I observed a part of the wall, where there seemed a regular fracture, running through the stones in nearly a square direction; I applied my hand to it, it shook under the pressure, and a large portion of detached rubbish fell at my feet. I felt inspirited; with the assistance of Michelo, I soon discovered, under a thin coat of plaster, that mouldered at the touch, a door, that had nothing else to conceal or to fasten it. I dragged it open, it discovered a dim cavity, barely wide enough to admit me. I entered it, stooping and contracted, and from its narrow dimensions (partly by feeling, and partly from the pale light the grating still afforded me,) soon discovered a kind of rude chest, disjointed and ill-secured. With an impatience which urged me to violence, I endeavoured to rend it open. From the loose and lumbering rattle of its contents, I had a shuddering suspicion what they were. I yet persisted; Michelo, who appeared animated by a sudden impulse of his own, endeavoured to assist me. With the feverish strength of eager weakness I succeeded. The decayed pannels gave way.

Ippolito, oh Ippolito!—my hand touched the mealy and carious bones of a skeleton! the dry limbs clattered as the pannels fell about. The light fell on the head, as it lay, and gave a deadlier hollowness to the cavities of the mouth and eyes. Panting and pale, I staggered back; the heat of exertion and pursuit was over; I had reached a terrible point of proof; the mute and ghastly witness before me spoke. Murder hurtled in mine ears, as I viewed it, yet still I was uncertain and disquieted. The crime was revealed, but the object and agents were still unknown.

Meanwhile I saw Michelo bend over the corpse, and examine it with attention; I saw him shudder, and clasp his hands. There is a state of mind, in which we only converse by actions. I hastened to him, and entering the den, surveyed the skeleton again. Michelo, with strong and speechless expression, pointed to one of its wasted arms; *the hand had been severed from it.* We looked on each other as conscious that each was brooding on his own convictions. At length I spake, and felt myself articulate with difficulty. "Michelo, does your knowledge of past events, suggest any thing that might explain this spectacle? If it may, oh forbear to wrong your own soul, and the soul of the murdered, by longer concealment." The old man smote his breast, and crossed himself. "I am innocent," he murmured, "I am innocent; but this object brings to my memory a report I had long forgotten, and which, when I had heard, I considered but as some tale which ignorance had invented to dissolve the mystery of that terrible night. It was whispered by many, that, on that night, some one had been privately brought into the castle, murdered, and interred in some unknown part of it; who he was, and for what cause, or by whom he was dispatched, none pretended to tell."

This account, though it increased my suspicions, did not diminish my perplexity. That some unhallowed deed had been done on that night, so often referred to, seemed certain; the hand that had done it, appeared shrouded from all human view or inquisition.—"Michelo! one question more, and I shall cease for ever to importune you: Do you believe this to be the body of my uncle, of Count Orazio?"—"From many circumstances, Signor, I should have been led to fear, this was the body of the late Count; but others would seem to contradict it.—But why should I wish to suggest to you, that he was murdered?"

"Here, it is said," he continued, "bells have tolled, and forms have moved.—Sometimes, long processions, with blazing lights, have been seen gliding past the windows; and sometimes a burst of voices, of no human tone, have been heard chaunting the funeral chaunt."

CHARLES MATURIN

"These are tales, Michelo, told and believed promiscuously every where by the vulgar and the timid."—"Aye, but Signor, I myself have seen"—"What have you seen?" "Things, Signor, that prevented my being much surprised at the discovery we have recently made. I have seen lights moving, and heard sounds issuing from those apartments, at a time when I knew no human cause could have produced either." "Were the appearances you mention, similar to those that occurred in the ruined chapel?" "Ask me no more, Signor," said the old man, "as far, and farther than was in my power to gratify it, your curiosity has been satisfied: let us quit this dismal place."

His words seemed to awake me from a trance. That momentary courage, which the emergency had invested me with, seemed suddenly to desert me. I looked around me; two lonely beings, shuddering over a discovery which conveyed nothing but terror to them, by the dim evening light, in the remote and long-deserted towers of an ancient castle, far from the comfort of human aid or presence, and feeling that they were unable to encounter an additional circumstance or object of fear, yet dreading lest, while they lingered, some other would overtake them;—two such beings I felt myself and Michelo to be, and started at the conviction. The confidence of the delegate of heaven was over: I felt myself a timid human being, encompassed by things, and the fear of things, which nature shrinks from; and only anxious to escape by a blind and hasty extrication from them;—like a child, that by shutting his eyes, and walking speedily past some spot of terror, imagines itself to be safe.

I turned from the revolting spectacle before me: I looked along the dim and narrow passage; I wondered at own temerity in exploring it. A few moments past, and I felt as if nothing could check my progress; at the present, nothing could impel me to pursue it. For a moment I wondered at myself, and almost ascribed the change to an influence that made part of the wonders of the place. But the lassitude that mixed with my timidity, dissolved the wonder. I discovered it was only the natural remission of over-stimulated feeling; and that if heaven was pleased to employ my agency, it would prevent the confidence of its instrument being inflated by presumption, by leaving him at intervals to the infirmities of his nature, to his common habits of impulse and cessation, to those usual ebbs and flows of mind, which prove to us, that our best frames are of imperfect influence, and interrupted length.

I assisted Michelo, by the light that yet remained, to fill up the cavity with the stones and rubbish we had removed from it, and then prepared to quit the stairs. As we returned, I endeavoured to forbear looking at its dark and silent walls; at the roof, where the light appeared so pale and so distant, it reminded me of that which streams on the hollow eye of a captive, through the bars of his dungeon. Nay, on the rude, uncouth steps themselves, that seemed just fit to be pressed by the assassin, stealing to the bed of sleep, or bearing away his prey to deposit it in some den such as we had discovered. But, wherever I looked, I found some food for sombre thought. I quickened my pace.

In our hurried passage through the cabinet and the chamber, we walked with silent and breathless fear, grasping each other, and endeavouring to fix our eyes on the floor; yet feeling they were every moment involuntarily raised to meet the approach of something we did not dare to intimate to each other. We had now reached the stairs, by which we were hasting to descend, when we distinctly heard, in the apartment we had just quitted, the loud tread of a foot that seemed to be pursuing us. Michelo, stupified by fear, was lingering at the top of the stairs; with a desperate effort, I dragged him along with me, and hurried down.

The tread came yet louder and quicker behind us; I dared not to look behind; I rushed on with headlong blindness, dragging my breathless companion with me.

The foot came nearer and nearer; I could feel the stairs bending under its pressure behind me; every moment I dreaded to feel the indenture of its "fiery fang." But we had now reached the door communicating with the passage—I dragged it open, and with that involuntary provision, which fear often makes against its objects, with averted head, I drew it after me, and locked it, while I thought I heard the murmurs of a voice within, but whether its tones were those of pain or terror, I could not discover. Whatever might be the power of our pursuer, he then ceased to exert it; no sound pursued us, and we encountered no object. We made a hasty and silent progress through the passage, and regained the inhabited part of the castle without observation.

By these events, I have neither been enlightened nor assured; I have been only perplexed and terrified. I have reflected, but without attaining conviction. I have debated, but without forming a resolution. Sometimes my exertion appears temerity, and sometimes my supineness cowardice!

CHARLES MATURIN

Am I the agent of heaven, or the dupe of fear and deception?—Was the voice I heard, intended to summon or forbid?—Has the arm been bared to beckon or to repel?—Shall I pause, or shall I proceed?

In this dark and turbid state, I look at the picture of Erminia—and taste a momentary, a delicious calm. Adio.

XI

Ut assidens implumibus pullis avis
Serpentium allapsus timet
Magis relictis; non, ut adsit, auxilii
Latura plus præsentibus—

—HORACE

Thus, if the mother-bird forsake
Her unfledged young, she dreads the gliding snake,
With deeper agonies afraid,
Not that her presence could afford them aid.

—FRANCIS

By the time this letter had arrived at Naples, Ippolito's habits of gloom and abstraction had increased. The scenes of passing enjoyment, he had some times permitted to checquer that gloom, he had now relinquished; and except the hours that he attended that summons, his whole time was occupied in feeding gloomy thought with solitude. When this letter arrived, none of the servants would venture to disturb their once-undreaded master; and Cyprian, who heard them debating, seized the opportunity of venturing into his presence. Ippolito had been for some hours alone in his own apartment: Cyprian, with the letter in his hand, knocked at the door; a voice, of which the tones had never been harsh before, demanded, "Who was there?" "I am afraid to answer to that voice," said Cyprian, "speak in another tone, and I will say, 'tis Cyprian." "You may enter," said Ippolito. Cyprian approached timidly. His master was extended on a sopha; his eyes were shaded by his hand; his attitude bespoke a wish to counter-balance mental inquietude with bodily ease. "This is a letter from your brother," said Cyprian, offering it with an unnoticed hand. After a moment's pause, he left it down, and placed himself before the sopha with folded arms. "Why do you wait?" said Ippolito, in a hollow and languid tone. "I know not why I wait," said Cyprian, whose anguish now burst forth in tears, and who hurried towards the door—"I know not why I *live;* there is neither joy nor use in me *now;* I know not why I live." Blind with his tears, he endeavoured in vain to open the door, when Ippolito, starting from the sopha, intercepted him. "Pardon me, Cyprian, I knew not it was you; I heard the tones of your voice, but I felt not you were near me. Pardon me, Cyprian. For many days past, my senses have been dull and distempered; the vigils of my nights have disturbed them. Even now, while I gaze upon you, you seem to me not as you ought; and should you change while I look upon you, to some strange shape, such as I have lately seen, I could scarce feel surprise."

"Oh, do not talk thus," said Cyprian, "what shapes and what sufferings are these you talk of? What dream of visionary anguish pursues and preys upon you? What invisible arm has torn you from life and enjoyment, and chained you down in a prison-house of pain and solitude? Are you persecuted by the power of the living or of the dead? I am importunate, perhaps, for I am fearless. Two days—two dreadful days, I have been deprived of your sight; your sight which is the very food of my existence. A thousand times in that period have I approached your door—listening for a cheerful sound or motion to encourage me to enter: with a breaking heart I wandered back, for I heard only your heavy groans. But I am so miserable; all fear of your displeasure has ceased; I will even support that, if you will not drive me from you; chide, and look sternly on me, if you can, but let me be near you: the sound of your voice will repay me for any thing it can utter. The image of your anguish, when absent, and imagined, is a thousand times more terrible, than present; or perhaps the sight of you, makes all suffering light."—

"You would be near me," said Ippolito, appearing to collect with difficulty what had been said; "You do not know, then, that misery is contagious?" "Misery!" echoed Cyprian, "whence, oh! whence, is this perverse repining of self-inflicted suffering? If *you* murmur, who shall not be suffered to groan? Oh, too lovely—too brilliant—too bright, as you are—more like the gay phantom of a youthful wish, than a human being, the destined partaker of infirmity and suffering—you seem almost without a wish, as without a fear. What is this sirocco of the mind, that bursts forth in the summer-noon of life, and blasts the freshness of its enjoyments? Why need I enumerate blessings you cannot be blind to—for of the distinctions of nature none are forgetful? Why need I remind you what, oh! what you are?" "You need not remind me what I am. I know, I feel it but too well. I am a pursued, a haunted, a persecuted being. The helpless prey of an invisible tormentor. Cyprian, a cruel, an inward fire consumes me. The springs of life, the sources of enjoyment, are dried up within me. I feel the energies of my mind seared and withered by the contemplation of a terrible subject, as the eyes would be, by being fixed on an object of intense and scorching heat; yet I cannot withdraw them. One subject, one only subject is involuntarily present with me—wherever I turn I behold it—whatever I do it is mingled with. Nay, when from the weariness of over-wrought suffering, I become almost vacant of thought or feeling, a dumb and sullen sense of pain mixes its leaven with those moments of unconsciousness.

You have wrung this from me, Cyprian, by your cruel pity, superfluously cruel to yourself and to me. Your sufferings may be increased by the communication of mine; but mine cannot be diminished by your participation of them. I bore the storm long to shelter you; now you have exposed your feebleness to it; and I can no longer enjoy the dignity of solitary suffering, or the aid of valid support."—"Oh, no," said Cyprian, "you know not the power and office of strong affection; it loves not to mix its beam with the summer-blaze of joy; to add its note to the choral song of flattery and pleasure; it reserves them for the dark, disastrous hour, when the amazed sufferer looks round on a desert world; when, what he thought he held, is dust within his grasp; when, what he hoped, to trust to, is a reed under his steps. Then is the power, and the hour of strong affection; then it rushes to him; it grasps him by the cold hand; it speaks words of comfort in his stunned and frozen ears; it clings to him with all the strength of its being, with powers stronger than suffering and death; it abides the conflict of the dark hour; and enters the valley of the shadow of death, with its companion. For such is its true nature and power; such emergencies only develope and realize them; among such only it expands it powers, it feels its existence; nay, it seeks its reward. Tell me not therefore of sorrow or of suffering; 'tis therefore I seek, and will not leave you. Something whispers me, this is an hour of confidence, not of dejection; that I can do much to serve and to save you; that I can perform something that will make men wonder at the energy of zealous weakness. Montorio, I love you, I love you; and to that name nothing is impossible. Montorio, I will examine your heart; and you will confess the cause, when I have discovered it."—"Forbear, my gentle, my darling boy, forbear; you spread your little slender branches to the storm that heeds you not; in passing it will lay you in the dust, and rush to me unobstructed. Cyprian, I have had a sore struggle; the enemy has assailed me with terrible strength once and again; my strength and my defences are declining; and he will yet prevail; yes, he will prevail, and have me yet in his dark thrall."

"Oh why do we thus magnify the trivial distresses of life," said Cyprian, "with words of such melancholy and mysterious import, that while we listen to them, we almost persuade ourselves we are suffering something humanity never suffered before, and claim such dignity from their support, or such wonder from their confession, that at length we begin to find a delight in misery. You have perhaps encountered some common evil, some visitation of human infirmity, or of youthful deviation; your mind, generous, noble, and fostered by long luxury, starts from the prospect of pain, or the recollection of error. But fear not yet; yours *must, must* have been a venial one; and if your own reflections have anticipated the censures of society, you may listen to *them* with the calmness of reestablished rectitude, nor suffer them to interrupt the even direction of the mind, that has regained the path of right." "And do I hear Cyprian," said Ippolito, "confounding the complexions of good and evil, and teaching an honourable mind to forego that susceptibility of praise from which it derives its best security, as well as its highest reward? Is this my monitor?" "Oh forgive me, forgive me," said Cyprian, "for *your own* sake; 'tis *you* have corrupted my judgment and my heart. My love for you has made me almost annihilate the distinctions of good and evil. When I look on you, Montorio, I cannot believe you guilty, your mind I cannot think less perfect than your form; and the dreadful deception practised on my own judgment, I endeavour, with guilty fondness, to extend to yours. How have I laboured to restore you to the paths of purity and peace, from which your lavish youth, and glowing temptations had caused a noble heart to deviate! How have I watched and warned! How have I toiled and importuned! How have I trembled and prayed for *you!* This one great point and object of my life, what could compel me to counteract? What, but the strong affection that compelled me to undertake it. I find I cannot bear to behold you suffer. I saw you erring, and I hazarded life; yes, hazarded life, to recal and reclaim you. But when I saw you suffer, I could only weep, and be guilty; I forgot the great purpose of my mission; I forgot I was your monitor; and remembered only I loved; forgive me, Montorio, for your own sake forgive me."—"I will forgive you every thing, Cyprian, but this waste of lavish love, on a wretch whom it wounds but cannot profit"—"Oh yet, do not say so: I have great resources; more than of hope or of advice; substantial resources.

What is this heavy load of mind? Montorio, I have marked your nightly wanderings. Have you been seduced to the feverish vigils of the gamesters? have you become the wretched thing of calculations and chances; the agitated sport of knavish skill; the ruined dupe of confederate deception? Oh thank the blessed saints for the wholesome lesson of your ruin. In that dreadful pursuit, to succeed is certainly to be lost; though to be ruined, is possibly to be saved. Be not yet dejected; the riches of your house are immense, and your father, though I have heard stern and severe, is proud, and will not suffer the honour of his family to be impaired by debt: or should your losses not require the fortunes of a house to repair them, I have resources, Montorio; resources, happily stored up against this hour of pressure; take them, my beloved, take all."—"Forbear, Cyprian, forbear; your conjecture is erroneous: mine are not the vigils of a gamester: miserable as I know them to be, I could almost wish they were."—"Oh what is this," said Cyprian, distressed and amazed, "what is this more terrible than misery and ruin? Do I read another cause in your pale and listless lip; in your darkened cheek; in your fixed eye? Such, they say, are the looks of those who love. Do you love, Montorio? Alas, is it possible you can love, and yet despair! Oh, no, no; too happy woman! too happy, methinks, for the indulgence of allowed caprice; too happy, for the petty, prescriptive triumph of her disdain; she cannot have punished herself to give you pain; or if she has, let her behold you now; now in this seducing shade of melancholy beauty; and she must—she will—oh why that groan, Montorio? Can you, oh can you be the victim of love, of lawless passion? Alas, what shall I say! I have heard of wretched, wretched women, who can love for gold; who would take deformity and decrepitude to their arms, instead of even *you*, if they could outweigh you in the price of their body's and soul's perdition; for such you cannot long languish: alas, what am I saying? Oh spare me, spare me, my beloved; make me not the reluctant agent of pollution; tear not from my agonized affection, its long, its last, cherished integrity. Alas, alas, such is the madness of my guilty love; I can bear to see you criminal, but cannot, cannot bear to see you miserable."—"Perplex yourself no more with this mental casuistry; torture yourself no longer with the superfluous remorse of imputed guilt; I cannot give you the consolation of thinking mine is a case of common suffering, or within the reach of ordinary relief; would, oh would I were the subject of any, or all the sufferings you could name, *rather than what I am.*"

Cyprian was silent from the perplexity of severe dismay. At every gradation of their conference, he had drawn closer to Ippolito, and now pressing his hand, he murmured feebly, "If that last, and dreadful guilt, the brand of civilized society, the dreadful imposition of an abitrary phantom, be yours; if you have hurried from earth, and from hope, your rash, offending brother; and if for a crime man could not forgive, you have sent him to answer for all before the Judge; his course unfinished, his task unfulfilled, his soul unabsolved, his salvation unobtained; if you have found that what society can palliate and pardon, conscience cannot; oh yet is there a dawn of hope! If the agents of justice or of revenge pursue you, let us fly, oh let us fly, this *land* of perverted and bloody manners; where the sore alternative of infamy or guilt, urges the revolting hand of virtue, to deeds, *its* praise cannot purify, nor its sanction expiate. Oh, let us fly, and the prayers of good and holy men shall be with us for good: there is a blessed virtue in those, and the offices of our holy faith, to obtain peace and remission for the soul so sore beset."—"Can murder then be forgiven? and if the bare crime, under strong temptation, and most urgent cause, hardly dare plead for mercy; what shall be said for murder, impelled by no motive, justified by no pretext, sheltered by no confederacy? For guilt, laborious, determined, inveterate? And this, oh all this is nothing to the shades of this dark vision."—"I understand not this terrible language," said Cyprian, who looked aghast. "If you have any thing to disclose, tell it quickly, for my senses are dull, and I am wearied with pleading." "I *have* a tale to tell, but it is not for your ears;" he rose hastily, he grasped Cyprian's arm, "wretched boy, why have you allied yourself to me, why will you cling to me with this helpless force? I am hunted and hard-pressed; every night, listen, Cyprian, every night a fire is kindled in my heart; a dagger is put into my hand; the midnight ministers of destiny are round me; they urge—they impel, me, onward—onward:—all around me is still—the stillness of dreadful preparation. My approach cannot be calculated; my blow cannot be averted; my victim cannot resist; my associates cannot betray; yet I linger—yet I would shrink—yet I would retreat: but my fate cannot be resisted.—No, no, no; my fate cannot be resisted." Cyprian listened in helpless horror.

Ippolito approached the window; he leant against the foliaged lattice; the breeze of evening blew back his dark hair. Cyprian gazed on him with that mingled pang of anguish and love, of which the bitterness is more than of death. In those visions in which the mind wanders for relief, under the pressure of suffering, but finds it only deepened and refined, he imagined he beheld those rich locks rent in distraction; that yet glowing cheek hollow and pale; that noble form wrecked and defaced by suffering; he felt a pang that must not be told; and scarce suppressed the cry that darted to his lips.—Ippolito leant against the casement; it looked into the garden of the palace; the breeze that breathed over groves of rose and orange, played on his cheek; the setting sun sent his beams through the twinkling foliage; they tinged with ruddy amber, they fleckered the waters of a fountain, that gurgled among them, and whose bason where the waters, that played in silver showers in the centre, lay still and deep, gave back the bright and lovely blue of the heavens, without a spot, and without a shade.—Ippolito remained silent long; at length, "I behold all this," said he, "joyless and unmoved; the burthen that sits so heavy on my soul, has oppressed my senses too. Or is it that I am already become a disastrous, discordant atom amid these elements of harmony and love. And am I already at war with nature? Oh how dreadful to be an alien from our own system and species; not to be able to drink the evening breeze; or glow with the setting beams of the sun; not even to know the pleasure those insects are tasting in his rays. To wish in vain for the quiet life of the fountain that flows, of the leaf that falls. But no, no, no; to be forced to agency; to be invested with dreadful responsibility; to hew out with groaning toil, the weight that is to crush me to atoms; is there no other task for me, amid the thousand, thousand lines of human life, branching and intersecting in endless motion, and infinite directions? Is there not one for me but this? And for me, whose heart never harboured a purpose of enmity to living thing; who knew not what men meant by hatred? In my days of childhood, Cyprian, I have forborn to disturb the insect that fluttered round me, to crush the reptile that crawled beneath me; and I must—must—and is there no repeal? And is there no retreat? Author of my being and of my fate! hear my groans! hear my despair!—Father, they are not the groans of a rebel heart! it is not the despair of daring outrage! but spare me; spare me."

He rent his hair by handfuls, he cast himself upon the ground. Cyprian, terrified, but unrestrained, fell beside him, and attempted to raise and to sooth him. In a few moments, he sprang from the ground; he stood erect, but tottering; his hair was dishevelled, his hands were clenched, his eyes were inflamed and wandering, his face was varied by a thousand shades; but a fixed and burning spot of crimson tinged his cheek. "Whither do you go," cried Cyprian, grasping him as he endeavoured to rush from the apartment. "To the theatre, to the

CHARLES MATURIN

gambling-house, to the brothel," he roared, "to floods of wine, to songs of madness;—this cannot be borne; off, release me, or will you accompany me, Cyprian, to dissipation, to frenzy, to ruin."

No prayers could pacify, and no struggles could withhold him: he seized his sword and cloak, and rushed from the palace, madly calling on Cyprian to follow him. The unhappy Cyprian paused; this moment seemed to him the critical one of his life and happiness. To be seen in the streets of Naples, was to encounter a certain and terrible death. He had so long considered life merely as a medium of service to his master, that this consideration would scarce have detained him to examine it. But what hope in pursuing the career of a maniac? What profit to Ippolito in witnessing those orgies he could save him from no longer? He lingered a moment; strong affection triumphed, and he felt the danger of exposing himself, and the despair of serving his master, vanish before that sad and nameless pleasure, which we feel from the simple act of clinging to the persons of those we love; even when aid is impossible, and consolation fruitless. He followed Montorio, but he followed him with tottering steps; nor could the impassioned strength of his feelings resist the shock he felt on being for the first time on foot, and unprotected in the streets of Naples. Feeble and terrified, he yet tried to keep up with the hurried pace of Ippolito; who, with that lightning-burst of generous feeling, that blazed even through the storm of his passions, turned to him, spoke some consoling but incoherent words, and then supporting him with his arm, hurried on. From time to time of their progress, Cyprian endeavoured to breathe a few soothing sounds; but the anguish with which the sight of Ippolito's fevered cheek, and fixed eye struck him, drove them back to his heart; or if uttered, they were so inarticulate, that Ippolito was insensible of them. They proceeded with astonishing rapidity, but without any apparent object, till Cyprian, with the provisional caution of fear, tried as he passed, to distinguish the windings of the streets, among which he feared, he might shortly be left deserted and alone. They reached in a short time the extremity of that part of the city where the Montorio palace stood; they entered a dark, lonely inclosure. Ippolito who appeared to have been lulled into vacancy by the hum and concourse of the streets through which they passed, now paused and looked around him eagerly, as if struck by the stillness and solitude of the place. "Why have we wandered here?" said Cyprian, timidly; "Because," said Ippolito, in broken tones, "because it is wild, and dark, and deserted, because it is meet for the hunt of ruin, and wretchedness. I love to gaze on this stilly gloom; to hear the hollow wind that stirs the trees:—would, the evening-shades would settle on this spot for ever; would, I could dose away being and consciousness here in stunned and stupid listlessness."

He leant against one of the trees; his cloak folded on his arm. Twice with a full heart, Cyprian tried to speak, but could not form a sound. Ippolito heard the murmurs of inarticulate distress near him. "Are *you* there still, Cyprian, will *you* still cling to me? Leave me, oh leave me to myself; to the dark fight I must encounter alone. Cyprian, you might as well attempt to stop the progress of the night that is spreading round us, as of that darker and portentous gathering that involves me; go from me, and be safe; why should I destroy you; sweet and innocent boy, approach me not, love me not. But for me, you might have flourished in stainless and joyful purity; but you *would* tempt the fate of a ruined man; you would go side by side with me in that dark untravelled path, which we must tread in suffering, and terminate in despair. Go from me, while I yet can warn you, yet can commiserate, yet can pity you; a moment longer, and I shall be wild and wreckless as the hunted savage that rushes on the weapons of his persecutors, and grinds them with his tusks."

"And is this then, indeed, our last hour of peace and goodness!—Is agonized affection summoned to her last trial-task? Will you indeed be Ippolito no more?—I have no more then to say, no more to suffer.—But with my dying hand I must hold you; I must cling to you with that strength which overcometh all things, with love, which is stronger than death!—I know not the fate which awaits you; it comes in mist and cloud; nor am I anxious to unfold them, to behold it. Suffice it, it is yours. Therefore, by strong necessity of love, it must be mine. Of my brief and unhappy life, the only object has been *you*—for *you* I have lived—and I *must, must,* die with *you*."

Blind with fears, stifled with convulsive sobs, he grasped Ippolito, who, breaking from him, with a wild unmeaning laugh, hastily rushed towards a building, which was recently lit up, and to which numbers appeared to be thronging. Stupified with astonishment, Cyprian beheld this change, but the instinctive fear of desertion impelled him to follow. When he entered the building, not even his ignorance could preserve him from discovering its destination. It was a gaming-house, apparently of the lowest description, numbers were already engaged in the pursuit of the evening; and Ippolito mingled among them with

CHARLES MATURIN

a bold and vivacious eagerness, which his companion beheld with additional anguish. His flushed and impetuous manner, his vociferous impatience, his noble air and figure—while they awed the majority, allured a few wily prowlers, who believing him to be disarmed by inebriety, marked him for a sure and profitable prey. Cyprian, aghast, alone, unnoticed, stunned by the lights, the confusion, and the jargon, objects as new as revolting to a mind of vestal purity, and almost vestal seclusion, yet retained his observation, which was only preserved by the strength of those feelings, that had exposed him almost to lose it. From these violent vicissitudes he collected, not that Ippolito's sufferings were too great for the powers of his reason, but that they were too great for the powers of resistance in a mind which, though not destitute of natural strength, had been so long accustomed to artificial resources of pleasure and consolation, that finding itself unable to adjust its present grievance, by the usual balance of extrinsic relief, it writhed under it in convulsive despair, and produced those throes of grief and fury, of gloom and madness, which had been almost as terrible to the witness as to the sufferer himself.

He had no long leisure for recollection, for Ippolito, whose success had been as rapid as it was unexpected, sweeping together the money which poured in on him from all parts of the table, scattered it among some Lazaroni who loitered round the door, and with a shout of triumph, flew from the gaming-house.

Cyprian pursued him with all the speed fatigue and fear had left him, but in vain; he called on him, but received no answer; he attempted to follow the direction of his steps; but found he was only pursuing a stranger. Then fear and anguish came on him;—a wanderer in a populous city, timid, alone, and exposed to greater dangers than he appeared to be threatened by, for one moment of his life he felt a pang in which his feelings for Ippolito had no share. He hastened on with faint and terrified speed through many streets and avenues, with a blind satisfaction in the thought of proceeding, yet with increasing alarm at every step, till he found himself again in the neighbourhood of the Montorio palace. Ippolito rushed on his mind—further pursuit of him was impossible, yet it was equally impossible to Cyprian to desert him. He suddenly bethought himself of going to the Alberotti palace, which he knew to be at a small distance, and of which he also knew the possessor to be Ippolito's uncle, of informing him of the late events, and imploring his interference. Wild as this scheme was, and obviously involving the dangers attendant on Cyprian's being recognised; he sprang forward, with new and eager strength to execute it. But on reaching the Alberotti palace, he found the avenues obstructed by carriages, and the portico blazing with torches; there was a conversazione, at which the greater part of the Neapolitan nobility were assembled; among whom, detection was unavoidable, and death was therefore certain.

From this last resource, he turned away, weary in mind and frame; he attempted to totter a few paces homeward, but the thought of Ippolito, abandoned to dissipation and depravity, stung through his heart; his limbs failed, he sunk on the steps of an adjacent house, and burst into that helpless flood of anguish, which bespeaks us equally unable to restrain, or derive consolation from them.

The sudden emptiness of the street, the mildness of the night, tranquillity, silence, and subsiding emotion combined to soften him into a kind of placid imbecility. The thunder-burst of passion was over, and he wept a soft and heavy shower of tears. Too much exhausted for acute or agonised feeling, the images that had passed before him, shed over his mind a gleam of melancholy sorrow, not the glare of madness and despair. Every image of former tenderness or brightness, every dream that had once dressed the thought of Ippolito in the tints of attraction, or the beams of splendour, now awakened with cruel contrast the sense of his present state; low in vice and in wretchedness, the abasement of his own feelings thrilled to his heart, and he felt the difference between those which accompany the tear of rapture, and the tear of humbled regret; between the being he almost bowed to worship, and the being he pursued to rescue, and stooped to raise.

He wept and was refreshed; he rose calm and sad, and endeavoured to return to the Montorio palace, with the feeble hope, that some intelligence of their way-ward master, might have reached the domestics. As he turned the corner of the Strada di Toledo, a lamp burning before the image of St. Gennaro caught his eye; and with a smitten eye he turned to pay his passing devotions, where he was conscious the perturbed state of his mind had too often withheld him from. As he approached the lamp, the figure of a man, muffled and moving hastily, passed him. But no disguise could avail.—"Montorio, oh Montorio!"—he almost shrieked;—he flew from the saint, and pursued the figure. It moved with a speed that defied pursuit; and the utmost exertion of Cyprian's could only keep it in sight. It followed a direction far from the palace, and Cyprian at length beheld it at some distance enter a spacious house, that appeared filled with company. Cyprian paused and doubted the evidence of his senses; he might be pursuing a stranger, and pursuing him where to follow was dangerous. He had acquired a kind of local courage in these frequent emergencies.

He saw at a distance two cavaliers of sober demeanour, he approached them, and in a voice of which the tones were like those of a wandering cherub, seeking the way to a purer region, demanded whose house it was, into which the cavalier who had passed them, had entered. The elder of the cavaliers looked at him for a moment—"Perhaps, Signor," said he, "I should, from principle, decline to satisfy your inquiry, but as your youth and appearance prompt me to hope 'tis not urged by a personal motive, I shall inform you, that is the house of Nerina di—the most celebrated courtezan in Naples." They passed on, and Cyprian remained alone. Stupified by the last intelligence, he had yet heard every syllable of it, and retained its full meaning.

Montorio, in the house of lewdness and shame; the last object of life frustrated; its sole hope extinct:—but though the prospect of good was lost, the fear of evil yet remained; the danger of his entering the confines of vice could not be averted, that of his remaining within them still might; yet Cyprian hesitated to follow him. But the delicate gloss of his feelings was now worn off; the shock of encounter had diminished the danger, or, when compared with Ippolito's, all danger seemed to disappear.

From the first moment he had fatally beheld Montorio, he had never been himself. He had patiently and successively assumed the complexion which Ippolito's character and fortunes had given him; his smiles or his sufferings were the uniform and necessary echoes of his master's; he had been the passive dependant of his attachment, whose happiness external circumstances might controul; whose fidelity, none could, ever. By pursuing him to the verge of ruin, he seemed to be only pursuing the course appointed to him; in plunging with him, from its final point, he appeared only to be fulfilling the severe, but absolute task assigned him.

These reflections rushed through his mind in a moment, and almost unconsciously, he found himself in an apartment of the house. To his inquiries for Montorio, no attention was paid; every one was busied in something that appeared remote from the purpose which had brought him there. Sick, faint, and terrified, he wandered from to room to room, still calling, still inquiring; the house was loud, festive, and tumultuous. His heart was oppressed, his senses ached, his limbs tottered. Half insensible, but still exclaiming, he rushed against a door, which opening discovered Montorio surrounded by some of the most licentious of the young nobility, revelling, shouting, drunk with licentiousness, and dissolved in wine. Among such a group, Cyprian, (whom some of them had seen at the Montorio palace) was beheld with delight, as an object of mockery and persecution. They surrounded, they overwhelmed him with derisive congratulations; they contended for the distinctions of doing the honours of the revel to him.

With a strength of mind and frame, which we sometimes owe to the partial absence of reason, Cyprian brake from them, and staggering to the seat where Ippolito reclined, clung to him, exclaiming, save me, save me; save your own soul alive—take me from this house of sin, or I die at your feet."

Ippolito, starting as if from a trance, protected Cyprian with his arm, and repelling his persecutors with a fierceness which awed even the rage of drunkenness, rushed from the house bearing his breathless preserver with him. They were pursued by the unheeded roar of dissolute malignity, but in a short time it was unheard, and they drank without interruption, the dewy freshness of the breeze of night; they saw the chaste and silent brightness of the stars; they caught that deep and stilly humming, so pleasant to the ear, that loves to listen by night.

They reached the Montorio palace in silence, and Cyprian with joy perceived Ippolito preparing to enter it.—They had now reached the portico, when the clock in the great hall was heard to strike "twelve." Ippolito started and paused, and by the lamps of the portico, Cyprian saw his eye roll fearfully.—*He turned*—"Whither, oh whither do you go? Have I sought, have I saved you for this?" cried Cyprian, clinging to him, with renewed and impatient anguish.—"Off, release me, I may not be held; longer than midnight I must not delay; there is no danger; whither I go, human good and evil cannot come; virtue and vice are negative things: at this hour, I am no more a mortal agent;— release me; my hour is come, I may not be delayed." "These are words of madness," said Cyprian, struggling, though hopelessly, to hold him; "whither have I not followed? and wherefore must I be repelled? Fear, nor danger, nor sin have deterred me! Oh let me not be left behind! What can I witness worse than I shall fear! What can I suffer so terrible

CHARLES MATURIN

as your danger?"—He pleaded in vain. Ippolito was gone with a speed which the fatigues of the *night* had rendered marvellous, and Cyprian entered the palace with a freshness of anguish which *its* sufferings had not exhausted.

XII

Tum demum horrisono stridentes cardine sacræ
Panduntur portæ. Cernis, custodia qualis
Vestibulo sedeat.

—Virgil, lib. vi

Then of itself, unfolds th' eternal door:
With dreadful sounds the brazen hinges roar.
You see before the gate, what stalking ghost
Commands the guard, what centries keep the post.

—Dryden

Letter from Annibal di Montorio

Whatever be the termination of these researches, I already lament the effects of their progress, nor can I review the circumstances I am about to relate, without many reproaches on my timidity and more on my obduracy. The feelings of doubt and uncertainty which had been suggested by my late visit to the apartments I communicated to Michelo, who, eager to adopt any thing that promised a remission of the task imposed on him, avowed it his belief, that the tenant of that tower had signified his displeasure of our intrusion by the signs we had witnessed, of which he declared our further misconstruction might expose us to dangers he dared not to name. I took counsel of his fear, unhappily for both, and believing, or compelling myself to believe, that one avenue was rendered impassable by a strength it would be impiety to resist, I resolved to repair at midnight to the chapel, and visit the tomb of Count Orazio, where the appearances, I determined to examine, were more frequent and obvious, and where therefore, some suspicion of their being produced by an agent such as myself, qualified the fear which in the tower I had found insupportable without such relief. Michelo, who had become as weary of deprecating, as I of importuning, made no resistance, and when (to compensate to myself for the timidity that had mingled in my design of omitting the tower) I determined to visit the tomb on that night, he promised to attend me.

He was to procure the keys, for he declined with so much terror the subterranean passages by which we had once resorted there, that I declined the proposal. Our few preparations were soon adjusted—long cloaks—a lamp carried in a lanthorn—and I determined to bring my sword. These arrangements were made with the whispering caution of fear, and we separated. During the remainder of the day, I felt myself involuntarily shunning the eye of Michelo, from a lurking apprehension that every glance we exchanged was observed and interrupted.

The night at length arrived; our dull and regular household dispersed; I retired to my apartment; my thoughts were occupied by the purpose of the night, and I endeavoured to banish from my recollection the circumstances that had attended my last visit to the chapel. They rose before me in strong shape and clearness; I saw them on every side, as I stalked across my chamber. I felt them, as I endeavoured to heave them off my breast, pressing on it, a thick and impalpable weight. With them came many a disastrous presage of uncertain evil. The whole ghastly troop seemed to be arraying for the encounter at midnight, in the tomb. My terrors increased, and though I felt that Michelo's arrival was but the signal for those terrors to commence, I yet longed for his approach, for the presence of a human being—This struggle of involuntary meditation was interrupted by a noise at the door; it was Michelo—"Hush, Signor, it is I; are you prepared?"—"I am."—"Then come, Signor, but speak and tread softly."—"Why this caution, have not the family retired?" "All, Signor, but the pages who are now assembling to watch in my lord's chamber. But then, Signor,"—"What then, why this hesitation?"—"There is one in this house," pushing his pale face close to me, and whispering, "one who never sleeps, or if he does, can do all the actions of of a living man; yea, and more, while he would seem to sleep."—"Absurd, Michelo, banish these dreams of fear." "Nay, Signor—but I am silent,—tread softly, however, Signor."

We proceeded through the gallery with cautious steps; we had now reached the stairs, when a distant sound was heard; "Hark," said I. Michelo turned round, and started on observing we were near the apartment of Father Schemoli. He communicated this in a whisper. "Proceed," said I. "I saw the confessor retire to his apartment an hour ago."—"Yes," muttered Michelo, "but heaven knows what apartments inclose him now."—We descended the staircase, muffling our lanthorn, and starting as the wind shook the casements, and the steps creaked beneath our tread. We reached the great hall, and stole through it almost without touching the pavement.

The deep and midnight silence, the dampness and dull echoes of the marble floor; the huge and dusky height of the walls and roof, over which our single lamp shed a dull, unpiercing gleam, made our passage appear like a progress through a vault. Michelo applied the key to the great door, and I wrapped my cloak about the lock to suppress the sound while he turned the key. Wonder not at this feeble minuteness; I cannot think of myself, creeping along in silence and in fear, without wishing you to accompany me; for sufferings, whether voluntary or not, we always expect some compensation, either of participation, or of pity.—We issued into the outer court, and I felt refreshment in the air of heaven, though it blew damp and sultry.

We now entered the chapel, and having reached, through many ruinous obstructions, the tomb of the late Count, we concealed our lamps, muffled our cloaks about us, so as to conceal as much of the human form (if seen) as possible; and lurking behind a projecting pediment of the tomb, awaited the event in a state of feeling difficult to describe.—There was nothing to relax its intense and severe controul. There was no external sound; no light, no motion. It was one of those nights, in which you feel, from time to time, a hot blast hissing past you, that sinks again into silence. A night, in which the dark and heavy clouds seem to be working with inward tumults; in which, from expecting a storm long, we begin almost to wish for its approach.

The moon, often struggling through the clouds, tinged for a moment their sombrous and surging masses, with a bright and sudden light that vanished in a moment; and the night-dews fell with almost perceptible damp and heaviness. On the dubious features of the structure, tombs and monuments, windows dusky with foliage, and arches shapeless in ruin, these bursts of light and darkness played with such shadowy influence, that he must have had senses not easily deluded, who could be convinced he saw nothing more there than might be seen by day.

I, however, felt that my situation required me to collect firmness, not to dissipate it, and I attempted to converse with Michelo. "Tell me," said I, "why, when the vaults of this chapel were already numerous and spacious enough to contain the remains of our family, why was a monument erected for Count Orazio, for one too, whose end, I have reason to believe, was obscure and tragical? And why, above all, was

CHARLES MATURIN

it erected in this ruinous and deserted pile, instead of that within the walls of the castle, which is still frequented by the family."

"There is a strange report, Signor," whispered the old man, "concerning this tomb, and the reason of its being built. Many things had concurred to drive it from my memory, but your inquiry has recalled it. It is needless to remind you, Signor, how much all your illustrious family have been attached to secret studies. But of all, the Count your great grandfather was most engaged in them. He devoted his entire soul to them; nay, some said so in such a tone, as if they wished to be understood literally. But, oh! Signor, what am I saying—rest his bones, they lie within a few steps of us." "Why this interruption, Michelo?"—"Is it not fearful, Signor, to speak of the dead, when we feel them to be so near us!" The effect of this observation on myself, I endeavoured to conceal, by urging him to proceed. "Well, Signor, (lowering his voice as if to deceive the dead,) be that as it may, no power could drag him from these studies; and at length it was said he had invented by his art, a glass, that could shew him every event and person he wished to see. It is certain, that after his decease, my Lord, your grandfather, spent many days shut up in his father's closet—examining and destroying his instruments and books; and 'tis said, strange and doleful sounds were heard to issue from the room while he was thus employed. But the task was an involuntary one, for I have heard the Inquisition were beginning to consider his proceedings as offensive, and had actually dismissed their ministers to examine into them, and to search the castle.

"A little before the old Count's death, he is said to have discovered by his wisdom, that there was a spot in the circuit of the castle, which would be the seat of calamity and destruction to the family. He immediately set himself to discover where this spot might be; and I conclude, that, if it required so much skill to find out that it did exist, it required still more to discover where. However, your great grandfather was in no wise dismayed, he pursued his point resolutely, and at length discovered the fatal spot to be the very one on which we now stand."—"What! the spot on which this tomb has been built?"—"The same, Signor. I have heard that the Count apprized his family of this circumstance, but the discovery slumbered unnoticed, till your uncle, Count Orazio, hearing of it, and being, as I have mentioned, much versed in those studies himself, ordered a monument for himself to be erected on the spot, hoping by this means to fulfil, and yet to avert the prediction—to defeat, yet not appear to defy it."

Few that connected what I had witnessed on this spot, with what I now heard, could blame the emotion to which I yielded for a moment. But, though the denunciation was terrible, there is a solemnity in whatever we suppose to be connected with our fate, that divests it of the hideous ghastliness attending other subjects of supernatural aspect, and that marks the bounds of awe and of horror.—Under *a decree,* the mind bends in controlled and gloomy passiveness, appalled but not convulsed—without the reluctance and revoltings of visionary terror. As the attempt to relax my feelings had been so unsuccessful, I turned for relief to silence and to meditation.—The bell tolled twelve.—

Michelo now, eagerly, but still whispering, said, "Look, Signor, look, through this chasm in the wall you may see—nay Signor, lower, yet lower—you must bend, Signor,—now do you see, Signor, a fragment of the castle, just above the great stairs?"—"I do see that part of the castle, which I believe to be adjacent to the great stairs."

"There, Signor, is Father Schemoli's apartment; that part of the tower, and that narrow window, in which you see a light burning, belong to his oratory:—now Signor, every night his lamp is to be seen in that window till midnight, and ever when the bell tolls it is said to disappear; nor, from that hour, can he be found, nor can it be conjectured, where or how he is employed:—this only is known, he is not to be found in his apartment. But his friends, it is said, are at no loss to find employment for him—Sometimes he holds a feast with them in the vault—and sometimes he mixes in procession with them, through that tower, and sings in their unholy mass at midnight." "What words are these, Michelo, and what is their import?" "Heed not me, Signor, mark the lamp; see, Signor, see, it grows dim, and more dim, and now it is gone—Holy Peter—it will be with us momently."

The emotion with which I had watched the extinction of the lamp, I endeavoured to resist, as the cause was utterly inadequate to excite it—"And what are we to infer from this, Michelo? The Confessor may be permitted to extinguish his lamp at midnight?" "Ah! but, Signor, (depressing his voice to its lowest tones,) 'tis from that moment, that strange appearances at this tomb are said to commence."—"Of the truth of that, we shall then soon be enabled to judge," said I, endeavouring to derive fortitude from the intelligence. The expectation which it suggested, scarce permitted me to draw my breath. I continued to gaze vacantly, but fixedly, for I knew not in what direction to expect the approach of this visitation. "Look, look, Signor," Michelo exclaimed,

CHARLES MATURIN

"look yonder,—now, Signor, do you believe, now do you beholds!"—As he spake, a light resembling that we had once before seen, a pale, dull light, appeared moving along a passage, which opens by an arch into the east wing of the chapel. In amaze I observed it issue from the lower end, where I knew there was neither door nor aperture.

I marked its approach, for it was slow: it seemed to have proceeded from the ground, gradually arising and advancing, and looking dim, tremulous, and sepulchral.

Michelo, leaning across the angle of the monument, grasped my arm; there was no sound; the very wind was still; I heard the beating of my heart. At this moment, the moon riding over the billowy clouds, poured a broad and sudden light through that passage. It played uncertainly through the rifted roof, and fell full on the arch communicating with the chapel. In that instant I beheld a figure standing beneath the arch; a dark gigantic figure; its form and attitude I could not discover; the light was brief and sudden, and the vision confused and imperfect; but I discovered, that, as if folded in its vesture, it held the light we had seen, and which, in the moon-shine, was diminished to a small, dull twinkle. I pressed Michelo's arm in token of observation, he returned the pressure; neither of us spoke;—all was dark—even that pale light had disappeared.—"He has seen us," murmured Michelo.—"Hush," said I, "let us await its approach in silence."—"Something is near," said the old man, "I feel the ground near me pressed, as if by feet."—"Hush," said I, "all is silent, a body cannot move without sound."—"There *is* something near," whispered he again, "for I feel the air driven to my face, as if some one passed me."—"'Tis the bat," said I, "that whizzes past you, or the wind that waves the ivy; I have heard, or felt nothing yet." "Oh no, Signor, there is a strange motion in the air; a rank and stifling chillness, as if something that was not good, breathed upon us."

There came indeed a blast across us, not like the blasts of that night, loud and feverish; but cold and noisome, like a charnel-stream. We shuddered as it passed; I felt some effort necessary, to resist the palsied feeling that was stealing over me: "Michelo, let us not be baffled a second time. This form, whatever it be, is probably approaching; before it oppress us with some strange influence, I will rush forth and meet it: and be they favourable or malignant, I will know its power and purposes."

Michelo's faint voice of dissuasion was lost in the wind that sighed hollowly through the aisles. I clambered out from my lurking place, and endeavoured to feel my way in the direction of the light and of the figure; for the central aisle was now totally dark. I advanced a few paces, I felt something rush past me—not with the distinct and alternate step of a human foot, but as if it glided above the earth, and was borne on without effort. I paused, and extended my arms—they encountered something that felt like a human hand, raised, and extended, and as it were, pointing onwards; I now called aloud to Michelo to turn the lanthorn, and to guard the door of the vault. By the noise that followed, I conceived he attempted to obey me, but at that moment a cry of horror burst from the tomb; the light disappeared, and the door of the vault, closed with a thundering crash.—All remained in silence and darkness.—I stood petrified; I called on Michelo, and shuddered at the echoes of my own voice—I attempted to move, but felt as if a step beyond the spot on which I stood, would be into a gulph. At length I broke from this trance of fear; I felt my way to the tomb—I called on Michelo again; believing him to have swooned. I felt all the pavement and pediments with the hilt of my sword—Michelo was not to be found; the tomb appeared to have opened her mouth, and swallowed him up. I applied my utmost strength in vain to the door of the vault, and though I almost expected it to burst open, and disclose a sight that would sear the eye, or unsettle the brain—I yet persisted to struggle with frantic force: no success attended my efforts, no sound encouraged them. Once I thought I heard a low and feeble moaning—but it was lost in that confused and humming sound, with which the effort to listen intensely, filled my ear. Fear and shame, and impatience distracted me;—to force the wretched, reluctant, old victim, to a pursuit from which he recoiled; to betray him into the very grasp and circle of it; to leave him expiring amid horrors, of which even to *think* was not safe; to do this, was to me impossible.

The being, at whose approach I had shuddered, I would at that moment have encountered and grappled with, to rescue his miserable prey; but there was no hope, and no power of assistance. I could not rend open the vault, and to alarm the castle, would be to draw on us from my father's resentment, consequences as terrible as any power could menace us with. More than an hour was spent in fruitless efforts and expedients; at length, I conceived it possible to rouse some of the servants who were lodged in an adjacent wing of the castle, and by rewards to secure their silence with regard to the object for which their services were required.

CHARLES MATURIN

It was when I moved from the chapel to execute this purpose, that I felt terrors of which I had been before insensible. Alone, at midnight, among the dead and their mansions, and probably near to some being, whose influence and image were the more terrible, because they were undefined and unimaginable; because they hovered, with a dim aspect of uncertainty, between the elements and agency of different worlds; because they could not be referred to any distinct or sensible point of fear, nor admitted of any preparation against them, such as men can always make against a human foe, and sometimes against an invisible one.

Haunted by these feelings, I yet moved on. The night was now still and dark; and in the massy line of shapeless darkness, which the castle spread before me, I would have given half its value to have discovered one spark of light; there was not one. In that deep stillness (which made the echo of my steps seem like the tread of many) the slightest sound was not lost. I had almost reached the castle-terrace, and was debating which wing to approach, when the hoarse and heavy grating of the door of the vault reached my ear.—I paused—I heard it close. Doubting, fearing, yet with a vague expectation of relief, I hastened back.—A light breeze waved my hair as I passed, and the volumes of cloud and vapour, floated back from the east, like a dark curtain-fold, and the moon stood calm and bright, in a deep azure field, tinging the fractured and shifting masses with silver as they retired. I blessed it, and wondered how often I had beheld that lovely light with apathy, or with pleasure, in which sympathy for the benighted whom it cheered, or for the wanderer whom it succoured, had no share.

I sought the aisle again. The moon poured a light as broad as day; through the windows. I saw the tomb of Count Orazio. I beheld a figure seated on it; I advanced in hope and fear. It was Michelo—he sat like a mariner, who leans on a bare and single crag, after the tempest and the wreck; he was haggard, spent, and gasping.—I rushed to him, but he appeared not to hear my moving; his head was raised, and his look fixed on the arched passage; the moon-light poured a ghastly and yellow paleness on his still features. I looked in his eyes, they were hollow and glazed; I touched his hand, it was cold and dropped from mine. I shuddered, and scarce thought him an earthly man. A moment reproached my fears, and I tried to address some words of comfort and inquiry to him, but I was repelled by an awe in which I scarce thought Michelo an agent.

"Woe, woe," groaned the old man, with a voice unlike a mortal sound, his arms raised and outspread, his eye wild and dilated, his whole form and movement rapt into a burst of prophetic ecstacy. I involuntarily retreated from him: "Alas, how is it with you, Michelo! let me conduct you from this spot; never will I forgive myself for having forced you to it. Haste away with me; my father may rouse in the night, the domestics may be summoned to attend his vigils in the chapel, and we shall be discovered; hasten back with me, Michelo."—"Woe, woe, woe," said the old man again, and bowed his head, and fell on the pavement.

I bore him from the chapel in my arms; tottering, for the weight of age and insensibility is heavy. The air seemed to revive him; and I saw, by the moonlight, something like colour, come to his dead face again. As I gazed on, and spoke to him, a shadow stronger than the waving of the cypress-boughs, crossed the spot. I looked up, I beheld issuing from behind the buttress, against which I leaned with my burthen, the dark, and shapeless form I had beheld.—(The moon disappeared.)— It passed me, and proceeded towards the castle. I gasped, but could not speak to it—I stretched out my arms, but had no power to pursue it—It floated onward, and with these eyes I beheld it enter the wall of the castle. It was at the solid buttress angle of a tower, whose strong line was visible in the shade; there was neither door nor aperture, but there was neither obstruction nor delay. The moon burst forth again as it retired, and Michelo unclosed his weak eye on its beam. He rose tremblingly; I supported him. We proceeded towards the castle; neither of us spoke, but he moaned heavily, and closed his eye from time to time. We reached the great hall, the door of which we had left open; all power or wish of inquiry died within me.

When we heard our steps on the pavement of the hall, and felt we trod in the house of the living, Michelo with a faltering hand made the sign of the cross, and swooned again. I had much difficulty in bringing him to my apartment, and often I thought I heard sounds that passed me, and felt a motion in the passages other than what myself occasioned; but I was in a state of mind in which it is difficult to avoid the illusions of fear. When revived and recovered, he implored to be led to his own apartment. His eye was yet wild, and his words were incoherent. I hesitated, but yielded to his earnestness.—"Lead me, Signor," said he, "to my turret, other hands shall bear me from it; lead me to my bed, a better rest than it shall give me, is near."

I attended him. I had forborne to importune him, but the wild resolution, the mystery of his silence, wrought with my abated fears of his safety, to excite a solicitude I could not resist. I seated him in his chair, I trimmed his lamp, and departing with a reluctant step, asked, "Michelo, what have you seen?"—"The secrets of the grave," said the old man, without a pause, and without a whisper. His boldness emboldened me. "And dare you relate them, Michelo?"—"And dare you listen to them, if I dare?" said the old man, fixing his eyes, which shone with strange light, on me. "I dare—so help me heaven, and all the saints, as no weak, personal concern or fear mingles in the spirit with which I await the development of these mysteries."—"No more tonight, Signor," said the old man, relapsing into weakness, "leave me tonight, leave me to silence, and to heaven. I have need of prayer and of preparation; my time is brief, and my task terrible. But come to the turret, and knock tomorrow, and if I be alive, I will answer you."—He fell before a crucifix, and prayed fervently. The lamp shed its light on his white temples and closed eyes. I retired, and when I closed the door of the the the narrow turret-room, I felt as if I had closed the door of a tomb.

THE PRECEDING LINES WERE WRITTEN in the remainder of that disastrous night, which had left me too much agitated for sleep; I have forborne to send them that I might add to them an account of our. . .

IPPOLITO, I AM DISTRACTED WITH shame and contrition. Michelo is indeed dying. The first domestic whom I saw this morning, told me, (what I endeavoured to listen to, as unexpected,) that Michelo was ill, and that he had sent for a monk of St. Nicolo, in Naples, to attend him. "Strange, Signor," said the servant, "that with so pious a confessor as Father Schemoli in the castle, he would prefer sending to the monastery of St. Nicolo."

I endeavoured to reconcile myself to this intelligence, that though Michelo might suffer by the shock he had received, it was unlikely those sufferings would be long or severe, far less mortal, and I determined to visit him in the evening, when delay would disarm suspicion, if any existed. But what was my consternation, when I heard the family physician declare that his patient would not probably outlive the day. The vital system, he said, had received a shock he could neither discover nor remove. "Michelo is neither dying of age, nor of disease, but he will not probably outlive the day." I have heard it whispered in the castle that my father, on this intelligence, desired an interview with Michelo, which was determinately declined. Strange condescension, and strange refusal! Twice today have I endeavoured to see him, but his confessor has not yet left him; they have been alone for hours. Hark! I am summoned—he will see me now. The monk has left the castle abruptly.—My spirits are solemnly touched. A moment ago, they were agitated, but this summons, and the expectation it has breathed through me, has hushed them into a severe stillness. Amid all my regret for this unhappy old man, whom I have killed as surely as if I had thrust my stiletto into his heart, there survives an impression of solicitude, of doubt, and of awe, which I am anxious to feed with strange intelligence. The hour, the place, the purpose, are most solemn; it is night—I go to the bed of a dying man, to learn the secrets of the grave! . . .

I AM RETURNED, AND THE impression I have brought with me, what shall efface? My mind is so completely filled, that I feel as if no other subject would ever occupy it, and I write, almost as I think, involuntarily.—I found Michelo in his narrow bed. A pale and single lamp lit the room, he held a crucifix in his hand, to which he raised his dim eye from time to time. There was another person in the room, whom, when I became accustomed to that faint light, I discovered to be Filippo, the nephew of Michelo. "Signor Annibal," said the old man, "draw near, I have many things to say; but my last hours are under that dark controul which has held them long, and till a certain moment I can utter nothing of import. Signor, you see me dying; this is the reward of my long and guilty silence. Alas I flattered myself, that silence was not participation; but a deathbed convicts all self-deceivers. The holy monk is now in possession of my last declaration; prepare you, Signor, for its consequences. You have sought a discovery, which will anticipate your efforts. Even I who would have concealed it, by partial communications, and pacifying expedients, am made an instrument of its disclosure. *I* see its approach, with the indifference of a man who has no more part in this world; but you, oh you, how shall I prepare you, young, noble, and impetuous, how prepare you for it! *The House of Montorio must fall!*"

Indignation and amaze kept me silent a moment; the dying man before me was no object for the former; but I fervently wished those words were uttered by some other mouth, down which I might thrust them with say sword's point. "'Tis well for him," said I, "your intelligence came from no living man; but even from the dead, I will not believe it true." The old man kissed the crucifix. "So may He to whom I am hastening, receive my soul." I paused, and trembled, and signified by a motion to him, to proceed. "Not yet, not yet, Signor; my hour is not come; and till that arrive, I cannot be released: but many are the signs that tell me it is near.

"I shall not linger long. Signor, tell me the hour, and tell me the moment." "But five minutes more," said I, "and it will be eleven." "Five minutes," repeated he, "it seems but a short space to one who has seen sixty-five years; yet I would they were over.—Look still, Signor, and count to every moment as it passes." I did so. The old man repeated the numbers as I told them. "And now, Signor, now," said he, "is the last arrived?" "The hand is on the last stroke; now it reaches it, and now—hark to the bell."—"It is eleven—Filippo leave us." Filippo retired. I drew nearer the bed.

The old man spoke feebly, and with many pauses. "I draw near the hour of my dissolution.—What I have known, or what I have concealed, will soon be published. That the disclosure will probably affect the fortunes and honours of your house, I presage too well. To prepare you for it, Signor, shall be the task of my last hour.—There is a being—he is no living man; his thoughts and movements are beyond our knowledge; yet he passes before your eyes, and moves, and speaks, and looks with a show and form of life. This being, I dare not name his name, has held me long in his controul. I dared not to speak or move, but as I was bidden, for he held power which man might not resist. But I am now released, for I am dying. I shall soon be as he is, and shudder not to meet him. But while I yet speak with a human voice, let me warn you of what impends over your house, Signor. *He is the evil genius of it*—he is the very power commissioned to act and to witness its destruction." "Who is this of whom you speak?" He crossed his brow. "I may not name his name; all that rests is to tell what he has told, and what he has told, shall surely come to pass."

"Many a night have I dimly beheld him—many a night have I felt his hollow whisper pass into mine ears: but, last night, I saw him—I saw him," said he, shuddering, "face to face!" "Whom?—where? delay this terrible intelligence no longer; what have you seen, and what have you heard?"

"I was at the door of the vault," said he, faltering; "you left me, and wandered up the aisle—I felt that unearthly thing approach; you called to me to expose the light; I tried to do so; but I was grasped by an influence that froze me up. The cold and bony hand was on me; the blood in my veins thrilled and crept like the cold motion of a worm; the door of the vault was rent open; I was dashed down it, as if by a whirlwind.—The door was closed on us, and I felt as if I was no more a human being.—I did not lose my reason; I knew I was among the dead, and with one I feared more than the dead; but I had a kind of ghastly courage. I felt as if the touch of that hand had made me like him that owned it. I was able to look around me. The moon-light broke through the rifts of the vault. I saw his form moving among coffins and bones; and in that dim, and shuddering light, it appeared to mix with them: then it seemed to sink into the coffin of the Count Orazio; and from thence there came a voice to me that said—" I listened with all bodily and mental ear—

"Woe and death," murmured a voice from beneath us. It was not like a human tone; it was like the moaning blast of midnight;—like the deep, long, hollow murmur of a distant sea; but the sounds it bore, were distinct and clear.

The old man's hair rose, and his eyes glared. "What did you hear?" said he. The truth was too near and terrible to be denied or concealed. "I heard a voice," said I, "that said, 'woe and death.'" He smote his hands, and sunk backward. "My repentance is too late:—that was the spirit's death-cry.—And I *must* die, and leave it untold; and I must die, and leave it unexpiated."

He fell—he gasped—he blackened. I knelt beside him in terrible enthusiasm. "Speak, I adjure you, while a breath is spared—while a moment is allowed you. Speak, as you would depart in peace—as you would go to glory." There came only a hollow rattle from his throat. I bent over him, agonizing for an articulate sound. He muttered deep and inward, "It is too late—Erminia—Orazio," (he added a name I could not catch) "murdered, murdered.—Their forms are before my eyes; their blood is on my soul." He shook; he was convulsed; he expired. I called Filippo to my assistance; but assistance was fruitless—Michelo is no more!

XIII

Tempus abire tibi est—

—HORACE

'Tis time for thee to quit the wanton stage.

At the Montorio palace all was confusion and riot. All the influence once obtained, and the concessions once exacted by Cyprian, were scattered and lost by this new sally of riot.

Ippolito returned to his former pursuits, with an avidity that promised to compensate for his short abstinence from them. His days were days of pleasure; his evenings, evenings of revelry; but his nights, remained nights of mystery. Every day he became more enflamed, more restless, and more intractable. His sense of internal anguish appeared to be more intense in proportion to his efforts to deaden it. And often, while he shook the dice, or swallowed the wine, his haggard countenance betrayed a heart far from holding alliance with a thought of joy or ease. The fatigues of his revels and his vigils combined, the fatigues of a mind that sought tumult even in pleasure, and banished ease from its very relief, preyed rapidly and equally on his frame and temper.

The high, romantic spirit, the vicissitude of tender and of lofty feeling, the carelessness of happy vivacity, the play of unlaboured mirth were gone; and, in their place, intervals of gloom and of fury, of spirits stimulated to unjoyous and fierce excess, or sunk to sullen dejection. His beauty only remained; for, whether flushed by the dark, fever-glow of riot, or pale with the gloomy weariness of his nightly watchings, he was ever most beautiful.

At such moments, Cyprian beheld him with that piteous and painful delight, with which we see the dim and altered face of a native dwelling, or the scarred, and dismantled branches of a tree, that has delighted us with its beauty, and refreshed us with its shade.

On one of those nights, that Cyprian, left to utter solitude, felt it only embittered by the thought of him who had once filled and delighted all solitude, he was informed that a stranger of rank demanded to see him. The demand was unusual and alarming; and Cyprian was at first about to decline complying with it, but his ever-wakeful solicitude suggested that the purport of this visit might relate to Ippolito, and he desired the stranger to be conducted to him. He entered. He was a Spanish officer, about the middle of life; the bold and imposing air of his profession was mingled with the stateliness of his nation; and he saluted Cyprian with that ease which bespeaks a familiarity with many modes of life.

"Signor Cyprian, I presume," said he. Cyprian bowed. "I am not ignorant, Signor, of your character and attachment to Count Montorio; my confidence in your zeal has been the motive of this visit. I myself know, and regard him; he is a young nobleman of worth and honour, otherwise," said he, touching his whiskers, "a Castilian could feel no interest for him."

Cyprian, warmed by Ippolito's praises, listened with a pleasure he had long been a stranger to. "It is therefore," said the Spaniard, "that I feel myself deeply affected by the state in which I see him plunged;—but first permit me to inquire, whether his domestic habits have undergone the same perversion with his social ones. You, of course, are well acquainted with them, and can pronounce whether he appears at home, restless, perturbed, and unequal; or whether those appearances are only the consequence of the excesses in which he is immersed when abroad." "Alas, no, cavalier;" said Cyprian, "a new and dreadful revolution has convulsed his whole frame of mind; it affects him at all times, and everywhere; he enjoys no repose at home; he is no longer Ippolito di Montorio." "The change is as violent as it is extensive then;" said the Spaniard, "he plays for stakes at which it would be madness to take him up; he plunges into frequent inebriety, a vice rare in your climate: he seeks every abode of licentiousness in Naples; his whole effort seems to be, to extinguish his reason, and to consume his health. Yet all this appears to be the result, not of a rage for pleasure, but of an impatience of pain; these excesses appear the dreadful alternative of anguish that is insupportable. Such vices," said the *liberal* soldier, "as I have described, might be forgiven in a young man of sanguine constitution, and splendid rank, but never should any excess lead a nobleman to derogate from his dignity, and the stateliness of high-born demeanour, and mix levity with licentiousness." Cyprian had sufficient knowledge of mankind to discover, that the motives to rectitude will always vary with the character and habits of the mind that forms them; though, therefore, he revolted from the distinctions of this worldly theory, he adopted the consequences drawn from it.

CHARLES MATURIN

"I, at first," said the Spaniard, "believed this to be only a sally of sudden impetuosity, the consequence of some casual disappointment of his views or his passions; but recent circumstances have induced me to think, that a mind of such noble and energetic powers could be perverted by no trivial cause; and I am confirmed in my suspicions by the event of last night." "Suspicions of what? What do you suspect?" exclaimed Cyprian, rising in agitation. "Suspicions," said the Spaniard, in the deepest tones of his deep voice, "of his being engaged in some bond of connexion, either hostile to his soul's or body's welfare, from which he tries to extricate himself, but tries either too late or too faintly. Were I less acquainted with Count Ippolito's honour, I should fear him to be associated in some dark design against the state; as it is, I believe he pursues some object of private hostility, yet often recoils: sometimes deterred by the magnitude or invidiousness of the enterprise, and sometimes by the danger of the means he must employ to accomplish it."—"Impossible!" said Cyprian, with the most animated action of enthusiasm, "impossible, that Ippolito's mind could embrace an object of guilty or obdurate rancour; or if he did, that danger could ever deter him from its pursuit."

"I was about to inform you," said the Spaniard, "of the circumstances that led me to that conclusion; they were his own words, sometimes dropt unguardedly, and sometimes extorted by a sudden pang; but they at best, are but inconclusive. I hasten to inform you, therefore, of the *fact* of last night, for I need not remind you, Signor, that no Castilian ever draws a rash or hasty conclusion."

Cyprian felt he had offended by his abruptness, but the emotion that had caused left him also unable to apologize for it.

"Last night," said the Spaniard, "a large party of us had assembled in a casino near the Corso; there was high and general play, and several strangers were mixed through the company, who were, several of them, as usual in masks. Count Ippolito was among the rest, in that perturbed and feverish frame we have lamented. He played for immense stakes, and stimulated his spirits by incessant draughts of wine. His vociferation, his eagerness, and his air and figure, which exhibited a kind of splendid and dissolute madness, had drawn all eyes on him. But they were diverted by the appearance of a stranger, whom I can no more describe, than I can define the impression his presence appeared to make on the company and on me. He was clothed in a long, loose, dark cloak, that completely concealed him. He wore a mask, over which the dark plumage depending from his hat, hung so as almost to hide it. He moved along with a slow stride, appearing to know no one, and to be known by none. His presence, though it did not suspend amusement, appeared to suspend all the spirit of it. The loud and eager voices of the gamblers were gradually softened almost into whispers; the loiterers deserted the places he drew near, and one old knight of Malta told me, he felt the air breathe a strange chillness, as this person past him.

"I should not have given credit to such effects attending the presence of a single, silent, solitary man, had I not felt myself, a strange sensation which I cannot describe, and do not wish to recal; a sensation, such as I never felt in the battle or in the breach. This person, after many movements, at length placed himself at the table at which Count Ippolito was playing, and stood, in a fixed attitude, directly opposite to him. I was near them—a superficial observer would have imagined, from the Count's manner, that he was insensible of his presence, but from the increased loudness, eagerness, and careless desperation of his manner, I at once drew a contrary conclusion. The eyes of all were fixed on that table. The stranger, after standing some time in silence and motionless, began at length to make some strange and unintelligible gestures, which were evidently directed at the Count. The only notice the latter took of them, was hastily to call for and swallow more wine, and to double his stake. The stranger then slowly raising his arm, and extending it from his cloak, pointed it full at the Count, it was naked, bony, and gigantic; some said it was spotted with blood; I saw none. The Count, bending over the table, furiously bid his antagonist, who had paused aghast, to attend to his play. They pursued it. The stranger spoke not; but drawing out a watch, held it opposite the candle which stood by the Count—the light fell on it—the hand pointed to twelve. Many, who stood on the other side, said that the reverse was inscribed with strange figures—I could not have seen them, if it had. Montorio eagerly pushed away the light. The stranger retreated, but all eyes followed him. He stood still opposite to the Count—he appeared to feel in his garment for something: a suspicion that he was an assassin, now arose in the casino, and there was a slight murmur heard. But it was quickly hushed by amaze. The stranger, drawing forth a dagger, marked with many a stain of blood, held it up, and waved it with a slow, but menacing motion at Montorio. At that spectacle his fierceness forsook him; he gazed a moment, then exclaiming, in a tone between a shriek and a laugh, 'Hell has triumphed,' rushed from the table. The stranger, concealing his dagger, slowly retired from the room, at every step turning and beckoning to Montorio, who followed him with faltering steps, with straining eyes, and with a shivering frame.

Such is the fact, witnessed by several of rank last night, in a crowded casino. They, who witnessed it, did not chuse to follow; and when inquiry was made of the attendants, they acknowledged they had seen them pass—but had immediately lost sight of them."

Cyprian listened in sore and fearful perplexity. "After consulting with some of Count Montorio's friends, we agreed that the circumstances we had witnessed, could only be ascribed to one of the causes I hinted at. We therefore determined to inquire whether the same change had been observed by his family, and if it were, to recommend the expediency of some steps to be taken, to discover and remove the cause of it. Your attachment, and the benignant influence you are said to exercise on the Count's habits and dispositions, pointed you out as the most proper object for this disclosure. With you, therefore, I leave it—and leave it also with you, in your discretion, to decide whether an application to his family, or to spiritual advice or authority, be most expedient on this emergency."

The acknowledgments Cyprian was preparing to make for this communication, were interrupted by loud clamours from the portico. "It is the Count returning from the Corso," said the Spaniard, "with some of his noisy associates. I was engaged to sup with them here, and took advantage of the invitation to introduce myself and information to you." "Stay then, I conjure you," said Cyprian, "stay with him this night, he is so accustomed at this hour to be abroad, that his return fill me with strange presages; perhaps this night he means to break that fearful bond that binds him. Oh, stay with him then, and let him not lose himself in the madness of the revel. You are a man of steady mind and arm—a man, such as I would lay hold of in my hour of peril, and bid abide with me. I will be in the adjacent room, and, oh! should any thing—only remember me."

The revellers were now ascending the stairs, the Spaniard retired to join them; and Cyprian hastened to a room adjacent to that where they assembled, where he remained struggling with hope and fear.

But he was soon agitated by feelings less remote:—the conversations of the banqueters soon reached his ear, and he listened with horror, which while it moved him to depart, rivetted him to the spot, to the impurity, the wickedness, and the wildness, that was poured out by those sons of mirth and ease. Gaiety, of which the happiest feature is fantastic lightness, appeared to be industriously excluded by the accumulation of every image, whose fulsomeness could disgust, whose depravity could offend, or whose profaneness, terrify. Often he wished for the wand of the enchanter, or the "wings of the morning," to bear Ippolito from pollution, in which his partial hope refused to believe him willingly immersed.

But Ippolito's voice was loudest in provoking, and circulating the frenzy of artificial joy; and Cyprian began to feel little consolation in the thought he had remitted his midnight visit; when, in one of those dead and sudden pauses, fictitious mirth is often compelled to make, he heard Montorio say, "If a stranger were permitted to view this joyous band, what would he conceive of us?" "Explain yourself?" said one of the cavaliers.—"Would he imagine there were among us beings who dared not encounter this hour alone, who rushed to this meeting, not for delight, but for shelter?" Of those to whom this question was addressed, many laughed, and all answered in the negative: "Would such a one imagine," continued Montorio, with increased emphasis "there were those among us, who were assembled here to shun a hand which follows, and fixes its grasp on them;—to fly an influence, that even here, extinguishes the lights, and poisons the wines, and makes the flushed faces around me seem as if they were seen through a gleam of sulphur-blue?" "No, no, no!" was again vociferated by the company.—"Would he imagine, that of these rioters, yet a few moments, and every voice will be hushed, and every cheek pale?" The negative was again repeated, but it was repeated by fewer voices, and in a fainter tone.—"Then," said Montorio, "he would judge falsely."—A pause followed this strange remark.—"What do these questions mean?" murmured the cavaliers. "You grow pale, Count Montorio?" said the Spaniard. "Do I? and wherefore do I?" said Ippolito, in quick and broken tones, "my hour is not yet come, let us be merry till the bell tolls, why do ye sit round me like statues, all silent and aghast?—Let me feel the grasp of your hands, and hear the sound of your voices. Laugh, laugh again: I implore you to laugh: I would laugh myself—but when I try, a raven seems to croak from my throat." He snatched up a guitar, and burst into extempore stanzas, which as he sung, he adapted, to a wild and varied melody:

CHARLES MATURIN

I

Fill, fill the bowl, the ills of life
I'll value not a feather,
No cloud shall cross my soul tonight,
Or shade its sunny weather.

II

I've sorrowed till my heart was sore,
And groan'd—but hence with prosing;
My last care dies upon this draught,
My last sigh's in this closing.

III

I'll revel with a bitter joy,
And mock at baffled sorrow;
Nor will I wreck how many a pang
Must waken with the morrow.

IV

'Tis a sweet flower, the late, late rose
That decks the sallow autumn,
And those the dearest beams of joy
That burst where least we sought 'em.

He threw down the guitar. "I am all discord—I have neither tone of mind nor of voice—But I must have music. Go, some of you, and call Cyprian.—Let him bring his harp, and hasten to us."

Cyprian, who heard every word, retreated in horror at these, and was hastening from the contiguous room; but the servants who had seen him going there, when the cavaliers entered in that hasty obedience which their master's wayward moods had lately taught them, threw open the door, and disclosed him. Ippolito clamorously called him forward; and Cyprian, whose compliance with that call, was mechanical and unconscious, advanced, though abashed and terrified. Of the cavaliers, many were intoxicated, and all had resumed the obstreperous gaiety which Montorio's questions had suspended. Some were calling for play, and some for more wine; but Ippolito, with lavish and boisterous praises of Cyprian's skill, called for a harp, and insisted on his gratifying the company with his performance. Cyprian, silently but earnestly, pleaded with his eyes for indulgence; but the demand grew more vehement, the harp was brought, and he sat down with sad and sore reluctance to an employment remote from its congenial scenery and spirits. He touched it with a trembling hand, its broken tones seemed, like him to mourn their altered destination. The times, when he had hoped the exertion of his talent would have cherished sensibility, and delighted virtue; when the grateful silence of praise struck more deeply on his delicate sense, than the boisterous delight, which rather terrified than encouraged him; when he hoped, the alternate sway of pleasures that refined, and of influence that rectified Montorio's mind, would have divided his life between the exercises and enjoyments of virtue; instead of lulling into vacancy, the intervals of Bacchanalian frenzy, with a despised and prostituted talent;—those times and hopes, struck on his mind, and tears fell fast on his hands, as he hurried over the strings.

But the emotion that shook him, added to the expression, what it denied to the execution, his eye was raised to Montorio, and the inspiration came on. He appeared to him, amongst that rout, like a frail and wandering spirit, seduced by the apostate host, and mingling in sad association; his brightness dimmed, but not lost, his nature "cast down, but not destroyed." The enthusiasm of genius was exalted by the intenseness of feeling, and he poured forth tones, that might have won such a spirit back to its original sphere and glory. All were suspended in rapture; the feast was forgotten; they hung all ear and eye on the minstrel. The clock struck twelve unheard. At that moment, a loud exclamation burst from Ippolito, who started from his seat, and stood bending from it, with arms extended towards the door. Every eye followed the direction of *his*. The servants who were collected round the door, hastily retreated; while emerging from it, was seen the figure which many of them had seen the preceding evening at the casino.

Its appearance was the same as the Spaniard had described; it was dark, shapeless, and gigantic; its face was concealed in a mask, and its head overshadowed by plumage. The cavaliers stared and murmured; Cyprian pressed close to Ippolito, and the figure stalked slowly into the midst of the hall. An utter silence succeeded; the very rustling of the cloaks of the guests, as they laid down their untasted wine, and turned to gaze on the stranger, had now ceased; and the sound of their shortened respiration, almost came to the ears; when the stranger turning from Ippolito, opposite whom he had planted himself, addressed the company—"I am here an unbidden guest; does no one receive the stranger? Then I must welcome myself."—He seated himself near the head of the table, while those next whom he placed himself, seemed doubtful whether to withdraw from him or not;—his appearance had amazed, but his voice had congealed the company. There was something so peculiar in its tone, so hollow, yet so emphatic, so distinct, yet so seemingly distant, that they who heard it, listened not to the words, but to the sound, and hung on its echo as on something that issued from an invisible direction.

Ippolito now sunk slowly back into his chair, with a face still turned, and eyes still fixed on the stranger.—"Pursue your mirth, cavaliers," said the figure again, in a tone that seemed to annihilate all mirth, "my business is alone with the Count Montorio."—"You shall not have me, unless you bear me hence in a whirlwind. From this night no power carries me, willing or alive, to your haunts." "You know my purpose and my power; delay not, resist not, retreat not."—"This is most strange," said Ippolito, recoiling in his chair, and grasping the arm of the Spaniard, and muttering in hollow and hurried tones while his eyes wandered eagerly over the stranger; "this is most strange—ye see how he sits there, in strong and visible shape, amongst us; every eye can behold, and every ear can hear him. This is most strange;—the forms that float before us, in our sleeping or waking dreams, or those more substantial ones that mingle in scenes of horror, in the solitude of midnight, in the vaults of the dead, in the chambers of sorcery; these can be banished as they are raised, by local influence, they can be dispersed by light, by human presence, nay by the effort of a recollected mind. But when they pursue us to the very hold and circle of our shelter, when they sit before us, amid our mirth and wine, in the blaze of lights, and the loud and comforting tone of human voices; when they do this, and will not be repelled, what shall we think?"—"Ippolito di Montorio," said the stranger, "delay not, resist not, retreat not; must I speak the words of power, must I produce the *seal* of your *bond?*"—"Summon your instruments and your powers," raved Montorio, with a shrieking laugh; "let them bear me off in their visible grasp; shake this house to its foundations, and amid the ruin, bury me, or bear me off; if ye will have me, I shall be no easy prey." The stranger rose, Cyprian shrieked, the cavaliers rose, murmuring and preparing to draw their swords—the stranger waved his arm; "Children of earth," said he, in a voice of thunder, "avaunt! For you there is neither task nor summons here; Ippolito di Montorio, I call on you; the bell has tolled; the hour is past. Ippolito di Montorio come with me."

Ippolito remained silent and unmoved. The stranger, as before, produced a watch, it was fifteen minutes past twelve. "Knowest thou this hour," said he, "knowest thou the deed which must be done at this hour? Ippolito di Montorio, come with me." Ippolito remained silent and unmoved. The stranger again produced the terrible dagger; the stains were numerous and livid; he waved it again before Montorio, whose eye seemed to lose all intelligence as he gazed on it. "By this dreadful instrument I adjure thee; by *his* blood which has rusted the blade I adjure thee; I adjure thee by those who saw it shed, whom thou mayest not deceive and canst not escape. Ippolito di Montorio, come with me."—"Liar—liar accursed," thundered Ippolito, "he lives, his *blood* is in *his veins*—no dagger has ever drained them. Why stand ye all round me in this dead distraction? Seize him, secure him; another moment, and his witcheries will chain you to your seats; or waft ye miles away; seize that dagger—I have discoveries to make." While he spoke, he and the company had surrounded the stranger; swords were now drawn, and arms extended to seize him—all was confusion and tumult; Cyprian, who had rushed forward, heard an eager contention of voices.—"Seize him!"—"Where is he?" "Here."—"There."—"*Gone!*"

The company gazed on each other with vacant and fruitless amaze. There were only two doors to the apartment; through neither of which had he been observed to pass. There was but a momentary pause, for Montorio exclaiming—"He that is not bereft bereft of reason, follow me," rushed from the palace. The company, partly in that perplexity which takes its omen from the first voice it hears, and partly in that solicitude to which any new object is a relief, accompanied him, and were attended by the servants, who seemed to have an ominous dread of remaining in the hall; and of the witnesses of this strange transaction, Cyprian alone remained in the deserted apartment.

When the pursuers reached the street, they perceived the necessity of adopting different directions. Among them was a nobleman, who had been intimate with the father and uncle of Ippolito; but whom his riper years had not yet taught to retire from the revels of youth. From the first appearance of the stranger in the hall, *he* had appeared uncommonly agitated. His attention to the figure, its voice, and its words, had been marked and earnest, and on the proposal to pursue different directions, he chose one that appeared most remote from the discovery of the object, and insisted on pursuing it alone. These circumstances were however but little attended to, in the mingled tumult of intoxication and terror; and the nobleman was suffered to pursue his way alone.

Two others, who had tried theirs without success, were returning to the rendezvous, when they heard behind the projecting tower of a church, through whose portico they were passing, voices which appeared to whisper, and sounds that resembled a struggle. They halted in that hesitation, in which the senses wish to assure themselves of their objects, and they then heard distinctly, in the terrible voice whose tones yet dwelt on their ears, "Release me, you know not who I am." "Then by these blessed walls," said the nobleman who had gone alone, "I will know, before I release you. Contend not with me, but tell me what you are, your life is in my power, if you are indeed a living man." A pause succeeded, which was followed by a loud and fearful cry, from the lips of the last speaker. The listeners now rushed, and found the nobleman, alone, and extended on the pavement in a swoon. They heard not the steps, nor saw even the shadow, of him they believed had been with him; but *had they*, their companion would have occupied their attention more powerfully, as they believed him to be dying.

The others who were dispersed in neighbouring directions, were collected by the noise, and assisted to support the Duke di—to the palace. Each expected abundant information on the subject of their pursuit, on his recovery, from the report of those who had been in the portico; but *that* recovery appeared long doubtful; medical assistance was procured, and the patient slowly regained the power of speech and motion. But when he did, it was only to aggravate the suspense of the listeners. From time to time, he murmured, "I have seen him, it is he"— and the weakness into which he relapsed, forbid further inquiry. Another object now engaged their disappointed attention. It was discovered by Cyprian's eager inquiries that Ippolito had not returned with the rest, and of the direction he had taken, all seemed to be ignorant.

The Duke was now borne, still partially insensible, to his carriage, and the convivial party separated, aghast, amazed, and unsatisfied. More inquiries, prompted by curiosity than solicitude, attended the bed of the invalid the next day. He continued virtually insensible; to his friends he made no communication, to his medical attendant, no complaint, to his spiritual, no confession. The words, "I have seen him, it is he," were ever on his lips. He lingered a few days in this partial delirium, and then expired, uttering these words.

The day following the feast, Ippolito returned, as usual, distracted and oppressed, but with unsubdued activity. He that day visited his companions, and solemnly intreated them to conceal the transactions of the preceding night. The request was easily complied with, for they could have told little but their own fear and uncertainty. And Ippolito returned without interruption or interference to his vigils.—In a few days a billet arrived from Annibal, of which the former part seemed to refer to some letter recently received from Ippolito.

Letter from Annibal

YOU ARE THEN AS I am—your letter describes an agency similar to that by which I seem to be led; what shall we think? By whom and whither are we conducted? I fear to follow, and I fear to pause; nor do I know whether these corresponding operations should remove or suggest doubt, should confirm the suspicion of deception, or of a power that extends every where, and blends characters and situations the most remote in the completion of its purposes. Either apprehension confirms my intention of pursuing my search and my inquiries; they must eventually lead either to the detection of fraud, or the discovery of truth. How do we flatter our motives. Were mine examined, perhaps, curiosity would be found the principal cause of my visionary heroism; yet I have witnessed things that render curiosity almost a duty. Filippo who has much attached himself to me since his uncle's death, often attends me with a face of busy significance, that seems to tempt an inquiry; but I should only be mocked by the grossness of vulgar superstition; he has nothing to relate, which I need wish to know. What Michelo concealed from me, he would not possibly communicate to him.

Night, 11 o'clock

The castle is in confusion—some extraordinary intelligence is said to have arrived; there was a messenger from Naples—he is gone; no one knew his errand or his employer. But every thing seems in silent, eager preparation. What may this mean?

Filippo has just been with me. "Have you heard, Signor, of the intelligence from Naples?"—"What have *you* heard, Filippo, for I perceive you wish to disclose something."—"I, Signor? nothing Signor,

CHARLES MATURIN

I assure you, nothing I can report as certain. Just now, I heard it said, indeed, there was some great visitor expected from Naples, for whom, preparations were to be made, and whose arrival it was said, surprised my lord, your father extremely. The cause of this visit, Signor," said he, glancing his shrewd, dark eye at me, "none of us presume to guess."— "Do you know who this visitor is Filippo?"—"There Signor, I scarce dare venture my information again; but it is said," lowering his voice, though we were alone, "it is said to be the Duke di Pallerini, his Majesty's confidential favourite; that is, Signor, not his ostensible minister, but as it were, a kind of trusty agent, who is always employed on secret and important services; you understand me, Signor."

The gravity with which I endeavoured to listen, silenced him: shall I trust this man or not? There is a shrewd promptitude about him, I like: will this visit bear any relation to the object of my pursuit? Beset as I am, with perplexity and fear, I lay hold on every thing for relief; and every thing deserts or deceives me.—

Noon

The Duke has indeed arrived. Have you heard any thing, in Naples, of the purpose of this visit? If it be an object of weight and of secrecy, I pronounce the man, from the first view of him, adequate to the trust. At first you perceive in him nothing but the suavity of the courtier; but a little observation discovers this to be only a veil to the other qualities of that character. His conversation is guardedly limited to indifferent topics, of which the charm of his manners conceals the insignificance. His very words seemed weighed in the balance of diplomatic decorum, yet you see an *object* ever directing his most trivial movements; he seems to me a mental assassin, who lurks in the shade of his purpose, to spring on the prey. But we often draw conclusions, not from what we see, but from what we determine to see. His presence has diffused something like life through this gloomy house. My father, my mother, appear to be gratified by this visit. The rest of the family with myself welcome it as a suspension of dreary monotony.

Filippo has been again with me—there was a secret in his countenance, which he did not suffer to burthen him long. "Does the Signor," said he, "recollect that there are certain apartments in the castle, which are supposed to have been unvisited for many years, and of which my late uncle had the keys?"—"I have heard of such apartments."—"And

I have heard, Signor, that since my lord your uncle's death, they have never been entered, never been opened, never even approached." "That," said I, almost unconsciously, "I know to be a falsehood."—"And so do I," returned Filippo, with quickness. "You," said I, astonished.—"And if my Signor will please to listen," he added, "he will hear something still more strange. Our apartments, Signor, are situated near that tower; mine is directly under a passage which is said to lead by a stair-case to those apartments; and often when I have lain and listened to the wind as it moaned so hollow down that passage, I have thought I heard other sounds mingling with it. Since a late period indeed, those noises increased, and often have I expected to hear the feet that fell so distinctly in that passage, enter my room and move round my bed, so plain and certain was their sound. But the danger which my mention of the adventure near the old chapel, incurred, taught me silence and fear.

Last night, however, Signor, it was my lord's order that we should feast the Duke's servants, and give abundance of wine to them; such store, Signor, was given out, even lachrymæ Christi was not grudged them;—close knaves they were, and shrewd. The more wine was poured down their throats, the more silent they grew, and at length they all pretended to sleep; some of them did so in reality; and then we saw huge stilettos peeping from under their cloaks. Strange, that one nobleman coming to visit another, should arm his attendants so!"—"And is this all you had to communicate Filippo?" "Pardon me, Signor, I was going to inform you, we separated late, and just as I had got to bed, I thought I heard the door of the passage open—I listened—it was a sound I had never heard before; for though steps had often trod that passage, they seemed to have issued from the wall, neither lock nor door had I heard ever till last night. It seemed to be opened slowly and cautiously, and many steps then brushed over my head. I sat up in my bed, and looked upwards, vacantly;—but the ceiling is old and shattered, and through the chinks I could see light passing, till it had gone beyond my room. I know not Signor, whether the wine I had drank, gave me courage, but I rose, and leaving my room softly, I went where a few steps lead to the door of that passage—I ventured up them—the door was open, and as I looked down it, I saw distinctly figures moving, and among them, one whose habit resembled a monk's. I staid till they disappeared, and then I heard other doors opening; and all night after I was disturbed by frequent noises in that direction; noises I might have mistaken for the wind, had I not seen what I did. But now, Signor, the strangest part of all, is, that recollecting the events of the night, I ventured, when the servants were in another direction, to examine the door this morning; it was still open. Twice since have I gone to it; it remains open—that is, Signor, closed but not locked: now if my Signor had any curiosity to visit those apartments"—I was struck by the circumstance he related. "You informed me," said I, concealing my knowledge, "that your uncle had the key of those apartments; who has obtained them since his death?"—"That, Signor, no one knows; nay, no one ever knew, but by conjecture, whether they were in old Michelo's possession or not. He never owned it; and the servants, would ask him for the keys of the tower, when they wished to torment him."

I mused for some moments; so many objects, and opportunities, and agents, all contributing their unconscious, but regular operations to the same point, all varying in the means and direction, but all agreeing in the end; all acting involuntarily, yet with an uniformity that suggested the idea of a superior influence; their agency neither obstructed by difficulty, nor deterred by fear; nor, as it should seem, dying with the death of their principal mover. All these struck me with a conviction of fatality, in the direction they pointed out, which I could not resist, and to which if I did, resistance would be vain. I submitted therefore silently, with awe, but not gloom; resigned, but not dejected. "Yes," said I, with an earnestness that appeared to surprise my attendant; "yes, we will visit those apartments; tonight, the servants wearied with attendance, and probably stupified with wine, will sleep sound and deep. Come, after the Duke has been conducted to his apartment, come to mine, and we will visit those apartments." Filippo assented with a pleasure, which flashed in his dark eyes.—Ippolito, I go again to the tower; often disappointed by partial discoveries, and fantastic hinderances, I go tonight with a solemnity of feeling and purpose, that tell me I shall not visit it in vain.

Adieu

HE WENT; AND, STRANGE TO relate, was seen no more by the inhabitants of the castle.

XIV

—But let both worlds disjoint
'Ere we will eat our meal in fear, and sleep
In the affliction of those terrible dreams
That shake us nightly.

—MACBETH

The cause of the visit alluded to in Annibal's last letter, may be explained by the following one, which had preceded the arrival of the writer one day, and which was directed to the

Count di Montorio

"HIS MAJESTY, THE KING OF Naples, ever attentive to the interests of his subjects, and peculiarly zealous of the honour of the higher orders, has received information that induces him to establish an inquiry into some events that are said to have occurred in the illustrious house of Montorio. With a confidence that their representative will completely exculpate himself from their imputed responsibility; and will view, not with resentment, but gratitude, the opportunity allowed him for this purpose by his gracious sovereign.—The Duke de Pallerini, to whom his majesty has been pleased to commit the inquiry into this delicate and important subject, begs leave to point to the Count Montorio, another instance of the royal benignity—the Inquisition is to be private; without the formalities of a court, or the publicity of witnesses and documents. The Duke de Pallerini proposes himself the pleasure of a visit to the Count's castle; from which he expects to return, with full proof, of the futility of the allegations he is appointed to examine."

This letter, the genuine production of an Italian statesman, who in the commencement of his letter, disguises the invidiousness of his office, by making the king the principal agent, who conceals the feeble and illegitimate character of the charge, by affecting to deprecate the offensive publicity of a court, and who prevents the possibility of preparation, by the concealment of his object, while he disarms the anxiety for it, by affecting to treat it with levity. This letter was brought by a courier, and presented to the Count; who, on reading it, continued to muse for an hour, and then desired the Countess might be summoned. The Countess followed the messenger; the attendants quitted the apartment, the Count locked, with his own hand, the door of the anti-chamber, and returning, pointed to the letter, which lay on the table; and covering his face, sunk back on his chair.

The Countess read, without uttering a sound, or altering a feature, and then with a movement which caution had made habitual, tore and consumed it. The Count raised his eye slowly, and fixed it on her; his must have been a steady aspect, that could have met it unrepelled; but hers sought and fixed it with a fuller meaning than its own.

"The storm has gathered," he murmured—"Then let it burst," replied the Countess, "what have we to fear, or to provide?"—"What have we to fear?" repeated the Count, "do you speak in despair or in defiance? What have we to fear? They who are compelled to trust or employ human agents, have ever to fear. The impotency of human power confounds and distracts us. The single arm cannot execute its own purpose. From those bold and daring conceptions, that swell the mind almost with a consciousness of its omnipotence, it must descend to the drudgery of means and agents; it must ask the aid of wretches whom it fears and hates; wretches, who are ever weighing the price of blood in one hand, against the price of treachery in the other. Commit the secret of your guilt to but one human being, let it be breathed but in one ear, ever so remote, ever so secured, ever so unassailed, and— tremble, as I do now."—"And wherefore do you tremble? Have we not secured, by oaths, by bribes, by mutual fear and danger, every being either conscious or partaking in our deed? Is not every mouth stopt, and every hand tied up? Nay, have we not, of some, the final, certain, terrible pledge of silence and safety?"—"Hush, hush, hush;" said the Count, waving one hand impatiently, while the other still concealed his face; "ever—ever those sounds—whatever words I hear, they are mixed with; whatever object I see, they are written on, and you must goad me with the repetition. Can you not speak without adverting to it; or, if you must, why advert to it so distinctly? Can you not speak like one ignorant of it; or, if knowing, one who knows it not so deeply? I need no remembrancer—no, I need no remembrancer."

"What is this weak and sickly waywardness, that shrinks not at the deed, but at the name. When the prevention of evil was yet possible, it might have been indulged; now that it is no longer so, exchange it for those views of advantage that prompted you to it. By absurdly inverting the places of desire and remorse, we lose both the tranquillity of innocence, and the enjoyments of guilt. If remorse may prevent guilt, let it precede it; but if guilt promises enjoyment, let enjoyment follow it. Ah! no, no, Montorio, this waywardness is not for us; strange deeds have made us familiar with strange language;—we must confer in the cold, hard terms of necessity." "If we must then—if we must talk like midnight assassins in their cave of blood—if it must be so—sit down by me, close and hushed; and let us consult from what quarter this danger approaches, and how its purpose and bearing may be discovered."

"There is but one quarter from which danger can approach us. The woman is secured, secured by her guilt; but Ascanio, Oh, Ascanio, that business, unfinished, unknown, unascertained, since we left Apulia, has haunted me with strange fears; it has tinged my thoughts, my very dreams."

"Would that were all that haunted mine," said the Count, inwardly. "That dark story, never fully told, in the wild fables of the Apulian peasants, I have often thought there might be some trace of Ascanio—then the monk of the mountains—the confession—the letters of doubtful menace you received from the prior of the monastery"—"Who is now," interrupted the Count, "the prior of St. Nicholo, in Naples." "Is he indeed, indeed, Montorio?" "He is; but why do you tremble?" "It was from that convent, that a confessor came to old Michelo, when dying." "True, true, he did," said the Count, smiting his forehead. "Oh, what a chaos is here! thought crossing thought, and circumstance clashing circumstance—yet nothing is certain, nothing direct. I have no motive for fear, but the consciousness of guilt. These circumstances might have happened in the common course of things. A maniac might have died—a monk might have attended his dying bed—the prior of a monastery might be removed, without danger or fear to me. But there is a coherence here—a consistency—a seeming order and form; as if some still, slow, invisible hand were busied in unravelling and displaying the train. Or, is it the curse of guilt to believe every common cause and agent in nature fraught with its detection—to see a tempest in the very blaze of noon? It is, it is;—the worm within me never dieth; and every thought and object it converts into its own morbid food,"

"Montorio, have I come here only to hear your complainings? If there be danger, the interval is short, and our preparation must be—Hush!—hark!—What sound is that? Did you lock the antichamber door?" "I did, I did; listen again. We are undone, there is a listener there." "And

CHARLES MATURIN

will you be undone? Have you not a dagger? Possibly there is but one, and he can soon be dispatched."

They had risen; they were rushing to the door. "What! more blood!" said Montorio, half recoiling, "must there be more blood?"

The Countess replied but by a look, and an effort to wrest the dagger from him; but the noise was occasioned by drawing back the bolts of another door, that which communicated with the confessor's, who opening it, suddenly entered the apartment. Montorio staggered to his chair, while his wife, with the involuntary movement of fear, held up the light to the stranger's face, to discover if indeed it were the confessor.

The monk spake in hurried and eager tones, but without the eagerness of discovery. "I know ye; I know the secret of your fear;—I know the purpose."—"Whom, and what do you know, and whence this intrusion?" said the Countess, passing with dexterous quickness between the Count and the confessor, to conceal the pale and fear-stricken visage of the former; on whom she cast looks of smothered fury, and muttered, "Shame!—shame!" through her shut teeth.

"It is in vain," said the Count, with a look of anguish and horror, "it is in vain, he knows it all." "I know it all," repeated the monk. "He echoes your words, will you prompt him yourself?—Or if he knows it all—have you not still a resource?" She pointed to his dagger; then turning boldly to the monk, to conceal the movements of the Count, again demanded of him what he knew, and wherefore he was there. *The monk laughed.*—The blood of Montorio and his wife ran cold to hear his laugh; they almost wished he had told his discovery.

"Lady," said he, "urge me not.—I know the deed—and the time—and the place—and the sign. I can repeat the signal of the secret. I have read the mark on the brow.—Do you remember your miserable agent, Ascanio? Do you remember the monk of the mountains?—the confession—secret—the letters of the prior—and how you trembled at their dark intimations?"

"Who, who is this?" said the Countess, in terror.—"Must I go on, or is your soul shaken yet?—Do you remember Orazio and Erminia—the betrayed—the distracted—the murdered?"

"Hold, hold, what, oh, what are you?" "Do you remember," said the monk, in a voice that froze them, "do you remember that night, that terrible night, when the thunder roared, and the earth was rent to appal you, in vain? Do you remember the north tower—the narrow staircase—the evening gloom?—Do you remember how your victim struggled?—Do you remember her dying curse—her dying scream?—Six strokes your dagger gave—I feel them all; at the seventh his blood rose to the hilt. You heard him chatter—you saw him convulsed—you felt him quiver—ha! ha! ha!—Go, comfort your pale husband yonder, he seems to swoon."

He released her arm, which he had grasped with violence; she staggered from him, and fell senseless on the floor. The Count remained petrified, holding his half-drawn dagger.

"Look to the lady," said the monk.—"I came not to terrify, but to save. You are in danger; I know its direction, its nature—nay its very degree. But fear you not; they can do nothing without me; you are safe from all human power, and all human vengeance. I am your dark, invisible shield. Be bold and reckless of them. Montorio, sad and fearful man, be bold. It is midnight now, and I must hence, on a far and dreary summons. Montorio, be bold and reckless."

He disappeared through the secret door. The Count raised and supported his wife. She recovered. She murmured, "Are we?"—"Alone," said the Count, "you called no assistance? None saw us." "None!" "Right, right," panted the Countess, "better death than discovery!"

She rose, feebly leaning on Montorio, the energy of her mind, contending with bodily weakness. She could scarce stand, but her eye and tone were firm.

"What fearful voice was that which spake to me?" "It was no fearful voice; it spake of strength and courage. Aye, and do I feel strange courage and strength within me since it spake." "Are you mad, Montorio? he knows our secret—pursue him, he is unarmed; he has not quitted the passage."

"Woman! woman!" scowled Montorio, "weak and daring;—but now you fainted at the name of blood, and now you urge me to shed it. I will not pursue him. Were he here, and at my very sword's point, I could not thrust at him. Zenobia! that man is the very agent of our fate. From the first moment I beheld his dark eye, and heard his deep voice, I felt my mind and genius in subjection to his. At our first conference, he appeared to be in possession of the burthen that presses on my soul: and he appeared to possess it, not in the vulgar joy of an inquisitive spirit, but with the deep consciousness and compassion that thinks not of the crime, but of the criminal. He has prayed with, and for me, in fervent agony the live-long night, till the big drops, like those of death, stood on his pale forehead;—but never till tonight did he own the extent of his knowledge, though he must have long been in possession of it. When I talk to him, events the most distant—the most secret—the most minute, seem all perfectly known to him; wherever I have been, he seems to have been—to have seen all I have seen—and to have known all I know.—His presence—his voice seem to act me like a spell. Either my spirit, weary of suffering, sinks into that lassitude, which precedes dissolution; or it bows to its arbiter, with conscious submission, and tells me to rest on him. And even now departing, he bid me be bold and fearless. I will not fear—I will rest on him."

"Montorio, you mistake the amazement of a harassed spirit, for the confidence of a controlled one. This is the monk of the mountains, whom your superstition would transform into the minister of your fate;—he holds the confession secret; which, perhaps, he only awaits the arrival of Pallerini to disclose tomorrow. And will you, will you, see the serpent crawling within your walls, and whetting the sting that is to pierce you, without an effort to crush him?"

"It is impossible to reach him now," said Montorio. "Impossible!" "Yes, when he came to reside here, he told me, I must never summon him at night, for every night he said, he had a task, which might neither be deferred nor suspended." "A pretence for an opportunity of prying." "No; often in my midnight-visitings, have I sent for him; but never was he to be found. The castle gates are locked every night; but he passes every where without noise or obstruction; he knows the secret avenues better than we do. I have seen him appear from walls, where no door was;—I have seen him in the passages of the—the—tower, but never at night may he be found."

"Your account almost tempts me to your own confidence in him. But what have we else to grasp at, it is the involuntary fortitude of misery, that converts its instruments of suffering, into instruments of relief.—At least, I am content to abide till tomorrow, for what can be done or known till then?" "Yes, tomorrow much will be known." "Did you speak, Zenobia?" "No, I was sheathing the dagger you had dropt." "I thought I heard a voice murmur, tomorrow; but I am often so deceived. Good night, Zenobia. Let the attendants return, and look you give orders for tomorrow's preparation with a cheerful tone."

The Countess rose to depart, but as she crossed, he grasped her arm; his eyes were cast upward; their lids quivered; his teeth were strongly shut; his frame rose and dilated with an intense and straining movement; he held her strenuously, but spoke not. "How is this, Montorio? Speak, what do you see, or feel, Montorio? speak to me—*must* I call assistance?" "Stir not, speak not," he hissed through his shut teeth. "What, and wherefore is this?" "There—there—there," he sighed slowly, while the influence that held him, seemed to relax. His eyes moved again, and the muscles resumed their tone and direction.

He sunk into the chair, still holding her arm, and almost dragging her with him.—"So, now, you must not leave me tonight." "Not leave you!" "No; the feeling has been with me; I know its deadly language; it tells me what shall befal tonight." "What shall befal tonight!" "Aye; ever when it comes, my eyes grow dim—my ears ring—my flesh creeps and quivers. Then I know that I shall walk in my sleep that night; and you must abide by me, Zenobia. From the strange looks of those who watch with me, I know I talk in those nightly visitings; you must abide by me, Zenobia; none but the murderess must hear the ravings of the murderer." "Yes, I will watch with you. This is the meed of our daring.— But how know you it will come on tonight?" "Whenever my mind is shaken by the mention of those events, then I know it will visit me. I have also a short, convulsive summons that betokens it;—you have seen me wrought by that; but now—prepare for the night, good wife; for what a night must I prepare!"

"How is the night?" said the Count, raising his heavy eyes to his wife. "'Tis almost twelve."—"Then my hour is very near; I feel its summons coming on; 'tis heavier than sleep, yet 'tis not like the drowsiness of sleep."—"Is there no means of preventing or of mitigating it; can you not turn your thoughts in another direction?"—"Can you!" replied Montorio, fixing his eye on her. "Is it not at least possible to repel sleep, and so repel this terrible companion?"—"No, no, no;" murmured he, with the heaviness of reluctant drowsiness. "I have tried a thousand ways, a thousand times, but never could I resist the lead-like weight of that unnatural sleep. Oh it were mockery to tell you, Zenobia, the childish, miserable things I have done to prevent these nightly visitings. I have wasted the day in fatigue, and the night in dissoluteness; but ever when it came, though the sleep that seized me were as deep as death, I rose almost as soon as my head touched the pillow. I have determined to watch at my casements, to mark the moon and clouds, their changes and shapes. I have turned my thoughts intently to one point and object, and still as it stole from my mind, I have tried to recal it. I have counted the sparks in the embers, the figures in the tapestry to force attention to wakefulness; but ever when midnight came on, I sunk into sleep, with all the horrid consciousness that it was not slumber, nor rest, but a living hell that awaited me. I have made my attendants read to me, varying their tone and subject, and bid them, if they saw me slumber, shake and rouse me up; but all in vain. When I have started from my dream, I have beheld them asleep with their books in their hands, and when I upbraided them with negligence, they fell on their knees, and declared, they neither could rouse me, nor preserve themselves from the influence that overcame them."—"Merciful heaven, and this, the moment your eyes are closed."—"My eyes never close," said Montorio, with a piteous ghastliness of visage; "on those nights; they continue open during the whole of my wandering."—"It will be a fearful sight for me to behold you."—"Aye; we must bear them though; we must learn to grapple with our fate, and all its terrible circumstance and feature. But mark me—however ghastly the sight, close not your eyes, close them not for a moment; if you do, sleep may overcome you; and the prying knaves of the chamber may listen or enter unobserved: no—though spent and affrighted, the wife of the murderer must not sleep."—"Fear me not, I shall neither slumber nor fear."—"However desperate my convulsions, my struggles, my sufferings, if my very hair stand upright, if blood gush from my nostrils, if I be drenched with the sweat of fearful agony, yet waken me not, Zenobia; let the vision spend its terrible force; for if wakened in its paroxysm, reason is irrecoverably lost.—Alas, Zenobia, by the light I see your eyes begin to wander, and your voice sounds faint;—rouse, rouse, you must not sleep, Zenobia; tell me the hour, and how much of it has our melancholy conference wasted?"—"The time-piece is beside you."—"Aye, but I want to see you move, and hear the sound of your voice answering me; tell me the hour, good wife."—"'Tis but a quarter past twelve."—"*But, but* a quarter! I thought we had almost dragged out one hour; when by some strong effort, I have resisted its influence for an hour, with what delight have I heard the bell toll one, and thought it was so much nearer morning; that so much of the terrible night was elapsed. But even that miserable respite is denied tonight. I feel that deadly sleep coming on me fast; speak, speak to me, Zenobia; let me feel your hand, or hear you move; no, no, no; all palsied, numb, and drowsy."—"Try to rise, and walk up and down your apartment; I will support."—"In vain, in vain;" he murmured, "I should sleep if rocking on a wave."—"At least retire to bed, before this oppresses you; perhaps you might get some sleep." "No, no; I will remain in this chair; even in my slumber, I feel the horrid motion of rising from the bed."

The last sentence was almost inarticulate; he shivered—he moaned—he fell backward; his eyes closed for a moment, but opening again, remained staring, motionless, and dead;—his hands moved with a faint tremour, and his heavy respiration sounded like a groan. The Countess, with involuntary fear, caught a cross that hung on her bosom, but dropt it again, while a terrible expression crossed her countenance; "What have I to do with thee," she half-murmured, and half-thought; she then seized a book that lay on the table, and began to read with fixed and vehement attention, studiously confining her eye to the page. She was disturbed by the louder groans of Montorio; she read aloud in the endeavour to drown them, but they became stronger and more terrible; she could no longer hear what she read, the book fell from her hand.

The groans were followed by some inarticulate sounds, and he then began to speak, in tones so distinct, yet so unlike human accents, that she thought the groans had not ceased.

"Zenobia, Zenobia," he said in a quick low voice, "where are you gone? What is this melancholy light by which I follow you?—the pale glow of embers!—Nay then, she must be near.—Let me draw the curtains of this bed;—Is this you, Zenobia? Ha!—lightning rive me!—Erminia!—let me, let me fly; no, no, no:—her eye has fixed, her touch has frozen me. Must I stand here for ever; rooted, congealed, gazing, face to face; touch to touch? I cannot move my foot, or withdraw my eye, or think myself away.—Ha, her cold shroud encloses me like a snow-cloud; her dead arms creep round; the icy dart of her eye numbs my brain.—Help, help me, Zenobia! I sink, I sink with her! Oceans of mist and snow! storms of icy sleet and shower! cold, cold; oh, cold."

His teeth chattered with frightful loudness, and the seat shook with his shaking limbs. "Whither, whither now!" he muttered; "aye, I know your haunt; I know, whence this dim unnatural light steals from! ye shall not drag me to the tower; it is in the castle, I know, and not in this misty bay. I will lurk in this gulph, and shun it. Ha! 'tis here; I move without feet, and without change of place; this is witchery! I will pray and cross me, and then no evil thing shall control.—Father Schemoli, cross me on the left breast, there—near the heart, for they say it is troubled and impure; I would do it myself, but my hands are bloody!—Ha! ha! ha! What hand was that which wrote on my breast? I bid it sign the cross—Orazio! Erminia!—Verdoni! in letters of burning sulphur.—

CHARLES MATURIN

Help, here!—Water!—steel! wash it!—erase it!—tear it out!—it eats into my flesh!—it drinks up my blood! Now they surround me!—save me, save me!—I stand their burning food!—Oh, their hot pincer-fangs! they hiss in my flesh!—Oh, rend out my heart, and let me have ease!— see, they divide it among them!—it spreads, it burns, upward, upward! my hairs blaze up, my eye-balls melt!—I burn blue, and green, and red!—I am a hell!—Fire, fire, fire!"

He roared with strong and horrid force, and started from his chair, and spread his arms, with the action of one who struggled with flames. A scream rose to the Countess's throat, she suppressed it with convulsive firmness. A dead silence followed this burst, and in its pause, the Countess heard the deep and heavy breathing of the sleeping pages in the anti-chamber. She felt there was something extraordinary in their torpor, but the security which it promised, balanced the fearful thoughts it whispered; and she listened to it with delight.

He advanced from his chair, with a slow but steady motion; he moved to the door; there he seemed to encounter some object, whom he addressed in low and pacifying tones.—"'Tis true, my lord, 'tis true, you must be satisfied;—there is reason for it.—Let me have the keys of the north tower.—Filthy knaves, why do you bring them smeared with blood, and twisted with worms?—Take them hence, and—ha! the doors open of themselves: 'tis a good omen, my lord;—enter first, I entreat you; nay, I would, but these old floors groan so under a man's tread, and if I entered first, you might think they groaned, because I trod them."

He went eagerly around the room, touching and pointing to different objects:—the Countess shrunk from every spot he approached. "See, my lord, see,—all is safe. Men will die—and they must be buried—and there will be a death-like steam, and a mist—a mist, my lord, but these things can be removed, and who will guess them then? Ha!" smiting with fury at the wall, "villains! villains! who has rent open this wall? Who points down that stair? Go not thither, Pallerini; nothing, nothing but a lumbering skeleton. Some dry, decayed bones, a sorry sight of mortality. It can tell nothing. Who has heard the dead speak? Ask it not to write, it hath not the means. See, I will touch it; 'tis a fearful sight, but a harmless one. Now, were I the murderer, the blood would gush from the holes of its skull:—ha! what is that! who raised its fleshless and clattering arm to smite me on my mouth?—again!—again! away— away, where the dead move is no place for us. But you heard yourselves, he did not say I did it."—He paused; he waved his arm with a slow, commanding air. "Prepare the feast—the wine—the music; but look there be no knives like daggers on the table; and let not the attendants wear those murderers' looks. Ho there, let us be merry!"

He sunk into his chair, and spread out his arms. "Give me some wine.—Ha! who is this? Ascanio!—Get thee hence, with that grim, sorry face. Ascanio, I have wished to see thee long, but this is no time, no place—avaunt! why dost thou stand grinning at me?—I tell thee this is no time. Noble Pallerini, I pledge you."

He writhed his mouth. "Ha! damned potion—what is this! Erminia's—blood!—Villains! why am I served thus!—and this! What's this before me!—a bloody dagger! Why do you all stare distractedly? Wherefore do you laugh, Pallerini? Ha! hold, the taper's here. Blasting lightnings! 'tis Orazio,—Erminia,—Verdoni, away—break up the feast, the dead are among us. The lights are sulphur; the music is a howl;—away—away;—who nails me to my chair?—The floor sinks under me!—down—down—down. Let me grasp at the air—will nothing hold me?—Sinking for ages—lower—lower—lower. My breath—my sense—my sight are gone!—Oh!—Oh!"

He staggered—he shrieked—he awoke. The Countess hastened to hold him. "Hush, hush, Montorio; all is well. You are alive—you are awake—you are in my arms." He shook and tottered in her grasp. His eyes were fixed on her; but he saw her not. Her voice was mixed with the voices of his sleep. Again she spake, again she soothed him in low, and cautious whispers. "Am I alive?—am I safe?—am I only a murderer still! Thank heaven! my hour is not yet come—my hour of flames and agony." "Hush, hush, Montorio; be yourself again. Are you unmanned by the fears that visit the infant's sleep—by the fantasy of a dream?" "And are you without fear or distraction? do you sleep all the long night? Have you no dark dreams, such as visit not an infant's sleep?" "Often; but I deride *them*, and *myself*. Often is my sleep broken with horrid starts of fear. Often do I see, through my curtains, forms with fixed eyes, and forms with none, that glare on me, in their emptiness. Often I hear, around my bed, those low, doubtful, moving sounds, which the ear can neither discover to proceed from itself, nor from outward objects. Then I shake my curtains, or trim the night-lamp, or mock the terrors that come too late for prevention, and too trfling for remorse." "Speak no more," said Montorio. "Words of comfort from the mouth of guilt, are like the prayers of the wizard, inverted as they are uttered. I

CHARLES MATURIN

would not live this life of horrors, but in the hope to compound for their mitigation in another."—

They sat in silence till near the morning. A light doze, which had fallen on them as they sat, was broken, by the opening of the secret door. Again the monk stood before them. They looked upon him, with that helpless stupefaction with which we view one who has the secret of our ruin, but over whom we have no influence to secure its concealment. "I have been far distant since," said he. "I have learned much. I would confer with you."

The Countess stared with reluctant amaze; but the confessor heeded her not. He prepared to speak; the Count pointed to a seat. "No rest for me; I would speak, and ye must hear." "Speak, then, but speak low; the attendants are in the antichamber," said the Countess, "and withdraw your cowl from your face, holy father, for my senses are dull and spent, with last night's struggles, and I scarce can hear you." "Wherefore that request?" said the monk, "none have ever seen my cowl withdrawn, none ever must, till."—

He paused. The Count and Countess bent forward with concealed faces, and fixed ears. The monk began his communications in a low tone, accompanied by violent gesture, and interrupted only by looks of silent ghastliness, which Montorio and his wife exchanged at different periods of it. The communication lasted till the watch-lights burnt dull and dim in the blue light that streamed through the curtains. The confessor rose from the chair, over which he had bent to whisper. "For this," said he, folding his dark drapery, "your preparation must be instant." "Fear us not; our demeanour shall evince nothing but ease and tranquillity." "Pardon me, lady, I never doubted your power of assuming what form or language you needed, but," said the monk, with unheeded irony, "I speak of another preparation. I speak of a place, hard to secure, and hard to conceal: of a place where the search of Pallerini might be directed, and where that search might discover a dumb, but fearful witness of our secret. Know you of such a place in this castle, lady?" "He speaks of the north tower, of the burial-hole, on the secret stair." "Why, why particularize it, with such hideous minuteness? Yes I know it well, holy father; we must anticipate all search there; that body must be removed." "When, and how, and by whom?" said the monk, in a hollow tone. "This following night," said the Countess. "And by you," added Montorio. "By me?" "Aye, by you. Contend not with me, I am

a man of wrung and harassed soul. I will not visit those apartments."
The few remaining points were adjusted in whispers. The monk retired.
The Count summoned his attendants, and the castle was soon employed
in glad and busy preparation for the arrival of the visitor—

A DAY AND A NIGHT passed in festivity. "I may expect then to meet
you in your apartment, at midnight, Count?" "I shall attend you, Duke."
But on that night, while the family were assembled in the hall, the
confessor entered, and whispered the Count, who, startled and agitated,
rose, and committing the entertainment to the Countess, retired. "You
will not forget your engagement, Count?" said the Duke, as Montorio
past him, with a solemnity so brief, it scarce seemed to borrow a
moment from the levity of his mirth. "I go to prepare for it," was the
answer. Montorio and the monk retired.

The Countess, who felt the necessary claim on her exertions,
redoubled them; though she would have almost exchanged her chair
of state for a rack, to have learned the cause of the Count's absence.
Midnight arrived; artificial levity could exist no longer. The Countess
almost talked to herself; and the Duke appeared perplexed and
suspicious, when one of the attendants acquainted him that the Count
was in his apartment. This was the signal of their meeting. The family
separated; the Duke retired to his own chamber, which, when he
conceived the castle was at rest, he quitted for Montorio's.

The Count and Countess were alone. The Duke entered, with
two attendants, in silence. The faces, the persons, the manners of
the meeting, had undergone a sudden and total change. There were
no compliments, no gaiety, no polished festivity; the countenances of
the group were only marked by different shades of suspicious or sullen
gloom, as they betokened the varied characters of the inquisitors and
the criminals. The Duke advanced. "Is it necessary," said the Count,
pointing to the attendants, "is it necessary that your lacqueys should
witness this extraordinary procedure?" "I trust," said the Duke, "you
will regard the circumstance I am about to acquaint you with, as
an additional proof of the consideration for *you* which is mingled
through the whole procedure. These persons are the officers of justice,
disguised as my attendants, and appointed to register the minutes of
the examination, I am commissioned to institute; others are dispersed
through your castle, in the same disguise, ready to execute any orders,
which the event of the examination may render it expedient for me to

issue. Under these circumstances, Count, you will observe opposition to be perfectly ineffectual, and I trust you commend the delicacy which suggested the expedient." "Proceed to your commission," replied the Count. "Will not the Countess retire?" said the Duke, "this is no place for female presence, nor will the terms and objects of our conference be pleasing to her." "The place where the honour of my family is discussed, is the fittest for the mistress of it," replied the Countess.

The secretaries seated themselves at a low table, in a remote part of the room. The Count removed the lights near which he sat, and the rustling of papers was all that interrupted a long and general pause. "You had a brother, Count." "I had." "He was married, and had children." The Count bowed. "How long is it since that sad and obscure end befel him?" "Twenty years." "And during that long period, has no inquiry been made? no solicitude excited for the fate of a brother?" "Pardon me, there needed no inquiry. I was well informed of its mode and circumstance." "And yet undertook no measure for the punishment of the murderer." "The murderer had punished himself; my brother fell by his own hand."

"How! this is contrary both to common report, and to the documents now in my possession."—"My brother died by his own hand, in a fit of despair, on the intelligence of his wife's death."—"Her death then preceded his; was it also a death of suicide?"—"No: she was pregnant; the terrors of the last eruption, which was twenty years ago, brought on a premature labour; she and her child perished."—"This can of course, be easily substantiated, a woman of her rank was certainly, suitably attended?"—"Her danger was too brief and mortal; she was only attended by the nurse of her children."—"Is she alive?"—"No; she did not long survive her mistress." "A strange fatality attended all the agents in this affair; the storm of that night had many victims, Count. But you mentioned children, how did they disappear?"—"They were conveyed that night to their nurse's sister, lest they should disturb the Countess; they died of complaints incidental to infancy."—"How considerate to remove them from the castle on that night! Doubtless their mother enjoyed repose soon after their absence; but, may I inquire, is the woman with whom they died, still living?"—"She is," interrupted the Countess, "she is now living in the Abruzzo; her name is Teresa Zanetti."—"The air of the Abruzzo is favourable to weak, infantine complaints?"—"We have reason to say so," observed the Countess; "our eldest sons, Ippolito and Annibal were nursed by that woman, and in that cottage, and they are strong and healthy young men."—"To return to the Count Orazio," said the duke, "I have heard he perished in Greece; was the suicide committed there, and by whom, if committed, was it witnessed?"—"A confidential servant was intrusted with the intelligence, but my brother started into madness on hearing it, and dashed himself from a rock, under which he was reposing on his return from a fishing party." "And of his numerous attendants, (for a nobleman would scarce undertake a journey into Greece alone,) were there none that could prevent this catastrophe?"—"He went alone, for he was fond of solitary recreation; Ascanio met him alone, and the efforts of madness which often defy numbers, were not to be resisted by a single arm."—"Of course, you soothed your grief for this melancholy event, by a public and magnificent memorial, your brother's remains were brought over, and his funeral solemnized by the family."—"Ascanio who knew what I would have suffered from the shocking intelligence that the body was so torn and scattered as to be unfit for interment, ordered a funeral, and pretended to bury the remains: I have since heard they were so mangled, *that* was impossible."—"Did no one but the *trusty* Ascanio, see those remains?"—"I was not concerned in the inquiring how many savage fishermen gazed on a carcase."—"You appear then by your own confession," said the Duke, while the secretaries pens went fast, "to be ignorant whether your brother perished or not; since to prove it, you have only the bare report of a solitary menial, who had neither witness nor evidence for his report, and who was capable of deceiving you in the most material part of the event itself. May I ask whether even this Ascanio is yet alive?"—"He has been dead some years."—"Did he die in your service?"—"No, he died abroad, in whose service I know not."—"Strange, the dismission of a servant so useful, so confidential, so considerate."—"If you expect from me the memoirs of every servant I have dismissed, I fear your commission will prove an unsatisfactory one."

A long pause followed; the Duke whispered with his secretaries. "You declare then you are utterly ignorant of this Ascanio; of his motives for leaving your service; or of any events which may have befallen him since."—"I declare it."—"Count," said the duke, "there are two ways of evading the issue of an inquiry, by partial answerings of an artful structure, or by a sullen and uniform negative; the latter mode is certainly the most safe; for subtilty may be ensnared, and guilt is apt to detect; but an universal disavowal is the shelter of obstinacy. Yet still

CHARLES MATURIN

I fear even this will not avail you; for I have not come unfurnished to this great commission; I have documents, Count Montorio; documents and proofs so powerful"—"That is false," said a voice behind him. The inquirer, the accused, and the attendants, stared in consternation. Beside the chair of the former, the monk was discovered standing; his entrance had been observed by none, his face was concealed, and after speaking, he remained so fixed and motionless, that the hearers almost doubted if the voice had issued from him. "Who is he, that is among us?" asked the Duke in a tone that spake the resolution of fear; "speak, whence are you, and wherefore do you come?" "Whence, and wherefore I come," said the monk, without moving limb or muscle, "it matters not; enough, that I know your commission, and your powers to the uttermost; you have no proofs—and he who has them, will not easily delegate them to kings or ministers."—"By what right have you intruded yourself into this presence?" demanded the Duke, "or under what powers do you pretend to dispute the exercise of mine?"—"The power under which I act," murmured the monk, "may neither be questioned nor controlled. The power which has commissioned me, does not act with the infirmity of earthly movements; it does not seek to supply a deficiency of proofs by confidence of assumption, nor make an extorted confession a substitute for the absence of witnesses; it does not leave me, as *your's* has left *you*, to shrink from a bold inquiry, and be abased by the up-braidings of falsehood; it empowers, as this moment, to acquit the Count Montorio, and to pronounce there is against him, neither witness, accuser, nor proof." "This is an excellent expedient, Count," said the Duke with indignation, "and your confessor, with the assistance of a secret door, plays his part admirably. But your next examination, shall be conducted in a place, secure at least from the intrusion of presumptuous ecclesiastics." As he spake these words, his eyes were directed to the Count; but the expression of unguarded astonishment with which the latter viewed his strange defender, undeceived him at once, prepossessed as he was with the belief of some confederacy between them.

"Why will you persist to contend with your conscience," pursued the monk, with dogmatical asperity, "I have told you, you have no proofs; *you have none;* they are distant, and deep; *where,* none can reach, and *such* as none can penetrate."—"You admit then that there are proofs," said the Duke, with the habitual spirit of availing himself of concessions, though hopeless of any favourable issue from this.—"Yes, there are proofs," said the monk; "but they are not for the sight of day, or the knowledge of man; there are proofs, but name them not; for there is a dignity in the supreme of horrors, not to be violated by the tongues of common men. For, the weak instrument of extrinsic and ineffectual agency, there is also a proof; a proof sufficient, that *you* have neither 'part nor lot in this matter;' that your time is not yet come, and when it does, it will summon you to no such task; such are only for spirits of high elect class. Follow me, and you shall behold this proof."

The Duke looked irresolute; the Count, and the attendants remained in mute astonishment. "Follow me," repeated the monk; "we must be alone."—There was about this man, a fearlessness, a careless and melancholy confidence, above humanity; he seemed to walk in a sphere of his own, in a cheerless, unsocial exemption from pain or fear, or every thing that can conciliate compassion or sympathy; and never to glance down on the ways or feelings of men, but with contempt for infirmity, or indignation for guilt. He possessed a commanding solemnity that infused enough of terror into his injunctions to render them irresistible; they who listened, could not but follow them; and they who followed, followed with a mixture of confidence and of fear, almost indescribable.

The Duke arose, but glanced at his sword, as if to intimate he was prepared for danger: the wild disdain of the monk's smile was lost in dark folds that concealed his face. The Duke and he passed slowly into another apartment. The emotion with which the Count and Countess had beheld this scene, and now awaited its conclusion, was such as cannot be described. They were restrained from expressing it by the presence of the secretaries, who amazed, and unknowing how to proceed, yet continued in the room. Of the interference of the monk, the motives that prompted it, or the modes which he had adopted to render it effectual, they were utterly ignorant; that he was acquainted with their guilt, to them was certain, and it was also certain that he appeared determined to exclude every one else from its knowledge or its prosecution. But in the miserable uncertainty of culprits, they sometimes thought he was only about to make the communication more certain and more terrible, by this mode of disclosure; and this fear, which their looks communicated to each other, as distinctly as language, was rendered almost intolerable by the impossibility of discussing it freely, or concerting any expedient that might delay or mitigate its danger; a glance or motion, indicative of solicitude, would have degraded that port of offended dignity, which they thought necessary to support before the assistants; but they listened, with dreadful intentness, to the sounds which they imagined, issued from time to time, from the adjacent room. This state, which they deemed of intolerable length, lasted but a few moments, for the Duke rushed from the apartment, with horror in his face, and scarce commanding breath to bid the attendants withdraw, made an abrupt and indistinct excuse to the Count for his visit and its circumstances. Every doubt, he faltered out, was removed, every suspicion dispelled, and nothing now remained, but to apologize for the disturbance he had caused, and to retire. This was done on the approach of morning, leaving the Count and Countess in security, mingled with amazement and fear.

XV

I have brought my harp," said Cyprian, "may I touch it?—Shall I read you those lines we found in the grotto of Posilippo?—I have coloured that sketch of the Castel Novo you praised, would it amuse you to see it?"—A dead silence followed each of these questions. Ippolito, to whom they were addressed, remained with clasped hands, and eyes fixed on a point, in utter silence.

"I am very wretched," sighed Cyprian, after a pause, which his companion's absence made to resemble solitude. "That is false," said Ippolito, "and when uttered he knew it to be so."—"Alas, what words are those," said Cyprian, "and to whom do you talk with such fearful earnestness of look and gesture?"—"Did you not say I was a murderer?" exclaimed Ippolito, starting up.—"Blessed Virgin, be calm! no one is here, no one speaks, but me."—"And is he not here?" said Ippolito, sighing, and gazing vacantly around; "I could have sworn by all the saints, I saw him, and he spoke with me but now. But he is ever near me; 'tis strange, Cyprian, but I see him in darkness, I feel him in solitude; he is ever with me."—"It may be so, dear Ippolito, our senses, are weak and deceitful organs; mine I believe, are failing too: even while I speak, you seem different from what you have seemed to me; your voice sounds not like what I have listened to, in dear and other hours." He wept and sobbed with uncontrolled emotion. "It is not true," said Ippolito, who had not heard him, "but let us change the subject. All power is limited by place and time; and the change of those may modify that power. I only say this,—because—if you should hear of my going to Capua tonight"—"Tonight! to leave Naples tonight!" exclaimed Cyprian.— "Yes," said Ippolito, "tonight, perhaps;" then added, "if the power that pursues me, can control the elements; if the hand that is stretched out over me, can indeed reach through every part of space; then I must be as one who can struggle no longer; I must shrink into its grasp; and be"—"Oh for mercy, for heaven's love, shake me not with these terrible fears; much longer I cannot bear them; what would you be, or do?—I will go with you; if you will fly, let me go with you."—"Go with me! never; so may all the visitings of a dark and wayward fate, be on my head, as your's escape it." He spoke with solemn tenderness, and laid his hand on Cyprian's head. But Cyprian felt his throat swell, and his head grow giddy; amid all his sufferings, the thought of being deserted

CHARLES MATURIN

by him he loved, had never been suggested to him; and when now it was presented to his mind, he felt as if he had never been unhappy before. An incapacity either to plead or to remonstrate, overcame him; with dim eyes and quivering hands, he attempted to follow Ippolito, feebly repeating, "I will fly with you; you said you loved me; take me with you, I will follow you barefoot and in beggary through the world! Did you not say you loved me?"—He spoke to the walls. Ippolito was gone; he remained stupified, gasping, and vainly trying to awake from what he felt to be like the spell of a dream. But it was soon dissolved; the clock struck twelve. The thoughts of Montorio's engagement at that mysterious hour rushed on him; he knelt on the ground, and prayed with fresh and fervent sorrow for him, for whom he began to fear his prayer was vain.

AT THAT HOUR—THE HOUR OF midnight; in a spot of which no one knew the site or direction, below the surface of the ground, and assembled by signals and avenues not to be discovered, were collected a number of beings whose appearance seemed to hold terrible alliance with the place and circumstance of their meeting. Of their forms many were distorted by those fantastic horrors, that startle the sleeper from his dream, and visit the eyes of the fearful when left in solitary darkness; and many were involved in a gloom through which the eye fancied it could trace shapes and shadowings of more unimaginable ghastliness, than light could reveal. All were silently and intently employed, but their gestures and movements were so different from life, that how they were employed, might not easily be known. A fitful and unsteady blaze of light played on them as they moved; it issued from a human skeleton, which stood in a recess of the vault, around whose bones a pale blue fire quivered without consuming them; and in whose eyeless sockets burned a deep and sullen flame. In other cavities of the walls, a dim, dull light appeared, supplied by tapers, which were held by shrivelled human hands, whose deadly yellowness became more visible in the light they dispersed. That light showed many other sights of terror; strange forms and characters were on the walls and roof, over whose dark and measureless extent, the eye sought in vain for a point or limit of distance. Some were in motion with a horrid resemblance of life; others were still, as the grave, from which they appeared to be but lately torn. At one extremity, if that could be called so, which was quite undefined, hung something that was intended as a separation between that and an interior vault, but of which the eye could not discover whether it was a curtain, or a volume of transparent wall, as its massive shadows appeared like the foldings of either. Before it was extended something that resembled an altar, on which a dark cloud brooding, concealed the deed and implements, through it, a dull and ghastly light was seen, across which moved the shadows of things still more terrible; and above it was extended the body of a man, blue, livid, and relaxed, as if but lately dead, but the eyes were open, and that glassiness which death only can give, lent them a strange light, like life; the right hand was raised, and the finger on the lips; and this posture, with the glazed fixedness of the eyes, gave a speaking and terrible effect to the corse. On a sudden was heard a sound which resembled what might be supposed to be the effect of a bell, tolled in the air, and heard at a vast distance under ground; suspense and doubt were visible in the aspect of the assembly, as they listened to it. All employment ceased; they looked dubiously on each other, and around them, as the deep tones died away, awaking echoes to a distance, that seemed never to have been visited by sound before. Their suspense was short—another sound succeeded, which was accompanied by the rush of a strong blast; the fires flared and bickered, as it swept them; their strong and sudden glow, making its noisome chillness more felt. In the dead silence that followed, nothing but the low hissing of the flames was heard; but the next moment, they caught the tread of a human foot, descending steps; it came nearer and louder—"He is ours for ever," exclaimed the band,—and Ippolito rushed into the vault! . . .

FROM HIS SHORT, UNEASY SLEEP, Cyprian had been often roused that night, by sudden noises in the palace; but they were so mixed with those of his sleep, that he believed both to be the same, and tried to compose himself again:—he was awakened from that late and heavy slumber, to which those who pass restless nights are accustomed, by a servant inquiring at what hour he preferred dinner, as it was near noon; with some surprise at the inquiry, he referred it to their master. "The Signor is gone," replied the man, "and we are ordered to take directions from you."—"Gone!" shrieked Cyprian, whither!—when!—how!—speak!"—"Whither, or how, Signor, none of us know," replied the servant; "he left Naples about two hours after midnight, attended by only one servant; you might have heard the noise of his departure, for we were all roused on his return; and—but perhaps, Signor, this letter

CHARLES MATURIN

which he left for you, will explain."—"I heard the noise of his departure," exclaimed Cyprian, "I heard, and did not feel he was going;—wretch, miserable wretch!" he opened the letter eagerly; the contents did not contribute to diminish his emotion.

From a persecution, which, though hopeless to escape, I am yet unable to endure, I fly, whither I know not, nor does it matter; he that drives me hence, can pursue me every where. I am hopeless of resistance or escape; yet I will fly, for I will be no easy prey. I will run to my chain's full length, and grapple with that, and make it a means of respite if not release. Some dreadful fate will befal me, cut off from the flush and joy of life, which never mortal loved as I did, and dragged to—Oh, that it were possible to compound for the misery and escape the guilt. Oh, that I might be a wanderer and a vagabond on the face of the earth, and never know habitation, or rest, or quiet of domestic dearness, so I might shun but that. I know not whither I go. I will write to you, but write not to me, for I shall probably remain in no place longer than a night. Besides, the direction might betray me. Alas! what does human device avail against him with whom I have to contend? Farewell, beloved Cyprian, my madness and misery have not left me one tear to shed, one tender thought to think of you. There was a time when I would not—but I am hot, and reckless, and insensate; yet oh! for your patience, your long-suffering love, your submissive and wife-like affection and fidelity, what shall I give you back? I am a heart-smitten and harassed man I cannot pray; I will not bless you, for I am cursed with a curse!

—Montorio

The servant, at the conclusion of the letter, informed Cyprian, that by the Signor's orders, the establishment was to be maintained for him in the same style, and his orders were to be absolute in the household. Cyprian heard him not. The whole of that dreadful day he passed in a kind of stupefaction, that did not yet exclude sensibility of pain. Montorio, his name and presence, had always seemed to him so necessary to his existence, that now he was, in his absence, scarcely conscious of life. He wandered from room to room, with a face of busy vacancy, that sought every where for an object, for whose absence it bore an expression of helplessness and dismay inconceivable.

Towards evening, in mere bodily weakness, he sunk on a sofa, and felt recollection return by increasing pain. It grew dark, and a servant entering, announced that a stranger was proceeding to the apartment, without informing any of the attendants of his name or intentions. Cyprian was alarmed, yet too feeble to make any inquiry or preparation, when the stranger entered the room, and motioned to the servant to withdraw. The light was dim, but Cyprian, in his striking air, discovered a resemblance to the house of Montorio. He advanced. "I feel that in this house," said he, "I ought to be secure; yet, I enter it in doubt and in fear." "In the house of Montorio, Signor cavalier," said Cyprian, "every man of honour is secure." "I have claims," said the stranger, hesitating, "which it were better perhaps to conceal; yet the tones of your voice bid me trust you. This must be Cyprian. I am Annibal di Montorio." "Annibal!" echoed Cyprian, wild with joy, "Annibal! Oh, fly, follow him, bring him back! Or have you found him? is he with you? Speak, speak, of him!" Annibal started. "Where is Ippolito? I came to him for shelter—where is Ippolito?" "Oh!" said Cyprian, retreating and sick with fear, "is he not with you? I thought—I hoped you had known his movements. You are his brother, and when I saw you, I—oh! do you not know then where he is?" "You amaze me—you alarm me. I knew not of his absence. I fled to him, for refuge, from danger, and extremity. I am scarce safe in his absence. Yet how shall I follow him, when you know not where he is? Tell me," collecting his habitual caution, "are the present domestics recently engaged? and are they natives of the city? "I believe they are." "Then I am safe, for some time at least. But I am worn and overwatched. I have lurked in the forest all day, let me have some refreshment, and let my own servant only, who has escaped with me, be employed about us; you shall learn all—all I know, and all I fear. My brother reposes unlimited confidence in you." Cyprian obeyed him, trembling with unsatisfied solicitude, and expected calamity.

Refreshments were procured, and Annibal eat his silent meal in secrecy and fear, attended by Cyprian, who could scarce suppress his inquiries; and by Filippo, who could hardly contain his communications, from the joy he felt at his own and his master's escape, as well as triumph in the dexterity he had exerted to effect it.

Lights had been introduced with the same caution, and Filippo had departed. Annibal rose. He examined the room, he secured the doors; he drew a stiletto, from his vest, and laid it with his pistols on the table. Cyprian beheld his preparations with an oppressing sensation of fear. Annibal returned; he traversed the room, listening to the steps of the domestics, as they passed through the rooms. The echo of the last had ceased—all was silence. Midnight arrived; Annibal looked round him with an expression of security, then resuming his seat by Cyprian, and pressing his forehead with the air of a man who struggles through weakness and weariness, to collect facts, whose weight burthens his faculties, said, "My brother's value for you justifies the communications I am about to make. No power but confidence could extort them from me. They are wonderful, dark and perilous; nor do I know what danger you may incur by becoming a partaker of them. But by comparing our mutual information on this dark topic, something may be known, which silence would have concealed. Or, perhaps, I am only yielding to the natural weakness of an oppressed mind. A dark and doubtful way is before me. I must tread it alone, without guide, and without companion; and before I go I would willingly leave with another, what my own tongue may never be permitted to tell. I would willingly think, that my memory may not be lost in oblivion, as my life will probably be. I will, therefore, relate the circumstances that have, within the last four months, befallen Ippolito and me. With the latter, he informed me, you were unacquainted; indeed, with both, except those effects which it was impossible to conceal."

ANNIBAL HAD PROCEEDED THUS FAR in his narrative, when he observed Cyprian had no longer the power of listening. In an agony of terror and devotion, he flung himself on the ground, and called on the saints to forgive and to plead for the unhappy wanderer. Annibal joined him with equal, though calmer devotion, mentally mingling his own name in his aspirations. "It is now finished," said Cyprian, as he rose from his knees, "it is all told? is it not?" Annibal shook his head. "Merciful heaven—what! more horrors! worlds would not bribe me to listen to them for another hour;"—"Not more than half an hour has elapsed since I began the narrative," said Annibal. "It has seemed to *me* a term of dreadful length," said Cyprian; "yet though I cannot listen to more, I can speak of none but him; let us sit all night, and talk where he may be fled."—"Where he has fled," said Annibal, it is now perhaps impossible to know. I had proposed, on my escape from the castle, to have come to him, and persuaded him to accompany me to France; the martial spirit of Louis the fourteenth, and of his government, holds out an encouragement to young and brave adventurers; and abroad, if the hand of heaven be not stretched out over us for evil, we might forget our country, our name, and those disastrous hauntings that seem to be inseparable from them." "And have you then experienced a similar persecution? Have you been driven also from your home? This is most horrible," said Cyprian; "is it a fiend that haunts your house?"—"It is a fiend," said Annibal, gloomily, "whom no power can chase from his prey; whom no exorcist can subdue; a craving fiend, who will have blood!"

He rose, and tossed his arms eagerly, and strode across the room. "Cyprian, horrid thoughts are besetting me; yes, I will hasten to France: I have relatives too, there!—my breath is choaked, my heart cannot beat here. But I must at least stay tomorrow; today I might say, (for see the dawn has broke upon our melancholy talk,) for I can only travel by night. If you are not yet weary of these things, wild and dark; things that defeat the reason, and make even fancy shudder; I will tell you a tale of such—I will tell you what has befallen me."—"Go on," said Cyprian, in a voice of hollow strength, "I can hear any thing now." "No, not now," said Annibal, shrinking from his own proposal; "I will now take a little rest; I will throw myself on this sofa. Lay those pistols near me, Cyprian, and loosen that dagger in its sheath; how you tremble! stay, I will do it myself."—He flung himself on the sofa, but starting up a moment after, asked Cyprian would he not try to sleep." "I am too anxious for *you*, to sleep" said Cyprian; "let me go into the anti-chamber, where the slightest noise will reach me, and I can sooner rouse you."—"This is a wretched substitute for sleep, for quiet, unsuspicious rest, to lie down, pillowed on daggers, and starting up to catch the step of the assassin."—"I doubt nevertheless, my short sleep will be calm and deep; I have a stern tranquillity within me, suited to the time." He permitted Cyprian to go into the outer room, locked the door, and composed himself again to rest.

XVI

Why do I yield to that suggestion,
Whose horrid image doth unfix my hair,
And make my seated heart knock at my ribs
Against the use of nature?

—MACBETH

During the day Annibal gave to Cyprian some papers, which contained an account of what had recently befallen him, after briefly sketching to him what was first necessary to be known, viz. the subject of his former correspondence with Ippolito. Where this is deficient, said he, at the close, I can supply it by narrative. It was written in solitude and durance; you must therefore expect a simple detail of lonely individual feelings; variety was precluded by the barrenness of utter solitude, and embellishment by the absence of all solicitude about a manuscript, which I thought would never become visible till its writer was no more.

It was on the second night after Pallerini's arrival at the castle, that I took the resolution Filippo had suggested to me, of visiting the tower. When I look back on the expectations I had formed of this circumstance and its consequences, and compare them with what has actually befallen, I can scarce be assured of my own identity. I can scarce think that the being then, whose mind was but partially tinged with fear and curiosity, whose expectations were balanced by incredulity, and whose credulity was again alarmed by experience—who was in that suspended state in which fear is not too powerful, nor solicitude too severe, can be the being now, whose mind is made up, whose feeling is tense, and the terrors of whose fate have appeared to him without cloud or shadow, without mitigation or medium—whose knowledge is without bounds, whose fear is without hope—who has no relief of human uncertainty, no shelter of natural obscurity. On that night we supped in the great corridor; it was intensely hot. I observed the Duke and my father deeply engaged in conversation, and quitted the table unnoticed. I went to my apartment, where I expected Filippo would soon join me; but he was there already, his dark eyes full of something. I had often seen them marked with curiosity and wonder; never before with fear. He anticipated my questions—"Oh, Signor, strange things are doing within these walls tonight—things that would never come into the thought of man are passing near us, frightfully near us: (drawing close to me and whispering,) you will scarce believe what I have seen, Signor." "What have you seen, Filippo," (said I, laying down the light,)—"The confessor—the confessor, Signor! I knew it long ago—I told the Count—would to heaven the inquisition had him—would to St. Agatha the Primate Cardinal of Naples had to deal with him. There was an old Carthusian in the village where I was born, who would feel the presence of a spirit before a taper had burned blue; and banished from his convent a stubborn imp who had defied holy water, and even Latin ever so long. Oh! would he were but to meet this monk, I warrant he would find him other employment than lurking in vaults, and mingling with the dead, and" . . . "Filippo, you must be composed; if you have any thing to relate, relate without wanderings and exaggeration: the time is a solemn one; nor do I wish my mind to be disturbed from the object I have fixed it on." "Signor, I will not exaggerate; I will tell you what I have really. . . but forgive me if I tell it with many starts of fear. Remember it is midnight; and that I am speaking of things fearful to think of, even at noonday; and forgive me. . . You know, Signor, how suspicious I have been of that father Schemoli, as he calls himself, though all that ever knew him say, they never saw father, or mother, or relative, or any one that owned him; but that, a few years back, when he took the vows in the Dominican convent in Gaeta, they talked of his having been first seen by some wrecked fishermen, after a terrible storm, all in a blaze of lightning, perched on a crag of a little desolate island in the Grecian sea; but this is nothing to the purpose." "I wish you could have remembered that, Filippo." "Well, Signor, I have always watched and feared him; and, after I saw him last night, visibly pacing down that passage to the north tower, I felt assured that he was connected some way with the strange noises and strange reports I had heard of that tower. So, Signor, all day I sought him through the castle; for I have a strange desire, Signor, to look into the eyes and face of one whom I suspect of any thing: I always think I discover something by it; but all was in vain. At length I bethought myself, and it was a bold thing, for some of the people of the castle would as soon enter the hole of scorpions as approach that room; I bethought myself of going to his chamber. I

CHARLES MATURIN

knew the partitions and doors there were crazy; and I thought, through some chink or crevice, I might get a sight of him, perhaps, strangely employed. Now, Signor, you have learning, and could perhaps explain your feelings better; but I had a strong thought, an audible voice, as it were, in my mind, that seemed to tell me, if I went it would not be in vain: it was as plain as if one of those pictures spoke from its frame to me: it was strange to me, and yet it gave me courage. I went about midday, when most of the family were asleep. I stole softly along, holding my breath, and looking round me, though there was no one near me; yet when I came to the very door, I could not help glancing behind me, to see if he were close to me; for I had a feeling, as if he had been stealing along with me the whole way, and would just gripe me as I came to his door. All was quiet; the passage empty; the door closed. I heard a little noise in his room, often ceasing, and often repeated, as if the person within was engaged in something that he would every now and then quit to prevent being overheard. I tried a thousand places to get a convenient view of the room; at length I fixed on one behind an old picture, in a waste recess; for all that part of the west turret is waste and dreary; and they say he therefore chose it for himself. I had a full view of him; he sat with his cowl thrown back:—never, but in my dreams, the time I had a fever, have I beheld such a face. One arm was extended, and I saw by his whole frame, that he was talking with earnest, and, as it were, angry gesture, (as he might do in the confessional, when reproving a penitent,) though I believed him alone. I changed my posture at the crevice to spy who could be with him; and I saw—yes, Signor, with these eyes I saw" . . . "Hush, hush, Filippo; more than me will hear your information."— "Then, Signor," creeping to me on tip-toe, "you must let me whisper, for I feel I shall shriek telling, if I do not." "Tell it any way, only proceed.—"I saw, blessed mother, a skeleton seated in a chair opposite to him, plain and erect, and with all that horrid quietness, as if it was the ordinary visit of a companion. My eyes grew dim. I had rather have seen him rending and abusing those dead bones, as they say the men of the unholy art do; for to sit face to face, in broad day-light, as man sits with man, with the decayed remains of the grave, with an object so loathsome to the eyes of flesh. . . Oh! it gave me a more ghastly thought of him than the night I saw him in the vaults of the old chapel. I could not bear to behold him. I stole away again and as I went, there came a hollow clattering sound from the room, as if that strange object was in motion. I hurried on, and scarce thought myself safe till I had got down the great stairs, and saw, at a secure distance, the little narrow oratory window, like a hole in a wizzard's den."—"It was indeed a ghastly sight, Filippo; but what is this to our present purpose; light that other lamp, and follow me." I was hastening away: "Stay, stay, Signor, this is not all; Oh these are fearful things to pass so near us, and to pass unnoted too; to think that we are in the next chamber to a being whose dealings are with the dead; for tonight, Signor, tonight again I saw him." "Forbear those gestures, Filippo, they tell of worse things than your story." "Oh! it was just so, Signor, I felt my arms raised, and my teeth grinding, and my very eye-brows stretched up to my forehead, when I saw him tonight coming along the passage from his room." "Why do you throw yourself thus in his way, if the only effect is fear?" "I could not help it, Signor; I felt I could not help it; I wished myself far off, but I could not move; he came on slowly, as if he were encumbered; he saw me not, those high windows give so little light, and I had shrunk just under one of them. I thought, as he passed, I heard other sound beside his steps: I looked after him, and under his garments the dead feet were peeping out. Oh! he is a creature, in whom are so strangely mixed, what belongs to the living, and what to the dead, that we know not who it is we see when he crosses us, nor what he will prove while we are yet looking at him. I followed him, though I scarce knew whither I was going, nor felt the floor under me. He went down some steps to the left, where you know, Signor, there is supposed to be a passage that has been long shut up, but where the wall is as blank and solid as this. Then I thought I should see something that would last me to tell of all my life, that the wall would open to receive, or the floor sink under, or a huge black hand be held out to him, or at least there would be a smell of sulphur as he disappeared."—"Well—well—but what did you really see?"—"I followed still, Signor; I know not how I felt; but I followed, when, suddenly turning on me—blessed saints!—it was not the monk:—a skeleton head stared at me—a bare decayed arm beckoned me backward. I retreated fast enough; but I dared not turn my back, while it was in sight least it should pursue me. It is more than an hour since I saw it, yet I see it still—every where—on the walls, on the ceilings; when the light falls strong, even I see it. I see it when I close my eyes; the deep, dark hollowness of the empty brow will never leave me."—"Filippo, is this your preparation to accompany me; to talk yourself

CHARLES MATURIN

into terrors about an object which, whether supernatural or not, has no connection with us, nor with our purpose to night?"—"Will you go to the tower tonight, tonight, Signor?"—"I am going Filippo." I rose and took the lamp; for I knew it was easier to work on fear by shame than by argument; and I felt a rising disinclination to going alone. Oh! we are all, in every state of existence, in every stage of intellect, the slaves of an inward dread of futurity, and its beings. The wisest of us, in the very pith and pride of our wisest moods, will suddenly feel himself checked and oppressed by an influence caught from the remembrances of childhood, the dream of sickness, the vision of night or solitude; from the story, the monition, the bare hint of the menial, or the crone, the humblest inferior in rank and in intellect, at the strength of which he laughs, shudders, and submits. Filippo followed me in silence, ashamed to repeat his fears, yet displeased they were put to another trial. Ippolito, (for to you I address these pages, though doubtful you will even ever see them,) you must yourself feel the hushed step, the stifled breath, the suspicious and lowered glance of eye that accompanies these movements, before their effect can be described to you. We came to the door of the passage; we tried, and found it open. At another time this circumstance would have struck me with surprise; but I was now so occupied by strange expectation, that I regarded it merely with that blind satisfaction which one feels at an object being unexpectedly facilitated to them. As we entered the passage, however, an unpleasant sensation arose within me. The first, and the last time I had trodden it before, poor old Michelo had been my conductor; the unfortunate old man, whom either my curiosity or my fear had actually killed. With an involuntary motion I raised my lamp to Filippo's face, to discover if my companion was changed; for I had felt a change in my own perceptions, that would prepare me for, and justify any strange appearance at the moment; and twice or thrice, not unconsciously, yet unwillingly, I heard myself call him Michelo.—"Do not call me Michelo, while we are here, Signor;" and I was angry and disturbed at his mentioning the name, though I had uttered it first, and giving him the pain he only wished removed.

With many such crossings of mind, sometimes resisted, and sometimes resisted in vain, we reached the apartments. The doors were open there too; but I endeavoured to withdraw my mind from every lesser notice, to still the flutter and variety of my thoughts, and fix them singly on the search of the apartments, and on the discovery of any circumstances that might attend their being opened and visited the preceding night. I passed through both apartments slowly, looking around me, but discovering nothing I had expected to see. Filippo followed still slower, with the lingering of fear, holding the lamp high, and confining his eye to that part of the room where the light fell clear. But in the second apartment I perceived the pannel removed. The circumstances of my last visit rushed on my mind: I moved mechanically towards it; but Filippo, when he saw me actually entering it, could contain no longer.—"Ah, Signor, how well you seem to know all these fearful places; and will you indeed go down that passage, that looks like a passage to the grave? (he shuddered,) If I entered it, I should think the door would close on me, and shut me into that dark cavernhole for ever. I should think (holding the light over it with a shaking hand,) to find the decayed bones of some poor wretch, whose end no one ever knew, thrown in one of those dusky nooks."—I was disturbed at his unconsciously reviving every image I wished to banish; for I felt that if I suffered my mind to pause over every fearful suggestion of memory or fancy, my resolution would be exhausted, and the moment of trial, if one was approaching, find me unprepared.

I took the lamp from him, and bidding him wait in the apartment, began to descend the steps.—"Pardon me, Signor," said he, following me eagerly; "if there be danger, you shall not encounter it alone." I easily persuaded him to stay, however, for I had no wish that he should witness all I had seen, or know all I knew. His mind was too quick and tenacious to see the object I had formerly seen there, without drawing conclusions, perhaps too strong; and I felt in the sense of his being so near me, a sufficient balance for dreary and utter loneliness.

I went down the passage alone; my lamp burned dim in the thick air. I would have hurried through it, without suffering my eye to glance beyond the limits of the light I carried; but I was come to search, and I felt myself impelled to do it. The opening of the panneldoor and the passage could be ascribed to no common cause. I soon found the place where I had discovered the skeleton; it was open and empty; the cavity remained in the wall; the rubbish appeared to have been lately scattered about; but there was no vestige of its former tenant.

I felt myself fixed to the spot. The current of my thoughts ran like cross-set streams, dark, and disturbed, and thwarting, and each perplexing me with brief predominance. I was yet hanging over the spot, indulging in doubt and fear, yet believing that I was dissolving them, when I saw Filippo above bending over the steps, and beckoning to me. I could not soon disengage myself, for my mind was intensely occupied, and I resisted his impatient motions, as the sleeper resists the effort to awake him; but before his fear could become distinct, I heard feet approaching, and saw other lights above. The steps were light and quick; I felt this was no spectre, and hastened up with a thousand feelings and intentions. They were driven back, crushed, silenced, in a moment. I beheld my father and his confessor already in the room. Oh, how many thoughts were with me in that moment's pause. My own situation and fears were forgotten. Michelo's hints, our joint discoveries, my father's character and habits, the well-watched secrecy of those bloody rooms. . . Ippolito, you are my brother; my suspicions have since been but too well justified, or I would sooner perish than write thus. But what have I known since? what have I yet to tell?—Though these thoughts were so busy so remote, yet I felt my eyes involuntarily, and even painfully fixed on his; their expression was terrible,—the monk was behind, holding up a taper in his bony hand; his face was in the shade.—"Annibal," said my father, with the broken voice of smothered rage, "why are you here?"—I was silent; for no language could relieve the tumult of my thoughts.—"Wretch, rebel, parricide," bursting out, "why are you here, and who conducted you."—I was roused by his rage.—"Why, is it a crime," said I, "to be here!"—"That you shall know," said he, fiercely, "by its punishment, at least."—He turned round, and turning, saw Filippo, seemed to start into madness, and drew his sword, and rushed on him with a force, which the other scarce avoided by a sudden bound; but the motion was so vehement, that the sword stuck in the wall, and remained fixed. Though disarmed, he again flew on him, and but for the monk and me, would have dashed him down the steps, or strangled him against the wainscot. Oh! it is horrible to hold the straining arms, and look on the bloodshot eye, and blue writhen lip, and hear the hoarse roar of a man rendered a fiend by passion.— "Villain," said he, foaming, and scarcely held, "'tis to such as you I owe my being thus persecuted, suspected, slandered—that my castle seems like a prison, and I tremble to meet the eyes of my own servants. You crouch over your fires, hinting treason to each other, till every owl that whoops from my battlements seems to call me murderer."—"Hush, hush, this is madness," said the monk, in a peculiar accent. "Follow me," said my father, resuming his sullen state.—"Where is my sword?"—His eye fell on the place where it was fixed; the light which the monk hastily held up, fell strongly on his face. For millions I would not have had within my breast a heart that could hold any alliance with such a face as his for a moment became. The sword was fixed in the wall where the stain of blood was so deep and strong. With an eye (which he seemed unable to withdraw or to close) terribly fastened to the spot, twice he said, faintly and inwardly, "Will no one give me my sword? will no one approach that wall?" The monk drew it out, and gave it to him. He turned away with the effort of one who would raise his head, and dilate his chest, and stride proudly forward; but his step was unequal, and his whole frame was shaken. He bid us follow him, sternly, and quitted the apartment. I had no means of resistance, and was so lost in thought, that of myself I thought not at all. The monk, who bore the light, lingered a moment, as if to see us quit the room. When my father called from the passage, "Come quickly, Father; I am in darkness, I am alone; Father, I say, come quickly." His voice gradually rose, as if something he feared was rapidly approaching him; it almost became a shriek. The monk hurried out, and we followed him. My father placed himself in the midst of us as we descended the stairs. I can give you no account of my feelings at this time—they were dark, mingled, strange. I believed there was danger impending over me; but what it was I could neither measure nor calculate. Ippolito, will you censure, or will you wonder at me? If I can recollect the state of my mind at that time the predominant sensation was pleasure; pleasure indeed of a doubtful, gloomy character, but certainly pleasure. The discovery I had formerly made, seemed so fully confirmed by my father's pursuit of us—his rage—his terror—and a thousand other circumstances I had remarked with the keenest local observation, that whether it was from pride in my own sagacity and perseverance, or from the resistless satisfaction that accompanies the final dissolution of doubt and perplexity, or from some other secret spring within me, I certainly was conscious of pleasure in no mean degree. Amid all this terror and danger, whatever I then felt was about to be terribly interrupted. We had come to the foot of the stairs without a sound but that of our steps. I turned involuntarily to the left, where the passage communicated with the castle. My father and the monk stopped. I read a consultation of blood in their dark pause. I turned to them. The lamp, held high, and burning dimly, from our swift motion, did not shew me a line of their countenances to read compassion or hope in. I grew deadly sick.—"This is the way," I faltered

CHARLES MATURIN

out, "from this tower," and pointed to the passage.—"It is a way," said my father, gloomily, "it will be long ere you find." I heard his words in that confusion of sense that retains the full meaning, though it mixes the sounds. I felt that danger was threatened to me, but I could not conceive either its degree or direction. My father went a few paces to the right, and, with difficulty opening another door, motioned me to enter it. I obeyed with a stupid depression, that left me even no wish for resistance. There was such a kind of dark alliance between him and this tower, that I felt him as the lord of the place, and of the time, and followed the waving of his hand, as if it were some instrument of power. In a moment the door was closed on me. The human faces were shut out. Their very steps seemed to cease at once; door after door closed at successive distances; but I did not feel myself alone till the echo of the last had utterly died away.

When I looked around me all was dim and still. The morning light soon broke, and shewed me a large desolate room, so buried in the dust of long neglect, that walls, and windows, and roof seemed to sleep in the same grey and mingled tint. No part presented a change: you might gaze till your eyes grew as dim as they, before the objects would refresh you with the least inequality: all around was dark, heavy, still. I had soon completed my comfortless survey. My thoughts turned inward on myself; I strove to drive them forth again; there was nothing to invite or to receive them. The sun rose, and the long, long day came on without object or employment for me. "Man went forth to his work, and to his labour," and I sat in cold stagnation. The monk's coming to me with food, relieved me from a thought that visited me with a sting of agony the moment before. He also brought preparations for a couch; and so miserably anxious is the mind for the relief of variety in such a moment, that I looked at them with a most desolate eye. The very thought of changing the place of my confinement, which I now saw there was no hope of changing, had been a latent comfort to me. He went and departed in silence, which no adjurations could break, nor even procure from him a look that intimated a wish or future purpose of speaking. He went, and left me alone. Solitary confinement!—may I experience any sufferings but such as those again! any other affliction supplies the power of its own resistance. There have been beings who have sung in the fires, and smiled on the rack; but the nerveless vexation, the squalid lassitude, the helpless vacancy of solitary confinement, when time flows on without mark or measure; when light and darkness are the only distinctions of day and night, instead of employment and repose; when, from the torpor of inexertion, man feels himself growing to, and becoming a part of the still senseless things about him, as the chains that have eat into his wasted limbs, have begun, from cold and extinguished sensation, to feel like a part of them—that—Oh—that to beings of thought, of motion, of capacity—what is it?—the uneasy consciousness of life, without its powers—the darkness of death, without its repose.

When the first tumult of my mind had subsided, and I felt I was really left to myself, I began to inquire what resources I had; for I shuddered at the idea of total vacancy. I had no books, no pen, no instrument or means of drawing. All I could do was—to think, to examine into my mind, and live on the stores of acquirement. I had read and thought more than young men of my age usually do; and the exclusion of outward things, I endeavoured to think, would rather assist than impede my efforts to plunge into the depth of thought. But a short time convinced me how different the employment is, that is sought for amusement, and the employment that is wooed for relief. I *could not think*. Whatever train of thought I tried to weave, whether light or solid, became immediately tasteless, and declined into absence. A monotonous musing that yet had no object, no point, nothing to quicken reflection, that hung sullenly on the objects around, without drawing image or inference from them, succeeded to every attempt at mental exertion. Here all extrinsic relief was precluded. He that is weary may throw away his book, or change his companion, or indulge meditation without the fear of vacancy; but *I* could not. *My* labour must be without remission or variety, or my dejection without hope. How long I strove, and how sadly I desisted:—I even tried to form an inward conference, to raise objections, and to construct answers; but my powers of reasoning sunk within me. I endeavoured to interest myself in the subject, to taste pleasure where I was conscious I had felt it before; to believe important what I had often contended for as so; but all was cold, shadowy, remote. I could bring nothing into contact with my mind; yet I felt that what interposed, I was interested in keeping as remote as I could. At length I spake aloud to myself, in hopes of forcing attention and interest. I tried to assent, and object, and interrupt, with a sickly affectation of the warm and vivid debates of society. The accents faltered involuntarily on my tongue; and while I was apparently talking with eagerness, my eyes and mind were mechanically fixed on the door and windows, whose height was so remote, so unassailable.

By design, I am convinced, the monk visited me but once a day; but once a day had I the satisfaction of seeing even that cheerless face, of hearing even that slow, unsolacing tread. There is no telling with what delight I waited even that, and how I listened to hear the rusty wards long resisting the key, that I might longer feel the presence of a human creature (as I believed) near me!—how I protracted the preparations for the meal he brought, that I might compel him to continue longer in my sight!—how I multiplied questions, hopeless of answer, merely because it was more like human conference, to see the person you spoke to!—how I rose from my untasted food to watch even his departing steps, and to pause, with piteous sagacity, whether it was the echo of the last, or the last but one I heard! But all this was tranquillity to what I underwent at night. During the day, I had the power of ranging through every part of my mind, and examining its gloomiest recesses without fear; but the first shadow on the deep arches of my windows, was the signal for my shutting out every idea, wild, and solemn, and fantastic; every thing that held alliance with such feelings as the place was but too ready to suggest. I measured the narrow circle of my thoughts, with the fearful caution of one who steals along a passage with the apprehension that an assassin is about to rush on him at every turning. When the dark hour came, which no aid of artificial light, no lingerings of grateful shade made lovely, then I ceased to look around me; for the dim forms so fixed by day, began to move in the doubtful light, and often I threw off my mantle, as I was wrapping it round my head, lest some other noise was couched in its rustling; but though the darkness around me was ever so deep, I felt there could be stillness without repose, and oppression without weariness. I could not sleep: I lay awake, to watch my thoughts, and to start with instinctive dread when any of them declined towards the circumstances of the last night. When I did doze, the habit was communicated to my sleep, and I started from my dreams when those images recurred in them. After the experience of the first night, I determined to earn sleep, at least, by bodily fatigue. The limits of my room admitted of many modes of exercise, and I, you know, am strong and active. At every hour, then, as nearly as I could guess, I rose to take exercise; and Oh! how dreary was it to rise to a solitary task! No stimulus of competition, of elastic spirits, any object proposed, or any prize held out, desired and contended for by others. I *did* rise and work myself into a fever of motion. I perceived, however, when I was in that tumultuous and bounding state, in which the movements are in a manner involuntary, that mine all tended to climbing. Once I had scrambled up the rugged wall with amazing tenacity; but I quitted my hold as soon as I was conscious of it, for of such a means of escape I knew there was no hope. But when I ceased, (the motion given to the spirits and blood, by violent exercise, seems communicated to other objects; and after it the performer looks around him, a consciousness of cheerfulness, that every thing else seems to partake—trees and fields dance and wave to the eye;) but when I had ceased there was no cheering voice. The echo of the noise I had made moaned long and heavily among the passages; and the walls looked so still, so dark, so unmoved, as if they scowled contempt on the puny effort to escape even the thought of their influence, to make the movements of health and freedom in a prison. I looked around me dismayed. I almost expected to hear a burst of ghastly laughter break on my ear. I almost expected to see the forms of those (if there be such) who love to haunt and watch the miseries of a prison, to scare the short sleep of the captive,—to shape to him, in the darkness of his cell, forms that wait for the hour of rest to steal on him,—to send to his grating, the faces and whispers of those he loves,—and, when he starts from his straw, to thrust to the bars some mis-shapen visage that makes mock at him. Oh! how pregnant with fearful imagery is solitude! At length, I bethought myself of the resources I had read of others employing in lonely durance. The thought of the little personal application with which I had read them was bitter to me. But, on the third night, I began to notch a pannel in my door with my knife, with the number of days I had been confined; but when the thought of my being thus utterly a captive, of my being so soon compelled to the very habits and movements of those who have wasted years in the sickness of deferred hope, the lingering death of protracted solicitude,—the knife fell from my hand, and I burst into tears. Oh! let none talk, henceforth talk, of the powers of which the mind becomes conscious in solitude; of the utility of seclusion, and the discoveries which an inward acquaintance delights us with. Solitary man is conscious of nothing but misery and vacancy; it is the principle hostile and loathsome to nature, the lethargy of life, the grave of mind.

Such was the general state of my feelings during my confinement. On the eleventh night, when they supposed me subdued by weariness, or impatience of confinement, as I was composing myself to rest, I thought I heard a step. I started up in hope and fear;—it came near. No words can tell the state of mingled feeling with which I heard it certainly approach—saw light through the crevices of the door—heard the key turn in it—and its hinges grate. Freedom could hardly repay me for such a moment—it was my father!

He approached with a slow, and, I thought, a timid step, holding up the light he bore, and glancing his eye around wistfully and intently. I thought I saw others without. When he spied me, he bore up proudly, and *I* endeavoured to rouse myself to the conference. "Annibal," said he, setting the light down, and fixing his eye on me, "you find I am not to be provoked with impunity." "I find," said I, "you can at least punish without provocation, or wherefore am I here?—For visiting a part of my paternal habitation? For going where I could neither intrude nor alarm?" "That it was my will these apartments should not be opened, should have been enough for you. From whom can I expect obedience, if my own children bribe my servants to transgress my orders? And what," said he, after a pause, "what have you gained by your rebellion? What have you seen or done that was worth risking my displeasure? Now, is your curiosity gratified? You have seen nothing but dust and decay—nothing but what any other ruin could shew you." There was such an unnatural calmness in his voice, that I was roused from my sullen negligence. I looked up. His eye was bent on me with a look so peculiar, as recalled at once his last words, and unfolded their meaning. I conceived at once that these questions were suggested to discover what I had seen and done, and discovered; whether I had found any thing which other ruins do not always conceal.

The discovery, that he was come, not to pity or to liberate, but to sift and examine one whom he believed confinement had tamed and enfeebled, at once depressed and strengthened me. My whole mind was roused and revolted by this treachery. He appeared to me not as a father, but an assassin, taking every advantage of a disarmed victim; and I determined to resist him with every remaining power, and send him back, abashed and defeated. Nor was I without hope of retaliating on him; for I had often heard of discoveries which it was the labour of thought to conceal, being made in the sudden confusion of rage, or the answer to an unexpected reply.

"Whatever discoveries I made," said I, "I should at least suppose your lordship was not interested in, and therefore could not suppose them the cause of your displeasure." "You have then made discoveries," said he, impatiently, "and why is it presumed that I am not interested in them?" "I should at least hope you were not," said I, with malicious pleasure;

"but as your lordship has informed me there *were* no discoveries to be made—that I *could* see nothing more than what other ruins might contain, I must imagine that all I beheld was either an illusion or a trifle, and in either how can you be interested?"

His eye kindled, and his lip shook. "Insolent wretch, you mock me; you exult in rebellion, because you imagine my power of punishing exhausted; but you are deceived. I have other terrible means—others that you dream not of. Drive me not to resort to them. Remember they will not be temporary, for they are not employed to extort confession, but to punish obstinacy. No; I need not your confession, foolish boy—I know every thing you can know, and an explanation of them which you do not know; but I wish you to confess, that I may have an excuse for forgiving you, and remitting your punishment. Tell me, therefore, how often you went with that lying dotard, whom death has fortunately sheltered from my resentment—tell me what he said to you, and what he shewed you—tell me—"

He stopped, as if he was betraying his expectation of too much. The impulse I felt at that moment I could not resist. I sat up, and fixing my eyes on him, "If I told you," said I, "you would either aggravate my confinement, or place me where there is a quiet exemption from all pain." But when the impulse was gratified, I felt that what I had said was dangerous and foolish; and I withdrew my eyes from him in confusion, "If," said he, in the voice of one determined to sacrifice his passions to his object, "if I am thus formidable, why do you not fear me? nor would you fear me in vain. Reflect how extensive my power is, and reflect you are within it. The resistance you have hitherto been enabled to make, you falsely ascribe to an imaginary strength of mind and principle, which, you conceive, no trial can subdue. Believe me, it is only owing to your trial having been not yet severe: (my heart sunk within me) you have been nursed in luxury, Annibal, and in the indulgence of a romantic spirit of contemplative seclusion. For you, therefore, solitude has no pains, while unaccompanied by those privations that ought to mark it as a state of punishment. While your food is plenteous and palatable, and your means of rest and warmth commodious, solitude will be employed to subdue you in vain. But if these stimulants of fictitious courage be withdrawn; if light, and warmth, and ample space, and liberty be denied you, you will find the courage which you imagined the permanent offspring of principle, the short-lived dependant of local causes, too mean to enter into the account of the high motives of a hero in chains."

My heart sunk within me as he spake. How keenly true was his remark! how superfluously cruel his irony! Oh! it is easy to resist those who are armed only with the common weapons of infliction; whose blows can be calculated and averted; who strike at parts that are exposed to and prepared for common and daily assault. But when the torturer approaches you, armed with a superior knowledge of your nature; when he knows exactly what nerve will answer with the keenest vibration of pain; what recess of weakness you most wish guarded and concealed, what are the avenues and accesses to all the most intimate and vital seats of suffering in your nature—then, then is the pain—then is the hopeless fear—the despairing submission. Such I felt, yet such I still wished to conceal.

"I know you," said I, "to have great power, and I believe you to have no mercy. Yet still I think I am not destitute of resources. My mind is yet unbroken, my resentment of oppression is inveterate, and my conscience is void of offence. This is my great stay and grasp. I will not declaim about the delights of innocence in a dungeon; 'tis ridiculous, and unlike nature. I shall probably undergo much; but what I shall undergo will, I am convinced, be rendered tolerable by the great aids I have mentioned. I will not sleep better on flint than on down; but, till my health is destroyed, I shall sleep calmly; nor will I be afraid, as long as my dim light lasts, to look into the nooks and hollows of my dungeon, rude and dark as they may be; nor, when I lie down, to listen to the changeful moanings of the wind, through its passages; to me it can tell nothing worse, than that the night will be dark and cold." As I spoke, a hollow blast shook the door, and made the light blaze bickering and wide.

"Will that be all?" said my father, in a voice that struggled to be free, "Are you sure of this?" "I will look around me," said I; for my impulse to speak was strong and elevating, "even with sport on the fantastic things which darkness and my weak clouded sight will shape out on the walls of my prison—perhaps my grave." The images were with me as I spoke, and I wept a few tears, not dejected, but sad and earnest.

"Fantastic," he murmured inwardly, "do you call forms like these fantastic?" "What forms?" said I starting in my turn. I looked up. His eyes wandered wildly round the chamber. He extended his arm, and again drew it back. He receded on one foot, almost shrinking within himself, and declining till he pressed on me. "What is it you watch," said I, "with such gesture?" bending forward with strange expectation.

"Have you eyes, and do not see it? 'tis you have done this; you have brought it here. Why will you talk of these things; their mention always does this." He reached his hand backward to grasp my arm, not for observation, but support—pointing with the other, and carrying it slowly round with the visionary motion he beheld. I was chilled with horror. It was the first time I had ever truly beheld a being labouring under the belief of the actual presence of a spiritual nature. My eyes followed his involuntarily, but I could see nothing but the dark hollow extremities of the room, darker from the dimness that came over me at that moment.

"Beckon not thus," he continued to murmur; "this is not the spot—no—you cannot shew it—here, in this room, I am safe."

Something too ghastly to be called a smile, was spread over his face. "In the name of all that is holy, whom do you talk too, or what do you point at?" "Who is near me," said he? "Ha! Annibal, why do you grasp my arm thus? What is it you look at so fixedly? there is nothing there—nothing, believe me." "I see nothing," said I, "but your language has amazed me." "Then look another way—you see there is nothing—I stretch out my arm, you see, and nothing meets it; but the shadows of these old rooms will often shape themselves into strange array." He passed his hand once or twice over my forehead. "Annibal, when my spirits are thus wrought, I will sometimes talk wildly. You must not heed me, or if you do, set it down to the account of the anxiety you have caused me; and let that operate with other considerations on your compliance. Annibal, disclose to me what you have seen and heard."

I was amazed and even incensed at a man's thus turning from the fearful punishment of guilt, to secure its concealment by the most abject wiles. I could not conceal my indignation. "I have seen and heard," said I, fervently, "but now what confirms all my former discoveries." These strong words roused him at once from his ghastly abstraction. "Dare you," said he, sternly, "dare you persist in this mockery of suspicion and insult: mockery it must be—you impose on your own credulity—you falsify your own convictions, that you may persecute and slander me:—you have no proofs—what you have seen in the tower would not be admitted as such by any but a wild and wicked mind, that would sooner accuse a parent mentally of murder, than want food for its frantic rage for discoveries." "You accuse me unjustly," said I, amazed at the distinctness of his references, but willing to avail myself of his apparent wish to expostulate: "what I have discovered was revealed to me by a train of events which I could neither control nor conjecture the issue of. By Heaven, I followed the pursuit with shrinking and reluctance, with more than the fears of nature, with a gloominess of presage and conviction, that I fear its consequences will verify on my head. The sights I beheld"—"Sights!" he interrupted, "there was but one—curse on the folly that tempted me to expose even that one. But who could have thought that cursed prying dotard would lead you to the very spot." All this was said with such involuntary quickness, I am persuaded he no more imagined I heard him, than a man does, who accidentally answers his own thoughts aloud; but every word came to me as loud and distinct as if he had been bent to force their meaning on me. I believe he saw horror in my face; for starting back, he said in a rage, "Your aspect is horrible to me; you would blast me with your eyes if you could. There is an expression in them, worse than those that glared on me just now. What matters it, that you and they are silent, when ye can look such things. But you are not as they are. No, you I can lay hold on, and compel to stay, and to suffer. And remember, in this contest of persecution, you will fare the worst. I have means of infliction beyond all thought, beyond all belief. The spirit that resisted darkness and solitude, may be bowed to scorn and debasement.—Wretch, you know not half my power. You know not that I am in possession of a secret, the disclosure of which would send you forth a vagabond and a beggar, without name, and without portion; scorn hooting at your heels, and famine pointing your forward view: that I have no tie to you, but a foolish one of habitual compassion: that tonight I might thrust you from my doors to want and infamy." "To want you might, but not to infamy. I would to heaven you would avow this secret, and thrust me out, as you threaten. Infamy may attach to me while bearing your name, and living in your crested and turretted slaughter-house; but were I suffered to make my own name, and establish my own character, I would ask only my honest heart, my strong hands, the sword you have deprived me of, and this precious picture, to animate me with noble thought."—In the enthusiasm of speaking, I drew the picture from my breast, I kissed it, and my hot tears fell on it. He bent over to see it, carelessly I believe; but, heavenly powers, what was the effect! The visage with which a moment past he had beheld, or imagined he beheld, the form of the dead, was pleased and calm, compared to the expression of mixt and terrible emotion! The horror and wild joy! The eagerness, and the despair with which he gazed on it for a moment, and then tried to tear it from me!—"Where!—How, by what, what spell, what witchery, did you obtain possession of this? Give it to me. I must have it.—'Tis mine. Wretch, how did you dare?—You kept it to blast and distract me. Struggle not with me, I would rend it from a famished wolf." "You shall not rend it from me," said I, holding it tenaciously; "it has been my companion in freedom and peace, it shall not be torn from me in prison; I care not who sees it, or knows how I obtained it; I copied it from a picture in that tower; the original is in my heart; the chosen and future mistress of it. I have vowed to seek her through the world, and I will keep my vow, if ever I leave this place with life." "Miserable boy, miserable, if this be true, you know not what you say." He smote his hands twice or thrice with a look of distraction, and spoke evidently without fear and restraint. "My crimes have cursed the world. The poison flows down to the skirts of our clothing. Beings of another generation shall lay their load of sin on my head. Annibal, Annibal, hear my words; you have sunk my soul within me; who but you has seen me thus humbled? I speak not in passion or revenge; such revenge as your ill-fated passion might prepare for me, I shudder to think of. I do not wish to plunge your soul into utter condemnation. Annibal, should you ever see the original of this picture, fly from her, from her abode, her touch, her sight; should her thought ever visit you, banish it as you would the hauntings of an evil spirit, as the tempting whisper of Satan himself; when it besets you, go to some holy man, and let him teach you penance and prayer of virtue to drive it utterly from your—remember this is the warning of him, who warns you in no weakness of love." He paused, for he was hoarse with eagerness. "Annibal, let me look on it, I pray you, let me look on that face, Annibal, 'tis but once more. I see it so often in flames and horrors, I would fain see it in peace, with the smile of life on it." He spoke this with the dreadful calmness of habitual suffering. I held it to him with a cautious hand. "Poor Erminia," he murmured inwardly; and looked at it with that piteous and anguished tenderness, with which we look on those, whose likeness recals their sufferings. "Poor Erminia," he continued to exclaim and to gaze. In the interval, I recovered my breath and my thoughts. "If," said I, scarcely hoping an answer, "the original be no more, what have I to dread from one who but resembles her? The original is dead, and in her grave; and I am to fly from her shadow." "No, no," said he in a low voice, "she is not in her grave." Again I perceived his eye fixing with that nameless and horrid vacancy, that bespeaks the presence of an object, invisible to the

CHARLES MATURIN

common organs of sight! Again, my blood ran cold. "I adjure you," said I, rising and holding him firmly, "I adjure you, be not thus moved again; I cannot bear the sight of it. Your attendants are without; go hence, before it overcomes you. I cannot bear it. I am a captive, a lone, fearful being.—Your ghastly face will be with me in every corner; it will be in my dreams." I could not move him. His limbs appeared stiffened and wound up; and the strong fixedness of his eye, nothing could turn away. He appeared to talk with earnest gesture to something that stood between him and the door; but his words were lost in inarticulate murmurs as he attempted to speak. My eyes followed his to the same spot; but though sharpened with fear almost to agony, they could distinguish nothing. "Aye," said he, in that low, peculiar voice, "I see it well enough! Ye are not of this element! But now ye rose from under my feet; and now ye muster round that door!—Not gone yet—nor yet!— No, they are larger—darker—wilder!" He paused, but his terrors did not remit, nor could I speak. Then he added, in a deeper tone, with solemn enthusiasm, "If ye indeed are real forms, that come with power, and for a definite purpose, stand, and I will meet you; will meet you as I may; for this hollow nodding and beckoning cannot be borne! Stand there, and bear up to me visibly; and I will try whether ye are truly as ye seem. I will meet you!—Now!—Now!" He seized a light in each hand, and rushed furiously to the door. "Gone, gone! I will gaze no longer, lest some other shape rise up before me." As he retreated, he said, "By heaven, they hear me without—they laugh at my folly—and you laugh, too, rebellious wretch! 'Tis you have brought me to this; your unnatural persecutions have subdued me to this weakness." He quitted the room, leaving with me a conviction that the plans of guilt are often frustrated by its terrors; and its cowardice is an abundant balance for its malignity. But all the use of this lesson was lost in the fearful recollections that accompanied it. If the purport of his visit was to punish, it was indeed fulfilled. The terrible spectacle of a being writhing under the commission, or the consciousness of a crime, oppressed my mind, almost as if I had been an agent in it: every wind that night brought to my ear, that low, strange voice in which he talked, as he believed, with beings not of this world; his wild, pale face was with me when I shut my eyes, when I opened them, it glided past me in the darkness; when I slept, I saw it in my dreams; but "joy came in the morning;" such joy, as no morning had brought to me since my confinement. Under the conduct of the monk, I was removed from that dreary room, and placed in another, in the same tower I conjectured, but more light and spacious; and, for greater indulgence, to my continued importunities, I received for answer, I should be supplied with books.

When he departed to fulfil his promise, I felt as if a new sense had been communicated to me; a new light of hope had fallen upon life. There is no telling the freshness and novelty of my joy on the possession of this long-withheld resource, which I wondered I had ever thrown aside in neglect, or in vacancy, or in caprice; which I wondered any one could believe himself unhappy, that was permitted to possess; which, above all, I wondered I had never felt the full value of, till that moment. During the hour that the monk delayed, I was too happy to glance at the probability of disappointment. I experienced a thousand glad and busy feelings. With the benevolence of joy. I wished I could communicate my frame of mind to the loungers, who yawn over untasted libraries, to those whose eyes wander over a book, without a consciousness of their contents. To me, my approaching employment seemed inexhaustible; I remembered the time, when I repined if I had not several books to make a selection from; but now, *one* appeared sufficient for the occupation of the whole day.

I can pause, said I, over every sentence, and though its meaning be nothing new, or peculiar, to think on it will waken some corresponding train of thought within me; I shall arrive at some discovery, some new combination, or resemblance in objects unnoticed before; at least, the pursuit will amuse me. I shall be intently, delightfully *employed;* and when I turn from my excursion of thought, to see I have yet so many pages to read; yet such a strong aid to interpose between me and the feelings of solitude, and the hour of darkness. Though reading had never been attended with such consequences, still my perceptions were so new, that I was confident I would enjoy all this, and more, on the possession of this new treasure, and I determined to husband my store with judicious economy, not to suffer my eye to wander over a single page carelessly; I determined to pause and to reflect, to taste and to digest with epicurean slowness. I almost wished my powers of intelligence were slower, that I might be compelled to admit more tardily, and to retain longer. At length, it came—the treasure—a single book—it was a library to me; I scarcely waited to thank my grim attendant. I opened the book, and the delusion vanished. So vehement was my literary appetite, and so long had been my famine, that I could no more restrain it, than the flow of a torrent; I hurried at once into the middle of my scanty repast, and found

CHARLES MATURIN

myself nearly half through it, before the execution of my deliberate plan would have permitted me to travel over a page. When all was finished, (early in the day) I reflected I had yet to read it over again; and I began again, but soon found that my pleasure was diminished, even beyond the power of repetition to diminish it; the uneasiness of a task was over me; I felt that I must do this to enjoy tranquillity. I could not raise my eyes with the happy vacancy of one, who knew he was not helplessly bound to a single resource; I knew what I was doing, I must persist doing, even in default of attention and pleasure, and therefore, I did it irksomely. Besides, as darkness was coming on, many passages of a visionary tendency, on which in the tumult of my first pleasure, and in the broad light of day, I had dwelt with peculiar satisfaction, I did not like venturing on now; and they presented themselves to me on the opening of a page; I scudded over them with a quick, timid eye, as if I feared they would assume some stronger characters while I viewed them.

On the whole, I even felt my positive pleasure less than I expected; my ideas were too confused and rapid for pleasure. I went on with blind admiration, and childish giddiness, swallowing passage after passage, without pause or discrimination. But even to reflect on this, afforded me employment, and employment was my object; of this I had abundance; the confusion of my ideas would not permit me to sleep; I turned from side to side; still I was repeating to myself passages I had read, and still I observed that those recurred which had interested me least. In a short time, all recollections became weary and tasteless to me from my feverish restlessness, and I heartily wished it all banished. When the castle bell tolled twelve, I listened with a momentary relief to the echoes, to the long deep echoes as they died away; the very recesses of my chamber seemed to answer them, and as they rolled off, I seemed to feel them spreading above, below, around; I listened to them, till my own fancy filled up the pause of sound. Would that it had never left my ears. At that moment, a voice, in strong, distinct human sounds, shrieked, murder, murder, murder! thrice, so near, that it seemed to issue from the very wall beside me. I cannot tell you the effect of this cry; whatever disposition I might have felt to assist the sufferer, to shout aloud in a voice of encouragement, to lament my confinement, and to tell them a human being who heard and pitied them, was so near, was al lrepelled by a sudden and inexpressible conviction, that the sounds I heard were not uttered by man. Whence this arose I could not explain, I could not examine; it would not be resisted, it would not be removed. It chained me up in silence; I could neither communicate, nor inquire into it. I could not even speak to my warden about it; I felt all day like a man, upon whose peace some secret is preying. I looked in deep oppression around me, on the walls and windows, and dark corners of my room, as if they possessed a consciousness of what they had heard; as if they could pour out and unfold the terrible sounds they had swallowed. In the midst of this dejection I recollected my book; I took it up, and with diligence that deserved a better reward, I read every syllable of it again, and paused over the very expletives with a superstitious minuteness, that made me smile when I discovered it. But it would not do. All power of feeling pleasure had ceased. I was like the vulgar, who, when they are affected with any malady, complain that it is lodged in the heart; all the attention I could bestow still left a dull sense of inward uneasiness, which I could not remove, and feared even to advert to. But long before night, I had finished even my book; still I was resolved not to be "tormented before the time;" I resolved by every or any act of exclusion, to keep the idea of what I had heard away, till midnight, till I could keep it away no longer. Oh, you have never known the sickly strivings of solitude! to dispose my scanty furniture in a thousand shapes, the most distinct from use that can be conceived; to endeavour to walk up and down the room, confining my steps to one seam in the flooring; and when they tottered from its narrowness, to look behind, lest some strange hand was pushing me from my way; to trace the winding veins in the old wainscot, that amused and pained me with a resemblance to the branching of trees and shrubs; to follow them where they could be seen, and feel them where they could not—these were the wretched resources of a situation that demands variety, yet deprives the spirits of all power as well as means to exercise it; and these wretched resources were a relief in the horrible state of my mind; nor could even that relief be long enjoyed.

The hour came. For many minutes I remained silent, gasping, as if I was watching for the sound I dreaded. My book was open before me. I did not see a word in it. I felt the slow, yet progressive motion that brings you nearer an object of horror. I felt my hairs rising up. I felt my pores open, and the cold, creeping consciousness of the thing we cannot name, spreading over me. I heard a hissing in my ears. My eyes were involuntarily distended. I felt as if all the dark powers were invisibly, but perceptibly close to me—just preparing to begin their

CHARLES MATURIN

work—just in the intense silence of preparation. The hand of a little timepiece, that had been brought to me, moved stilly on. Worlds would I have given for a sound when I saw it just touching on the hour. The castle bell tolled. It was but a moment; for I could have borne it no longer; and the voice again shrieked, murder! It was, if possible, more horrible than the preceding night; there was more of human suffering in it—more of the voice of a man who feels the fingers of a murderer on his very throat; who cries with the strength of agony, stronger than nature; who pours all his dying force into the sound that is the last living voice he shall utter. Even he who hears such a sound feels not what I did. Man, the actual sight of man, in the most dreadful circumstances in which man can behold or imagine him, is nothing to the bare fear, the suspicion, the doubt, that there is a being near you, not of this world. Between us and them there is a great gulph fixed, on the limits of which to glance or to totter, is more terrible to nature than all corporeal sufferance. Of this mysterious sensation it is impossible to describe the quality or the degree. Its darkness, its remoteness, its shapelessness, constitute its power and influence. Whether my mind was wearied by its own motions, I do not know; but I soon fell into a deep sleep. I know not how I was awakened; but I recollect it was so suddenly and thoroughly, that I started up as I awoke, and became sensible in a moment. The monk was sitting opposite me. He sat at the table, on which stood the time-piece and the lamp. His head rested on his hands, and he watched the timepiece in silence. My recollection came to me at once, and fully. I felt that at such an hour, such a visitor could have but one purpose. Oh! who can tell the gush of horror that comes to the heart of the being that, lone and helpless, is wakened at midnight, and sees around the hard blank walls of his prison, and, beside him, the face of his murderer, pale with unnatural thought, by his dim lamplight.

I sat up with the impulse, but not the power of resistance. I gazed on him earnestly. He neither raised his head nor spake. I was amazed by his silence. It seemed to cast a spell over me. I had no power to break it. I could not speak to him; yet my eyes remained fixed, and my thoughts seemed rapid in proportion to my inability to utter them. A thousand causes for his silence were suggested to me. He might be waiting the arrival of some assistant, who was to overpower my struggles, or help to thrust my corpse into some dark, remote hole, where no search would ever follow or find me; where the foot of a brother might tread over my dust, without a suspicion of my fate. Perhaps he was awaiting a signal to rush on me; perhaps, till some new and horrible means of death should be brought in, and administered to me; perhaps—that was the worst of all—some such means had already been applied, in my food, or while I slept; and he was come to watch its operation, to witness the bitterness of death, the twisted eye, the writhing feature, the straining muscle, without giving the aid which all that retain the shape of man alike expect and afford.

While these thoughts were yet in their height, the hand of the time piece pointed to one. The monk extended his hand to it—it touched it—and he raised his head. "Now I may speak," said he, fixing his large heavy eyes on me. My former suspicion recurred. "Then," said I, "I shall know my fate. Oh! I feel that you are come to announce it; I feel that you are come to murder me." He waved his hand with a melancholy motion. I had but one construction for all his motions. "Speak," said I, "I conjure you; your eye is dark, and I fear to read it, or look into it. What is your purpose?" "Death," said the monk:—"Then I am to be murdered, murdered in this dark hole, without a chance, or struggle, or straw to grasp at for life? Oh! merciful Heaven, Oh!" "What is it you fear?" said the monk rising:—"my business is death; but not yours. What do you fear? Look at this hand; years have passed since it held a weapon; years have passed since blood has flowed in its veins." I looked at his hand. I involuntarily touched it. It was deadly cold. I was silent, and awaited some explanation of his appearance or his words. "My business is death; a business long deferred, longun finished. Under its pressure I have been called up, and kept wandering for many years, without hope, and without rest. I have had many pilgrimages without companion or witness: no one knew me, or sought my name or purpose. But my term is closing, and my task will soon be finished; for now I am permitted to come to you, and speak to you." He spoke so slowly that I had time to collect myself. I marvelled at his strange language. "I know not what it is you mean, nor to what business you allude," said I. "If my senses are not impaired, you are Father Schemoli, the companion of my father." "I am," said he, in a peculiar tone, "I am your *father's constant companion*." "I know you well; you look pale and strange by this dim light, yet I know you. But what is the purport of your appearance at this hour, or of the words you have uttered, I know not." "And do you only know me as Father Schemoli? Have you seen me under no other appearance? Do you remember the last time you saw me?" "I remember it well: it was in the west tower; you bore the light; you accompanied my father; I remember you well." "Had you never seen me there before?" "Never; whatever I suspected, I never saw you there before." "Beware—beware. What spectacle did you behold there, buried and mouldering in one of the passages?" "I saw a terrible sight there," said I, shuddering; "but it was removed on my last unlucky visit to that place." "No; you saw it, though in another form—saw it as plain as you see me now." "I know not what you mean. Your voice chills me, but I do not understand you." "You will not understand me; look on my eyes, my features, my limbs," said he, rising, and spreading himself out, "the last time you beheld them, they were fleshless, decayed, and thrust in a noisome nook; yet still the strength of their moulding, and shape, and character, might strike an eye that was less quick, and gazed not so long as yours." As he spoke—was it fancy, or the very witchery of the time and place?—his eyes, his mouth, his nostrils, all the hollows of his face became deeper and darker; as the sickly glare of the lamp fell on the skin of his shorn head, it looked tense and yellow, like the bones of a skull, and the articulations of the large joints of his up-spread hands, seemed so distinct and bare, as if the flesh had shrunk from them. I swallowed down something that seemed to work up my throat, and I tried to resist the effect of his words and appearance; for it outraged my belief and my senses to a degree that no local terrors, no imposition, or fantasy of fear could justify. "Is this mockery or frenzy? Is it my ears or eyes you would abuse? If I understand you, you mean something that could not be imposed on the belief of a child, or of superstition itself. You would make me believe, that you, whom I have seen exercise all the functions, whom I have seen going in and out amongst us, are a being who has been dead for years—that you now inhabit another form—that the flesh which I felt a moment past is not substantial. Do you think that durance and hardship have debased me to such weakness? Do you believe my mind cramped and shackled like my body? Or, do you believe, even if it were, that my senses are thus enfeebled and destroyed—that I cannot hear, and see, and feel, and judge of the impressions objects ought to make on those senses, as well as if it were not now midnight, and in this dark hold, and by this single dim light? Away! I am not so enfeebled yet." He heard me calmly. "You, who wish to judge only by the evidence of your senses, why do you not consult that of your hearing better? Have you never heard this voice before? and where have you heard it?" "Yes," said I, with that solemnity of feeling which enforces truth from the speaker, "Yes, I feel I have; but whether my perceptions are confused by fear, or my memory indistinct, I cannot recal when. I hear it like a voice I have heard in a dream, or like those sounds which visit us in darkness, and mingle with the wind; yet I feel also it is not the voice with which you speak in the family."

I was gazing at him while I spake, as if I could find any resemblance in his face, that could assist me to recal the former tones of his voice. He fixed himself opposite to me—he turned his eye full on me. "What voice," said he, "was that which bore witness to Michelo's fears in the west turret, that your father's *vengeance was terrible?* What voice passed you on the winds of darkness, when you watched at the tomb of Orazio? What voice rung in the ears of the dying man, 'Woe and death,' when you knelt beside his bed? What voice shrieks, 'Murder,' every night, from a depth never measured even by the thought of man since these walls were raised? Is it not the voice which speaks to you now?" His voice had been progressively deepening till its sounds were almost lost; but in the last question it pierced my very sense with its loudness. His form was outspread, and almost floating in the darkness. The light only fell on his hands, that were extended and almost illuminated. All the rest was general and undefined obscurity. I was lost in wonder and fear, such as can only be felt by those who suddenly find their secrets in possession of another; who find all that they had thought important to acquire or to conceal, the sport of another, who sports with it and them.

"Blessed Virgin! who are you? where were you concealed? how did you follow me? who uttered these sounds, or if it was you—?" "You cannot admit things that would outrage the credulity of an infant, or of superstition; you cannot believe that I have assumed other forms than that I now bear; you are prepared with your reasons, and your answers, and your arguments, physical and sage, and able to solve all appearances and objects you may witness." He pursued derisively—"You can tell me, then, what form every night visits the burial-place in the old chapel? Whom did you behold when you ventured into the vault? Whom did you see in the passages of the west tower? Who waved the shadowy arm, and pointed the eye of life from the dead wall on you? Who shut, and you could not open, the door of the vault? Who, when I discovered your pretence for breaking into the secrets of the dead, was but a weak and unhallowed curiosity—who removed with steps not unseen, from that tower, to the dark and unblessed lair, from which my cry every night reaches your ears? And if you cannot tell this, what is he who can?"

CHARLES MATURIN

When I heard these words, fear, and every other sentiment they might have inspired, were lost in the prospect they opened of satisfying my doubts, my wonder, my long, restless, unsated curiosity. I cannot tell you the effect this enumeration, so distinct, so well-remembered in its parts, produced on me. The predominant feeling of my nature revived and arose within me. Images so remote, so obscure, never recalled without perplexity and doubt, were now with me as if just bursting into light. A hundred inquiries were on my tongue, a hundred wishes were in my heart. I was all restless, glowing expectation. Who, to see my ardent eyes (for I felt them kindle in their sockets) and out-spread hands, who could have believed I was addressing such a being—a being formed, in his most favourable aspect, to repel, not to attract; and now arrayed and aggravated in the mist, and dimness, and shapeless terrors of a supernatural agent.

"Have you indeed this knowledge? Are you indeed the being Michelo's suspicions pointed to, and my own hopes, and fears, and doubts have so long been seeking? Can you make these rough places, I have wandered on so long, plain to me? Shall my feet stumble on the dark mountains no longer? Will you tell me all—all I wish to know— all (you can discover) I want to know? If you can do this, I will believe you, I will worship you, and revere you. Take me but out of this house of darkness, and durance, and guilt; give me but to know what it has been the torment and the business of my existence to know; let me learn if I am the dupe of fear and credulity; or, as a better confidence has sometimes whispered, set apart for something great, and high, and remote; let me know this, and I will bind myself to your service, I will, by all that is sacred, I will bind myself by some tie and means so awful, that even you, with all your awfulness of character and purpose, shall hold it as sacred, and tremble to hear it."

In the eagerness of speaking, I did not perceive my declining lamp. I was drawn to it by his eye. "You do not speak," said I, "my lamp is going out. Oh! speak before it goes out; for then, perhaps, I shall tremble to hear your voice, and wish you away; speak, I conjure you: it is a dreadful thing to be left in darkness with such feelings stirred within me; satisfy them before you depart: are you going? or does the dying light deceive me?"

I could only see his eyes and his hands, that beckoned with a fitful motion in the flashing light. "That lamp warns me away. I must go to my other task: I must go to watch at your father's bedside." The tone in which he uttered this convinced me he did not speak it in his earthly capacity. The lamp went out. I saw him no more, nor heard him more. He disappeared in the darkness, without the closing of a door, or the sound of a step.

Gracious Heaven! what a sensation came over me when I felt myself alone after what I had heard and seen! I shrunk into my cloak. I wished sight, and hearing, and memory utterly extinct. I felt I had acquired a strange treasure. I felt that the visit and the communications I might probably receive were supernatural and marvellous; but I feared to look into my mind; I dreaded to think on them; they were all too wild and darkly shaped to be the companions of night and solitude. I wished to think deeply of what I had witnessed; but not till morning. I longed for a deep, heavy sleep, to ease my dizzy head, that throbbed, and whirled, and rung, till, grasping it with both hands, I tried to shut every avenue of thought and sensation. It was a dismal night. I heard the clock strike every hour. Morning broke; and when I saw, at length, the sun, bright and chearful, shining on my walls, I lay down to rest with a confidence, a satisfaction of mind, that I believe I never shall again feel going to rest at night.

Father Schemoli visited me, as usual, in the day. There was not a trace of last night's business in his countenance. I shrunk when he entered, yet soon surprized at his silence and unaltered look, I spoke to him, spoke of last night, first with questions of general import. These received no answer. I became more anxious; I inquired, I demanded, I intreated in vain. After staying the usual time, he departed, without relaxing a muscle, without uttering a sound, or indicating, by look or gesture, that he even understood me. He departed, leaving me in that unpleasant state in which you begin to question the evidence of your own senses, and doubt whether the objects of your solicitude were not the shadows of a dream.

The day passed on. Evening came, with a train of sad and dusky thoughts. I could not exclude them. I ceased to attempt it. My mind had either sunk under the languor of a long and vain resistance, or had become familiarized to objects once so strange and repulsive to our nature. They seemed to me the proper furniture of my prison. I hung over them in gloomy listlessness, without shrinking, or repelling them as I first endeavoured. Of a mind in this state, no wonder the sleeping thoughts were as dark as the waking. Indeed, all my thoughts, at that gloomy time, floated between vision and consciousness. I have often started from a point where their pursuit has led me, and asked myself, Was it the dark object of a dream? That night, weary with the watching of the last, I threw myself on my narrow bed as soon as it was twilight. I had scarce closed my eyes, when I was invested with all those strange powers which sleep gives, beyond all powers of life.

I thought Michelo was still alive, and that he led me to the apartments of the west tower. They were decorated gaily and magnificently, and filled with crowds, who turned their eyes on me, as if something was expected from my arrival. I passed through them till I arrived at the chamber, that chamber whose ominous stains told me of dangers my curiosity or my fortitude defied. It was more magnificent than the rest. At the head of a sumptuous table sat my uncle and his wife, such as I had seen them in their portraits, gay, and young, and splendid. At a distance, they appeared to be smiling around them, and on each other; but as I drew near them, the smile was altered into a strange expression. It seemed an effort to conceal the sharpest agony. I came still nearer, and fear began to mingle with my feelings. As I approached, my uncle seized my hand, and drew me to him, then, withdrawing his gay vest, shewed me his breast pierced with daggers, and splashed with blood. I shuddered; but while I was yet gazing on him, he snatched one of the daggers from his side, and plunged it into that of his wife. She fell, dying, beside him; and, with one of those sudden changes, that in dreams excite no wonder, he suddenly became Father Schemoli, his head shorn, and his habit that of a monk, and chaunted the requiem over the corpse of his wife. It was echoed by a thousand voices. I looked around me; the company, so gay and festive, were changed into a train of monks, with tapers and crosses, and the apartment was a vault. As I gazed still, the lights grew blue and pale; slowly, but perceptibly, the body decayed away, and became a skeleton, wrapt in a bloody shroud. The band of monks faded away, as I looked on them, into a ghastly troop, with the aspects of the dead, but the features and movements of the living. Their eyes became hollow, their garments a blue discoloured skin; the hands that held their tapers, as yellow and as thin as they. Still I gazed, while they all around me, and standing on a single point of ground; I beheld them all go down, their forms deadening in the gloom, and the last sound of their requiem coming broken, and faint, and far from beneath. The whole scene was then changed, and I found myself wandering through rooms, spacious, but empty and dreary. From the floor, from the wainscot, from every corner, I heard my name repeated, in soft, but distinct accents, Annibal, Annibal. It came to me from every side, Pursuing it, but yet scarce knowing the direction, I followed it from room to room. At length, I was in one that had an air of peculiar loneliness in it. The voice ceased; and there ran a hissing stillness through the room, as if its object were attained. I looked around me, expectingly. On the centre of the room a sumptuous cloak was spread. I approached it, conscious that this was the point and end of my wanderings. I knew not why—I raised, but dropt it again, shrinking; for a bloody corse lay beneath. I was retreating, but the garment began to move and heave; and the figure extending a hand, seized mine—I could not withdraw it—and drew me under that blood-dropping covering by it. The floor sunk down below us, and I found myself in a passage, low, and long, and dark. The figure glided on before me, beckoning me to follow. Far onward I saw a dim, blue light. I followed the mangled form. We came into a place resembling a chapel. I again saw my uncle standing beside an altar. The tapers on it burned with that strange light I had seen. There was a fearful contrast between the furniture of the chapel, which was gay and bridal, and the figure of the cavalier, and that of a lady who sat near the altar, wrapt in a shroud and cearments; the cavalier approached her, she rose, my uncle advanced, and began to read the marriage service. The cavalier held forward his bloody arm; the lady extended her hand— it was Erminia. I said mentally, "Is this a marriage?" I rushed forward with a wild feeling of jealousy and fear. The lady saw me, she shrieked, she darted from the altar, and catching my hand, led me to my uncle. He gazed at me a moment, then clasping me in his arms, I beheld him again changed into father Schemoli. I shrunk from his embrace, twisting myself from him with motions of horror and reluctance.

I awoke with the struggle, and beheld the monk again seated opposite me; and watching the time-piece, by the lamp that was not yet extinguished; with the full wakefulness of horror, I bent forward to see if my hour was yet come—it was past twelve. I felt a satisfaction at it, that even the presence of my visitor could not check. He spoke not, as on the former night; and his silence again bound me up. It was a strange and solemn form; we gazed on each other intently: I had no more power to withdraw my eyes from, than to speak to him. Whoever had beheld us, would have believed me bound by a spell, till his dark eye was turned to me, and his finger extended to dissolve it. The images of my dream were with me still, so strongly, that he scarce seemed to make a stronger impression on me by his real, than his visionary presence; he ceased to be an agent, but appeared come to be an interpreter. Again, as the hand of the timepiece pointed to one, he raised his eye, and said, "Now I may speak." "What is it," said I, familiarized to his appearance, "What is it forbids you to speak till this season? You seem to have a strange freedom given you at this hour. I adjure you, to speak to me in the day, when our conference will be more natural, and like that of man; but you love to glide on me in darkness and sleep; to look on with strange eyes, to talk to me with the voices of sleep or of fancy." "That is, because in this form, my powers are limited; I cannot speak when I would, nor to whom. I am only permitted that at a certain hour, and to but one human being. This heavy vesture I am wrapped in, presses on me, and checks my movements; but 'tis but the weeds of a pilgrim-spirit, and enough has at times glimmered through it, to give token of its strange tenant." "What is it you speak of—what it that restrains and presses on you?" "This form of seeming flesh and blood, that bears about an imprisoned and penanced spirit." Gracious heaven, how he looked at that moment; so sad, so dim, so visionary. My eye scarcely fixed his form, that seemed to mingle with the darkness that surrounded it. "Penanced, indeed," said I, shuddering with partial belief, "if immured in such a form. But how wild, how monstrous a fiction would your words intimate. Gracious heaven, preserve my reason while I look at you; save me from credulity, that would deprive me of the very use of my senses; that would make me the victim of a horrid, and impossible dream. What might I not be impelled to do, if I could believe you? You might make me a murderer, were I resigned to your influence. No—this midnight visiting, and the terrors with which you would fill me, are but the beginning of sorrows, my unnatural father threatens me with. I see the malice of this persecution. Solitude and confinement, and the privation of all that attends my rank and time of life, have been employed, and failed to subdue my mind; and now he sends you, you, whom nature or habit has indeed made fit for a messenger of horror; he sends you to depress and terrify me; he causes voices to shriek in the passage; and sends a face, like the visage of the damned, to stare at me, when I start from my sleep. Gracious heaven," said I, rising, and stung with heat and anguish of increasing fear, "how I am beset; these are not his last resources; he will persecute me to madness. I shall shriek existence away in this den; my eye-strings will burst at some horrible sight; I shall die the death of fear, and die it in solitude. Oh, turn your face away; I see, I feel, a smile of mockery and torment through all your silence. I know it, I know you will be here tomorrow night; I shall hear your shrieks rising through the darkness, and winds of night. Then you will stand beside me in some altered shape, or perhaps drag me from my sleep." I had worked myself to a frame, that felt and witnessed all it described. "Away," I cried, dashing myself on my bed, and hiding my head eagerly in my cloak, "away, I will shut mine eyes, and not look upon you." "If this was intended," said he calmly, "why did I not do it before, when the impression would have been more forcible from its being unlooked for? And why do I throw a veil over the visioned form of my nature, and confer with you, as man with man? If my purpose were to terrify, would I have acted thus?" "I know not; 'tis your office and habit to deal in mystery, to torment with perplexity; if it be not, why will you not explicitly declare your purpose, and begone. This chamber is dark enough without your presence.—Yet do not," starting up, and grasping his hand, "do not tonight; tomorrow, speak to me tomorrow at noon, and I will listen to you." "Tomorrow at noon I cannot; I shall be laid in my dark and bloody lair; I cannot walk in the light of noon, nor utter a voice that may be heard by man." "Your outward form," said I, "will be here." "It will be but my outward form," said he. "But why this necessity for night and solitude? Are you an owl, or a raven, that must haunt in ruins, and hoot by moonlight only." "I have a darker tale to tell than the owl that sits on the desolate ruin; than the raven that beats heavily at the window of the dying." "Then forbear to tell it, for I will not hear it, and leave me; the terrors of solitude, and my own thoughts are enough." "You did not think when you forced old Michelo to the West tower, to watch with you at the tomb, when you pursued me from haunt to haunt, and almost saw me at the task, which may not be seen." I was not then," said I, "confined in this prison;" "and therefore I was not permitted to speak to you." "Strange being, who can at once lead on and repel; who can so qualify fear with curiosity; who just know when to strengthen while you seem to remit all influence. I feel I can resist no longer. You are possessed of every avenue to the human mind; you can make me fear, and desire, and retreat, and pause, and advance as you will; even when I think I dread you most, you can make an appeal to some secret and cherished object of pursuit or desire, that distracts me with curiosity, that subdues me to concession and intreaty. I feel my heart, and mind, and fate are at your disposal, or your sport. You have been with me in solitude; you have seen me, when no eye saw me; you have over-heard my thoughts, when they were not uttered. Go on, tell me what you will; tell me what I am to do, or to know—go on; I fear, I feel I must believe it all." "'Tis twenty years since I was what you are now, a mortal, with mortal passions and habits. 'Tis twenty years since my blood flowed, or my pulses beat with life; when they did, their current was keen and fiery; I lived the life of sin and folly. Heaven and holy things were far from my thoughts. The power whom I forsook, forsook me: I was given over to a reprobate mind. My life was passed in a blaze of wickedness, and cut off with an end of blood. I was dragged to the grave by murderous and unhallowed hands; hands, like my own, on fire with wickedness, and drunk with blood; hands that I am appointed to see every night held up for pardon, and to tell they are held up in vain. My body was thrust into the hole where you found it, and my soul—" "Where did it go? I adjure you, stop not there;—tell me, where did your soul depart to?" "I must not tell, nor could you hear the secrets of the world of shadows; my taskers, who are ever around me, would flash upon your sight, and sweep me away before you, if I told their employment. The bare sight of them would shrivel you to dust, and heap this massy tower in fragments over your head; you must not cross me with these questions, nor interrupt me while I speak; my time is short, and my words measured to me; but of this be assured, no visions of moon-struck fancy; no paintings of the dying murderer; no imagings of religious horror have touched upon the confines of the world of woe. After a term of years, (during which it was a remission of sufferance, to ride the nightmares through the dark and sickly air; to hide me in the foldings of the sick man's curtains, and slowly rise on his eye, when his attendants withdrew, till he shrieked to them to return; to wail and to beckon from flood, and fell, and cavern, till the wildered passenger, or wandering child of despair, plunged after me, and with dying eye saw who had waved them on to do the loathed service of the foulest of fiendish natures, the incubus, and the vampire, and the goule; to bring them from the various elements which have swallowed them; their unutterable food, our own corrupted remains: to see the very worms conscious, and dropping from the prey; to feel the pain of our own flesh devoured with mortal sensation not all extinguished, like the faint feelings of pain in sleep, just vexing our dreams, and warring on the outworks of sensation)—after a term of years thus passed, one night, when the evil ones were lording it in the upper air, driven on by the flaky forks of the lightning, the sharp-bolted shot of the hail, and the hollo, and shout, and laughter of the revelling host of darkness, I shrunk into the recess of a mountain, and called upon its riven and rocky bowels to close upon me; but I was driven still onward; the sides of the mountain groaned under the fire-shod and hooky feet of my pursuers. I pressed on through the dark passages, through secrets of nature never seen by sun, clogged by the dews, parched with the airs, seared with the meteor fires of this dungeon of the fabric of the world; till through an aperture that would admit all the armies, I flew into a vast plain, in the centre of the mountain, where piles of smouldering and charmed rock, inscribed with forbidden names, repelled the escape even of a disembodied spirit. I believed this to be my final bourne, and almost thought with hope, that the last thunders would dash even this adamantine prison to dust; but I was deceived, yea, though a spirit unblessed, I was deceived by hope. This had been a vast plain, whereon, in elder time, stood a vast city, with all its inhabitants; they were idolatrous and wicked, and invoked the powers, and studied the arts of the dark and nether world.

Therefore, the supreme power had in his wrath caused a vast body of volcanic fire to rise out of the centre of the city, which had consumed it, with all its inhabitants, in one night, while the stones, and mineral masses, and solid fire spreading around, and arching over it, formed a mountain around it, and hid its name, and place, and memory from man for ever and ever. It was now the favoured haunt of unclean spirits; none others could find their way to it, and live. There I saw forms that must not be named, nor how employed; I shrunk into a recess, from the abhorred lights; but there I found that my flight had been involuntary, that nothing was less meant than a respite from pain, and that even the sport of devils must have malignity. In that recess, a volume of fire, fed with other substance than earthly fire, sent up its long, flaky spires, of green, and purple, and white; around it, impressed on the rock, and flashing out in its shifting light, were the forms of men in solid sulphur, or molten mineral, or those fused and mingled bodies, the monstrous birth of volcanic throes; they were a company of sorcerers, that were met to do their dark rites on the very night that they were caught, and blasted by fires from the nether world. They remained fixed around a magic fire they had raised, each in the very form and attitude in which punishment overtook them, melted into the walls of the vast temple of magic, where they were assembled and which was now a cavern in that inward region; each still bore the frown, and the awe of the potent hour in their smouldering faces; each still was armed with sigil, and teraph, and talisman. In the heart of the fire, lay a human body, unconsumed for two thousand years; for they had but partially raised it for some magic purpose, when they were destroyed; and till the spell was reversed, the body must continue there for ever. But they were now compelled by a stronger power than their own, by the power of my companions, to waken from that sleep of horrid existence, to renew the unfinished spell, and to raise the corse that lay in the flames. They obeyed, for they could not resist the words of power; and they felt that their crime was become their punishment. It was a sight of horror, even for an unblessed soul to see them. Rent from the smoking rocks, that they wished might fall on them, and hide them; their forms of metallic and rocky cinder, where the human feature horribly struggled through burnt and blackening masses, discoloured with the calcined and dingy hues of fire, purple, and red, and green; their stony eyes rolling with strange life; their sealed jaws rent open by sounds, that were like the rush of subterrene winds, moving around the fire, whose conscious flakes pointed and wound towards them. The spell was finished—the corse was released, and the living dead re-inclosed in their shrouds of adamant. Then words were uttered, and characters wrought, which no man could hear and live; and I, for further penance, was compelled to enter the body to which the functions of life were restored; and to which I must be confined, till my term of sufferance was abridged by the interment of my bones, and the punishment of my mortal murderer." "Stop, stop," said I, vehemently, "I can listen no more.—My head is reeling—my eyes are flashing—while you continue to speak, while I look on you, my breath is lost.—Can man believe these things?" I repeated to myself, "can man believe these things? But, Oh," again I said internally, "can man invent these things?" "Yes," it continued, "these are massive bones of the elder time; this tawney skin was darkened by a sun two thousand years older than that which lit you yesterday. It was the body of an inhabitant of that ancient city, that was raised to be employed in the dark doings of witchery, on the very night of its destruction. Oh, think what it is to be again pent in sinful flesh, without the power or desires of life; to look on the world through the dim organs of death; to see men, as shadows moving around me, and to be a shadow amongst them; to feel all the objects and agents of life striking on my quenched perceptions, as faintly as the images of sleep—but to be terribly awake to all that imagery, those motions that are hid from man—when I sit among you, to see the forms, and hear the voices I do; to converse with the dead, and yet wander among the living; how can I lose this dread sense of another state of existence? It can be acquired by no living being, but can never be lost by the dead—if any dead are tasked like me. I cannot tell you what words are whispered to me, nor what shapes are beside me now."

Alternate bursts of enthusiasm and fear were visiting my mind, like the alternate rush and ebb of an ocean-wave, as he spoke. I had uttered my last words under the influence of fear, and now, I spoke alike involuntarily, under the other impulse. "You can, you must let me behold those froms; I must hear those sounds. Are the secrets of another world so near me, and cannot I lay hold on them?" "You cannot; these things man may not behold, and live." "I would hazard life itself," said I, with frantic eagerness, "to look on them." "Mortal, perverse and fond, you would throw away life to feed an unhallowed curiosity; and you listen, without emotion, to a spirit in despair, that cries to you for remission and rest from the pit where there is no water." "Me?—to me this appeal? Who cries to me?—What must I do, or how am I involved? Oh! do not call on, do not come to me. I fear the snares of death are gathering about me, while I confer with you. Be satisfied; you have filled me with horrors; you have kindled in my mind a fire that can never be quenched.—Be satisfied, and depart. This is a wild hour, full of dark thoughts, and hauntings from the power of evil. Leave me. I have heard too much; I have thought too much." "No I cannot leave you; I must not leave you. Every night my visit must be repeated; every night my tale must be told perhaps by other voices than mine. Long was the name of my deliverer withheld. I was driven around the world for years, the sport of the elements, the outcast of man, unknown by, and unknowing all, yet compelled every night to visit the place where my bones decay, unblest; and measure every night, with groans that would thrill a spirit to hear, the ground to the chapel, with my strange load, rend up the earth with my own hands, and place it in an unhallowed grave, while the fiends, who watch the lost souls in those vaults, with howl, and charmed tapers, mocking the absent rite, would cast it forth again, and bear it with laugh and ban to that blood-sprinkled hole where it cannot rest. It was a weary way for me to wander every night to that spot, though the sun had set on me in the deserts of Africa. At length, I was permitted to enter this castle, in a character that procured me exemption from the persecution of frequent notice, and of being compelled to mingle much with human beings; yet, secluded as I was, the domestics noticed, feared, and watched me, and were punished for their curiosity. Here I learned who was to free me from my dark thrall. Annibal di Montorio, it is you. You must collect my unburied bones; you must lay them in holy earth, with needful and decent rite, with bell, and blessing of holy men. Annibal di Montorio, your task does not end here. From the groaning ground, from the ground where my murder was done, there comes a voice, whose cry is, "Blood for blood."

"Stop, stop, before I run wild; I must not hear these words, and deserve to live: I know their terrible meaning: I know whom they point to; but it is impossible, it is unnatural, it is perdition; I must not listen to you, I dare not; you are indeed," (my thoughts sinking into solemnity), "you are indeed, what you say you are, an evil spirit. Such things as you have told me, man could not conceive, man could not relate. I believe it all, and I believe you are a tempting spirit, a spirit of lies; full of horrible suggestions. Oh, Maria, my brains wheel round; but, to think on what you have darkly led me to!—Away from me—avaunt, thou adversary! Whatever you are, you savour strongly of the power that prompts you. A moment, and I shall see you fly shrieking and defeated, surrounded by hooting imps, goaded with talon and fang. Oh, look not at me thus! I pity you, by heaven and all its saints, I pity, and will pray for you. All offices of grace and love, mass, and prayer, and pilgrimage shall be done for you; your bones shall lay in holy earth, with cross and relick, and holy water, and ceremonies to drive away the power that has you in dark durance: all things that may do peace to a parted soul, shall be done for you; but further, name it not, hint it not; I will not hear you speak again. Do not look at me with that dark, meaning eye; I know who he is; I know all—but some other hand—Who made me an angel of vengence, to ride air in the terror of my purpose through the bowels of nature, through the shriek of mankind, through the blood of a father?"

Ippolito, if, from these broken sentences of fear and aversion, you cannot discover the meaning I ascribed to the words of the phantom, I dare not tell it more explicitly. He understood me well.—"You perceive my purpose, then; with the purposes of destiny, it is the same thing to be discovered and obeyed. But you are full of the flesh, and fleshly fears. You have not yet attained that sad and lonely exemption from mortal feeling, which is *marked on the brow* of the agent of fate. You have not stood in the thick cloud of your purpose, from which the lightnings and thunderings issuing, terrify the congregation of mankind. But we shall meet again." "Never; Oh! never. By every holy name, if holy name have power over you, I intreat you to depart; haunt me no more; you can drive me to despair, but never to guilt. Begone, I adjure you, and command you. We must meet no more. I know not to what the terrors of your presence might drive me. Madness, or worse than madness threatens me while I look at you. Your words have sunk into my soul. Nothing shall ever remove them. Your appearance and your tale can never be forgotten. There is no need to repeat them. If you value the welfare and salvation of an immortal soul, leave me, and never see me more."

He shook his head mournfully. The motion continued so long, and was accompanied with a look so disconsolate, that twice and thrice I rubbed my eyes, and doubted that their weakness gave a vibrating motion to what I saw. At length he spoke. "My visits are involuntary. I was constrained to wander over the earth, till I found the being destined by Fate to give rest and atonement to my corse and spirit; and now that I have found you, your own shadow, your own limbs, your own consciousness, and heart, and soul, cannot be more intimate and ever-present companions to you, than I and my terrible tale shall be. I will visit you every night: I will hover round you all day: my whispers shall never leave your ears, nor my presence your fancy. Fly from me, plunge into other scenes and employments, change your country, your character, your habits—I will follow you through all space; I will live with you through all life; the eternal will has wedded me to you. Suspend the swelling of the sea, arrest the moon in her course, change all things beneath the throne of heaven, and then, despair of driving me from you. The powers of both worlds are alike armed against your impious opposition. Hell will not remit its torments, nor heaven reverse its decrees. I may haunt you in more terrible shape; I may speak to you in a voice that resembles the seething tides of the lake that burneth with fire and brimstone; your reason may desert you in the struggle, but I must pursue you till my body and soul are at peace. Then when the great blow is struck," (his eye rolled and his figure spread,) "and the thunder, the long with-held thunder of heaven, is smiting into dust these dark and blood-steeped towers—then, once, and for the last time, you shall see, in my original form, bestriding these blasted battlements, a giant-shape of fire, rending up the vaults where murder has slept for ages, and pouring out to day, the guilty secrets of a house, whose records of crimes and of disasters shall end in me."

I attempted to interrupt him, or to forbear to listen to him, in vain. I might as well have interrupted the ravings of the Sybil, or arrested the

CHARLES MATURIN

storm of heaven. He rushed on the ear and soul with a flood of sound and thought, that left the hearer, gasping, bewildered, staring around to see had the voice issued from above, from beneath, were the walls around him in motion, or was the ground beneath him heaving and yawning with those terrible sounds. Till he had ceased, so suspended was my mind, I did not perceive I was in darkness. This circumstance, which I had determined to watch tenaciously, again escaped me in the confusion of my thoughts. I held up the glimmerings of my lamp. They shewed me his figure dimly retiring, but in what direction I could not discover, in the wide blackness of my vault. Quitting my lamp, and extending both arms, I felt around me, calling on him till the echoes of my voice, so fancifully aggravated, and modified to a thousand wild tones, in those long passages, came fearfully back to my ear; and, with a sudden impulse, I drew in my arms, lest I should encounter his, or some other strange touch, freezing up my limbs with its chilling gripe.

When I retreated to my bed, I expected a terrible night; but I found that the energy of my feelings was a balance for their wild agitation. I was too much out of the sphere of human nature to be assailed by its fears. To every start and stirring of uneasy thought I felt myself replying with a power of resistance and careless defiance I had never felt before, and that now I wondered I felt. I slept heavily for the remainder of the night, undisturbed by dream or start of fear.

The next day, when I awoke, I looked around me with a new sensation. I spread out my hands, and said to myself, almost audibly, I am a new creature. I rose, and strode across my room, with the proud step of one who was elevated above the feelings and claims of nature. I felt that I had held communion with the inmate of another world, of that world, so awful to our fears, so remote from our conceptions. I felt a shadowy dignity spreading around me. A feeling of pride, without the grovelling and precarious qualities of earthly pride, bore me up. I felt myself superior to kings, and all the mighty ones of the earth. What is their power? said I, internally; It lasts for a few hours, and worms like themselves tremble beneath it. To secure it they consult with man, they arm men, tremble for its preservation, and are annihilated by its loss. But the power with which I am invested, extends to a future and unending state. Dependent on me is the state of beings, whose substance is indissoluble, and whose duration is eternal. To solicit my aid the laws of heaven are changed, and the veil of the temple of eternity rent in twain. I can fix in passiveness, or bind down in torment, beings who could, if they were let loose, scatter and ravish the system and elements in which I live; and I can do this, by powers beyond the most magnified powers of my nature—powers peculiarly and exclusively entrusted to me, and for a period beyond that of my own life, perhaps beyond that of mankind.

The ghastly character of these new powers was lost in these contemplations, or rather in that strong flow of renewed spirits with which every creature enters on another day, occupied by a peculiar train of thought, and illuminated by a bright and morning sun. When I did look around, the few external objects the circuit of my prison furnished, all became, to my grasping and expanded frame of feeling, converted into fuel for them. Their impressions diversified my thoughts without diminishing them. I looked on the sun, or rather on the reflections that, chequered with the heavy casement work, fell on the thick arches of my windows. I looked on him as if I could have controled, and turned his beams backward. I thought with contempt of his task, employed in lighting myriads of half animated creatures to quit animal sleep for mental lethargy, a night of drowsiness for a day of vacancy; in calling up beings exactly the same, since he first dawned on earth, through exactly the same tasks, and to exactly the same repose.

And I thought of myself, set apart by the hand of heaven to work a secret and sublime purpose; to open the hidden book of crimes, and read them to an appalled world; to gripe, like Sampson, the main props of the fabric of iniquity, and bear it to the ground, crushed under its huge and scattering ruin. I thought, that to the record of my life, the heart of man would cling, by its most vital hopes and fears, by its fond interest in life, and its trembling solicitude of futurity; while the histories of nations, and kingdoms, and chiefs, the ephemeral bubbles of time, mouldered away in their hands. I looked on the walls of my prison with a contempt, a secret, invidious contempt.—Yes, said I, ye may frown and lower; ye may deepen your shadows, and make your fastenings ten-fold more strong; every wind of heaven may blow on you, till your cement hardens into solid rock, and your pile is as a pile of adamant. But before the arm of Him, who beckons me to his strong bidding, ye, and all earthly obstructions, shall pass away like smoke. Ye may look grim on other prisoners; children of earth may languish out their unmarked and valueless lives here; they may look up, shuddering, to your iron roof, and say, from hence is no redemption; but what are ye to me, whom the Power that leads, can bring from the bottom of the ocean; can snatch from the crater of the volcano; can bid the elements fall back; yea, can make the very grave give up again, "because he hath need of me?"

I paused over these reflections. My mind was filled with a terrible courage, a daring elevation, a wild and gloomy sublimity. The sensation of fear was the ground of all my feelings; but it was fear purified from all grossness of earthly mixture or infirmity. I was the associate, not the prey of unearthly beings. I was no longer grasping at a shred of the falling mantle of the prophet; but sailing up in his fiery chariot, careering through the extent of space, and bending the forms of the elements to my progress and my power. For hours I walked up and down my prison, which was spacious and lofty, but whose limits seemed to drive back my breath—my velocity increasing, my frame mantling and throbbing, my mind soaring at every step, till the hour of my attendant's appearing was long elapsed.

This scarcely produced an impression on me. At length, I heard a step approach, and a key inserted in the door. My senses had been so quickened by the habit of intense observation on the trivial circumstances that exercised them, that I perceived at once, from the slow and irregular manner in which the key was turned, that it was not held by the usual hand. I had scarce time to notice this, when it burst open with an impetuous movement, as if my gaoler was incensed at the delay, and Filippo, half-sobbing, half-shouting, was at my feet. I never experienced, never will again experience, perhaps, so strong a proof of the mutability of human feelings. In a moment all within and around me was changed. I was rejoiced to compound between the dark and cloudy elevation of my mind, and the warm, humble, sheltered feelings that the sight of a human creature, my fellow in the flesh, its infirmities, and affections, and who appeared to have some kindness towards me, excited. I rejoiced to descend from the precipice of aerial existence, and claim kindred with man. For some time I permitted his emotions to flow on unrestrained. I was soothed and delighted by feeling his warm tears and kisses raining on my hands, my vesture, my knees, with rapid and impatient delight. I was only moved to disturb him by the consideration, that we were perhaps observed, and that the unequivocal marks of his regard might expose him to danger. I endeavoured to raise him. He understood and answered my fears. There was no one near us, he said; no one dreamed of watching or suspecting us; all was trusted to him, thanks to the blessed saints, and, above all, his patron Filippo, that enabled him to deceive my father, and even that fiend-monk, as he called the confessor, with vehement bitterness.

I could not suppress my astonishment at his appearance and his information. I had believed myself shut out from all the world, from the approach or sympathy of man; least of all did I believe, that one exposed to the persecution which had immured me, should be permitted to visit me in freedom; but it was in vain to pour question on question. Filippo's eagerness and delight overbore and actually silenced me for the first half-hour, and scarcely even then could I obtain from him a coherent account of the means that had again brought us together.

"Oh! Signor," said he, "do you remember that last terrible night when you paused at the foot of the stairs, and threw open that dark door; and you entered it so pale, I thought I had beheld you going into your tomb; but I had scarce time to think of any thing, when I was thrust back, as I attempted to follow them, and the key turned on me in the passage. I knew not what they intended. I feared all things that were terrible. But there was a heaviness over me, whether it was the consequence of the sudden amaze that had seized us, or the watching, or the strange doings of the night, I know not, but I sat down on the ground, and wrapped my head in my mantle, and continued still, but not insensible; it was a strange mood, Signor, now that I recal it. I felt no fear; I uttered no complaint; yet I believed I had not long to live. I listened stupidly to steps approaching, though I thought they were the steps of some appointed to dispatch me. But when I heard them coming yet nearer, and felt that I must raise my head, and look on what was so near me, I uttered a loud cry, though without any distinct notion of pain or danger. It was the monk. He raised me roughly by the arm, and bid me follow him. Queen of heaven! thro' what places did he lead me! What a prize to the inquisition, or to a banditti, would this castle be, with its passages and vaults, and chambers in the solid wall, without window or loop-hole, or a single avenue of human comfort, and air that our lamp could scarce burn in—air, like the breathings of a vault! I felt I should die, die a certain and miserable death, if I were left there, even without violence or hardship; but I tried in vain to obtain from the monk the slightest hint of what he intended to do with me. Often I thought I was as strong as he; that there was no one near to assist either of us; that if I even extinguished the light, and trusted to the windings of those vaults for concealment or escape, it would be better than to go on, like an ox to the slaughter. These thoughts often came to me, and often I half-raised my eye to the dark face beside me, to see, was it assailable, was it like the face of man that is liable to weakness or danger. But Oh, Signor. I drew it away again without hope. There is nothing like man about him. I fear no man. I could cling to life, and grapple for it as keenly, if I knew my weapons and my compeer, as any man in Italy; but when I am near that monk I feel—Oh! I know not how. The air that comes from him is chill; his large dead eye fixes me; the tones of his voice come over me, like the roll of distant thunder at night, when we half fear to listen, and half to shut it out. Is he not a strange being, Signor?" said he, turning suddenly, and fixing his dark eyes, distended with fear, on me. "He is indeed," said I involuntarily; "but (after a pause) proceed Filippo." "Do you believe him to be indeed a man like ourselves?" he continued, with increased eagerness, and visage still lengthening. "I know not; I cannot tell; I beseech thee to speak no more of him; go on with thy own narrative, but mention him as little as possible in the course of it." "Well, Signor, I passed four days in darkness and solitude; but how shall I proceed, if I am not permitted to mention the monk? He was the only person I thought of, the only person I saw, except you. Oh! Signor, think what it is to pass four days in total solitude, in total darkness, except when he visited me with my scanty portion of food; and then, by the dim light he carried, I could partly see the vast and shapeless darkness of my vault. 'Twas strange, Signor, but I saw it better in his absence. When the light was brought into my prison, a mist seemed to hang over every object; a kind of tremulous, blue dampness spread all beyond the edges of that pale lamp; but no sooner was it removed, than all the dark nooks and corners, which I had never seen, came strong and clear before my eyes. It was in vain that I wrapt my head tight and tighter in my cloak; in vain I said to myself, I am in the dark; these things are not before me; I am in a close, sheltered corner, where nothing is approaching me, and from which nothing is moving me—yet still—still would I seem to myself wandering on, thrusting myself down some steep, dark descent, rooting in some gloomy nook, following some strange light that glimmered and flitted before me, till, all on a sudden, some haggard face edging the dark corner, would grin and chatter at me. Then I would feel myself shrinking back to my straw, and still it would pursue me, and still it would seem to rustle through my cloak, and peep at me in every fold; for still I seemed to see, though my eyes were closed, and though I was in utter darkness."

Melancholy as this account was, I yet was delighted with human communication, and with an opportunity of comparing feelings different from my own, in a similar situation.

"Ah! Signor," said Filippo earnestly, "how happy are gentlemen of learning, learned Signors, that can search into their own minds, and recal their reading, and frame conversations, and have all they ever knew or loved with them in their captivity and loneliness, by force of mind. I thought I should never feel that deep and heavy solitude, if I could recollect something to think of, something that would take me out of that dark place, and set me among things and people that I once was happy with. Heaven help me! I knew nothing to drive that lonely feeling from my heart. All I could do, I did. I repeated all the prayers my uncle Michelo had taught me, whenever my food was brought; for I had no other means of knowing the hour, and I tried to recollect, as well as I could, some verses of Ariosto, which I had heard a *recitator* at Naples pronounce. I found my memory marvelously improved by darkness and solitude; many lines I had long forgotten came fresh to my mind. I repeated them over and over again; nay, I even added some to them, very unlike the original indeed; but what would not a solitary prisoner resort to, and find interesting? Still there was a loneliness, an emptiness within me, a want of employment and of thought. I envied even the grim and silent being that came with my food. He had doors to lock, and passages to pass, and something to be employed in. And Oh! how I envied such as you, Signor, who have a power of filling up all solitude, of reading over your books, and conversing with your friends, though both are far from you."

When Filippo said this, I blushed involuntarily. I recollected how little of this praise of felicity belonged to me; and I felt how much it is in the power of circumstances to reduce minds to the same level, to strip us of the trappings of locality, and shew what a kindred vein of suffering and weakness runs through the breast of us all, if the removal of outward distinctions permits us to detect and to trace its affinities.

"But proceed, Filippo, the period of your total solitude was only four nights, you told me." "Yes, Signor, it was on the fourth evening, that the confessor, after bringing food, and waiting till I had finished it, told me to follow him, and prepare to quit the vault. He has so absolute a manner with him, that all power of inquiry or resistance dies within me when he speaks. I followed him without a word, and knew not, as he led me on, whether it was to death or life. I began, however, to

CHARLES MATURIN

mistrust that it was the former, when I perceived he was conducting me to your father's apartment. It was evening; but the tapers were already lit, for your father hates the darkness. When I entered the room he was standing. There was another figure there which I saw but dimly; for my eyes were weak, and my limbs reeled under me. Your father looked at me with astonishment. "Is this Filippo," said he, turning to the monk, "this spectre, this shadow, is it Filippo?" I was subdued to a childish weakness by my confinement. His voice sounded compassionately. What voice would not be delightful after a silence of four days? I attempted to supplicate. I believed him touched by the spectacle he had made me; but my voice failed me, and I stood, trembling and silent, before him. "Filippo," said he, "you see the consequences of disobedience; you feel that I have a power to punish, which it is vain for you to provoke or to oppose. I know you to be not incapable of reflection, not of a vulgar mind, and therefore I deign to reason with you. If romantic boys and inquisitive menials are permitted to rove about, discovering, or inventing wonders, what family can repose in honour, what individual can rest in peace? I am not admitting that you can discover any thing that would tend but to your own confusion; but even the misfortunes of an illustrious family, if extensively known, involve a species of disgrace, from the prejudices of society; at least they are unfit for a domestic's tongue to sport with, and to scatter around."

All he said appeared candid and condescending; the voice of gentleness, of human feeling, was rare and delightful to me; I felt it convey shame and conviction to me; I inwardly condemned myself for curiosity and disobedience; I attempted to falter out an excuse— he interrupted me. "It is enough," said he, "I meant not to crush, but to correct you. You have suffered enough; but as long as the influence of your young master might expose you to repeated danger, I should be to blame for your second offence, if I exposed you to it. Go hence, therefore, and if gratitude can bind you, you are bound to me. Marco here will conduct you to the house where my Apulian steward will call in a few days, to bring you with him to my estates there; he has my directions to settle you there in a situation little inferior to his own, where you may learn habits of regularity and obedience. Do not oppress me with your thanks—I—I do not wish to hear them." I attempted to utter some incoherent sounds of gratitude; but he repelled me with impatience that confounded me. "I will have no more of this—I cannot bear it. Will you not take him from me, father?" I forbore to speak.

"Set out immediately," said he, "night is the best time: tomorrow will bring you to your journey's end; and Marco will be your guide." He retired, attended by his confessor. "Come, fellow traveller," said Marco advancing, "shall we set out? night is gathering fast."

I now saw him distinctly for the first time; he was a strange, ferocious looking fellow: I marvelled to see such a one in the Count's apartment; among whose virtues, condescension was never very distinguished; but every thing around me was marvellous, and the sight of Marco, as he was called, was forgotten in the condescension of the Count, and the suddenness of my own deliverance. I said I was ready to attend him; but he saw me totter, and look weak; he approached the table, where stood a flagon of wine: "Come," said he, "this glass to your safe and speedy journey; swallow it man, you will have need of courage." I took the wine from him, and looked on him as I took it, with the vacant eye of weakness; but the look of his features rouzed me, weak as I was; it was a strange expression; I do not like to think of it, even now. We went out immediately; he took care I should not be seen by any of the family. We went to the stables. I felt myself inflamed by the wine I had swallowed, and we rode off together in high spirits. In a short time, however, my companion became silent and gloomy. I asked him a thousand questions about my journey, its object, and its termination; I could get no answer from him, but a short and general one—"Your journey is short and easy; tomorrow night will end it." Then I spoke of the Count, and his condescension to me; but I observed, that as I spake on this subject, he became more dark, and more restless; then I began to inquire how long he had been in the service of the Count Montorio. "I have served the Count," said he, "many years." "Yet I do not recollect seeing you before tonight," said I. "It is very possible; I am not always visible to the family, though few, I believe, can boast of being more constantly employed, or of having rendered more useful service to his Excellenza." "Secret ones, it should seem," said I, half jestingly. "Very likely, but not the less useful," said he, sternly.

We went on in silence, and lay that night at a shed, in a vine-yard in the Campagna: those sheds, you know, in which the watchers guard the grapes during the vintage, are constructed of straw, and branches, and other slight materials—this was our lodging; I did not soon go to rest, for my mind was tossed by the circumstances that had preceded the journey; and soon after my companion lay down, I found all thought of rest was vain. He talked to himself with such loudness and vehemence, you would have believed that armed men were fighting in the hut, and blood was spilt, and bodies were falling like withered leaves. Sometimes he would cry out to wipe those daggers; sometimes to hide those bloody garments; sometimes, "What, struggling still! Press your knee firmly on his breast, and gripe the skin of his throat! Aye, that will do; now close his eyes, and wipe that bloody foam off his mouth." Then starting up, he would cry, "There, fellows, there, he has fled, he has escaped; fly after him, pursue him; my lord the Count will buy his blood with half his lands."

These were strange words; but I confess, that while I looked at the bright and blessed moon, and caught the breeze through my casement of leaves, so fresh and cool after the damp heats of my dungeon, I listened to them rather with vacant curiosity, than fear. As I looked on the clear heavens, I thought I saw the very star, that when I used to be returning through the woods to the castle, I would see just rising over the battlements of the West tower. It would glimmer among them, Signor, just like a feeble taper at a casement; and when I saw it rising over the dark hills of the vintage, I thought of the castle, and of you. Though my companion and my journey were so strange, myriads would I have given you were along with me, and I determined as soon as I had reached Apulia, to discover where you were, and to liberate you if possible."

"Filippo, I believe this is a gratuitous addition to your narrative. In the sudden joy of liberation, could you think of me?" "Could I, Signor? Ah, you know not with what keenness the mind, just escaped from suffering, reverts to images that awaken and contrast its former state. To think of myself was to think of you; for to think of myself, was to think of a lonely being, a solitary being, a confined and pining being; therefore I thought of you. All I had so lately felt for myself was transferred to you; it was not sympathy, Signor, but strong remembrance—remembrance of the dungeon and the darkness, the dim lamp, the meal that I scarcely saw, the strange faces staring me out of sleep, and the toads that I shook off as I awoke: all this I thought of, and how then could I forbear to think on you?

Early in the morning we set forward again; we rode through a wild, woody country all day, only baiting to sleep in the hollow of a chesnut during the heats of noon. At the close of evening, we were in a thick wood, the tracks were perplexed, and appeared as if they were not much frequented. Marco often paused, and looked around him with uneasiness and distrust; he often checked his mule, and looked between the trees, and listened often, as the wind that now began to rise, moaned among the branches, sometimes resembling the sounds of a human voice. It was to no purpose to ask questions; his utter silence, and the gloom of the evening, were beginning to make me feel strangely, when on a sudden, after muttering to himself for some time, he spurred his mule on violently; then turning round, and bending his head low, he gallopped on me so quick, that I had scarce time to spring out of his way, and ask what he meant. "It was a spring of my mule," said he, "cursed jade," lashing the animal, and falling behind me. "I had better keep out of your way," said I, crossing into another track. "Aye, aye, you had better, if you can," he muttered. Then darting forward, he disappeared among a thick tuft of brushwood on the right. I was startled for the first time, at this motion, and followed him as fast as I could—it was in vain; he had a better knowledge of the wood, and its dark ways; still I pursued him, though in a short time I could not even hear the sound of his mule's feet. But the wood opening suddenly to the right, I saw a large ruinous building, that appeared like the remains of a good dwelling, fitted up for the residence of a woodman; there were no offices about it, no appearances of any country business being exercised by the owner, it looked strangely dreary. Marco was at the door, dismounted, and talking to an ill looking man; both advanced when they saw me, with an appearance of satisfaction. "This is your host," said Marco, "this is Venanzio. You were rarely frightened when I gallopped away and left you in the thicket—but I knew you would follow the track; few can miss it, that have once set out in it."

"It was cursed foolish, however, to leave him," said Venanzio discontentedly, "he might have got away, and all pursuit of him be vain. Come, young man, alight, you will not be sorry of a good bed, and quiet rest after your ramble today." I alit, and followed him into a large, dreary room. A flagon of wine was on a large rustic table, around which sat one or two men, meanly dressed, with that peculiar staring wildness of face which great indigence, and remoteness of situation combine to give the inhabitants of a deserted country. They seemed undetermined whether or not to go away when we entered; but Venanzio, with an air of command, bid them resume their seats. They sat down again, eying me surlily. There was a miserable old woman in the room, busied in a dark corner of it, who also looked at me from time to time, with a peculiar expression, of which I could not tell whether the meaning was hatred or fear.

CHARLES MATURIN

"It was cursed foolish, however, to leave him," said Venanzio discontentedly, "he might have got away, and all pursuit of him be vain. Come, young man, alight, you will not be sorry of a good bed, and quiet rest after your ramble today." I alit, and followed him into a large, dreary room. A flagon of wine was on a large rustic table, around which sat one or two men, meanly dressed, with that peculiar staring wildness of face which great indigence, and remoteness of situation combine to give the inhabitants of a deserted country. They seemed undetermined whether or not to go away when we entered; but Venanzio, with an air of command, bid them resume their seats. They sat down again, eying me surlily. There was a miserable old woman in the room, busied in a dark corner of it, who also looked at me from time to time, with a peculiar expression, of which I could not tell whether the meaning was hatred or fear.

We sat round the table, and drank; little was said; and that little was broken and distant, full of allusions I could not understand; but which the rest seemed to consider as very significant. Marco, drawing back his chair, measured me with a slow and steady look, from head to foot; and then nodding to Venanzio, began twisting his fingers into a knot, and drawing them afterwards with a straining motion together; Venanzio only grasped the hilt of his stiletto firmly, but both desisted suddenly, when they beheld me looking at them.

There came a boding sickness over me; I struggled with it, for I knew not why I felt so. I attempted a conversation, for we had sunk to monosyllables and silent looks. The name of Venanzio I thought was familiar. "Certainly," said I to the host, "I have heard your name before, though your name-sake does not do it much credit." "Very possibly you might," said he. "The person to whom I allude," said I, "was a famous assassin, in Messina; his atrocities were the most numerous and extraordinary I ever heard of." "Why do you say *were*," said one of the fellows, "I hear he is alive, and as wicked as ever." "Oh, curse him," said another, "I could forgive him anything, but cheating his comrades, as he did, when they had so handsome a price for their work."

Venanzio looked surlily; "Perhaps," said he, "he was ill paid himself." "You seem to mistake me," said I, "the person of whom I speak, was no mechanic; he was an assassin." "Well," said one of them, "and don't you know, that such a one must have assistants; aye, and pay them well too (darting an angry look across the table), and must have work too—aye, bloody work, tearing work! ah, ah, ah!" (cutting out large splinters of the table with a clasp knife, and forcing a horrid laugh). "But of this man," said I, though I scarce knew how to proceed, "I heard he baffled every pursuit of justice, and after numberless murders and assassinations, being traced to the very sea-shore, hid himself in the tackle of a fishing vessel, and when the poor fisherman had begun to coast along the shore by night, with a lamp at his stern (for that is the mode of fishing there), Venanzio started up, and compelled him to put out, and stand for Naples; and on their arrival, immediately murdered his unfortunate pilot, lest he should betray him; and interring him in the sand, changed his name, and betook himself in disguise to the woods—this I learnt was his last exploit." "No, no, this will not be his last exploit, friend," said one of them, "take my word for it." "You seem to know him," said I. "Too well." "Have you been a sufferer by him?" "Incalculable," said he, shaking his head. "Do you ever see him now?" said I, pursuing him with simple importunity. "As plain as I see any one at this table," said he. "And do you believe him to be alive still?" "As sure as our host there is alive," said he. "Come," said Venanzio, abruptly, "enough of my namesake; perhaps, like many others, he is driven by want to blood; without doubt, he repents by this time being entangled with ruffians, who suspect, and watch, and insult; but of whom he may one day get rid, as he has done of other incumbrances." Two of them began to growl in a lower key at this, and the third, whose face was peculiarly savage, said, "Aye, aye, few men know how better to throw off incumbrances than Venanzio; his life belongs to the hangman, his soul to Lucifer, and his honour to the first man that will offer him a dollar to cut his own father's throat."

He ended this sentence with a burst of wild sound, so unlike laughter, that it chilled the blood; yet it evidently spoke defiance and contemptuous hatred. "His honour," said Venanzio, uneasily, "is unimpaired; he never betrayed or threatened his comrades." "No," said the other, eagerly, "he is content to use them so ill, that it is not in his power to threaten; and to rob them so unmercifully, that it is not worth his while to betray them." The others joined him in the conclusion of this sentence, with emphatic bitterness, yet with a kind of forced and savage derision; their visages were inflamed, and their voices hoarse and broken.

Our host seemed to pause and bethink himself for a moment, then suddenly resting his arms on the table, and looking them stedfastly in the face, he said in a quick, decisive voice, "I'll tell you, comrades, one

CHARLES MATURIN

thing of this Venanzio, which shews he was a sensible, clear-headed knave:—there were two or three dogs, that he kept sometimes to bark, and sometimes to bite; now and then he threw them a bone to pick, which they did not think was enough for their services. They took particular care, whenever he had any *business to do*, to howl, and snarl, and disturb him; if a stranger came into their kennel, the whole set were in an uproar; all were raving to gnaw his bones, and lap his blood, before Venanzio had time to carve him, and give every one their share; whereat," (said he, stretching his brawny arm at full length on the table), "he one night addressed them thus: 'Look'ye, ye blood hounds, if ever I hear ye again open your throats, by the holy cross, I'll stop them with cold iron. Don't ye know, with a curse to you, that I am the life of you, that my name only preserves you from the pursuit of justice, lodges you, feeds you, employs you; that if I am lost, ye are undone; that no one will employ such miscreants, but as spies, and then strangle them for their information. Where will ye go then, or what will ye do? Your chain is galling, and your food is bad; but what can such mongrels as you expect. No one would employ you, but to misuse and maltreat you; no one would keep you but to trample on you. Your only employment would be to fly at beggars, and mangle women and children; and, if ever you stole from your haunts, fire, and sword, and poison, and curses, would pursue you, and blast and scatter you, till the very crows and vultures would clap their wings in despair, as they flew over you. Do you not know this, dogs? Hounds of blood and hell, do you not know this, and will you dare to growl?"

His fury was terrible. He rose erect; he stamped; his hairs bristled; his eyes flashed; his voice was a roar; he smote the table with a violence that made the pannels start asunder. "I heard the dogs grew quite peaceable after that," said Marco. "He watched them still, for he knew they were but dogs," said Venanzio, with wrathful and venomous bitterness. His speech was so sudden, so vehement, so voluble, that I listened with stupid astonishment; I tried in vain to follow the metaphor, for his passion had broke it; I knew not at whom the torrent was directed; it seemed to awe the souls of every one present; all that had heard him shuddered, and were silent.

But in, the pause that followed, when the thunder of his voice died away, I began to comprehend, slowly and painfully, the meaning of all I saw. But the sting of agony was so piercing, so sudden, that I shook off the thought, as I would shake a reptile from my hand. It was too terrible to be believed—a gush of heat came over me, and then a deadly cold; my teeth chattered, though my cheeks were burning; cold, big drops of sweat stood on my forehead. I swallowed my glass eagerly, and then another, and still I was like one in a dream, who sees a hideous face, and tries to shut it out, but feels it spreading, and growing on him, and staring at him from every side, till it seems actually to get within his eyes, and mount into his brain, and madden him. So I felt that thought; still I resisted it, yet still it was in my mind.

"I am tired, I would be glad to see my room," said I, rising, with that hopeless effort that looks for relief in the mere act of motion. "You shall *see it*," said Venanzio, rising. "Ho! Bianca, bring a light." The old woman brought a light, which she held close to my face as she passed me. Her own resembled that of a sorceress. Her earthy skin, her sunk red eyes, her ragged hair, with a peculiar look of glaring malignity, blazed full on me as she passed. My heart sunk within me. I followed Venanzio up a flight of narrow, ruinous stairs. He opened a door to the left, and led me into a room, like the rest, dark and wide. The bed was in a remote corner of it. Involuntarily, I glanced at the windows that were high, and well secured. They were the only part of the building that seemed in repair. "This is your room," said Venanzio, "I wish you quiet rest in it." I turned to him as he spoke, to read hope or fear in his face; but he held the light so high, that I saw only his dark head and brows as he bent over the bed.

"Stay," said I, as he was quitting the room, "I will go down and take another flagon with you." I was unwilling yet to be alone, though I had every thing to fear from these men. Yet still their presence gave me a kind of nameless refuge. I had a faint hope too, that I might have misinterpreted doubtful expressions or unpromising faces; and to the hope that flatters us with life, who would not cling as long as he can? Venanzio did not resist my going down. I was descending the stairs, when the old woman called out to me, that I had left my cloak in the chamber. "Go you and fetch it for him," said Venanzio. Grasping at every omen that accident might give, I soon passed the old woman, who seemed to halt on purpose, and entered the room. I searched for my cloak all around it in vain. The old woman called out to me to examine a particular corner. I did so; and by the lamp, that I still held, I perceived that corner was dyed in blood. My own seemed to flow back on my heart. Venanzio called loudly for the light. I tottered down stairs; but he was gone. My eyes were dim, and when I reached the foot of the stairs, I no longer distinguished the passages, they were dark and intricate. I wandered along without perceiving the direction I took, till I was startled by the peculiar dreariness and loneliness of the part of the building I had reached. The wind whistled after me with a boding cry, and the ruinous casements rattled as if they were shaken by some forcible hand. I paused. The thought of escape came into my mind. All around me seemed deserted; and I felt, that if I could once get into the forest, I should have wings like a bird. I stepped on quick and lightly. The passage terminated in a low door at some distance. I approached it. It was open. But as I drew near, I distinguished voices within, the voices of Marco and Venanzio. I had rather have heard the hissing of a serpent. Oh! 'tis a most dark and soul-sinking feeling, when you know every human being near you, every one who could help or comfort, who could understand or unite with you, is armed with a mortal purpose against you; and, secretly or forcibly, will, and must overcome you. Hopeless of escaping in any other direction that communicated with the more inhabited parts of the building, and anxious to gather what I could from their conversation, I lingered at the door. They spoke in that low, muttering tone, that it is terrible to listen to; but my hearing was so quickened by apprehension, that I did not lose a syllable.

"Where is he now?" said Marco. "He is above, not half-pleased with his apartment." "He will be less so, when he finds it is to be the last he shall occupy; but why wait till he retires to rest?" "I am afraid your retreats are suspected. I have observed more travellers passing near it than could have business in this wild wood; and I wish to have no voice or struggling till it is dark, and no traveller near. 'Twas for that reason I blamed your leaving him in the wood. He might have escaped; he might have taken a hint from that gloomy visage of your's, and fled; for, after so many years residence, a child might baffle me in the windings of this wood; and then the first intelligence we should have got of him, would have been a stiletto in your heart for suffering him to escape." "How could I avoid it? By my soul, I was as much alarmed as you, your not meeting me at the place, owing to Nicolo's blunders. Besides I had almost forgotten the track. The fellow is almost as able as I am; and, I'll warrant, would have grappled fiercely for his life. Once I was in the mind to have put him out of pain. I found my mule full a-head, and galloped on him; and if I could have thrown him to the ground, I would have dispatched him with a few strokes of the stiletto; but he sprung on one side, and avoided me." "And did he continue to ride with you still?" "He did; he seems to have no suspicions, or Zeno and the rest would have alarmed him with their hints, and you with your fury in the chamber below. Ha! ha! ha! I could have laughed to hear him question so gravely, a man, about his own existence, and telling him stories of himself. Or do you think he was beginning to discover who you were, and tried that method to certify himself." "I know not. He appears simple and inapprehensive. Yet just now, in the chamber, I thought I saw a dark shade cross his countenance. His cheek was white, and his lip shook. But my eyes are none of the best. Strange things sometimes seem to pass before them; that cursed old hag too—but I may be mistaken. I thought she left his cloak purposely in the corner where the monk was murdered, that he might take notice of the blood." "Aye, that was the business that incensed Zeno and the rest." "Aye," repeated Venanzio, angrily, "the rapacious dastards—they think, if they cut the throat of an unarmed peasant, or burn a hovel now and then, they have a right to the same rewards with men that have been employed by the first nobility, that have made princes keep them in humour and in pay, that have dispeopled a whole country by their mere name—the villains! because I have been hunted to this dark den, where I live in poverty and fear, and am sunk to the cutting the throat of a wretched, single domestic—they think"—"Hush, hush, was that the wind? it sounded like a human groan: what dreary sounds come along these passages!" "Ha! ha! why, your cheek is as pale as your fellow traveller's. It would cure you of these fancies to live as I do here, listening to the sounds that sweep through this old building, and to others, of which I dare not think whence they come." "In the name of heaven, are you so beset? Why, it were better to follow our business in the heart of a populous city, as we did at Messina. There, we were only posted in the corner of a street some dark night, and when we had disposed of the body quietly, in some vault, or ruinous building, we could resort to jollity, to some house of entertainment, and drink away the memory of the night's work, as soon as we washed the blood off our hands." "Aye, aye, but here, in the deserted haunts, in the dark forests, thoughts come to me that never came to me in Messina. I am not the man I was. 'Tis not that I repent. No. By the mass I am no flincher. If the fathers of the Inquisition were preaching to me, they would not get me so much as to mutter a pater noster, or to sign a cross, though often, often I do it unawares, through fear, and in the weakness of the moment. But yet I know not how I feel. Marco, you know I am no visionary. Will you believe me, when I tell you what I saw the other evening, as I sat in this chair, when the wind moaned through the chesnut trees, just as it does this evening?" Marco changed his posture to listen to the story. I moved away mechanically. It was not that I had a distinct fear of his presence. I believe had they both rushed out on me, I could neither have resisted nor deceived them. I could not think a thought; but I staggered away, as from an intuitive and mortal sensation of dread at the sight or step of the murderers. I know not how I got down the passage, nor up stairs again; but I did so, and recollect leaving my lamp on the floor with the same quiet regularity as if I should ever have occasion for its light again; but then all sensation appeared to leave me. There was no doubt, nor shadow of hope; no refuge in thought for me. I knew all, and knew it all at once, and the worst at once; I should never leave that apartment; a few moments were all I had to live; death, sudden, unexpected death, what a desolating thought! how it sweeps the whole soul of man, with every resource of strength or hope, away. My eyes darted fire, visibly. I felt the sparks. My teeth chattered. Every pore was so wide, that I felt the cold, thick drops of sweat that every one sent forth. My hair rose, every hair sore with distinctness, and hissing on my head like a serpent. I gasped for breath. It was true and proper death that I thought was overtaking me. I tried to stir, but every limb was palsied. I tried to speak, and could only make a faint inward croak in my chest. The lamp, the ceiling, the floor, became tenfold and a hundred-fold in a minute; and then disappeared at once. I know not how long I remained in this state, but surely, whenever I die, I shall twice taste the bitterness of death. I recovered at once. I was so fully awake, so conscious of all I heard and knew, that I sprung on my feet lest they should enter and take advantage of my helpless posture. I looked and listened around me. All was still, save the wind, that was now becoming tempestuous, and whose hollow rush came along the passage of my chamber like the sound of garments and footsteps, and waved the tall trees, whose shadows crossed the casement, making strange motions to a fearful eye.

As I listened still, though hopeless of hearing a sound of comfort, I thought voices beneath the casement came scattering on the wind. They might be travellers in the forest; they might be those of whom Venanzio spoke. With the eagerness of sudden hope I climbed into the window-seat, and, holding by the bars, looked below. There was a dim moon, often hid by the clouds that were driven along the sky; nor was twilight wholly gone. Below, I could at first see nothing but the tuft of trees; but as I looked closer, I saw a man, whose cloak, ruffled by the wind, I had at first taken for a branch. He held something in his hand which I could not distinguish. In a short time he was joined by another, whose head was bare. Their voices came up distinct and clear. The latter was Venanzio.

"What are you doing here," said he, "always loitering when work is to be done." "I have not loitered," said the other, sullenly; "look at this mattock, and then look at the stubbed, tangled roots of this pine. Do you call it loitering to have dug the grave in such ground as this?" "It is not long enough," (stooping to measure it: Oh! I saw every motion he made). "Lengthen it yourself, then," said the other, throwing down the mattock, "a man were better work for the devil than you. Can I not dig a grave now? I was captain of as bold a band as ever trooped at a signal, when you were pitching up ducats in Messina for a coward's blow, and a flight in the dark." "Well, well, we need not quarrel; we both have seen better days and better work, than butchering a sorry lackey; and yet that fellow appears inclined to give us work too. He will require your bony arms, or Zeno's, to give him a firm gripe by the throat." "Will you not stab him, then?" "No, I'll have no more blood spilt; it stains the rooms, and gives strangers hints that it would be our wisdom to hide from them. You know how suddenly the pilgrims left us the other evening, of whom we thought ourselves sure. List, Nicolo, I'll have him strangled as soon as he is asleep. We will go and have another flagon in the room under him, and watch till he has lain down." "By my soul, I would rather meet a man armed with a dagger, and strive with him hand to hand, than strangle a sleeping man. I am not myself for a month after. The black and staring face, the set teeth, the forced-out eyes, are with me wherever I turn. Maria! do you remember the last man that perished in that room?—still, how he struggled, and gasped, and tore out handfuls of Marco's hair in his agonies! he was horridly strong; the worse for him; there was no crushing life out of him. He heaved as we laid him on the ground; his eyes have never been off me since; I see them in the dark. Holy mother! they are glaring on me from that pit—look—look—Venanzio." "Away you fool; and what if they were? Can the eyes of the dead stab you?" "They can, they can; take that mattock; I would not look into that hole again for the whole price of this night's work." "Ha! ha! listen to the blast that howls after you. Is that the dead man's cry? Ha! ha!"

He pursued the scared ruffian with an hideous laugh. I let go the bars in utter agony and helplessness of soul, and fell on the floor. I

CHARLES MATURIN

had heard my death determined. I had seen my own grave dug; a sad sight, that few living men behold. Before the lamp burnt out, before the blast died away, before another hour, I should be a corse, swoln, and stretched, and stark. My mind ran with astonishing swiftness through every circumstance of the past days. Oh! how I cursed your father's barbarity, for one offence, so trivial and easy to be prevented for the future, to send me to a distance, where no cry could reach a human ear, to be butchered by cannibals; to disarm me by such promises and condescension; to keep me immured till I was weak and pliant; to leave me without the means of resistance or escape. Oh! how I cursed my own folly to trust him; not to profit by the many hints my dark companion gave; to go on like a sheep to the shambles. I recalled every circumstance that had escaped them, hinting the past possibility of my safety; I could have fled into the wood; I could have struggled with Marco, "I was almost as able as he:" nay, yet—yet I might escape in the windings of the wood, if it were possible to reach it. All these thoughts, and a million more, came to me so clear, so keen, so stinging, that I was almost mad. Oh, the bitterness of feeling life lost by one moment's folly, and not to be recovered by the fullest stretch of thought and action after.

I seemed to myself to have thrust away my safety with both hands, and to have hunted and pursued away every chance of life, and run headlong into the snare that closed on me, and shut me round for ever. After a moment's sober and severe pain, I started into actual phrensy; I ran round the room, striking the walls, and grappling with the windows, and gnashing my teeth with the rage of madness. I am astonished they did not hear the uproar I made at length, I began to look round me more calmly; but still with the fiery penetration, and glaring eagerness of real insanity. I am convinced I was mad, yet one idea was still so clearly present and powerful with me, that I felt I was capable of exerting every force of my soul and body, while it continued to stimulate me. There was no furniture in the room; nothing that could present either a weapon of defence, or means of escape. Despairing, but still with forcible and unremitting intentness, in the dusky walls and floor it was not easy to discover any object; but poring on the latter by the light of the lamp, I discovered a pannel, with a ring in it; it resembled a trap-door. I had little doubt of the use of such an instrument in such a place, and as little hope, that I could long lie hid in any place to which it might conduct me; yet still active from the restlessness of misery, I began to raise it, and succeeded.

There was a dark cavity below, that I judged ran between the flooring of one room, and the ceiling of that below, which might possibly continue to some distance, or be connected with other cavities and passages. I got down, and scrambled to some distance in it; it was filled up with rubbish, which I struggled through, half stifled with the dust; but I soon found my passage obstructed; some soft substance was presented to my hand; slowly and cautiously I withdrew it, and crawling backwards, brought it out with me; the lamp was still on the floor, and by its light, I perceived I held a heap of bloody and decayed garments, pierced with more holes than those of decay. As I gazed on it, a wild blast shook the door, and raved round the walls; the flame of the lamp shivered, and blazed athwart and overblown.

I looked around in terrible expectation of the wearer of the garments, that told a dark story, appearing to witness the discovery; strange shadows played on the walls, as the lamp burnt clear. After many bickerings, I replaced the garments, and again endeavoured to grop my way through the passage, in which I discovered a light, on my second attempt; I crept on, and found by the sound, as well as the light, that it came through the broken ceiling of the room below, where the whole group were assembled, and seen distinctly through many an aperture. I heard my name often repeated, and saw some motions horribly significant when it was repeated. The blast was now so loud, and howled so fiercely through the broken rafters, over which I leaned, that I could not distinguish any thing of their discourse, but my name; nor perhaps, even that, had not my senses been quickened to that exquisite keenness, which the solicitude to overhear a conference about your own life, can alone produce.

In a short time, I began to think I might perhaps make a better use of this passage, than merely to overhear a conversation, of which I already knew the probable purport but too well;—I crept on therefore with breathless caution, and found, to my inexpressible joy, that I had passed the room where they were assembled. The apertures were now more numerous, and I conjectured I was near some ruinous, and perhaps neglected part of the building, from which escape might— might be possible; my obstructions grew fewer too, and the passage itself wider and I had no doubt of its being purposely constructed, and having therefore some certain outlet. As I crawled on, I again perceived a faint light beneath, supported between two beams; I applied my eye to the largest hole near me, and perceived it proceeded from a dim lamp that burned at some distance below; the light it gave was so faint, that it was long before I could distinguish it burned in a large desolate room, in the corner of which lay an obscure figure, stretched on a palle I gazed long before I could discover so much, and it was not till the figure turned, that I had a view of the most wasted, and ghastly form I ever beheld, covered with rags that were steeped in blood. As the wind howled round his comfortless bed, I could distinctly hear his groans mingling with it. For a moment I believed him to be some victim of the ruffian-band—but why then should his life be spared? At all events, I perceived this wretched object was in no condition either to resist, or even to give an alarm to the rest: the cries he uttered, were the weak tones of one worn with pain; if therefore, I could let myself down into his room with safety, I had little doubt of escaping. His apartment must be near the extremity of the building, and I heard the casements shake in the wind. I felt such a resolution must be achieved in a moment; the murderers were now drinking, the storm was high, and the sufferer incapable of opposition; yet, not one of these circumstances might continue to favour me a moment longer.

I began to examine the largest aperture, through which, when sufficiently opened, I was to descend; when I was checked by a loud noise from below—I desisted—a door opened, and one of those I had seen below entered with a lamp and some provisions, which he placed near the sick man, who appeared to decline them. The other spoke a few words of encouragement to him, from which I discovered, that the sufferer was one of the band who had been wounded in some late attempt, and who was now lingering under the festering tortures of his wounds without relief or hope, as they were apprehensive to procure assistance was to hazard discovery. After some careless consolation, he who brought the food was preparing to depart; but the other, in the infirmity of suffering, besought him to stay a few moments. "I cannot," said he, surlily, "I must be gone, we have business on our hands tonight. There is one lodged near you, who in half an hour must change his resting-place for a cold and bloody bed in the forest." (In half an hour! Who that has not heard his death denounced, and felt how dreadful it is to know and measure the approach of death can tell what I felt at these words?) "Oh, Saviolo," groaned the penitent villain, "talk not of those things to me; how can you mention them, and look on me stretched here, and think how soon the judgment of God may visit you for these things, as it has overtaken me." Saviolo replied only by a muttered oath at his lamp, which a blast of wind had almost extinguished. "Oh," continued the dying man, "if I could but have the benefit of some holy man; if I could but see a crucifix, and be taught one short prayer before I go hence—dark and dreadful things are on my conscience; no one knows what I know; I have more than the petty murders of an obscure villain to unfold; I was engaged in a horrid conspiracy against the peace and honour of a noble youth; Oh, there were things once, that would deceive the devil, to deceive and ruin him, and I fear they have succeeded." Again Saviolo cursed his lamp, which was almost extinguished, and looking around fastened his eyes on the ceiling, through whose many holes the wind rushed in every direction.

I saw him eye it suspiciously, and I drew back for a moment, terrified at the delay which his observation occasioned, for a half an hour's chance for life, who would lose a moment? and till he left the apartment, no attempt could be made. He was again preparing to depart, when the sick man shrieked to him to stay; "Oh, stay," said he, "for the love of the mother of God, stay with me a moment, he is coming, I hear him in the wind." "Who is coming," said Saviolo, stopping, and turning pale, as the light he bore glared on his strong visage. "The wicked one, the wicked one; he is with me every night; sometimes he stands beside me, and sometimes he rises through the floor before me; Oh, he is ever—ever with me, and soon I must be with him."

"Peace, peace, you driveller, turn to the wall, and close your eyes, and try to rest; and look, if you should hear any cries within half an hour don't come crawling from your bed as you did the last time, with those bloody swathes scaring us all before the work was well done." "Oh, Saviolo, dear, good, blessed fellow, do not leave me for a moment—for one moment; I see a hoof coming through the curtain."

Saviolo rushed out of the room with a curse, that shook it, and the conscience-smitten wretch shrunk under his rags. Now was the time; one was gone with precipitation, and the other would probably shrink from any thing he might see or hear moving near him. I had but half an hour to work for life. I began quietly, but swiftly to remove large flakes of plaster, which were so dry, that I found little difficulty in removing them, and the thin laths to which they were attached. In a short time I had displaced enough to admit an arm or leg: I was afraid of making too wide a breach, as the materials were so infirm, I feared they might sink under me, and supported myself on a beam while I loosened them. I tried to let myself down; the breach admitted me easily, and the beam supported me firmly. In the delirium of my joy, I was unable for a moment to proceed; I was obliged to wipe away the tears of joy, that prevented me from seeing my progress. I now measured the distance cautiously. I had at least twelve feet to fall, for the room was lofty; such a fall, however, could neither stun nor hurt me. I only dreaded the noise might alarm the ruffians; this however, was not to be avoided. I determined immediately on my descent to rush across the room, and spring through the window, or if possible to prevail on the wounded man, who appeared averse from blood, to inform me, in what direction I might escape.

I now let myself down silently, but expeditiously. The wounded man gave no sign of notice; I neither heard him star nor moan; I had sunk on the beams, till only my elbows were supported, and was endeavouring to detach those, and let myself drop, when by some untoward motion, a large heap of the rubbish I had removed fell through the hole with a loud noise, and part lit on the bed. The frighted wretch screamed aloud, and continued his cries so long, that though my intention was to leap down, and implore him to be silent, I heard steps approaching before I could execute it, or draw myself back, almost, into my hiding place.

Saviolo re-entered, as usual, with a curse in his mouth; but I found the purport of his return, was not to sooth, but to threaten the sick man; and with horror I heard him say, "Curse on your clamours, you will waken the man that is to be murdered, and give him a hint of where he is; and then we shall have a struggle, instead of finishing him as he lies." The terrified creature averred with earnest repetitions, that some one must be in the room, from the noise he had heard, and from the violence the roof appeared to have sustained. Saviolo appeared little inclined to believe him; the noises he said were imaginary, and the roof had been shattered by the storm; "For just over your head, there is a passage between the stories of the building, with the extent of which none of us are acquainted, and through which the wind rushes with terrible fury; but at all events," he continued, "as they will not want me in this business, I shall stay with you, and prevent you from crying out, till it is over; they will have struggling enough with him, there is no occasion to wake and put him on his guard."

Oh, blessed virgin, and St. Philip, with what agony I heard him cutting off my last retreat, shutting up my last narrow breathing hole of life. He would stay, and it was impossible to descend; he was a brawny, resolute fellow, a weaker man struggling for life, might indeed have overcame him, but I was unarmed; he had a poniard, and pistols stuck in his belt, and the very mode of my escape would expose me, as in descending I should probably fall. I lingered a few moments in the mere vacancy of despair, and then heard him tell the sick man, Zeno was about to go up, and discover whether the stranger was asleep, and that if he were, he was to inform the person appointed to strangle him, who would dispatch him immediately.

At this terrible intelligence, I was almost ready to dash myself down, and trust to a desperate chance of safety, for every probable one had disappeared; I was enclosed on every side, death actually stared me in the face. The immediate danger, however, I felt an irresistible impulse to escape from. If any of them should visit my room, and find it empty, he would quickly discover my retreat, and I should be butchered in that dusky hole without a struggle; back therefore, I crept, without a single hope to direct the motion; but with a blind resistance of inevitable evil, half smothered by the dust and rubbish, I scrambled through, crushing at every touch the eggs of the little domestic serpents, and displacing the nests of lizards and toads, whose cold slime made me shudder, as I crawled amongst them.

At length, I reached my own apartment, and as I raised myself out of the trap-door, and caught the lamp that burned still beside it, I almost expected some hand would push me back into the cavity. The room was empty, and no one had been there in my absence. After a moment's debate, I rose, shut the trap-door, placed the lamp on the table, and threw myself on the bed, concerting with calm desperation my last plan of deliverance. I had scarce lain down, when I heard a slow, heavy tread on the stairs; though I had arranged something like a means of escape, and though part of it was to admit Zeno into the room without resistance, as his intentions were not immediately murderous; yet there is no telling the agony with which I heard him approach—certainly approach, nor the miserable watchfulness with which I struggled to distinguish whether the steps were real, or whether I was deceived by the wind, whose force had made the ruinous stairs creak all night—it *was* a step, the step of the man who came to see was I prepared for murder. He came up softly, and I heard him pause at the door, and withdraw the bolts slowly, like one who fears to disturb a sleeper; I heard him in the room, I felt him approach the bed. I counterfeited deep sleep; as he came nearer, I experienced a horrid sensation, like that which accompanies the oppression of the night-mare; it was the struggle of nature within me; my resolution was to lie still, but nature moved within me to struggle or to fly. He came close to me, I heard him keeping in his breath; he bent over me, holding his lamp almost close to my face. I thought this might be a trial whether my sleep was counterfeited; but I dared not stir. I would have given the world to have looked at him under my eye-lids at that moment; to have seen the expression of his face, whether there was compassion or any relenting in it; but I dared not. Yet at this moment, while I yet doubted but he was examining whether he could not do the deed himself, and that, in the next instant, I should feel his stiletto in me before I even saw it drawn. Even at that moment, will you believe me, Signor? an irresistible propensity to laughter spread itself over my face; over my face I say, for in my heart was nothing but despair; yet was it irresistible; my features relaxed into something that felt to me like the motion of laughter, but struggling with the perturbation of fear, and the paleness of expected death. It appeared so different to him, that muttering inwardly, "Poor wretch! he sleeps uneasily," he withdrew his lamp and quitted the room. I did not even dare to turn on my side, or unclose my eyes till he had shut the door. I counted his steps down stairs, and then rose instantly. I had no refuge now but in myself. All that intervened between me and death was removed. The next visitor was to have my blood.

I hastened to the door, and secured it as well as I could. This was a means of delay, if not of defence. I then extinguished my lamp, and descended through the trap-door, and scrambled on to my former station, after drawing the trapdoor after me as close as I could. As I crawled over the ceiling of their room, I ventured to peep downward. They were still sitting; but, as I looked, one of them prepared to rise; then I durst look no longer. I crawled onward, till I came over the room of the sick man. I looked downward. The sight was beyond the most sanguine calculations of my hope. The sick man was quiet; the lamp still burned; and Saviolo was asleep. There was not a moment to be lost. I let myself down as quietly as I could through the hole in the ceiling till I hung only on the beam with my hands. After suspending myself for some time, till I felt my own weight, and was released from all obstructions, I commended myself to St. Philip, and let go my hold, and fell with less violence than could be imagined. The sleepers did not move. I looked around me for some time, without venturing to stir, to be assured of the reality of my descent, with so little noise or danger, and that the tranquillity about me was not counterfeited. All was still.

I rose; and creeping with that caution, which none but such a situation can give or imagine, I began to explore the room. There was but one window; the lamp burned in the hearth, before which Saviolo was sleeping in a chair. Scarcely touching the ground, I proceeded to pass him. When I was opposite him I involuntarily stopped, and, with an impulse I could not resist, looked full at him. His eyes were wide open, and intently fixed on me. My terror did not conquer my reason. After a moment passed in the stupor of fear, I perceived he made no use of his observation; he neither spoke, nor offered to stop me. I ventured to look at him more closely, and I perceived, from the fixed and filmy glare of his eye, that he was still asleep. A moment's thought confirmed my confidence. I had often heard of people who slept thus, particularly those whose minds are gloomy or perturbed. I now withdrew myself quietly, and placed the lamp at some distance, lest its light should act too strongly on the exposed and dilated organs of sight. I glided across the room to the window. It was a large casement that appeared, from its structure, to be moveable; but with most distressful apprehension I perceived, that to reach it I must step across the pallet of the sick man, nay, actually step on it. After what had happened, however, without disturbance or discovery, I had some hopes that a light step would be unfelt and unheard. I rose therefore on one foot, and, reaching across the bed, laid hold of the frame of the casement. A terrible blast that rushed against it that moment, almost made me fear it would be shattered in my hold. I released it for a moment, and looked round me with fear. I heard only the heavy breathing of Saviolo, and the groaning of the old and ruinated ceiling, as the wind swept over it. I felt these delays of fear would be endless; and, resting my knee on the frame-work, and holding it with both hands, drew my foot from the bed, when the sick man, with a faint cry, like that of weak surprise, extended one arm, and caught me by the ancle. In tha scene reason, life, seemed to forsake me. I neither felt nor thought; I neither struggled nor spoke. I grasped the frame with a force that shook it, and fixed my hollow and bursting eyes on the hand that held me. For my liberty, for my life, again, I would not live over the two moments that elapsed, before I perceived that he had grasped me in the agonies of pain, involuntary, unconscious, and yet asleep; that he had laid hold on the first thing that was next his hand, and held it without being sensible of the act, or of any relief from it. But this discovery consoled me but little. He might hold me till escape was impossible; and to liberate myself by a

CHARLES MATURIN

struggle, would be to wake him. With anguish therefore, (such as none but he who counts but a moment between him and death—death, aggravated by the near chance of safety, and the certain increase of suffering, has ever felt,) I awaited the dissolution of his hold as my only hope of life. In two moments, with the same suddenness of motion, he released me, and, with some inarticulate moans of pain, turned to the other side. The instant he released me, I felt such a gush of heat through me, that I almost relinquished my hold of the casement from weakness. In a moment, however, I collected myself, and attempted to open the casement. This was done with difficulty; yet I dared not look behind me, lest I should see Saviolo's eye upon me. It *was* done however, and I looked out on the free air and the open woods. The night was now utterly dark, and the tempest terrible. I could hear the roar of the forest below; but knew not whether I should be in the forest on springing out of the window. For deliberation there was no time; nor could it teach me any thing. Around, above, and below me, were only tumult and darkness. I threw myself out of the window. I alighted, after a rapid descent, upon something solid. This gave way under me, and I felt myself falling again, with more pain, and through more obstruction than before. At length I reached the ground, sore and bruised. Every thing about me was soft and damp, otherwise, I am convinced, I must have broken my limbs with my double fall. At a little distance from me, I heard the growling of a dog, and the rattling of a chain. I did not dare to stir, nor even to examine whether I was hurt or not, lest he should betray me by his barking. In a moment, however, I began to reflect, I had gained but little beside bruises and danger, by throwing myself out of the window. I could be as easily discovered and murdered in a shed, which I believed my present abode to be. I rose therefore as quietly as possible, but sunk down again from utter inability to stand. I found I had either sprained or broken the limb on which I alighted. Another thrill of agony ran through me at this discovery, keener than the pain that followed my vain attempt to stand; but however reluctant or perturbed, I was obliged to sink down upon the damp straw that was spread over the ground. In a few moments, the moon broke thro' the clouds, and shining with strong light, discovered every object around me. I was in a large shed, rudely constructed of mud and the branches of trees, and covered but partially with straw. I could not see whether it was connected with the principal building; but it was open every where; yet I could not escape. The roof was broken through where I had fallen, and through the fracture I had a view of other parts of the building, rude, and ruinous, and dimly seen, from amid dark clouds and masses of forest shade that were spread around them. The anguish of my mind would, I believe, have again risen to madness, had it not been qualified by a kind of stupid satisfaction at the idea of being so far from the persons and weapons of the murderers, and a dream of impossible hope that I might be concealed by being where it was not probable any would search or suspect, from its nearness to the house. Thus pacified by contrary expectations, of which, nevertheless, the love of life rendered both probable, and compelled to reconcile myself to remaining where I was, since, to stir was impossible, I sunk down, but still kept my eyes fixed on the building, still listened eagerly for a sound. In a short time, I beheld a light moving slowly up a part of the building just opposite. It was so dim, and proceeded with such frequent pauses of mischief-meaning delay, that at once I conceived it was the person employed to murder me who was ascending to my room. I attempted to stand upon my feet; but the impulse was unable to contend with pain and infirmity. The light stopped, and disappeared for some time. In a moment after, the whole building echoed with cries of astonishment, and quick voices that called and answered each other, and lights darted and disappeared at every window in my sight. All this I interpreted aright. He had gone up to my room, found it empty, and was now alarming the rest to pursue and discover me. All this I was obliged to know, with a consciousness, that if any chance should direct them to where I was concealed, I was inevitably lost. After half an hour's intolerable suspense, during which every part of the building seemed to undergo a search, I distinctly heard them going out in another direction, apparently that by which I had entered the house, and which was opposite to the part of the building where the sick man lay. This was an intimation of safety to me; but still, how precarious was that safety! Any of them might take the direction where I was. A casual impulse, a motion unaccounted for, might bring one of them to my shed. Their voices, however, became more and more distant, and their whistles and hollows echoed from the remotest parts of the wood, as the wind bore them faintly to my ear. The hope of life revived within me, when I heard that devil, Saviolo, (who, it appeared, had been awakened by the uproar in the house, and joined with the rest in searching it for me,) bending from the window just over me, exclaim, "Here, here; this way; he must have escaped through this window; it is

CHARLES MATURIN

open, search for him here." I drew in my breath, and listened in despair. There was no answer; they were out of hearing. I heard him cursing their stupidity, and muttering something, as if he was about to descend himself. I tried to rise, and found, with the surprise of unspeakable joy, that my hurt had been trivial. I was now able to stand and to walk, but feebly. Any degree of recovered capacity was matter of hope to me now, though I was still unable to make any considerable exertion for my safety. I crept towards the mastiff who was chained near me, and whom I had some hope of making serviceable to me. He growled fiercely at me; but as I drew nearer, to my utter astonishment, he stretched out his neck, and fawned on me with the utmost gentleness. I knew him almost as soon. He was a dog I had in Naples, who followed me every where, and fed from my hand; and though it was four years since I had lost him, he knew the first tones of my voice. Surely this was the providence of St. Filippo.

I had scarce time to slip off his chain, when a door opened near me, and, thro' the chinks of the shed, I saw Saviolo approaching, holding up a lanthorn, and looking round suspiciously. His drawn dagger was in his hand. He came up to the shed slowly, but directly, and, entering it, saw me instantly; and, with a yell of joy, rushed towards me. I had formed my plan; and, urging the dog with my voice and hands, the faithful animal flew at him like a tyger, and, fastening in his cloak, dragged him to the ground, and held him there, as if waiting my orders. Saviolo, with a cry of horror, and the visage of a fiend in pain, begged his life with the most abject language of fear and agony. I told him I had no intention to destroy him; that I wished to fly from destruction myself; but that my safety required me to secure him, till I could effect my escape. I desired him, therefore, to throw away his dagger and his pistols. "You will murder me if I do," said the villain, with a horrible mixture of fear and malignity in his face; for he had no thoughts but of treachery and blood. "I will not," said I, "nor I, for worlds, be a wretch with such murderous hands as you. Throw away your dagger and pistols, and you are safe: keep them another moment, and that dog shall tear you to fragments." He threw them to some distance. I took them up, and armed myself with them. He watched me with a fearful eye. He could not comprehend that any one could have another in his power without making a sanguinary use of it. I then compelled him to tell me where I should find the horses of the band; what direction they had taken; and whether they had left the house. I dared not ask him the way thro' the forest, as he would probably have pointed the way of danger. I now called off the dog, who released him in a moment, when the wretch, snatching a short knife from his breast, plunged it into my preserver's throat, who instantly expired. The vehemence of his motion was such, that I scarce perceived him turning on *me*. I closed with him, and, after an obstinate struggle, wrested the knife from him. I could scarce forbear burying it in his heart when I got it. I struck him to the ground in my rage, and when he rose I bound him, with some ropes I found in the shed, to a post in it, and left him, grinding, and gnashing with his teeth, and spitting at me, with the contortions and fury of a demoniac.

I found the horses where he told me, and immediately mounted one of them. From the circumstance of their not being employed by the band, I could only gather, that they believed me to be at no considerable distance. They were therefore probably all around me; but if I could get beyond the immediate region of the house, I believed I should be safe. I went out in the direction opposite to theirs. I need not tell you of my wandering in the wood; how often I quitted the track, and concealed myself in the thicket, which I quitted the next moment, from the fear of what had impelled me to seek it; how I dreaded to proceed, and was yet unable to stop; how I listened in horror to the wind, and the hollow whistle that ran through the wood, mixed with it; how I thought the whisper of murder was in the underwood, as it hissed in the breeze; and how often I recoiled as the tossing branches of the trees flung a sudden shadow across the way. I got out of the wood, after all my terror, safely, about the morning dawn; but I was no sooner freed from one danger, than the fear of another, as urgent, smote me.

Whither could I go, or to whom? I had escaped miraculously from your father's hands; but I knew they could reach me in any part of Italy. Where could I fly, that money could not purchase my blood? He might list a whole army against a single wretch; and, on a long chase, I knew St. Filippo himself could be no match for him. I believe, Signor, you will think the result of this debate was actual madness. I pursued my way eagerly to your father's castle determined to go directly to him, to present myself before him. At a distance from him I knew there was no safety; but I felt that this strange confidence might ensure my safety with him.

Without further danger or adventures, I reached the castle that very evening. The servants, who did not appear to know the plan about me, admitted me without surprise. I desired immediately to see the Count. I was conducted to him. He was alone when I entered; and the tapers which were but just lit, burnt on a table near him, so that he could scarce distinguish me till I was close to him. He then sprang almost off his chair, and continued to stare at me, for some moments, with a look of vacant horror. During that time I could not speak. I could not recover myself; the temerity of my purpose appalled me in the moment of execution.

At length, I said in low and hurried tones, "My Lord, you are surprised to see me here. The villain with whom I travelled had designs upon my life. I discovered them, and escaped. Listen to me, my Lord. You have suspicions of your son Annibal; no living creature but myself can verify them. Whatever knowledge I possess will be lost to you if I perish; and whatever may yet be gained from your son, can be gained only by me; for I possess his confidence, and he believes me attached to his person. I can serve you more effectually by my life than by my death. I can serve you more effectually than any of the villains employed to murder me. Mark me, my Lord, my death may ruin you; my life may serve you. If I were this moment dragged from your presence, or stabbed before it, a thousand tongues would tell it. If I were even immured in your dungeons, and poisoned, and buried secretly there, my disappearance would excite suspicion, and that suspicion would persecute you to the end of your days, and perhaps abridge them. Let me live, then. I will be faithful from fear and from gratitude. No villain, hired by the price of murder, can be so faithful as he who serves for life—for life restored and confirmed. While at a distance from you I might have saved myself by flight; but I fled hither, because I knew my life was important to you, as well as to myself."

Was not this a bold effort for life? I knew it was my only one. I knew, besides, (and believe me, Signor, even in that painful moment, I felt the force of that consideration,) that my success might be of the most material consequence to you; that, if I was believed, I would be admitted to you, might talk with, plan with, perhaps escape with you; that your sufferings would certainly be mitigated, perhaps your life preserved.

The effect produced on the Count was what my hopes had anticipated. He was overpowered by the suddenness of my appearance and language; and whatever attention the hurry of the moment allowed him, was impressed by what I said, by the promises of present discovery, and of future services. He waved me, however, to leave him. I urged him still for a promise of safety. He gave it on his honour; and I departed satisfied.

As I left the room, I could not but wonder at myself; my very existence seemed a prodigy to me, what no power of body or mind on their fullest stretch could have effected for me; one effect of lucky rashness produced for me, the pacification of an enemy, powerful and inexorable; the escape from a danger that threatened me every hour of life, and in every part of the world. I mixed among the domestics, and wondered they did not feel the same surprise at my living appearance that *I* was conscious of, without reflecting, that of my disappearance they did not know the cause, nor would perhaps ever have known it.

In a short time, I was again summoned to the Count. I found father Schemoli with him, that sight of evil omen. The looks of both were fixed on me, as if they would search my soul; a moment after, they exchanged looks, that seemed to express I was too much in their power, to be an object of dread to them. I approached, and was instructed in what they expected from me. I did not understand till then, how my offers of service were understood; it was then evident that I was to be employed as a spy; that my having been honoured with your notice and confidence, was to be made a means of extorting from you some knowledge, which they did not describe very clearly, but of which they seemed determined to get possession. My attachment to you made me shudder at this proposal, till I recollected, that to appear to enter into their measures, was the best way to defeat their mischief; and that to betray my indignation and horror at them, would be only to sacrifice my powers of serving you, to an unseasonable display of my zeal. I listened to them therefore in silence, and by holding down my head in a posture of deep attention, concealed the changes that my countenance underwent. I never knew so much of the iniquity of the human mind; I could not believe so much had existed in it, as I heard manifested in the directions given me for acquiring the knowledge of this secret they believe you to possess. The object was simple; but the means were crowded with such superfluous, and complicated knavery, the lessons of falsehood and deceit ran from them with such facility, that they seemed, compared with their usual habits of speech, like foreigners, who are suffered to speak their own language, and who compensate by their sudden volubility, for long restraint and silence. They seemed to speak a new and natural language. I promised strict obedience, and affected to profit by their documents; and at length was dismissed with an assurance, that my fidelity was the only security of my life; that on the discovery of the slightest tendency to duplicity, my punishment would be what I could neither conceive nor avoid. I was then given these keys, with a direction to visit you, and all plans of escape were banished by the thought of seeing you; but I am permitted to be often with you, to attend you in place of the confessor—nay, to pass hours in your apartment. These are my instructions, and it will be strange, if with such advantages both for planning and executing, we should continue long in durance.

I was as willing as Filippo could be, to let the satisfaction of the present moment supersede all provision for the future. I dwelt with a pleasure I did not try to restrain, on his simplicity, his strong attachment, his miraculous escape; and felt that whatever might be the success of any plans we might form, my mind, spent with unnatural force, would find relief in their discussion; or even in the circumstances that made their discussion possible.

I collected myself, however, enough to remind Filippo, that the present juncture required the most dexterous conduct; that it was not impossible, even the present indulgence was only a stratagem of deeper mischief; that it was necessary for him at all events to amuse my father by promises of success in his employment; otherwise, his visits would be obstructed, and probably his life sacrificed to their disappointment, or their suspicions; that he must frame his reports so as to bear a due relation in point of time to the execution of any measures we might have adopted, so as neither to compel us to precipitate or delay them, but just gain the proper time for their adjustment. Above all, I charged him, with an earnestness he did not understand, to observe the confessor, and repeat to me every instance of his deportment he could remark or remember. Our conference extended to a late hour, and I was compelled to drive him away; for something like hope began to flutter within me, and I determined not to sacrifice its promises to a casual indulgence.

He was hardly gone when I wished to recal him. The terrors of the hour that was approaching I shrunk from meeting alone. As my visitor threatened, every night his appearance was becoming more terrible, and its expectation more insupportable to me. I dreaded in what this might terminate. He had darkly spoken of the possible subversion of my reason; I felt all the horrors of this prediction. There is no evil like the expected or approaching loss of reason; there is no infliction that cannot be tolerated in imagination; but that which sweeps all power of provision, resistance, or mitigation of any other. Even in the present state of my mind, this sensation was exquisitely painful, as it in a manner verified what, of all things I was most unwilling to believe true; viz. the agency and power of that singular being. I shuddered inwardly with reluctant conviction, with that irksome feeling, that cannot dispute the evidences; yet hates to admit the conclusion. One circumstance relative to his appearance, (which might in a great measure assist me to judge of his unnatural pretensions), I believed myself abled to discover still—the mode of his entrance into my apartment. If, as it seemed, he was a being that could glide through walls, and overcome material obstructions, I could resist no longer the belief of whatever he might disclose. If he required the assistance by which human beings pass from one part of space to another, I rejoiced in the hope of discovering his imposture, and obtaining a triumph over this wonderful being, whose superiority to humanity, mingled envy with my astonishment. While I was occupied by these thoughts, a strange drowsiness crept over me; I resisted it at first, without an apprehension of its influence being so strong; but in a short time, I felt all power of thought gliding from my mind.

Half angry at so unseasonable a weakness, I rose, and began to walk about the room; it was in vain. In a short time, from utter incapacity of motion, I was obliged to throw myself on the bed, where a deep sleep fell on me. It did not continue long; I awoke I know not how. Before I was fully awake, I felt my eyes were in search of Father Schemoli; they discovered him, as usual, sitting by the table on which my lamp was burning still.

Without betraying any emotion, without uttering a single word, or interjection of fear, I continued to gaze on him, expecting something more than I had yet heard, to proceed from him; the idea of his supernatural power involuntarily mixing with my own thoughts, produced a full conviction in me, that he was acquainted with the real object and topic of Filippo's conference with me; and I awaited his declaration of it with as full reliance, as if he had been present at our conversation; but he spoke without allusion to that, or any subject, but the constant one of his visits. On that, he poured forth a flood of supernatural eloquence, which I no longer attempted to resist, or to interrupt. It was terrible to hear him—the admiration that follows impassioned oratory, was lost in more strange and awful feelings; there was evidently something of the power and evidence of another world about him. Delight was checked, yet heightened by terror; and attention was often suspended by the wonder, how man could hear him and live. The mind rose to the level of the speaker, I felt myself upborne and floating on the pinions of his voice over the confines of the invisible world, over the formless, and the void. I felt it with a wild and terrible joy—a joy that made me as strange to myself, as every thing around me was; a joy that from the very giddiness of its elevation, precluded me from measuring the height to which it had raised me—the remote point at which I stood from the common feelings and habits of human nature. I know this was a strange and wayward frame; I wonder at myself; I can hardly describe or render it probable; but I have heard of beings, who, with unnatural strength of feeling, would hang on a bare and single point of rock to see the ocean in a storm; would rush out to cross the forky lightnings in their dance, or howl to the storm as it bent the forest, or shook the mountains to their base. I have heard of such, but scarce believed such a feeling could exist in a human breast, till I listened to this strange being, and listened with pleasure as strange. But this night, whether encouraged by my silence, or whether in the progressive fulfilment of his commission, he spoke more openly of its object, he dared to tell me I was doomed to be a murderer. A murderer did I say? Compared to the crime, which he affirmed I would perpetrate, that of murder might be termed a benefaction, an honour to society. In language of horrid strength, without pause, or limit, or mitigation, again and again he affirmed it; nay, described its mode and circumstance, the process of preparation my mind would undergo, the gradual induration of my heart, and sealing up of my mind and conscience with that penetrating and emphatic minuteness, that proved an intimacy with the inmost heart and spirit of man, from which I shrunk in vain—in vain tried to shelter myself by arguing from the futility of his reasoning and descriptions, to the futility of his prediction.

But though I could not work myself into incredulity, I tried to work myself into rage; I endeavoured to awe or to repel him by my fury. I demanded how he dared to impute to me such crimes? Was I not a free agent? Had I not the power of choosing one mode of action, and declining another? To the perpetration of such horrors as he predicted, nothing but insanity could drive me, and insanity would relieve me from the burthen of consciousness, as well as the guilt of volition. I charged him in my turn, successively, with being an impostor, a maniac, and lastly, an evil spirit, embodied and empowered to work my eternal woe, and confirm his own by his infernal triumph. I abjured all further commerce with him; I heaped him with reproach and malediction. I stopped my ears, I closed my eyes against him; only my voice was free, and with that I cursed, and bid him begone. When the bellowings of my rage had ceased, and the echoes of my prison were still, he burst into a laugh; my blood curdled to hear him, and when I raised my eyes to him, he was gone.

The impression he left with me was stronger than any preceding night; but it was more tolerable; the sense of oppression or persecution wakens us to rage and to resistance. There was something so determined and tenacious in these nightly hauntings, so persevering and obtrusive in his mention of the subject I had abjured and refused to listen to, that I felt it like a challenge to my powers of resistance, and I met it with my full strength of mind. There now appeared to be an obvious and definite ground whereon we were to contend; a trial of powers common to both; his, of importunate persecution, and mine, of unremitted opposition. I pleased myself in collecting the forces of my mind, and ascertaining the ground and point of our conflict. I resolved if I must yield, not to yield without a vigorous struggle. I forgot, that by all this I only confirmed the identity of my torment; only gave it form and substance, instead of endeavouring to dissipate it as the vision of solitude, as the dream that floated on the heavy vapours of my dungeon.

They must repose great confidence in Filippo. They have this day permitted him to bring me materials for writing. These were indeed welcome, like others. I trifled with my indulgence for the first hour. I scrawled the paper over with strange figures; but when I examined them, I was struck with the number of instruments of death and punishment I had described among them: how strong a tincture my mind communicates to trivial and indifferent things!

Filippo tells me, they continue to importune him with questions about me, and the knowledge he had obtained from me. "I have told them," said he, "a plausible story about your former visits to the tower, and about the communications you are daily making to me. But I take care not to make any extravagant or momentous representations, lest they should expect some verification of them, from your movements or sentiments, which it would be impossible to give. In the mean time, their suspicions are eluded, and time is obtained, which is all we require."

CHARLES MATURIN

It is obvious to you, that in his narrative and conversations, I have always *translated Filippo's language.* The vulgar often express themselves with force, particularly in descriptions; but they are insufferably tedious, and abound in repetitions. Nor, since I retained the substance of his narrative, was it necessary for me to retail his idioms and vulgarisms.

He sits by me, and talks of plans for our escape—talks merely—for even his sanguine disposition cannot trace a vestige of rational hope in any he has yet proposed. The castle is too well guarded; filled with domestics all day, and every passage locked at night. He believes it to be full of subterranean passages and secret recesses; but even if we reached them, we might perish in them by fatigue and hunger.

I have now begun my journal; and, within these three days, wrote the preceding account. You must henceforth only expect it in fragments.

Filippo often looks at me with unspeakable solicitude. He confesses to me, I am so altered, so reduced, and haggard in look, and abstracted in manner, that he cannot believe such a change to be produced merely by my confinement. He importunes me with an earnestness I often find it difficult to resist, but must not yield to. He would either think me a maniac, or a being leagued with, and under the power of some evil spirit. The very name of Father Schemoli (of whom he has notions justly terrible) would inspire with terror, and perhaps even his attachment might not be proof against the aversion which the idea of our intercourse might produce.

"Signor," said he, "there was a man in a village where I was born, who believed himself haunted by the evil one, and that the object of the temptation was to make him commit murder. He told this in confidence to some one who pressed to know the occasion of his constant melancholy; and he told it to another, and in a short time every one shrunk away from the poor wretch, as if he had been a real murderer. No one would meet him alone; no one would pass near his house at night; no one would sit near him; for whether they believed him really beset, as he described, or only visionary, it inspired them with a dread and a suspicion, that made every one shun him as some evil thing. After lingering some time in utter solitude, he at length disappeared, and strange things were whispered about his departure.

"Some months after that, however, we heard of an extraordinary murder committed at Venice. The murderer had had no enmity to the person he killed, nor even any knowledge of him. He had inquired his situation in life; and, on learning that he had no relations who would suffer by his loss; that his character was good; and he had come that moment from receiving absolution—he exclaimed, 'That is my man,' and immediately stabbed him. He then surrendered himself to justice; said he was perfectly sensible of his crime, and desired no mercy; but had taken care that his offence should be attended with as little injury as possible, either to society, or to the sufferer.

"When we inquired the name of this extraordinary man, we learned he was the very individual who had left our village. Now Signor, you must forgive me; but no human being ever looked as that man did but you. You have exactly his dark, fixed eye, and that peculiar contraction of the forehead, and hollowness of the cheek. I saw him the morning before he disappeared. He was tracing some lines in a bed of withered leaves, over which he bent; and, as you hung over your paper just now, drawing those melancholy lines, you were the picture of him. Do, Signor, tell me, for the love of grace, what it is thus presses on your mind. It is something else than your confinement, I know. When I speak of that you are quite easy and resigned, and listen to all I can say with composure; but if I mention night, or solitude, or the confessor to you, your countenance changes, that I scarce know it."

You may conceive with what pain I heard him. The sympathy the unfortunate subject of his story had met with, taught me what I was to expect from a similar disclosure. I silenced him as soon as I could; but, as he left the room, he murmured something about father Schemoli. Is my persecution written on my forehead? Can the very menials read that I am tempted to murder? If so, 'twere almost better committed; there would be less suspicion, and less of "fear which hath torment."

His visits are unremitting, and his persecutions increasing in force and frequency. He now names the object of it directly, proposes means, and, without remitting his mysterious character and language, discusses them with a familiarity that chills my blood.

What shall I do? I am strongly beset; I am sore pressed and straitened. Would to heaven I could make my escape from this durance. Even if he has the power of pursuing me, may not that power be diminished or increased by the circumstances of time or place? He hinted that himself. He talked of his power being limited to a certain hour and spot. If I could but fly from him; if I was to hear the terrible voice no more; to lay my harrassed head where *one* night would be unbroken by these visits of horror. He has no longer the power of feeding curiosity, or of fascinating imagination. My only sensation at his presence is unmixed

CHARLES MATURIN

aversion, mortal repugnance and fear. It is not to be wondered at. No human mind can longer endure the pitch mine has been strained to lately. It must relieve itself by insanity, or by a deep and motionless stagnation of its powers. The objects that have occupied me are not the natural topics of human meditation; the mind can only bear to see them remotely, and partially, and transiently; it cannot confer with, and be habitually conversant with them, without changing its properties, nay, its very nature. The distant cloud, whose skirts are indented with lightnings, and whose departing thunders roll their last burden on the winds, we can bear to follow with the eye, and feel our hearts quelled and elated with the fluctuations of grateful horror; but who could bear to live for ever in the rage and darkness of the tempest; to sport with the lightnings that quivered around him, and grasp at the bolt that rushed to blast him. My mind is utterly changed. I shrink from these things, and would fly back to life for shelter, if I could. I feel a kind of indignation at the perversion of my powers. Why should I be shut up in this house of horrors, to deal with spirits and damned things, and the secrets of the infernal world, while there are so many paths open to honour and pleasure, the varieties of human intercourse, and the enjoyment of life? I struggle to regain the point I have quitted; to feel myself a man, and amongst men again; to "confer with flesh and blood."

What are these bodings that oppress me? Must I never return to life, never be myself again? 'Tis but the involuntary recollection of his words. I cannot dismiss, but I will not believe them. He tells me, my first stirrings of curiosity, my conferences with Michelo, my visits to the tower and to the tomb, were a series of acts which I could neither produce nor forbear, which belonged to that great chain of agency that bound me to him, and him to me indissolubly—a chain which I could neither forge nor break; of which one link could neither be added nor detached by the power of all nature. I will not believe this; yet how consistent is it with the process of my feelings! how suddenly did I rush into the pursuit, without any preparation of mind, or of circumstance! This was not natural nor right; nor did I feel any surprise at the greatness or suddenness of the transition from quietness and indifferency, to the rage of sudden zeal, the impetuosity of resistless activity. This was not natural either. How do I heap up arguments to my own confusion! How do I set out resolved to disbelieve an assurance, yet employ myself only in collecting proofs of it, and observing the repugnance I pretended to confirm! Curse on the impulse, whether fated or voluntary, that first led me to the pursuit. What motive summoned me to it? My conscience was clear and my rest quiet. Who made me an inquisitor of the secrets of blood, a searcher of the souls of men? What had I to do with it? No voice called on me; no hand beckoned to me; I was warned neither by dream nor vision; my officiousness was wilful; my obstinacy was incorrigible. What if I had heard these dark reports, had I a right to investigate them? If a pit opens at my feet, am I to plunge into it to examine the cause? Could I not have walked over the unsafe and suspected ground I was led to, with the quiet fear, the shrinking caution with which a child passes over the place of graves? Whatever secrets may be around and beneath him he cares not, so he may get safely through them. He trends lightly, lest he should break their tremendous sleep; he will scarce breathe, least it should sound like a call to them; he will scarce name the divine name in the stifled prayer of fear, lest it should have some unknown power in that place of awe.

Oh that I had thus glided past this pursuit! The fatal affectation of supernatural dignity; the conscious pride of the agent of Heaven; the chosen instrument of Him, (to be the dust of whose feet is above all earthly power); this, this undid me. It is a sensation rarely felt; the modes of life seldom admit it; the heart of man has scarce room for it; but it is of surpassing and magnificent power. Would I could exchange it for the most timid humility, for the most servile ignorance, for the most impotent superstition that ever depressed the human breast. Such are safe from danger by the excess of fear, instead of being, as I am, mated and leagued with these horrors, blended in unhallowed intimacy with what it is frightful and unlawful for human nature to know. Would I were the gossip-crone, who, shivering over her single faggot, crosses herself to hear such things named, and trembles to see her dim and single light burn blue, while the tale goes round; or the child that seems to sleep at her feet, lest he should be sent to rest before it is finished, and imagination fill it up too well when he is alone, and in darkness—would I were one of those. Their fear, their ignorance is their security. Heaven never selects such instruments for its higher purposes. They may eat their humble bread, and drink their water in peace, while the servant of heaven, who tarries on his way, is torn by a lion. They may remain, like their own rustic hills, covered with useful verdure, and content with quiet beauty, while those, whose deep roots extend to the world beneath, whose feet have supplanted the foundations of the earth, are impregnated with fire and destruction,

CHARLES MATURIN

blast all the region around them, and are rent and ruined by their own explosion. Why did I assume this fatal responsibility? What were the crimes of others to me? The whole world might have laboured with some prodigious discovery; yet I might have passed my life in it, unsolicitous and unconscious of it. These things do not come in quest of us; 'tis our fatal curiosity that removes the natural barrier of separation. The earth on which I trod might have quaked and groaned with untold secrets; every breeze might have brought to my ears the cry of an unappeased spirit; the tapers that burned before me might have been tipt with blue; the very dogs might have crouched and shivered with a consciousness of invisible presence; I might have set every step upon an untimely grave, and slept every night in a chamber stained with secret blood, so I had known nothing of it, my sleep would have been quiet, and my mind undisturbed. I would have passed through life as calmly as the sea-boy sleeping in the shrouds, while the spirits of the storm are mustering and hurtling in the blast that lulls him to rest. A search into the secrets of crimes we have not been privy to, is like an acquired faculty of seeing spectres. Before its attainment, all was safety and innocence; after, solitude becomes uneasy, and darkness terrible. The consciousness of guilt is as bad as the commission. He who obtains the knowledge of another's crimes, shares their burthen and their torment; he is either summoned to expiate them, and forced from the quietness of life, and the natural current of human action, to a line of daring and desperate adventure, which he pursues without sympathy, and without reward; (for the feelings, attached to that state, are too uncommon for participation, and its termination is not his own exaltation, but the punishment of others) or he sinks into the partaker of another's crimes, by forbearing to disclose them. He suffers more than the real agent; his painful consciousness is the same, his dread of detection the same, and his sense of the injuries of the sufferer, and the consequences of discovery are greater; for he fears to be found wicked, only from the love of wickedness, without the motives of enmity, or the temptations of reward. To a personal action, if brave and daring, nay, if egregiously flagitious, the wonder of mankind involuntarily attaches some degree of honour; but the gratuitous villain, who was not guilty, not because he *dared*, but because he *feared*, is deservedly heaped with the contempt and maledictions of all. To such an alternative has my fatal curiosity reduced me; an alternative, aggravated by circumstances of peculiar horror to me. Whatever be the object disclosed to you,

Ippolito, can it be so terrible as that which my hints have told? Do you understand me? Involuntarily I hope not; yet you should understand me, to estimate the struggles of my mind aright. A month past, I would have believed my heart contaminated by the casual visitation of that thought which is now its constant inmate. I dread lest it should lose its salutary horror of which this habitual contemplation must divest it. And what shall I do? What security shall I have then? A villain in theory, is half a villain in action. Habit is as strong a security for our virtues as principle; to a mind beset as mine, perhaps stronger: 'tis impossible for the purest mind to dwell long on villanous and murderous thoughts, even as indifferent and neutral, without feeling their pollution not only infecting its frame, but partially influencing the actions; impulses of malignity, of mischief, of revenge, will be felt unchecked, and unrepented. I feel it myself—I feel the fiend growing strong within me. What, oh what will become of me, Ippolito? I can hardly breathe, I can scarce hold my pen; these are the last lines it shall ever trace; you will never behold them, they will be buried with their writer. I shall not outlive this night. Filippo is weeping beside me—I cannot describe circumstances; the shock of death is too forcible for my mind. I know not what to think, or almost where I am; but I feel what I must shortly be.

About an hour ago, Filippo rushed in with horror in his face. He fell at my feet, and gasping and speechless looked up in my face. When he could speak, it was only in broken tones and howlings of despair, to tell me I was "to die." "I had but a few hours to live." I listened with the incredulity of amazement. The mind cannot readily admit the thought of death—of death so near and so sudden. At length, his agony excited my fear. I then spoke unheeded in my turn, for he was unable to hear, or almost to speak. With difficulty and many interruptions, at last, he told me, "He had of late, observed my father and his confessor often engaged in conferences from which *he* was excluded; that his suspicions were awakened, as hitherto he had been a principal agent in their consultations; that this evening, owing to my father's abstraction, he had succeeded in concealing himself in a part of the room, as the confessor entered. It was a dangerous experiment, but he felt such a peculiar, boding sensation on his entrance, that he could not resist making it.

"They conversed in whispers at first," said he "and with such long intervals, that I could collect nothing; at length, the Count, as if many things had been proposed, and none had satisfied him, throwing himself back in his chair, said aloud, "I know not how to dispose of this incumbrance." "An incumbrance," said the monk, "is only another name for something we want resolution to be freed from." "I do not want resolution," said the Count, "but I know not what means to employ." "He who does not want resolution, could not hesitate to employ *any* means," observed the confessor. "But my own son, father," said the Count. "His crime is therefore aggravated by disobedience," said the monk. "But in my own castle," said the Count. "You can therefore be more secret and secure," replied the monk. "But another—another—another"—said the Count in a piteous tone, and as if unable to force himself to finish the sentence—"Another is rendered necessary by those that have preceded; the first movement is voluntary, all that follow are consequential and inevitable," urged the tempter. "By my soul," said the Count, apparently answering his own thoughts, "I am neither safe nor secret within these walls, witness"—he stopped suddenly. "Our success depends as much on the choice, as on the use of means," said the monk. "When we employ violent passions as our agents, their explosion will often extend to ourselves; but there are still and unsuspected means." "Do you know of such means, holy father," interrupted the Count. "I do," said the monk. "And are you acquainted with one who would apply them," asked your father, in a lower tone. "I am," said the confessor. There was then a long silence; the children of satan appeared to understand each other without speech. I could have rushed out, and pierced their false hearts with my own hand.

The Count seemed to force himself to break the silence, and said in a hurried manner, "Good father, it is needless to observe to you, that this must be done so, so—as neither to excite suspicion nor disturbance. You have of course witnessed many proofs of the efficacy and expedition of what you propose." "I heard many proofs," said the monk, evasively. "But," continued your father with increased eagerness of tone and gesture, though almost whispering, "they are such as leave you in no doubt of its certainty." "Would you have me doubt my senses?" said the monk, impatiently. "Pardon me, father," said the Count, "you did not mention any thing of seeing a proof of its operation." "But is not hearing one of the senses," said the confessor, recollecting himself. It struck me, Signor. when I heard them conferring thus, that leagued as they both were in wickedness, each of them felt a wish to be possessed of some knowledge of the other's previous iniquity, that might supply an influence over him at some future period. To such a motive I attributed your father's anxiety to draw an ocular confession of the power of these means (which I suppose to be poison) from the monk; for though the guilt of either could scarce be developed without implicating that of the other, yet the fears of wickedness are perpetually impelling to provisional caution, and security for the subordination of its associates. The monk rose to depart, "You must not go in anger, father," said the Count. "Pardon me, I mean to set about it in cold *blood*," said the monk, in a peculiar accent. "Go then, but send my attendants to me quickly—quickly, father, and throw open all the doors as you go, that I may hear the sound of your steps till I see *them* approaching. I cannot be alone a moment—I am a miserable man!" This last direction was fortunate for me, for I glided out from behind the hangings through the open door, and reached your apartment in a moment.

Having told his tale, he again fell at my feet, and wept. It had been more merciful to have let me die without this intelligence; for die I must. The poison will probably be conveyed in food, undistinguished by any peculiar taste; its operation will probably be like the approach of sleep; I should not have tasted the bitterness of death; the interval of expectation and agony. He has suggested a thousand plans for escape or resistance; they are wild; it is not a single enemy, or a single emergency I have to contend against; they have me utterly in their power, these walls must bound my struggles. If I resisted violence, they might leave me to perish by famine; this is horrible. Oh, for a single weapon to grasp in mine hour of need. There is none; death comes on like the night, shutting up all creation in darkness, hopeless and impenetrable—I have driven Filippo from me—driven him almost by force; his clamours disturbed me. I would think if I could; my mind is wonderous heavy and beclouded. I am stunned and blasted by this stroke. Death, death— What is death? Men talk of it all their lives; and the wise will talk well and smoothly of it; but who hath understood it? Who has seen it approach so near, and measured it with their full power of mental vision, described and embodied its just dimensions, and said to it, now I know all thou canst be, or bring to me. No, it is impossible; if speech could be obtained in the last agonies, we might know something of it; if they could even make signs to signify the gradual obscuration of sense, and exclusion of the world and its objects; if they could intimate at what moment they let go their hold of the life of sense, and feel the dawn of their new perceptions. No, I was born to die—I have seen many that died; yet I know nothing of death. Great and invisible being, whose name is to be uttered by silence, where am I going? all conjectures of reason, all illuminations of faith fail me now. I could talk of these things like others, and believed my notions of them clear and authentic; but now all around me is tenfold darkness. A mountain rises between the regions of life and futurity; through it, or above it no power can obtain for living man a glimpse or a passage; clouds are seated on its top, and its centre is mantled over by darkness. I sit at its feet, and look upward in vain; I tremble in ignorance, I gasp in expectancy. Whither am I going, or to whom! How many fears of flesh are compassing me round! How much am I a mortal even at this solemn hour! The dread of pain, though it is the last I shall suffer, the throbbings of curiosity, though I shall never be sensible of their gratification, are I think more strong within me, than all other feelings. The mode and circumstance of death are more terrible to me, than the act itself; of that, I have no conception; but of the possible pain and agony of the struggle, I have too, too clear an idea—Will it first affect my intellect, or my senses? Shall I feel my mind obscured and declining, or mine eyes growing dim, my pulses fluttering, my hearing mixed and dizzy? Oh, what will be the first symptoms, that the pilgrim is setting out on her journey; the first faint beat of the march, that calls the coward to the last great conflict; and when I try to "go forth, and shake myself as at other times," to scatter these faint assaults of infirmity; to feel, to know that no power can arrest or subdue them; that, feeble as they seem, they are the beginnings of that wondrous process, that in a few moments will change my body into dust, and shut out my spirit to wander in a state new and unknown; of which, the conception can only commence with the existence?

I will wrap up my head, and think no more—it will not be. Shall I suffer much pain? Will my struggles be long? How do we know but the approach of death is pleasurable? None have returned to tell us; perhaps our fears are all that invest it with pain. Oh, no, no, the aspect of the dead bears no expression of pleasure; the pointed nostril, the grim and rigid mouth, the distended and bursting eye, the hair bristling and erect, like resistance—these are not the features of one who is at ease. No, death is every way horrible. I have heard, too, that the young and those in health are more susceptible of severe pain, and longer struggles, than the weak and aged. They cling to life with terrible force, and repeated blows, and hard butchering violence must rend them asunder. Yes—death is every way horrible to me! Almighty powers, can this be possible? Have two hours elapsed since I was told I must die? It appears that I have heard it but now. Oh, who can think life long who knows he must die? Who can slumber over the hours, whose lapse lead to futurity? How fast, how fast, even to the eye, the hand of this timepiece travels—even while I write it changes its place! If it were arrested for an hour, what injury would the world sustain for an hour?—It might stop for a day, for a year without mankind being sensible of it; and, if it should, its termination would only find me, as now, lapt in terrible conjecture! To prepare for what is indefinite, no time would be sufficient—all around me is wondrous, as if I had but just begun to live. This little instrument, can its minute workings lead to an effect so stupendous? Can the progress of that small line precipitate an immortal spirit into futurity? I have heard of the current of the stream before; but now my eyes see it, I have felt its force, and measured its rapidity; nothing may turn it back or withstand it. A few moments more, and—was that a step? It was a step; I hear it—they come! I must die! Gracious heaven, is there no help, no respite? Oh, for the swords that are playing by the sides of the idlers of the world this moment! Oh, that I were in a forest, and could rend the branches from the trees for my defence! Can I not tear out the beams or stones of these giant-walls to cast at them? By heaven, I will not hold out my throat to them. I will fight for life, and that terribly. I will make a weapon of something; or they shall feel that the naked hand of despair can scatter firebrands, and arrows, and death."

Here the manuscript ended, and Cyprian, when he had finished it, looked with wonder at Annibal to behold him yet alive. Its termination had indicated death, aggravated by hopeless resistance. Annibal pursued the narrative verbally.

I wrote those last lines with many intervals of fear and of meditation. It was long after midnight, that I heard a step approaching. After a struggle, which neither my power nor voice can describe, I started up, and stood fixed opposite the entrance; my only instrument was a massive chair, which in my frantic strength I wielded like a wand. I am convinced I would have crushed to death, the being against whom I lifted it. The step came nearer. I set my teeth close, and rose on my feet, and my sinews felt like iron. The door was unlocked, and before I could raise my arm, Filippo rushed in. There was no time for inquiry or explanation; he was gasping for breath, and only beckoned me to follow; that motion calmed me in a moment. I seemed to understand intuitively it was a sign of safety and freedom.

CHARLES MATURIN

I caught up the lamp, and followed him. On quitting, the room, I was about to turn down the passage, but he graspt my arm, and though still unable to utter more than interjections, gave me to understand we must take another direction. He passed before with quick, but steady steps. I held the lamp low, lest our speed should extinguish it; for the passage into which we had entered, appeared longer and loftier than the other, and the air, though damp and still, was strong in its current. I was amazed at the apparent incaution of Filippo's movements; for he walked as he would at noon day; but at the end of the passage, he suddenly stopped, and taking the lamp from me and shrouding it with his cloak, stepped forward with breathless and shivering slowness, motioning me to do likewise. I did so; but in the room we entered, I could discover no reason for this sudden caution; it was spacious and desolate, and as the half veiled light threw a partial and thwarting gleam upon it, I could only see masses of dusky obscurity. As we drew near the opposite door, Filippo contracted his steps with increasing fear, and I now threw round me a glance of serious inquiry. I discovered then with difficulty, a dark heap in the corner we were approaching; it was too dim and shapeless to suggest any cause for the caution he betrayed; yet his eye as he drew nearer it, rolled in horror, and his steps almost faltered. I leant over him to view it more closely, and in that moment I thought I beheld it move. Filippo murmured something between a groan and an exclamation of affright, and darted forward so quickly, that I found myself alone and in darkness, almost before I perceived he was gone. I followed him, but know not why I shuddered as I passed that strange dark heap. Just as I reached the door, it moved again; I heard it distinctly rustle in the darkness. I sprung past it with the quickness of real fear. My perceptions were entirely changed; but a moment past, and I dreaded nothing but the terrible monk and his poison; but the sudden and causeless appearance of Filippo, the dim light that led me, this still and fantastic gliding through passages of unbreathing desolation, and the last strange object I had beheld, combined with the confusion and horror of my recent feelings, had rendered me as susceptible of momentary and local impressions, as if I had no other, no personal concern; as if I was not flying for life—for life hardly held and hourly threatened. Still, under the influence of what I imagined I beheld, I eagerly questioned Filippo, whom I had now overtaken, and who had renewed his swiftness. "That chamber," said he, incoherently "ask not—hurry on; your life depends on a moment—he is quiet."

I obeyed him in silence; we crossed other chambers and wound through other passages I had never beheld before, or knew this vast fabric contained; but as I passed, I could not help glancing a thought of horror upon the numberless victims of the guilt or cruelty of its former possessors, so far from the knowledge or sympathy of their fellow creatures, though under the same roof, and within the same walls; that it was perhaps unknown to their nearest relatives where they existed, or what they suffered; that the groans they uttered, might form a part of the respiration of a friend or a brother, without conveying to them, that the lips from which they issued were so near. We now appeared to have traversed that wing of the castle. We had entered a large hall whose doors had a loftier moulding than any we had passed, and which seemed from the bolder and simpler character of its structure, to be near the extremity of the building, and probably to communicate with the court of the castle.

Here Filippo paused, and uncovering the lamp, began eagerly to examine the doors: at several he shook his head with the impatience of disappointment. I followed him mechanically; at length, he darted towards one, that lay deep in the shade, and vehemently applied to it a key, which he snatched from his bosom. By the delay, and the imperfect sound that followed the application, I knew its success too well; the sound struck upon my heart. Filippo the next moment withdrew the key, and disappeared down a dark arch, which I had not seen before, bearing the lamp with him. I remained in utter darkness. My mind had been weakened by trials and sufferings both real and fantastic. The moment he was gone I became the victim of visionary terror. I recollected his sudden appearance, almost impossible to be effected by human means; his strange swiftness and silence, his look so wild and unnatural, his few words so ominous, his disappearance without noise or preparation; I recollected the strange warnings given to those who were near their dissolution, by those who had already undergone it; I recollected how probable it was Filippo had exposed himself to danger, even mortal, by his zeal for me; I recollected with horror, the mysterious heap in that dark chamber, at which he had seemed to pause with portentous shudderings; its dimensions and shape were like those of a corse. I felt it impossible to nurse these horrible imaginings long; they were invading my last half-rallied remains of reason; there was a more probable cause for his desertion; but my habitual reliance on him long resisted that.

I looked around me, to see if any hope remained from my own exertions; the clouds of a heavy night, appearing at the high and pillared windows, excluded every gleam of light, and prevented me from conjecturing, even in what part of the building I was.

As I gazed around, a faint noise came to my ear. I listened, it was the mixt sound of a voice that whispered, and steps that hesitated. I stood motionless betwixt hope and fear. "Hush," said a voice at some distance; willing to believe it Filippo's, I answered in the same accent. "Is it you," said the voice more articulately, "I have been in search of you." As the last words were uttered, I perceived the voice to be that of my father!

I neither exclaimed nor moved, I was stiffened and speechless; to have felt a stiletto in my breast, had been almost a relief to me at that moment. The steps drew nearer; the blood which appeared to have deserted my frame, now rushed back with a sudden and feverous glow; strange and accursed thoughts were with me. We were in the dark; I remembered the visitation of the spectre monk; I remembered words never heard by man, but me—never to be heard. My eyes grew dim; a blaze of purple light quivered through the hall, yet I could see nothing by its glare. My limbs tottered under me; but the influence whose terror would have betrayed me, abated. The steps were evidently receding; and as they retired, I thought I heard curses hissing along the walls. I remained gasping for breath. The air of the hall grew cool again, and though the darkness was not diminished, its shades, I thought, were less dense and oppressive.

On a sudden, I felt myself grasped with violence. I struggled to free myself. I heard the voice of Filippo. I believed him treacherous, and all the mystery was solved. "Wretch," said I, grasping him in my turn, "you have betrayed me" "What madness is this?" he whispered in low but vehement tones, "for the holy Virgin's sake, follow me; but speak not." "You lead me to death," said I; yet I followed him without resistance.

I now found we were in complete darkness. After descending a few steps, we stopped. I was urgent in my whispered inquiries; but obtained no answer. I became impatient of fear and expectation, and almost remonstrated aloud, when I heard a noise near me, like the opening of a door; and, in the next moment, Filippo led me into the court of the castle.

It was the air, the free, open air, the blessed air of heaven. I breathed it in freedom; it was no dream of transitory freedom. I opened my bosom to it; I extended my arms, as if it were tangible and material. I was delirious with sudden and incontrolable joy.

When my senses returned, I found we were in a ruinous enclosure, surrounded by buildings I had not remembered to have seen before; but which, from their appearance, I judged to belong to the servants of the castle. In one or two of the turrets, that were grotesquely perched here and there on the blank and giant walls, I still saw lights twinkling. Filippo, stooping to the ground, raised up the lamp, which he had dexterously hid behind the fragment of a fallen battlement; and we crossed the court in silence, with steps often obstructed by the ruins that were scattered over it. We glided thro' other arches, whose darkness was partially broken by our half-hid light; and at length reached a low door, which opened on the rampart. Here still greater caution was necessary. This has been long in a ruinous state; our steps were confined to a narrow ledge of rocky path, and our only hold of support was the projections and weedy tufts of the dismantled wall.

At length the glare of the lamp flashed upward on a rude and ruined arch, which appeared once to have been connected with the remains of a drawbridge. We crept under it, and, clinging to its rugged and indented sides, which the bickering gleams of the lamp carved into fantastic shapings, descended to the moat, which the fragments that had fallen from above, had almost filled up beneath the arch. We crossed it; descended the mound; and reached the wood in safety.

I now heaped thanks, inquiries, and applauses, in the same breath, on Filippo, who was too busy crossing himself and praying to his patron to heed me.

At length, as we lay behind a tuft of chesnut trees, for he would not permit us as yet to proceed, I procured from him the intelligence of the means.

"When you drove me from you, Signor," said he, "and seemed determined to die, I left you with a resolution to do something desperate. I was resolved you should not perish unaided. This was necessary for my own safety, as well as yours. I could not imagine they would spare *me*, who was permitted to live, only as a means to betray you, when it was no longer necessary to employ that means. I went back to the Count's apartment; I found him preparing to quit it, in order to join the family in the hall, where they usually sup.

"I could not observe any change either in his looks or his language. He suffered my attendance, as usual, without notice. I followed to the hall, and mixed with the other domestics. On this night I observed the confessor had joined the family. Through the air of deep abstraction he always wears, it was impossible to discover his thoughts, or whether the frame of his mind was habitual or peculiar.

"As he approached, where the family were not yet seated, I observed him bring forward, as usual, a small vial of lemon juice, which he mixes with water, and which constitutes his only beverage, and place it beside his cover. I was near him. The motion of his arm shewed me another small vial in his vest. I grew deadly sick as I beheld it. I had no doubt I saw the instrument of your death. As he turned round he displaced his girdle and rosary. He observed it and began to adjust them. In order to do so, he found it necessary to place the other vial on the table, to which his back was turned. This was the critical moment. The vial of lemon-juice was on the right; the other on the left. With the quickness and silence of thought I changed their places. He turned round; put up the first vial into his vest; and emptied the latter into a glass of water that stood beside his cover.

"When I had done this, I reflected that I had only gained time; that it must be soon discovered that the monk was poisoned, and that you had only swallowed lemon-juice. If, therefore, I could not devise some means of escape in the interval which I had gained, I felt it was unavailing, except so far as to punish an intentional murderer; but the success and promptitude of my first movement suggested a flattering omen, which I accepted, not unreadily.

"In the mean time the family assembled. The Count and his confessor whispered often. With unspeakable delight I saw the latter employ the vase that stood beside him. Towards the conclusion of the meal, the Count desiring the chamberlain to be summoned, spoke some words to him in a low voice, on which the latter detached a rusty key from his girdle, and gave it to the confessor, who lodged it in his vest. I understood every motion. It seemed, that for some reason, probably that of concealing the corse, the monk had found it necessary to procure the key from the chamberlain. I had glanced on the size and shape of the key, and though it was nothing remarkable, I guessed from the former, and from the apparent intention with which it was procured, that it belonged to some external door of the castle, to which, if we could procure access, our safety was assured. I therefore resolved to watch the monk silently. I concluded, from the conversation that I repeated to you, that the poison was of a rapid and quiet operation. I doubted not that the monk would soon feel its effects, and if I could be near him at the moment, and secure the keys, all was well.

"The family now separated. The monk retired. I watched him at a cautious distance, and saw him enter his apartment—to that terrible apartment, even at noon day, I knew not what force could have compelled me; but now, at night, alone, and in darkness, save the dim and solitary lamp that burned in the passage, I knelt at the door, and watched every sound within. It was now past midnight, when I heard him advancing abruptly to the door, as if a sudden thought had smote him. I retired with speed. He came out. I saw him first bend forward from the door; and, holding his lamp high, look far into the passage. Not a sound breathed along it. He advanced; and I thought I heard him sigh. He then went rapidly forward, so rapidly, that I was alone in the passage. His steps, however, were a sufficient direction for me in the deep stillness of the night. He took a direction to your apartment. Every moment now I expected to see him falter, or to hear him groan, as I glided after him on tip-toe, led by the taper that streamed distantly on the darkness.

"He proceeded, however, without hesitation, till he entered a large hall, not immediately near your apartment. It was empty, and far from any inhabited part of the castle. I almost shuddered to follow him so far; but the thought of you inspired me. I paused in the passage which led to the hall. When he entered it, I heard him groan audibly. He stood a few moments in the centre of the room, and then advancing to a picture at the opposite end, held his taper close to it. He gazed long; and, as he turned away, the light fell full on his countenance. I never had beheld it before so singularly impressed. There was a look of human agony in it I never before had seen, or believed him capable of feeling. He then laid the taper down on a marble slab, and sat down, with his arms folded, beside it.

"I eyed him intently. There was neither change in his countenance, nor weakness in his motions. I grew sick with fear. He was not like a man that had swallowed poison. I doubted, and I trembled. I recollected all I had heard of him, and some things I had seen. I condemned my own temerity in supposing him assailable by the modes of human destruction. He was evidently incapable of being injured by them; and if he were not, what must befal *me?*

"While these thoughts beset me, I will confess to you, I was only with-held from flying away, and relinquishing the whole in despair, by the thought, that if he were indeed a being not of this world, all distance of space would be ineffectual to protect me from him. While I yet debated and trembled, he rose suddenly, as if from an impulse of pain. I leaned forward, breathless with fresh hope. At that distance, I could not observe any change in his features; but, as I gazed, methought a yellower tinge mixed with the paleness of his visage. In the next moment all doubt was removed. He gasped, he shivered, and he fell.

"I now came forward with confidence. I approached him. His eyes were glazed and reverted. He was evidently in the agonies of death. I did not wait for the mere decencies of humanity. I searched his vest. I found the keys. I hastened back to your apartment, unable to speak or to explain. I hurried you to the hall where the corse lay; for I knew, by his pausing there, it must be in the direction of some outward passage or door. I followed the track, partly from conjecture, and partly from memory; for I had traversed that part of the castle before, and succeeded in my pursuit.

"And now, Signor, adieu to dungeons, and poison, and monks. We are safe on the outside of those grim walls; and if ever we enter them again, St. Filippo will have a good right to disregard our prayers for deliverance."

Such was Filippo's narrative, to which I listened with wonder and thankfulness. I readily admitted the interposition of divine power for our safety; yet it was not without horror that I thought of the monk and his sudden and terrible fate. A degree of involuntary incredulity mixed, and still mixes itself with my feelings on that subject. He appears to me a being above the vicissitudes of humanity—a being who does not, in a mortal sense, exist, and who, therefore, cannot, in a mortal sense, perish.

The impression received in the chamber of my confinement at Muralto, nothing has yet effaced. I mentioned to Filippo the voice I had heard in the hall, when he left me so abruptly. This he ascribed to fancy; and perhaps that was its only cause. His own hasty departure was owing to the sudden recollection of a door in an adjacent passage, which he wished to attempt without agitating me by probable disappointment.

I now inquired why we did not proceed; and was told, that the man who brought ice to the castle, and who travelled at night to avoid the heat, was probably on the way which we were to take, and that it were better to avoid being seen till we reached Naples.

While we lingered in the wood, I raised my eyes, not without awe, to the castle, whose huge and massive blackness strongly charactered itself, even amid the gloom of night, and the dusky confusion of the forest and mountains. Far to the left, I saw the ruined chapel, that spot which awoke so many terrible recollections. It stood in shapeless darkness. As I gazed on it, I almost expected to see that mysterious light wandering along its walls, and gleaming on the dark tufts of wood and shrubs that invest it. As I still looked in vague expectation, a light indeed appeared, which I watched, not without emotion; but discovered it to be but a star, (the only one that twinkled through the darkness of the night) just appearing beneath the arch of the shattered window.

At this moment, steps passed near us, which Filippo affirmed to be those of the person we waited for; and we pursued another direction with our utmost expedition. When we had penetrated about a mile into the forest, a bell from the castle sounded in the air above; and, on turning, I saw distinctly a light, that, pale at first, as if seen through a casement, grew suddenly brighter, and poured a broad glare on the darkness of the upper wood. I believed this to be only an indication, that the person who had passed us, was admitted, by some one at the castle, from whose taper proceeded the light we had beheld; but Filippo, under more serious apprehensions of pursuit, persuaded me to hide in an intricate part of the forest, as it was impossible we could reach Naples before our pursuers would overtake us. Subdued, but not convinced, I consented to conceal myself in a pit, the mouth of which was mantled over with tangled and briery shrubs. The event was only a day wasted in watching, solicitude, and famine. No step passed near us; no sound or signal of pursuit was heard in the forest. Towards evening we quitted our retreat, and reached Naples in safety, which, since I perceive there is no immediate persecution excited against me, I shall quit with some hope of safety.

I distrust this calm, however; it is unnatural; but while it continues, I may take advantage of its influence, to escape from danger that is only meditated and distant.

I shall leave Naples tomorrow. 'Do you then hold your intention of going to France?" "I do; but first I shall go to Capua. There is an uncle of my mother's, a wealthy ecclesiastic, from whom I expect assistance and protection, as he has long been on terms of enmity with my father. The present contents of my purse would scarce convey me to France; and it is necessary for an adventurer to conciliate credit by his appearance, as my peculiar circumstances exclude other recommendation. Poor Ippolito! would he were with me; but the tumult of my own feelings and situation has not allowed me to waste much sympathy on him. When you write, Cyprian, tell of my unhappy circumstances; but do not mention my disappointment on discovering his absence; for that would only aggravate his own." "And the inquiry, begun and terminated under circumstances so extraordinary, do you intend to pursue it no more?" said Cyprian, timidly. "Name it not; the sound is hateful and terrible to me. I abjure the idea of spectres, mysteries, and disclosures. I will fly from ruins and the gloom of antiquity, as I would from the mouth of hell, if it yawned at my feet. I will chuse the airiest structures for my abode, the lightest topics for my conversation. My companions shall be those whom levity can easily procure, and folly can amuse. The being who indulges in the dreams of vision, and courts, whether with intentions pure or foul, the communion of the forbidden world, makes himself a mark for the imposition of mankind, and the malignity of infernal ones. He is a fit and willing subject for the machinations of hell; he is given over to them by the power he has offended by seeking them. I am convinced that Satan is permitted a greater latitude of temptation, and fierceness, and frequency of assault, on such a being. The pursuit must tend to subvert his reason and deprave his heart. No, no; whatever I have witnessed or been engaged in, whether it be true or false, whether it be solemn or futile, I here renounce it. Let them find another agent for their purposes of horror; let them harden, by familiarity of temptation, and assimilate to their own demon-natures, by frequency of communication, the alien and apostate soul, that seeks their secrets or their presence. I shall heal and sooth my distempered mind by images of softness and beauty; by the agencies of humanity, and the enjoyments of nature and life."

As he spake, he drew forth the picture he always bore in his bosom; kissed it, and gazed on it with complacency. Cyprian, who saw it too, with strong emotion, begged to look on it more intently; and, while he held it in his hand, his tears streamed fast upon it.

"Do you know that picture, then?" said Annibal in amaze: "How is it possible you should know it?" "Ask me not; it is impossible I should tell; yes, I know it too well." "What mystery hangs over this picture? All that see it seem to know it; yet none will communicate their knowledge." "There is a mystery, and it is inscrutable." "Does the original of this picture, then, live? Do you know her? Tell me but her name: I will not ask by what means you obtained the knowledge of her, nor will I endeavour to solve the mystery of resemblance between one so long dead, and one who lives; of resemblance without possibility of connection." "The original of this picture lives, but not to you. If you love her, seek not to disturb her quiet or your own, by a search, of which the success is hopeless. She never can be your's." "This is beyond all comprehension; the influence pursues me still; my whole life is to be overshadowed by mystery."

After a night of fruitless inquiry and exclamation, Annibal took leave of Cyprian; and, accompanied by Filippo, set out for Capua.

XVII

These men, or are they men, or are they devils,
With whom I met at night?—they've fasten'd on me
Fell thoughts which, though I spurn them,
Haunt me still.

—Miss Bailie's Rayner

In the mean time, Ippolito, without any object but that of flying what was inevitable, had quitted Naples with a single attendant, and no other preparation for a journey, than an utter indifference to its vicissitudes or hardships. On the first evening, without having pursued consciously, any direction, he found himself on the banks of the Lake of Celano. It was now the close of autumn, and as the wind swept over the dim waters of the Lake, and the mists moved in fantastic wreaths over the remote and rocky shores, sometimes giving the forms of ancient structure to the cliffs and headlands, and sometimes shapings still wilder to the scattered fishermen's huts, and villas on their points; Ippolito mechanically looked around for some place to which he might retire for the night, without the hope of repose.

"These winding roads," said the attendant, "Signor, are so wild and lonely; the nearest town to which we can resort, is that of Celano, a good mile further." Ippolito, too weary of spirit to communicate with his servant, silently took the direction pointed out to him towards the town of Celano, which they reached at the close of evening.

They entered a wretched inn, to the many defects and inconveniences of which Ippolito was insensible, since he procured in it, the only luxury he could enjoy—a solitary chamber, against the very casement of which the waves of the lake were beating.

Here for the first time he thought on what direction he would pursue. Many were suggested, and many rejected, till Ippolito, wondering at his own fastidiousness, began to examine into its reasons, and discovered, with a sensation nearly amounting to horror, that there was spread over his mind a sense of invisible and universal persecution, which impelled his thoughts in their flight from place to place, with the same velocity that its actual influence would have chased his steps. When this conviction struck him, in utterable anguish he started from his chair, and paused for a moment between the impulse of fright, and the torpor of despair. That this influence should have attained this absolute dominion in his mind, and asserted that dominion in the very moment when the change of place had flattered him with partial victory, was not to be borne. His distraction almost applied to the stupendous frame of the Psalmist, when he exclaimed, "Whither shall I go from thy presence?" Of the latter clause he felt the truth too forcibly, "If I go down to *Hell*, thou art there also." As he stalked about the room, some persons in the next spoke so loudly, that he was compelled to hear them without any effort of attention. As he listened to the voices, he recollected the speakers were a party of vine-dressers and labourers, who were returning to their native territory—the Abruzzo, from the neighbourhood of Naples, whither they had been allured during the summer, by the hope of higher wages. They were now drinking in the adjacent room with the landlord. "It is a strange business," said one, addressing the host, whose name was Borio, "nor do I like speaking of it much. I never liked to have Satan's name often in my mouth; for, *Christo benedetto*, one is so apt to think of him, when one is alone. When I have to cross the mountain near our village by night, or to watch the grapes in the hut alone, I never listen to stories such as those in the day; I always fill my mind with store of good hymns; but when there is a good number of us together, as we are now, I feel that I have as much courage as another. And so, comrades, as I was saying, they talked of nothing else all over Naples. Some said that the cavalier had devoted himself, body and soul, to Satan; and that he met him every night in some place underground, *where* no one could discover; that his servants never could trace him further than the portico of the palace; and that some who attempted to follow him, were all invested in a glare of blue fire, and their torches were dashed out of their hands by a hoof of red-hot iron.

Others said, that it was not the young cavalier's fault, but his great-grandfather's, who had sold all his posterity to the old serpent, for a great heap of treasure he gave him; but that the purchase was not to be claimed till this generation, and that it was forfeit at the time of the last carnival; when the fiend appeared to the unfortunate youth, habited like a minstrel, and playing on a harp, whose strings were the guts of necromancers. 'Your time is come, you must away!' and that all the grove where he glided along, has been blasted and bare ever since." "Now by what I have heard," said the host, "the fiend has more Christian

CHARLES MATURIN

bowels, an uses the Cavalier like a man of honour, for I hear he has given him permission to wander over Italy for a year and a day; and if he can get a priest to give him absolution, he quits his claim on him for ever." "Ha, ha," exclaimed another, in a tone of superior wisdom, "do you, friend, take the devil to be such a fool? no, no, rely on it, if he quits him on the simple score of witchcraft, he will stick his claws fast in him on an action of bond and compact. It is marvellous, neighbours, how simple ye are; why it is just in the world below us as it is here; witchcraft is like contracting a debt, but a compact is like a bond—if once Satan is able to produce it in open court against the defendant, the inquisition itself must acknowledge it; nay," (exalting his voice with his argument), "his holiness the pope himself must sign as a competent witness."

All seemed struck by the force of this argument, and a pause of general meditation ensued, till one of the party, whose voice was that of an old man, said with an apparent diffidence of his own sentiments, "Now were I to give an opinion, it would be that the Cavalier was neither devoted to Satan by himself nor his ancestors. Ah, neighbours, did you see what a goodly and noble youth he is to look at, ye never could believe he dealt with any thing evil—no, no, as long as Pre-member, or as long as my father could remember, the Montorio were a great, proud, wicked family; they did deeds of mischief enough among themselves, without the aid of Satan; they were always threatened with discoveries; and dying assassins, employed by them, confessed terrible things, it was said. Now perhaps something of this kind is about to be disclosed, and the Cavalier's noble heart is breaking to think of it, and he cannot bear to stay in Naples any longer, to witness the ruin of his family."

At this mild construction of Ippolito's flight, every one uttered a murmur of disapprobation. The love of the marvellous is too jealous for its gratifications, and too irritable for its credit, to yield to incredulity so easily. And the former speaker, elated by his success, was anxious to preserve the popularity it had acquired him. "Old man," said he, "you are much mistaken; if the Cavalier be permitted to traverse Italy, rely upon it, 'tis for the purpose of bringing others to his master's service, in order to escape better himself; for that is the way Satan always deludes those poor wretches. He promises reward and honour to those who are zealous in his service; and when they have seduced souls without number, and finally lost their own, then he rewards them after his own manner, which any one knows that has once seen the great picture near the shrine of St. Antonio, at the Church del Miroli, near Naples.

There, all the degrees and kinds of punishment that ever were invented are exercising upon the hosts of ruined spirits; one would think the devils had been all in the Inquisition, they are so clever at it; you could swear you smelt brimstone, and felt a heat like that of a furnace, breathed over you from it; but only to tell you of one group in it, there are three figures—"

Here Ippolito heard the clustering sound of his hearers drawing more closely around him, his misery became suddenly intolerable, and he groaned aloud. Terrified at the sound, they all desisted to speak or to listen, and without venturing to comment on the cause of the disturbance, the last speaker said in a voice of fear, "I believe we had better cease to speak on this subject, unless some ecclesiastic was in the house with us." "There is a convent of Dominicans near these walls," said the host, who was anxious for the conclusion. "How near," said the other, whose desire of exciting wonder was contending with fear. "You may hear the vesper bell from this," said the host, evasively "But how near, friend Borio, tell me precisely how near?" "'Tis a long mile," said the host, reluctantly. The speaker declined to finish his story on this security. "The devil's in it," said the host in his disappointment, "if the toll of that bell, and the chaunt of the monks at vespers, are not sufficient to frighten the devil, if he were in this room."

His companions reproved him for profaneness, and the host, to, retrieve the credit of his sanctimony, said, "Whatever be the cavalier's intentions in this journey, I would not be the host to receive him for the wealth of the Vatican. I warrant, the smell of sulphur never would quit the room he lay in; and if I received a single coin from him, I should expect it to turn into a burning coal in my hand." "You had better be on your guard, friend Borio," said another, in the mere wantonness of wisdom, "I hear he was seen to take this direction." "By the holy saints, there came a cavalier to my house this evening."

There was now a general commotion of fear, followed by a whispering consultation. Ippolito's first impulse was to quit the inn, but he recollected that would only confirm their suspicions, and perhaps make his further progress difficult. Another expedient occurred, but his proud heart long struggled with the necessity of deceit. At this moment he heard his servant passing under the window; he called him, and without specifying his reasons, desired that he would on no account, mention his name or rank in the house, nor during any future part of the journey, which he must be in readiness to pursue as soon as possible.

The man, proud of a charge that resembled an approach to confidence, readily promised to observe it; and that his fidelity might not want the merit of resisted temptation, immediately repaired to the room where the vine-dressers were seated with the host.

They had just resolved to send for him, in order to discover whether his master was the Count Montorio, and now received him with the overcharged welcome, that suspicion gives to hide her own purposes. "Pray friend," said the host, after they had drank some time, "what is the cavalier, your master's name?" "His name—his name"—said the man, who in the determination to conceal the real, had forgot to provide himself with a fictitious one. "Aye, his name," continued the host, "I suppose you have lived with him but a short time?" "I have lived with the Signor several years," said the man, in his eagerness to prove he was not unprepared for every question, and to retrieve the ground his embarrassment had lost. "You have lived with him several years, and yet do not know his name; that is strange indeed, stranger than any thing I have yet heard?" "Why what have you heard of the Signor?" said the man, glad to become the inquisitor in his turn. "I have heard he sometimes walks at night," said the other, significantly. "To be sure he does, and so do all the cavaliers in Naples," said the man triumphantly. "Aye; but do you know where he goes?" said the host, lowering his voice. "No; nor does any one else," said the man, betraying a material part of his intelligence, in his solicitude to prove that no one was wiser than himself. "You never attend him on those occasions?" pursued the host. "Santa Maria, no," said the man shuddering. "What would you take, and accompany him in one of his nightly wanderings?" said the host, pursuing his victory. "Not the wealth of Loretto," said the man, who recollected the terrible stories he had heard of his master at Naples, and who had answered his own thoughts, rather than the questions addressed to him. "Then it is all true," said the old man. "Holy saints! what a pity!" "What is a pity?" said the lackey, roused from his abstraction by the exclamation. "What you have just confessed about your master!" said the host. "I confess?" said the man; "I would not confess if I was torn with pincers; I confessed nothing." "Nay; it was not much either," said one of the men, a shrewd fellow; "you only acknowledged your master was one of the Montorio family." "I will be torn in ten thousand pieces first," said the man, with increased vehemence; "you are a horrid and atrocious villain to say I acknowledged it: I never did, and never will." "Come, come," said his wily opponent; "you need not be in a fury; perhaps I mistook you; but you must confess, that if he is not one of the family he is remarkably like them." "To be sure," said the man, again sacrificing his cause to his power of answering a partial objection, "to be sure; there is a strong *family* likeness among them all."

Here a general cry of triumph arose, which drowned even the angry exclamations of the servant; and Ippolito, distracted by the consequences of his folly, and the superstition of the rest, silently quitted the chamber, remounted his horse, and pursuing the first track he discovered, with all the speed that darkness and weariness permitted, was many miles from Celano, before the party had resolved whether to summon the Dominican brethren to their aid, or to send express to the Inquisition at Naples.

The hardships of his wanderings, rather than his journey, were lost in more painful subjects of meditation. The secret of his soul was known—that deep and eternal secret, that he believed buried in the bowels of the earth. It was known; and the tumult of his thoughts forbid the conjecture by what means it was known, or how its further diffusion might be prevented.

The only sensation that prevailed in his mind, was a confusion undefined, and unappeasable, that could neither trace the forms of danger, nor discover what way of flight from it was to be pursued. He trembled, though he scarce recollected what was past; he deprecated, though he knew not what was to come; he fled without an object in flight; and he increased his speed, as the motives of fear became more and more obscure to his mind. The darkness and remoteness from human resort or notice, in which the transactions at Naples had passed, had utterly excluded all suspicion that they were known, or could be known to any individual but himself. And such was the abstraction and intentness of mind with which he was engaged in them, that had such a suspicion occurred, it could not have suspended the pursuit a moment. Along with the circumstance itself, all consequences, remote or obvious, were equal strangers to his mind. When, therefore, the fact itself, with all the consequences that the suspicions of ignorance, and the rage of superstition could attach to it, rushed on his mind, unforeseen and un-weighed, without a power of preparation or resistance, he staggered under the shock; it blasted and astounded him. For a moment, visionary and remote fears were banished by substantial and imminent terrors. The anguish of terror that cannot name its object, and of guilt that cannot ascertain its danger, gathered over his mind. A sensation of rare and excruciating influence; the sensation of all our measures being anticipated; our progress measured aud ruined; the exact reach of our boundary calculated and shadowed out; the inmost recesses of our mind violated and laid waste; and Omniscience engaged on the side of our enemies to destroy us, overcame him. No murderer, at whose feet a sudden whirlwind would dash the witness of his guilt before unsuspecting thousands; no traveller, at whose naked breast the lightnings are aiming, before a cloud has been seen to gather in the heaven, ever gazed around them, so transfixed and appalled.

His immediate impulse was flight. He urged his horse to his utmost speed; and still all speed sunk under the velocity of his thoughts. His mind was rather irritated than appeased by the tumult of motion. An imaginary line seemed to run beside him, which he could neither measure nor out-run. His speed left nothing but space behind; and his progress seemed nothing but an approach to mischief.

Towards morning he found himself in a part of the country, whose wildness and savageness insensibly poured quiet and confidence on his mind. It was man he dreaded; and here there was no trace of man. Rocks and waters, whose wreathed and fantastic undulations, almost resembled the clouds that hovered round them, melting their hues and shapes into their own unsubstantial forms of misty lightness, presented a range of scenery, more meet for the haunt of an aerial genius than a mortal inhabitant.

Far to the left, as the fuller tints of morning deepened and defined the shadowy characters of the mountain landscape, Ippolito descried a dim cluster of cottages, perched in the hollow of two hills, whose antic and spiry pinnacles seemed to have been cleft for its reception. The opposite features of its wild and sheltered situation presenting a contrast that divided the feelings between awe and pleasure. To the inhabitants of a place so sequestered, Ippolito believed he might safely apply for food and refuge.

Thither therefore he directed his course, and found, that whatever wonder he excited, was occasioned by the appearance of a stranger in so remote a region. Here he reposed for some days, like a bird that, chased and wounded, regains her nest amongst inaccessible rocks, and spreads her torn plumage to the winds of freedom. He was excited to personal exertion to render existence tolerable. Here were no artificial resources, no expedients to disguise the waste of time, and renew the spirit of enjoyment. He was impelled to vigorous bodily exercise, at first to exhaust the throbbings of inward pain, and afterwards to gratify a newly-acquired sense of pleasure. An extraordinary vigour of frame, which the voluptuous indolence of Naples had enervated, was renewed by his mountain habits; and the change was in some time extended to his mind. He was at first soothed by the dash of the cataract, the hum of the winds in the mountain caverns, the masses of rock, bold, abrupt, and detached, that often assumed the port of some ancient Gothic structure; their marked and storied ascents and towery summits, shaping out the fantastic forms of its architecture; and the beams of the setting sun, reflected from a surface, resplendent with hues of verdure and stains of marble, aptly portraying the illuminated windows, glorious with the colours of blazonry.

By these he was at first soothed, and weaned from painful remembrance; but in a short time, he visited them with positive pleasure, not for the sake of what they took away, but of what they gave.

It is impossible for a mind, not conscious of great crimes, to be conversant with nature, without feeling her balmy and potent influence. The quiet magic of loneliness, the deep calm of unbreathing things, the gentle agitations of inanimate motion, poured themselves into the very recesses of his soul, and healed them.

At first, when he rushed into these solitudes, he mentally resolved to devote himself to the contemplation of his situation, and of some bold, gigantic effort by which he resolved to free himself from his thraldom; but as weariness and distraction were the only result of his deliberation, he suffered it gradually to steal from his mind, and balanced between the reproaches of indolence, and the refreshment of tranquillity.

He was amused in his solitude by some papers of Cyprian's, which, in the hurry of his departure from Naples, he had unintentionally taken along with him. They related to that mysterious story which he had left unfinished. Ippolito had almost forgot, that the object of it had been attached to him. The other extraordinary circumstances of the narrative, strange and remote as they were, Cyprian's enthusiasm had thrown a shade of incredulity over; and Ippolito read it as a representation of events that had never existed.

In the papers he now read, the author's mind appeared weary of the ordinary modes of language, and progress of narrative. She had selected different periods, as eras in her melancholy history, and written a few lines on each in the language of poetry.

They were monotonously melancholy. It was a passion apparently unbroken by an interval of tranquillity, unillumined by a single ray of hope. She had loved as none had ever loved, and suffered as few had suffered. Nor would Ippolito have understood the reason or possibility of such despair, had he not recollected to have heard from Cyprian, that the unfortunate female had been a nun; that she had not seen the object that fascinated her, till she was under irrevocable engagements; and that though her "love, stronger than death," had survived in these posthumous lamentations, it had not the power to make her transgress the barrier of religion, by a disclosure of it while she lived. The first appeared to have been written when passion had lingered long enough to know it was hopeless; when the first clouds of melancholy began to gather over her feelings—it was written on a second accidental view of the object of her affections.

Once more I caught thy form—'twas but a moment—
A moment! passion lives an age in moments.
Feeling can trace the boundless range of being,
Each maze of fancy, each abyss of thought.
Joy's rose-twined bowers, and memory's pictured cells
Recal the past, anticipate the future,
Exhaust all forms of life, and dreams of vision
Within a moment's lapse.
So Mecca's seer, as the wild legend tells,
On the supernal wing of vision soared;
Explored the star-strewn paths of Paradise,
Drank the rich gale, that laps her pearly gates,
And swept the circle of the seven-fold heaven
Ere mortals marked a moment's flight below.
So bright, the while I caught thy passing form;
So brief, or ere I lost it.
Chance, 'tis thy checkered influence to dispense
The hour that gives him to my visible eyes—
The hour that memory treasures; but I boast
Beyond thy sport or spleen, one solace yet,
One last, one dear, one sad—Oh, 'tis when eve
Dispreads her dew-wove veil, when no rude eye

Marks my wan cheek, slow step, and start abrupt
(Pale passion's guide, the weeds of fancy's thrall),
To wander and to muse unmarked, unknown,
To trace the thought, no breast has e're conceived,
To heave the sigh, no ear has ever drank,
And thine *must, never*—thine *of* all *must, never*—
Oh, 'tis to wish impossibilities!
Yet start to think them real, 'tis to trace
My sad tale in these sands, while aimless hope
Points the approaching in th' imagined hour;
Wooes to the storied spot thy wandering eye,
And all's disclosed. Oh, then I fly! deface,
Disperse them quick, lest one surviving trace
Should tell the tale, I'd—give a world thou knew'st.
'Tis oft to pour the secret yet untold
In lines like these, of love's despair that hopes,
Then rend the fragments, give them to the winds,
Tremble, lest one be wafted to thine hand,
While dreams th' extinctless hope, "Perhaps it may."
Oh, 'tis to waste my life in prayers to see thee,
And when thy distant form re-lumes my view
To hide me, and to fly; then, when thou'rt past,
To kiss the light-pressed path, th' imagined spot
Thy shade has crossed and hallowed—oft my soul
Sunk in voluptuous vacancy, resigns
Herself to float down fancy's fairy stream,
(Unconscious and unheeding of its lapse).
Oh, then, how bright the dream; its magic tints
Paint passion possible, and nature kind.
Thee, thee, I see, I hear, I touch—hark, hark—
The vesper-bell—it tells me of despair.

Of the next, whatever the execution might be, the subject was perhaps the most interesting that could occur in poetry: it purported to represent a mind deeply sunk in passion, yet alive to a feeling the most painful and hostile to passion that can exist; a conviction of the unworthiness of its object. The struggles of reluctant conviction, and the anguish of involuntary fondness, were portrayed as in a narrative; but Ippolito easily discovered the sentiments and situation of the unfortunate nun.

CHARLES MATURIN

——————*He died—living he died.*
Living, but dead to her, whose ceaseless toil
To win him from the weary paths of sin,
Long with vain essay strove; but when she found
That on a mind so weak, no lofty precept
To virtue's lore, wrought with incitement high,
That on a soil so light, instruction's seed
Fell fruitless; like the exiled Hagar of yore,
(Who wandering in the wilds of Beer-Sheba,
Saw the last morsel of her pittance spent,
Saw its last drop scarce wet her babe's parched lip,
And seeing, said, with hopeless anguish bowed—
Let me not see him die!—and went far off
And wept): so went she to a spot remote,
And wept—ceaseless and silent wept; no gleam
Of tremulous light played on her evening hour,
No sheeny phantoms of the tints of morn
Wove to her eye the painted visions of joy,
Or struck their airy harps far heard. Her life
Was lone, her purpose strange, but never brake.
She reared an antic structure, wild and simple,
Like some lone eremite's tomb, and called it his.
She watched beside his tomb, in patience, pale,
With sunk and tearless eye, and lips that moved
In inward prayer for him, whom she deemed dead
To all worth living for. She hung that tomb
With garlands, fancy-wrought, and dim of hue;
They were as wild as mountain-spirits' song,
They mocked all rule, and scorned all art—and yet
No child of feeling true, might see that wreath,
Nor wake their waning colours with a tear.
Far other employ she hoped *for them—with these*
She would have strewn his path, or wreathed his brow,
Or decked the polished hours of virtuous life.
But little did he reck of virtuous life,
Or aught but the loose flow of dance, and song,
And roar of midnight revel—sad she heard,
And still she sat in pale and pined constancy;
Yet not without impulse of natural sorrow,

(Strong throes of anguish, cleaving still to life),
She thought on her last hopes, her withered heart,
Her youth departed, and her mind decayed.
Yet still she loved—yea, still loved hopeless on.
Infatuate passion desperate, still lit
Her hollow eye, still warmed her fevered lip—
The memory of her first love, like rich music
Sung in her witched ear. She was condemned
T' outlive the object, but the passion—never

The author appeared to have had a knowledge of the unhappy life of the person she was attached to, deeper than was necessary to furnish the garniture of poetical sorrow. She appeared intimately to feel, and to deplore with the mingled zeal of religion and love, the evil habits that had overspread and abused a noble heart. Such were the feelings intended to be portrayed in the following lines:

I

That tempting fruit, how ripe it hangs,
How rich it grows on high;
And there I reach my helpless hands,
There fix my straining eye.

II

Oh, not for me, those gay tints rich
Its mellow cheek adorn;
Ah, not for me, its odours fine
Vie with spring's bud-wreath'd morn

III

Oh, but to taste those nectar'd sweets,
That I a bird might be;
Oh, that I were the common air
Uncheck'd that blows on thee.

IV

How o'er thy ripe cheek's glowing down,
Would I my soft tale sing;
How faint amid the sweets I fann'd,
With rapture-dancing wing.

V

How would I chase each reptile rude,
That saps thy wasted bloom?
How would my whispering pennons play,
To wake thine hid perfume.

VI

Enough for me the joy, to view
Thy purer beauties glow,
Bid unrestrained those odours rise,
Whose sweets I ne'er must know.

In these lines Ippolito discovered an attempt made to express a strange and complicated feeling, that often occurs in real love, when existing under a desparity of circumstances—'tis that feeling which arises from a mixt sensation of moral debasement, and worldly rank and splendour; of which the effect is partly to awe by magnificence, and partly to interest by compassion.

The unfortunate vestal seemed to be betrayed by the very feelings on which she depended for her defence; she was evidently fascinated by the rank, the spirit, and the excesses of the man she loved, as well as by the qualities by which love is more properly excited; she was dazzled by the glare of the very vices she affected to deprecate; she was struck with involuntary admiration of splendid dissoluteness, and tumultuous grandeur—yet often the sentiments of these lines spoke merely the sighs of desire, such as are poured out in the involuntary excess of the mind, and without a reference either to hope or to despair.

Such were the following:

I

I wish I were a vernal breeze,
To breathe upon that cheek of down;
Then I might breathe without a fear,
Then I might sigh without a frown.

II

I wish I were a burnished fly,
To sport in thine eye's sunny sheen;
There wing my raptured hour unheard,
There dazzled droop, and die unseen.

III

I wish I were a blushing flower
Within thy breast one hour to reign;
Then I might live without a crime;
Then I might die without a pain.

Sometimes amid this blaze of luxuriant fondness, a sudden cloud of remorse and horror would intervene, as in these lines.

I

Oh, come to my arms, whose faltering clasp
Is still folding thy phantom in air!
Oh, visit mine eye, whose fancy-wrought spell
Is still raising thy form in its sphere!

II

Oh, let my languid head sink on thy breast,
Other refuge or rest it has none!
Oh, let my full heart once heave upon thine,
And its throbs, and its tumults are done!

CHARLES MATURIN

III

And I'll lose, while my swimming eye floats on thy form,
All thought, but the thought, it is thine;
And I'll quench in the nectar that bathes thy red lip,
The fever that's burning in mine.

IV

And lapt in the dream, I'll forget that a voice
Would recal, that a fear would reprove—
Till I start as the lightning is lanced at my head,
And wonder there's guilt in our love.

With these alternate struggles of passion that could not stifle conscience, and of principle too weak to contend with passion, many others were filled. One arrested Ippolito's attention, from having the following sentence in prose, prefixed to it: "The disguise I have assumed, supplies me with many an hour of weak indulgence. Sometimes I pass almost close to him, catch the sounds of his voice, linger at night near his dwelling, drops of slow poison each—but how fatal-sweet! Last night, I touched the very railing on which I saw him lean but an hour before, as he descended the steps—touched it! Ildefonsa reproached me; but I have resisted other reproaches than her's—Why should I yield to human monitions, what I have refused to those of my own heart, and of heaven?"

I

'Tis vain—'tis vain my lips to move,
'Tis vain my arms to sever;
Thou hast my everlasting love,
And thou shalt have it ever.

II

Oh, why to tempt my doubted faith,
Those dread recitals borrow?
Know, trifler, they who dare to live,
Dread not to die of sorrow!

III

Why tell the pangs of vows unheard,
The woe of hopes undone?
To weep was all my vows e'er woo'd,
To weep was all they won.

IV

I asked to view thy heaven-lit eye,
Till these weak eyes were blasted;
I asked to view that bliss-bathed lip,
Till mine with wishing wasted.

V

No soft reward of blameless love
E'er sooth'd mine unheard wooing;
For oh!—a glance was phrensy's fue,
A touch had been undoing.

VI

Not mine to love with florid art,
I wove no poet-willow;
My inward tears prey'd on my heart,
My hush'd sighs scorch'd my pillow.

VII

No cherish'd hope of rich return
E'er sooth'd with promised pleasure:
Love rifled all my native store,
But gave no added treasure.

VIII

The tear that seeks the shade to fall,
The sigh that silence breathes;

And this fond moment's wilder woe,
Are all that love bequeaths.

IX

Chill emblem of my iron fate,
Yet guiltless, I may grasp thee;
Woo thy cold kiss without a blush,
And wildly, fondly clasp thee.

X

Then take, oh take this feverous kiss
To meet his lip vain burning;
And take, oh take this smothered sigh,
That wooes no fond returning.

XI

And crush, oh crush this harass'd breast,
No more to wild hope waking,
And take (oh, would it were the last)
Throbs of a heart that's breaking.

XII

I'd rather breathe these hopeless sighs
Than vows of sanctioned duty;
I'd rather leave this lost kiss here,
Than press the lip of beauty.

XIII

But oh, the bitter—bitter thought
That thus it must be, ever
To woo thy shade, to watch thy step,
But nearer—never, never!

XIV

To feel my lips unbidden form
What they must never say;
To feel my eyes in gazing fix'd,
In gazing waste away.

XV

Of vision'd days, and restless nights,
A weary length to roll,
With passion on my fever'd lip,
And anguish in my soul.

XVI

Yet some relief to weep and vow,
What time can frustrate—never,
Thou hast my everlasting love,
And thou shalt have it ever.

Ippolito had perused these lines, stretched on the mossy roots of an ash in a wild dell; when he had finished the last, he perceived that the evening had already gathered round him. He rose, and remounting his horse, which was fastened to an adjacent tree, rode homeward to the hamlet.

He lingered in the way, for the images of sadness, had combined with the hues of evening to pour a voluptuous melancholy over his soul. Within a furlong of the hamlet, he entered a woody defile, where the branches of the tall, thick trees meeting above, excluded light even at noon-day, and now deepened the gloom of gathering night. Across the high banks and matted wood-path of this dell, the roots of the trees branched into a thousand antic ridges and curvings; while above, the foliage, so thick and bowery, scarce admitted the wind to whisper through its leaves, or the birds to find their way to the nests, that seemed woven into a verdurous wall. Ippolito paused as he entered it to mark the rich gleam of western light its opposite extremity admitted. At that moment a face appearing beside him audibly pronounced, "Why do you linger here? your fate may be forgotten, but will not be long unfulfilled." It seemed to pass him as it spoke, and was lost in the gloom of the wood.

It was the voice, the face of the stranger; in darkness, in midnight he would have known it. He lost not a moment in thought; the very force of his fear gave him speed like a whirlwind; calling, commanding, adjuring him to stay or to return, he plunged into the wood, and while he could trace his shadow in thought, or the vestige of motion, or sound that followed him, he pursued it with a speed that seemed to make all human flight unavailing. It was in vain; in an hour he was many miles from the dell in the wood, but had not obtained a a glimpse of him he pursued. His feelings were too tempestuous to weigh circumstances, or pause over doubts; he had but one object—to discover if this dreaded being could really pervade all space, and overtake all flight. If he had in vain called on the mountains to cover him, and hid himself where even the jealous rage of superstition had failed to discover him. He paused on a rising ground, to catch the last remains of the light, as they faded over the wide prospect before him. He saw at a distance what he at first believed to be a young tree, whose branches were tossed by the wind; but his eye, sharpened by fear was not long deceived—it was a human figure, tall and dark, that moved onward with amazing swiftness, and whose outspread and streaming garments were flung to the wind, like the foliage of a tree. Again he called, again he hastened forward, but his voice was only echoed by winds and woods, and his speed only led him to wilder haunts, and remoter distance.

He rode all night with unabated eagerness of pursuit, and towards morning, first felt his confidence decline on seeing before him a town, from whose numerous avenues, roads branched in every direction. But though not successful, he yielded to the weariness of the noble animal that bore him, and entering the first inn he saw, summoned the camariere, and inquired, had a person of the stranger's appearance, which he described shuddering at his own precision, passed through the town. The man listened to him with a look, which Ippolito thought might be owing to the stern earnestness of his own; but replied without hesitation, there had not. Ippolito then dismissed him, and wearied by the wanderings of the night, sunk into a perturbed and broken sleep.

When he awoke, he perceived he had devoted more hours to repose, than his time admitted; the day was far spent, and he called impatiently for his horse. No plan of pursuit was suggested to him, but he determined to follow the open track of country through the principal towns, and inquire for the stranger as he passed through each.

As he quitted the inn, a servant appeared with his horse; a rustic was leaning carelessly against a post of the shed from which he had been just led. Ippolito observed as he sprung into his seat, that the servant eyed him intently, and inquired the reason. "You are very like a cavalier I have seen in Naples, Signor," said the man. "And what of this cavalier?" said Ippolito, pausing. "Nothing, Signor, but that I should not like much to see him in this house—I do not think I should ever sleep in it again." "Has the cavalier the power of banishing sleep from the houses he visits?" "It is said, he never sleeps himself, Signor; he has other employments at night." "What may those be?" said Ippolito. "Pardon me, Signor, I dare not speak of him or them." He crossed himself with signs of strong fear. "But I would wish you to be more circumstantial," said Ippolito, who readily comprehended whom he meant, and who wished to know the probable extent of his danger, and become familiar with its terrors. "I should wish to know him, should it be my chance to encounter him." "You will easily know him by yourself, Signor," said the man retiring, "he is just your stature and figure."

This comparison suggested another idea to Ippolito—the stranger and he were exactly of the same stature; he pressed his inquiries on the man, adding, "It is of importance to me to be acquainted with the description of this person. I am in pursuit of one myself, whom perhaps it may assist me to discover." "The person of whom you are in quest," said the peasant, who had not before spoken, "is already gone before you, Signor; he is by this time at Bellano." Amazed at this intelligence so abruptly given, yet unwilling to expend time in inquiring how it was obtained, Ippolito hastily asked the distance and direction of Bellano. The peasant informed him, and Ippolito was hasting away, when a suspicion of this strange intelligence crossed his mind, and he waved his hand to the peasant to approach him. The man lingered with a reluctant air. Ippolito again signified his wish to speak with him, and the man advanced slowly and irresolutely. "From whom had you this intelligence?" said Ippolito. "I do not know, Signor." "How—not know? Is it possible you could converse with a human being, and not know to whom you spoke?" "I know not, if he were a human being," said the man. "What is it you say, what manner of man was he that spoke with you?" "Why do you ask? I pray to the virgin I may never see either of you again—you know him well enough, I dare say he is beside you now, though no Christian eye can see him." What insolence is this; or is it phrensy rather? Slave, do you know to whom you speak?" said Ippolito. "Slave," repeated the man, with strong resentment, "'tis you are a slave, and to the worst of masters; I would not change with you, though this shed is my only dwelling, were you on a throne of gold. Poor, wretched, deluded creature, your grandeur is lent on hard conditions, and for a miserable moment of time! I see even now melancholy appearing through those noble, beautiful features you have assumed. I wonder all those gold trappings do not blaze up in rows of sulphur, while I talk to you. But I have discharged my conscience. I dare not say farewell to you; but I trust to see you soon in the dungeons of the Inquisition, and that is the best wish a good Catholic can give you."

Ippolito, overpowered by the impassioned tones in which the man poured out his horror and aversion, and by his fears of more general and serious persecutions, retreated without remonstrance, and hastily took the road to Bellano. He understood too well the suspicious hints of the groom, and the open rage of the peasant.

There is no country in the world where pursuits, such as Ippolito's, are observed with more jealousy, or abhorred with a more "perfect hatred," than in Italy. Ippolito saw all the horrors of his fate, and cursed his visionary imprudence too late. The innocence of his intentions, and his exemption even from the transgressions to which it might be supposed to lead, it was useless to avow to himself; and who else would believe him? To have sought the secrets of the other world, as a diversity of levity; and to be conversant in them, without sacrificing our spiritual welfare, was what could not be easily, nor indeed probably believed. But all excuse or vindication was too late. Suspicion haunted his footsteps; the relentless vigilance of superstition had an eye on him for evil, and not for good. Once excited, her persecution was inexorable, and her rancour mortal.

His dark and secret trials were known; and, instead of exciting compassion, and ensuring shelter and protection, they had only awakened hatred and fear. It was little consolation to him to reflect, that the conversations he had heard had passed among the rustics of obscure villages. The rage of the vulgar is more deadly and indiscriminating, less liable to be pacified by representations, less assailable by any medium of rational vindication, and more apt to vent itself in sanguinary violence, than that of the higher orders. Besides, the knowledge that had reached them must have been first diffused through every other rank in society.

A dreadful feeling of abandonment and proscription began to overshadow his soul. The rudeness of the scene—rocks and waters seen in a cloudy twilight—fed the dark tumult of his thoughts. As his consciousness of the hatred of mankind increased, a sense of hatred to mankind increased along with it. He wished, in the wildness of the hour, for some banditti, or mountaineer to cross his path, or rush from the hollow of the rocks upon him; his tall dark figure, and waving sabre, like the pines which bowed their branches almost to his saddle-bow, as he passed them. He wished for some object of enmity, some struggle of violence, to exhaust the eager beatings of his fury; to quench that aversion to mankind which he felt their persecution had already kindled in his heart.

Impatient of solitude, he contended with nature and the elements; he spurred his horse to passes that seemed inaccessible; he delighted to gallop up precipices, to ford streams, and to wind along the giddy and pointed ridge of rock, where the heron and the crane were first startled by the foot of man; he pushed right against the blast when it blew with vehemence; and held on his path where, for a mile, the foam of every returning wave of a lake beat against his horse's mane.

It was now the close of evening, when he descried Bellano. A few scattered huts, interspersed with larger buildings now in ruins, overspread the view to some distance. From what this desolation proceeded Ippolito could not discover. The soil was fertile, though neglected; but in the houses and their inmates, there was an appearance of staring wildness, and of squalid dejection, such as he had never yet beheld. He looked around in vain for an inn, or any place where he might either procure repose for the night, or information on the object of his journey.

As he passed slowly through the narrow streets for the first time, he imagined that the eye of all he saw was fixed on him; that his name and fortunes were legible on his brow. Whatever knowledge of him had been betrayed before, was communicated in hints and whispers; was avowed with timidity, and murmured round till it was lost in the fears of the speakers. But now he seemed to feel that a general spirit of inquisition had fastened on him; that every one either pursued him with suspicion, or shrunk from him in terror.

Wearied, dismayed, and disappointed, he struck into the skirts of the town. They were now dark and lonely. He flung the reins on the neck of his horse, and loitered on without object. At this moment, the figure of the stranger visibly passed him. He paused a moment; and then, throwing himself off his horse, adjured him, with the most earnest and solemn supplications, to appear, and inform him, in audible words, why he was thus pursued and persecuted. Not a sound followed his adjurations; not a step crossed him.

After following an imaginary track for some time, he found his progress checked by a rising ground, on which stood a large edifice, dimly seen in the evening light. Its buildings, spreading over an extent of ground, presented a range of shadow, heavy, sombrous, and solitary. It bore no mark of habitation; no smoke ascended from the roof; no step echoed round the walls. Ippolito gazed on it irresolutely; yet with a strong impulse to enter it. It was certainly the point of termination to the direction he had pursued; and the direction was what the stranger, if he moved on earth, had probably taken.

At a little distance, he saw a peasant approaching, who seemed, like himself, to linger near the building. There was a promising confidence and simplicity in his manner. Ippolito thought it best to preface his inquiries with some vague observations on the desolation around them. "Yes, Signor," said the peasant, "something has happened to the place: I think it looks as if it were cursed." "But what has been the cause of the indigence and loneliness I see prevailing here, not only among these ruins, but among the inhabitants of the village?" "They are wretched and oppressed, Signor. A strange suspicion hangs over this place. There is a horrible tale told of it. I do not like to relate the circumstances, I have heard them related so differently; but since they happened, the inhabitants of this place, which was then flourishing, have been scattered and desolated." "What are those circumstances so strange, that could depopulate a country, and leave such marks of ruin behind them?" said Ippolito, glad of the relief of local curiosity. "They relate," said the peasant, "to a murder committed, or supposed to be committed, on a man who was entrusted with some affair of extraordinary import. The murderer was never discovered, nor his motives for the action even conjectured; and however the circumstances are told by a hundred mouths, the wise seem to imply, none of them in fact ever transpired." "But is it possible no steps were ever taken to trace this mysterious affair?" "I know not, Signor. There was a great, powerful, wicked family, said to be concerned in it. They had influence to crus all inquiry. No one that contended with that house ever prospered. They do not want power for outward means, nor villainy for secret ones. So, whoever opposes them fares like the inhabitants of Bellano." "Was the whole village then implicated in this strange transaction?" "They were punished as if they had been, Signor. Good night, Signor. I do not like lingering near the spot at this hour. This is the very house in which the deed was done."

The peasant retired. Ippolito surveyed the structure. He saw it was safe, from solitude and fear. In the village, wild and deserted as it seemed, he dreaded discovery; he dreaded the unknown effects of the stranger's machinations. Weary of persecution, and impatient for gloomy quiet, he thought with pleasure of plunging into the recesses of a solitude, from which even superstition, that haunted him in every other retreat, would recoil with shuddering.

Again he surveyed the building, and, ascending the rising ground, traversed the dismantled wall that enclosed it. It was spacious and ruinous. The dark lines of the building were strongly defined on the deep blue of a clear autumnal sky, in which the stars, faintly emerging, tipt here and there a battlement, or a turret with silver. He found the principal doors fastened; and, as he examined the wall more closely, to discover some means of admission, he thought a figure started and disappeared in the same moment, from behind a projecting angle of the building. He pursued eagerly, but vainly. Yet as he turned away, something like a sound issuing from the interior of the building, struck on his ear. He listened; all was still. He now renewed his search, and soon discovered a low door, which required but little force to open, and which admitted him into a passage, lofty, and dimly lit. It conducted him to the principal hall, from which doors and passages branched in every direction. All were alike dark and deserted. No foot seemed to have trod there for many years; and their long perspectives led the eye to a shadowy depth it feared to penetrate.

As Ippolito gazed around him, a shadow, faint and undefined, passed along the other extremity of the hall. He would have looked on it as one of the imaginary shapes that seem to people the shades of obscurity; but the next moment he heard a sound too distinct to be the production of fantasy, that seemed to die away in distance.

He sprang forward, and found himself at the foot of a spacious staircase, over whose broken steps the darkness made it difficult to proceed. As he ascended them, he loudly and repeatedly called on the person whom he imagined he had seen, assured him he had nothing to apprehend from violence or malignity; that he was himself a lonely traveller, who was willing to unite with him for mutual security in that solitary mansion, and to whom it would therefore be more prudent to disclose himself. No answer was returned to his remonstrances; and he was checked in their repetition by the loud clapping of a door in a remote part of the building. That this dreary place had inhabitants, he had now no doubt. Who they might be, or what was their purpose, he resolved to examine, with a boldness which was the offspring of desperation. He was delighted with a summons that seemed equal to the powers of his mind, and did not threaten to taint him with guilt, or blast him with infamy. The stranger was not here to demand from him the energy of a hero, and then predict to him the fate of a villain. The event of this adventure might perhaps exercise his imagination or task his courage, but could scarcely affect his peace, his principles, or his character.

He had now ascended the stairs, and paused for some moments in a gallery which seemed to communicate with several chamber; from one of them a light appeared to issue at intervals. He entered it, and was surprised to see some embers of a wood fire, dimly burning on the hearth. From their blaze, which rose fitfully and expired, as the wind hissed through the dismantled casements, waving the feeble fire, he discovered an apartment like the rest, spacious and dreary. Not a vestige of furniture, or any circumstance but that of the fire, indicated the presence of a human being in the building; his eye wandered over walls, ceiling, and floor; not an object struck them, but the damp, misty obscurity of decay. The room was chill, he approached the fire; the blaze became more strong, and by its increasing light, he discovered in the wall opposite him, a narrow grating; the dusky bars gleamed in the fire-light, and, as he continued to look on them, a human countenance appeared distinctly on the other side. Ippolito started; he advanced to the grating; the face disappeared, and a piteous cry issued from within. Ippolito now earnestly demanded who was concealed in the apartment, threatening, with serious anger, to punish any one he might discover, unless they avowed themselves, and the causes of their concealment.

The grating was then thrown open, and the servant by whom Ippolito had been so imprudently betrayed at Celano, threw himself at his feet. "Oh, Signor," said he, after a long and unintelligible vindication of himself, "why did you leave me at Celano?" "Why did you compel me to do so by your folly, in exposing my name?" said Ippolito. "It was not my fault, Signor—it was not my fault; I never travelled with a wizard before, and I could not know." "A wizard, idiot!

you will drive me mad." "Illustrious Signor, I kiss your feet, be not angry with me in this dreadful, solitary place! alas, I have suffered enough for it since; those devils at Celano were near tearing me to pieces, and when I escaped from them, I lost my way returning to Naples, and after wandering about in this wild country, dreading to make inquires, lest I should be discovered and sent to the Inquisition, I crawled in here tonight, to sleep in one of these waste rooms, and pursue my journey to morrow, and little thought I should have the ill luck (good fortune I mean), to behold you again." "But why," said Ippolito, "did you fly from me on the stairs, you surely must have heard my voice, and when have its tones denounced danger to you?" "I did not fly," said the man, "I was not on the stairs." "'Tis but now I pursued some one to this very apartment," said Ippolito. "By all the holy saints, I have not quitted the room since I entered the building," said the man. "This is most strange," said Ippolito, musing, "I am pursued by a power that seems to possess more than human resources—resistance is vain; I am spent in this struggle. But how was it possible you should conceal yourself, if you did not fly from me?" "The door by which you entered, Signor, is under the windows of this room, and when I saw you, I concealed myself, and have not quitted this room since you entered the door below." "And why did you conceal yourself?" said Ippolito, "to me, in the same circumstances, the sight of you or of any human being would have been most welcome." The man hesitated. "Why did you conceal yourself," repeated Ippolito, "you knew me, and knew that from me you had nothing to fear." "I knew you indeed," said the man, shuddering, "and therefore I hid myself. Ah, Signor, it is well known for what a purpose you seek these solitary places, and whom you are accustomed to meet in them; I thought the roof shook over my head as you came under it. He crossed himself with the strongest marks of fear. "Mother of God," exclaimed Ippolito in agony, "is it possible? Am I so utterly lost? Do my own species tremble at my own approach? Hear me, my good fellow; you who have lived with me, who have known me, who have been lavishly nurtured with every indulgence a generous master could afford, can you believe the horrid tales that are told of me? I attest the blessed name I have just mentioned, and every saint in heaven, that I am as innocent as you are. I have entered into no compact with the enemy of souls; I am no dealer in witchery; I am a crossed and care-haunted man; a restless and unhappy spirit is within me; it has driven me from my home, and instead of being soothed and

CHARLES MATURIN

healed by the compassion of mankind, it is aggravated and maddened by the brutal rage of ignorance, till existence has become loathsome to me."

In the ardour of his appeal, Ippolito had laid his hand on the man's shoulder; the man recoiled from his touch. Ippolito felt it in every nerve, and was again about to expostulate with him, when a strange hollow sound seemed to issue from a distance, and approach the room. "I will believe it, I do believe it all," said the man eagerly, "but say no more now Signor, this is no time or place for such subjects." "Can this place have other inhabitants," said Ippolito, pausing from his remonstrance to follow the sound. "Surely it has," said the man. "Have you seen or heard any thing since you entered it, any shape or sound like this?" "I have indeed, Signor; just before you entered, the shadow of a dark figure passed the door, and I am convinced I afterwards heard heavy steps on the stairs; but in these old mansions, the wind makes such strange noises, that unless one's eyes assure them—"

Here the man's face underwent a convulsion of terror, and flying on Ippolito, he held him with the strong grasp of fear. "What have you seen," said Ippolito, supporting him, "or what is it you fear?" "A hand beckoned to me from that grating," said the man, in inward and struggling tones. "'Tis this bickering blaze deceives you," said Ippolito, stirring the embers with his sword, and looking at the grating; "the light it flings on these mouldy walls is so pale and fitful." "No, no, Signor, I know this place, and its history well; I marvel that its inhabitants have taken so little note of our intrusion yet; but they will not long neglect us." "You know this place is inhabited—and by whom?" said Ippolito. "By the spirits of a murderer, and its punishers," said the man, rolling his eyes fearfully around him. "Why do you pause with so many starts of fear," said Ippolito, "speak plainly and fully what you have heard of this place, and of the cause of its desertion." "You know them perhaps, better than I do, Signor," said the man. "How is it possible I should know them, it is scarce an hour since I entered these walls?" "Because they relate to your family." "To my family?" said Ippolito, as recollection faintly wandered over his mind; then added in an evasive tone, "there are many circumstances relating to my family, of which I am ignorant." "Do you wish to hear what is told of this mansion, Signor," said the man, pursuing the subject. "If your courage is sufficiently recovered to relate it," said Ippolito, wishing to suggest an excuse to him. The man proceeded in his narrative.

"It is some years back, Signor, since this was an inn, and as the town was flourishing, and in good repute, I suppose the inn was so likewise. It so happened that this inn was full of company on a night, and they were all employed speaking of some strange mysterious business that was about to be disclosed shortly, that they said would involve one of the *first families in Naples*; I know not whether it was a monk, or an assassin that was to make the discovery; but, whatever it was, the import of it was expected to be most singular and terrible. So, as the guests were all conversing, and each giving his conjectures and reasons, a person was ushered in, accompanied by a guard of soldiers, not as a prisoner, but in order to defend him on his journey; he spoke but little, and seemed dejected and terrified, like a man labouring under a great secret.

It was immediately whispered about the house, that this was the person who was to make the discovery, and many inquiries, and hints of advances were made, to learn what it might be; but the stranger was so distant, that, one by one, the guests all dropped off to their own rooms, and left him to go to his about midnight. So he did—but never was seen to return from it, Signor; no trace of him was the next morning to be seen, nor ever since.

The house was examined, the guests were detained, the host and his family committed to prison, from whence they never emerged. Then the fury of the law fastened on the town; the wretched inhabitants were sent, some to the Gallies, and some to the Inquisition, but no intelligence of the stranger was ever procured; but ever since that night, this place has been visited with strange appearances. Tenant after tenant quitted the house; and at length it was deserted, and left to decay, as you see. The very last inhabitant told me, that as he was sitting one dark evening about the close of antumn, it might have been in this very room"—"Hark! hark!" said Ippolito and his servant to each other at the same moment.

A pause, deep and breathless, followed. "Did you hear a noise?" said Ippolito, in a suppressed tone. "I did, Signor; it resembled, methought"—"And I see a shape," said Ippolito, springing forward; "it glided past the door that moment; I saw it with these eyes; I saw its shadow flitting along the gallery."

He was rushing out. "Holy saints!" cried the man, clinging round him, "you will not follow it." "Away, dastard!" said Ippolito, snatching a brand from the fire to excite a stronger light. "I shall die if I remain here alone," said the man. "Then follow me," said Ippolito, who had

CHARLES MATURIN

already reached the stairs. He looked around. All was dark and stilly. The flaring and uneven light of the brand quivered in strange reflections on the walls. As he still looked down the gallery, the shadows at the farther end seemed to embody themselves, and pourtray something like the ill-defined outlines of a human shape. He held up the light, and it vanished with visible motion. Ippolito impetuously pursued. The passage terminated at the foot of a narrow and spiral staircase. As he ascended it, the echoes of another step were heard distinctly above; and something like the brush of a vestment, floating between the shattered ballustrade, almost extinguished the light.

Encouraged, not repelled, Ippolito sprung upward with greater velocity, and soon reached the top of the staircase. A figure, strongly visible, but still obscure, now appeared at some distance; and, waving to him with shadowy gesture, disappeared to the left without a sound.

At this moment, the last blaze of the brand quivered and expired. Ippolito stood lapped in uncertainty. A step from below approached. It was the servant, who, binding two of the faggots together, advanced with a stronger light. "Come, quickly," said Ippolito; "it disappeared here—here to the left." The man followed him, aghast and reluctant; but dreading solitude more than even the apparition they were pursuing, they entered a room, the only one to the left. The figure he beheld appeared to have vanished through the walls. Ippolito examined the wainscot and the casements; the latter commanded a view so extensive, that he discovered the room was situated in one of the turrets of the building. All was silence and desolation still.

"By what mysterious agency," said Ippolito, "does this form hover over space, without being confined by it?" A sound, like the fall of some ponderous body—a sound that seemed to shake the walls, and sink into the depths of the earth, roused him from his musing. The concussion was so violent, that it flung open a low door in the wainscot, which had hitherto escaped his notice.

Ippolito approached it. Within, he beheld an apartment, the extent of which was lost in shades, that were, for a moment, dispersed by a pale blue light that fluttered over them, and then disappeared.

Ippolito, taking the light from his servant, whose countenance spoke the very despair of fear, entered the room. "This," said he, as he waved the light above his head, that slowly broke through a gloom of frowning and peculiar blackness, "this should be the very seat of those marvellous operations. There is a depth of shadow, a majesty of night and horror here—here I pause—that wandering shape rested here—here he will either return, or appear no more." "What is that dark mass in that corner?" said the servant, who had crept after him. Ippolito approached the spot he pointed to, and discovered the remains of an antique bed. "Make haste, Signor, and quit this apartment, the brand is almost extinguished," said the servant. "You must go down and relight it; I shall not quit this spot tonight," answered Ippolito. "Go down—by myself! blessed Virgin! no; not for the Pope in person," said the man. "Did you not come up by yourself?" "Aye, but, Signor, I was coming to you, I heard your steps, and thought of you the whole way. But to go to an empty room, to feel every step I am getting further from you, and at length to venture into the very hold and haunt of other things than myself! no, Signor, not if I were to get a Cardinal's hat for it." "We must then remain in the dark till morning. I shall on no account quit this spot." "Then, Signor, I shall throw myself at your feet, and wrap my head in my cloak; and, for the love of grace, speak no more till you tell me that morning has dawned, and that you have seen nothing all night." "I subscribe to one of the conditions; the other, perhaps, it will not be in my power to observe."

The man threw himself at Ippolito's feet, who, glad of an opportunity of silent meditation, leant against the wall, fixing his eye on the dying flashes of the brand, which he had placed in the hearth. Its broad glare danced on the ceiling, transforming the characters of damp and decay into forms as fantastic as the lines of magic, and now, shrunk into a point, scarce shewed the rude and blackened stones on which it was consuming. In the veering light, Ippolito once thought he saw a form in a remote part of the chamber; but the next moment it expired, leaving a thousand imagined shapes to darkness.

At this moment, the servant, half-raising himself, whispered, "Signor, I hear a person breathing near me." "You hear *my* respiration probably," said Ippolito. "No, Signor, no; it is the breath of one who breathes with difficulty, as if he were trying to suppress it—there—there—it passed me now—blessed saints, how near! Signor, if I live, I felt the rushing of a garment past me that moment." "Hush," said Ippolito; "you will not let me distinguish if any one is in motion near us." They both paused some time. Not a sound was heard. "I am stifled holding in my breath," said the man. "You may draw it in peace," said Ippolito; "no one seems inclined to molest us; and if there should, against visionary assailants I have innocence, and against corporeal ones, a sword."

He spake the latter sentence aloud; for the objects he had witnessed were such as human power could easily produce; and he endeavoured to resist his strong propensity to search for supernatural powers in every object above ordinary life. In a short time, the servant forgot his fears in sleep; and Ippolito, exhausted by recent fatigue, slumbered, as he leant against the wainscot. The visions of his sleep were like the spirits whose agitation had produced them, wild and perturbed.

He dreamt he was kneeling at the altar of a church, which was illuminated for a midnight mass. Around or near him, he saw no one either to partake or administer the right. At length, a figure advanced from the recesses of the altar, and approached him; at the same moment, he perceived his father and brother kneeling beside. A deep stillness spread over him as he gazed around; he experienced that sensation so common in sleep—the consciousness of some mystery we are unable to penetrate; but of which we silently expect the developement. The figure distributed the consecrated element. His father, on swallowing it, shrieked "poison," in a tone of horror, and fell back expiring. At that moment, the figure, throwing off his monkish weeds, discovered the person of the stranger, arrayed in a voluptuous and martial habit.

He gazed with a fixed eye of horrid triumph, on the contorsions of the dying man, bent over him to catch his groans; and, as his dim eyes wandered in agony, presented himself in every point to their view, exclaiming, "Behold." The vision suddenly changed its scene and circumstances—Ippolito found himself in a vaulted passage, lit by a few sepulchral lamps; Annibal was beside him, and the stranger bearing a torch, and in the habit of a funereal mourner, stalked before them.

As Ippolito slowly seemed to recover his powers of observation, he perceived he was in a part of the castle of Muralto, he remembered to have traversed before. The stranger, waving them to follow, entered an apartment hung with the insignia of death; he remembered it well—it was the last of the chambers that communicated with the tower so long shut up. In the centre of the room, stood a bier, covered with a pall: the stranger withdrew it, and pointed to Annibal and Ippolito, the corse of their father beneath. Ippolito, retaining his natural impetuosity in sleep, snatched the torch from the stranger, and held it over the countenance of the dead; they were fixed in a kind of visionary sleep. As he still gazed, the lips began to move; and at length uttered some words of extraordinary import, which Ippolito vainly tried to recollect when he awoke. As he still gazed, the body extended one hand to him, and another to Annibal, seized on both, and drawing them under the pall, lapt them in total darkness. He shuddered and awoke.

The light had long expired; it was succeeded by moonlight, dimly breaking through the discoloured windows, and figuring the floor with the rude imagery of their casement work.

He looked around him to dissipate the forms that still flitted before his eyes; on a part of the floor, where the light tell strongly, he observed a dark spot he had not beheld before, whose shadows by their depth seemed to fall within the floor. He approached it, and perceived a chasm of which he could not discover the depth. He examined it with his sword, and found there was a descent by steps within; he tried to follow them, but found their depth extended beyond his utmost reach. Here he paused for a moment, but his resolution was soon taken to descend and explore it.

There appeared to be something designed to tempt and to baffle him in the circumstances he had witnessed, that tempted his courage as strongly as his imagination; they were circumstances beside, such as human power and contrivance could easily produce, and such as human fortitude could easily cope with. The jealousy of imposition operated more powerfully on his high-toned mind, than even his appetency for the marvellous; and of the latter too, there was a lurking impulse that expedited his resolution.

His servant still slept, and Ippolito wished not to disturb him, as he would be equally clamorous at either alternative of accompanying him into the vault, or of remaining in solitude; his sleep would probably continue till the morning, and at morning he might depart in peace. He therefore commended himself to all the saints, and began to descend the steps. They were winding and irregular. He soon lost the faint reflections of moonlight, and for a few moments advanced in total darkness. He paused, for to advance in darkness, was to encounter superfluous danger, when a flash of sudden light from below played on the dank, black walls, and shewed him the rugged steps winding downward to a depth it was giddy to think of. The paleness and flitting disappearance of the light, indicated the distance from which it issued; but as Ippolito, encouraged by this dubious omen, eagerly proceeded, frequent flashes of a stronger light convinced him it was stationary, and that he was approaching it. He advanced; the light increased; it seemed the faint gleam of a lamp struggling with darkness. In a few moments he perceived it glimmering at a determinate distance, and sending up long streams of abrupt light on the upper darkness. A few steps more brought him to a level; he entered a vaulted passage low and black, hoary and chill with damps; at the entrance of it a lamp burnt feebly. He disengaged it from the wall with difficulty, (it was iron, of coarse and ancient structure), and proceeded with it slowly, extending his sword before him. In the deep blackness of the perspective, no object near or remote could be descried; the air seemed almost materially thick and dark. A dim atmosphere of bluish light spread round the edges of the flame Ippolito carried, which shivered almost to dissolution, though he advanced with the most cautious slowness, dreading lest its extinction should leave him wandering for ever in darkness, or its motion should kindle the foul and pent-up vapours to a flame of which the explosion would be fatal. As he glided onwards a sound, he paused to distinguish, came to his ear. He listened—it was a human groan; it was repeated; it was like the expression of mental anguish, more than of bodily; it seemed to issue from an immense distance. Ippolito called aloud in accents of encouragement; the sounds ceased. As he turned in the direction from which they had proceeded, his foot struck against something which he stooped to examine; it was a rosary and crucifix of wood, they were corroded by damp, but their shape was yet distinguishable.

As he examined it with that disposition which desires to look for proof in casual things, another light twinkled like a star in the passage beyond him, and a figure dimly defined, appeared and vanished with the swiftness of a shadow. Ippolito with alternate cries of menace and intreaty, adjured it to pause, or to approach. It hovered for a moment on the remote edge of darkness, as if doubtful whether to obey him or not; but as he hastened forward to urge his importunity, it disappeared. Its motion was so evidently human, that Ippolito felt inspirited with a hope of success as he pursued it, till his progress was suddenly entangled by something that lay on the ground. Impatiently he endeavoured to remove it with his hand—it was a heap of dusky and decayed garments, of which the shape was indistinguishable. As he threw it from him, the clank of a human bone rung against the vault.

He was now irresistibly checked, and holding down his lamp, tried to discover whether any memorials of horror were near him that might be avoided in his progress. Shuddering, he perceived the remains of a human skeleton scattered to some distance around him; the skull had dropped from the garment that was entangled round his steps. As he gazed around unwilling to linger, and unable to depart, the lamp darted a bright and tapering flame upward, and then sinking down, quivered as if about to expire.

For a moment he believed the fluctuation of the light was owing to an influence connected with the object before him; but on looking upward, he discovered an aperture of which his eye could not measure the height, in the roof of the vault, through which the air rushing had almost extinguished the lamp. Comparing this circumstance with the spectacle before him, he immediately conjectured that the unfortunate person had been precipitated through the chasm, and dashed piecemeal by the fall, as the bones were scattered at various distances.

All thought of further pursuit was for a moment repelled; and in the interval, as Ippolito was withdrawing his eyes with the slowness of fascination from the object before him, the other light appeared approaching from a distance. Through the thick vapours of the vault, Ippolito could scarcely discover that it was supported by any visible hand; but as it approached, he perceived it was the stranger who bore it! He had no time to collect his faculties; the stranger was already beside him. They viewed each other for some time without speaking a word, while the lights they held reflected to each, the visage of the other as pale and fixed as that of the dead. At length, "Wherefore are you here?" said the stranger. Wherefore am I here?" repeated Ippolito. "Is that a question? What other shelter have you left me? Where can I fly without persecution and danger? I have been torn from life, and from society, from the objects and occupations that are congenial to my age, my spirit, and my fortunes. I have been banished the presence and the sympathy of my own species; I hear nothing around me but the hiss of suspicion, or the mutterings of hatred. You have written a character of horror on my brow, that my own menials read and fly from. You have poured a poisonous atmosphere around me, that blasts and wihers the feelings of every human being that approaches it. In the whirlwind of your pestilent progress you have rent me from my own soil and station, and flung me on a bare and isolated precipice, where I stand the sport of every storm, shivering at my own desolation. You have done this, and dare you ask me why I follow you even here? Why I pursue you to the very verge of being, to ask you for myself?" "You do well," said the stranger, "to harbour amid such scenes as these, to such your fate is about to lead you; and you are right to habituate yourself to them; you are in your proper abode. Child of despair, I greet you well. Do you see these walls? Such shall soon be enclosing you; what the

CHARLES MATURIN

object at your feet is now, such you shall shortly be." "Away with this horrible jargon," cried Ippolito, "I will be duped by it no more. I have grovelled under you, till I am weary of suffering and submission. These struggles are not of despair, but resistance; I have fled, not to shun, but to pursue. Mysterious and inscrutable tormentor, I have too long been your vassal; your power was illusive and imaginary—it was borrowed from *my* weakness; my visionary folly arrayed you in the attributes of imagined terror, but it can strip and mock you for its sport. *My* triumph shall have its turn now. I will change in a moment the parts my abject folly assigned us; you shall fly, and I will become the pursuer now. Yes—I will haunt you as you have haunted me. I will proclaim you to the vulgar—to children I will proclaim you; your shadowy movements, your mysterious dignity shall be the tale of beldames. Horror shall be dispelled by familiarity, and contempt shall mock at the detected imposture. I will pursue you with an army of persecution, malediction, and ridicule—the horror of the virtuous, the hatred of the vulgar, the jealous fury of superstition, and the awful resentment of justice. You shall find what it is to drive a soul to despair. I will pursue you from place to place; I will chase and scatter you over the earth; on no part of its surface shall you rest; at no depth below it shall you be safe. Human power shall urge you to the limits of this world, and the vengeance of religion shall pursue you to the next. Ha! ha! what an ideot have I been. Yes! 'tis a glorious thought—to be revenged of you; to dash your sceptre of iron, your scourge of scorpions, from your hand, and to wield them against you; to deliver myself; to deliver the world; to do a service to heaven. Methinks I breathe a new element. The ground on which I tread bears me up since I have conceived the thought. The very activity of motion, the energy of pursuit will be congenial to my nature, and a relief to my spirits."

The stranger listened without resentment, and paused long before he answered. "Unhappy boy! you grapple with a chain of adamant. You may run to its utmost extent, but what will that avail you? I hold it in my hand. I have measured its length, and numbered every link. If you were capable of reason, would you not perceive that this restlessness of mind, this appetite for vehement struggle and rapid pursuit, is but the oppressive sense of unaccomplished destiny. You feel that you have a task, of which you imagine inventing another will destroy the remembrance and the responsibility. You are approaching a precipice with silent but gradual swiftness; and you imagine that short deviations, and momentary sallies, will alter the direction, or intercept the fall. Do you not already perceive your power of resistance diminishing? Do you not perceive your excursions are shorter, and your progress more perceptible. Recollect, when to mention this subject, was only to excite a torrent of rage and malediction. Now you can definitely talk of its enormity; and the next step will be to consider that enormity as modified and palliated, till you contemplate it with horror no longer. Recollect, that when the former thought of it tinged your dreams, you would awaken with the force of horrible conceit, and practise every expedient of childish fear to sleep no more that night. You dreamed of it tonight, yet no waking consciousness of horror broke through your slumbers; no cold dew gathered on your brow; your teeth did not gnash, nor your limbs heave and quiver; your waking was the effect of accident—of an extraordinary accident. Recollect (and acknowledge the power that reads your heart) that your intended persecution of me is prompted by an irresistible desire to discover the motives which prompted my suggestion of the action; the means that would have been applied to its accomplishment; nay, its very form and circumstance, all horrible as they are. Such is the purpose with which you would pursue me; and how absurd to deprecate the contemplation of what it is the burning and inward thirst of your soul to satiate itself with the knowledge! What we desire, from curiosity or fear, to contemplate, we will soon be habituated to; and what we are habituated to, soon ceases to be revolting. Thus you impose on yourself by the very means you take to avoid imposition. Your flight from evil is circular, and brings you to the very point from which you commenced it. The impulse, upon whose tide you float so triumphantly, is ebbing in its pride, and will bear you back to a depth and distance greater than even that you have emerged from."

"Mother of God!" said Ippolito, "I see I am lost." He staggered and gasped. "Human force cannot contend with this enemy. You are something which thought is unable to reach. You blend the familiarity of human temptation with the dark strength of the fiend. I am weak and cannot contend; I am weary, and amazed, and all strength has failed me. Had I the power of an angel in my arm or my brain, what would it avail? I stand before him naked and helpless as infancy. I think, and he tells me my thoughts. I deliberate, and he anticipates my resolution. I move, and my motions are measured and bounded. I fly, and my flight is overtaken and arrested. Night cannot veil, nor the bowels of the earth hide me. I look upward, and the shadow of his hand is over me. I look downward, and I am thrown before his feet."

He mused in the stupor of horror, and murmured inwardly, "If the great blow to which I am urged, could deliver me from this; if it could be struck, and all this terrible siege he lays to my soul, cease with it—would it not be well?"

A dark smile passed over the stranger's face, as the last words were spoken. Ippolito burst into rage again, as he noted it.

"Devil, I see your triumph. You think I am parleying with guilt; you think you see the balance held with a trembling hand; you hope that despair has driven nature from her hold, and fixed her black banner in the very centre of her works. No; your infernal wisdom has deceived you. You are deep in the mysteries of iniquity; but your knowledge becomes foolishness when it has to deal with a human heart. You might as well predict the tossings of an earthquake as the struggles of a high-principled soul goaded to phrensy. I am indeed strongly beset. The enemy has had power over me, such as is seldom given him over man. These thoughts are often with me. My powers are shaken by a thousand impulses to evil. But hitherto I think I feel my actual abhorrence of guilt is undiminished. I think so. If I admit the thought of it more frequently and patiently, 'tis not because I am reconciled to it; but because—no matter; it is better not to think of the cause. I am sure I shall be upheld—I trust so; yet I am dark and lorn. Evil is gathering round me like night, night unbroken by a single ray of light. I would willingly cleave to nature and to my fellow-men. I would call to them for comfort; I would lay hold on their hands for help; but they reject and abhor me. This is one of the fiend's subtlest devices; this is the very pith of his dark power. Yet still I am not cast down. I stand, though sore shaken. Yet, Oh! when shall I be able to curse him, and bid him depart?"

"There is no need. I am gone; but what will that avail you? The power you dread and deprecate is within you, where its gradual workings shall lead you to the very act for whose mention you curse and proscribe me. I attest night and this vault, the witness of untold things; I attest these mouldering bones, and this dagger, on whose blade the gore you shed is yet visible—three months shall not elapse, till you do the deed, whose visioned horrors were disclosed to you in the chambers of our secrecy. My task is now finished, and my office has ceased. When next you behold me it shall be in another form, not to predict your fate, but to witness it."

As he said these words, with the solemn sadness of human feeling, he slowly retreated. The unhappy young man was stung to madness. For a moment all was mist and cloud around him. When he raised his eye again, the stranger was scarce visible in the dark distance. With a cry of despair, Ippolito rushed after him. In a moment he was at the extremity of the passage. Here several others branched off, losing themselves in the darkness. In none of them could the stranger be traced by sight or sound. The very light he bore had disappeared. It was impossible that, in a few moments, he could have traversed passages of such length. But Ippolito had long since ceased to judge of him by the measure of man, and now plunged into the passage immediately opposite him with the blindness of desperation. No object was visible, as he glided along, but the hoary and frowning arches of the vault; no sound was heard but the echoes of his steps, half-heard in the thick, damp air.

He had proceeded with a rapidity that left him no time to think of the distance he had traversed, till he was checked by actual weariness, and then perceived, for the first time, that of these winding passages there seemed to be no end. His mind was in too tumultuous a state to recognise this circumstance, further than as it was connected with the length or difficulty of the pursuit. He was like a man, who, waking from a fearful dream, seems still to hold conference with forms of fantasy, peoples darkness and vacancy with shadowy crowds; and is scarce recalled to the objects of life, by discovering that all around him is solitary and silent. It was this deep stillness, this interminable darkness, that first checked Ippolito in his pursuit. The stranger, his appearance, and his words, seemed to him as a vision, a shadowy imagery, that floated on the vapours of the vault. That he could have disappeared thus suddenly and entirely, was a contradiction to his actual presence; and Ippolito, almost distrusting his senses, began slowly to look round him to discover some means of extrication from this maze of passages.

From the moment he looked around him with this object, the length and darkness of the vault became intolerable. He would have been delighted to discover the slightest change in his progress; he would have been delighted to observe the walls more rugged and fractured, or the ground more uneven.

At length, the objects around began evidently to assume a different aspect. Large masses of stone, rude and dark, projected from the walls and roof, as if they would crush the passenger. Around some of them Ippolito observed dusky and stunted weeds were entwined; and once he thought a pale reflection wandered through a chasm over his head, as if light was stealing on him from the world above. Still his progress appeared endless.

He now walked on with steady swiftness, not admitting the suggestions of the hour and place to overshadow his mind, or benumb his exertions. Moving, with the rapidity of one who was approaching a definite object, while his eye vainly hung on the darkness to discover one, sometimes stung with an impulse to return, he would pause till the perplexity of the passages wildered his brain in the effort to retrace them. Thus he passed on, dreading to look behind, and scarcely hoping, as he looked onward. In this state of mind, he suddenly found his progress checked by a wall that terminated the passage. Neither door nor window was perceptible in it. He examined it with his lamp, and at length discovered a grating that, almost decayed with rust, ran for a considerable length in the wall, parallel to the ground. From its form and direction, Ippolito conjectured it had been a part of a door, that was now inclosed in the wall.

Here was something like a means of escape, though in other circumstances, it would rather have resembled an obstruction; but Ippolito, with his natural impetuosity, believed that nothing could resist his strength, stimulated by danger, and already felt himself liberated from this dungeon of famine and darkness. As he laid down his lamp, for the purpose of examining the bars, he perceived through them a light so faint and remote, that he almost believed it a star. As he gazed on it, it became more distinct, and he at length perceived it was a light in motion, though by whom it was borne, or through what space, it was impossible to discover. As it flung a tremulous and misty gleam through the thick air, he could see after some time, a flight of steps at a vast distance, that wound beyond the sight, and of which partial fragments appeared through chasms at a still greater, feebly tinted with the moving rays of the light. And now as it advanced down the steps, he could see it was borne by a tall, dark figure, who preceded another still more obscure, bearing in his arms something that was enveloped in white. They descended from a vast height at the extremity of a vault, over whose extent the torch as it approached, threw a transient flash without exploring it. As the vast masses of shadow varied with the motion of the torch, Ippolito thought he could discover objects that resembled the furniture of a place of sepulture scattered around the vault before him; but the light was too faint and partial to give them distinctness. The figures at the other extremity had now descended the steps, and entered the vault. One of them laid down his burthen for the purpose of adjusting it, and while the other held up the torch to assist him, the strong light that fell on his visage, discovered the stranger! The other was in the habit of a monk.

He resumed his burthen, and was proceeding with it when the stranger producing a dagger, fastened it in the monk's girdle, pointing with appropriate gesture to the object in white, and giving him the torch he bore, retired up the steps, where Ippolito could see his dark figure gliding past the chasms, through which they wound, and sometimes bending from them, as if to mark the motions of his agent below.

By what means this mysterious being was present in every scene of horror, and active in every purpose of mischief, (for such the present appeared) filled Ippolito with new wonder. He seemed to glide from place to place, like the very genius of evil, with a dark suggestion for every mind, and a dagger for every heart.

The monk proceeded with slow steps across the vault, till he was nearly under the grating where Ippolito stood. The paleness of guilt and of fear was in his face. As he held the torch low, to direct his steps over the broken pavement, Ippolito could distinguish it was strewed with the memorials of the dead. He stopped where the ground was recently disturbed, and a stone appeared half raised from it; and seating himself, while the torch burned on the ground, withdrew the covering from the burthen in his arms—Ippolito discovered a female form, folded in a shroud, whose relaxed limbs and pallid face resembled those of a corse. The monk looked around, though not a sound was near, and then unsheathing the dagger, surveyed it wildly.

Ippolito no longer doubted that the object in the shroud was living, though it seemed determined she should be so no longer. The monk now raising his hand tremulously, and half averting his face, seemed to wind himself up to the blow. Ippolito, in an agony of rage and horror, struggled with the barrier between them, and uttered a cry so terrible in the conflict, that the assassin, dropping the dagger, remained petrified with fear; his fixed and strong eyes not daring to seek the direction from whence the sound had issued.

Ippolito grappled with the iron in a phrensy of rage; bar after bar, loosened by age, and shaken with supernatural force, gave way. The stones in which they were fixed yielded along with them, till an aperture was formed, through which Ippolito forced himself, and leaping downward a descent of which he did not feel the depth, burst into the cemetery. The monk, whether in the confusion of his fear, or determined to effect his purpose before Ippolito could descend, had struck at the female with his dagger, but with a hand so uncertain, that it scarce rased the skin; he then fled, bearing with him the torch, which however he extinguished in his flight, and fled up the stairs, his dark garments fluttering through the apertures above.

Ippolito supported the lady in his arms, he perceived that she breathed. The feelings that her beauty might have inspired, were repelled by her helplessness and her danger, and Ippolito bent over her with solicitude merely fraternal. To escape from the cemetery, was the first object of safety; but to do this it was necessary to wake his companion, and procure some information from her; for he had no knowledge of the place, or of the direction to which the steps might lead. All attempt however to wake her was in vain. "This is not the sleep of nature," said Ippolito, "some pernicious means have been employed to reduce her to this state." He looked around him in consternation; the steps at the other extremity of the vault, appeared the only mode by which he could escape from it; the rest were buried in shapeless darkness. The lamp which he had left in the place from whence he had descended, threw a faint and shadowy light from above, which threatened every moment to expire. There was no time to balance means and expedients. He raised the lady in his arms, and pursuing the direction the monk had taken, began to ascend the steps. He looked around in vain for direction or assistance; the steps were broken and irregular, and but for the dim light that still issued from the lamp at the other extremity of the vault, had been utterly dark.

Ippolito knew not whither they led; it might be into the very centre of danger—but no choice of directions was left him, no other means of flight from the cemetery were visible. As he still ascended, wondering at his own safety, he could distinctly hear the steps of the assassin retreating before him, of which the sound was sometimes lost in the echo of doors closing, and in the rush of wind that accompanied their opening. The light that still burned in the vault, was now too remote to afford him assistance; he saw it but at intervals, as it twinkled through the chasms; but above him, a light almost as faint issued through an opening. Several steps were yet to be surmounted; he collected his declining strength, and with one vigorous bound reached the summit of them.

Pausing for breath, he now looked upward; the light issued through a trap-door in the roof, which the monk in his flight had neglected to close. Part of his habit which still clung to it from the struggle of his fears in effecting his escape, assisted Ippolito to ascend through it with the only arm he had at liberty, the other supported his still insensible burthen.

On emerging from it, he looked around him—he was in a cloistered passage, that appeared to belong to some ecclesiastical building. Through the windows, dim and few, a faint moonlight was poured on the checquered floor, the clustering pillars, and the pointed arches of the roof. Far to the left, Ippolito thought he could still distinguish the dark figure of the monk as he flitted along, though his steps were no longer audible; and still further a gleam as of distant lamps, trembled through the obscurity, warning Ippolito to shun the direction, where, as there were probably inhabitants, there was danger. With only this conjecture to direct him, he immediately turned to the right. The passage terminated in a door, feebly secured; but as Ippolito laid down the lady to force back the bolts, he looked behind him with an eye of wonder, to mark was there no sound of pursuit or of danger following them. Exhausted as his strength was, he found some difficulty in removing the fastenings of the door; it opened on a covered walk, through whose pillars, that still bore the form of cloisters, he beheld a garden on which the moonshine flung its rich and tremulous flood light. On Ippolito, panting from the vapours of a dungeon and torches, no object could have had such sudden power of refreshment and renovation, as the beams of the moon, and the breezes of night.

As he supported his companion, he perceived with delight, that the current of the air had recalled her spirits; she spoke not, but her limbs heaved, and her eyes unclosed, though without a ray of intelligence. As he now hastened with her through the vaulted walk, he distinguished all the features of the building to which the passages were attached. The high tufts of pine, and larch, and cypress concealed the lower parts of the fabric; but above them he could see the row of small convential windows, with the antic carvings of the battlements above; at their extremity, the great staircase window, stained with a thousand colours, that gave their rich, romantic tingings to the moon-beams, and the trees that waved around it; beyond, features still more characteristic of the structure appeared; the niched and figured walls, the angles of the buildings surmounted with crosses of grey marble, and further still the spire of the convent rich with the fantastic profusion of gothic embellishment.

As he still gazed, though he hastened onward, he could see tapers gleaming in different parts of the building; and once he thought he beheld a figure passing among the shade at the opposite extremity of the garden. The walk which he had traversed, by this time, terminated in a portico, whose light pillars were connected by trellis-work, and mantled over with luxuriant shrubs; he crossed it, and beheld before him an aperture in the garden wall, whose fragments lay scattered around, through which he beheld the open country in all the magic of moonlight. He darted through it with an impulse which annihilated weariness and fear, and found himself on a rising ground, whose gradual slope, skirted with tufts of arbutus and magnolia, led to the brink of a stream, whose waters reflected the turrets of the convent. Ippolito hastened to the bank, and depositing his unconscious charge beside it, sprinkled her with water, and unfolded her vesture to the air.

While she slowly recovered her intelligence and speech, Ippolito gazed on her form, lovely even in the semblance of death. Her long, dark hair that fell over her face and bosom, like the foliage of the cypress over a monumental marble, informed him she was not a religious; yet the building from which he had borne her, was evidently a convent. Her first emotions on recovery, which were terror and surprise, as Ippolito had expected, he endeavoured to calm, by the most respectful assurances of safety and protection, delivered in a tone so humble and soothing, as inspired her with a confidence her strange circumstances opposed in vain. When at length her perceptions became clear, and her language collected, Ippolito supplicated her to inform him by what means she had been involved in a situation so strange, as that from which he had rescued her; of which, however, he took care to suppress the circumstances he judged too terrifying to be repeated to her.

At the mention of the cemetery and the convent, the lady shuddered, and, apparently too much agitated to answer his inquiries, fell at his feet, and with a torrent of tears, avowed her innocence and her helplessness, and implored him to protect her from the horrors prepared for her by the persecutions of mysterious enmity, leagued with the oppressions of religious cruelty.

Her appeal was made in a language now little understood—the language of chivalry; of which no other ever possessed the power, when addressed by a beautiful and helpless woman, to a young man, noble and brave. Even at that period, this language was much disused; and though Ippolito felt its energy in every fibre of his heart, yet he could easily observe, that the manners and conceptions of the lady were utterly remote from those of ordinary life. He raised, and assured her, with impressive fervency, that while he possessed a weapon or an arm to wield it, no power should molest her; that he would defend her with the zeal of a lover, and protect her with the purity of a brother.

He then, while he conducted her along the bank of the stream, casting around his eyes in quest of some means of escape, of safety, or concealment, again implored her to explain the circumstances that had led to his discovering her.

The lady shrunk from the familiarity of a conference. Her timidity faltered in every accent, and shivered in every limb. She scarce accepted the assistance necessary to support her steps, and in vain endeavoured to raise her eyes to his, and discover if they confirmed the confidence his words inspired.

"I ought to trust you," said she; "nay, I must trust you; for I am destitute and defenceless; but if you are indeed a cavalier of honour, as your demeanour and voice bespeak, conduct me to some matron-relative, some female protector; and, till then, pity and forgive the fears of one, timid by nature, and by habit; fears that scarce give me breath to thank you for my life."

Ippolito was distracted by this appeal, which he could neither answer nor resist. "Lady," said he, "I am wretched to afford you protection so imperfect. I am a wanderer myself, and all the safety I can promise you is borrowed from your innocence, and my own courage. I am, like you, a lorn and luckless being, without friend to appeal to, or assistance to claim."

The lady was again in tears as he spake; but they seemed excited by a cause different from that which her last had flowed from. "It is his voice," said she, with impressive emotion; "it is his very language. Are all men unhappy? or are the brave and noble only persecuted? You, cavalier, are but the second I have ever seen, yet your language is exactly like *his*, whom I would I had never, never seen." "And why, Signora;" said Ippolito, "is he unfortunate?" "He said so." "What is his name?" "He told me never to disclose it, but that it was noble. I know but little myself of ranks or titles. Are you noble, cavalier?" "There are few names more illustrious in Italy than that of Montorio," said Ippolito, forgetting his habitual caution in the pride of the moment. "Montorio!" shrieked the lady, in the wildest tones of joy: "Oh, then, I am safe. I must be safe with you. He is a Montorio too; and, though he is unfortunate, he is the bravest, the noblest, the loveliest"—"What, what is his name?" said Ippolito, eagerly. "His name is Annibal." "Annibal! how came he here? He was at the castle of Muralto. Where is he now? Wherefore did he come, and where has he gone to?" "I know not," said the lady, mournfully; "but he is gone where I never shall see him more. They who separated us will never permit us to behold each other again. Oh, that I knew where he was. I think, I almost think I could fly to him." "Lady, all you utter is mystery; but there is, I fear, no time for any thing but consulting our safety; if, indeed, there remain enough for that. The moon is setting; and I see tapers gliding about at the windows of the convent." "And hark, by that chime the bell will toll for matins in an hour. They chaunt their matins an hour before sunrise. I see the vigil-lamp burning in Mother Monica's turret. Oh, Signor, where, or how shall we fly?"

To discover this, Ippolito debated, if tumultuous anxiety can be called debate, in vain. His horse he had left behind him at Bellano, to which he knew not even the direction. Of the country into which he had emerged, after a subterrene passage, he could not be supposed to know any thing; and his companion, though a resident in it, was equally ignorant. All she could inform him was, that she had heard in the convent, Puzzoli was at no great distance from it. This, though contrary to Ippolito's topical conjectures, gave him, nevertheless, some definite object to pursue, though it supplied no means of attaining it.

As they wandered along the bank in quest of some track that communicated with that they intended to pursue, they descried a small boat, that was moored in a thick bed of rushes and watery weeds, and fluctuated lightly on the tide of the stream. "This is fortunate!" exclaimed Ippolito; "we shall be safer from discovery on the water, and shall probably reach some obscure fishing-hut in the windings of the river, where it will be easy to procure assistance without suspicion or delay."

The lady's reluctance to venture in a bark that had only one oar to navigate it, was overcome by her more immediate fears; for at that moment a sound was heard, which, she believed, was that of pursuit, issuing from the convent. Ippolito, who thought otherwise, concealed what he thought, lest the aggravated terrors of his companion should render her unable to proceed. They hastened thro' the willows and osiers that hung over the bank against which the bark was beating; but, as Ippolito was reaching for the oar, his companion called to him to observe an extraordinary appearance in the trees which suddenly seemed to bend towards the river, and then retire again, while their branches quivered with a strange vibration. Ippolito looked up for the confirmation of his fears, and, at the same moment, the convent bells rung out a quick and terrible peal, and its spire and turrets rocked with a motion perceptible in the reflection of the water.

The lady, screaming with horror, clung to Ippolito, who, combining in the moment, calm reflection with the fullest sense of danger, assured her they would be safer on the water.

As she yet hesitated in the distraction of fear, Ippolito sprung into the boat, and, extending his arms, implored her to embark while yet the ground supported her; but, as she attempted to follow him, the stream suddenly receding, flowed backward to its source with such rapidity, that Ippolito, when he recovered his sight, no longer knew the banks between which it was flowing. Around him all seemed in motion; the shrubs, the trees, the rocks, gliding past him with the undulating swiftness of a fluid; while, before him, the tide on which he floated, separating from that below it, left the bed of the river, black and bare, heaving up, as if the waters from beneath were rushing upward, with wreathed heaps of foam, that sparkled to the meteorous and misty sights with which the air was filled.

Amid the tumultuous sounds of mischief and terror, that now arose on every side, he listened with feeling agony for the voice of the unfortunate female, from whom he had been severed; but all power of discrimination was lost in another agitation of the river, which rushed into its former current with a velocity that left every known object behind it.

As he was borne along, Ippolito could see the turrets of the convent, of which he knew not whether the rent and tottering appearance was owing to the vibration of the air, or to the real injury they had sustained; but no vestige of his companion remained. The ground on which he had stood appeared to be converted into a marsh, in which were only seen the upturned roots of the willows and osiers, nodding where their branches had waved a moment before.

The confusion was now general. Amid the concussion of rocks, the crash of buildings, and the hollow and tumultuous rushing of the earth, Ippolito could distinguish a thousand piercing tones of human distress,

CHARLES MATURIN

more terrible than all; the objects from which they issued, he was spared the sight of; but every murmur of inarticulate terror, was associated with the images of social or individual calamity in his imagination. He was still borne on with irresistible rapidity, till a third concussion checked the current with a shock so violent, that Ippolito was obliged to grasp the stern of the boat for safety. The stream moved to and fro with uncertain undulation, while a deep murmur trembled beneath its waters, and eddying whirls of a blackish hue boiled upon the surface, spirting out globes of foam and sand, and bodies from the river's bed, all sunk and subsided. The river resumed its natural course and level; and the slender bark glided on in safety between the banks where solid and firm-seated substances had changed their places and forms with the levity of the atoms dancing in the wind. Ippolito now employing the oar, navigated his boat with all the dexterity in his power, but such still was the fluctuation of the river, that he found himself unable to make either shore; the current still bearing the boat onward with a force he found it fruitless to contend with.

In spite of the recent and dreadful commotion he had witnessed, Ippolito found it impossible to withdraw his feelings from his own situation, so strange and forlorn. Of all who contended with the terrors of the elements, who had so little to fear from danger? for who had so little in life to hope or to pursue as he? The rived earth, and the heaving flood had swallowed many a being that night, whose dying thoughts clung to life with the energy of hope, and the fondness of desire; while they had spared one, who would willingly have sheltered his head from the dark conflict that beset it, in the gloomiest grave their chasms presented.

The inextinguishable persecution of the stranger, the jealous malignity of society, the gloomy presages of an irresistible fatality, and that mistrust of our own power; that sinking of soul which anticipates the issue of long and sore temptation, began to settle over his mind, making it night within him. He had fled from Naples to avoid the presence of his mysterious tempter, he had met him in the solitude of deserts: he had pursued him, and found him again in circumstances, of which no conjecture could furnish an explanation; they were separated again; but where might he not appear as suddenly as in the vaults at Bellano, or the cemetery of the convent? Distance of space, or strangeness of hour, were no obstruction to him; he might emerge after a subterranean journey, at Puzzoli, or appear again at Naples. But one expedient presented itself, the same which under similar circumstances had been suggested to Annibal, that of flying to another country. To abide the fixed and regular assaults of the stranger, was not tolerable even to thought, as its continuance would not only expose him to aggravated suspicion and danger, but to the greater mischief of familiarized guilt, at which he shuddered, for he had already begun to feel its influence.

The morning now began to pour a pale light through mist and fog on the landscape, and Ippolito looked back on the events of the night, as on the business of years. That a few hours only had passed since his arrival at Bellano the preceding evening; and that into those few hours, so many circumstances should have been compressed, almost exceeded the belief of reflection. As objects became stronger in the strengthening light, he discovered that the ravages of the late shock had been partial, and almost confined to that part of the country he had quitted; all around him seemed tranquil and uninjured. At a distance he beheld along the banks, the huts of fishermen, scarce peering from among the tufts of the thick embowering trees, that love a watery soil, and here and there the sails of their early barks flitting on the distant waves, like the pinions of the white fowl that skim their surface.

He now endeavoured to moor his boat on the shore opposite to that he had embarked from; and at length, though destitute of any skill in the use of the oar, succeeded. He debarked near a small cluster of huts, where he procured the necessary information with regard to the distance of Puzzoli, from whence he resolved immediately to return to Naples; and there make the necessary arrangements for passing into France. He had some faint idea of communicating his project to his brother Annibal, who seemed like himself, the thrall of a wayward fate; but of whose wanderings he knew nothing, except that he was no longer at the castle of Muralto.

While in this hamlet, a horse was procured for him with much difficulty. His soiled, though splendid dress, and his mingled air of grandeur and distraction, excited a curiosity, which he was compelled to appease by a plausible fabrication. As he endeavoured to utter this with fluency, a sting of anguish and proud shame darted through his whole frame: he remembered the stranger's prediction of his gradual immersion into vice and falsehood, and cursed the power that rendered an habitual violation of truth, a part of his existence.

A thousand times in the bold movements of an open heart, he was about to avow the truth, till he recollected that it might be attended with many evils, but not one advantage; and that in his present progress, it was less necessary to consult his heart, than his safety. He was informed when, to repel inquiries, he began to inquire himself, that the concussion of the earth the preceding night, had been felt but partially; that the river had undergone some extraordinary fluctuations; but that they were in daily terror of some great shock, such as those they had lately experienced, usually precede; and that they had understood Vesuvius had been unusually turbulent for some time. "And these are the omens of my return," said Ippolito, as he set out for Puzzoli.

The day was now advanced, and he pursued his way with the guarded and vigilant firmness of a man who is prepared for danger and interruption. He looked around with an eye, which habitual fear had fixed in sternness, for the form of the stranger, or some other portentous shape to rush across his path, or glide dimly before him. His spirits seemed collected for their last effort; their energies were patient and stern, prepared to resist without violence, or to submit without desperation. Bodily weariness combined with exhausted solicitude, to produce that deep and unbreathing stillness of soul, in which the acting powers are not extinct, but in repose. It was that frame into which every mind sinks after violent struggles and repeated defeats, and which usually precedes the last conflict it is able to support—it was that frame of which the force is indeed great, but the continuance doubtful; and the defeat, if there be one, total and decisive. It is too simple and absolute for variety of expedients, or renewal of contest; its impulse is single and collected; if it fail, it fails without hope, and without effort— it was that frame, in which he whose intent was to deceive, would be least willing to encounter his victim. It resists the visions of imagination, it questions even the representations of the senses; but its gloom is a balance for its strength and capacity; it doubts, it resists, but it despairs.

No object occurred in the way to Puzzoli; those that presented themselves on his approach to the city, were in unison with his mind. It is a magnificent theatre of ruins. Antiquity has impressed her bold, gigantic charactery on their remains; she seems to sit among them like a sovereign, at whose feet distant ages and departed nations pour the tribute of their former greatness in their tombs, their temples, and their palaces. They lie scattered as around her footstool, in confused tints and shapeless grandeur. The great Domitian way filled him with awe as he entered it; he felt the interests that agitated him, disappear like the vicissitude of the life of an ephemeron, at the bare thought of the myriads that had trodden that way since its erection, with thoughts as tempestuous as his own, who had passed away without leaving a trace in the history of mankind.

The temple of Jupiter Serapis, and the ruins scattered around it, detained him till the heat of the day becoming intense, and operating with his sleepless and eventful night, of which he had only dozed a few moments in the turret-chamber at Bellano, he eagerly turned to the first inn the street presented, and after a slight refreshment, threw himself on the bed, and endeavoured to repair his strength for future encounters.

On awaking, he found evening had arrived; and a secret and half unconscious dread of returning to Naples, induced him to determine the remaining for that night at Puzzoli. He wished besides to discover whether the suspicions entertained of him were universal; if there was no place where he could appear in safety and innocence; whether the polished and enlightened habits of a city, might not promise him protection from that superstitious malevolence, to which he had been exposed in the more remote and savage parts of the country. He arose therefore, and went out, but with dejection in his countenance, and distrust in his heart. His eyes wandered vacantly over the many objects of curiosity and delight that encountered them; but hung with supplicating and intense solicitude on every human visage that passed him.

In an Italian city, the great church and its avenues are usually the places of principal resort. As Ippolito slowly, and with agitation ill-concealed, passed through one of those, two persons of ordinary appearance followed him at a distance he judged suspicious, till he observed they were conversing on indifferent subjects. "'Tis true," said one of them, "so extraordinary a circumstance has never occurred within the walls of Puzzoli; I could not have been persuaded of it, had I not witnessed it. It outdoes all the miracles ever performed within the walls of church or convent—it is a few steps from the confessional, in the principal aisle, and just beneath the window which bears the blazonry of the Mirolo family." The other assented to the singularity of the circumstance, and added, that he concluded no stranger could quit Puzzoli without visiting the great church, and beholding with his own eyes, so remarkable an object.

Ippolito, easily excited by the mention of the marvellous, and glad of the relief which an object of curiosity promised, repaired immediately to the great church. The antiquity and vastness of this awful structure scarce arrested his step as he entered it; he passed on to the principal aisle, and discovered a group collected round the spot the person had described. A boding of some dread, disastrous thing; some evil unmeasured and unexplored, darkly hovered in his mind as he approached them. He resisted its effects with the feeling of a man, who conscious that something terrible is approaching him, and determined to meet and encounter it, receives the intimation of evil as an appropriate and natural presage, and is confirmed, not repelled by it.

As he advanced, he observed they were gazing in different points of view on an inscription in the wall, of which the characters seemed to have been traced in blood. The group gave way as he drew near; he raised his eyes—the characters were large and legible. He beheld with horror the very lines which were inscribed over the portal of the subterrene chamber at Naples, which *then* surrounded with more terrible imagery, he had scarce noticed; but of which he *now* recognised every impression with a tenacity that appeared to have slumbered in his mind till that moment. All caution, all power, of reflection forsook him at once. It seemed as if the lines were visible in their real character to him alone—to him alone it seemed as if they were charactered with lightning that seared his eyes. In the excess of ungovernable horror, he turned around, and fiercely demanded, "Who had done this, by whose means it had been placed there?" The spectators stared aghast, till one of much suavity of address advanced, and inquired what had discomposed him. Ippolito in the hoarse and breathless tones of passion, repeated the question. "That inscription," said the stranger, "has not been lately placed there." "It must have been," said Ippolito in the wildness of his emotions, "it is but lately that I beheld it in another place myself. Every movement around me seems to be conducted by witchcraft—how may this have been?" "Your knowledge of the place where you last saw, or imagined you saw it," said the stranger, gravely, "may assist you to form a probable conjecture on the movements that brought it there, without doubt."

Half recalled by this speech, yet still confused and distracted by this unexpected witness of his secrets, Ippolito made an imperfect apology for his vehemence, and added, "That the sight of circumstances so extraordinary had disturbed him." "They are indeed extraordinary," said the stranger. "Are you then acquainted with them?" said Ippolito relapsing, and staring wildly at him. "Am I known even here?" The circumstances relating to yonder inscription are undoubtedly extraordinary," said the stranger, "but how far you are interested in them, I cannot presume to say." "I implore you to relate them," said Ippolito, "heed not me, or my interruptions; I am a wild, unhappy being; I am feverish from fatigue of body and mind; heed not what I may say, or how I may look as you repeat them. I am innocent—in spite of those damning characters, I am innocent. The stranger half shrinking from his wild, appealing glances, proceeded in his account.

"This cathedral church, Signor, is of high antiquity, and frequently memorials of the classic ages, and perhaps of others more remote have been found within its walls. The inscription before you," (the stranger need not have referred to it, for Ippolito was unable to remove his eye from it) "is of such remote antiquity, that it is supposed it was originally graven on the stone before the building was erected, as there is no tradition of its recording any event since that period; it is therefore concluded to have been a fragment of ancient stone, accidentally employed in the first construction of the church. There have been many conjectures on the subject of its meaning, but it is unfortunately in a language which the literati of Europe are utterly unable to recognise. The words you see are barbarous, though the characters are Greek. The most probable conjecture I have yet heard, is founded on the two last words, KOTΣ, OMΦHETΣ. Ancient authors have acknowledged that these words were employed in the Eleusinian mysteries; they have also admitted that they were words barbarous and unintelligible to those that used them, but were supposed to have some secret reference to the mysterious purposes of that institution. Is it not probable therefore that the whole inscription is the admonitory formula of the mysteries of which the words were admitted to be foreign; but of which the characters would in transcription be probably Greek, as those before us are? but while the learned had their conjectures, the superstitious had theirs also. There was a tradition connected with these characters, that whenever the fate of a distinguished family in Naples was approaching, the wall of the aisle of the great church at Puzzoli would weep blood. This was repeated from age to age with the partial wonder of imperfect credulity, till lately, when a circumstance occurred that revived its recollection.

It was about a month past that a stranger, tall and closely muffled in a dark habit, arrived in Puzzoli, and immediately repaired to the great church. It was the time of vespers: the stranger planted himself opposite

CHARLES MATURIN

this inscription. The congregation assembled, vespers were performed, the congregation dispersed, the stranger stood unmoved!" (The speaker, during his narrative, kept his eye intently fixed on Ippolito.) "It was the vigil of St. John the lesser; the service and offices were renewed every hour of the night, and mass was performed at midnight. Numbers of ecclesiastics came from other churches to assist, and the faithful were passing and repassing at the different hours of service the whole night, so that probably every inhabitant in Puzzoli had successively the opportunity of seeing this extraordinary person, who remained in one posture, silent and motionless the whole night, gazing on the inscription. Towards matin service, one of the lay-brothers going to extinguish the lamps which burned dimly in the dawning light, observed as he passed through the aisle, that the stranger had departed; and as he proceeded to replace the tapers which were nearly extinguished at the shrine yonder, he suddenly was heard to give a cry of horror, and exclaim, That the wall of the aisle was weeping blood! Several monks hastened to the spot. Whether they confirmed the lay-brother's report, I do not presume to say, but it is certain, that ever since that period, those characters which were before of the colour of the stone, have retained the appearance of blood.

"Such are the circumstances, Signor, which you must acknowledge to be sufficiently extraordinary." "Pardon me," said Ippolito, with a sudden and unnatural mildness of tone, "nothing to me appears extraordinary." "You must then be *conversant* with such circumstances," said the stranger. "Perfectly conversant—oh, there is no telling how familiar I am with them!" said Ippolito, with a frightful laugh. "You will then gratify me by some conjectures on this singular subject," said the stranger. "It is more than conjecture," said Ippolito, answering his own thoughts. "Have you any idea of having seen the extraordinary personage I have described, before," continued the stranger. Ippolito was silent. "Can you form a conjecture where he is at present," pursued the wily stranger. "He is *here*," answered Ippolito, in a tone that transfixed him. "Here," repeated he, trembling, and looking around. "Yes, here," replied Ippolito, with eyes still fixed on the inscription—"see him," he murmured, "yes, I see him always; I see him now, I hear him; blindness cannot shut him out—I have lost myself, but I cannot lose him."

The stranger who had at first raised his eyes in wonder at Ippolito's unqualified confessions, now examining his countenance, beheld it fixed in the fiery stare of madness. Improving this appearance, according to his own conceptions, into demoniacal possession, he retreated with the precipitation of fear, unnoticed by the wretched young man, who was utterly careless of the construction put upon the expression of his misery.

He continued for some time gazing vacantly on the wall, and at length sunk against it, in helpless stupefaction; but it was a stupefaction merely of the senses. The operations of his mind were active and acute; he counted every drop of the tempest that was poured out upon him; as the lightning blazed around him, he seemed to dissect its fires with a prism, to concentrate its burnings, and measure their aggravated fury.

The prediction which he applied to his family, whose peace and honor would be for ever blasted by the deed he was tempted to perform. The appearance of the stranger (for he had but one archetype in his mind, for all beings of mysterious appearance and agency) and the obvious, though inscrutable connexion between the characters on the wall, and those he had seen in the vaults of the scene of blood at Naples, rushed on his mind with a force condensed and complicated, and for a while swept away all power of resistance.

He hung over them with his mental powers benumbed and impassive. He saw them as it were with a mental eye glazed and opaque, that can suffer a body to touch its very organ without feeling it. The intellectual frame, shocked by violence, had folded up its fine texture, and no further assault could compel it to a capacity of suffering. Real and proper absence of reason succeeded; substantial forms faded from before his eyes. He thought the persecuting *stranger* was again beside him forcing into his hands a dagger, which he endeavoured to refuse. The stranger, with a terrible smile, desisted, then retreating a step, held up the dagger, and pointing to the bloody drops which stained if, waved it over his head. The dead and crusted blood dissolved as he moved it, and dropt slowly on his face and hands; he shuddered in vision, and struggled to wake to free himself from the terrible imagery. He awoke and felt it still; he started—looked around; his hands were bedropt with blood; he touch-it—it was warm, it flowed from his temples, which as he fell against the wall, had been wounded by the pediment of a tomb, and now streamed with blood, unfelt. He wiped it away without a groan, and quitting the church, hasted back to his apartment at the inn.

Here he strode about for some time in agony of thought. The persecution that hunted him, was aggravated tenfold by his personal feelings and character: too noble minded for the bare admission of a criminal thought, and too impetuous for the slightest restraint on his actions or movements, he saw himself invested by the most noxious characters of a criminal, and circumscribed in every motion by his inexhaustible pursuer. He had contended, and his struggles had only wearied himself: he had fled, and his flight had been measured and accompanied; he had endeavoured to retire from the conflict in silence, and he had been rouzed again to phrensy, by fresh instances of the presence of his impassable tormentor. To sit down in sullen despair, was equally hopeless. His pursuer was not content with negative malevolence, he contended with him when he resisted, he excited and goaded him, when he was passive, he followed him in his motions, and he was present with him when he was at rest. There is no thought more overwhelming than this; it disarms the soul of every power of resistance, yet leaves it nothing to hope from submission. "Oh, that he were human!" Ippolito exclaimed, in the bitterness of his soul, "that he were an assassin, and I a lone and naked traveller in the depth of a mountain-forest; that he were an inquisitor, and I a prisoner in his grated and airless dungeon; that he were an earthly tyrant, and I the meanest of his slaves who had incensed him, and stood before him, surrounded by the ministers of torture; then I could measure the power I had to contend with, and prepare my own for resistance; then I could know exactly to what they could extend, and where they *must* terminate. I could image to myself that point where exhausted cruelty could not compel another groan; where nature would mock at the impotence of power. Oh, that he were even of an order of beings above me, whose powers could be recognised and limited; then I might know how far his commission to punish might reach, and insult him with its imbecility. Definite misery cannot be intolerable to an immortal being. Though he pursued me with the rage of the dragon, I would yet know that the key of his pit was kept by an angel; though his commission were to last a thousand years, that thousand years would be to me, but as yesterday. But how can I contend with an inaccessible enemy, whose power is undefined, and whose duration is unimaginable? I know not yet if he be man or demon. His goadings and suggestions drive me to phrensy; to resist them is becoming impossible, and to obey them, is to devote myself to destruction, body and soul."

The echo of his loud and agitated voice at this moment coming to his ear, he suppressed it; and at the interval, he thought he heard voices whispering at his door; he stopt, and listened; for fear had made him suspicious of trifles. A voice then articulated, "This must be his apartment—that was his voice." After a moment's pause, another whispered, "He is silent now—did you mark his words?" Several other sentences were uttered in suppressed tones, and he then heard steps retiring through the passage that led to his room.

He hastened to the window, and saw three persons of ordinary habits pass into the street. It was a dusky evening in the close of autumn; he could neither distinguish their persons nor their faces. He was recalled from his conjectures, by the voice of his host, who passing near the door exclaimed, "I cannot conceive who they are, unless they may be ministers of the Inquisition? St. Iago be my protector. The sight of them makes me tremble from head to foot." He then passed into a hall adjacent to Ippolito's room, where others were apparently assembled, and eagerly repeated his suspicions and his fears to them.

The whole company were in commotion. The name of the Inquisition operated like that of pestilence or the sword amongst them. "Alas," said the host, "what have I done, that they should honour me with this visit?" "Perhaps this visit is meant to some of your guests," said a strange voice, "do you know who is at present under your roof." "You are the only stranger," said the host, "and you, Signor, look too like one of themselves, to be in any dread of their visit." "Are you sure of this?" said the other voice, "Is there no stranger under your roof but me?" "Santo Patrone," said the host, "sure enough there is a strange cavalier in the house; but he has remained in his chamber since he entered it, and I had quite forgotten him." "Has he remained alone?—*that* appears suspicious; you should observe him." "Observe him! not for the world; I would not take the full of this room of gold; and watch a heretic, a criminal of the Inquisition! How do I know but the very sight of him would make me as bad as himself?" To this wise observation the other assented, apparently with a view of aggravating the fears of the simple host, which were now extreme and oppressive. "Alas," said he, "what an age is this for good catholics to keep inns in! It was but lately, an inn-keeper at Celano, as innocent as myself, lodged a cavalier, from Naples, a strange man, who, they say, never sleeps at night; and of whom things are told, that would make the hair of a good catholic stand upright." "Have a care," repeated the stranger, "that the same person be not within your walls at this moment." "Jesu Maria forbid," said the host, crossing himself. "If he be under your roof, you are answerable for his appearance," said the stranger. "It cannot be he," said the host, eagerly, vindicating himself from the imputation,

CHARLES MATURIN

"for these plain reasons—" Here he enumerated several circumstances relative to Ippolito's appearance; every one of which tended to confirm what he meant to disprove. "I tell you," said the stranger, exalting his voice, "he is within these walls. Look to him, as you will answer it to the most holy Inquisition."

For some moments after this terrible sentence, the whole company seemed stunned into silence. Ippolito, partaking of their sensation, remained listening, rather from an incapacity to exclude the sound, than any positive effort of attention.

"Who was he that came among us?" said the host at length, in a voice of fear. Every one alike disclaimed any knowledge of him. Some withdrew from the spot he had just quitted; others looked fearfully towards the door. All agreed that he had entered unperceived; that he had mingled in the conversation before they knew he was present; and that he had departed without sound or visible motion.

They then began to examine the few words he had uttered; to compare their descriptions of his appearance, and their ideas of his real character and purposes, till, almost petrified with fear, they scarce ventured to raise their eyes to each other's visages, or to trim the lamp, which the imagination of each had tinged with vivid blue.

At length, their consultations took a less abstract turn, and they jointly determined on the expediency of apprising the holy Office of the character of their guest. But Ippolito, obeying the impulse of nature and despair, with a bold and rapid movement, threw open the door between the rooms, and stood amongst them. The group at this time were the host, the females of his family, their confessor, the monk of an adjacent monastery, and some Campanian travellers.

"I am Ippolito di Montorio," said he, with a disarming voice; "but I am not the monster you dread." In the energy of the preceding moment, he had conceived an appeal of resistless strength and eloquence; but his powers of utterance failed him. He tried in vain to collect the scattered images; they swam darkly before him; their force only oppressed and stifled him. He stood with extended arms, and a form whose expression, with the female party at least, amply supplied the place of elocution.

The party, astonished and dismayed, remained silent, stealing, at intervals, a glance of doubt and fear at the spot where he stood. Their silence chilled and repressed the unhappy Ippolito. With violence he could have contended, and with remonstrance he could have reasoned; but what was to be done with hopeless silence?

At length, the flush of his first impulse utterly fled, and his spirits dispersed and weakened, in a faltering voice he addressed the host, intreating him not to accredit the wild and unauthentic suspicions of the vulgar, nor lightly to admit charges so terrible against a being, to whom no means of purgation were allowed, and against whom no definite proof could be urged.

His ardour augmented by what he mistook for the stillness of attention, he proceeded to call Heaven to witness his innocence. He attested every saint that he was a firm believer, and a good catholic. "This is indeed," said he, "the time for me to cleave to God, when all his creatures desert and abhor me." He told them his sufferings arose from a dark and untold cause, that was locked with in his own breast; "But those," said he, "who do not solicit confidence, are not therefore to be excluded from compassion."

He was proceeding with the increasing warmth which our own vindication seldom fails to inspire, when he was checked by a deep and universal murmur of detestation. Wizard, infidel, and "Eretico damnabile," were echoed from every mouth. "I implore you," said Ippolito, struggling with emotions that made utterance painful, "to retract those horrible words, or at least to reflect on them. Be not so inconsistent in inhumanity; be not so wanton in persecution. Did I possess the powers you ascribe to me, would I stand here to plead for reputation and honour to such a tribunal? Would I supplicate beings from whom I never expected to hear a sound myself but in supplication? Would not my resentment shiver you to atoms? Would not my *sport* scatter you to the winds? Would I not myself mount on their wings, and fly to regions where persecution would not reach me?"

"Stop your ears!" cried the host in horror; "he is uttering some spell. He talks of the winds as familiarly as of a horse. Signor, whoever you are, I implore you to quit my house. Only quit it before the roof falls on us, and then you may mount the first wind you meet, and ride to the devil on it too if you like, with my best prayers for your speedy arrival." "Oh!" said Ippolito, descending, in his distress, to the plainest language; "talk not, I conjure you, of driving me from your house. I have often afforded shelter, but never asked it before. The protection of your roof is but little for a son of the house of Montorio to beg; but misery is humble. I feel if I am driven from your doors no other will be opened to me. It will be the sealing of my fate. I shall cease to have strength for any further conflict, or spirits for any further appeal. Will you be the first to raise the outcry of savage pursuit; to blast the victim of imaginary infection? I claim the common privileges of a traveller. I am spent and overworn with weariness. Many days have past since I have sat at a domestic board, or stretched myself on a quiet bed. My wanderings have been restless and incessant."

"So they may well have been," said the monk, who thought it time for him to interpose: "Fac, ut illi similes sint rotæ." "Sit via eorum cæca ac periculosa, angelus autem Domini profliget eos."

"Do not," said Ippolito, with patience almost exhausted, "do not overwhelm me with this blind and sottish severity. Ye have but one standard to judge of criminals by, and ye make it a bed of Procrustes, to all alike. Ye have but one formula of execration, and you fulminate that without thought or discrimination. Is there no difference between offenders? Are there no gradations in evil? Is suspicion to operate like conviction, and is conviction itself to exclude humanity? Do you reckon as guilty alike, the stubborn villain, from whose barred and brazen side your shafts rebound as they would from a rock, and an erring brother, to whom the bare glance of a reproachful eye is as iron that enters into his soul? Do you reckon lost alike, him who has gone down so deep into the gulph, that to follow him would be to sink along with him; and him who yet shivers on the verge, and who can be pushed from his hold by despair?"

"If you repent, and make expiation for your enormities," said the monk; "the church is an indulgent mother, and will absolve you on your confession and penitence."

"And is it then impossible to procure the privileges of humanity, but at the price of pouring out your whole soul to men, who can neither judge of its sufferings, nor heal its breaches; who will dismiss you with the cold, professional look of the Levite, but sprinkle neither oil nor wine upon you? Is it not possible that a man may retain his integrity, and yet cherish some secret he cannot disclose? Can you not believe him possessed of resolution to bear up against some sore and inward trial, unless he forfeits that resolution by detailing its exercise? Is there no compassion for the shame of suffering? Is there no garment for the writhings of a naked and wounded mind, to whom the very air and light of day are torture, and who feels it is exposed, not to compassion, but to curiosity? To complain is, to me, hateful and uncongenial; but to complain to the incredulous, to the unpitying, to those who debate whether you are a criminal or a madman, while they listen to you— must, must, this be done? Or, may I not be reckoned a fellow-creature?"

"By my holy order," said the monk, "he blasphemes the church and her sacraments." Ippolito turned from him indignantly. "You," said he to the females, "have the habits of women: Oh! have you not the hearts? Judge of me in the gentleness of your natures. I am not what cruel and bigotted men have told you. I am like yourselves. I differ only from others in my sufferings. I am no wizard, no sorcerer, no heretic. How can you credit such absurdities of one so helpless, so supplicating, so persecuted? I am like yourselves. I have, like you, a dread of persecution, a hatred of oppression, a reputation to be blasted, a peace to be destroyed, feelings to be wrought to frenzy. Feel these hands I hold out to you; they are warm with life and feverish blood. Put your hand on my side. Feel my heart; it is beating, it is bursting with agony. I would it were broken this moment." Overcome by anguish, he staggered, he fell backward. A few burning tears fell from his eyes; but they neither gave him relief, nor the power of utterance. "Christo benedetto," said the women, bursting into tears, "how beautiful he is! Ah! madre di Dio, what a pity!" "It is no pity," said the monk. "Satan can transform himself into an angel of light. I have seen him more than once myself, in the shape of a white pidgeon."

Ippolito, swallowing down his tears, sprung, with a convulsive impulse, to the knees of an old man, who had hitherto sat silent, and whose mild and venerable aspect seemed to announce an exemption from the resentments of nature. "Father, father," said he, "your looks promise me confidence and compassion. You are already almost an inmate of that world where prejudice and passion are unknown. By your white hairs, I adjure you, if you have a son like me, believe me, acknowledge me, commiserate me. I am innocent, I *am* innocent; and to leave that impression on such a heart as yours, would be well purchased by the suspicion and abhorrence of a thousand such as those around us."

The old man, who had vainly struggled to free himself from Ippolito's earnest hold, at length exclaimed with vehemence, "If I had a son like you, I would pray to heaven to make me childless. My grey hairs are defiled by the appeal you make to them. I have lived three score and eight years, and I had thought to have closed my eyes in peace; but the sight of you has prevented it. I have lived too long, since I have lived to see you. I had heard of such wretches before. They were old, and withered, and miserable, and might almost be forgiven for resorting to forbidden sources to seek from them what nature and this world denied them. But you, Oh! you, so young, so beautiful, so exalted, what temptation, what excuse, what plea could the destroyer of souls prevail with, to make you seal your ruin, body and soul? Release me; my heart is breaking to see you look so. Why have you not the visage of a fiend as well as the spirit? I might grow a heretic myself looking at you. Let me go; my blood curdles at your touch. I said I had lived too long; but I will not think so till I have heard of your terminating your horrid existence in the dungeons of the Inquisition."

The old man spake with the energy of virtuous abhorrence. He shook in every limb, and marked himself with the cross wherever Ippolito had touched him; but his failing voice bespoke a lingering of humanity, which his zeal contended with in vain.

Ippolito retreated from his last appeal. The fountain of his heart seemed dried up and sealed. The vitals of humanity were parched and withered within him. He extended his arms, and looked upward. "Then I am outlawed of nature. I am divested of the rights of being. Every ear is deaf, and every heart is iron to me. Wherever I tread, the sole of my foot dries the streams of humanity. I have done; but you, Oh, you! may you one day know what it is to knock at the human heart, and find it shut! May you know what it is to fly from the hellhounds of superstition, and hear their howl double on you at every winding! May you feel, with me, the malignity of men united with that of demons, to chase and scatter you! and may the shelter to which you fly, drive you forth, as you have driven me, to despair!" He rushed out of the house, and ran wildly into the street, reckless of expected danger, and only seeking to subdue the sense of anguish by impetuosity of motion.

"Heaven be praised!" said the monk, "his smooth words did not seduce us to listen to him. He shewed his cloven foot, departing, however." "I saw no cloven foot," said the host, rather angrily. "He went away, to my mind, just like a cavalier in a passion." "Just," said the women; "he did not go away a bit like a sorcerer; there was no blue flame or earthquake; nor did he carry away a stone out of the wall with him." "How!" said the monk; "will you presume to say he went out of the house like a catholic?" "To be sure he did," said the host; "and, after all, I shall have nothing to tell of tomorrow in the town." "His presence has infected you," said the confessor: "will you deny that he was followed by a track of sulphur, in which you might see imps flitting up and down, like motes in a sunbeam." "Holy father, be not incensed," said the wife; "I do think there is indeed a smell of sulphur." "I begin to perceive it myself," added the host. "Let us pray," said the monk, &c. &c. &c.

Ippolito traversed the streets with rapid steps. Evening was not wholly closed; but he could perceive that his presence every where anticipated the solitude of night. Children fled from their sports as he passed; and the few passengers he met darted eagerly into another direction. The influence of the stranger seemed to surround him, like the spell of an enchanter, converting every human being he met into a silent shadow, and making him a shadow to them.

It was then he felt the extent of his misery. To be alone on earth; to forget the language of man; to lose the vital functions of nature; to be amerced of his humanity; to find "those cords of a man," by which the human race are drawn together, relaxed and severed by a power that was not death; to feel, like the Mexican victims, his heart, the seat of life and sensation, taken out, and held before his eyes, yet panting; to die mentally, yet still feel the burdens and sorrows of the flesh. A deep and utter desolation shadowed over his soul. He loathed life, but knew not how to die.

He still continued to walk, from mere hopelessness of rest or shelter. Night arrived. He loitered on without approaching a door, or addressing an individual. The blast scattered his dark hair; his feet began to falter— when three persons, suddenly surrounding him, commanded him in the name of the most holy Inquisition, to follow them.

This was expected; yet he felt thunderstruck when it actually arrived. To an Italian ear, that name speaks unutterable things. It is associated, in their imagination, with every idea of horror and ruin, eternal confinement, undiscovered oblivion, solitary and languishing death, and all shadowed over with a mist of superstitious fear, such as the fancy believes to hover round the cave of an enchanter, and which is suggested by the peculiar mysteriousness of the proceedings of that tribunal.

Ippolito looked wildly on the men, and half-drew his sword; but, after a moment's conflict, folded his arms, and followed them. At this period, the Inquisition was not so fully organized in its several departments and motions, as it has since been. Its principal seats were then Rome and Naples. In the other cities it only maintained agents, who, with the help of the secular arm, observed, apprehended, and dispatched their several offenders to the principal seats of the office. The present agent at Puzzoli, was a Signor Giberto Angellini, a man of intelligence and humanity.

There was no regular prison in the town; but the number of suspected persons had lately increased so much, that they had been compelled to repair and fortify an ancient structure, that had formerly been a Roman fort, and which stood on a mole on the western shore, whose waves beat against its hoary bastions, murmuring sounds of woe to the sufferers within.

Thither Ippolito was conducted. At another hour his mind would have thrilled and dilated with awe, as the dark features of his prison emerged to his view, in the windings of his long approach to it. The rude, gigantic portal, of a form elder than what was called ancient centuries back; the long perspective of arched passages, over which the torches of his conductors threw a flaring and shadowy light, fringing with deep red the tufts of weed and dusky grass, that wound through their clifts; and shewing the bold irregular shapings and fractures of their unhewn walls; while often, as he passed among them, he caught bright glimpses of the distant sea, quivering in the moonshine; or of the sky, whose deep, clear blue was strongly marked by the black indentures of the walls, whose edges it spangled with stars, finer than points of dew—the dark habits, the gliding steps, and the muffled visages of his guard, giving almost a visionary solemnity to their progress.

They arrived at length at a larger and more regular apartment of the building. Ippolito observed, in its dark extent, grated windows, and arched doors, that bore proofs of modern repair. His guard here bowing profoundly, resigned him to a person of solemn appearance, who advanced from the opposite extremity of the hall, and silently lighting a torch at a lamp suspended from an iron chain in the roof, beckoned to Ippolito to follow him.

They began to ascend a flight of stone steps. The cold wind, issuing from a thousand crevices, chilled Ippolito; yet he saw neither door nor window. The ascent seemed endless. His conductor glided on in unbreathing silence. Ippolito stopped. The man stopped also, by way of inquiring, without words, the reason of his delay. "I listen," said Ippolito, "for the relief of some sound beside the echo of my own steps." The man paused for a few moments, as if to convince him no such relief was to be expected, and then glided on as before. They now reached an arched passage, where guards, fully accoutered, stalked backwards and forwards, in silence also. They bowed to the person who conducted Ippolito, but at *him* did not even direct a casual glance. The sullen habits of their office seemed to have extinguished all human feeling, even curiosity, the last that might be supposed to linger within the walls of an Inquisition.

His conductor now led Ippolito through a dark, narrow chamber, to another, more spacious, but equally gloomy; and lighting a lamp attached to the wall, and pointing to a pallet scarcely distinguishable in a distant recess, silently disappeared. Ippolito threw himself on it, and, reflecting that the influence of the stranger was excluded here, sunk into sleep.

He was three days in confinement before he was summoned to attend the Inquisition. During that period, the solitude and silence of his prison; the noiseless step and mute visage of his guard; the few and monotonous sounds that reached him from without; the toll of the bell; the chimes of the night; the whispered watch-word of the guard; and the hoarse dashing of the sea at the foot of his tower—had tranquillized his mind, and poured into it a still and patient melancholy, not destitute of vigour, but utterly distinct from sternness.

On the third day, he was conducted to Signor Angellini's presence. Through the passages he traversed, he perceived day-light gradually diminishing, from the thickness of the walls, and the narrowness of the grated apertures. It was almost twilight, when they reached a low door. One of the guard touched it with a staff he held, and it opened. Ippolito was led into a room hung with black, and lighted by a lamp. The inquisitor and his secretary were seated at a table at the upper end. The guard withdrew. There was little of the grim formality of an inquisitorial examination observed, save that Ippolito was seated opposite the agent, the prisoners of that tribunal not being permitted to stand during the examination.

When the inquisitor raised his eyes, he seemed involuntarily struck with Ippolito's form and expression: and surveyed his wild and woe-tinted countenance with a feeling, Ippolito thought proscribed within those walls. "Be so good, cavalier," said he, "as to inform me whether you bear the name of Montorio?" "I did not know," said Ippolito, "that it was part of the business of this office to inquire the name." "In this case it is necessary," observed the inquisitor, "as part of the depositions laid before us refer to the actions of a person named Montorio, and part state, that you are that person; this point, therefore, requires the first consideration."

Ippolito had heard much of the subtlety of the proceedings of this tribunal. He determined to make no concessions he could avoid, and to give no information he could withhold. "If your information be accurate," said he, "you need not inquire my name; if it be not, it becomes you to seek from a more authentic source. I shall not disclose my name." "I must then proceed as if you had," said the inquisitor; "that is the rule of our office in such cases; but I must observe, few are thus anxious to conceal a name they have done nothing to dishonour." "To dishonour it," said Ippolito, with dignity, "would be to avow it in such a cause; to prostitute it to the refutation of absurd and malevolent charges." "You are then acquainted with the nature of the charges urged against you?" said the inquisitor, with surprise. "How is it possible I should be ignorant of them?" said Ippolito; "they assail me from every mouth, at every step. The solitude of deserts, and the sanctity of churches protect me in vain. They pursue me in society; they haunt me alone; they have poisoned my existence; they have subverted my peace, almost my reason." "If you were conscious of innocence," said the inquisitor, "why did you not apply to the church, or the secular power. No unoffending person can be thus persecuted with impunity in a civilized country."

Ippolito gnawed his lip, and was silent. He perceived that the stranger, with the malignity and art of a demon, had snared him in his favourite pursuit; that he had involved him in guilt, which to conceal, was no longer possible, and to avow, in such a country, was fatal.

"Were you ever in Puzzoli before?" said the inquisitor. "Never." "Did you witness any remarkable object on your arrival there?" Ippolito hesitated. The question was repeated. "I saw an extraordinary inscription in the aisle of the great church." "What was the reason of the emotions you betrayed on beholding it?" "The emotion of surprise was too natural and general to require an individual to assign reasons for it; many others expressed the same, whom I do not see here." "You were observed to use some remarkable words." "Were my words then noted by casual observers?" said Ippolito, shocked and overwhelmed at this discovery. "Those around you were not casual observers," said Angellini; "your motions and your expressions have, from the moment of your quitting Naples to the present, and for some preceding time, been in the possession of the holy Office."

At this terrible intimation, Ippolito sunk back in his seat, and hid his face with his hands. He felt like a man, who, believing he has eluded the pursuit of an assassin, traverses a long and dreary path with hope, and just as he approaches its termination, perceives that his pursuer has only sported with his destruction; that he has followed him step by step, and is prepared to spring on him as he reaches the last. The inquisitor seemed slightly affected by his appearance, but renewed the examination.

"Had you," said he, "ever beheld that inscription before?" Ippolito, within whom all power or impulse of resistance began to fail, admitted he had. "When, and under what circumstances?" said the inquisitor. Ippolito hesitated, but was too dispirited to construct an answer, till the question was repeated with solemnity, "Ask your informer that," he replied, "and his answers will betray another victim to the holy Office; his confession will unfold a horrible tale."

"He has already unfolded it," said the inquisitor. "What—is it possible that he has surrendered himself to the judgments of the church? Has he disclosed the mystery of his iniquity? Is it possible that a vindication awaits me?" "Of whom do you speak?" said the inquisitor, "there appears some mistake here." "Of whom!" said Ippolito with vehemence, "of the evil one that haunts and troubles me; of him who has blasted my existence, who has defiled my conscience with horrid thoughts, who has hunted me from society, and chased me into the talons of the inquisition." "You speak then of one I am a stranger to," said the inquisitor, "my informer was an individual of unquestionable innocence." "It is impossible," said Ippolito, "he could not have obtained his information if he were; none but agents were witnesses of the transaction." "Have a care," said the inquisitor. "If it be impossible that a witness could be innocent, what are we to think of you?" "You confound, you overwhelm me," said Ippolito, "is this an examination? I say, whatever guilt is supposed to be attached to me, the person who informed you of it, must partake; for where I was an agent, he was the same; if he is innocent, I must be innocent also." "You accuse me unjustly," said Angellini, "I extort no concessions, I equivocate myself into no unhappy man's confidence; I desire to abide by the plain and direct meaning of your words. And to convince you of the candour of my proceedings, I give you to understand, that the charges exhibited against you are of so important a nature, that nothing but the most irrefragable documents should substantiate or refute them; I have therefore compelled the personal attendance of the principal witnesses, who are not yet arrived. This I inform you of, lest you should be terrified into a confession on the usual apprehension instilled by inquisitors; that they are already in possession of every thing which confession can inform them of. You have now time to arrange your thoughts, and prepare your defence. I only wished by this private inquiry to discover if you had any wish to be spared the shame of involuntary confession, and being confronted with positive testimony. You may retire; I lament your apparent obstinacy. I warn you—you have to do with a tribunal with whom the heroics of affected defiance will avail just as little, as the sullen retreat of an universal and positive negation."

Touched by this open address, and wrung by the thought, that the only sentiment even the generous seemed to have for him, was a doubtful compassion; Ippolito would have paused, and appealed—but it was too late; the guard, on a signal unperceived but by themselves, advanced to reconduct him to his apartment, and the inquisitor and his secretary silently vanished in the obscurity of the chamber.

He was led back to his solitary tower, where he had abundant leisure for the preparation the inqustor had recommended to him; but he had now no resolution for it. His mind was weary with misery; his powers weakened by continued sufferance, were now relaxed to that frame, which, out of great events and ample ranges of view, selects only the recent and proximate points, and dwells on them with minute partiality. Of his various and eventful life he only remembered and revolved his conference with the inquisitor. But by what means the stranger could reveal the transactions at Naples without acknowledging himself as a principal, or any other person could obtain a knowledge of them, he conjectured in vain. Yet even this state of uneasy debility and helpless fear was not utterly without relief. The varying colours of the sky, and aspects of the ocean, the wild scenery of rocks and ruins, that indented the bold curvings of the shore, and the endless varieties their shapes and hues underwent from the transitions of morn to noon, of evening to moon-light, with imperceptible gradations, too soft for the quaintest pencil, or most curious eye to follow; all these were with him in his prison. The influence of the stranger could not change the eternal forms of nature, nor prevent their gleaming through the high-grated window of his tower. At intervals, he even perused the fragments of Cyprian's strange story, which had been spared in the search he underwent on his entrance into the Inquisition.

As long as the faintest ray of light trembled over the water or the shore, Ippolito lingered at his casement, studiously confining his thoughts to external objects, pleased even to observe the distant tokens of involuntary sympathy, that were paid to his situation, or its imagined tenant. To observe the fishermen pausing on their oars, as they glided round the vast projecting buttresses that propped the rock on which his tower was perched, and shake their heads, as they threw a scarce perceptible glance at its steep and impassable height. When the guard silently lit his nightly lamp, Ippolito producing his manuscripts, would pore over them with unrelaxed attention; not to procure pleasure, but to exclude pain.

Yet some of these excited his sympathy, exhausted as it was with personal claims. They marked out regular periods of life as well as passion, and therefore conciliated a degree of substantial sympathy and vivid belief, not always accorded or sought in such performances.

In the fragments he now perused, the writer seemed to have exhausted every drop of the bitterest draught ever held to the pale lip of human affliction—disappointed passion. She seemed to delight herself with imaging the last distress that could be now inflicted or with-held,—that of separation from the object she had loved in vain. Whether this separation was voluntary or compulsive, imaginary or real, could not be discovered from the lines themselves; but to Ippolito, they seemed like the struggles of weak resolution, (such as might be supposed to linger in the breast of a vestal crazed with love,) torturing itself with *more last looks* at an object it could not accomplish, and could not renounce. The first of these fragments appeared an attempt to blend the warmth of passion with that of devotion. Yet the passion was neither sanctified, nor the devotion softened by the union.

I

'Tis past! my anguish'd heart proclaims
The mortal conflict o'er;
This silence speaks what words can't tell;
We part to meet no more.

II

Do not, I pray thee, shed one tear,
Let no sigh reach my cheek,
Or my o'er-labour'd sense will fail,
My o'er-fraught heart will break.

CHARLES MATURIN

III

I've wound my fainting courage high,
And struggled hard for breath;
Oh, let me bear away this smile,
To deck the face of death.

IV

Is it not near, the blessed hour,
When, fleshly suffering o'er,
We'll glow with spirits' sinless loves;
We'll meet to part no more.

But who can tell the last farewell of passion? It appeared impossible to tear her from this subject. Her mind seemed fixed on a point from which the object never lessened to her view. The next denoted a state of mind strange and rare. It was that in which all the corporeal parts of love have evaporated, and only the spirit lingers behind, to mourn over the remains, in which the decay of passion is lamented, not as a cessation, but a source of woe. In which the total decline of feelings, which have already begun to wax cold and hopeless, is anticipated, in which the "loosing of the silver cord, and the breaking of the golden bowl," is expected with an anguish, which the loss of acknowledged calamity can scarcely be believed to inspire, except in the visionary mind of love.

I

Good night, good night, my journey ends,
The night-shades are closing fast;
But one faint ray prolongs the light,
Nor long shall that faint ray last.

II

Still, still while it gleams, must my steps pursue,
Still rove by that witching ray;
But not long shall I follow the false path it points,
But not long shall the wanderer stray.

III

Light the landscape no more, thou fairy beam;
But fade in the face of the west;
And let all be cold as the bed of my home,
And dark as the night of my rest.

IV

For when mine eye views thy meteor sheen,
The way's long toil seems won,
And hope's quick pulse wakes my withered heart,
And my failing steps urge on.

V

Thou unnamed one, on whom while I gaze,
Mine eyes swim in dews of delight;
'Tis thou art my lone way's setting star,
In solitude and night.

VI

But thou whose eye lit my early hope,
Come, witness its last gleam o'er;
Come, catch the least, weak, struggling sigh
Of the heart that can love no more.

VII

For I raise my eyes to that madding form,
That once made their senses fail;
And I twine my languid arm in thine,
And unchang'd is my cheek so pale.

VIII

And that soften'd tone, to which rapture danced,
Its nameless spell is o'er;

And that eye, to whose beam the day was pale,
Darts fire and madness no more.

IX

It is not that thou art less lovely, love,
Or less bright thy noon-tide high;
The sense still might bask in thy sunny cheek,
The soul still be lit by thine eye.

X

But I am cold, and a deathly chill
O'er each frozen feeling creeps;
And, cold, the flow of the fervid fails,
And, hush'd, the loudest sleeps.

XI

The master-hand wakes their song no more,
And their sound of accord is low;
And my wearied pulse is dead to pain,
And my fevered heart beats slow.

XII

Then wonder not that my sighs are still'd,
And the cold tear congeals in mine eye;
'Tis nature fails when passion fades;
And love only with life can die.

XIII

For I have lived till each lost hour
Has floated down passion's stream,
And loved till Heaven's immortal light
Was quenched in thy brighter beam.

XIV

My time, my health, my mind, my peace,
Were tribute to its sway;
And when each humbler offering fail'd,
I pined my life away.

XV

Then wonder not, my heart's lost hope,
At its scanted homage weak;
But read the cause in my sunken eye,
In my wan and woe-stained cheek.

XVI

But shouldst thou approach the solemn bed,
Where fluttering life is stay'd,
To pour its last look on thy form,
Or for thy peace to plead;

XVII

May I not at that hour, when anger is dumb,
My heart's deep wound unfold;
Oh, may it not fall from my dying lip,
That tale of horror untold.

XVIII

Oh no, for ere then will the fine nerve be broke,
That should raise my closing eye;
And all that would prompt my trembling tongue,
Shall be hushed as its last, low sigh.

But the tranquillity promised by the farewell to passion, was mere temporizing. She still lingered over the remembrance, and endeavoured to describe the desolation of life after its spring and hope are extinguished for ever. Compared to her former feelings, those she was now possessed

CHARLES MATURIN

with appeared like those of a departed spirit, hovering over the deserted abode and memory of its human agency. Her love darted a spent and feeble ray through mist and vapour. Its direction was unaltered, but its lustre gone.

I

There was a ray that lit my life,
It has sunk in the west so pale;
And once ere mine eyes that sight might see,
I hoped their sense might fail.

II

There was a path of pleasantness,
In which I was spelled to stray;
I would I had died ere I lost that path,
Though wild and lorn my way.

III

There was a voice which did discourse
Sweet music to mine ear;
And (oh that I live to hear mine own)
That voice I no more must hear.

IV

The ray that lit my life is sunk,
The voice is stopped with sand;
And o'er that path forbid, high Heaven
Doth wave a flaming brand.

V

And I must wend my way alone,
Despair's last curse to prove;
To pine o'er passion's vanished dream;
To live, yet not to love.

But these pursuits soon failed to diversify the monotony of confinement. The repose of solitude soon degenerated into apathy—listless, depressing apathy. He began to remit the habits of watching at the window for objects; of taking the exercise the limits of his apartment allowed; of making those petty provisions against utter vacancy, that every one makes on the first apprehensions of it; but which gradually decline as its influence increases.

Dreading the total enervation of mind and body, which the progress of this habit menaced, he almost welcomed his second summons to attend the inquisitor. There are few who could imagine such a message would communicate joy; but Ippolito longed for the sound of a human voice; for the excitement which human conference supplies. He longed to try the powers of his mind, and the organs of speech, to the exercise of which confinement had made him almost a stranger. The shadows, that silently presented him food and light at stated hours, had nothing of human but the shape.

He was again conducted in utter silence to the same apartment, from which he again found the light of day excluded at noon, and supplied by torches which shed their smouldering and funereal light on darker hangings, and sterner visages than he had seen on the former examination.

The depositions which Angellini had collected, had appeared to him so momentous and extraordinary, that he had applied for assistants from the holy Office at Naples, which were granted to enable him to make a more full and deliberate report of the charges against his prisoner, before he was referred to the supreme cognizance of the tribunal in that city. There was more of form on this occasion than the preceding; and more of that appalling preparation, that dark pomp of mystery and fear. Quaint habits, mute assistants, silent signals, and whispered consultations, by which the office obtain an influence over the firmest minds, utterly distinct from the sense of the awe of their authority, or the uprightness and ability of their proceedings.

The examination, which lasted six hours, consisted entirely of questions drawn from the various depositions made before the inquisitors, relative to Ippolito's supposed character and movements both before and after he quitted Naples. Ippolito collecting the utmost energy of his mind, and inwardly not displeased at the trial of it to which he was summoned, at first objected in a moderate, but earnest manner to the process of the examination. He demanded the names of his accusers. He was informed it was totally contrary to the practices of the institution, to declare them. He then demanded a copy of the accusations, and time to prepare a refutation of them. He was told with this also it was impossible to comply; that if the charges urged against him were groundless, no length of deliberation was requisite for him to disclaim them; and if they were just, the less evasion and delay in admitting them the better; so that in either case, a categorical affirmative or negative was all that was expected from him. This was the sentence of the Neapolitan assessors; but on the representation of Angellini, they consented to let the depositions relative to which he was examined, be read to him before they proceeded.

Ippolito listened to them with a solicitude, (which even his dangerous and disastrous situation could not repress) to learn the various opinions and conjectures excited by conduct so extraordinary as his had been. Nor could he even resist the visionary vanity that inflated him, while he heard himself mentioned as a being whose character and purposes were only to be known by fearful conjecture; who moved before the eyes of men in a cloud of mystery, through which they only caught passing glimpses of a form and movements more than human. The information laid before the holy Office of his conduct while in Naples, appeared to be the testimony of men who had watched it with wonder and suspicion; but without sacrificing either their judgment or their senses. They stated generally, that he had been observed to wander out at night unattended, frequently with gestures of gloomy distraction; to proceed to a certain spot, where he was met by a person of extraordinary appearance; that almost immediately on each meeting, they both disappeared; nor could the minutest search discover a trace of their persons, or their direction from that moment. To this extraordinary circumstance they added no fantastic comment, no wild exaggeration; but they strongly noticed the obvious and consequential alteration in the Count's temper, habits, and pursuit, which from being gay and open, had become severe, unsocial, and gloomy. In addition to these were the informations communicated by the servant, who had accompanied him from Naples, and the peasant he had seen at Bellano. These were as monstrous as fear, falsehood and superstitious malevolence could make them.

The wretch, whose folly had betrayed him at Celano, and whom he had afterwards forgiven, and condescended to vindicate himself to, when they met in the deserted inn, at Bellano, stated to the Inquisition, "That his master was a sorcerer; that he had endeavoured to seduce him to his iniquitous art; that he had fled from him to avoid his persecutions; that they had afterwards met in that untenanted house, whither the Count had resorted to confer with the spirits that were known to possess it; that supernatural voices had called him from room to room, and shapes of unimaginable horror had crossed and overshadowed him; that terrified at a situation which no human courage could sustain, he had swooned, and just before his senses forsook him, had seen Montorio sinking in a fiery cloud through a chasm in the floor, from which a host of huge, black hands, armed with claws of griffins, were extended to receive him. The peasant whom he had met when wandering round the building, deposed that he had seen him assume different forms while he spoke with him; that at the end of their conference, he suddenly sprung upon the highest turret of the building, where he appeared, mounted on a black horse, who breathed fire, whose feet were cleft into talons, and whose mane scattered lightnings; that goading this terrific courser with a large serpent he held in his hand, both disappeared, leaving a train of bluish light behind them." If this information proved any thing, it proved that he had not entered the building at all. The inquisitors crossed themselves with devout horror as they listened to it, and Angellini hardly suppressed a smile that struggled with indignation and pity.

Ippolito observed with astonishment, that not an article of this information had been supplied by the stranger; nor was there any mention of the terrible transactions of the vault at Naples, which he believed had been divulged by him to the Inquisition, and would have constituted the subject of his examination. As it appeared, however, it must be partially known to them, by the process of the first examination, of which the subject had been the recognition of the inscription, he concluded that its present suppression was only a device of inquisitorial subtlety, which concealed the extent of information, in order either to lead to it by a chain of evidence, it would afterwards be impossible to retrace or disentangle, or to anticipate it by confessions drawn from the prisoner in the course of examination. He resolved therefore to admit nothing but what they already possessed; of which its absurdity was the easiest refutation.

At the conclusion of the depositions, he was solemnly exhorted to confess, by the principal inquisitor. "What have I to confess?" said Ippolito, "what mockery of equitable investigation is this? You urge accusations too monstrous for the credulity of an ideot; and you hope by affecting to believe them, to impose their belief on one whose conscience and memory disavow them; to make him doubt the testimony of his senses, and the events of his own existence; or to lead him in the fictitious heat of vindication from imaginary charges, to the mention of real ones." (At this ill-timed observation, he saw the inquisitors exchange looks of grim intelligence; but he was exasperated, not checked by it, and hurried on.) "Confession! Of what use were confession to me now? If I should even convince you of my innocence, can you restore to me its purity and its praise? Can you restore it to me without suspicion, and without reproach? Impossible. He who has once entered your walls, never can regain the estimation of society—never can regain his own confidence and honest pride. Whether acquitted or convicted, it matters not; he is held in the invisible chains of suspicion for life; the damps and dews of his dungeon form an atmosphere of repulsion around him for ever; the shadow of your walls darkens over him like a curse. Of what avail would confession be to me? It cannot recal the past, it cannot unmake me a prisoner of the Inquisition. Your dreadful policy can neither reverse its proceedings, nor remedy its evils; it rushes through society confounding, subverting, and trampling; but it cannot pause to raise or to repair; and if it could, it were in vain. The wounds it inflicts are mental, and therefore cannot be healed; the brand impressed by irons red from the furnace of superstition, can never be effaced, and ache at every breath of heaven. No reputation of habitual innocence, no actual evidence of universal integrity, can protect your victims. A single suspicion, a whisper, a look, can dash them from the height of human excellence into the dungeons of the Inquisition; the most abject villain may blast and destroy the most exalted of mankind. Though unassailable every where to the view, the most trivial of his motions, the very *heel* of his moral frame may be reached by the shaft of clandestine malignity, and the wound is mortal. Of what service is acquittal to such a man; is the world into which he returns, the same as that he quitted? No; while he slept in the lethargy of confinement; the vestal fire of his honour, which it was the business of his life to guard, has gone out; and he sees its ashes scattered and trampled on. How are these evils to be anticipated by confession? Confession itself is an engine of mental torture, which none but an inquisitor would use; it is possessing yourselves, under the name of religious authority, of the means of gratifying carnal and selfish curiosity. It is, where your natural forces have failed, to lurk in the *horse of superstition*, and enter in dishonourable triumph. The thoughts and actions of the purest lives cannot bear this universal scrutiny. There is no human being fully known to another; it is only by partial ignorance, that mutual esteem is preserved. To the wife of his bosom, to the friend of his soul, to his own consciousness and recollection, a man will not dare to reveal every thought that visits his mind; there are some which he almost hopes are concealed from the Deity. When a man exhibits his mind, he shows you a city, whose public walks and palaces are ostentatiously displayed, while its prisons, its cages of unclean birds, its hold of foul and hidden evil are concealed; or he exhibits it as he would the sovereign of that city, when he stands on the pinnacle of his pride, and looks round on the ample prospect of his own magnificence, not as when he flies from the resort of men, and herds with the beasts; when his power is lost in degradation, and his form buried in brutality.

And why confess to *you*? What claim have you from nature, or from confidence for the demand, or do you ground it upon the absence of all? Are we to repose in you a trust, withheld from all mankind beside, because you have less motive of solicitude, less claim on confidence, less power or wish of sympathy than all mankind? Are *you* like the ocean, to engulph in silence and darkness, the treasures intended to be shared with affection and sympathy? is confidence like the ebony, the growth of subterrene darkness, the nursling of a dungeon? No, it is your greedy, furtive, serpent curiosity, that longs to wind itself about the tree of knowledge; 'tis the ambition of a fiend, counterfeiting the aspirations of an angel, like the impure priests of a pagan idol, ye love to prey on violated purity, that as yet has never sacrificed to nature or to passion, and to call it a rite of religion."

He would have proceeded, for the inquisitors listened with the most unrelaxed composure; but Angellini, shocked at his impetuosity, that offended without advantage, interrupted him by observing with severity, "That a vague and rhapsodical declamation was no defence; that a definite charge had been read in his ears, and that they were prepared to listen to his vindication; that on the wild expressions he had used, no construction could be put that could tend either to the information of his examiners, or his own exculpation." This was said with the benevolent intention of dissipating the injurious inferences that might be drawn from the careless vehemence with which he poured out his thoughts.

"Vindication," repeated Montorio, "from what? From charges you do not, you cannot believe—from charges of which my present situation is the fullest refutation. Who can believe such powers as they ascribe to me, to belong to a being whom they themselves hold in durance and dungeons? If I possess these powers, why do I not exercise them for my own preservation? If I can remove the barriers of nature, and sport with the opposition of the elements, why am I here? Have I more pleasure in terrifying a solitary peasant, than in extricating myself from persecution and danger? Why do I not mount in flames? Why do I not cleave your walls at this moment? Do these powers desert their possessor at his hour of need alone? No, it is impossible you can be thus deceived; no habits of suspicion and bigotry could reduce minds to such a level in judgment; it is impossible such weak instruments could impel you to distrust the experience of your senses, the course of nature, and what should be more unquestioned than either—the honour of a noble house! No, your informers and your information are of a higher class; 'tis no dream of a lying menial that has brought me here." "You are conscious then of some more important causes which the holy Office have had for their proceedings relative to you," said one of the inquisitors. "I did not say so," said the prisoner. "You implied it," said the inquisitor.

At this observation a new object rushed on Montorio's mind; that of turning his defence into an accusation. He found that it was impossible to contend against the evidence of his dark pursuits they were possessed of; all that could be done, was to make their confession fatal if possible, to the minister of evil who had betrayed and destroyed him. The terrors and dangers of the fate that probably awaited his confession, disappeared, when he thought of his enemy trembling before the same tribunal with himself; his visionary person and claims, either reduced to a definite and vulnerable substance, or analysed and dispersed to their original element. His natural vehemence, his curiosity, his despair of exclusive vindication, urged him together to this bold movement. The toils that invested him he could neither rend nor unravel; but with a lion-bound, he broke away and bore them with him. "I am conscious," said he, in a firm tone, "that other and more momentous information has thrown me into the prisons of the Inquisition; but I am also conscious, that he who supplied that information, is dyed a thousand fold more black and deep in its implications than I am. If there be guilt, he has been the framer, the prompter, the minister of it. Summon him here, if you can. Confront me with him. Let his business be unfolded with a solemn and deliberate hand. When we stand as criminals together; then will I speak, and tell a tale that shall amaze your souls. Till then, I shall only speak to arraign the justice of the procedure that treats a supposed offender as a criminal, and an actual one as innocent. He could not accuse me without condemning himself. Why is he not then here along with me? Can he alone, like the Messinean assassin, stab invisible and unpunished? Can he only shake off the viper of sorcery from his hand, and feel no hurt? Can he like the fabulous ferryman, convey souls to the infernal regions, yet never enter them himself?"

Angellini again interrupted him to assure him the conceptions he had formed of this character, were totally erroneous; that he was an innocent individual, who had not even a personal knowledge of Montorio, and whose only motive in giving information to the holy Office was a disinterested zeal for the Catholic faith. Montorio persisted on the other hand in the most emphatic assertions of his positive guilt. "He is a sorcerer," said he. "He is an ecclesiastic," replied Angellini. "He is a murderer," pursued Montorio. "He escaped with difficulty from the fangs of murder," said Angellini. "He is a fiend," repeated Montorio, gnashing his teeth, "and his office is to betray the souls of men." "His office," said Angellini seriously incensed, "has been to rescue a human soul from its betrayers." "Prove your charges," said the inquisitors, "prove that the person who informed against you, is obnoxious to the power of the holy Office, and here we pledge our faith, that he shall be cited to our tribunal." "Reverend fathers, he knows not what he says," said Angellini. "I know what I say, Signor," said Montorio, "and I also remember what I have said; I remember that I pledged myself to prove the guilt of your informer, in the event of your summoning him to your tribunal, and confronting him with me." "And on what information shall we cite him?" said the inquisitor.

Again Montorio was silent from confusion and fear. He found it necessary to criminate himself in order to the bare citation of the stranger. In the moment of his hesitation, Angellini again interposed. "Reverend fathers," said he, "here is some profound mistake. The prisoner is evidently ignorant of his real accuser. Permit me to relate the circumstances under which I received the information on which he was confined; they will perhaps remove his errors with regard to the person of the informer, and assist us to examine this intricate and mysterious affair." The inquisitors hesitated, till one of them reminded the rest, that by doing so they might discover the person against whom Montorio's invectives had been directed, and that the discovery might furnish further matter of cognizance to the holy Office. They therefore permitted Angellini to proceed in his narrative, to which Montorio listened with the breathless, fixed attention of one whose existence and vital determinations were suspended on the words of the speaker.

"It is now near a month," said Angellini, "since I was informed, one evening, that a stranger desired to speak with me on affairs relative to the holy Office. I desired him to be admitted. He was in the habit of an ecclesiastic. His figure and face were remarkable; but of his voice, I never shall lose the memory of the sound as long as I retain my senses. The singular degree of awe, almost amounting to repugnance, which his appearance inspired, was removed by his entering on the subject of his business, with unusual promptness and intelligence.

His narrative was extraordinary, but perfectly probable. He mentioned that he had been travelling from Padua to Naples; that his direction was to a convent in the western suburbs of that city, where he had not arrived till the approach of night. That his ignorance of the avenues of the deserted part of the city, combined with the lateness of the hour, at length suggested some apprehensions of his personal danger, which were confirmed when he saw from the projections of a ruinous building which he was to pass, two figures occasionally leaning and retreating when they perceived themselves observed. He could distinguish indeed that their habit and appearance was utterly unlike that of assassins, or indeed any class of men he had before seen in any part of Italy; but he knew not what disguises assassins might assume in Naples, and he felt it was probable there could be no common motive for their partial and hurried concealments. In the first impulse of his fear, he dismounted from his mule, and ran to shelter himself under a dismantled arch, which he did not conceive to be connected with the building from whence they had appeared to start. He had hardly done so, when he heard their steps approaching his retreat, and saw their tall shadows projecting from the entrance of the arch. He rushed desperately forward. In the tumult of fear and flight. Little accuracy was to be expected from him with regard to the passages he traversed, or the objects he witnessed; otherwise perhaps deserving the minutest attention.

His perceptions, he confessed, were only exercised to discover whether the steps of his pursuers were advancing on him. He perceived they were, and sprung headlong forward with the rapidity of one who fears no danger, but the obstruction of his flight. The steps of his pursuers gained on him. He perceived he had reached a flight of steps, and he rushed down them without any other object than of escape. Occupied only by his fears, he did not perceive the vast depth he had descended to, till he was in utter darkness. Terrors of equal magnitude now beset him, and he endeavoured to retrace his former steps, or discover some means of relief and assistance. While he was thus employed, he perceived a faint light in the vast distance of the darkness that surrounded him. He approached it through many obstructions he described with the strength of personal suffering, but which I need not repeat, and at length discovered that it twinkled through an iron grating in the wall of the passage he was traversing; he applied his eye to it, and beheld within, figures employed in actions which suspended every faculty of mind and sense, as he gazed on them. In the first impulse of horror he would have fled; but after a moment's delay, found himself rivetted to the spot by the very feelings that at first would have hurried him away. He remained long enough to observe the agents and their strange deeds, with that tenacious and indelible feeling which the very reluctance of horror impresses on the mind. He reported them to me with strong, but evidently real emotion, such as none but the recollection of actual objects could inspire. In consequence of this information, I proceeded with regard to the holy Office, and to its prisoner, as you have seen; I also communicated the mode of his escape from the vault, and his extraordinary reasons for laying his information before me, instead of the tribunal at Naples." "They were extraordinary," said the inquisitor, "but fully justified by the event."

Montorio had listened with the profoundest attention; but remained unconvinced. A secret mistrust of the stranger's agency, bound up his mind as if by a spell of incredulity. He addressed himself to Angellini. "I have little," said he with solemnity, "to offer in support of what I say, but my own convictions. I cannot be supposed armed with a regular refutation of positions I now hear for the first time; yet there are no words of sufficient power to express the firmness of my belief, that the circumstances you have just now mentioned, are only a new device of subtlety and malevolence, which I have found exhaustless; they are incongruous, fictitious, impossible." He paused to search his memory for some circumstance to substantiate his assertions. After a long silence, he said, with a severe smile, "You will form a judgment of the strength of my convictions, and my earnestness to impress them on you, from my being led to confess circumstances no other power could have extorted from me. The vault of which your informer pretended he commanded a view, had neither grating nor aperture; it was on every

CHARLES MATURIN

side inaccessible but to those who visibly entered it. In this point I feel I cannot be mistaken. No lapse of time, no intervention of other circumstances, however numerous or important, can efface from my memory, the few and minute notices it retains of that place. I have counted every stone in its walls, the curve of the arches, the depth of the shadow, the peculiar hue of its blackness, are written on my soul for ever. You see I do not deceive you, when I venture on defences so distinct. Reverend fathers, it is impossible that any being could have approached from without the place, your informer specified. He must have been the instrument of another's ministry—the channel of higher intelligence. I again repeat my adjuration, that you will compel him, from whom you received your information, to attend the tribunal of the holy Office, and confront him with me personally."

"This incredulity is affected," said an inquisitor, "we have more than the bare assertion of the witness for his extraordinary information; we have proof, such as none but the most intimate knowledge could supply, and such as artificial obduracy will resist in vain. Must we remind you of the mysterious inscription over the portals of the vault? Could that have been recognized and reported to the Inquisition by one who had never read it?" Montorio trembled; he thought he felt the toils of evidence tightening around him. "Must we remind you," said the inquisitor, in a thrilling voice, "of the bloody dagger that is for ever shaken before your eyes, and of the deed its sight recals and punishes—that deed unseen, unspeakable, wrought in central darkness, lapped in the very skirts of the nether world. I see you tremble—I tremble myself." He sunk back in the seat from which he had risen in the force of speaking; the attendants hid their faces with visible shudderings of fear. Montorio, in broken and inaudible tones, said, with frequent intervals, "I cease to feel for myself—to speak for myself; I have no longer any power of defence or of resistance. I speak without hope of belief or conviction; but I speak it with the solemn firmness of despair. I am a prisoner without a crime; I am a visionary without intercourse with forbidden things; I am a murderer without the stain of human blood."

He stopped suddenly. A hollow, broken sound succeeded. The inquisitor motioned to the attendants to lower the lamp that was suspended from the ceiling, that they might observe the changes in his countenance. It was then perceived that he had fainted. He was conveyed to his apartment; but the inquisitors entered into a consultation that continued till midnight. When Montorio recovered, the operations of his mind were decisive and rapid. Danger was no longer indefinite or avoidable; but in proportion as it became certain, his terrors were diminished, or exchanged for other feelings. The temper of his soul became at once rigid and vindictive. His sensibility of suffering was appeased by the hope of teaching another to suffer; and the horrors of the Inquisition only served to exalt his prospect of revenge.

On the next appearance of his guard, he signified his wish to be supplied with pen and ink, and to be undisturbed for some time, in order to prepare some documents for the inspection of the holy Office. His request was complied with, and he devoted himself for somedays to writing; but as he proceeded in his task, he was often checked by suggestions of repentance. The goaded and unnatural vehemence of mind that prompts to extraordinary movements, soon fails us, if their execution be not instant. This occupied some time; and during that time he often debated the possibility of some intermediate measure, often lamented the necessary violence of motion the emergency compelled him to; and was only urged to the completion of his task, by the recollection that he was pledged to its performance, and that the danger of confession in his case, admitted neither degree nor diminution.

On the third day it was completed; and he then put it into the hands of Angellini, who received it with a look of mournful solicitude, which his judicial gravity vainly resisted. Montorio gave it to him in silence, a silence which the other's deep feeling did not permit him to break. He was quitting the room, when Montorio waved his hand. Angellini heard the sound this slight motion occasioned; and turning eagerly round said, "You wish then to speak with me?" "No, Signor," said his prisoner, "no; I have now neither wishes nor fears. Let the holy Office be acquainted as soon as possible with the contents of these manuscripts." "And for me," said Angellini, with emotion, "you have no charge for me?" "Yes," said Montorio, after a pause, "to reflect on the horrors of that fate, to fly from which I have plunged into the dungeons of the Inquisition."

Angellini quitted the room. For an hour after he left it, the prisoner remained fixed in his seat, his clasped hands resting on his knees, his head declined, his eyes fixed on the ground, which he did not see. The sun set, and it grew dark; but he perceived no change of light or object.

At length, he felt a step in the room, and dimly descried a figure which stood opposite him. He saw not whether it was human or not; nor did he raise his eyes till he heard, addressing him, the voice of the *Stranger*. "You now," said he, repeating the words he had uttered at

Bellano, "behold me in another form, not as a forteller, but as a witness of your fate." Montorio beheld him steadfastly. He was now in the dress of a monk, which he wore with the ease and freedom of an habitual dress. "It is he," said the unhappy young man, speaking to himself; "it is he, but I will not see him." "You can no longer avoid it," said the stranger; "here are no resources to palliate the deceptions of sense. We are alone; nor is there any human cause or object to hide from either of us the real character and purposes of the other." "I will not look up till he is past," said Montorio, still speaking inwardly; "this terrible shadow will soon disperse, and I shall be a whole man again." "Look up, look up," said the stranger; "it is no shadow that stands before you; it is the form of him who has followed you so long, who must follow you for a term still; of him, from whom it is folly to fly; for your flight has only been into the clutches of the Inquisition." "Better a thousand-fold than into yours; better into the hands of man than of you, whom I will not call a demon, lest I should wrong superior depravity. Yes, I have fled hither; and therefore it is, that I can bear to behold and confer with you. Look round, and tell me what has an inmate of this mansion further to fear. I stand upon the utmost verge of nature. I shall see or hear my own species no more. I am a prisoner of the Inquisition for life. I have reached the bare and desolate crag, and the wave of vengeance bursts at my feet. Here I am safe in despair. You did not calculate this last giant-spring. You did not know that life is easily thrown away by him to whom it has lost its worth. You did not know that a soul can wrestle with its chains of darkness; aye, and do deeds with them beyond the pitch of mortal implements. Fool! how I have mocked and baffled you! how I triumph over you this moment! How did you enter this prison? By all that is good I am rejoiced to see you. Hark! I have intelligence for you. I have told every thing to the Inquisition—every thing, by my immortal soul! I am a prisoner for life; I know it; I triumph in it. Better their chains for ever, than yours, in thought, for a moment." "What do you call my chains? I never forged or bound them on you. I unfolded their connexion as far as was visible to humanity. Mine is a hopeless task—to reconcile nature to suffering, and pride to shame. But weariness will not excuse it. I, whom you think the sole and voluntary mover in this business, I am myself impelled by a hand whose urgings never remit or rest. The central seat of our mysteries at Naples; the solitary heights of the mountain; the vault at Bellano; this chamber in the prison of the Inquisition—are all but parts of a progress that is incessant and interminable; though it mostly holds a direction invisible to the human eye. I know your folly in disclosing your secret to the Inquisition. I knew it before I entered these walls. What have you gained by it? The publication of your guilt, the certainty of your condemnation. Were all the armies of the earth summoned together to hold you from the commission of that deed, it were in vain. They would only witness what they could not prevent. To resist the agency of the invisible world, you might as well employ a broken reed, a gossamer, a mote, as the whole pith and puissance of the earth. To conduct your steps in silence and without interruption, I threw over them a veil of mystery. You have rent it open; and what have you gained by it?—Exposure without commiseration, and confidence without assistance."

"I will not," said Montorio, "be pushed from the proof by words. The trial-hour is arrived; the power with which we are to contend is extrinsic and impartial. I have strove darkling with you; but the light approaches at last. These walls are indeed the last retreat man would fly to; but they will protect me. I feel here a gloomy strength, a defiance of those devices by which you have deluded my senses. You cannot crumble these towers into dust; you cannot fight with an institution whose source is in the power and vitals of the church." "It were better for you that I should; but your ingratitude and obduracy deserve that I should resign you to your fate." "What is it you mean?" said Montorio. "Do you then know so little of the Inquisition? Do you imagine that they can believe the tale you have told—that they will not consider *it* as an attempt to delude and mock them, and you as an audacious and obdurate enemy of the faith. No; should you disclose to them all you saw and all you imagined, they would never believe your confession, full or sincere; they will look on you as a hoard of dark secrets, which can never be exhausted; and they will for ever continue urging you to confessions when you have no longer any thing to disclose. Shelter in the Inquisition! Yes, they will give you shelter safe and deep; your bed will be burning coals, and you will be pillowed on pincers and searing irons. No declarations of ignorance will avail you; and no resources of fiction will shield you from their endless persecution." "There is yet a resource," said Montorio; "I can die." "Die! you know little of the Inquisition. Oh, they have horrid arts of protracting life; of quickening the pulse that vibrates with pain; of making life and sufferance flow on together like two artificial streams of which they hold the sources. They inquire to what precise limit nature can support their inflictions, and precisely to that limit they pursue them; and then remand their prisoner to his cell, to renew his strength for the next conflict. You will waste away in their dungeons, like the lamp that glares on your agonies. You will never, never escape their hands, till you are unconsciously enlarged to do the deed you fled into them to avoid in vain." "This impossible," said Montorio; "the grave will sooner yield up its dead than the Inquisition her victims. Here, I am safe. It is a dreadful immunity; but I welcome it. I will stretch myself on my burning bed. I will gripe the irons of torture, for they will protect me from you. To preserve my life and innocence is perhaps impossible; but it is at least possible to purchase innocence with loss of life." "You are deceived. It is indeed in your power to aggravate your sufferings by fruitless resistance; but not to remove their cause. The deed you are fated to do, you may delay, but cannot decline. Respiration is not more necessary to existence, or consciousness to thought. You might as well contend to reverse the past, as to resist the future. Your struggles may work the torrent into foam, but cannot repel its course. The dungeons of the Inquisition, and the summit of a mountain afford you equal shelter. For proofs of the power with which I, the weakest minister of your fate, am armed, I can, at this moment, bid those bars of iron dissolve. I can lead you forth through every passage of your prison, under the eyes of your guard, in the very presence of the Inquisitors. Will you be wise? Is your arm strong? Is your heart set and bound up? Will you do the deed tonight? Within an hour you shall be on the spot; your path so secret, a leaf shall not rustle beneath your feet; your blow so certain, no groan shall follow it. Shall this be the hour—the hour of enlargement—aye, and the hour of fame. A pestilence, an earthquake, a volcano live in the histories of men, when sunny days, and drowsy prosperity are forgotten."

His manner, as he spoke, changed beyond all power of description. It was bold, animating, daring; but mixed with a wildness that appalled, with a demon-greatness of wickedness and strength that exalted and terrified. He placed his hearer on the extreme point of a precipice, shook him over the abyss, and laughed at his shudderings. Montorio looked at him for a moment with a fixed but speechless eye, and then said inwardly, "If my passage be only thither, there is a shorter way."

As he spoke, he sprung up with a violence neither to be foreseen nor resisted; and, rushing past the stranger, dashed himself against the massive and studded barrings of his iron door. He fell to the ground. The stranger raised him, and perceived he breathed no longer. He bent over him. He received in his hands the blood that gushed from Montorio's forehead and mouth; and, holding it out, murmured, "Drink, drink, if thou hast any mouth; but do not haunt me with those famished eyes. Yes, yes, anon I shall sup with thee, and we will feast it well."

As he spoke, his eye fixed on a remote spot in the darkness; and he shrieked in agony, "Oh, hide, hide the scourge—thou seest I am about it."

XVIII

The evening was dark and gloomy, Angellini and the principal inquisitor were seated over a dim fire of wood embers, in a remote part of that vast structure, it was a lone detached turret, against which the dark waves of the autumnal sea were tossing. They talked of disastrous tales, of events known only to the agents of the Inquisition, such as made their prisons seem the abode of more crimes and miseries than the day ever looked on, when the inquisitor requested Angellini again to repeat to him the extraordinary circumstances of the confession of Montorio. "I have not," said Angellini "all the papers in this closet, but *one single perusal* of them has made so deep an impression on me, that I can easily continue the narrative, where the manuscript is deficient." They examined and secured the doors, and Angellini depressing his voice, proceeded thus:—

IT WAS ABOUT THE MIDDLE of last summer, that Count Ippolito was returning from an evening excursion on the shore of Naples. He arrived at his palace, and was about to enter the portico, when a stranger, whose figure and aspect were concealed by the swiftness of his motion, said to him in a low voice, "Signor, has your *nativity ever been calculated?*" Ippolito started,—the inquisitor was out of sight. The servants declared they had seen no form, and heard no voice. Most would have regarded or remembered this circumstance, as merely exciting temporary surprise or curiosity; but the words of the figure contained an appeal to Ippolito's favourite science, and that appeal was irresistible. That evening he was engaged to an assembly at the Alberotti palace; the images of expected gaiety, had almost banished other musings, and he was ascending the steps of the palace, when he was entangled in a dispute between two cavaliers. In the crowd, he observed a person who stood without any motion or share in the disturbance. Ippolito's eye was fixed on him by this circumstance, and a moment's glance of his quick eye discovered the person who had that night addressed him. He turned eagerly on him; but the stranger, anticipating the movement, turned on *him*, whispered, "Signor, remember my question," and was lost in the crowd. At the assembly, Montorio was absent and dejected— he quitted it early, and returned home. The door of the carriage, in which Montorio was leaning back musingly, was thrown open by the servants, who were bowing with Italian obsequiousness as they waited for him to alight, when a face was suddenly thrust in at the opposite side, and that voice, of which the first sound could never be forgotten, repeated, "Signor, answer my question." Then Ippolito, alarmed and incensed, sprung from his carriage, and calling to his domestics, endeavoured to pursue his tormentor. Every direction was explored in vain. The unknown appeared to have communion with the powers of earth or air, and to be aided by them in his movements. Montorio, on his return to the palace, gave signs of that perturbation and alarm which had so *terrified his page,* who had not accompanied him.—(Of this young person, Montorio speaks with strong affection; what may be his endowments and virtues, I know not; but their friendship is as tender as that of brothers, and among his own calamities, Montorio enumerates the distress of his page for his disastrous fate.)

His perturbation, however, proceeded not from fear, but from disappointment and curiosity; disappointment, which had even mortified his pride; and curiosity, whose pampered appetite had met its first repulse. That day was spent in vain search, at night he found the following billet on his table:—"Montorio, do you remember the person who questioned you last night? are you interested in the inquiry he made? would you venture to know and to explore it? Then meet him, but meet him without mistrust or futile preparations, in the church of San Piero, in the north aisle, behind the fourth pillar from the confessional, when vespers are over, and the congregation dispersing. You may see him if you will; you may confer with him if you dare." The letter was anonymous, and the hand unknown. Whether Montorio would have neglected the appeal it contained to his curiosity, that, in the last line, to his courage, was peremptory; and he repaired to vespers with the mingled satisfaction of feeding his curiosity, and exerting his fortitude. The church was lonely and remote—he dismissed his attendants, and paced the aisle almost in solitude,—the service was nearly over;—through a narrow door he caught a view of the service, and of the priests as they bowed round the high altar with the imposing solemnity of public worship:—a pause followed—and the organ burst forth, accompanied with the loud and deep chauntings of the monks, and mingled with them came the toll of a bell that called them to service in another part of the convent. Ippolito listened, touched and subdued; but endeavouring to shake off an impression which he felt to be merely local, he examined the congregation as they dispersed, and from time to time turned to the pillar, toward which he momently expected some one of them to glide. No one approached it, all had departed, and to the noise and stir of their departure had succeeded the solitary passing steps of the monks and attendants of the church. Vexed and impatient, Ippolito again turned to the pillar, and thought he could observe a deeper shade than it had before projected round its base. He advanced—a figure stood in the shade erect, motionless, and almost appearing a part of the column. Amid the joy of this discovery, Montorio could not avoid recollecting, that no person, since his entering the aisle, had visibly approached that spot. He advanced, purposing to address the figure, but its unmoved and utter stillness repelled him. He passed close to it, and fixed his eyes intently on it;—the habit was that of a man, but dark and confused, the stature tall, the face concealed. Montorio passed and repassed him, pausing each time, but without obtaining the smallest notice, or indication that the figure he beheld had sense or life. Convinced, at length, that his silence was stubborn and affected, Montorio making a full stop, addressed him in a low, but resolute tone—"You have summoned me here; what would you have with me?"—"Nothing," replied the figure, in those tones with which, though heard so lately, he was well acquainted. "Why, then, was I brought here? Do you know aught concerning me?"—"Every thing," replied the stranger. "Speak, then," said Montorio, "I am here," and he rested on his sword. "I have not power—I am now as other men,—I am weak as a broken wave; but the hour cometh that has in it the force of unutterable things, and I await it awed and still."—"Why was I then brought here?"—"Like me you must await that hour, like me you must be borne on by it in dreadful submission,—when it arrives you shall hear from me."—"I will not leave this church unsatisfied," said Montorio impetuously; "whatever you are, or wizard, or impostor, I will know before I quit you; remember the mockery of last night." The figure glided away—Ippolito eagerly followed. It entered the confessional, where the prior sat engaged in the holy service of the place, and he determined even to wait its termination, in order to see the stranger again. This resolution his impatience rendered intolerably tedious; he remained in the aisle, counting the moments, and expecting at the lapse of each to see the unknown issue from the confessional, when with astonishment he beheld departing from it only the prior, who quitted it with the air of a man engaged in solitary prayer. Montorio, in astonishment, now addressed one of the monks who was passing: "Is it usual," said he, "for penitents to remain in the confessional of S. Piero, after the confessor has quitted it?" The monk beheld him with surprise. "I have but now," he eagerly explained, "beheld a person enter the confessional; I waited the end of his confession, and now I see the prior quit his seat alone."—"You are deceived, Cavalier," said the monk; "I myself saw the last penitent this evening quit the confessional, and afterwards the church: it is the devout custom of our superior to continue some time in solitary prayer, after his penitents depart, and this necessarily implies he must have been alone." Montorio, hopeless of giving conviction to the mind of another, while his own was oppressed by perplexity, yet endeavoured to explain what he was assured he had beheld, when the prior, whose attention, as he passed though the aisle, was arrested by his gestures and exclamations, paused, and said, "There is no penitent in the confessional, Cavalier, nor has been since the conclusion of mass."—"Reverend Father, pardon my impatience," replied Montorio, "I have reasons for examining this affair—reasons peculiar and important. Immersed as you were in the consideration of divine things, you might not have heard the entrance of him who is now lurking in the confessional; permit it but to be examined, and I shall depart happy, if even convinced and pardoned for my misconceptions."—"I should not hesitate to reject your petition," said the prior, "if I thought any person was concealed there, for penitence should be as sacred as devotion; but I comply, because I know there is not." The door of the inclosure, where the penitent kneels, was then thrown open, and it was empty. Montorio, after some apologies, which his confusion rendered inarticulate, retired, and passed the rest of the evening in fruitless attempts to hide his solicitude from himself by dissipation; he returned home, perplexed and disappointed: but his visitor had anticipated him. The following letter was on his table:

"Thou wast not prepared, nor was I, for this night's meeting. But why seek to pierce my retreat? When I would be, I am invisible, and where I would be, I am present. I mock at the means and power of man; I am alone in the world, yet I move in its paths, and mix in its agency. Again, I walk with man side by side, day after day; yet I am in utter solitude, for no man knows me; my presence is not seen, but felt; my motion casts no shadow, but the substance is there. From detection and pursuit, I stand aloof in dreadful immunity; pursue me not, therefore, but meet me, when summoned, and when we meet, ask not, but listen. Tomorrow, at midnight, there will be a funeral in the church of the convent S. Antonio; be there, and I will appear to thee. Dost thou tremble at the taper and the bell, the corpse and the shroud? If thou canst meet me, fear not to meet the dead."

Ippolito, by this letter, was fully confirmed in his pursuit of this strange being; all the irregular desires which had fed his fancy with temporary food, were now exchanged for a distinct and definite object, whose pursuit interested more feelings than those of curiosity, and whose attainment promised more than their gratification. At midnight he went to the church of S. Antonio; it was the funeral of a person of rank, many of the laity attended with ecclesiastics. The melancholy pomp of midnight worship was deepened by every circumstance which the genius of our church, and the policy of her ministry, apply so successfully to the enthralment of weak, and the local captivation of even strong minds. The bells tolled at measured intervals; the masses performed at the different altars, mixed their deeper tones with the audible and fervent aspirations of the devotees; the tapers poured a pale and steady light on the tonsured heads, the dark drapery, and the sepulchral faces of the monks; and here and there disclosed a ghostly figure, that knelt and wept before their patron's shrine, while the torches poured a blaze, yellow, and broad, and bickering, on the stronger features of the structure; the dark recesses of the cloisters, the dim imagery of the roof, windows, whose burnished picturings blazed and disappeared in the waving light, and walls obscurely traced with flourishes and inscriptions, the achievements of forgotten worth, and the memorials of departed superstition. Though there was a crowd, no one felt the cheering effect of human presence, each was to himself, solitary and subdued; all communication was in whispers, and even that was involuntarily suspended at the low, tremulous tones of the organ, and the first, faint, distant chaunt of the monks, that rose with it, a flow of solemn and undistinguished sound.

Ippolito, in a remote part of the church, stood with recollected feeling, which the general awe deepened, but did not divide. It was his fate at these meetings to be suddenly encountered by him he was watching to see; for, as he looked around him, he felt his cloak touched by a person, who passed on without speaking. Montorio, with momentary conviction of the identity of the person, followed him. They quitted the church, and traversed many aisles and passages of the convent, with which his silent conductor seemed perfectly acquainted; they seemed to have at length got beyond the reach and sound of the human inmates of those walls; their single and measured steps had succeeded to the deep murmur of the church, and to its illuminated walls the pale and solitary lamp that partly lit the passage, which to Ippolito seemed endless. They now descended several steps, and reached a door, low, and apparently leading to some subterraneous apartment. It opened at the stranger's touch; but Ippolito half receded when he saw the dark stairs beneath, that dimly lit, and, winding beyond his sight, seemed to hold communication with the receptacles of the dead. The stranger beckoned—Ippolito paused;—the stranger beckoned again—then Ippolito spoke with firmness:—"Whoever you are, wherever you are leading, do not tempt inevitable danger: fraud I will detect, and force I can resist; my arm is as strong as yours, and my sword is by my side." The stranger turned, and, for the first time, partially uncovering his face, fixed on Montorio a look of melancholy conviction, of which, as of all his looks and movements, the effect was resistless; it seemed to convey a depth of knowledge, and compassion for some foreseen and inevitable evil, such as could be attained or communicated by no creature of limited and earthly powers. Montorio, silently subdued by that look, followed him down the descent, with an obscure but intimate sense of influence that could not be repelled, and of evil that could not be averted: it led to the vaults of the convent. They wandered for some time among those dreary passages in silence, till they saw a stronger light in the vault than what issued from the damp and misty lamps which twinkled through shade and vapour; it proceeded from torches, which burned in a new opened vault, opened for him whose funeral was celebrated that night; around it stood some assistants, who were waiting for the corpse, and on whose dark habits and rugged visages the torches threw a yellow and smoky glare, that terrified imagination to find a resemblance for. The stranger started from their view, and lighting some concealed preparation at a lamp which hung from the low arch, entered another passage, which, but for that faint light, was utterly dark. Montorio, who had no longer the power of retreating, followed,—the stranger turned;—his aspect was melancholy, but not ghastly; his voice hollow, but not terrible:—he paused;—the echoes of a clock, that struck one, were heard distinctly from the cloisters above. "It is the hour," said the stranger, "and dost thou dread to meet it?" Montorio, whose courage was inflamed by impatience, motioned onward;—they proceeded;—the stranger turned again, and something like human feeling was in his melancholy eye. "Yonder is thy fate, and dost thou shrink to behold it?"

CHARLES MATURIN

The noble disdain that flushed from Ippolito's eyes was his only answer. They turned a dark angle in the vault, and his conductor, in muffling the lamp he carried, let its light fall on a bier, where lay the body of a man, suspected of murder, but who had died in prison under the terrors of his expected fate. Montorio approached; the event and the person had been known to him; he looked up—he read a dreadful interpretation in the gesture and expression of his companion, who stood over the bier, embodying in his look all we conceive of those instruments, who are said to prompt the crimes they predict; to realize uncertain evil by the suggestions of supposed necessity; to breathe the first thought of blood into the predestined murderer, and lead the devoted mind, through the horrors of anticipated guilt, to the daring abandonment, the convulsive energy, the high wound and horrid pitch of determined distraction. Montorio shivered; the influence of his habitual pursuit became in one moment serious and painful, he endeavoured to wrest his mind from its hold; he could not; and while he yet struggled to reason himself out of involuntary oppression, the light disappeared, and its mysterious bearer was seen no more. Left in darkness and among the dead, a new object of fear succeeded; he called to his companion, he stretched out his arms in the direction where he had stood, and recollecting the dimensions of that part of the vault, he felt with the most accurate search every quarter that his hands or his sword could reach,—in vain; he encountered no object, he heard no sound, and was only recalled from his dream of pursuit by the entrance of the attendants with the corpse, into another part of the vault; the light directed him to them, and he eagerly inquired if his companion had been seen by any of them, adding the closest description that fear and haste permitted him to give. The men stared with astonishment; and on his urging the inquiry, averred with one voice that no human being had that night visibly entered the vault but themselves. "Did he render me, as well as himself, invisible?" thought Montorio, as he returned amazed and unsatisfied.

A letter, in the hand writing he now well knew, was again left in his apartment. "Your probation is over; you are without fear and without weakness; may command my power and knowledge to their extent, beyond the reach of nature and thought, beyond the dream of enthusiasm, even in the wild and wishing hour you may command them. *May*, have I said? alas! you *must* command them. Mine is no voluntary service. Oh, that worlds might purchase my exemption! But they cannot; and when worlds shall end, my task will have but begun.

As little voluntary is the spirit of inquiry that now impels you, and whose impulses you believe to be casual and free. Would you know more? I have no longer a right to conceal aught from you; then be in the west colonnade of the church of S. Piero, with no arms but fortitude, no companion but midnight; and when the bell shall toll, I will stand beside thee." In the intervals of these summonses, Montorio had often inquired into the means by which they were conveyed into his room; the domestics, on examining them, declared no such had been left at the palace, or given to them for their master; but when dismissed, after a fruitless inquiry, they talked much among themselves of a person that was frequently seen in their master's apartment, and who, it was said, disappeared when any one entered it. By this account, if he was more perplexed, he was yet more excited, and he awaited with impatience the appointed hour; it arrived—he hastened to the church of S. Piero; it was a clear and lovely night, the moon fleckered the columns with streaks of silver, and gave a more thin and pointed brightness to the wrought edges and tracery of the pediments and friezes. Montorio at every turn examined his watch, and with a beating heart and suppressed breath, perceived it wanted but a moment of twelve.—Now it struck, and the stranger stood beside him. "Are you prepared?" said he, in a low but firm tone. "It is Ippolito di Montorio to whom you speak, there needs no other answer," said Montorio proudly. "Youth," said the stranger, lay aside these weapons of fleshly warfare; where you are called to contend, pride of soul and force of arm avail not; lay them aside, with the sword and the dagger, the strength of flesh, and the arms of mortality; take with you only fortitude, that will shut out light without a sigh, and firmness that will bear to behold what it must bear to undergo." A voice issuing from the grave could not have delivered this monition in more chilling tones; Montorio felt their influence in every nerve, and followed his conductor with an awe which preserved his curiosity from levity, and divested his expectation of impatience.

They went on with silent speed, but the stranger sometimes paused, and looked upward, and Montorio once thought he beheld a tear in his eye as he raised it. They reached a remote and unfrequented part of the city; they stopped; the stranger seemed shaken with many emotions, there was no local cause for them; the quiet loneliness of the place; the moon, that seemed stationary for very brightness; the sea, whose checkered and sparkling waters just rose to the eye, and whose murmurs rose and fell with lulling measure, all seemed to speak peace to the spirit

CHARLES MATURIN

that had one peaceful element. "Oh, youth!" said the stranger, "the hour is come; thou, or I, may shun it no longer; and these struggles, these cold drops of inward agony, are for thee. The hour is come; and amidst a power that rules or reverses nature, I am as a worm of the dust, a thing of nought, confounded and dismayed. Oh, youth! it is for thee I have prayed that this task might not be mine; but he, whose hand hath made the thunder, will consign it to whom he will, and he must wield it, though its fires blast him."—"By whatever power you act," said Ippolito, "you have excited in me wonder and amazement; hasten, therefore, that I may know whether I am not, as often, the dupe of a vicious sensibility of the marvellous, or whether these impressions are, indeed, the movements and intimations of my fate." The stranger produced a bandage—"With this," said he, "your eyes must be bound; and take with it a caution, whatever you may see or hear, be silent, be motionless, and be fearless." Montorio suffered him to fasten the bandage, and was then conducted by him through many ways, of which he in vain tasked himself to remember the direction. They now ceased to tread on the pavement, and Montorio felt, from the change of air, that they were in some building; in a short time they began to descend steps; as they descended, the air changed again, but it was the chillness of subterranean damps; the echoes were dull and protracted, and no longer mixed with those sounds of life which they had heard in the open air. The descent seemed to be endless. Ippolito in vain tried to appease the irksomeness of involuntary blindness, and perhaps other unwelcome feelings, by reckoning the steps. The echoes became more hollow, the damps more dewy, and Montorio felt that even the misty and impalpable light that the bandage had not utterly denied him, was now obscured by intense darkness. He had often spoke, but received no answer, and now grew weary of the echoes of his own voice, unmixed as they were with any other sound, and giving an idea of utter solitude, which he was almost glad to recur to the pressure of his arm, and the sound of his conductor's steps, to repel. An hour had now elapsed since they left the haunts of men, and Montorio almost imagined this passage was intended to penetrate below the bottom of ocean, when he felt himself checked by the hand which led him. A sound then succeeded, which was so multiplied by the echoes of the place, that its distinctness was lost, and he found himself in a moment descending, with a swiftness so rapid, so breathless, so astounding, that he sickened with very giddiness, and gasped for the recovery of sense;—the motion ceased—he knew not how he had descended: he was again led forward; many sounds met him in his passage; some descended from above, and some brushed near him; blasts of different airs crossed him, some so hot, they felt like floods of flame, some so cold, he shivered in their parching blight. A sound, as of the ocean in its strength, was then heard; it came nearer and louder, and Ippolito almost expected to feel its waters bearing up his feet. All sound and motion then ceased, and he felt himself slowly invested in a garb, of which the form seemed to be unlike any usually worn; his hands were unrestrained; he examined the garb with them— it was the garb of the dead. But this was no time for resistance, and he believed his only means of safety was the observance of the stranger's caution: prudence was for once combined with his courage, and he remained silent. A voice then, deep and distant, repeated the service of the dead; the responses were echoed by multiplied myriads of voices. Montorio heard the solemn words pronounced over him, which no living man hears; he felt the shroud and the crucifix, he heard the bell and the requiem; he remembered his conductor's words, and expected to see the light no more, when his bandage was dissolved, and he was hurried forward.

What objects or circumstances he witnessed there, he has not told; whatever intimations are given of them, are casual and obscure, extorted by a sudden exclamation of pain, or involved in the train of other confessions, but from such intimations I believe them to be of a nature too horrible to be told; what I have learned has been principally collected from letters which passed between him and the stranger, and of which I have copies; at these meetings, it should appear no word was uttered, and whatever required explanation or discussion produced a letter, which was, as usual, left in his apartments, by means none could discover. Of the first of these the contents are as follows:

Letter from the Stranger

"WHAT CAN DISPEL YOUR SUSPICIONS? What can obviate your doubts? You have already had every assurance I am no pretender, that I seek neither aggrandizement nor influence, that I am unanxious the impressions you receive should convey any thing to you but a conviction of the genuineness of their cause and object; for myself this is superfluous, I need neither consciousness nor proof of my commission. Ages have I strove in vain to lose the dreadful sense of it; it is on you I seek to make

CHARLES MATURIN

a single impression—that I am the certain and commissioned organ of your fate, that I bear a power and office, which I must neither decline nor qualify, which you may neither resist nor change. Recollect how you have complained of the rapacity of former pretenders, wretches, whose mercenary ignorance blasphemes the awful name and objects of the other world, (whose visitation often and judicially punishes their presumption, by the infliction of madness and idiotcy, the natural extremes of a brain overwrought with gloomy and cumbrous contemplations,) and whose quaint fooleries are as easily detected as their needy avidity. What has been my pursuit of you? What have been my claims on you? The very dreadful instruments of our preparation, the form and circumstance of our meeting, are such as human hands could not collect without toil and pain, if you can indeed believe them to have been the collection of human hands; and what demands have been made, but on your acquiescence and conviction. Here is a proof, a native and intrinsic proof of the reality of my office and power, which no sober mind can well gainsay, that a number of beings should conspire to condemn themselves to toil, and pain, and horror, unexcited, unsolicited, unrewarded, merely to persecute and perplex another being, over whom they seek no other influence, and who can neither punish nor please them, is an outrage to the credulity of even a Montorio. Again, an impostor might perhaps stimulate your feelings by artificial and well-measured delay, but he would beware of protracting this beyond its due term of operation, of suffering solicitude to fret itself into impatience; but he whose power is beyond and unswayed by himself, must await its ebbs and its flows, the rush of its approach, and the lingerings of its suspension, in passive expectancy, hushed and still. Do you remember last night? Many times have you trodden that place, which only your own human feet have ever entered; before you had been even summoned there, I told you I could foreshew every event of your life, yet—even yet—I have not the power to declare it. How many nights have now witnessed those unuttered and terrible things, which once obtained a knowledge and potency for me, now inscrutably withheld. Last night, moved by the danger to which your impetuosity opposed you from my ministers, (whose services I command, though I cannot repress their power or malignity,) I had recourse to those deep and dreadful extremes, which I once believed no human cause could demand the use of, or no mortal witness; but in vain, the master-agent of our movements would not be tasked: the earthquake, the whirlwind, and the fire were there, but he was not there. I wrestled with these terrible engines of his coming, I writhed in convulsed and fervent agony, and were mine the life of nature, the struggles of last night had ended it. It was in vain you departed with rage and imprecations that you would return no more. Was this then voluntary and artificial? An agent, whose power and movements are his own, exerts them without producing any effect, but fruitless toil and angry disappointment!!! Is this credible? I collect these circumstances that they may certify to you, what the levity of your mind, and your experience of repeated imposition, tend to conceal, or render indifferent to you; that my power and commission are extrinsic, are involuntary, and are real."

To this, only part of Ippolito's answer appears: "Whatever was the complexion of my mind, when I formerly pursued similar objects, it is now totally changed; though ever grasping at the secrets of another state, and pursuing their attainment under every form and colour of probability, I recollect rather feeling towards them expectation than belief, rather seeking to discover, *if* they were really within mortal reach and capacity, than seeking them, *because* they were.

"I think I recollect seeking to these professors, and awaiting their fantastic exhibitions, in a mixed and not unpleasing state of suspension, where the awful solicitude, from which no mortal is exempt, was tempered by the natural jealousy of deception, by the experience of disappointment and imposition, and above all, by the native and inherent scepticism of *negative experience*, which is perhaps the only balance that renders the terrors of such expectation supportable, and even grateful. I was, therefore unconsciously prepared for every event of such meetings, and I attended them with a fortitude, in the cause of which many deceive themselves. I had curiosity to excite me in the pursuit, and possibly to support me, had it been successful; I had vigilance, taught by experience, to scrutinize into imposition, and I had a shade of levity over my mind, the offspring of natural and involuntary incredulity, which disposed me to laugh at detected folly and fraud, with the same facility with which I would have shuddered at the terrible discoveries the other event of the meeting would have prepared for me: above all, when I had received any impression from the strange objects which some of them were able to summon or to create, I examined and sifted it with a tenacity, of which probably the motive was curiosity, but of which the end was uniformly the discovery of deception, of the force of local emotion, or of the assemblage of fearful or unwonted imagery.

Thus, therefore, I continued to pursue it, hopeless of attaining success or certainty in the original object of my search, yet gratifying an appetite for the marvellous, which repeated indulgence had rendered restless, and fastidious, and insatiable, and of which the sensation resembled that which urges us to the theatre, where we gaze, delighted by vision and sound, but not deceived into reality.

From my first conference with you, the frame of my mind was totally altered; the severity, the simplicity, the high and remote modes of language and action I witnessed, struck me with a complicated feeling of fear and confidence, of wild joy and supernatural dread I cannot describe: all I saw was unlike all I had before seen. Instead of being mocked by fantastic jargon, I was restrained by solemn silence; instead of being plundered with vulgar rapacity, I was taught that all human influence, whether of force or of insinuation, was nugatory there; instead of commanding, I was commanded, and that by an influence viewless, and impassive, and unsearchable. Of all this, the effect has been the irritation of my feelings, almost to madness, the inflammation of my curiosity to a pitch and point, which I believe nothing but its very strength and vivid force enables me to endure. By all this terrible preparation, a weak mind might have been depressed and subjected, and have relinquished its object rather than encounter the horrors that invested it; but mine is an elastic one, and it rises with a force and spring proportioned to the pressure it has been urged by. I feel all subordinate desires and objects absorbed by one—the desire to obtain that long-withheld and mysterious something, which I seize with such a comprehensive grasp of expectancy, that it has no distinctness of form or name in my thoughts—the desire to know all you can disclose, or cause me to know. It utterly absorbs me; I cease to inquire into the truth or evidences of your commission or pretensions; you are anxious to press their examination on me—I am indifferent to them. Were it proved to me this moment that you were an impostor, that all I had witnessed was the very fooling of my fear, I would still pursue you with unabated anxiousness, to supply my feelings with that food for which their appetence is famishing and delirious. Talk no more of delays and proofs, and the cold exercise of my faculties; I tell you I am mad—mad, till I am gratified! By what means you have attained this influence, I know not; perhaps it is a part of that strange power you say is forced on you; but exert it no longer to torture—I am miserable—my day and night are one delirious dream; my burning eyes have not tasted sleep for many days; the images of the night are ever around me: often I smite my arms and breast, and rend out handfuls of my hair to deaden or distract that pain, whose gnawing and fiery keenness seems to survive all change of time, and place, and motion, to sting me in my broken sleep, and live through every hour of life. Have mercy on me! If you can do any thing, do it, and let me have ease. Montorio."

Many such letters appear to have passed between them, most of which contain repetitions of what I have now read: on the one side claims to some undescribed and mysterious power, of which all direct proof was, however, withheld, and on the other a continuance of complaint, and entreaty, and remonstrance. Whether relief was delayed, because it was out of the power of the stranger to bestow it, or suspended, because he judged suspension would answer his purpose better, it is certain that purpose was fully attained. Montorio's mind was wrought to an intense and desperate state of feeling; all thoughts, and passions, and objects were swallowed up by one; his whole day was passed in obscure expectation of the events of the night, the night in disappointment of that expectation, and the following day in the renewal of that dark and feverish hope, which, while it tormented his existence, seemed to constitute the very principle and spring of it. I have very imperfect documents of these melancholy times; but it should seem that one night Montorio contrived to signify to his conductor, that his mind was burdened with many things, which haste and confusion would prevent him from committing to paper; that he was anxious to discuss them in a personal conference; and that if the stranger owned the power he professed, he could indulge him with that conference under hours and circumstances that would prevent the possibility of intrusion or discovery. "I will go," answered the stranger, "because your importunity proceeds from a suspicion that I cannot comply with it. I will go, therefore, to convince you that no time or place have a power in them to repel me." Ippolito wondered mentally, for he felt this had been the real motive of his request.

On the following night, Ippolito had been detained unusually late by an engagement; he returned with the childish joy of a truant; his valet lit him to his apartment, but both started back on observing a stranger in the room, in an uncommon garb, who sat with his back to the entrance, and who did not rise on their approach. Montorio, immediately discovering his visitor, dismissed the terrified servant, and advanced, with some expressions, I suppose, of complacency, which his surprise rendered incoherent. "You have forgotten your appointment, Signor, but I have not neglected mine," said the stranger, with a smile somewhat grim. "I am glad you have not," said Montorio, "I have long wished to see you here."—"I am," answered the stranger, "a constant though unobserved visitor; nor would you, perhaps, be pleased to know how often I have trod this room, and drawn your curtains, and beheld you sleeping in that bed; nay, how often I have passed in the broad light of day, and almost touched you as I passed, and you beheld me not."— "Oh!" said Montorio, tossing with impatience, "is it ever to be thus? am I to be ever abused and mocked by a power that is extensive and resistless only to torment me? can you thus control nature, and yet not give an individual that intelligence which the meanest pretenders to your art will endeavour to give at the first conference?" "Because they are pretenders," said the stranger sternly; "their very facility proves it; your mind, its habits and faculties, have been so vitiated by marvellous indulgence, so outraged by lying inconsistency, that you cannot easily admit the bare forms of reality, the cold solemnity of truth; you have been accustomed to the jargon of astrology, the fooleries of the wizard, the phosphoric blaze, and the spectre of gauze; you can digest the idea of beings who can mount in cloud and fire, who can yoke the spirits of the blast, who can be served by the forms of the elements, and discover treasures that nature never owned: that such should lurk in the hovel of indigence, should depend on plundered credulity for their subsistence, should shrink from the cognizance of earthly power, and when detected, want a single friendly familiar to save them from ignominy and punishment; you can digest *this;* and therefore, to you, he that speaks with the simplicity of truth, must appear as one that mocketh." "I am, indeed, mocked," said Montorio impetuously, "mocked by my own timidity, by my own folly; but, by the living God, I will be mocked no more!" He started up, he grasped the stranger wildly—"Either satisfy me this moment; tell me who and what you are, for what purpose you have fastened on me to haunt and to madden me, or you never shall quit this apartment. By that tremendous name I invoked, I will never relax my hold till you have told me whom it is I speak to." "Who I am," said the stranger rising to the question, "who knows, and who can tell? Sometimes I do not know myself; yet often I am as other men, and do with them the deeds of common life. But when that hour cometh, when the power is on me—then" said he (and his visage lightened, and his frame dilated) "the torrent and the tempest shrink from me, the ocean in his force retires from me, the foundations fail from under me; then I ride on the horses of the night, I pass from region to region like the shadow, I tread the verge of being alone;—that is my term of punishment, and its control is terrible; then am I left motionless, wasted, annihilated, on the mountain top, in the desert, on the ocean; I feel the earthly air breathe on me again, I feel the beams that give light to man falling soft on me; then I begin to live again.—But I hear the feet of my taskers, and I spring onward before the moon has set."—"Unimaginable being," said Ippolito with strong emotion, "shall I worship thee as a deity, or shun thee as a fiend? What are those goblin shapes that are with you every night? and what is it ye do in the bowels of the earth?"—"Some of them are my agents, and some my punishers; we are a race of beings, of whose existing many have talked, many have read, and none believed; we can be only known by our properties, for our nature who shall tell? the meanest of us are employed in the mischiefs of creation, the meanest of us toil in the mountain and the mine, yell in the tempest, and lash and furrow the flood, edge the lightning points, and mix and watch the seeds of the pestilence; but we who are of a higher class, Oh! who shall tell the height of our punishment? It is ours to watch over a frame a million times more corrupt and distempered—the heart of man, and his life, and his actions. There is not a deed of blood, there is not a deed of horror, there is not a murderer, there is not a being whose fate and circumstances make his species shudder to hear or read, but it is ours to lead and to prompt, to harden and to inflame, to sear the conscience and to steel the arm."—"And is it for such a purpose I am thus haunted?" interrupted Montorio wildly, "and am I to be—what must I be? a murderer! a being whose fate shall make mankind shudder! Tell me," he exclaimed, seizing the stranger again, and almost shouting with vehemence, "only tell me, and I forgive you."—"What your fate will be," said the stranger, "I can only intimate from the eagerness and tumult of the preparation that accompanied its disclosure to me. I was," said he, fixing his eyes and planting his feet, "in the very central core of the earth when I received it, and I stood beside you at night."—"And yet you cannot disclose it, even now—" he paused a moment; "Does this delay intimate any thing beside your power of suspending your victims?"—"I dare not flatter you, I have ever found this supernatural delay precede the disclosure of something of uncommon horror—at least I recollect it to have been so in the case of your ancestor, Muzio di Montorio, who lived in the troubles of Massaniello."—"In the troubles of Massaniello, why they were 200 years ago!"—"They were."—"And you knew Muzio di Montorio, who lived at that time?"—"I did; my knowledge of circumstances, which could be known only to a contemporary, will prove it. He was a man proud and irritable; one of the Girola family had obstructed his success both in love and fortune; a deadly hate to this man fixed on Montorio's mind: from that moment it became my office to tend and observe him. I bore another form then; my prognostics of his fate, which were tempting and partial, rouzed his curiosity; I was with him day and night, as I am with you, but his fate it was not permitted me to tell expressly. Weary at length of suspended expectation, and disgusted with Naples, where the constant presence of his enemy occurred, he prepared to fly from Italy; but he could not fly from me: he thought he had, however, and proceeded with satisfaction. On the dreary hills between Pisa and Lucca, he was benighted at a small inn on the borders of a forest; he inquired if he could pass the night there, and was told all the rooms were occupied by the Count Girola and his train. Muttering curses on the name, he was preparing to pass the night in the forest, and brave the violence of an approaching storm, sooner than enter the roof of his foe, when the host recollecting himself, informed him he might have an apartment, for he had heard the Count say he would pass the night at a kinsman's of his, whose castle was about a mile distant, and where his train, after passing the night at the inn, not to incommode his kinsman, might join him in the morning. The image of his enemy, in a lonely forest, unattended, unprepared, flashed like lightning on the mind of Montorio. I was beside him at that moment. He bid his attendants halt at the inn, and plunged into the forest with blind fury. The storm came on; he saw not who rode behind him in it; he saw not what shape was in the ghastly light that shone round his horse, as the heavy sulphur clouds rolled over the forest. But I and others were near him—near!—we were above, around, within him. He lurked in a thicket, a dark, matted, briery thicket, where by the glancing of the lightning he saw a cross erected, in memory of murder recently done there. As he beheld it, I heard him groan, and I believed my office was rendered void (for a moment); but in the next he heard a voice which made his teeth grind and his flesh shiver; it was the voice of Girola, desiring his page, who was on foot, and his only attendant, to hold his torch lower, as the forest track was dark and tangled. Montorio rushed forward; the page fled shrieking, and dropt the torch. Girola was afterwards found near the thicket, horribly butchered; his skull alone had seven deep wounds in it, as if the hand that struck him was resolved to hunt and extinguish life wherever it might linger. Muzio was also found by some messengers from the kinsman's castle, and by Girola's train, bareheaded, leaping, and raving, for the rage of his revenge had deprived him of reason; he was brought back to Naples, tried for the murder, and condemned. In prison I was again with him, for human hindrances are nought to me; he knew me, for his reason returned, and acknowledged the truth of my intimations. I was with him in the last terrible hour, and wished my being frail and finite like his. But it must not be; with me time is ever beginning, suffering is ever to be. But I talk of myself, and no wonder, for every mode of human misery revives my own, which mixes with all, partakes of all, and yet is distinct from all, by a dreadful exemption from solace, or mitigation, or end."—"This is passing all belief." said Ippolito, who was musing and speaking inwardly. "If we yield to these things, if we do not rouze up our minds, and put them to the issue, we may at once resign all power and exercise of reason." He paused, and fixed his eyes earnestly on the stranger. "The circumstances you have related are such, indeed, as none but a contemporary (or one versed in secrets I thought hidden from all strangers) could know; yet still I listen to you, mazed and reluctant; but," rising and eagerly advancing, "if you can give me one proof, one solid, *masculine* proof, that you witnessed the transactions of times so distant, I will yield, I will believe every thing, I will submit to every thing, I will crush every thing in my mind that rises against or resists you."—"I can," said the stranger, rising also, "the portrait of Muzio is in the next room, take that taper and follow me; survey that picture, the left hand rests on a marble scroll; do you see the ring on that thumb?"—"I do."—"Nay, but remark it, 'tis most remarkable, so much so, that it was always worn by the owner, and faithfully copied in the portrait; it was an antique, found in a vault in the demesne of his friend, Cardinal Lanucci, a man well known in the consistory those days, and presented by him to Muzio; you have observed it, now look here." He showed the ring on the forefinger of his right hand; "you must often have heard of this ring, you must have heard it disappeared with Muzio, and that your family deplored the loss of it; he gave it to me almost in his last moments, for I was with him then; and now," said he with an unutterable look, "now he is with me." Ippolito was so absorbed in wonder at the circumstance, of which it was not easy to dispute the evidence, that he even forgot the constant subject of his solicitude and inquiry, and suffered him to depart

CHARLES MATURIN

without question or delay. As he was quitting the apartment, which looked into the street, a number of monks passed along, who were going to visit a dying man, and who elevated the host for adoration as they went; Ippolito, scarcely waking from his trance, paid the short form of habitual worship, but the stranger turned away disconcerted and perturbed.

Ippolito felt delight at his departure; this last circumstance impressed him with the terror that attends the doubtful presence of something not good; and he leant from the window, half expecting to see him dissolve in air or flame as he quitted the palace. But it was now broad day, and he saw his strange visitor pass with slow and visible motion down the Strada di Toledo.

But the impression which the conference was intended to convey soon revived, and Ippolito describes it as most strange and peculiar. He writes, that when he awoke from his noon-day sleep (now the only one he took), the first sensation he experienced was a consciousness of new agency, a new view of existence, a clear and thorough perspective, in which the modes of life lay before him, not as they appear to the human mind, mixed, uncertain, and obscure, possessing an eternal power of exciting expectation by novelty, and tempting solicitude by doubt, but all equally near and familiar, and, as it were, in the same plane to his mental eye, as if by some optical deception all the distant objects of a long journey were at once rendered equally large, and striking, and palpable, to one who had but just set out on it.

But the effect of this extraordinary approximation was not to make him satiated by the nearness, or weary of the familiarity of these objects; no, he felt his mind as it were hedged up and pressed on by them, with a force which no other could interpose between or remit; his powers seemed not to be occupied, but compressed, not ambitious of enlargement, but incapable of dilation; to *him* there was but one course to be followed, but one act to be done. He felt like one whose fate is already told, and to whom no future discovery can reveal any object of toil or of solicitude; there was therefore within him a strange passiveness, that yet did not exclude the highest degree of busy excitement. He felt some great event was not to be wrought, but to be waited for; all the dullness of lingering expectation was superseded by this great event being as it were placed in contact with his mind, in place of tumultuous preparation; there was therefore an earnest awaitment, and amid the most vigorous mental emotions he possessed an entire animal calm.

When he arose and went abroad, and looked around him, those whom he met, and their pursuits, appeared to him indescribably vague, and trivial, and hollow. He mentally wondered how men could be engaged in pursuits whose attainment was not certain, or in views whose objects were distant and indefinite. A million of times in that day he said to himself. "How can these beings exercise such alacrity and zeal for they know not what? they cannot see the events of another hour, yet they push on with eagerness in their eye, and activity in their motion. How dreadfully flat and vacant would such pursuit be to me! in me the clear and certain view of supernatural disclosure justifies the utmost energy of motion, as well as the utmost patience of expectation." But when his mind had partly recovered from the glare which this new light had poured on it, and the artificial nearness in which it had placed the objects it disclosed, he began to inquire *what new light had indeed been poured on his mind,* or *what new object had been discovered by its help?* NONE! The intimation of his fate had been conveyed in the most general terms of doubtful prediction; something had been revealed, but without circumstance or connection; all that can prompt inquiry, or distinguish between our own conjecture and the information of others, was concealed. But enough had been told to fill the high-minded and romantic Ippolito with delight while he thought of it; his fate was to be no vulgar one (by the agent employed to announce it); he was not to fall with the unknown, nor lie with those that are not remembered: something great, terrible, or tragical was to mark the close of his course.

Before the day ended he had mentally rehearsed, and compared, and applied all the circumstances of high and distinguished endings of life he could remember; calculated what relation the most probable of them could bear to the period of his own; and, clothed in the array of visionary heroism, beheld life and death pass before him with indifference. Such was his propensity to the romantic and the marvellous, and such his thirst for distinction, that the gratification of these primitive feelings of his nature was not only a balance for the view of near and expected dissolution, but even for those more dark and disastrous intimations which the stranger suggested relative to the usual complexion of the fate of those to whom he was appointed to predict it. The triumph of these high-wrought and vivid feelings was short; he was about to exchange the pride of gratified solicitude, the stirrings of noble expectation, the dream of high-fated and heroic visionry, for doubt, which he believed to be gone, and for remorse, which he thought never would arrive.

CHARLES MATURIN

I do not know whether for some days after this visit he saw the stranger; I rather imagine not, for he had again leisure and relaxation of mind sufficient to mingle in society: such is the power of habit over minds even in the highest state of excitement. This I collect from his next page, which, though sufficiently incoherent, informs me he was engaged to a fete at the villa of the Countess Verano, near the foot of the mountain. The villa was not sufficiently large to contain the numerous company, who intended to stay for some days, and most of the cavaliers passed the night in temporary buildings which were scattered through the demesne, furnished with refreshments in the day, and illuminated in the evening. To one of these Ippolito retired; but the balmy moonlight and air that came mingled like one element through the bowery lattice of his hut, refreshed him more than sleep, and he arose and feasted silently. He had not been long at the window when he thought he saw the figure of a man, whose habit and gesture were strange, advancing from the trees, and moving with caution and fear. Whether his mind was fatigued by dissipation, or whether he saw no resemblance in this object to any that might excite an apprehension, he observed it and saw it disappear without an inquiry. Soon after he retired to his rustic bed; the lamps had been long extinguished; but the moon shone full through the foliage of the casement, and once accidentally raising his eyes, on thinking that light obstructed, he fancied he saw the face of a man at the casement, looking in earnestly: even this made only a momentary impression on him, and he was soon asleep. We are utterly the creatures of time and place; had the day been passed in solitude, had his dormitory been at a distance from the habitations of others, had there been an impression on his mind, like the expectation of some fearful thing, much slighter appearances would have rouzed him. He slept not long, however, he was awakened by a glare of light and a pressure on his breast; he attempted to rise, but could not, and when he was able to distinguish objects, he saw the stranger bending over him; there was a wild force in his expression and gestures, and a combination of the fantastic and horrible in his appearance that made Ippolito shrink as from a spectre. A long, dark robe was his only covering, on which the characters and emblems were, some of them too obscure, and some too wild for examination. It was fastened by a cincture, on which the word "mystery" was inscribed; his long arms were bare, his long black hair streamed around him, but the temples were bound by a circle of fire, whose points blazed in the eyes of Ippolito as he looked upward. "Awake, arise, Ippolito di Montorio, arise and come with me!"—"Who are you? and wherefore are you come? and whither must I go?"—"The hour is come, stay not to question; the power, which nothing can resist, is come; stay not to question." As he spoke, he disappeared. On what a subtle hinge do our motions turn? Had the stranger but waited to repeat his injunction, or allow time for expostulation, Montorio would probably have been checked by the delay, and forborne to accompany him; but his departure had an air of independence in it that impelled Montorio to follow him involuntarily. He had lain down in his vest, and now wrapping his mantle round him, soon overtook his conductor; the latter proceeded with a speed that did not move but glide. Ippolito with all the vigour of youth and expectation scarcely could keep pace with him; wherever they went, all seemed buried in sleep, and without exchanging a word, or remitting their speed, they reached the suburbs of Naples. The bandage was again put on, and Ippolito conducted to the subterranean passage. What his feelings were at this moment, he probably had not leisure to remember or describe. A man who, inflamed by dissipation, is roused from sleep, and plunged among objects of terror, can only tell of a mixt and tumultuous state, in which, though all was unpleasant, nothing was distinct. The first clear impression that such a person would experience, would probably be from an object affecting not his mind but his senses: and consistently with this, he says, that when the bandage excluded from him the distraction of external things, when the echoes of that passage smote his ear, and his breath was driven back by the dark and heavy air, the mist that had obscured his mind and senses seemed to disperse, and he became suddenly and keenly capable of reflexion. His first sensation was delight, a proud and eager delight, that welcomed an object so remote and long desired, not without an awe, such as his present circumstances suggested, and such as the romantic mind loves. But while he was yet in the confusion of sudden joy, a strange feeling came to his heart, a doubtful terror, such as he had never before known, was on him; to bodily fear he was a stranger. He spoke of this sensation as the inward and sensible motion of a power above him, a power that impressed the evidence of its own agency by a resistless consciousness, an intimate peculiarity, which cannot be communicated but cannot be mistaken. The stranger felt his steps faulter—he paused—"I am out of breath," said he, "and this air suffocates and repels me."—"That is not your motive for pausing," said his conductor; "I acknowledge it is not,"

CHARLES MATURIN

said Ippolito, "there is a feeling within me, such as no time, or place, not even this, with all its circumstances, ever suggested to me before; it tells me to return, it tells me to visit these haunts, to proceed in this business, no further. I wonder at the sudden change of my mind and views, I wonder at the gulf that seems to have opened between me and my most vital pursuit, at this utter dampness and despondency that has struck to my heart's core; it makes me an astonishment to myself: but I believe it to be the intimation of a power either within me or above me, and this hesitation is, not to obey but to ascertain it." The stranger paused for some time. "The sensation you describe, you do not know the cause of; nor would any hour or place, but those in which we now are, justify me in its disclosure; it is part of the influence of this most signal night, part of the influence felt by all, by the traveller in his lonely journey, who hurries on at this moment, he knows not why; by the retired man, who trims his lamp to repel the solitary feeling that comes to his heart; nay, by the very child, who waking now shudders a prayer, and tries to hide itself under sleep. The influence of this hour is felt by all, and misunderstood by all; they judge of it by their various superstitions of time and place: it is the presence of our master that hangs in the elements, darkening the night, and sending fear into the souls of men. This influence is now felt by you, but mixing it up with your habitual feelings, you mistake it for a monition from a power that reaches not here."

This new appeal to his curiosity made Ippolito at once forget his doubt and hesitation. "Who is your master, let me look on him?"—"He has neither name, nor form, nor symbol of existence."—"How then can you know that he is present with you?"—"By signs, which cannot be told to man."—"And is it his presence you have required so long, and will it now enable you to reveal my fate to me clearly and faithfully? is this the great opportunity so long withheld? shall I know all tonight?"—"Whatever is to be known, must be known tonight; though uninvoked and invisible, he is present with us, and all things are possible. I have neglected nothing to prepare me for the business; you saw me surrounded by fires, the relics of the grave, and the blood of dead men; but what hands arrayed me in them," said he in a deeper tone, "you could not see."—"Proceed," said Ippolito eagerly, "if indeed you have such power, and this be its hour of exercise; if I shall learn tonight what no mortal power can unfold, it is the very pitch of my enthusiasm, the very point and sum of my visionary ambition, and I will follow you, though my steps faulter, and my mind sicken with some unutterable presage; but if this be a night of disappointment, by him whose name I dare not name in this den of sorcery I will enter it no more."

His conductor enjoined silence, and led him onward; they descended. Ippolito endeavoured to collect all the strength of his mind for what he believed to be a signal, even if a fictitious struggle; but such were the terrors of the place, and such the impression, utterly distinct from deception or professional imposture that attended the words and movements of his companion, that he sought in vain for that relief which the belief of having only to do with beings like ourselves always affords to the terrors of such an encounter. He endeavoured intently to recall to his memory impressions of former awe, expunged by discoveries of former deception; but there was no resemblance either in the modes or agents to qualify his present emotions with the suspicion that they were excited in vain, and he continued his silent progress in that unpleasant state of mind in which receding expectation is pursued by advancing fear, and the apprehension, having gone too far, is aggravated by the doubt that it is possible to return. They went on, however, without interruption until they arrived at that place of which I could get no description except from sudden starts and exclamations of horror. The bandage was removed. Ippolito observed, that every object bore a different aspect on this night from any he had seen on his preceding visits; whatever strange appearances used to meet or greet him on his entrance, were now removed or silent. As he passed through the vault, the former ministers of fear were stretched around him in deep sleep, and as he walked among them (the blazing and up-pointed hairs of his conductor his only light), some of them shuddered and some moaned, some of them laughed and some gibbered inarticulately, and pointed towards him. "Of those forms," said the stranger, "the living spirits are now absent; for, ever before they meet their master, they have a short space of rest and remission; it would weary the imagination to follow their flight now, where they are contending with contending elements, or shooting on the track of the meteor when he careers beyond this bourne of earth, and suspends them over the unknown vast, 'without form and void.' Of those that haunt the habitation of man, it is easier to guess the pastime; some are weaving the dim and ghastly visions of the sick, some are searing the sleep of the guilty with sounds of remembered voices, and forms that they thought sleep would shut out; some hide in ruins, from which they send wailing voices, that seem like bodings of

CHARLES MATURIN

fearful things to the belated passenger, or lights that lure him to the den of the robber, or the brow of the precipice; and some in the dwellings of the dead, where they do things, such as crazy superstition, or the howling maniac never dreamed of." On Ippolito's mind, this assemblage of terrible imagery produced no additional effect; he had wound it to a fearful pitch, even to that of all others to our nature the most repugnant, which, laying aside all the softnesses and levities of life, prepares to look upon the unclothed and unqualified, and near-brought nakedness of death. He said, he felt within him a dark strength, a stubborn and horrid force of mind, as if he were determined to be revenged on any terrors the discoveries of the night might prepare for him, by contemning and defying them, for so strong was the impression of the reality and certainty of what was about to be disclosed to him, that he had no more idea of resisting or evading it, than if a voice from heaven had declared it to him. In this ferocious sullenness, therefore, his mind took shelter, and though he endeavoured to exchange it for that resignation of which he had heard moralists talk, and which he felt to be the more appropriate feeling of that crisis, yet still the natural resentment of an oppressing force, the native abhorrence of having our liberty abridged, and our path hedged up and carved out for us, (even by a superior power, and of the knowledge of whose precise operations our pursuit has been eager and incessant,) filled him with emotions gloomy, perturbed, and rebellious. What were the peculiar rites of this signal night I know not, nor whether the presence of the evil one superseded the attendance of his ministers, who were absent on their goblin devices, but after describing his feelings in lines of which the tremor is yet visible, Ippolito went on to tell me he was left alone and in utter darkness, in some remote part of this immense space, (which he described as a *territory* under ground,) with injunctions neither to speak nor move, but to see, and to mark what he beheld. By what means he was to see in utter darkness, he could not conjecture, till at a distance he beheld a small blue flame rise before him, it spread and enlarged gradually, and ascending to a vast height, stood, without any of the flickering or volatile appearance of fire, a fixed and voluminous curtain of vapour. Its light, though strong and distinct, but partially discovered the extent of the vault, its dusky and ill-defined roof, and those parts of it whose limits pressed on the edge of the flame, were faintly visible; into the recesses of deeper darkness that spread around him, Ippolito felt not inclined to look. Meanwhile, the body of the flame, slowly diminishing and dividing, was suspended in a luminous arch, within which appeared a black reflecting surface, which filled the whole interval, and which Ippolito compared to a mirror of black marble. He gazed intently; several undefined forms chased each other over the surface, and were lost in the columns that formed its frame. At length, a full distinct form appeared directly opposite to him; it was in a modern garb, the face was concealed, the gestures indicated distraction and dismay; Ippolito, as yet unconscious of the intelligence they were to convey, watched its motions fixedly. Had the figure availed itself of every mode of speech and expression, it could not have conveyed more powerfully the idea of a being impelled by a power resistless and invisible, to some deed or object, from which it shrunk, sometimes with humility of deprecation, sometimes with devices of evasion, and sometimes with convulsions of resistance, still the power that acted on it appeared to increase in strength and effect, and its progress towards this event appeared more rapid; its motions were now most strongly indicative of fear, irresolution, and reluctance; like the animals who are said to be within the sphere of fascination, it shivered, and parleyed, and retreated, every motion a start, and every limb in a struggle of aversion that protracted the misery it endeavoured to shun in vain. At length with a vehement impulse he snatched the dagger, to which its hand had been often involuntarily directed, and threw it from him with the force of one who wishes to remove from him an object of temptation, and appeared to regard it for some time as a respite from internal persecution, but in a short time the influence appeared to operate again, again he appeared to make the faint yet desperate struggles of one who knows that all struggles are bootless. With a quivering and yet a straining motion he approached the place where the dagger lay; often receding, his feet bore him to the spot; often wincing at the touch, his hand at length grasped it strenuously; but then all further power or means of delay seemed to cease. The figure rose severely erect, as if every nerve were forcibly dilated, and the whole man wretched and wound to a pitch of unnatural energy, and then moved away with a motion, which an effort at swiftness, struggling with the warped and contracted state of the muscles, rendered frightful. The figure and his motions conveyed one idea so powerfully to Ippolito that, on his disappearing, he exclaimed aloud, "he is going to murder some one!" Almost as he spake, a cry came to his ear, not like the cry of individual agony, but as if all the terrors of a last dying groan were mixed with the shriek of those who look upon some direful thing. Ippolito's hair stood erect at that sound. The figure reappeared, his actions now were the savings of despair, his garments were splashed with blood, and he held the dagger with the gesture of one whose horror has rendered him insensible that he holds the witness of his condemnation. A confused sound was then heard, and several dim figures appeared on the tablet, Ippolito heard the rattling of chains, mixed with the toll of a bell, and that hum of preparation which accompanies some event of moment, the agonies of the phantom seemed to redouble, and Ippolito instantly comprehended that the punishment of his crime was approaching. In a short time, figures in the habits of executioners surrounded him, in the struggles of despair he broke from their gripe, and falling on his knees and stretching out his arms with the gesture of one who addresses heaven, not to appeal, but to accuse, the covering fell from *his face*, and Montorio darting towards him beheld *his own*. The figures disappeared, the sheet of blue fire closed over the tablet, and sinking into the floor with a faint hiss, expired. Ippolito was silent for some moments, from the struggle of feelings that almost suffocated him; at length rage, and amazement, and horror, found vent in a storm of execration and fury. It is impossible to conceive with what abhorrence his mind, so high-toned, so ambitious, even romantic in virtue, and impracticably rigid in its system of honour, with what abhorrence it must have struggled with the idea of undergoing the vilest of punishments for the vilest of crimes. There is a delicacy too, taught by early luxury, and the indulgences and exemptions of rank, that shrinks from the *debasing circumstances* which attend the commission and the punishment of a crime, with as much native antipathy as virtue feels at the crime itself, and which is often a security for the forbearance of evil in minds where the purer principle is absent. Ippolito was all outraged, and inflamed, and revolted, and the appearance of the stranger, on whose entrance the vault was lit again, only gave his rage an object. "Monster," he roared, "was it for this I was drawn hither, to be abused by a wizard lie, a damned prediction, which no heavenly power could doom! nor you, nor all your host of fiends, nor Satan himself, could tempt me to realize? Was it for this I watched and waited, was it for this I resigned the peace of my existence, and the welfare of my soul, that I sought the haunts I believe of demons, and yielded myself up to *you*, their leader, thou Archimage, thou Beelzebub, prince of the devils, to be told that I am—that I must be—Oh! it choaks my utterance, it blasts my Jungs to speak it—what?—a murderer; a skulking murderer; dragged from his hiding-hole by the hands of the common executioner, that does his vile office on the beasts of the people—monster!"

The burning tears of rage burst out in spite of him, the stranger stood unmoved. "Whom do you accuse? You *would behold* your fate, and you *have* beheld it."—"Impossible! wretch! liar! impossible!—Do I not know myself? Would I not search out and stab with my sword, my very heart's core, if it could harbour a thought of depravity? Had I been represented struggling with an open, armed foe; had I been represented acting in the fever of passion, (though even so I could not wound the unprepared,) had it been aught but this, I would have borne it, though the perspective was filled with racks and fire. But this—what pretext—what device—what excuse?—I have not an enemy on earth; no, by heaven! I am as void of hatred as I am of fear. But why do I linger? Let me from this cursed den; the very air breathes lies and witchery; I am infected while I stay here; the very consciousness of a crime is stealing on me; I am tempted to do something vile and guilty; and may all the horrors, the indignities, the low-sunk depravity I am menaced with, fall on me, if I ever from this night enter your haunts, or have intercourse of any shape or circumstance, or any pretext or temptation with you or your associates, be they fiends, or impostors, or what they may; nay, if I do not from this night renounce all pursuit or search of this damned art, that curses alike with suspense or certainty."—"Go," said the stranger, still sternly calm, "go, and the fulfilment of your curse go with you, for from henceforth it shall ever seem as if this vault indeed engulphed you, as if your view was bounded by its darkness, and your thoughts filled with its terrors; what you have seen or heard this night shall never leave your mind's eye; wherever you are you shall remember me."—"I will lose my memory first, in drunkenness or madness; I will drink mandragora and opium, I will have a drum beat on my head when the thought of you is there."—"That is but temporary, you will remember me in the hour of your guilt."—"Liar!"—"You will remember me in the dungeon."—Ippolito stopt his ears.—"You will remember me on the scaffold, and the image of him you have murdered will be scarce more terrible than the image of him you have belied and spurned."

"The image of him I am to murder!" said Ippolito, who had in vain endeavoured to shut out the deep voice of the stranger, "Where is it? Is it near me?"—"It is," replied the unknown, "with myriads of other unclothed embryos of future horror; here the shapes of things untold are assembled; spirits that tempt, and spirits that punish, are here awaiting their task, and howling for their prey in these untravelled spaces. You cannot see their form, nor hear their sound as they sweep past you; yet how many are gathered around you now! For, on this signal night, myriads are assembled to attend their master and mine." Ippolito, who was quitting the vault, though he knew neither passage nor direction, hesitated; his mind was in that state when the violence of its agitation is favourable to the most improbable and contradictory impressions, but in which it always seeks a relief to its distrained and overwrought frame in an extreme, and therefore if it deviate from one, certainly declines to another. At such a moment, the temptation of his habitual curiosity so critically suggested, and the near prospect of its gratification, combined with the impression of sincerity, which the stranger's unyielding calmness involuntarily conveyed to him, wrought a strange and sudden change in the whole frame of his feelings. He returned slowly, and faultered out, "Can you indeed shew me the form of him whom I am doomed—" he could not say to murder. "*That* I know not," said the stranger, who during their conference had never changed his posture or expression. "Unfeeling and unyielding that you are," said Ippolito, relapsing into passion, "is this my answer? Is this the way you relieve the wretch whom you upbraid for leaving you? Why should I stay? You have poured fire into my brain, and poison in my heart, and now when I turn to the only resource you have left me, you mock me with a cold, lingering, doubtful answer. By whatever power you serve and fear, I adjure you, adjure you earnestly, terribly, by the convulsions of a broken spirit, by the ruins of a mind which none but you could bow down to weakness, I adjure you, grant me this last, wretched boon; let me grow familiar with the wickedness of my own heart, nor feel these revoltings, as if the motions within me were caused by the possession of a demon."

The stranger spoke not, moved not, saw not, his arms were uplifted, his head thrown back, the whites only of his eyes were visible, and though not a limb moved, the folds of his garment rose and spread as if they partook of some inward motion. Ippolito, almost insensible of what he saw, and possessed but by one object, repeated his importunities with aggravated vehemence; again and again he grasped the unknown by the arm, and shook his garments, and shrieked his petition in the agonies of delirious impatience. "Away!" groaned a voice, that seemed to come an immeasurable distance; "away! I am with my master now; he comes, he comes, where space neither measures nor reaches, through the viewless and the void." Ippolito, inflamed not deterred, only raised his voice, and redoubled his eagerness; his feelings became frenzy, his voice a roar, he supplicated, he menaced, he cursed, he defied with daring provocation, the presence of the masterspirit, and threatened with extermination the stranger, his ministers, the haunts of their resort, and every agent and instrument of their accursed doings. At this outrage the stranger shivered, and half starting from his trance, looked around with a glazed, unawakened eye: "Who hath brought him here?" he murmured; "The terror of his presence be upon *him*."—"Let them be upon me," raved Ippolito, "let me have something to confront and to contend with; I dare him; he shrinks from me; let him come; if he be more terrible than these dens of horror have yet shewn me, if he be what I can but behold and die, if he blast my eyes with the livid lightning of hell, let him come; I dare him; does he hear me? yes, I dare him; let the echoes of his temple bear to him my shout, my laugh of defiance." He burst into a horrid laugh.

At these last sounds the stranger shrieked; his shriek, so wild and unearthlike, was echoed from a hundred parts of the vault, and all the crowd of strange shapes, and many he had never before beheld, surrounded him in a moment; the cavern rung with their cries, a commotion like an earthquake shook every place and object, self-moved lights darted through the darkness; a sound like the moans of the dying, borne on the wind of midnight, rose, and increasing as it spread, filled the vault, till the maddened ear sought in vain the cause of its torture in the dizzy roar that oppressed it: Oh, there is no telling the terrors of that hour; if a being could be supposed to be plunged for a moment into Tophet, and retain his vital powers and reason, such I believe, would he describe it on his return, if the power of description remained to him. I recollect some expressions of Ippolito's which described it with the energy of personal suffering. "The very dead forms and characters that were on the walls, at this moment came to a horrid state of partial existence, they crawled and shuddered with a motion like life; the very reptiles, of size and form such as is never seen in the upper world, seemed endued with a strange consciousness, and rose erect some, and some uttered sound, and some looked and stared with ghastly intelligence."

Amid this scene what an object must Ippolito have presented, the bold and beautiful outline of his figure appearing amid the fires and darkness, and witched shapes of that meeting, his sword drawn, his habit thrown back, his eye and cheek kindling into frenzy, heightened with the peculiar wildness of supernatural terror. The stranger awoke from his trance; he arose; he grasped his arm, and looking on him with an eye that seemed to see other forms: "Come," said he, "you who compel the powers of the night, and of the nether world, come with me."—"Swear then, that you will shew me that form, the form of him who is to make me a villain; if I can but behold him, I will sit down in passive wretchedness, and resist no more; shew me but that form—" "You shall behold him."—"Lead me then where you will."

Again he was led to a space so remote that it seemed as if the immense extent of this place was suddenly become doubly immense, yet their motion was so quick that the rage and uproar seemed to have ceased at once. No sound was near them, their steps did not seem to emit any, the damp and foggy dulness of the coarse medium which could scarce be called air, seemed to absorb every impression; the single light the stranger bore, did not permit them to penetrate into the thick darkness, more than the arm could extend. They proceeded in utter silence; there was a chilling remoteness from life, within and around them. Ippolito had no consciousness of any thing, till he found they had stopped and entered a dark chamber, or rather another rude recess in these endless passages. Some object, dark and muffled, lay in a corner; but Ippolito's sight had been too long stimulated by glaring and unnatural impressions to regard it. "In a few moments," said the unknown, "you will be cursed, like the rest of your species, with the fulfilment of your own wishes; what, in compassion to you, I would have withheld, I can now withhold no longer. The lord of the night, compelled by outrage and defiance, has come, in the fullness of his terrible potency he *has* come, and I am forced by that presence to deal with you without the mercy of reserve or delay."—"Therefore," said Ippolito with eager weariness, "I pray you be speedy; soon let me know what is yet to be done or suffered. I tell you I am in the very weakness of desperation! Do not therefore speak, for I can no longer hear; my head is hot, and my mind wondrous heavy. Let something be done, and quickly, while I am yet equal to it. I could, methinks, grasp at fire, or drink fresh blood, as if I were in the common ways and habits of nature. How long this searing of the mind will last, I know not; make your tool of me now, I am in your power."—"There is something yet to be done," said the stranger drawing very near him, "to recognize and to propitiate the presence of our master, a deed must be done, a deed without a name, which sounds foully in the ears of nature. Have you not sometime heard that the power with whom we deal requires the spilling of blood as the test?"—"I have heard of these things before," said Ippolito speaking quick and low, and fixing his eyes on a point; "and the dreams that used to terrify childhood, are they become the acts of the man? those things so dark, so distant, are they indeed brought so near to me? Be it so: here is my sword, from what part are the drops to be drawn that seal this mystery of iniquity?" He bared and held out his arm. "Not that," said the stranger, "it is not that; the sacrifice is already prepared, and you are not to be the victim, but the one who must offer it. Such victims with us are common; credulity or fear supplies them every day."

As he spoke, he approached that obscure object, and drew off part of the covering that concealed it. Ippolito beheld a naked human breast, the rest of the body, head, and limbs were concealed in a dark drapery, that fell also over the rude block, on which it appeared extended and fastened as on an altar. "Here is the victim prepared," said the stranger, "he cannot fly or resist, he cannot discover or upbraid; the movements of the dead are not further from the light or knowledge of life than what is done in this vault; here is the weapon," giving him a small dagger, "strike firm and sure, the presence of our master requires this attesting act, and all shall then be known."—"Never," replied Ippolito, awaking at once to the keenest and most exalted sense of feeling and reflexion, "never; what future horrors my fate may prepare for me I know not, nor what dreadful preparation a goaded mind and a devoted consciousness may steel me with; but while I have sense, and can hold a weapon with the steady hand of one who can aim, or who can forbear, never shall such an accursed deed be done by me."—"Rash boy!" said the unknown, "you know not what depends on this moment; you know not whose presence makes these insensible walls burst out in an ominous dew, and this prepared taper burn tremulous and blue; you know not who beholds you now, summoned hither by the outrage, and now dismissed with the capricious infirmity of a mortal, *his* wrath will be terrible, my power will fail before him, his fangs will scatter your flesh like chaff, his breath will blast and shrivel your substance to an atom, you will be borne alive to his horrible haunt, the mock of his taloned imps, the torn, shrieking, and yet living feast of fiends."—"I hear your words," said Ippolito, "but my ears are stopped with horrid things, and I cannot distinguish them, nor am I longer able to speak or to reason. I will not do that accursed thing; I will not harm that miserable object, though he can neither resist nor upbraid; for myself, I am in *his* hands, whose hands can reach even here."—"Think, oh, yet think," continued the unknown, "of the alternative that awaits your obstinacy, if the more direful and violent extremity should not overtake you; you must never quit this vault again—never. No human force or art can ever find or free you; here you must linger on the confines of the outer darkness, feeding despair with fearful shapes and sounds, so very near the nether world, that the horrid familiarity will make you forget your nature; and even while yet alive, and in the flesh, feel yourself becoming a demon, till on such a night as this you shall be nailed to a block like *him*, whom similar infirmity has brought here, to be put to a death you can neither see nor struggle against; and then to lie here, your rotting bones made instruments of such unhallowed doings, that their dead juices shall creep and curdle to be so abused, while no friend weeps or knows your end, and your miserable soul unabsolved, unblessed, unappeased. Oh, think of this!"—"I have thought—it is in vain; if one of your goblin ministers were howling temptation in my ears, while these horrors leave me a glimpse of will or reason, while I can draw a dagger, or not draw it, I will not be a tame, resigned, voluntary villain."

"'Tis possible," said the tempter, "the malice of mercy may spare you to a worse fate; 'tis possible you may be dismissed from this chamber to linger out a long life of horrible expectation, for such it must be, with the consciousness of future guilt. You will neither have the preparation of definite knowledge to enable you to dare it with firmness, and to suffer with dignity, nor that partial reconcilement which long familiarity must produce with the most revolting objects, and which, if it do not leave the mind satisfied, at least renders it calm. No—instead of this, conscious that you must be guilty, you will try many modes of guilt, partly from curiosity, and partly from a vain hope to evade your allotted one; thus will you become hardened in evil, familiar with varieties of vice. Your mind, from its habitual contemplations, will be degraded ed below that of an assassin or a robber. The contagion will extend to your manners and habits; your whole character will sink into a squalid misery, a depraved dejection, a desponding meanness, a ruffian abandonment. Never knowing when you arise that the sun will not light you to a shameful death, you will bear for ever about you the curse and blast of existence, the self-watching torture of fear, that dreads to wake and dreads to sleep. In the morning you shall wish for evening, and in the evening you shall wish for morning, anxious for the day to pass that you may see it over without a crime, yet cursing it when it is past, that it has brought you nearer to inevitable misery. In every wind you will hear cries of pursuit, in every eye you will see a spy or an accuser, every straw that crosses your path shall seem like a weapon offered to you, the infant and the sleeper shall suggest to you a whisper of temptation; your character, your feelings, your nature changed, low in vice and in wretchedness, you will crawl with conscious revoltings to the end of a long, long life, you will rush, shrieking with precipitate reluctance, on its guilty close, and you will perish in the sin for which the horrors of uncertain anticipation allowed you no time for repentance, and the degradation of your heart forbid the praise of fortitude or the solace of compassion. Such must be your life if you quit this chamber without seeing the face of your victim. But it is now in your power to command that sight, and if you do, its appearance will suggest to you so many circumstances of time, and place, and action, that you will have means to collect your powers; your arm will be strong, your mind bold and awake, your energies collected, keen, intense; you will be undisturbed by the rage of ignorance, the stupid curses of the vulgar; you will walk with a steady step to the end of life, and quit it with the mysterious dignity of one who, possessing a knowledge above nature, was enabled to act a part above it; who, knowing more than mere man could know, acted as mere man could never have acted. And is not this worth the struggle of a moment?"

While he spoke, he had insinuated the dagger into Ippolito's hand, who, in the unconscious workings of his mind and body, grasped it intensely. The strong picture of wretched life was before his eyes, his heart was hot, and desperate, and wreckless. Before he knew the direction his hand had taken, he felt the blood gushing about the hilt of the dagger; he heard the stifled, and broken, and peculiar moan of death; he staggered, and shut his eyes; he felt as if they were forced open again; he looked, but could see nothing—there was a dead silence. At length Ippolito stammered out, "I have done it! now fulfil what you promised, now let me see that figure."—"You shall," said the stranger in a voice whose tone made itself felt, even in that most horrible moment, "withdraw that covering and you shall behold it."—"Where! what! I am mazed! my head is throbbing—speak—quickly." "Withdraw that covering, and you shall behold the face of your victim."—"Are you mad, or am I? What connection can there be between this miserable object and him whose form I was to see?"—"Look, and you shall see the very object, self, and form; not express, but actual." With hands that did not feel their own motion, he withdrew the covering from the face; it was dimmed and altered by the struggles of death—but he saw it; in that pale light, and with eyes that were seared and flashing, he knew it."

"What did he see?" demanded the inquisitor. "I know not; whenever he but approaches the mention of it, his hand becomes illegible, his expressions grow wild. It is in vain to importune him for that name, he could as soon bring himself wittingly to do the deed itself, as disclose the object or circumstance of it, even to a brother."—"What change of sorcery," said the inquisitor, "what dark dealing is this? How could the sufferer in the wizard's vault, and the being he was doomed to destroy at some future time, be the same? or how—" "And still more strange," said Angellini, "from allusions in subsequent passages I can collect, that the dying face he saw in the vault was the face of a living man, a man yet living in this world, in no expectation or chance of death; nay, one who could by no means be supposed to be in or near that place, one who is yet alive and well known to him. Though he had felt his hands stiff with his blood, though he had seen the drawn features, the close set teeth, the broken and reverted eye, with all the terrible charactery of actual death upon him."

"It is all a riddle, dark and fearful. But still, was not his mind lightened by the thought, that what had passed that night could be but in vision? that if his victim was yet alive, he could not have perished in that dark chamber? Did no hope of deception, of imposture, of the infirmity of his senses spring up within him?"—"Oh, no; it was only misery heightened by anticipation, and confirmed by certainty! He had read, and so have I, when perhaps our motive to such studies was curiosity, of some potent workings of that art, by which the spirits of the living are, with unheard of anguish to the sufferer, brought to the place and the power that requires them, and there are made, or seem to undergo in vision and mist, whatever can be inflicted on the real corporal agent; and during this fearful divorce of soul and body, that the latter remains as in a deep sleep, which nothing can disturb or interrupt till its suffering tenant is restored by the power that divided them. Such things have we heard, and what would make the hair stand upright, if told, of the tortures of the more subtle part, whose powers of sensation are rendered inconceivably acute by this unnatural dissolution, to whom the state itself is a state of dark, dream-like suffering, through which they labour with a feeling of oppression feverous, and dim, and dense, such as accompanies the presence of the nightmare. To such a cause he persists to ascribe the appearances in the vault; for he firmly believes that terrible stranger a being not of this earth. Nor have I any means of contending with his belief; his actions and character, so far as I have been told them, have lapped me in wonder."—"Oh, Blessed Mother! Blessed Mother, have mercy on him! heal his mind and forgive his sins! Holy St. Agatha, have mercy! Holy St. Rosolia, have mercy on him!" He beat his breast and crossed himself, and Angellini joined in his aspirations. "These papers," said he, after a pause, "I have since received, are all sudden starts of pain and terror, without connection, without subject. See how they are written; how the hand must have trembled that wrote these!

Fragments of Letters from Ippolito to Angellini

"MY MIND IS BECOME UTTERLY waste and desolate; existence lies before me without form or colour. I am the man whose fate has been made known to him, who has no part in life but its close; whose thoughts bear him over the whole earth, without a passing glance, and set him down before the grave. And mine, where shall it be dug? Aye, there is the sting of death! I must lie in the dust, in the shadow of the gibbet and the wheel! Dying villains shall pray that their bones may not be thrown near mine! Oh, if this must be, that I could wrap my head in darkness, in deep deathlike sleep, and pass away the term without a thought till my hour came on! and then to rush with blind arm, with headlong blow, that is struck before it is felt, and at the same moment to feel it returned home to my heart, sure and firm, before recollection return, while I am yet in the doubt of a horrid dream! before I hear the wonder, and the cry, and the tale; before I feel the cursed gaze of mankind on me, straining to see the murderer. And then to lie down, forgotten for ever, clean passed away from note or memory of man; my name unknown, my grave in the sands of a desert. Oh, that it might be thus! for though I must perish by a ruffian's fate, I have not a ruffian's heart. No, it is the very omnipotence of fate to thwart, to humble, to crush, to mix opposites that loath each other; to bid the proud heart become acquainted with pollution and abject wretchedness. Never was a heart that kindled as mine did with the love of all that is dear to the young, the ardent, the high principled mind. My race of pleasure and

CHARLES MATURIN

glory seemed to be endless; it was but next spring to quit the levities of Naples, to enter as a cadet with an assumed name into the Spanish service, and never to avow that of Montorio till the commandant should ask the name of the youth who had done some distinguished service: this was my purpose. And I must perish on a scaffold, or in a dungeon, where lives are crushed out in silence and darkness! No, here there is no hope; no dignity can be given to an end like this; no decent pride of death. To die for some act that was the burst of passion, the excess of erring principle; to see among the multitude a thousand whose hearts are with you, who weep, and pray for, and bless you as your firm step ascends the scaffold; nay, to struggle madly for the chance of life, to grapple with the executioner, to spring over the edge of the platform, to dash with chains through the guard, to trust to the sympathy of the sheltering crowd for your escape; to do this, while only conscious of erring as many have erred, would be to me more delightful than life. But, pitiless heaven! must I be dragged with the meanness of guilt, the villain-visage, in whose lines I shall hear them, as I crawl along, tracing the characters of vice; my felon hands tied behind, while the confessor, shuddering at the monster, can hardly bid him not despair. This—this— Oh, blessed heaven! let me run mad! Will he not take these burning tears, this scattered hair, this broken heart, and spare me but the foul deed, spare me but the shame, the public curse, the public gaze, and I will bear the pain, silently, deeply, while nature will bear it—!

"I AM MUCH IN SOLITUDE; when I am forced to go amongst men, I often feel myself examining their faces with a suspicion that makes *them* shrink—and *me,* too, when I am conscious of it. I am, therefore, much in solitude; for who can bear the sight of the human face when once it has become offensive? Horrid thought is my only companion! the worst of that came to me last night. Was it only a passing thought of fear, or was it one of those dark intimations that latterly, I think, often visit me? A mind in my state may well be conceived a fit medium for the agency of unearthly natures. I thought, for a moment, I was possessed; I did, for a moment, think it! In truth, there are such fightings within me, I feel I am yet so unlike what I am told I must be, my head has so many thoughts so like my former self, my heart has still so many pulses that are yet alive to the love of grace, that I almost doubt if ever I can wittingly do the unnatural deed—if ever I can have the heart to be a wretch. When these thoughts rise in me, I try to crush them; I shriek, I stamp, I beat my head; I say with a horrid laugh—these are no thoughts for the murderer! I must be wild, wreckless; hard as the rock, rough as the storm. I try to chase these cruel lingerings of my former nature, and be thoroughly, inveterately, the wretch I *ought* to be. It was in such a struggle last night (that almost drove me to pray for the consummation of my wretchedness); for a moment I thought I was possessed; that the evil one had *not utterly* prevailed; that I would feel him hourly growing stronger within me, drying up the springs of nature, searing my conscience, and shutting up my soul, till—Oh, language cannot follow that thought! I was standing when it came to me, and I feared to look into the glass opposite me, least I should see my breath inflamed, or my eyes glisten with strange intelligence, or my hairs pointed and tipt with fire, or my foot—Oh, this cannot, cannot surely last much longer!—

"I THOUGHT THAT I FELT the worst; that long anticipation had made me familiar with all horrors; that in thought I had drank the dregs, and wrung them out. I was deceived; for our capacity of bearing pain is always deceiving us. Whom could I have believed who would have told me what I could support a short space back? Last night I had thought long on it; I went to bed; I slept. I dreamt that I had done it, that I had in very deed done it. Every hair on my head I felt distinctly upright; every nerve and muscle was strained and stiffened out; my eyes were coals of fire; my fingers were distended into talons; I was drenched with the sweat of deadly agony. Even in my sleep I felt I said, "Oh, reverse time, but for one moment! let this be *but to come*; let me be the thrall of horrible expectation for ever!" Sleep could not long continue. I awoke, awoke in transport, awoke exclaiming, "I am not a murderer!" It was long before my senses returned perfectly; but when they did, I remembered ere long I must feel this, and seek to waken from it in vain. Oh, then, I wished to pass life in such a dream, so I might never waken to such a conviction! My reason is much obscured; mine eyes are strained and burning; mine ears have a roar in them, like that of ocean, that is never diminished. Nature is dark to me, and mankind a spectre. Yet, yet, my sufferings are but begun!—

FOR SOME TIME PAST I had a wretched resource, such as wretches have. Even that has failed me utterly. The events that have befallen me, the objects that surround me nightly, bear so little resemblance to

CHARLES MATURIN

reality, that often they appeared to me the images of a dream, a dark, haunted dream. For a moment I dared to think I was not doomed to be a murderer! In the morning, those objects were as clear and palpable as any action I had ever witnessed or performed; at evening, with the help of wine and high play, to which I forced myself, they became doubtful, and sometimes disappeared. What must that be to which the rage of drunkenness and of gaming is a relief? But last night and the night before, he appeared to me amid crowds to whom I had run for shelter in vain; he reminded me of the hour, he shewed the dagger, he scared all around, he bore me away. Oh, when I saw him break the last fence I had against him, I felt like the wrecked wretch, who at nightfall lights his few faggots to deter the wild beasts from approaching him, and sees by their blaze the tiger couching to spring over them and seize him. I have no power of resistance, no hope of escape; I am the prey of the powers of darkness! Oh, how terrible is this sinking of the soul, this closing round of the utter darkness!"

Angellini was proceeding to examine more of these extraordinary papers, when he and his companion were startled by an unusual sound that murmured near them. They listened not in apprehension, for within the walls of the Inquisition there are no listeners but in curiosity. At that moment Angellini observed a remarkable change in the appearance of the sea, which was flowing beneath their windows; it suddenly retreated to a vast distance, leaving its bed bare and heaving, and stranding in a moment the numberless small vessels which were sailing or anchored in it in total security, and whose bulged and scattered fragments were spread over the surface as far as it was yet visible. Angellini and his companion were too well acquainted with the climate to be ignorant of the purport of these dreadful phenomena, and if they had, the loud and terrible cry that rose from the city and the shore would not have allowed them to be long so. They now could see distinctly crowds of people rushing to the shore from every quarter, they ran for refuge and safety, for in their houses it appeared impossible to continue longer; but when they found the beach naked, the vessels destroyed, and the sea receding almost from their view, they stood aghast, and eyed each other in speechless despair.

Angellini, endeavouring to subdue the terrors of nature by the discharge of his official duties, recollected that unless the shocks were unusually violent, it was probable the fabric would resist them, and that at least while any work of man remained, a pile which had stood for centuries would be safe. While he was yet debating the probable direction of the next shock, he was stunned by a sound, which he in vain endeavoured to believe proceeded from the multitude on the shore; it was the ocean returning in its strength, in a strength that seemed to threaten the bounds of nature. In the next moment they beheld it approaching as a mountain, the black concave of its waters darkening on the view like a cavern. Angellini, who was hastening from the room, stood riveted to the spot for an instant of horrible expectation. It burst, and he felt the building shake to its base. It yet stood, however, and he rushed out to order the guard to remove the prisoners, who were lodged in chambers hollowed out of the rock beneath the foundations of the fabric, where he feared the sea, in these convulsive workings, might penetrate, and the inhabitants of them perish miserably. He gave his orders eagerly to the proper officer, who bowing profoundly, assured him "the prisoners were perfectly safe."—"Safe!" repeated Angellini, "they are safe, indeed, from the power of man; but I wish to put them in a capacity of avoiding the most deplorable of all modes of destruction."—"With submission, Signor, I apprehend it would be better policy to leave them where they are," said the officer. "Policy!" said Angellini with some indignation, "this is rather a moment for humanity."—"Of that I do not pretend to be a judge," said the officer; "but were the prisoners of my mind, they would rather die where they are, than live to perish at the stake."

Angellini had but just time to repeat his orders, when a second and a third shock made the walls around him vibrate visibly, while a large aperture yawning in that opposite him, he beheld through it the towers of the fabric tottering, and the inner court strewn with fragments of battlements and columns. All was now confusion and horror; the cries of the sufferers from the town were audible amid the tumult of destruction; but on the ministers of the Inquisition, callous from habitual misery, and frozen by a life of monotony, the effect was much diminished in point of terror and consternation: they moved with that stalking silence with which they traversed the passages on ordinary occasions. The prisoners whose situation exposed them to danger were by Angellini's direction placed in a court, where, though guarded, their motions were at liberty, should they be necessary to their own safety. Angellini, when half an hour had elapsed without a renewal of danger, began to examine the structure, whose gigantic strength had resisted a shock that had almost laid a city in ruins. The tower alone seemed shattered by the concussion; its inner front, which faced the court, was marked with some traces of injury, but the outer wall seemed shaken into ruins, for Angellini saw the bare and pointed ridges of the roof, and caught the gleams of the outer sky through the gratings which light had never penetrated before. He hastily demanded, had any one been confined in that tower? and was told it had been the prison of the young nobleman from Naples. He instantly ordered some of the officers to ascend the remains of the staircase, that hung fearfully pendulous, and visible on the outside of the fractured wall. They obeyed him, but after some delay returned with horror in their faces, affirming that of the prisoner there was not a vestige in any part of the building; they averred also, that it was impossible for him to have escaped by human means, for their own approach to his apartment had been only rendered practicable by the falling in of part of the building as they were ascending the stairs, which had enabled them with some difficulty and danger to reach and find his chamber empty.

From the looks and gestures which accompanied this information, and the whispers with which it was continued, the prisoners conjectured that it contained other circumstances still more extraordinary. Angellini, when it was concluded, raising his eyes to the ruin, so fearful and impassable, thought with a mixture of horror and compassion on the mysterious fate of this unfortunate young man, and for a moment submitted his strong mind to the belief of the marvellous things superstition had told of him.

I am now come from gazing on the sight:
From bank to bank the red-swoln river roars.
Crowds now are standing upon either shore
In awful silence, not a sound is heard
But the flood's awful voice, and from the city
A dismal bell heard through the air by starts.

When Annibal, still attended by Filippo, arrived at Capua, he learned that his relative resided at Puzzoli, where he had been removed for the enjoyment of a distinguished benefice. Disappointed by the delay, and alarmed by the danger of exposure, he nevertheless was compelled, by the exigency of his finances, to pursue him to Puzzoli with this relative, who was his mother's uncle. Annibal had from his youth been a favourite, and what was of greater consequence, his father had long been the reverse, in consequence of some family disagreements: both from his fondness and resentment, therefore, he hoped for assistance, and, at least, believed himself secure of confidence and protection.

He therefore hastened to Puzzoli, and rested on his way at a small town in its neighbourhood, purporting to reach it the following day. Slight shocks of the preceding earthquake had been felt in the country, and a considerable degree of alarm prevailed among the inhabitants, which, as usual, they endeavoured to appease by ceremonies and processions. A river, that flowed near the town, had lately undergone such extraordinary changes, had swoln with such sudden violence, and then subsided without any apparent cause, that the people were not only terrified with the expectation of what these changes indicated, but with the more obvious danger it threatened to their lives and habitations. Annibal, who was shewn into a room of the inn which commanded a view of the river, saw not without solicitude and fear the rush of its dark, turbid waters, sometimes wrought into eddies, and sometimes checked by invisible obstructions, its roar often mingled with other sounds, of which the causes were unknown, and its waters flushed with the sullen sanguine hues of a sun, setting amid the clouds of a gathering storm. "Illustrious Signor," said the host, entering with preparations for supper, "you have arrived at the most fortunate time imaginable; we have had threatenings of an earthquake and inundation these four days."—"You flatter me highly," said Annibal jocularly. "May I perish if I do, Signor," said the man earnestly; "I think it by no means improbable that this roof may be in ruins over your head tonight."—"You must explain the mystery of this good fortune to me," said Annibal smiling, "I confess I am unable to comprehend how being buried in the ruins of your house is a subject on which I can congratulate myself."—"Why, Signor, is it possible you can live in Italy, and not know that whenever we are threatened with danger the abbess of the Ursuline convent and the prior of our monastery unite in a solemn procession to the river, and produce all their relics to prevent an inundation; and that ceremonies are performed, and crowds collected, and such a multitude of strangers and spectators pours into the town to witness it, that if the inundation swept away half the town, the remainder are happier for it all their life. It is quite a jubilee, I assure you, Signor, only that it occurs somewhat oftener; if Providence continues to favour us, as it has done of late, I expect to see scarce a house standing."—"You will allow me, however," said Annibal, "to quit yours before so desirable an event occurs, as I should be equally unwilling to prevent or to partake its good fortune."

Shocked at the man's insensibility, and determined not to augment profits thus iniquitously desired, he quitted the house and wandered towards the river. It was now night, deepened by the darkness of a cloudy sky, and Annibal's mind, under the influence of time and place, involuntarily adopted a subject of congenial meditation. He thought of his strange fate, of events no conjecture could solve, and no contemplation could divest of terror; the precise frame of his mind was critical and dangerous, perhaps even more so than his brother's. Ippolito was always accustomed to act from impulse, Annibal from conviction. But impulse is more variable than conviction; and therefore, though Ippolito's emotions were more vehement, his mind was much more disengaged than his brother's. He had no distinct belief of the character of his persecutor, nor any clear impressions of the influence exercised on himself; he had never seriously debated whether it was the production of human or superhuman powers; he resisted it merely because it was painful and atrocious; instead of bending his mind to discover whether he was the victim of imposture or the agent of destiny; he expended his energies in sallies of rage and convulsions of resistance. Into the deeper mind of Annibal, one conviction had radically wrought itself, that of his being visited by the inmate of another world. What relief he had enjoyed under this terrible impression was merely local and furtive, produced by change of place and vicissitudes of action, violent and sudden: but the impression remained slumbering, but not extinct, ready to resume its force and character whenever the cause that had produced it should recur. Hence, while Ippolito was almost in despair, his very violence of nature formed a security against the object he dreaded, as poison is often expelled by the convulsions it produces; while Annibal, whose tranquillity seemed almost unimpaired, nourished an unsuspected tendency to the very deed, from whose remote apprehension the frame of his mind flattered him with a treacherous immunity. He walked alone. His mental debate, which occupied some hours, might be reduced to the following propositions: "I have seen a departed spirit, an inhabitant of those regions which are invisible to man; I cannot resist the evidences of his appearance and ministry; I draw them as much from the circumstances that preceded and followed, as from those that accompanied it. There was a regularity of disposition, a subordination of parts, a progress of developement, which indicate the agency of an intelligent being; and if intelligent, certainly not human. He prompts me to a crime, revolting to nature and fatal to my own life, reputation, and perhaps immortal interests. I have resisted him, for it requires no debate to reject evil so positive and heinous; I have resisted him hitherto; but who can tell how long he may resist a being whose powers are the powers of another world? nay, who can tell how far he is right in resisting him? Distance of place has in a measure relieved me from this persecution; but should he pursue me where I am flying, I feel I have no further resource, no remaining powers of defence; the evidence of his character, the truth of his commission, it will then be no longer possible to resist. Far be that day from me, Oh, heaven! In my present state my misery is solitary and incommunicable; I have no associate, I *can* have none; for unimaginable distress there is no sympathy; he who has felt as I do might pity me; but where shall I find him? What being is there who holds communication authentic and avowed with the world of spirits? None! The tenderest friend or relative must regard me as a visionary, a madman, or an impostor, and to my other sufferings I need not voluntarily add contempt. To implore the aids of the church is equally hopeless; the consequence of confession would probably be immurement in the Inquisition! they would listen to me, not as one for whom something was to be done, but from whom something was to be learned; they would listen to the tale of suffering or of guilt, only for the sake of considering how far the interest of the church might be promoted by the issue of the affair. I should be ever afterwards to *them* an object of vigilance and suspicion, they would presume on my distress to predominate over my freedom and my intellects; they would macerate my body and enfeeble my mind; and, after all, if my persecution be not a visionary one, they would fail to protect me from it, and if it be I am able to protect myself."

He was pleased with the result of his meditation; for though he had not adopted any resolution, he had appeared to think with the vigour of resolution: he had, in fact, anchored without a bottom, but the increasing crowds and noise would have prevented any further exercise of mind, had he been disposed to it. He found, according to his host's account, multitudes assembled, and multitudes more assembling, though it was now near midnight, and the appearance both of the sky and the waters was menacing. *They* heeded it not, the triumph of seeing their saints acquainting the river in the rage of inundation, "that thus far should he go and no further," was heightened by the increased wealth and consequence which this confluence of strangers gave their town, and both were exalted by that love of pleasure, and sensibility of external objects, for which the Italians are distinguished, and which the desire to gratify must be incalculaby powerful in a people, who enjoy but few spectacles of splendour, or opportunities of festivity, but what religion affords them. Annibal was drawn along by the crowd, and learned among them that the Abbess and her train were to come from a neighbouring convent, with relics of peculiar virtue; that they were to be met at the entrance of the town by the religious orders who inhabited it, and that both were to march with united forces to the very brink of the river, and pronounce a solemn interdiction of its further outrages. Annibal, who was a good Catholic, believed his mind would be refreshed, as well as his senses delighted, by this act of religion, and therefore willingly mingled in the crowd, amused even by the preparations for the ceremony, by the murmur and concourse of so vast a multitude, over whose visages, tinged with various shawdowings of confidence and fear, the torches by which they were seen, flung an expression wildly animated and picturesque.

Through the darkness of the night he could see distinctly the lights that twinkled from the convent, and often he listened to catch the chaunt of their solemn service, as the low, intermitted gale breathed past him, but could only hear the roarings of the river, which filled up the hushed murmurs of the crowd, with a sound strange and deep; at length a bell from the convent, which was caught and answered by those in the town, gave signal that the procession had set out. The crowd pressed forward to meet and join it, and Annibal was borne on by the rest. It was marked by every circumstance of fantastic splendour, by which the unhappy inmates of a convent try to diversify hopeless monotony, and employ the talents which are denied their proper and social exercise. All the wealth of the convent was displayed, several nuns were arrayed in the habits and characters of those whose relics they bore. The Abbess herself, assisted by four lay-sisters, supported an enormous piece of tapestry, embroidered with the life of their patroness, St. Ursula, whose figure in wax, larger than the life, and blazing with jewels, followed in the rear of her own atchievements. But the multitude forgot every other object when the procession closed with a figure, such as their eyes never before had beheld: it was a lay-sister, habited as the genius of martyrdom, and bearing a relic of more value than the whole wealth of the convent, it was the head of St. Catharine, which by particular providence had found its way from Alexandria, where it had been severed from her body, in the reign of the tyrant Maximin, to Italy. This saint had a special antipathy to inundations and earthquakes, which she took care to manifest in so spirited a manner, that the river had upon all former occasions paid the highest deference to her hydrophobia, by instantly retreating to its natural current. This inestimable relic, set in gold, and placed in a crystal case, never had attracted the attention of the faithful so little. They hung upon, they blessed, they almost worshipped the beautiful representative of martyrdom. She was placed aloft, on a car of curious construction; it was entirely composed of racks, crosses, and instruments of death and torture, woven with such skilful intricacy as to preserve their distinct forms, and yet form a spacious vehicle; at due intervals imps of temptation and punishment were peeping at the genius with faces of ugly malignity, and derisive grimace. She stood in the centre of the machine, in the attitude of trampling on the terrible apparatus, on which she cast from time to time looks of contempt, such as the serenity of angelic beauty may spare. A robe of white floated round her like a cloud, one hand held the head of St. Catharine, the other waved a branch of amaranth, her locks were wreathed with a coronal of palms, and her eyes were upturned to a resplendent figure, which, bending from the canopy of purple, extended to her a crown of gems, and pointed her view to heaven. Her form breathed immortality,

CHARLES MATURIN

her vestments seemed to emit light as they moved on a face pale with early confinement and habitual sorrow, the murmurs of adoration, the awakened consciousness of beauty, and the enthusiasm of religious drama, had kindled a radiance that seemed borrowed from the regions her view was directed to. The faithful felt their devotion exalted, and the libertine was converted, as they beheld her. By a singular chance her face was concealed from Annibal as her car passed the spot where he stood. He was again borne on by the multitude, who hastened to the river, on the bank of which the religious orders were already assembled; the solemn sound of their chaunting mixing with its roar, and their line of dark forms, so diversified by the shadowy picturings of torch-light, here heaped in tumultuous darkness, and there flashing out in abrupt and fantastic light, that the eye sought in vain for a resemblance to known or common objects, and struggled to believe itself in the regions of life. After prayer and hymn, the various relics were exposed, that of St. Catharine was reserved for the last. At length the genius descended, and through crowds that prostrated themselves before her in doubtful devotion, advanced to the brink of the river. After a short prayer she exposed the sacred head to the waters, and waved it with a gesture of inspiring command. At that moment, the night and the dark surface of the waters were swept by a glare of sudden light, a meteor low-hung and lurid passed over the upturned visages of the multitude, and disappearing in the darkness, left a train of bluish sparkles behind. The crowd, in the joy of confidence, believing it to be a signal of divine acceptance, burst into a shout of triumph, and the genius, flushed with the radiance of inspiration, turned to ascend her car, with a step that seemed to discard the earth. Her veil floated back with the elevation of her motion; Annibal beheld her face, without a shade or interruption, it was the face of Erminia, the original of the picture cherished by fantastic passion, and preserved without a hope of discovery. Carried beyond himself, he rushed through the crowd, he called on her in a voice the murmur of thousands could not suppress, he addressed her in alternate rapture and awe, he invoked her as an angel of light, and supplicated her as the beloved of his heart. The crowd, incensed and astonished, collected round him in numbers, which he strove to break through in vain, but still he contended, expostulated, and intreated, and holding out the picture, bid them behold a resistless witness of the truth of his passion, and the identity of its object. The crowd still surrounded and repelled, but he still spoke with more vivid eloquence, more animated passion, for he could perceive, at this moment, that the object he addressed, amid the pomp of procession, and the triumph almost of deification, had paused, and beheld him with a look in which surprize was quite unmixed with anger. Emboldened, he burst from the crowd with sudden strength, and implored her but to pause, but to listen. His story was wild, but true; he had seen her picture where she had perhaps never been. He had devoted his heart to the resemblance, and his life to the pursuit of her; he had unexpectedly, miraculously found her, and again he poured out before her, in tones no woman could hear unmoved, his passion, heightened by visionary feeling, and romantic discovery.

But at this moment the murmurs of the crowd, and the angry interference of the ecclesiastics, were lost in an universal roar of horror, and a rush of sudden flight, that, like the torrent it shunned, bore every thing before it. The river, with no physical cause, but subterraneous and invisible convulsions, suddenly rose with the rage of a tempest, and bearing down bank and mound, poured a waste of watery ruin on every side. There is a darkness of distress, a helplessness of resistance, an obscurity of fear, in the dread of perishing by water, such as are not found in even more terrible modes of destruction; but here, where safety was obstructed by multitudes, and the horrors of desolation were aggravated by recent triumph, where the eye dreaded even darkness as danger, and the foot knew not in what element its next step would be plunged; the confusion and terror were beyond all power of description, and Annibal felt himself hurried into involuntary safety, while his eyes were yet strained to discover the situation of her, to perish with whom was the only thought of the moment. The torrent of flight, however, which he resisted in vain, never ceased, till he was almost in the centre of the town, where the bed-rid and diseased were at that moment lamenting their absence from a ceremony from which they never could have escaped with life. Here the crowd paused to be assured of their safety, and Annibal, taking advantage of the first power of voluntary motion, hastened back to the spot which he feared he would now visit in vain. He was often obstructed by groups of fugitives, who still ran, though they were far from danger, but when he came near the brink of the water, which was now extended to the suburbs of the town, all was desolation, still and dark, save for the hoarse dashing of the waters, contending with obstructions it had not yet removed, and the solitary, intermitted shriek of some wanderer, whom even the terrors of the scene could not drive away from calling on the names of those they could hope to see no more, and pausing to distinguish was it the cry of death, or only the sullen rush of the water that answered them. He had wandered along the margin of the waters, sometimes climbing over the remains of half-demolished buildings, and sometimes wading through shallows, encumbered by corses. He had no name to call on; and over the dark and tossing waste before him, no power of sight could discover any thing but occasional streaks of light, where the yet unextinguished torches blazed on casual eminences, or were suspended from casements to assist the sufferers. At length, on a bank he descried a number of people who appeared to have forgotten their personal sufferings in some object of distinguished distress; when he reached the spot he discovered it.

The ruins of a bridge, which had once joined the shore, were now scarce seen in the midtide of the stream; arch after arch had yielded to the force of the torrent, and but a segment of the last yet remained, over whose rent and tottering fragments, every successive burst of the flood left a trace of foam higher than the last, a form was visible on the extreme ridge. Sometimes it was seen with a despairing hand, to wave a part of its garment towards the shore, from which it was only answered with outspread arms and fruitless cries. Annibal, bending from the bank, gazed on it; his sight, quickened by fear, could not fail: with a cry, in which anguish was wildly mixed with joy, he tore off his mantle, and plunged into the stream. He was a dexterous and bold swimmer, but had never before encountered such difficulties. The currents were adverse and irregular, the depths uncertain, and the obstacles (arising from fragments of trees, buildings, and human corses, which floated on the tide, or rose in eddying masses,) were such as neither skill nor strength could easily contend with; but as he struggled onward, every moment stimulated his efforts, for every moment the form became more distinct, and the distress more acute. With incredible exertions, he had reached the single and tottering arch; he grasped its projecting fragments, which he felt loose in his grasp, and in accents scarce audible, besought her to throw herself into his arms, while yet it was possible for him to save her. In the stupor of fear, she appeared to listen without a capacity of effort, till fragment after fragment crumbling from her hold, and the dashing of the spray rising to her breast, and Annibal's despairing adjurations almost lost in the deepening rush of the waters, she ceased to cling to the ruin, rather from weakness than energy, and sank into his arms. He received her with a mixture of joy and terror, but when he saw the dark waste he had to repass, his strength diminished, his burthen encreased, and the roar of the waters deepening round him, his heart sank within him, and his efforts became the blind strivings of despair. Still, however, he struggled onward, but obstructions increased; he had no longer any definite point to fix on or to reach; the shore seemed removed to an endless distance. He plunged on without regular effort or object, till anguish succeeding to hope, and courage exhausted on invincible difficulty, all recollection forsook him, and he dimly remembered, as in a dream, that he still held *her* he could no longer save, even when the waters were closing over their heads, and, to perish together, was all that hope could promise.

When he recovered his faculties, he believed himself in the regions of death; all was dark, and cold, and silent: he lay for some moments in strange expectation, till he felt the warmth of life returning, and was assured that he still existed. He arose, he felt his limbs stiff and drenched, but capable of motion; he felt his way before him, and his hands touched walls that were damp and stony; he called aloud, but his voice was repressed, as if by low roofs and a contracted space. As he still proceeded, he distinctly perceived steps retreating before him; he again called on the person he believed so near him, and was answered by a faint cry of fear, from a voice that made him pursue it as if he were winged. At that moment, the vault he was traversing, opening above his head, the first beams of a wan, beclouded moon fell through the chasm, and discovered a female figure standing near him, in an attitude of flight and terror. Annibal advanced, and the female again attempted to fly, though evidently scarce able to stand. Annibal flung himself on his knees, and throwing away his sword, addressed her in a voice and attitude to disarm all fear; he adjured her not to fly from one who had lately hazarded life to preserve her. He mingled the tenderness of passion with the strength of reason; told her that amid danger, to fly from protection was madness, and whispered that to convert that protection into a duty, and to sanction love by religion, had been the purpose that animated his search, and that even *now* made darkness and terror delightful, since they favoured the opportunity of urging it. The lady made no reply, but listened with that gracious silence, more flattering than speech to the pleadings of a lover. Annibal now venturing to rise and approach her, implored her to permit him to lead

CHARLES MATURIN

her to some place of safety, and to avail herself of the opportunity yet afforded them, by disclosing her name and circumstances. "By those long and beautiful tresses," said he, venturing to touch them, "I perceive you are not yet a nun; flatter the boldness this moment teaches me, and tell me you never will be one. If your vows are not irrevocable, my rank is high, and my family has influence to absolve you from ordinary engagements." As he spoke, he ventured still nearer, he wrung the wet from her dripping hair, and rending off his vest, wrapt it round her, and as still she shuddered, almost supported her in his arms. Though trembling at her own temerity, she neither shrunk from his touch, nor rejected his services, and at length murmured in a voice of music, "I am not a nun, I am a novice in the Ursuline Convent, I am unhappy, but I scarce knew it till this night. I know I should thank you for presreving my life, but the effort to address you deprives me of all power of speech; and I scarce regret it, when I recollect that perhaps I have already said too much."

On Annibal's mind, the effect of these few words, delivered with pause, and tremor, and hesitation, was beyond all he yet had heard of language, or imagined of eloquence. He prepared to answer her but found that the tremor of which she complained, had extended to himself. But to the speechless tenderness of passion, which would expend hours without an articulate sound, there was now no time; the waters were yet rushing over their heads, and they perceived that the place to which they had been thus miraculously conveyed, would afford them shelter no longer. They hastened therefore to quit it, and perceived that they were among baths in the extremity of the town, which had been deluged in the first fury of the flood, which was now departing from them, and whose retiring tides yet terrified them, though a pledge of safety. They emerged from them with some difficulty, and found themselves about the dawn of morning on the verge of a spot which had once been a vineyard, but which was now a shapeless marsh. A little further boats were plying amid recent gardens, and often entangling their oars in the vestments and corses of their owners; and near them a group of ecclesiastics were employed, some in offering rewards for gems and relics that had been lost the preceding night, and others with impotent superstition, displaying those that had escaped, to check the further progress of mischief. A band of these, among whom was the confessor of the Ursuline convent, recognizing the companion of Annibal, hastily advanced, and reclaimed her. Exhausted with fatigue and emotion, she sunk into the arms of the monks, and Annibal in vain watched to read in her closing eye, an invitation to pursuit, or a promise of hope.

Spent with the struggles of the night he was now returning, but the streets were yet full of wailings he could not hear without pausing, and of miseries he could not pass without an effort to relieve; he therefore continued to wander amid the scene of devastation, affording all the assistance his strength yet could spare, and when that failed, directing those whose distraction had rendered their exertions desultory and inefficient. As he was thus employed, he observed a person at some distance, who sprung from crag to crag, and from ruin to ruin, with a giddiness that seemed to mock at danger, yet apparently without any definite object. His gestures were so wild, and his velocity so restless, that Annibal for a moment believed him to be some one, whom the late disasters had bereft of reason. He was not mistaken in the conjecture, though his senses, impaired by fatigue, had failed to recognize the object; it was his faithful Filippo, who, frantic at the absence of his master, had flown from place to place in quest of him all night, till his exhausted strength scarce sufficed to bear him to Annibal's feet, to gasp out the joy, the expression of which almost killed him. They returned together through the remaining streets. Of the inn, where they had arrived the preceding night, there was not now a vestige, and it was with difficulty they procured from the dismayed and scattered inhabitants, the refreshments their fatigue and weakness could no longer want.

In the dream which visited the long and placid sleep of Annibal, the angel form of the novice floated in a thousand lights and attitudes. Sometimes she moved before him in majesty, and sometimes witched him with a smile, sometimes he caught the skirt of her robe, which was luminous as a cloud, sometimes a tress of her hair, and sometimes her milky arms, whose softness seemed to bend at his touch. Lapt in the luxury of vision, he almost resisted the return of his faculties, till he remembered a resolution he had formed on separating from her, of immediately repairing to the convent, to learn her name and rank, and interpose, if possible, to prevent the obstruction her situation threatened to his hopes and his passion. It was evening when he arrived at the convent; much of the day had passed in repose, and much in preparation to wait on the Abbess, for he had no credentials but his person and address, which, in spite of recent fatigue and previous suffering, were still powerfully conciliating. But when he arrived he found the community engaged in a solemn service, of which the object

CHARLES MATURIN

was to deprecate the continuance or repetition of the late terrible visitation, and implore forgiveness for the sins for which it had been inflicted. Annibal lingered near the walls, in hope of distinguishing the voice of the beautiful novice amid the solemn swell of sound that rose at intervals on the stillness of evening.

In the interval of his next visit to the convent, he had sufficiently subdued the impetuosity of his feelings to recollect, that to alarm the Abbess by precipitate inquiries, and eager admiration, would be only to defeat or delay his pursuit; when he was admitted, therefore, on the following day, he confined himself to asking with ill-affected indifference, the name, rank, and relatives of the novice, who had at the late festival, personated the genius of martyrdom. The Abbess answered with a trepidation, which shewed that she endeavoured to conceal under embarrassed silence, her knowledge of a subject secret or important unexpectedly revived. She informed him that the novice was named Ildefonsa Mauzoli, that her birth was mean and shameful, that she had been consigned to a monastic life by authority she could not resist, and that she was now in the last week of her noviciate. Annibal, shocked at the near prospect of his loss, now disclosed his rank and his passion, but still suppressed his name, he warned her not to trifle with his feelings by false intelligence, or imperious measures; he told her of his high ecclesiastical interest, from the influence of which he had no doubt of obtaining a dispensation from the vows of Ildefonsa, even if she were a novice; he indignantly demanded by what power could she be devoted to a conventual life, exclusive of her own consent, and refused to credit the particulars of her birth, fortunes, and monastic choice, unless confirmed by herself. The abbess, incensed in her turn, demanded by what right a stranger broke into her sanctuary, to affront her veracity, and dispute her jurisdiction; she blamed herself for the condescension which he had abused, and sternly refused to permit him to see or speak with Ildefonsa. Annibal, alarmed for the consequences of power united with malevolence, began to mingle apologies for his vehemence, with continued intimations of his rank and influence, and of the danger of proceeding with precipitation, which that influence might make her repent and reverse. "Away, Cavalier!" said the abbess, "and when next you disturb the peace of consecrated walls, let it be with pretences at least less shallow than a tale of rank, you cannot even confirm by the disclosure of your name, and a menace of influence, which, whatever be its power, can scarce annul the ties between a recluse and her God."

As she spake she rose to depart, and Annibal quitted the convent tormented with that peculiar fear which dreads secret malignity and unconjectured machinations.

A thousand times he lamented the precipitate harshness of his language to the abbess, yet reflected that whatever had been his language, the intelligence would probably have been the same, that still she would have delighted in the exercise of petty tyranny, and the infliction of arbitrary misery. His future conduct he knew not how to direct; he dreaded the idea of quitting the neighbourhood, least some advantage might be taken of his absence; yet to stay was useless, for from personal influence nothing was to be hoped. Amid all his plans he was astonished at his own temerity, thus disposing of life, while of life he was almost uncertain, and meditating the liberation and possession of an object to whom he yet knew not but he might be an object of indifference. But that his hopes were romantic, was no discouragement to him; he took a flattering omen from the extraordinary events in which he had been engaged; he thought that in every thing strange and difficult there was a spirit congenial to real passion. He would not purchase the prize it promised him but on terms of difficulty and enterprise, as the children of an ancient nation were not permitted to taste their food till they had earned it by the effort of bringing it down with their arrows from the summit of a tree. But immediate decision on his movements was necessary, and he decided with all the judgment he possessed.

He dismissed Filippo to Puzzoli to his uncle, with letters in which he explained, but not fully, his situation, excused his absence by stating his apprehensions for the safety of the lady, and intreated his uncle's interference with the abbess, and the bishop of the diocese, or, if necessary, with higher authority, to prevent devotion to a monastic life in an object of whom he strongly suspected the reluctance to it, and whose loss would consign him to despair. The strange and hasty vicissitudes of his life from tranquillity to danger, and from death to love, he endeavoured to palliate without revealing what he believed of the crimes of his father, or what he knew of his own dark persecution. When he had dismissed Filippo, though it was now night, he hastened back to the convent, to gaze on the walls that enclosed Ildefonsa, and enjoy that nameless delight which passion indulges in being near those it yet cannot see. The night was dark; he wandered round the walls at an unsuspected distance, till grown bold from security he approached close to them, and as light after light disappeared from the narrow windows, delighted himself with thinking he could discover the habitation of Ildefonsa, or imagine her employments, among which be dreamed a thought of *him* might sometimes steal upon the solemnity of mingled worship, or the lonely orisons of the cell. As he yet lingered, the noise of something falling lightly at his feet aroused him; he stooped, and picked up a flower, which as he held in his hand he perceived to contain a small paper buried in the petal. He in vain endeavoured to distinguish the writing, but convinced that it contained something more than fancy had yet promised, he hastened back to the inn, guarding the paper by a thousand superfluous precautions, and calling for a taper, locked himself into his apartment, and sat down to feast in solitude.

The billet, which was intricately folded, contained the following lines: "Whether I am wrong in writing thus, I know not, but I fear I shall scarce condemn myself if I am. If I do not misunderstand your expressions, they intimate that I am to you the object of a passion which I yet know only by name, but of which I fear I shall not much longer be ignorant. Thus dangerous is it to see you; but greater dangers beset and terrify me. I am surrounded by enemies and by snares, which alone I resist in vain. Helpless and dismayed, I fly to the first arm that is extended for protection. Should you betray me, remember there is no honour in oppressing solitary weakness. The same reasons impel me to fear and to trust you. Heaven protect me, I know not what I do! At the extremity of the west wall of the garden there is a breach, occasioned by the late commotions, which has not been repaired; it is almost concealed by laurel and arbutus, but tomorrow night there will be a moon, and you can discover it. I will be there, for liberty to walk in the garden till a late hour is still allowed me. I write by stealth and with difficulty; I dreaded least this note should escape you, and enclosed it in a tuberose to ascertain its descent. At the same hour tomorrow evening, in the same place, a tuberose will fall at your feet, if it be possible for me to repair to the garden, if not, I shall drop a cluster of violets from the grating. But is this a dream, such as sometimes float on the mists of my cell, or shall I indeed see you there, and forget while I see you that I am the persecuted, the disowned, the oppressed Ildefonsa Mauzoli."

Over these lines, perused a thousand times, and folded next his heart, Annibal vainly tried to sleep. He rose, and lighting the taper he had extinguished, to read it, sat down again to its perusal; while he held it in his hand, he felt as if he had a treasure which the lapse of ages could not exhaust; yet when again impelled by unsated curiosity, he again read it, he felt that its contents were brief and ineffectual.

The day passed in anticipations of delight, and when the moon rose he hasted to the convent. He reached unobserved the foot of the turret, where he had stood the preceding night, and had not been there many moments when a tuberose fell at his feet; he scarce gave himself time for an exclamation of rapture, and hastened to the appointed spot. There is no telling but to lovers the tumult with which he watched for her steps amid the murmurs of the foliage, and the eagerness with which he sprung forward when the tremulous glittering of moonlight falling on the light leaves of an acacia, made him believe he saw her white garments floating near him. At length she arrived. The first meeting of youthful lovers may well be imagined; the inarticulate murmurs that spake more than language, the looks still more eloquent than they; the sighs of vestal beauty breathed through the fragrance of a moonlight bower, her cheek kindling in its ray, her eye wandering but not withdrawn, her steps hesitating yet lingering, timidity flushing into confidence, and sudden tenderness checked by timidity, her whole frame trembling in the alternate sway of fear and love. And, on the other hand, a young man, unlike any of his species she had ever before beheld, with all the animation of courage, and all the attractions of beauty, who promised liberation and who whispered love, it was not in nature to resist it; the time, the place breathed to them such thoughts as were perilous to hear; upon love confidence is soon engrafted, and Ildefonsa related her wild and simple story to Annibal before they separated.

"My infant faculties must have developed soon," said she, "for while almost unable to walk, I recollect perfectly being every day caressed by a lady whose form and mien were so different from those of the inmates of the cottage where I was nursed, that I invented in infantine endearment a new term to distinguish her, and the sensations with which her presence always inspired me. As I grew up, other circumstances caught my attention. The lady's visits were always in the evening, they were passed in tears and lamentations, and ended in a hurried departure. I also observed my dress and food to be different from those of the people with whom I lived, whose attention, though always assiduous and affectionate, was redoubled on every visit from the lady. When I was about five years old, I was also visited by a cavalier, who lavished on me the same tenderness and grief as the lady. At length I was suddenly removed, and for some time wandered through the apartments of a magnificent castle, where solemnity and sorrow reigned in every room, and where I saw the cavalier and the lady for a few moments together; they stood at opposite ends of the room, surveying each other with looks of which I still remember that the anguish was mixed with distracting fondness. Their souls seemed rushing into their eyes; looks were all they durst indulge in; each looked as if to speak was to be undone; it was in vain I ran from one to another, endeavouring with childish blandishments to soothe the distress I did not understand, and could not bear to behold. Children are apt to be impressed by clamorous grief and violent exhibition, but on me this scene of silent agony made an impression never to be effaced. After this I returned to the cottage, and was visited and caressed as usual, till one night, one terrible night, never to be explained or forgotten, the cavalier came to the cottage with an air of distraction, and placing me before him on his horse, plunged into the forest at the close of evening. My thoughts were disengaged, and though disturbed I was not terrified. I employed myself in observing the furniture of the horse and his rider, which were sumptuous and warlike. We were now within sight of the turrets of a castle, which, tinged with the last light of day, rose over the dark forest tops, when several ruffians rushed on the cavalier from a thicket we were passing through. They were no common murderers, it was no common spirit of vengeance and horror that flashed from their visages and deepened their howl of wild delight. Afterwards I remember nothing distinctly. Mine eyes were blinded by the glare of steel, mine ears were stunned by sounds which I echoed in convulsions of fear, around me were only the cries of slaughter and the strife of despair. I was thrown aside as one who was neither remembered to injure or to spare: the horrors of the struggle I do not recollect clearly, but he must have fallen before so many assailants. When my faculties returned, I found myself again in the cottage; I cast my eyes around timidly, and saw one of the bloody forms of the forest bending over the embers of a fire. I closed my eyes, and tried to be insensible again. I was delirious the remainder of the night, and only roused to recollection by sounds of such terror as insensibility resisted in vain; they were the voices of the murderers which muttered all night around my bed; I heard also the steps and voices of others, whom I feared to look at through the darkness, lest I should see realised the shapes which imagination poured on me when my eyes were closed.

"At intervals I saw lightnings of blasting force and brightness flashing through the casements of the hut, and heard sounds rolling over the roof, which I afterwards heard were the thunders of a volcanic eruption. In the morning, when I at length ventured to inquire and to complain, I was checked by words and looks of prophetic sadness, and the woman to whom I was intrusted often began to speak to me, but suddenly broke off without power to proceed; whether distrusting the levity of childhood, or resisting the violation of confidence, I know not. A few days after I was conveyed to a convent, where I was placed to board, and from which I was removed, as afterwards from others, with much hurry of trepidation and many stratagems of concealment. Parent, relation, or inquiring friend I had none; the life that had begun in calamity proceeded in mystery. At every place where I resided, I was indeed told of a friend by whose directions my life was managed, but whom I was never to see: this friend I was exhorted to conciliate by silent reverence and remote submission. I felt little complacency towards an invisible benefactor, by whom I was supported just above indigence, and hurried about from place to place without any communications of affection or confidence.

At length I was some years ago placed in this convent, where I was told at my entrance I must prepare to take the vows, and seclude myself from the world for ever. Solitude and ignorance had left me little power of choice, and little temptation to resistance. At first, therefore, I heard this with little reluctance; but as I grew up, strange visions floated before me, of that world which I was to resign without having known. Sometimes I delighted to imagine the world a region whose gales breathed felicity, and whose soil poured forth roses spontaneously, whose inhabitants melted in bowers of balm, or sparkled in palaces of amethyst; and sometimes it appeared to me as in the dark dreams of that visioned night, every hand armed with the weapon of blood, and every visage flashing the flames of hell! Yet even over this picture of terrors was shed a light of romantic splendour and wild adventure, which, modified as it was by length of time and weakness of childish perceptions, left on my mind an impression of curiosity, mingled with awe, indeed, but not remote from desire. Whether my meditations on the world were just or not, the result was a determination not to quit it thus ignorant and incurious. I communicated my resolution to my abbess, who heard me with a burst of indignation, which when I had suffered to pass over, I found her arguments not equally forcible. I resisted her, therefore, respectfully but tenaciously. When she was weary of contending with one she could neither convince nor punish, she wrote to this person whom she represented as the arbiter of my fate, and whose interference she looked on as irresistible. Her appeal was followed by a haughty command to take the veil, without opposition, which would only prove the impotence of my contumacy, and the imbecility of my helplessness. I was now roused to resistance; for whom will not oppression rouse? I demanded by whom I was detained and dictated to? I demanded to be restored to my natural protectors, and affirmed it was impossible there could be a human being so destitute of support and protection as I was represented to be. The answer was short, but decisive: 'Your birth is infamous; your parents are dead; you must take the veil or perish.' Four years have since been wasted in oppression without the right of command, and of resistance without the hope of triumph. I have often resolved to fly, but where can I fly, to whom the world is a wilderness? I have sometimes meditated to submit, but how shall I submit, to whom a convent is worse than a tomb? The sight of you has given a new spring to hope; when I think of you other thoughts mix themselves with the joys of liberation; the world, since you have said 'I love,' is no longer a dream of imaginary felicity; yet the same sounds would, I think, sooth and sustain me were they never to be repeated beyond the echoes of a cloister."

When Ildefonsa had finished her short narrative, Annibal, whose thoughts while she spoke were busied in remote events, drew from it this conclusion, that she was the concealed and persecuted heir of honours which were usurped by murderers. The rest of the interview passed in a retrospect of the fearful events that had introduced them to each other. Ildefonsa, with many others on the first alarm, had attempted to reach the town by a bridge, which gave way while hundreds were on it, and to the ruins of which she clung without a hope of safety, till rescued by Annibal. They had become insensible when near the margin of the stream, to which they had been wafted by its fluctuations before they recovered. On parting, many plans of liberation were proposed, of which that which Annibal had already adopted appeared the most judicious, to employ the interest of a powerful ecclesiastic in removing Ildefonsa from monastic restraint, the oppression of which he encouraged her to bear with tenderness that lamented what it advised. They were now separating, when they were startled by a noise; both trembled and looked round; a shadow, so faint that to Ildefonsa it was scarce visible, passed before them. "What did you see?" said Annibal in a voice of fear. "I heard a faint sound," said Ildefonsa answering vaguely. "What did you *see?*" said Annibal impatiently. "I saw the shadow of a tree," she replied, terrified by his voice. "I saw the form of a fiend," said Annibal gloomily. "What do you say?" said Ildefonsa still more alarmed. "That I am destroyed!" said Annibal, and he rushed from her with unconscious wildness.

Filippo was detained four days at Puzzoli by the indisposition of the prior, to whom he at length presented his letters. The prior, a man of strong passions and extensive power, proud of patronage, and ostentatious of authority, immediately espoused Annibal's cause, wrote to all he could command or importune, sent to Annibal a magnificent present, and invited him to reside with him at Puzzoli. This intelligence was sufficiently inspiriting, and the progress he had continued to make in Ildefonsa's affections was such as might animate a less sanguine imagination. Yet when Filippo returned, he found his master plunged in a gloom which nothing could explain or dispel; in vain Filippo watched him with the mute assiduity of humble affection, in vain he exhausted all the flatteries of his eloquence in painting his approaching happiness and distinction, the resistless austerity and munificent affection of the prior, the disappointment of the abbess and her secret employer, and the triumphant liberation of the Signora Ildefonsa, with part of whose story he had been entrusted. Annibal remained silent, or only replied by interjections, which proved his mind was far from the subject on which he spoke. He still resorted in the evening to the convent, but for the evening he also appeared to have some other employment. His despondency increased every moment, and Filippo, who at first pretended to be his counsellor, had now little business but to watch his looks silently in the day, and count his groans sleeplessly all night. Ildefonsa perceived the change also, but in the precarious and distressful state of their passion there were so many reasons for melancholy, that, judging of his feelings by her own, she ascribed them to the same cause, and endeavoured to inspirit him with hopes she scarcely dared to indulge herself.

It was in one of these melancholy hours, which were half devoted to fear and half to love, that Filippo, who watched at the extremity of the wall, rushed forward with terror in his countenance, and motioned to the lovers to separate. Ildefonsa retired through the garden in haste, and Annibal retreated with Filippo, who hurried along his master with looks and broken interjections of fear, till they had reached a considerable distance from the convent. "Signor," said Filippo, "I have seen him!" Annibal made no answer. "Signor," said Filippo stopping, and turning the light of his lantern full on Annibal, "I *have* seen him!" Annibal moved onwards silently: they reached the inn. Filippo, emboldened by mutual terror, entered the room along with him. "Signor," said he, gazing in his master's face, and not speaking till he was near enough to whisper, "Signor, I have seen him tonight!"—"I see him every night," said Annibal gloomily. Filippo retreated. "Yes, Filippo, every night. He is not dead, poison cannot kill him; he crosses my path when I move, he lurks in my chamber when I sit, he pervades all the elements, and whispers audibly in my ears even when their senses are closed."—"Signor, what is it you say?"—"I know not what I say; once I hoped my heart would have burst before I could have uttered thus much, but it is in vain, human resistance is in vain. I know him not, through mist and vision my mind grasps at him in vain; but I feel that though his character is shadowy, his influence is substantial; I feel that I am—did I say his victim? Oh, not yet, not yet!"

He fell on his knees, and prayed in agony; Filippo sunk beside him. "Oh, Signor! you break my heart. If the terrible being I have seen be yet alive, the guilt is not yours, nor is it mine. I had hoped, indeed, he had perished; nor would I have felt so much fear from his spectre, as I did from his living presence this night. Oh, Signor, he is not a being our hands could reach! we are sinful men, Signor; let us confess to some holy man, and beg the aids of the church; we are sinful men, and our offences visit us in these shapes of terror—I never recollected them so distinctly as I do this night!"—"Filippo," said his unhappy master, "I have yielded to the weakness of nature once and the first time, no one has seen me thus subdued before; dismiss your fears, *you* are in no danger; this business requires other agents, leave me to encounter it alone. I believe I am for the dark hour and the unutterable task; I believe I am resigned by my better angel; a blast has spread over life, and the organs with which I behold objects are seared and discoloured. Go from me, I no longer wish to feel any thing human near me; it enfeebles me, and my nerves should be of iron now. I should be mantled in midnight, and armed with serpents—I would I were; I would I were muffled in blindness, or hissed into stupor. Filippo, do not heed me; I struggle no longer from conviction, but from despair. Filippo, do not heed me. The enemy of souls, it is said, has great power over melancholy spirits; I have been melancholy from my youth, but this is reality, terrible, overwhelming reality; here is fact and consequence! Filippo, why do you gaze thus? Do not heed me."

Filippo, ignorant of the real cause of the convulsions of Annibal's mind, and ascribing them to the dread that the being he had seen was the spectre of the poisoned monk, endeavoured to console him by the hope that he had escaped the effects of the poison, and was yet alive and uninjured. "I know, I know he is alive!" said Annibal distractedly. "There is then nothing to fear or to be reproached with, Signor; I will get absolution for giving him the drink, and we will go to the holy prior happily."—"And who shall give me absolution?" said Annibal. "For what, Signor?" asked Filippo, confounded by the question. "Villain!" said Annibal, starting into frenzy, "do not name it, do not utter it even mentally; would you tempt *me* to speak it? would you feast your ears with my ruin? You are one of his emissaries, bribed to haunt me in his absence, and shut up every breathing hole of remission, every glimpse of quiet."

Filippo, astonished and dismayed, forbore to speak, and Annibal soon after perceiving him about to quit the room, desired him to sleep at the foot of his bed that night. Filippo obeyed, and Annibal, throwing himself on the bed, closed his eyes. Filippo rose, and bending over him, watched if he slept. His master, starting with the quickness of habitual fear, demanded why he had risen? "Be not displeased, Signor, these are relics of power and sanctity, every one of these crosses has touched the shrine of Loretto; I was going while you slept to lay them under your pillow, so that no evil thing might hurt you." Annibal silently suffered him, and again tried to rest, but Filippo again rose, and began to tie something about the pillars of the bed. "And these, Signor, I have but thought of this moment, they have power against all wizards and unholy things that walk the earth in the shape of men, but are not; this is a shred of the cloth in which the head of St. Januarius was wrapt when it was first discovered: while this is on your bed you are safe from spell and wizardry."—"It is indeed a relic of virtue if I am," said Annibal heavily; "but where did you procure them, Filippo?"—"My uncle Michelo gave them to me on his dying bed, he had purchased them from a Dominican."—"Take them away quick, the haunting of that name will not depart from me all night; let not Michelo touch me, it brings back a thousand images; dark and disastrous thoughts are with me when he is named. Lie down again, Filippo, and speak not till the morning." Filippo obeyed, but twice started up in the night, from an apprehension there were others in the room: so loud were Annibal's exclamations and struggles in his sleep.

To these nights the occupations of the day sometimes afforded relief. The presence of Ildefonsa soothed both his melancholy and his passion; the variety, too, and spirit of adventure which the circumstances of their interview were diversified by, occupied his mind and his imagination. Sometimes the signal of their meeting was the low tones of Ildefonsa's maudoline breathing from among the moon-lit foliage; sometimes that of disappointment was a cluster of withered flowers dropt from the grating of her cell; once he heard her utter sounds of a tone different from those of common tenderness, and paused before he approached her to interrupt it. The lines were these:

I

We meet no more—oh, think on me!
Though lost to sense for ever,
Yet faithful Memory's record dear
Whispers—we shall not sever.

II

No, by that lip of richest sweets,
Oh, never press'd by me!
No, by that soft eye's humid fires
I must remember thee!

III

Each passing object's casual light
Shall oft revive its power;
Even you, pale beams, shall wake the though:
They lit our parting hour.

IV

And then I'll think I see that form,
In ardent beauty glowing;
And at the thought a tear shall wake,
As fond as now 'tis flawing.

Annibal advanced from his concealment; Ildefonsa discovered him, and said in faultering accents, "Those lines were suggested to me when I had seen you once, and expected to see you no more."—"And was it possible," said Annibal, "you could think such a passion could exhaust itself in one night's rapture and conflict?"—"Were it not better that it should than to have lingered through a few nights more only to expire?"—"What do you say, Ildefonsa?"—"That where there is no confidence there can be no passion. Annibal, Annibal, are these like the sweet hours of early love? is this the mixture of soul and feeling you have talked of? Your eye is wild, Annibal, and your cheek is pale; you will not tell me the cause, yet you say you love me."—"If you love me," said Annibal vehemently, "mention this no more. Can the communication of misery and guilt endear affection or increase happiness?"—"Of guilt, Annibal!"—"Yes; is there not mental guilt? may not a man be a murderer, a parricide in *thought?* do you think that the hardened wretch whose hands reek every night with blood, unrepented and unremembered, suffers like *him* over whose soul the image of anticipated guilt sits for ever, the absence of commission more than balanced by the horrors of feeling and remorse? Oh, Ildefonsa! the anguish of a mind unwillingly depraved, to which evil is aggravated by the bitterness of compulsion and the revoltings of innate integrity, such a state was to be *imagined* in the list of human sufferings till it was inflicted on me."—"What do you mean? Blessed Mother! what do you mean by those words?—"Nothing, I know not myself; let us talk of your liberation. How did we wander to this subject?"—"It was my fault, and I should have forborne it, for I perceive it always laps you in waywardness and musing; it was my fault; but my mind was strangely touched tonight. I again saw that ominous stranger, whom when I see I believe in my fear every thing I have heard of one that watches over my life for evil"—"Who? what stranger is this? why did you not tell me of him before? what manner of man is he?"— "You startle me, Annibal, by your vehemence. He is a monk; I have observed him some days past in consultation with the abbess; I know not of what convent he is, or what brings him to ours, but I feel a wild awe as he passes and looks on me."—"His name, have you heard his name?"—"I think I heard the abbess call him Father Schemoli; but I will watch him more closely, and learn—" "No, no, no, approach him not, touch him not, it is unlawful to hold converse with him. Ildefonsa, my innocent love, beware of intercourse with that being; it is not good to hold it; once I joined my hand to his, and his grasp has never been relaxed since."

Ildefonsa now terrified to tears, terrified Annibal by her distress. He attempted to sooth her, but every effort to diversify their melancholy conference was rendered ineffectual by involuntary recurrence or gloomy abstraction. "There is a spell over *me* too," said Annibal, with a painful smile, "*my* mind has has also been strangely touched. I ascribe it," said he, forcing himself to proceed, "to a prediction I recollect relating to myself, which sheds a gloom over me I cannot dispel."— "What is the purport of it?" said Ildefonsa. "That I am to be flattered with a prospect of the completion of my wishes, never to be verified; that the object I love is to be torn from me at the moment of possession; and that life is to change its complexion at the period when its aspect becomes brilliant with joy and hope."—"The prediction is so general, it must have been uttered in infancy," said Ildefonsa. "Possibly long before it," said Annibal, heavily. "Has it been so long in circulation?" replied Ildefonsa, endeavouring to evade the application. "I only heard it last night," said Annibal with emphasis. "It is a melancholy one," said Ildefonsa, yielding to the complexion of the hour and the conference. "There is an alternative," said Annibal. "I would embrace any alternative preferably," said Ildefonsa, heedlessly. "Would you,—would you indeed?" said Annibal, with sudden eagerness. "I would, assuredly," she replied, "unless—" "Unless what?" "Unless it involved a crime—or—" "Aye, aye, I know all you would say," said Annibal. "Would the degree of the crime make any difference?" said he, after a pause, then again interrupted her with "But that is of no consequence to me." From a conference thus wildly broken, neither could derive much pleasure; they separated, uncheered by a promise of speedy return, for Ildefonsa informed her lover, that attendance on a peculiar ceremony would detain her for three following nights.

This interval Filippo observed his master to pass in unmitigated wretchedness, and overheard him in solitude and in sleep, perpetually repeating to himself the ominous sentence which he had communicated to Ildefonsa. On the morning of the fourth day, letters arrived from Puzzoli of the most momentous import. They contained an order from the Bishop of the diocese for the removal of sister Ildefonsa Mauzoli, of the Ursuline convent, to another in Puzzoli. This the prior informed Annibal in another letter, was only a preparatory step to her being declared free to adopt or reject a monastic life. The letter concluded by pressing Annibal's removal to Puzzoli, where the event of his love and fortune seemed to demand his presence. The order was brought to the convent by a messenger of the prior's, who was also an ecclesiastical officer, and presented by him to the abbess; Filippo accompanied him by the order of Annibal. The delivery of the order was attended with some formality, and witnessed by a number of attendants.

Hour after hour, Annibal counted the delay of the messenger with impatience, which was at length discoloured by fear. Unable to communicate the cause of his agitation, and agitated by other causes, he wandered on the margin of the river, now dark and wild with winter, and tried in vain to expel from his thought the dolorous sounds, which his lips were incessantly forming, while he struggled to forget them. Late in the evening Filippo returned breathless, with strange intelligence, which at first he could only vent in exclamation; compassion for his master's solicitude, at length made him coherent, and he related the events of the day, but his peculiar manner, and numerous interruptions may be spared in the narration.

He had pressed with many other attendants, into the apartment where the messenger of the prior was introduced to the abbess. She received the paper with submission, but on receiving it, crossed herself with marks of grief and dismay, and then addressing herself to the messenger, said, "This order comes too late, except to renew our grief for the loss of a departed sister; Ildefonsa Mauzoli is now beyond the reach of earthly power, she expired yesterday."

The messenger, with strong expressions of concern, and some of distrust, quitted the apartment, where the clamorous distress of the nuns, which seemed to wait a signal for its renewal, contended in vain with the loud murmurs in which the attendants testified their suspicion and resentment. But Filippo, whose first impulse of concern was superseded by his penetration, determined not to quit the convent thus incuriously. He dreaded his master's despair; he mistrusted the malignity of the Abbess; and while the attendants were dispersing, he glided through the passages of the convent, and repaired to the chapel, where he dispensed his prostrations with such unction, and examined the relics with so profound a visage, that he attracted the notice of an old, deaf, crippled nun, who usually loitered in the chapel to tax the faith or charity of devout visitors. By this sybil he was led about from one saint's nail to another's eyebrow; he was shewn the dust that dropt from the crayons of St. Luke, and a tile which fell from the Holy House of Loretto, in its aerial journey from Palestine to Italy. In the course of his enquiries he

CHARLES MATURIN

satisfied himself that *she* was almost completely deaf, and nearly blind; he now therefore reconnoitred the chapel with some degree of confidence. Through one of the upper arcades, he observed the nuns passing with such frequency, that he immediately conjectured it opened to the gallery where their cells were ranged. To confirm his conjectures, by the gratuity of a few zechins, he prevailed on the nun to repeat a certain number of prayers for him, at a shrine which owed the distinction more to the distance from the place of his devotion, than to his belief of its uncommon sanctity. When he had made this arrangement, (in the prosecution of which he very soon had the satisfaction of seeing the aged nun fast asleep) he cautiously approached the part of the chapel under the arcade; he knew not in what manner to convey his presence or his purposes. A small portable stringed instrument, which he had purchased on the way from one of the attendants, in hopes of soothing his master's gloomy solitude, presented itself as a lucky medium of unsuspected communication. He touched it, but the old nun, awoke by so unusual a sound, tottered forward to demand the reason of it, at the same time assuring Filippo that he had been so unfortunate as to disturb a vision in which St. Ursula was just about to promise her any favour she could ask for the young visitor, on condition he applied for the situation of gardener to the convent, "For our gardener," said the nun, "has *grown so old*—" "Venerable mother," said Filippo, "return to the shrine, doubtless you will be favoured with a continuance of the vision. I myself received an uncommon accession just at the moment, which, with the help of your prayers, may improve into an actual call to become gardener to St. Ursula. With regard to this instrument, venerable mother, I was once, when wandering over the *Andes* (which are a ridge of high mountains dividing Germany from the Island of Africa,) chased by a band of bloody, unbelieving Moors, I had no instrument of defence but *this*, on which I was inspired to play a hymn to St. Ursula, the effect of which was so sacred, that the whole troop was converted, and remain good Catholics to this day. I made a vow on the spot, that on this very instrument I would play the same hymn at the shrine of St. Ursula, as soon as I arrived in Italy; I beg, therefore, reverend mother, you will do me no disquiet in the performance of my vow." "Heaven forbid!" replied the religious, "I never heard a more glorious recital, it is exactly like the legends which the confessor reads to us on the vigils of the saints."

She then returned to the shrine, where she was soon wrapt into another vision on the call of the young gardener. But however the deaf nun might be dismissed without much cost of dexterity, he knew not how to lull the vigilant sisters. It was a lucky hour, *that* allotted to private devotion, which most of them were resigning to sleep. He recollected an air he had heard Annibal sing in suppressed tones near the garden, while he waited for Ildefonsa; it was plaintive, and might well pass for a pilgrim's song. He touched a slight prelude on his instrument, and then sung the following words, *mezza voce:*—

> *If she who weeps a lover's woes,*
> *Yet linger near these conscious walls,*
> *Of absent love the song she knows,*
> *She hears its fond, though timid calls.*

He paused—all was still. He repeated it in a voice tremulous with disappointment, and a light vibration, (low and brief as a sigh) of Ildefonsa's well-known maudoline, came to his ear, filling him with confidence and joy. His recognition of this signal was without doubt or fear, for he had heard his master say, that Ildefonsa was the only inmate within the walls that touched the maudoline. He rose joyfully, and was quitting the chapel without disturbing the old nun, to learn the success of her second conference with St. Ursula, when a sound near him arrested his steps. He knew not to what direction to refer it; it seemed that of a human voice, yet it issued from under his feet! He listened—"There was no sound," said a voice from beneath the shrine, "it was fancy; the chapel is empty."—"Then let us ascend," said a female voice, "for I am suffocated with these damps. Is your apprehension of discovery sufficiently removed?"—"Perfectly;" answered the first, which Filippo discovered to be that of Father Schemoli. "Discovery *cannot* penetrate where you have led me. Tomorrow night, then, reverend mother, this serpent shall be crushed in the dark! May I rely on your assistant?"—"As firmly as on your own resolution, father."—"*That* has never failed:" said Schemoli, emphatically.

The time which they took to ascend, and enter the chapel by a concealed grating, in the pavement of the shrine, gave Filippo an opportunity to screen himself behind the profuse volumes of drapery that enfolded it; but when he saw the confessor and abbess of the convent, for that was the female, ascend from the shrine, and pass the spot where he stood, he ceased to hope for life. They passed him, however, and drawing near the door, observed the nun; the abbess awoke her; "Why are you sleeping?" said the abbess. "I was not sleeping," replied the nun. "Strangers might have entered the chapel," said the confessor. "That is impossible, while I am here," observed the nun. "Are you sure no one has been here *since*," asked the abbess. "There was one young pilgrim," said the nun, exalting her voice, "who went through the pannelled door, behind the drapery at the left pediment of the shrine of St. Ursula." Filippo took the hint as dexterously as it was given, and gliding through the door which he had not till then observed, retreated silently through a remote passage. "You were very particular in observing the manner of his exit," said Schemoli. "To tell you the truth, I let him out myself," answered the nun. "She is foolish," said the abbess, retiring with Schemoli, "but strict and faithful."

In the mean time Filippo hasted to his master; he informed him of the supposed machinations of the abbess; he did not conceal from him the presence and agency of Schemoli, he averred it his belief that the Signora Ildefonsa did exist, though he feared it was determined she should not exist much longer. All personal interference was now fruitless, as he would probably be excluded from the walls of the convent, but as the following night was assigned for the celebration of her funeral, at which strangers would of course be present, he advised Annibal to repair thither with the officer who had brought the Bishop's order, to state the circumstances which had occurred, and of which he (Filippo) would avow himself a witness, cover the abbess with confusion, and interest the spectators and the ecclesiastics in the restitution of Ildefonsa. Every thing indeed, that courage or ingenuity could propose, was anticipated in the advice of Filippo, which Annibal prepared to adopt, with a heart he was delighted to feel beating with human passions once more.

The funeral of a sister of the Ursuline convent was always attended with peculiar solemnity, from the abbess's wish to impress strangers who were permitted to attend it, with an opinion of the sanctity of her retreat, as well as to spread over the minds of the inmates a deeper shade of religious awe and submission. The office was to be performed in the chapel at midnight: two hours before which every avenue was filled by strangers, among whom Annibal and his attendants found no difficulty in mingling. His spirits were solemnly touched; the idea of Ildefonsa associated with the persuasion and imagery of death, (though from death he believed her sufficiently distant) the gliding steps, the dim light, and the low requiem, repelled the tumult of expectation, and stilled and saddened him. While the crowd were examining the devices with which the passages of the chapel were arrayed, Annibal, from an upper arcade, beheld a group of nuns assembled round the bier, which stood in the centre of the chapel. The tapers were not yet lit, but a torch burned dimly at the foot of the bier, shewing the pale, evanid forms of the sisters, who from time to time breathed the low, lulling tones which compose the office for the dead, and which were soon to mingle with the chantings of the choir and the rich thunders of the organ. Annibal, visionary by nature, and melancholy from habit, listened, entranced in sadness, and almost wished himself lapped in the deep rest which was soothed by the breathings of such holy harmony. Of Ildefonsa, even if he possessed her, he dreaded his possession would not be long, and though armed for her liberation, he already wept her as dead.

Meanwhile midnight approached, an ecclesiastic of rank attended to perform the service. The abbess and the nuns were ranged in their galleried stalls, the crowd below, pale with religious awe, filled the aisle and chancel. The service of the dead was chanted; the roar of the organ ceased, the prior, rising, advanced to the bier, and spreading his arms, breathed a benediction over the pall that covered it. The attendants raising it, bore it towards the narrow door of a subterranean cemetery, preceded by the sacristan, whose torch flared over the dark and arched entrance. On a signal, the nuns were about to renew the requiem, whose last echo was now dying on the ear, when Annibal, who had wrought himself to an energic burst of rage and enthusiasm, called aloud to them to forbear, and appealing alternately to the prior and the spectators, demanded justice on the abbess, for deceiving them by a fictitious interment of a nun, whom, if alive, she had immured in the recesses of a dungeon. This bold outcry was followed by terror and confusion. The attendants paused in dismay; the nuns ran shrieking to their cells, the prior advanced in amaze, and the crowd, variously divided, awaited the event of this extraordinary appeal.

Annibal now briefly, but vividly, related the late events, which were corroborated by Filippo. He urged the prior by his awe of episcopal authority, and he interested the spectators by a detail of the helplessness, the persecutions, and the beauty of Ildefonsa. By this time the abbess had descended, and appealed loudly in her turn, against the insult offered to her character and her sanctuary, by a wandering fugitive, of whom nothing more was known than, than that he was an enemy to the Catholic Faith, a seducer of vestal purity, and a calumniator of vestal sanctity. Annibal, who perceived the auditory fluctuating, hastened to bring the contest to a speedy and obvious test, and throwing himself at the feet of the prior, besought him to command the pall to be removed, and the bier to be examined. "If," added he, "Ildefonsa be living, she is not on that bier, if she be dead, the appearance of the corse will justify my charge, and blast her murderers with conviction."

To this proposal the prior, moved by strong personal curiosity, consented, nor did the abbess seem to decline it. They moved with difficulty through the chancel, now obstructed by the crowd, tumultuous with curiosity. The attendants invested the bier, the prior himself held a taper as he bowed over it, the pall was removed; with a spring of agony Annibal threw himself on the object it disclosed, on the *corse* of *Ildefonsa*.

He started up, revived by frantic hope, he examined the hand on which his burning tears were dropping; it was no waxen effigy, it was cold and relaxed, but it was human flesh. He looked with straining eyes on the face, there was no sign of violence; he knew them well, there was neither streak nor stain, neither discolouration nor contraction, she was calm and lovely, as in sleep. He was stirred from his trance, by a sound which he heard, without comprehending it, it was the loud rage of the abbess and the spectators, who, on this visible proof of the falsity of his charge, would willingly have torn Annibal to pieces, without patience for his explanations, or a sympathy for his misery. But his mind, embittered by persecution, and goaded by a conviction of crime or imposture in the present event furnished him with such sudden eloquence of vindication, such a flow of passion, (which described himself as bereft, by monkish fraud and cruelty, of the only hope that soothed his existence, and heaped together such fearful stories of monastic oppression and religious murder) that the lower orders of the auditory, always favourable to the depression of dignity, again adopted his cause, and demanded loudly an inquisition into the affair. The abbess, enraged, addressed the crowd, and warned them how they upheld a wizard, a sorcerer, one that was leagued with unholy spirits against the cause of the church and its votarists; she told them, the stranger was a *Montorio*, one of the dark race, whose deeds of horror extended beyond the limits of earth, and the catalogue of human crimes.

From this accusation, Annibal, unused to the persecutions of Ippolito, was defending himself with the vehemence of genuine horror, and looking round the multitude, demanded who dare approve the charges on himself or his house, when his eye, as it swept the circle with a look of command, rested on the dark face of Schemoli, standing directly opposite him, and regarding him with a look of fixed sternness. Annibal was transfixed to the spot; his eye became hollow, and his lip quivered. He bent forward with a broken sound of fear, and retreated without a power of collecting thought, or uttering a word. The abbess screamed with triumph. "See," said she, "the wretch, arrested in the very moment of his false defence, by the power of conscience! See, does he utter a word? Look on his haggard face—his eye is bent on air—but doubtless he sees forms from which the eyes of the faithful are veiled."

Annibal springing through the crowd with a vehement impulse, called him by name to stay, then retreating, with his eyes still fixed in the direction where he had glided away, said inwardly, "See where he flits along; he is no creature of this earth!"—"Whom do you speak to?" said some around him, in fear, or in curiosity. "Ask me not," said Annibal wildly, "I dare not tell; his form is human, but be not deceived, he is not one of us." The few who pressed around him, were driven back by these wild words, and the zealous and terrified crowd now as loudly pressing for his arrest and detention, as they had a moment past to hear and to favour him. The prior advanced, and informed him is conduct and expressions had been so extraordinary, that he conceived it his duty as a churchman, to take cognisance of them. He then commanded his attendants to secure and guard him. On the unhappy prisoner, neither his address, nor the consequent movements appeared to make any impression; he was in the calmness of fixed madness. From time to time he uttered the words, "See where he glides away," to the great terror of his guard, whom he however made no attempt to resist.

Terror, disastrous passion, and disappointed revenge, had indeed impaired his reason, but his madness was without violence, for his strength was exhausted. The remaining rites of sepulture were hastily concluded; the crowd, still murmuring with wonder and doubt, dispersed, and the prior recollecting, that in the ruined town, there was now no place to secure the prisoner, consulted with the abbess, who agreed that he should remain secured in some outer apartment of the convent, and watched by the attendants. There was little need of security; Annibal remained calm and passive, but from time to time, uttered words, which, had his hearers been acquainted with the late events of his life, would have suggested ideas more terrible than the outrage of a convent; but terrified by the ramblings of delirium, which some interpreted as possession, and some as prophecy, his guards, one by one retired, each alledging the departure of the last as a reason for his own, and each dreading as he saw a companion retire, that *he* would be left alone with the maniac. It was solitude, silence, and chillness that recalled Annibal to his reason. He was in a deserted room that had once been the sacristy; the pale, faint light of the moon almost setting, fell through mist and haze, on a narrow window. Annibal for a moment recollected the events of the night, and then, in the confusion of returning sense, endeavoured to exclude them by shutting his eyes; for the late privation of reason had been accompanied with imperfect vision, and he wished to retire for shelter to insensibility again. It was impossible; every thing recurred with a force more vivid than reality, and again he started up to prevent the attendants from carrying the bier of Ildefonsa to the vault. He found himself in a lone and narrow apartment, the door of which was secured, but from without he thought he heard whispers as of men in consultation. He now implored release or information respecting the fate of Ildefonsa, by every topic that he thought could operate on compassion or fear, and in every tone of passion, from the whisperings of supplication, to the hoarse, broken, inarticulate roar of rage and menace.

He procured neither freedom nor answer, and at length feeling his brain again unsettle, and dreading the loss of reason as the extinction of his sole means of hope, he retreated to a seat, and hiding his head in the folds of his mantle, and pressing his temples firmly with his hands, he tried to exclude the forms that were every moment enlarging in size, and quickening in motion before him, and to breathe a broken prayer for the preservation of his reason. He grew calmer, but when he ventured to look up, he again mistrusted the faithfulness of his senses. Every object around him seemed in motion; and the blue and shadowy light quivered so fitfully and wild, that a kind of fantastic animation seemed to pervade the very walls and cieling. Again he closed his eyes, but the motion was palpable, for though he could no longer see any object, he felt the seat shaking under him. Before he could rise, he heard the bells of the convent pealing out with that confused and dolorous sound, that the wretched inmates of countries visited by earthquakes understand but too well. The thought of perishing without a struggle was horrible. Again he rushed to the door, and implored to be at least allowed a chance for life, which in that hour of horrors is not even denied to the most abandoned convict in his dungeon. He implored in vain, his cries, even to his *own* ears, were drowned in the increasing tumult and distraction of the convent. He heard, indeed, many voices, but none that answered him; he heard steps passing close to his door, and some even that faultered as they passed, but they faultered from the terror of their own flight, and though they echoed his cries with involuntary impulse, they yet seemed not to hear them. At length a crash was heard, which seemed like the toppling of the whole structure, and the next moment a mass of ruinous building falling against the door of Annibal's prison it was shattered to atoms; and through the chasm he beheld the walls of the convent shaking, figures, in the infatuation of fear, clinging to the rent and heaving fragments, and a copper-tinged and flaky sky, peering through the crushed roof, whose crags and ridges, tinted with the glare, seamed the mass with portentous shapes, that seemed to the fugitives below, like dragons perched on their spires, or hippogriffs breathing sulphur through their shrines. Annibal started from his prison, and the next moment saw its walls rolling together like a scroll, and its place lost in a cloud of dust, and sparks, and sulphurous smoke. Half blind, half stifled, he struggled on, and perceived that the fall of the principal tower, which had shaken the walls of his prison to dust, had also forced its way through the pavement of the cloistered passage on which it descended, and which now only presented a number of chasms, whose darkness or depth the eye could not measure, and whose crumbling edges were but just visible in the light of the funeral lamps which had burned in the cloister that night, some of them yet unextinguished in the fall gleamed to some depth in the chasms, shewing their rude, dark prominences, and playing ineffectually on the thick darkness in which their depths were lost. He noted all this with perceptions quickened by fear, but the impulse to advance was irresistible to one so lately in durance. He advanced, therefore; he was on the edge of a cavity; on the opposite side was a door, through which a steady light appeared, as if that part of the building was not yet in ruins. He attempted to spring across it, but either his senses were false or his strength impaired, for he plunged into darkness and emptiness, and his breath and recollection failed him in a moment. He recovered, but after what interval he had no means of knowing; he felt himself sore and stunned, but not incapable of motion. He rose and attempted to discover into what place he had descended. The floor was damp and stony; it was evidently the floor of a vault, but the utmost extent of his arms could not discover the walls, nor encounter any intervening object. He groped on in cautious and breathless fear, till the dread that he was only treading the same dark circle, the dread that he was plunged into an abyss, over which was heaped a mountain of ruin no hand could ever remove; the dread that he must wander in darkness, uttering cries that must never be heard, and imploring aid that never could reach him, till he must suck the dank and flinty ground in the madness of thirst, or gnaw his withering flesh for food;—the dread of this rose like a burning tide of agony in his throat; and sending forth a cry that might make itself be heard, even amid the uproar of that night, he sunk on the ground. He sprung up again, for his cry was plainly repeated by other sounds than the echoes of the vault; again it was repeated, and Annibal, to whom even the imaginary tenant of darkness would scarce have been an unwelcome visitant, called aloud and repeatedly, and springing on one foot, listened with every faculty on the stretch. Again he heard a voice so distinct, so well known, so unhoped for that, bewildered and laughing with convulsive joy, he said to himself, "It is impossible, it is illusion, it is a sleight of the enemy! Oh! when will the cool, clear light of the morn come, and all this vanish?" He was answered in tones he could no longer misunderstand, "It is, it is I; stir not, move not a step, I must approach in darkness; but stir not limb, or joint, or thought, till you feel my hand in yours." Again believing his senses failing, he closed his eyes: it was fortunate he did so. The next moment he felt the soft hand of Ildefonsa lightly touching his. With a sensation inexpressibly delicious, he suffered himself to be led a few steps by her in darkness. He dared not yet trust himself with sight; he felt as if there was a treasure near him, which to discover too soon was to destroy; he dreaded that to open his eyes would be to banish the delicious dream of her voice. At length a strong light fell on them; he looked around; Ildefonsa was beside him, and a torch burned at the foot of a cluster of pillars, against which she leant apparently exhausted with emotion.

For a long time their questions were asked and answered by looks, by lips that moved but could not articulate, by eyes from which they smote away the tears that obscured the sight of each other for a moment. "Oh, Annibal!" said Ildefonsa, speaking first though feebly, "my preserver, I have preserved you in turn! When I discovered you, you were suspended on one foot over a vault, of which the depth is—Oh, Santa Madre! it opens beneath my feet when I think of it; another step and you had been dashed into atoms, into ten thousand atoms! Had I called you would have moved, had I approached you would have moved, had I displayed the torch, in the giddiness of sudden sight you would have moved, and a motion was death. I concealed the light; I called to you not to move; I crept over to you, dreading the sound of my own foot; I saved you, and now save me, for I can stand no longer."

She tottered, and the wound (which Ippolito had bathed in the stream and bound up) bled afresh from the violence of her emotions. Annibal, grasping her in his arms, looked round with anguish and distraction. In a vault of vast extent, dimly lit by the lamps of a distant shrine, and strewed with the relics and emblems of the dead, he looked around in vain for relief or for hope. Ildefonsa's eyes wandered, and her lips were pale, but she was yet capable of conveying her meaning by gestures, and now pointing vehemently to the left, Annibal bore her thither, still carrying the torch, and still looking around without a glimpse of deliverance.

The direction to which she pointed appeared only more dark and rugged than that they quitted; but as he advanced (the torch burning dimly from the damps of the vault) a faint blue light seemed to hover in the distance. He stopped and gazed; Ildefonsa murmured an audible sound of encouragement. The light became more distinct, it issued through an aperture in the roof of the vault, which here was so low, that Annibal was compelled to bend as he approached it. A fragment of something resembling a piece of drapery floated through it, and a voice which at first breathed a few faint timid calls from above, now bursting out in a torrent of lauds, blessings, encouragements, and entreaties, accompanied by a figure eagerly bending from the cavity, discovered Filippo. It was no time for inquiries, though the situation suggested a thousand. Filippo, with equal strength and dexterity, fastening his mantle, which he tore into stripes, to the edge of the cavity, drew up Ildefonsa with Annibal's assistance, who was himself aided by its projections to ascend after her, and beheld, with mind and senses revived, the morning sun dawning on the placid course of the river, which had the preceding evening reflected the turrets and groves of the convent, but whose water snow glided by dismantled walls, and were fringed with inverted trees, patches of verdure dotting naked rocks, and beds of sand and slime poured into the bosom of gardens. In the sudden joy of liberation, they almost forgot the circumstances of danger and distress by which they were still surrounded, till recalled by the necessity of immediate shelter for Ildefonsa. A perplexed consultation was held. It was dangerous to remain near the convent, though in ruins; it was dangerous to return to the town. Of any local resource nearer than Puzzoli, Annibal and his servant were ignorant, and there it was impossible, in Ildefonsa's exhausted state, to proceed. They were relieved by Ildefonsa herself, who recollected a retreat where neither pursuit nor accident was likely to betray them. Thither she was borne by Annibal, who felt, while watching her dim eye, and listening to her painful and broken respiration, an agony of domestic intimate distress, such as had never accompanied the high and strange events in which he had been lately conversant.

It was a hut rudely built of sods, cemented by the intertwisted roots and foliage of the verdure with which they were covered, and roofed with wicker, over which the trees that surrounded it had shed a profuse covering of leaves. They were not surprised to see it yet standing, for they knew that slight structures often survive those shocks which overturn palaces. "This," said Ildefonsa as they supported her into it, and strewed their vests over the bed of moss on which they placed her, "this was the habitation of a recluse. His habits were solitary and gloomy; the peasants believed him a being conscious of some great crime, or engaged in some dark pursuit. They dreaded to approach his hut while living; he has been dead some days, and their reluctance to visit it is probably greater. Here we are safe, for superstition secures us from every intruder."

Annibal groaned incredulously. The care of every further arrangement was left to Filippo, who planned with his usual address, and executed with his usual caution and spirit. He resolved, as soon as the confusion of the disaster had somewhat abated, to return to the town, and there, with the clamorous grief of a domestic, to bewail his master, whom he was to represent as having perished in the ruins of the convent; at the same time he was to learn the reports circulated concerning the causes of *his* and the Signora Ildefonsa's disappearance. He was to remove from the house where they had lived every article that might either lead to a discovery of his master's name, or minister to their comfort in their woodland abode; and whatever was yet necessary during their sojourn there, he was to procure from another village, which he purposed to visit in disguise. Annibal, satisfied of his talents and fidelity, suffered him to arrange his plans without interruption, while he hung over his pallid love, and saw with more anguish her forced and patient smiles, than the expression of pain and weakness with which they contended ineffectually.

Filippo in about an hour set out, and Annibal was left alone with Ildefonsa. During this interval he experienced new and peculiar feelings; he felt he had opened a new page in the history of human misery. His rank had been exalted, and his youth was passed in the downy repose of luxury; his wishes were anticipated by the diligence of a hundred domestics, and of *wants* he had formed conceptions as clear as the inhabitant of the torrid zone may have of the cold, and darkness, and wintry horrors of Greenland. His distresses were wholly intellectual and imaginary; he had yet to learn that there were such evils as cold, and want, and destitution, and on this day he learnt it with bitter force.

To spread over Ildefonsa's couch every garment he could spare; to close every cranny of the hut with the driest leaves and moss he could find; to vary her scanty furniture a thousand times, and still find something to be rectified in every change; to solicit her lost appetite with the late and tasteless forest fruits—all this he *could* do. But to read in her dim eye wants he could not satisfy; to know that assistance was so near, yet not dare to implore it; that there were ten thousand alleviations of pain and weakness for which she languished, and which the wishes of solitary affection could never bring; that he had often scoffed at and wasted as superfluous what now he would welcome as a treasure—this he could *not* do; it was insupportable: he almost reviled the elements as voluntary ministers of mischief, and was only restrained from violence of complaint by the fear of alarming the sufferer for whom he trembled.

Filippo returned tottering under a burden of every thing that inventive solicitude could provide. A plenteous meal was prepared, and a fire kindled, which they recollected, if seen, might confirm the superstition of the peasantry, and throw a stronger spell of fearful security around their wild abode. The intelligence of Filippo corresponded with their conjectures. Annibal was supposed to have perished in the fall of the tower which had freed him; no suspicion of his escape existed. Of Ildefonsa he had heard nothing, but the same opinion respecting her prevailed in the convent; for the monk who was employed to assassinate her, dreading the rage of Schemoli and the abbess, averred that she had perished by the blow he gave her as he fled; and as the convulsions of the earth had ravaged even the subterranean apartments of the convent, breaking up vaults and overthrowing shrines, the disappearance of her corse excited neither surprise nor suspicion. Seated now amid comparative abundance, while Annibal saw or hoped he saw the wan cheek of Ildefonsa grow warm in the ruddy light, and Filippo, with characteristic vivacity, laughed, shouted, and bounded round his master and the Signora (for no influence could prevail on him to sit or partake the meal with them); each of them recounted the extraordinary circumstances under which they had again met, after being separated by the rudest shocks of both natural and moral violence.

The escape of Annibal has been already related; that of Ildefonsa (who after being preserved from assassination by Ippolito, was afterwards separated from him by the shock of an earthquake) was owing to the numerous subterranean passages of the convent, which extended to the brink of the river, and into one of which she had been precipitated by the vaulted roof opening beneath her feet, and enclosing her with such expedition, that Ippolito saw her no more. She had descended with little hurt, and soon discovered where she was by the lamps which glimmered before a subterranean shrine of St. Ursula. At this she was prostrating herself for protection, when another chasm yawned over her head, and she beheld through it, when her terrors permitted her to see, Filippo, who extended his arms, and called on her in tones of encouragement. She was about to avail herself of his plan for extricating her, when the voice of Annibal, whom the windings of the passage excluded from the light, reached her ear, and lighting the extinguished torch which her assassin had dropped, she pursued the sound, and discovered him suspended, as she related, over a cavity, into which a step had been destruction. On concluding their narratives, both turned to Filippo, whose account was brief and simple. On learning the imprisonment of his master, he had in vain supplicated to be permitted to share it with him. He had been driven from the convent with violence; "but no one," as he said, "could drive him from sitting down beneath its walls." Here, though he knew his presence was no protection, he yet dreaded there was danger in his absence, and continued therefore to linger and to lament, till he was astonished by the sight of two figures, one of whom he knew to be Ildefonsa, descending from the gardens of the convent, and gliding along the brink of the river. His mind was at first clouded by fantastic fear, but when he could no longer doubt that the figure he saw was "the real and living Signora," he prepared to follow her, assured of safety from the protection that was extended to *her*. Just at this moment a commotion of the earth separated the figures he was observing; the lady sunk into the ground, and the cavalier was wafted down the stream with a rapidity that mocked the sight. The lady, however, was Filippo's principal object. He observed that the shocks were slight and partial, though the convent, situated on an eminence, almost excavated by subterranean recesses, and mined by the lapse of a river, was shaken to ruins by it. When personal danger therefore had ceased, he examined that part of the bank where Ildefonsa had disappeared. The hollow sound of his steps convinced him there was a cavity beneath; the apertures made by the earthquake were but slightly and irregularly closed with masses of earth and stone. He removed with his hands those which obstructed the spot near which he beheld her sink, and by the lights which twinkled in the cemetery far beneath, he discovered Ildefonsa prostrate at the shrine of St. Ursula. From thence her liberation was easy.

The evening was passed in congratulations on their marvellous escape, in anticipations of future security and happiness, and by Annibal in regret that his brother had been so near, unseen by him, and had probably perished in the disastrous commotion of the night. This regret was increased by a disappointed wish of meeting and conferring with Ippolito, between the cause and object of whose persecution and his own he began to trace a resemblance, pregnant with singular suspicions. Filippo promised, if possible, to procure some intelligence of him in his next excursion; and Annibal then retiring to the porch of the hut, left Ildefonsa, with *unprompted delicacy*, to the sole possession of her humble apartment.

As Ildefonsa's wound was slight, and her weakness local, she recovered rapidly; and the assiduous tenderness of Annibal was aided by the vivacious intelligence of Filippo, who related with strong humour the conjectures of the superstitious villagers about Annibal and Ildefonsa, of whose disastrous passion they imagined that the figures seen dimly on the brink of the river were a visionary representation; and *they* had more than the praise of common courage who would venture at night near the spot where the shade of the ill-fated votaress was supposed to seek the sanctuary of consecrated rest, and that of her tempter to be wafted down the current in a bark into which he was inviting her, and whose progress tracked the waters with furrows of flame.

Of Ippolito, Filippo failed to procure any intelligence, as he had been apprehended immediately on his arrival at Puzzoli by the order of the Inquisition, and the secrecy which marks the proceedings of that tribunal rarely permits a vestige of its victims to be traced beyond the precincts of its walls. That the brothers were so near without meeting was not surprising; Bellano, and the village where Annibal resided, though near the convent, were in opposite directions, and Ippolito had delayed at the former only one night.

Ildefonsa's health was now so far restored, that her care was transferred to Annibal, whose attendance on her she feared had impaired his strength and spirits, and she urged him repeatedly to excursions in the forest, whose "wild and woodland scenery would breathe freshness on his mind and frame." He declined her importunities, or, when he complied it was for a short time and with reluctance. "Why will you not," said she earnestly, "go out and wander in the forest for an hour?"—"*Why* will you press me thus?" said Annibal, who appeared to have reasons for his reluctance he could not avow. "Because it is now the hour, and—" "The hour! who told you *this was the hour?*" said Annibal wildly.—"Do I not know that night is the time for *you.*"—"Why, what is the meaning of this? why do you thus *dwell on night?*"—"Because it is unsafe to walk by day, and expose us to discovery."—"True, true; was that all?" said he vaguely. "That was all, in truth."—"Perhaps," said he after a gloomy pause, "there is still less safety by night than day."—"I do not understand you."—"So much the better," said he impatiently. "But why," said Ildefonsa with fond tenacity, "why will you not wander for an hour along the path you described so vividly to me the other evening, where the trunks of trees and lingering foliage are tinged with colours richer than summer, and the pale gleams of sky between the branches, intersected with spray and fibre, resembled, you said, the narrow shafted lights of a cloistered passage: you described it so forcibly, I thought I saw you there?"—"*Saw me there!*" said Annibal starting, "Heaven forefend! No, no, impossible; you did *not* see me there."—"I would I were able," said Ildefonsa, reverting to her indisposition. "I tell you, you *would not be able,*" said Annibal emphatically. "And will you not wander this evening?"—"No; I dread that I should *lose* myself if I did."—"I think I could discover you if you did."—"Discover me?"—"Yes, discover you. Is there a den or a labyrinth there?"—"There is, and it is dark and horrible."—"You drew *me* out of one that was indeed dark and horrible, and I think you have tended me so well I should have strength to extricate you."—"I fear you have not," said Annibal in a hollow voice, "no power can avail to reach or to raise me."—"Heavens! you talk and look as if you had fallen into it already."—"Not yet, I have not yet," said he absently; "but do not press me to walk in the forest." She ceased, for she perceived he was answering his own thoughts; nor did she venture to mention the subject again; for though on all others Annibal spoke with the fervour of a lover, and the chaste solicitude of a husband, yet the slightest allusion to the forest, or to his nightly excursions there, at once overshadowed him with a gloom, which was only interrupted by starts of moody abstraction.

Yet she observed, that when unsolicited he often stole forth, and returned with the quick step and startled eagerness of one who feared or fled from pursuit. At length Ildefonsa found herself no longer compelled by weakness to retard their journey to Puzzoli, for which Filippo set out to make preparation. The joy this intelligence inspired she shared in an eminent degree herself.

In spite of the high and well grounded confidence she felt in Annibal's pure and noble love, her timidity was terrified by her dangers and adventurous prospects, and her delicacy retreated from being the daily associate of men who, however generous, tender, and respectful, repelled her from the very circumstance of their sex. Her confidence resembled the image of Cybele, which resisted every effort to remove it till it was drawn along by the *zone of a virgin*. Her feelings, delicate, vivid, and evanescent, resembled the Peri of the eastern mythology, whose subtle essence is subsisted by perfumes, and whom a grosser aliment than the fragrance of flowers would confound and destroy.

Early in the evening of the day previous to their departure, Filippo, who had exerted more than usual diligence, arrived at the hut of the forest, with every requisite for their journey. He had engaged horses and a guide, whom they were to meet in the morning at the skirts of the wood; and with the natural joy of a domestic, who believes where there is splendour there must be safety, he described the munificent affection and superb palace of the prior, where he expected soon to behold them blazing in magnificence and fortified by power, scarce remembering the mischiefs of vulgar malignity at the distance to which they were removed, and dispensing pardon or punishment to the wretches from whose dungeons they had recently emerged themselves. Annibal and Ildefonsa listened to his sanguine promises with confidence, tempered by remembered sufferings; and satisfaction, exalted by the benevolence of mutual passion. "And shall we," said Ildefonsa, "remember the hut that sheltered us in the forest, and the cluster of pine under which we met in the garden of the convent?"—"I shall," said Annibal, "for there you first owned you loved me."—"And I," said Ildefonsa, "for I past every interval of your absence I could spare on that spot. Will you forgive me, Annibal? I thought those hours even pleasanter than those to whose remembrance

I devoted them. There is a nameless charm which the places where we have met those we love derive even from the loss of their presence, I can delight in, but I cannot define it. 'Tis the faded wreath, 'tis the dim light of the banquet that has ceased, but whose luxuries still linger on the sense; 'tis the fairy circlet, that prints the field with *brighter* green when the elf-dance is done, and the whisper of their music is low."—"You are an enthusiast, love!"—"I am, and I am glad of it, for you are gloomy; life and reality have not joys enough for you, and I have power to draw them from another sphere, even from that where I sought them before I knew *you*. When the wayward fit is on you, I will spread wings you have not yet seen, and fly into other regions; and there, like the sylphs I have imagined I saw in a summer noon, employing a hundred tiny pencils to paint the rose leaf, and fluttering their fairy plumage to give coolness to the breeze, or diffuse the breath of the lily; so will I flutter about, collecting stores of mental sweetness and beauty to pour over your head, like the balm of the enchanter, that dissolves the sullen spell of sleep. I have heard of masquerades in the world, I will put my mind in masquerade for *you;* I will call up the airy shapes of existence, *past, future, impossible;* I will invest them in shapes now sportive, now solemn, now wild; I will feast you with forms of visionary beauty, brighter because unseen by the world's eye; I will bid them pour strange music in your ear, sweeter because none but yours ever caught it."—"Sweet, sweet love!" said Annibal kissing her hands with unresisted fervour, "you witch me with your blandishments; will you be thus lovely, thus enchanting in the world? will your fancy flutter thus wildly, and warble thus sweetly in the gross atmosphere that shall soon enclose it?"

"I do not know; I have heard that the world is fatal to mental pleasures; that few who mix in it preserve their fancy, and fewer still their sensibility. But granting that my feelings were sometimes the victims of deception or disappointment, and selfish levity derided what; it never experienced, still, as those feelings withered, my judgment would ripen, and the tears that flowed over my young mind's wasted prime would be assuaged by the lesson that their fall had ameliorated my heart." Annibal, who had fallen into the "wayward fit" as she spake, now interrupted her with conjectures relative to the picture which so strongly resembled her, and the mystery which overshadowed her birth and infancy, so strangely under the control of a nameless persecutor.

"Nay, if you are for a romance," said Ildefonsa playfully, I will call for Filippo's maudoline, and sing you a sad tale of a lady and a knight, so very deep in love and woe, none ever resembled them but the *Fugitives of the Forest*." At this moment they heard Filippo touching his maudoline in the porch of the hut, and caught by the wild prelude, listened to a ballad he had learnt from some woodland minstrel.

I

Oh, far he fares! though his step is light,
His heart is heavy, sore;
And dank around fell the sweepy shower,
And shrilly the wind did roar.

II

Oh! was it a flash of lightning blue
That lit the briery dell,
Or rush from cottage lattice low,
Or taper from hermit cell?

III

Whate'er it be he faster hies,
Whate'er it be he draws nigh,
And down in briery dell so dusk
A circled dance did spy.

IV

And round about, a vassal rout,
And some that descants rung;
Too wild, I wis, for mortal ear,
Too sweet for mortal tongue.

V

"What cheer, what cheer, my revel feere?"
This seely wight did say;
"I joy to see your featly round,
And list your roundelay."

CHARLES MATURIN

VI

"And who art thou (bold wight we trow),
That hearest the elf-voice sing;
For we be nightly fays that here
Do dance amid the ring?"

VII

Then all by unknown impulse strange,
Amid the rout ran he,
While round about the changed shapes
Did dance with shrieking glee.

VIII

And every form, ere now so fair,
Grew grim and ghastly to view;
And thin as mist were their shadowy shapes,
And dim their spectre hue.

IX

And the taper's light was quench'd amain,
And the music a howl became;
Then shook the ground, and the dancers round
Were wafted in veering flame.

X

Then his heart beat quick, and his breath grew thick,
And he sunk to the ground outright;
And with a shriek the shadowy crew
Evanish'd from his sight.

XI

Beware, beware, all ye that hear,
As my harp's wild chords I ring!

Beware ye stray through briery dell
Where nightly fairies sing.

They were pleased with the wild melody of this ballad; but when Ildefonsa began her tale of "love and woe," Annibal listened as to the inmate of another region. She had always the power of recalling other times, and pouring around her hearer the imaginary *scenery* of her song; she looked the very genius of romantic minstrelsy; her voice was like the sound for which fancy listens amid ruins; her song woke a beam of memory to play on faint and distant images, as the moon, hailed by the nightingale, advances to shed a melancholy light on the mouldering forms of antiquity.

The Bower of Rose and Eglantine

I

Come, sit with me in twilight bower,
The bower of rose and eglantine;
For this still light and evening hour,
Best suit with such a lay as mine.

II

'Tis moonshine all, the lattice fringed
With rosiere rich, the garden pal'd;
And the green path, touch'd by that light,
Glistered like sheeny emerald.

III

'Twas silence all; deeply she sat
On terrass'd tower, and crested spire,
Hush'd the low rippling of the moat,
And woo'd the moonshine's stilly fire.

IV

'Mid those fair scenes, Oh! who so fair
As she with pearly coronal?

She leads along a stately knyght,
Whose dark form gleams in ebon mail.

V

Like knyght and ladye fayre they seem,
Who meet for love in moonshine bower,
Yet sadde was seene that ladye's cheare,
And sadder was her paramoure.

VI

She had him through the garden's maze,
Where faery-rings the green bank studde,
Where opal hues of shadowy light
Dimm'd orient flower and rubied bud.

VII

She had him to the margent trim
Of fountayne that in moonlight played,
Where garden-gleams, and tremulous bowers,
And silver sleepe of veiled flowers,
Like land of faery seemed, throughe mist,
Its soft and shadowy archings made.

VIII

But when she had him to the bower,
The bower of rose and eglantine,
How fail my harp's sad tones to tell,
Oh! woeful knyght, that look of thine!

IX

He shook the mail on his harnessed side,
He shook the dark plume on his crest,
He dared not on that ladye look,
Though she hung and wept upon his breast.

That ladye was as bright of hue
As ever shone in princelye bower,
All pale for grief, but sure more fayre
Than if she blushed in beautye's flower.

XI

For she had loved that statelye knyghte,
In bowers of rose and eglantine,
*And left him for a royal love,** *
Whose gawds around her coldly shine.

XII

And fickle woman's worthless pride
Drew tears that o'er her wan cheek fell,
And sorrow and shame had marred her prime,
And stained the charms she prized too well.

XIII

And still the thought of her first love
Did hurt her mind with sweet annoy,
It lit a dream more bright than hope,
It woke a grief more dear than joy.

XIV

For it was not hope, and it was not joy
That woke her sunk eye's wandering fire,
'Twas memory, wooing passion's shade,
'Twas grief that glowed o'er dead desire.

---

* Mary, sister to Henry the Eighth of England, was attached to Charles Brandon, Duke of Suffolk, one of the most accomplished knights of his age; she married the King of France.

XV

As half she sunk into the bower,
The fleckered bower so tremulous bright,
And her wan cheek, like winter rose,
Show'd through the bowery foliage light—

XVI

"Oh come with me into the bower,
The bower of rose and eglantine,
And be my spirit's paramour
'Mid scenes that say—Thou still art mine.

XVII

"I do not think of thy burnished eye,
Or ringlets of thy dark brown hair,
Or curved brow of ebon quaint,
Or cheek of summer's sunny paint,
Love's forms are faded from my mind,
And, but its soul, nought lingers there.

XVIII

"Like spirits that in moonshine meet,
We'll talk of love's evanished bliss,
And mingle memory's shadows sweet,
With parting passion's last cold kiss.

XIX

"And far and faint, as cloudy tints
That still through westering twilight show,
Dim blazon of departed day,
Forgotten forms of bliss shall flow.

XX

"Then come with me into the bower,
The bower of rose and eglantine,
And be my spirit's paramour,
'Mid scenes that say—Thou still art mine."

XXI

The moon was on her tear-bright eye,
The moon was on her breast of snow,
He turned him from the witching sight,
And faultered faint, and deep, and low.

XXII

"I cannot come within thy bower,
I cannot melt in moonlight grove,
All these fair scenes are dark and lorn,
For, lady, I no longer love.

XXIII

"Yet still I see how fair thou art,
Too well I see thou'rt wond'rous fair;
As the lone pilgrim's parting feet
Still turn the twilight fane to greet,
Though long my heart has left thy shrine,
Mine eye still loves to linger there.

XXIV

"'Twere perilous in secret bower
To parly with a form like thine,
And list that bland and breathed spell
That woos the woven eglantine.

CHARLES MATURIN

XXV

"I am a knight of faith unstain'd,
And thou art an high and royal dame,
We may not love like chambered page,
Nor tempt the losel's wanton shame.

XXVI

"Oh! lady, lov'd so passing well,
In dear devotion truly held!
Why was thy love so light and weak?
Why was thy heart by folly spell'd?

XXVII

"When my nerved arm was first in fight,
When hoary eld my voice rever'd,
When honour plumed my youthful crest,
When ladies loved and warriors fear'd—

XXVIII

"Then thou, like a most blighting frost,
Didst come upon my glorious youth,
O'erthrew my valour's stately stem,
And nipp'd the buds of vernal truth.

XXIX

"My wane of life comes sadly on,
My voice is heard in halls no more,
My lance has rusted by my side,
The pride of knightly thought is o'er.

XXX

"And would'st thou now—Oh! lady cease,
Tempt not my dark and dreamless rest,

I'll bear my load of silent woe,
All, but the fear thou art not blest.

XXXI

"The diamonds sheen that bind thy brows,
Are mock'd by clouds that sadden there,
And they again are dimm'd by tears,
To me than gems more rich, more rare.

XXXII

"Thou art not blest—Oh! that thou wert,
For by my heart's evanish'd joy
So might not false love taint thy bloom,
And late and vain regrets, annoy.

XXXIII

"I'd doff this mailed coat of pride,
Wind round mine arm the rosary,
'Vail to the cowl my helmed head,
And breathe my life in prayer for thee.

XXXIV

"Thy dying love's forgotten lair
Should be some hermit's tapered shed,
Thy buried love's untrophied tomb
Some sainted valley's lowly bed.

XXXV

"But oh! that pale and pined cheek
Bids e'en that hopeless wish be vain,
That wish whose wild, unselfish aim
Now sooths with joy, now stings with pain.

　　　　　　　　　　　　　　　CHARLES MATURIN

XXXVI

"Oh! come enchantress, from thy bower,
I may not, must not, talk with thee,
Come but to tell me what I feel—
Tell—is it joy, or agony.

XXXVII

"Still on its light, dew-spangled spray
Hang my warm tear-drops unremov'd,
And still those breathing roses seem,
Oh God!—as sweet as when I lov'd.

XXXVIII

"Oh! come enchantress, from thy bower,
I may not, must not talk with thee,
But I can tell thee what I feel—
The bliss *of love's strong agony."*

XXXIX

He led her from the bowery shade,
A tear was in her humbled eye,
He led her to the palace-pile,
No ear might catch their unbreath'd sigh.

XL

But vestal stole, and penance pale,
That lady's woful ruth did prove,
When told the knell of the requiem bell
That lovely knight had died for love.

To song again succeeded "converse sweet," and Annibal, whose thoughts had been occupied by the wonders of recent safety and escape, now enquired by what means the extraordinary appearances at the funeral (when he believed her dead,) had been produced and conducted.

"Of that strange transaction," said Ildefonsa, "I can know but little, but believe that as my death was determined on by my invisible enemy and the abbess, so it was resolved to impose on those who might presume to inquire and examine, by a funeral; in which I was to assume the aspect of a natural death. Had any violence been used, this had been impossible; from the effects, therefore, I conjecture I was lulled by an opiate into the resemblance of death, and in this state I was exposed as a corse, and in this state (after the tumult occasioned by your interposition had ceased) was conveyed to the cemetery of the convent, where your brother rescued me from assassination. It is probable the operation of the drug was limited to a certain period, during which no violence could rouse me; for of the tumult at my funeral, or the wound given me in the vault, I have not the slightest remembrance, though when my faculties returned, they returned without disturbance or imperfection. This is all I am able to tell or to conjecture, except that I believe the malignity of my enemies was accelerated by the report of your attempts to liberate me; and that therefore my existence is of more consequence than they have been willing to allow me to believe."

Annibal was about to join her in this conclusion, when Filippo grasping his master's arm, pointed with eager silence to the chimney, down which a dark object was slowly descending. They caught it as it fell into the flames, and examined it with eyes that doubted their own evidence—it was the *hood of a Monk's habit!* With an immediate impulse, Annibal rushed out, and at the same moment called to Filippo for his carbine. Filippo, who hastened to him, found him already plunged far into the forest, while Ildefonsa, with fruitless precaution, extinguished the light, and awaited their return in terror that hardly breathed. They returned after some time pale and spent; Filippo could not, and Annibal would not, tell any thing. He begged of Ildefonsa, in a voice of perturbation, not to be disturbed, and breathed every moment an impatient wish for morning. Morning, however, was yet far distant, and Annibal examining again the charge of Filippo's carbine, withdrew to the porch of the hut, where he watched in silence. About an hour had elapsed, when a loud shriek from Ildefonsa recalled him. She averred earnestly, that she had seen the face and part of the figure of a tall man in dark drapery, who for some time continued at the casement, viewing her intently. She confessed herself much enfeebled by her fears, and rising from her couch, intreated Annibal not to quit her for the remainder of the night.

The porch of the hut was secured therefore by an immense log of pine, that had been the table of the recluse, and the party endeavoured to obtain such rest as can be snatched at intervals of fear. In a short time, however, Ildefonsa, whose spirits were too much agitated for sleep, observed Annibal rise, and go to the casement, where with a variety of silent but earnest gesture, he appeared to confer with some one without. She watched him till her terror could no longer be repressed. "Annibal," said she gently, "why will you not sleep?"—"I had rather never sleep, than be visited by such dreams."—"I fear they are melancholy, indeed."—"How do you know? What have you heard, or *fancied* you heard"—"Thrice I have heard you in your broken sleep repeat those mournful words which were the last I heard from you in the garden of the convent."—"What words were those?"—"I cannot repeat them, they were about some *prediction*."—"True, oh true! Are you sure you heard nothing more?"—"Nothing more."—"If you should, Ildefonsa, do not believe it; imagine it the voice of fancy; do not think it proceeds from me; men cannot answer for what they utter in their sleep; but *should* you hear any thing, remember to tell it me, and then forget it as soon as you can."—"I will."—"Do not deceive me."—"Deceive you?"—"Yes, what can I trust, when my own senses are false?"—"Trust *me*."—"Ah! many have been betrayed by those who watched their sleep; I will not sleep again; would it were morn."

Ildefonsa for the remainder of the night counterfeited fleep; in the morning they were conducted to the opposite verge of the forest, by Filippo, where the guide with horses and mules awaited them. Filippo had suggested the policy of taking a circuitous road to Puzzoli, (in order to avoid the vicinity of the convent, or the village) which in consequence of this arrangement they did not expect to reach till the close of day. They stopped at a small village at noon, and proceeded on their journey in the mild decline of a genial winter day.

Security and happiness were now so near, that it was perverseness to distrust them. An emersion from dungeons and death, from struggles with the devastations of nature, and a rude shelter in the recesses of a forest, into the pomp of wealth, the luxuries of art, and the beneficence of affection, and this illumed by the rich and radiant light which youth and love shed on the perspective of life, such a prospect was enough to dazzle mental sight even stronger, and better accustomed to the fluctuating objects of life than theirs. They inwardly congratulated themselves on their distance from dangers they would not now mention to each other, and listened with complacency to the garrulous gaiety of Filippo, and the vaunting prolixity of the guide, who, by his own narrative, had encountered and escaped more dangers, than Hannibal ever met on the Alps, or Cambyses in the Desert.

"I do not like that man," said Ildefonsa, "there is a mixture of weakness and fierceness in his face I have seldom seen."—"I have *seen* no face but yours since we quitted the hut," said Annibal. At this moment the guide suddenly turned in a direction opposite to that they had expected. "Where is it you are going?" said Filippo. "Where I was *hired* to go," said the man. "But this cannot be the direction to Puzzoli," said Annibal. "Will you not permit me to know the road better than you, Signor?" replied the man. "I will not permit you to know the points of East and West better than me," said Annibal. "But you—you forget, Signor, that I am obliged to take a circuitous road."—"It is not necessary," said Annibal, "since we have quitted the vicinity of the forest."—"It is more so than ever," said the man. "I repeat, it is of no consequence," said Annibal. "It is of as much consequence to *me* as my life," replied the man. Annibal believing he alluded to the necessity of his safe and faithful conduct as a guide, ceased to contend with him, and quitting the high road they pursued a heathy track, whose limits were skirted by a distant wood. "Do you conduct many by this road?" said Ildefonsa.— "Not lately, Signora," said the man, "but I have in my time conducted a number."—"It is at least a secret one," said Filippo—"There can be none more so," replied the guide. "And safe and certain?" said Annibal. "Perfectly certain, Signor."—"Its gloom oppresses me," said Ildefonsa. "I never heard a traveller utter a complaint of it, after his journey was done," observed the man. The track now terminated in the wood, in which no continuance of road or path was visible, but the guide entered it without hesitation, and they followed him. Here they wandered for some time amid the entanglements of an untrodden wood, when the guide suddenly stopped. "I fear I have lost my way," said he, growing pale with unaffected fears. "How!" exclaimed the travellers. "*They* are not here," said the man, with unrepressed terror, "and I am lost."— "Villain, you *are* lost," said Filippo, levelling a carbine at him. "Hold," said Annibal, who, though in despair, was deliberate, he rode up to the man, and griped him by the throat, "Villain, you have betrayed us, and betrayed yourself, you have sold both body and soul to perdition. Hear me, villain, you have but one chance for existence—conduct us from this forest, and conduct us safely; my servant and I will ride on

CHARLES MATURIN

each side of you—come here, Filippo—on each side of you, villain! each with a loaded carbine at your head; and, by my immortal soul, if I but see you faulter, or wince, or *think* awry, (for I shall see your very thoughts) that moment your brains shall be scattered about the road, and your soul be the prey of him who has tempted you to murder!" The man listened, half dead, to his menaces, and turned tremblingly to quit the wood, but at that moment a shrill whistle pierced their ears, and a number, with whom it was madness to contend, poured around them. Annibal and Filippo turned on them in the fierceness of despair, and the party enraged at the appearance of resistance, prepared to fire. Annibal, at the same moment, discharged his carbine, and then rushed forward with his sword, when a shot from a villain, whom he had wounded, grazed his wrist, and compelled him to drop his weapon; endeavouring to recover it with his left hand, he lost his balance, and falling to the ground, was stunned by a blow from one of the assassins' horses, who was terrified at feeling his rider fall beneath his feet. In the mean time Filippo, who, in the impulse of a just revenge had discharged his carbine at the head of the wretch who had betrayed them, before he had time again to load it, was assailed with such determined fury, as made it evident his life was the object of the ruffians. He defended himself with courage, but when he saw his master fall, and the lady, who had fainted, surrounded by the band, his arm grew weak, and he perished almost without aiming another blow.

XX

Thou must speak that which, in its darkest hour
Pushed to extremity, 'midst ringing dizziness,
The ear of desperation doth receive,
And I must listen to it.

—Miss Baily's "Rayner"

When Annibal's senses returned, he found himself extended on a bed. He looked round, he was in a low, mean apartment, dimly lit; it was night; a lamp burned near him, and as he distinguished objects, he thought he saw a dark form moving in the distance. Nothing was plain or palpable either to his mind or senses; be felt as if a motion, a breath would dissolve the objects around him, and plunge him again into insensibility, or the darkness and dreadful imagery of the forest. But when he recognized the figure which advanced on hearing him move, and stood fixedly beside him, he dashed down his head, and hiding it in all the coverings he could catch, exclaimed, "Let me be lost again!" His persecutor, however, would not suffer him to relapse into insensibility. Cordials were prepared, and when they failed an irresistible stimulant was applied. He mentioned the name of Ildefonsa, and Annibal instantly started up, quickened to the most keen and vivid perceptions of misery. But to awake or satisfy inquiries on the subject of Ildefonsa was not the purpose of the tempter; he only mentioned *her* to introduce the prediction concerning their ill-fated loves (which he had uttered in the garden of the Ursuline convent to Annibal), and to appeal to its fulfilment. "The *object of your* love," said he, "*has been torn from you at the moment of possession*, and *life has changed its complexion at the moment it was becoming bright with hope and joy.* Am I a deceiver now?"—"You are a fiend," said Annibal. "You rave still," said Schemoli. "No, my faculties are *too* perfect; this is night, we are in solitude, you are Lucifer, and I am your prey."—"My *minister*, and in vain have you sought to shun me; though you take the wings of the morning, I must follow you. Annibal, never can I leave you till the deed for which I am doomed to follow you be done by your hand; the chains which bind a spirit in paiu, I know your weak human hand trembles to unlock. *I* should plead to you for relief in vain; but think on *yourself,* think on your wanderings, your persecutions, your fear-spent, spectre-ridden life. The hand that dissolves my chain, shall also dissolve that which binds in unnatural union a human and a departed spirit. Free me from jeopardy, and you free yourself from *me;* resist, and you drag about with you a restless wanderer, whose shadow shall darken you at noon, and whose feet shall be planted by your midnight bed." Annibal was silent. "What signifies that waving of your hand; can it reverse the laws of the nether world? You have resisted them, and what are you now? a fugitive, an exile, a dependant, the outcast of your family; the imprecations of your father pursue you; you are blasted in hope, and love, and fortune. What are you now?"—"I AM INNOCENT!" said Annibal. "Yes," said the tempter, "if to resist the laws of destiny be innocent."

Their conference continued all night. It appeared from several passages of it, that since his first visits to the convent where Ildefonsa resided, he had been incessantly haunted by Schemoli in his usual and undisguised form. He met him near the convent, he crossed him in his evening wanderings, he even appeared in his chamber at the house where he lived, ever upbraiding him with his wayward and foolish flight from what it was equally impossible to avoid or to destroy; ever maddening him with the suggestion of that subject so dark and horrible, which had been the topic of their conferences in the prison chamber at Muralto. Annibal's dejection (visible both to Ildefonsa and Filippo) had kept pace with his gloomy acquiescence in the belief of an influence exerted over him, with which to contend was alike impossible and impious. This dejection he had eminently betrayed in his last conference with Ildefonsa in the garden of the convent, when he repeated to her a prediction with which his shadowy tormentor had menaced him but an hour before. He had also betrayed it when Ildefonsa pressed him to wander into the forest; for in the forest he had beheld his persecutor, and in the forest he had again been tempted to that crime, whose imaginary burden sat so heavy on his soul. All the predictions of evil were now verified, and the objects whose presence had suspended the powers of his mind from dwelling on the subject perpetually obtruded on it, were now removed. He had no longer any powers of resistance or disbelief; he saw before him a being who, he had every reason to believe, had a power and commission not to be disobeyed. *Poison* could not suspend his existence, nor distance of space his agency. His tale, to a superstitious mind enfeebled by recent calamity, was irresistibly imposing; and his injunctions, horrible as they were to nature, were justified by his tale.

Annibal's mind was indeed naturally strong, and sluggish in its operations; but its strength was misapplied. It pursued visionry and falsehood with the conscientious energy of truth, and when it had found it, embraced and adhered to it with a vigorous tenacity that might have honoured virtue. Thus he was betrayed by his very virtues. The stern activity of his intellect had only been employed in the acquisition of dangerous principles, and his unbending firmness of heart only insured that the blow he struck would be unerring, whether its impulse was derived from vice or from virtue. Such was Annibal in his best hours; but now, enfeebled by bodily suffering, distracted by mental pain, his superstition aggravated by his conscience, and his primitive and intimate bias of mind confirmed by external impressions, such as the soberest intellects could hardly oppose, he yielded without resistance of reason, but not without struggles of passion potent and terrible. The last convulsions of the human mind, the dissolution of the *moral principle;* the utter abdication of the *influence* of reason, while her *power* is retained only to abuse it; the frightful misrule of passion, assumed as a principle and exalted into a virtue, *this* it cannot be expected to exhibit; and if expected, it is not possible. Those dreadful revolutions of the mental system oftener occur in silence, rarely express themselves by groans or gestures; and if they ever employ words, they are only exclamations and inarticulate cries of passion, such as nothing but reality can faithfully represent, and if really represented, would be fled from in horror.

The *unhappy young man yielded!*—But when he had yielded, he exclaimed in agony, "If there were but a parallel in the history of human nature for mine, if there were but another human being like *me* beset, and lost like *me*, I would not utter a murmur!"—"There is," said Schemoli. "It is impossible," said his victim. "I will produce him to you," said Schemoli. "It *is* impossible," repeated Annibal. "He is *your brother*," said Schemoli.

A long pause succeeded this tremendous disclosure, during which Annibal's mind, traversing the distant and connecting the remote, arrived at the conclusion which a *meeting* with his brother might have long ago supplied. He rose from the bed on which he had been tossing in agony. "Who, then, are *you*? answer, while I have breath to ask you—answer, who are you?"—"I am the *stranger of the vault!* I am the *spirit of the prison chamber of Muralto!*"—"And my brother!"—"His course has been parallel with yours, and its termination will be the same."—"Was this the deed to which he was fated?"—"It was."—"And has he consented?"—"Let himself tell you," said Schemoli quitting the apartment.

Annibal did not seek to employ the interval of his absence in recollection, for he was now in a state of mind in which reflection was impossible and solitude insupportable. Had Ippolito been disclosed to him in a blaze of lightning, or been dashed at his feet by a whirlwind, it would scarce have drawn from him an exclamation. In a few moments Schemoli returned, accompanied by Ippolito. It was Ippolito, but what a change! Annibal, who had beheld him but a little before he set out for Naples, in the richest glow of beauty and flush of enjoyment, now beheld him a skeleton, meagre, keen, and fiery, the very image of *spirit* wasting and preying on the ruins of *matter.* Grey hairs were profusely scattered amid his bright locks, and a wild, restless fire wandered in his sunk eye. They looked at each other without speaking for some time; but Schemoli perceiving the dawn breaking through the narrow windows, hastily closed them, secured the door, and trimming the lamp, retired, after having excluded every gleam of daylight.

The two brothers were left alone; there were no starts of passion, no sallies of tragic violence; they were beyond them now: no two men of this world, sitting down to confer on their joint business in the cold terms of life, ever discussed it more dispassionately. They now discovered what might have been discovered long before, that under different forms and trains of suggestion, they had been led by the same hand and to the same point. But this discovery suggested no fear or *hope* of deception, the *single* exertion of such powers appeared beyond the reach of man; *united*, therefore, it was an evidence that the being who exerted them could not be human.

Ippolito repeated to his brother the circumstances that had occurred to him since his quitting Naples. "On the day," said he, "that I was visited by the stranger, as I have called him, in the prison of the Inquisition, in Puzzoli, an earthquake shattered to atoms the tower in which I was confined, and liberated me. At that time I would have leaped into fire, water, earth, to have escaped from him. I am not so weak now as to believe that mortal elements can protect me from him. I sprung out upon a mole which extended from the island rock, upon which the prison stood; half the surviving inhabitants of the town were crowded on it, embarking in vessels, barges, any thing that would bear them from the land. I leaped on board the first I saw, it was a small trading vessel bound to Sicily. The steps of a fugitive, and the looks of a madman, were no wonder, and no disqualification in that hour of distraction. I had money, too, as I since found, for I scattered it last night among a group of pilgrims who were going to beg absolution for one of their body who had committed a *murder!* As I sprung on the deck, the last words of the stranger rung in my ears. 'Bury yourself under a mountain, and it shall roll back from you! rush to the *ocean*, and *it* shall throw you on the shore again! plunge into the grave, and the grave shall break up and resign you to your fate!' We stood out to sea; I paced the deck all night; I knew not the omens which the seamen knew. I saw them pale and shivering, and asked them what they feared, since they had left the *enemy* behind? and forgot their answer, if they *did* answer me. As I stood among them, a ball of fire settled on the stern, where it glowed blue, and red, and white; and then gliding down the decks, disappeared without singeing a rope. The sailors shook their heads; the surface of the sea was dark and still. It was now night, but we could distinctly hear the cries of destruction from the shore; *they* could, they said, and many a distracted soul on board echoed the imaginary wail of father, and wife, and child. I heard but one voice; it was that which spake to us just now."

The wind fell; we became quite becalmed. A luminous sheet spread over the surface of the sea, whose particles looked solid and distinct, and sparkling like stars: a rope let into the waters was drawn up dripping with liquid fire. The passengers bending over the sides said they saw strange things in the deep; wrecks of ships long lost, and shapes of others that were to be, and forms that lay like dead men at the bottom, and others that beckoned to them with blue swoln fingers, and called on them in voices like the roaring of waters. I looked also, and saw nothing but the recesses of the vault, the damned flitting of its impy forms, and the bloody heaving breast, and the *eternal* dagger. I could look no more. There came a sound upon the waters, not like thunder, for it was more terrible, it seemed as if its force alone rent the mast and sails, for they fluttered around us in fragments. The vessel flew before it like a gossamer upon a summer breeze. It stopped; the ocean tossed and heaved, and its whole bottom came surging up, with tides of sand, and surf, and wreck; and bodies that had lain there rooted in the bed of ages, things that dreamt of rest till doom's day, they rose whirling above us, mixing with the strife of upper air a chaos of elementary wrath

CHARLES MATURIN

and ruin; then pouring down, deluged us with tides of solid fire, and melted stones, and boiling sand, and sulphurous rain. The vessel half on fire, half buried in the water, staved into a thousand fragments; on those fragments the shrieking crew dashing themselves, tried to reach the shore, which was not two miles distant. I was the only one who reached it alive; fate was careful for none but me; the world was not to lose its spectacle and it scourge. I was thrown on a bare solitary point of shore, about half a mile from Puzzoli. The stranger was standing there; lightning hissed around his head, and the ocean burst at his feet; neither could hurt *us*. I fell, spent and breathless, at his feet, and he said to me, "rush to the ocean, and it shall throw you back on the shore again." From that hour I became *his;* he led me to this desert hut, where I have past two days without food, or sleep, or prayer. I drink abundantly; my dreams are terrible, they last all day; but reality will banish them. No waking can be so fearful as this sleep; mine eyes are open, but my soul is in a trance of heavy restlessness, of conscious suspension, in which it is undisturbed by *human* thought, to which even the human voice is an alarm."

Here Schemoli interrupted their conference. He came to prescribe the mode and form of the deed they no longer shrunk to hear named; he unfolded his plan, arranged every part with cold and dreadful precision, without either weakness or sanguinary vaunting; he debated what was important, and he adjusted what was subordinate. He was no longer opposed or interrupted. In consequence of his plan, it was settled that Ippolito should go for that day to Naples, and that Annibal should depart to the seat of the transaction. They were to meet at night.

They were now rising to depart, when Ippolito, in whose heart the yearnings of nature lingered, turned and looked on his brother. Annibal extended his arms, Ippolito sunk into them, and they wept on each other's necks, and kissed each other; their last fraternal, their last human tears fell on each other's dry, wasted cheeks. But they knew their *task*, and smote away the warm drops, and set their teeth, and drew their breath hard, and tried to belie God's work and look like villains. They turned for relief to Schemoli, and met amazement. *He was on his knees*, in agony of prayer; the sweat drops stood on his brow; his body was wound into the dust! They gazed without comment, for they were deprived now nearly of all power of wonder, or any of further fear.

Had they not, the attitude of Schemoli would have inspired even *fear*. To see Lucifer surrounded by livid lightnings is less shocking to the imagination than to see him in the garb of an angel of light. They separated, and found horses prepared to convey them to Naples and to the neighbourhood of Muralto.

XXI

Hic quos durus amor crudeli tabe peredit,
Secreti celant calles, et myrtea circum
Sylva tegit; curæ non ipsâ in morte relinquunt.

—Virgil, Æn. vi. 442

Not far from thence the mournful fields appear,
So called from lovers that inhabit there.
The souls whom that unhappy flame invades,
In secret solitude and myrtle shades,
Make endless moans, and, pining with desire,
Lament too late their unextinguish'd fire.

—Dryden

I ppolito arrived in Naples about dusk. To the servants at the palace, who hardly knew him, he addressed neither question nor order. He hastened to his apartment, around which he looked vacantly for some time, and sadly *on the bed;* be then rushed into the garden, where Cyprian now spent almost all his time in a little hermitage, where he was entirely occupied by devotion. He saw Ippolito approach, and shrieking with the wildest voice of joy, remained riveted to the spot. Ippolito entered the hermitage; Cyprian flung his arms around him, but the next moment started from him, and gazed on him in silence. "Do *you* shudder at the sight of me, too?" said Ippolito. "It is his voice, it *is* his voice!" said Cyprian; "but for that I could not have known you."— "You have scarce seen yet how much I am changed; you have not seen my heart."—"Oh! where have you been, and why have you tarried so long?"—"I know not where I have been; never from Naples in *thought.* But *you*, Cyprian, gracious heaven! where have *you* been, measuring your grave? Is it this dim rising moon that deceives me? you look as pale as the dead, you are wasted to a shadow!"—"Am I? I believe I am; I am spent and worn watching for you; I am very ill, my eyes are almost wept away."—"And why are you in this cold vault-like hut?"—"'Tis my only abode, Ippolito; 'tis a structure I raised in memory of one you have perhaps forgotten, but who never forgot *you.* Here I have past my days and nights, thinking on you, and praying for *her."*—"And this little mound with the cross on it is her grave?"—"It is; and this inscription is to be laid on it when her remains are brought there." Ippolito read the lines by the light of the moon.

The Inscription

"IN EARLY YOUTH SHE HAD sensibilities that were strong, and an imagination that was stronger. Her mind, therefore, fluttered in pursuit of ideal happiness, and ideal happiness was all she was ever doomed to know; for she loved, she loved where to hope was madness, yet to be disappointed was to be lost. From that moment life was darkened by a shade, which the gleams of passion's wild and wayward joy sometimes *chequered*, never *dispelled*. She sat down in lone and unsuspected misery, and wooed a dream for comfort. But there is a place where the wailings of sorrow cease, and even the pulse of passion is cold and still; there the foot of mortal pilgrimage turns in hope; there the world weary spirit reaches and rests; *there* she rests at last with her beloved, her heart moulders near *him* for whose love it was broken, her lip wastes near *his* for which it withered with pining. There she rests at last with her beloved, and none can now divide, and none will now condemn her. Let those who would arraign her errors think upon her sufferings: those who *can* weep for her sufferings will feel they were repaid by her end."

"It is sad," said Ippolito; "but I have no time for sickly sorrow now, I came here only to depart, I must begone this hour."—"Begone! where, wherefore, where is it you must begone?" said Cyprian. "I know not whither; into some country dark and unknown, into some land that is very far off; but still I know not yet where I go."—"Oh! why is this? Oh, my heart sickens to hear you!"—"I have done a thing against which the laws are strongly armed; the world frowns upon me, fortune has nothing good for me; I must be gone tonight."—"Oh, God! what is this that comes in clouds and darkness? let me see it, let me but see it. *What can* you have been tempted to that can expose you to danger? The laws in this country are not so rigid to the rich and powerful. What is it you have done?"—"What is that which chases a man from his country, which marks him with horror and reprobation wherever he is followed and discovered, which—" "Oh, I cannot tell! horrid thoughts are crowding on me too fast to utter; but if it be all I fear, the habits of society are but too favourable to such offences, you need not fly for killing your enemy in a duel."—"I did not kill him

CHARLES MATURIN

in a duel, he was no enemy of mine; in cold-blooded malevolence I butchered one who had never offended me, with such circumstances of horrid fiendish cruelty, that nature would make the very stones of the hall of justice cry out against me if I were acquitted."

Cyprian fell to the ground, Ippolito approached to raise him. "I am strong, I am well, I am, indeed." He struggled to say, "This is but folly, nothing; let us begone this moment, I am strong and ready to go."— "You are strong! Ah, Cyprian, I knew it would be thus, I knew I was a cursed wretch, forsaken by nature and affection. No, you cannot go with me, you cannot *bear* me; those sunk eyes, those shaking hands, those open and bloodless lips, they all speak your natural, your virtuous horror of me. I have done a deed that puts me at an immeasurable distance from human sympathy; I am so far *out*, that even you who stand last and longest on the shore have ceased to see me in the distance."

"Oh, cruel, cruel!" wept Cyprian, crawling after him on his knees. "Oh! if you could *but know*, and when you *do* know, as *shortly* you *must*—I not follow? *I* not bear you? Shew me the hand that did the murder and I will kiss it, if you will not drive me away; I will follow you in quiet misery, I will smile on you as in our days of innocence, and only weep when you are at rest. I will wander with you, beg with you, famish with you."—"You draw every picture of misery; you will wander, you will famish with me! Am I so very lost? is there no one bright speck or atom in futurity for me? must we be thus wretched?"—"Oh, no, no!" said Cyprian eagerly, "there is a hope for penitence; there are gracious and humble joys unknown to the proud that have never erred. Let us go hence to decent indigence and retirement, to some place remote from the din of folly, that is never necessary to happiness, and always unfavourable to virtue. I will go with you to the vallies of Switzerland or the mountains of Spain. Many a melancholy pleasure dawns upon me in our hermit haunt of penitence. Conference when you are cheerful, the sound of my harp when you are pensive, the consciousness of safety when disposed to repine, and the remembrance of error when tempted to passion: these will be with us in our valley of sorrow, and who that has these can be dissatisfied?"—"Is it then possible for a murderer to know peace?"—"I will pray for your peace," said Cyprian tremblingly. "But *is* it possible that a murderer can have peace?" said Ippolito vehemently. "All things are possible with him whom we have to do with," answered Cyprian fervently. "May I, indeed, be forgiven?"—"If the penance to which I here devote every hour of my remaining life can procure you peace or pardon, you shall," said Cyprian, falling on his knees and kissing the crucifix that was on the tomb. "Keep your vow," said Ippolito in a fearful tone. "What is it you mean?"—"You have eased my soul of its burden, you have taught me there is pardon for a murderer. The deed is not *yet* done; but if it can be pardoned, why should it be delayed?"—"Oh! what words are those? Oh, plunge not your soul and mine in wilful, unresisted ruin! There can be no pardon for premeditated guilt; there is no mercy for the presumptuous offender who offends in the confidence of forgiveness, and converts the long suffering of heaven into the minister of sin."

Ippolito was gone. He had spoken peace to his conscience by the wild sophistry of despair, and drawn from the abused lips of purity an unintentional encouragement to guilt, and pacified by this wretched device, he rushed from the palace.

Of him whom he left behind, no more was heard, Cyprian was beheld no more. Affection had no more to contend with, nor had sorrow any further power of suffering. His existence was rendered vain by the frustration of the purpose to which it had been devoted, and for which alone it had been supported; and he felt how dreadful it was to hope no more, to have in life no further worth or use, aggravated by the recollection that his had been voluntary choice: his, therefore, was merited suffering.

ANNIBAL WAS CONDUCTED BY SCHEMOLI to the neighbourhood of Muralto; he was led into a hut and supplied with refreshments, and pacified with the promise that he should be disturbed by no intruders. To all this he listened in silence, and Schemoli was preparing to leave him—"Whither are you going?" said Annibal. "I am now going to the castle, I shall return at night and bring your brother with me; I will then lead you both to the *very apartment*."—"And am I to remain alone till night?"—"You must."—"Impossible! I dare not trust myself; do not *you* trust me. I shall be mad, incapable of doing the work that is fastened on me; incapable of any thing, even of mischief. What! to be six hours alone, with such thoughts as mine! you are mad to propose it."

Schemoli appeared disconcerted; at length he said, "If I bring you to the castle, you must consent to remain alone and silent till the hour arrives."—"Yes, I can remain alone and silent in the castle, for the sounds of life will be around me; but lead me not to any apartment I

CHARLES MATURIN

have before been accustomed to; let me see no place I have inhabited while my heart was light and innocent."

Schemoli led him to the castle unobserved; such was its extent, and so many parts were ruinous and uninhabitable, that this, though it was only twilight, was no matter of difficulty. The apartment to which he was conducted he had never seen before, nor did he examine it now; he paced up and down, listening for the sound of steps or voices, of which he heard but few and distant. It was not impossible, that had he devoted even this interval to recollection, he might have recalled his direful resolution; but it is the curse of a desperate state of mind to consider the exclusion of reflexion as a species of duty, and his resolution, therefore, continued unaltered because unexamined.

Night approached; through a pannel in the door he saw light twinkling; he believed it was Schemoli approaching, and determined to meet him at the door, not *to be called* and *chidden to his task.* He therefore hastened to the door, without perceiving it was not the door by which he had entered. It gave way, and through it he saw a suite of apartments, in the last of which lights were burning. With an impulse for which he did not seek to account, he entered them; all was still and deserted. He reached the last, and paused to examine the strange diversity of objects it contained. It was furnished even with modern elegance, but repelled approach by an oppressive smell of medicines. Silver branches sparkled on a table of marble, on which stood several phials; beside it was extended on a sopha a lady apparently asleep. Annibal advanced, and beheld *Erminia*, her very self, as he first beheld her in the picture of the secret apartments. The sylvan robe of green velvet, overspread with her long loose tresses, and clasped with diamonds, the veil of gold gauze falling over her face reached the ground. Her sleep was uneasy, she moaned often, and at length throwing aside her veil with a quick motion, which yet did not wake her, she discovered the face of *Ildefonsa!*

Her face presented the same strange and frightful contrast as the furniture of her apartment; the deep fixed colour that burned on her cheek was evidently artificial, while her wan and purple lips seemed withering in the parched breath they exhaled; her bosom, decked with pearl and shaded with ringlets, was displayed with a meretricious excess, yet the cold drops that trembled on her forehead seemed forced out by the approaches of dissolution. All power of exclamation was denied to Annibal. He felt nothing but wonder, saw nothing but witchery; the presence of her he believed lost, her solitary pomp, the mixture of emblems of death and magnificence that surrounded her, had she slumbered till the day of judgment he could only have gazed on her. But after a few inarticulate murmurs of painful sleep, she started, and awoke and beheld him. Even then he could not speak; he knelt beside her, he grasped her hands, he gazed earnestly on her face. "I could not die till I saw you, my beloved," said Ildefonsa. "Die!" repeated Annibal in a voice which cannot be described. Ildefonsa pointed to one of the phials, and sunk back on the sofa, Annibal reached it to her silently; her face was convulsed, she swallowed it, and then another. "Will this," said she, "give me breath to tell you how I have been brought here, and what I have suffered?" Again her speech was impeded. "Oh, no, I cannot! all that remains of life is scarce enough to tell how I have loved—how, dying, I love you still! We were not doomed to be happy here, this earth has no good things for us; the storm has been with us, but its roar comes far and faintly now, and where I am hastening it shall not be heard any more for ever. Oh, my love! my gentle love! distract not my dying hour by this violence! rend not your hair, nor gnash your teeth thus! I was calm till you came; it is an hour in which I had rather think of you than behold you."

Again she was convulsed, and sunk backward. Annibal supported her with that firmness of silent and terrible strength, which seems to the sufferer himself like the effect of a spell, and which he dare not breathe lest he dissolve. During the remainder of the night she was sometimes convulsed, sometimes quiet, but never articulate or lucid; in calm desperate agony he had to watch the slow expiration of sense, the long, severe strife of nature in extremity, grasping at relief fitfully, and again relaxing its grasp. He had to behold her die, without relief and without discovery of her murderer!

In her struggles he thought at times he heard her name his father. He continued to gaze on the corse till the clock struck twelve; the sound smote on his soul, he caught up the taper and rushed from the apartment: in his own he found Schemoli and Ippolito. The brothers communicated not, by word, by groan, by look. "It is the hour," said Schemoli; "all is still; I will dismiss the attendants." He departed; he was absent for an hour, during which not a word was uttered by his victims. They could not have heard each other; there was a storm, a storm which rocked the castle, and which they did not hear.

Schemoli returned; they did not *see* his altered expression till his motions compelled their notice. He dashed the lamp from his hand, he fell at their feet, he wound himself round their knees, pushed back their drawn swords, and then bared his own breast to them. Insensible to everything but the terrible purpose of the hour, they scarce saw him at their feet. Still unable to speak, he gasped, he writhed, he howled, he pointed to the apartment to which he was about to conduct them, till believing they were abused by the mows and grimaces of a fiend, they broke from, and left him extended on the floor. His pointing hand instructed them too well, and his shadow seemed to flit before them to the very door of the apartment.

XXII

—Ere the bat hath flown
His cloister'd flight, ere to black Hecate's summons
The shard-born beetle with his drowsy hum
Hath rung night's yawning peal, there shall be done
A deed of dreadful note.

—Shakespeare's "Macbeth"

My senses blaze—my last, I know, is come;
My last of hours. 'Tis wond'rous horrid! now—

—Lee's Mithridates

O n that night it was observed by the attendants that the Count was
remarkably agitated. His confessor had been twice summoned to
him. On his quitting him for the last time, he desired the Countess to
attend him, and when she came, the attendant, as usual, quitted the
apartment. They were two hours in conference. His spirits were usually
calmed by the stern energy of his wife, and by the influence she had
acquired over him from the superior strength of her character; but on
this night her influence failed, and after two hours vainly spent in the
sophistry of guilt and palliations of misery, he remained gloomy and
agitated. "Why do you walk up and down in the dark corners of the
room, listening to the wind and looking on your shadow?" said the
Countess. "Sit down by this ruddy fire, I have trimmed the tapers, and
every thing is bright and cheerful."—"Are they, indeed?" said the Count.
"They are; come, sit on this seat beside me, and be calm."—"No, no;
when I am in the darkest corners of the room *I know the worst.* I can
look upon no part of the chamber that is not brighter than that I am in;
but when I sit in the circle of the light, I dare not look beyond it; the
shades are all in terrible motion beyond the very edge of the taper!"—
"Why will you bend your mind to these sickly fancies?"—"*They* bend
my mind to *them.*"—"What is it that oppresses you tonight?"—"That
which oppresses me every night."—"There is something unusual in your
agitation tonight; your looks, your very language are altered."—"Are
they, indeed? in truth, are they? Nay, 'tis no wonder; man's ordinary
frame would sink under one hundredth part of what I daily or nightly

undergo; yet my strength is unimpaired. Not a hair of my head is changed. My mind seems to have absorbed all power of suffering into itself, and *its* faculty of suffering, we *are told*, is immortal. I have much to harass and disturb me of present and imminent fear. How do I know what danger that *fugitive* may be preparing for me in the remotest region of Italy? or his brother, who has hurried from Naples, no one knows whither?"—"Do not suffer yourself to be dejected, the confessor will discover them be sure, and then we will have nothing further to fear."

"Have I not perpetually before me a remembrancer, a living remembrancer, who combines the imagery of fancy and reality, who recals at once the living and the dead. The roof of my castle seems to shake over me while she is beneath it."

"And was it not your own fond fantasy to deck her up in that array? Like a child you run from a mask you have yourself painted; but whether real or fantastic, your fears may cease tonight: she has sunk into a sleep from which she will probably wake no more."—"What have you done?"—"That which must be done, and which therefore they who do soonest do best. Would you be ruined by the babbling waywardness, the whining love of a girl?"—"*I* could not have destroyed her."—"Weak and inconsistent! what would you have? you tremble in danger and you pine in security. What would you have?"—"Ask me not what I would have, I would have what no power can do for me; I would have time turned backward, and deeds *undone;* I would have impossibilities; I would have peace, and ONE night of unbroken sleep!"—"That is impossible."—"I do not want to be told so. Secure! my security is like the fortress of a giant, moated round with blood; it is like the tower of the Persian tyrant, a pile of human skulls. I am become a wonder to myself. I could not (once) have borne to think what I now must bear to be. In the first stage of my progress, I saw but a single act necessary to success. I revolted from its first view; but habitual contemplation, and, above all, the facility of repenting, *one solitary act* of guilt bribed me to its perpetration. Had it been joined in the remotest bearing with another crime; had but another link of the dark chain been shadowed in my mind's view, I had never been guilty. But it is the policy of Satan. I had scarce dipped in blood when I found I must swim in it. Another act but led to another; to retain what I had acquired demanded more of the means that acquired it. I found myself tottering on a point which I deemed the central hold of success; I tried to rise, and found myself tottering still. I look back now on a length of crimes that sear the sight, I look round and feel I totter still. I look upward, and see the point of safety remoter than ever, and that I have been lost, and trebly lost for nothing! Where will this end?"—"In safety and eminence at last," said his dauntless wife; "in a height from which we shall look down on envy and danger alike, and feel no sacrifice too great to obtain."— "Safety!" said Montorio growing pale, "how can you talk of safety and hear the yelling of the blast? Hark, how it bursts, wild and horrible! the casements will give way; and now it sinks again, and wails away so faint and distant. Oh, that dolorous, sobbing, spent sound! could it be the wind, Zenobia? What if it were?"—"For shame! will you run mad listening to the wind? will you conjure the innocent elements into phantoms of fear? Listen, it is gone already; it whistles over the cottages beneath your castle, and does not wake a sleeper there: it is fallen now, the night will be calm."—"Do you think so, good wife; do you indeed think so? I pray you look out at the casement, and tell me the shape and waftage of the clouds, and whether the wrack flies swift, and *where* the winds are chasing it."—"Look abroad yourself, you are near the casement, and the flitting clouds will amuse you."—"*Amuse* me! Oh, if you knew what forms are riding in the darkness when *I* venture to look out, aye, flitting across the casement with palpable motion, and when I start, beckoning from the ridgy clouds, but not like *them*, gliding away: if you saw this!"—"Are you the slave of such fantastic folly? I would sooner tear mine eyes out than let them abuse my reason thus."—"If my eyes were torn out I should see them still."—"Oh! these are the dreams of fearful solitude; the very whispers of the place and season. I should run mad with apprehension if I shut myself up in a lone tower, and listened to the wailings of the wind."—"Aye, 'tis the wind I shrink from. Whenever the storm howls round my castle I think of the night when— hark, hark, how loud it is now! Just such was the sound, and such was the season—" "You mistake, it was at the close of autumn."—"I do not mistake; it is spring, and summer, and winter, and autumn with me; I hear it in every wind that blows."

"Let us go then to Naples, I know not why we came to this house of horrors; let us go to Naples. I will go with you, and we will have feasting and jollity. In the tumult of festivity you will forget these thoughts that ride your fancy like the hags of vision; you shall go forth, and enjoy your state like a magnificent noble, and all shall be well."—"No, I cannot, it besets me THERE; and how can I trust myself amid a crowd, who dread

CHARLES MATURIN

to be discovered to my own lacqueys? My life is wasted in watching a secret. When I was last in Naples they dragged me to some assembly. I saw it *there;* aye, you may gaze, but I saw it plainly as I see you now. As I crossed the portico it stood opposed to me for a full minute, and looked on *me:* looked! no, no, it had no eyes; but still it seemed as if it saw me, and I saw *it.*"—"Saw what?"—"Do you not know?"—"No, in truth, you have so many visions and fantasies."—"Why, then, not to avoid its sight again could I utter the name."

He sat down sullenly, and remained silent for some time, then starting up again listened to the wind. "Did you not tell me," said he reproachfully, "that the storm had ceased?"—"I am not to blame if the elements will not be at peace."—"And who is to blame," said he, striding up and down gloomily, "that I am trembling here with every change of them? It is destiny's, not mine. If I were a conqueror, a ravager of the earth now, I should lie down in peace; if I were one who had slept after the carnage of thousands, whose bare word had swept off more in one day than all the petty villains of earth would stab darkling in their lives; if I were one who had flung infants and pregnant mothers in the fire, and rested every night lapt in the colours of victory, and stunned by the thunder of my drums; if it were thus, I would be at peace, I would be called a hero by the world, and lie down at last lulled by the acclamations of mankind. Oh, if it were thus! Yes, it is this cursed domestic sensibility of guilt that makes cowards of us; the deed that makes the hero damns the man. I am lost, because I am pent up in the walls of a castle, and mark myself with the sign of the cross; the magic chain of evil is the fear."—"I have never seen you so wrought by fear and dismal thought as this night."—"'Tis true; this night has a presage with it, I cannot, cannot—" "Has the confessor been with you?"—"Twice." "And has he given you no comfort, as he is wont to do?"—"Aye, marvellous comfort, solitary penance for an hour; and so good night, Zenobia. Zenobia, do you pray at night?"—"I do."—"Indeed! and fervently, truly?"—"Aye; but I do not trust to prayer alone."—"What do you mean?"—"Look here," said the Countess, and withdrawing her vest shewed beneath an iron band that encircled her waist, and was closed under her breast by a spring whose point entered it. "Who devised this most horrible penance?" said her husband. "They who could execute it could alone devise it."—"The infliction is most sharp and agonizing, but the consequences are worse. Remove that dreadful zone, Zenobia; the corrosion of the iron—" "Will produce a cancer, I know it."—"And the consequence must then be—" "A terrible operation; I have sustained it already. Eight months I wore it on the other side, it terminated as you suggest. I submitted to the operation without discovery and without a groan, and when it was over I removed the sharp point to the other side."

Montorio smote his hands together. "What have we become? what have we made ourselves?"—"That which I would bear this, and tenfold this to be, great and powerful, one of the eminent on the earth. Let any curse be mine but that of high-born, high-thoughted beggary; the habits of a noble, the spirit of a sovereign, and the fortune of a mendicant. Oh my earliest view of life I saw but one thing that it was good to be; the price was high, and the conditions difficult; but since it is accomplished, I will not affront my pride by thinking I gave for it too much. I am the possessor of rank and magnificence; all that is seen of me is great and splendid. Let the world be deceived and I must be happy; yes, I *am* happy."—"And will the other world also be deceived?"—"No; but it will be pacified, if our priests tell us true. They say St. Peter's keys are of gold, I have one of IRON that cannot fail. If penance can avail, what can be so powerful as that I voluntarily do?"—"I know of but one mode more severe."—"More severe! what is it?"—"*That* I must undergo tonight."—"What! is it the scourge, or iron?"—"No."—"Do you rend your flesh with sackcloth?"—"No."—"What can it be?"—"An hour of solitude," answered Montorio, turning on her with the visage of a fiend in woe.

The Countess was retiring. "Hold," said he, "are you going, already going? am I alone? does he make me undergo this that I may think less of my final mansion? I cannot bear it, no, I cannot be alone, Zenobia; send the confessor to me, I will confess to him; that expedient we adopted to pacify heaven, and avert the cause from our house. I have not confessed that yet, I have never told it; perhaps it may move him to mitigate my penance."—"Perhaps it may, he shall attend you."

She retired, and the confessor was again summoned. Their conference was long, and marked with singular emotions. In the progress of it, the Count avowed that secret with which he had fed an inward, doubtful hope of palliation for many years. The monk was sitting on the chair when (in the posture of the confessor) he received it; he started, as if his soul was smote within him. In a voice, whose tones were convulsed with unknown emotions, whose tones were audible from the bare strength of their meaning, almost without aid of

CHARLES MATURIN

articulation, he demanded a repetition of the confession. His penitent, overpowered he knew not how, hesitated. The confessor repeated his demand in a voice not human; the Count again faultered it out with mechanical fear. The confessor paused, as if to assure himself of what he heard; the seat shook under him. The Count looked up in his face with amaze, his cowl had fallen over it, and in his agitation it remained untouched; and his figure thus dark, silent, and shaking with unuttered thoughts, was more like the phantom of a terrible dream than the living and actual form of man. At length, spurning aside his chair, he rose and was rushing from the apartment. "Father," called the Count, "you have not given me absolution."—"Nor ever will," yelled the monk, "nor ever shall myself seek or obtain it." He was gone.

His penitent, long accustomed to starts of passion resembling insanity in the confessor, believed that he was only overcome by the discovery of a new link in that chain of crimes which had for four years been gradually unfolded to his view, without a prospect of their dark termination. Believing, therefore, that the event of this conference would scarce have ended in the mitigation of his penance, he prepared to undergo it, mentally resolving, however, that if after the experience of some moments he found solitude what he feared, he would summon his attendants to the antichamber, and at least hear their steps, and see their lights through the crevices of the door while he performed his task. He had scarce time to explore the terrors of solitude.

The issue of those dark hauntings by which the brothers had been beset so long, may already be conjectured. The secret crime, so often suggested to them by visionary temptation, they now proceeded, under the influence of visionary terror, to perpetrate. The secret door through which the monk had rushed to deprecate it, in vain, was still open; they advanced through the passage with feelings, which he who knows human feelings will hardly inquire or willingly hear. They entered the apartment of their victim; he was on his knees, in that agony of prayer which hears no sound but its own murmurs. They approached unseen; they dared not look at each other; but so intense and single was the impulse, that at the same moment their swords met in their father's body! He expired without a groan.

The noise of the body falling on the ground alarmed the attendants, whose habitual vigilance was easily aroused. They rushed in; there was no outcry of inquiry or conjecture, for the parricides stood, frozen and senseless, still grasping their red dripping weapons. The body was raised and examined, but when they discovered it was stone dead, their faculties were restored, a wild burst of inarticulate horror rung through the apartment, and every one applied himself to a different purpose with the precipitation of sudden, momentous discovery. The murderers were secured, unresisting and unconscious; every tower in the castle blazed with lights, and resounded with hurrying feet; the alarum bell rung out, quick, and loud, and terrible; the sound was heard at Naples the live-long night, wafted by the howlings of the storm. The family, whose inquiries were only answered by ghastly silence, rushed to the Count's apartment. The daughters threw themselves in agony upon the body, the sons demanded the means and circumstances of the murder. The Countess stood beside the couch to which the corse had been removed, and covered her face with her robe.

At this moment of distracted questions and incoherent answers, a number of the officials of justice arriving from Naples, entered the castle, and without disclosing the cause of their appearance, required that the criminals should be delivered into their custody. This was performed. The family had often turned, in the midst of their lamentations, with looks of appealing agony to the brothers; but their voices were drowned in a fresh burst of woe, and they could not ask what probably had been asked in vain. The attendants, however, whose grief began to yield to wonder, interrogated the criminals repeatedly, on the motive and object of the dreadful deed they had done. They obtained no answer; the unhappy young men were once heard to ask for a little water, but from their fixed and blood-shot eyes, their staring hairs, and mute ghastliness, it was rightly conjectured that of what was passing around them they heard or noticed nothing.

In about an hour something like order was restored, and the criminals, of whose guilt so obvious there was scarce an official inquiry, were about to be removed, when the confessor rushed into the room. The attendants, who had beheld with calmness the terrible spectacle of a violent death, faultered and shrunk at the sight of him: there was nothing human to which he might be compared, nor any thing beyond or below it that could be imagined like him. He flew with the speed of a demon to mischief; he paused as if he saw the desolation of the world. He gazed for a moment around him, and then approaching the officers, demanded that he should be secured by them as the real agent of the crime of which they were appointed to take cognizance. The supernatural wildness of his aspect, contrasted with the calmness of his address, stupified the officers. They listened to be assured that the sounds they heard proceeded from the object before them. He repeated them in a voice that chilled them; but while tremblingly they secured him, they almost expected to see the fetters with which they bound him disappear, or his whole form dissolve into vacancy. His demand, however, was incontrovertible; no one had accused, no one even had mentioned him; his surrender was voluntary, and no one inquired its reason.

The family now separated with the dumb solemnity that attends events too great for complaint. A few attendants renewing the half-extinguished lights, prepared to watch by the body of their Lord, over which was extended a black pall; and the carriages in which the officials had travelled, conveyed them and their prisoners away about daylight.

The crime of the night, in all its circumstances, was so new and horrible, that even the ministers of justice, grown old in the history of human depravity, felt amazed and outraged by the event. Their attention was fixed strongly on the prisoners, as hunters would gaze on the motions of a monster, such as their search had never before discovered. The brothers were totally silent, and on their arrival at Naples, were found to be plunged in a sleep so deep and heavy, that they were lifted out of the carriage by the attendants (who shuddered to touch them) without awaking. Schemoli kept his head enveloped in his cowl, through which his heart-drawn groans were every moment audible. On alighting from the carriage his face was involuntarily uncovered, and his eyes for a moment fell on the young men; and for that moment the expression of his visage was such, that the attendants scarce thought themselves safe till it was concealed again. In consideration of their rank they were allotted apartments in the castle of St. Elmo, where Schemoli immediately demanded implements for writing, a small portion of bread and water, and undisturbed solitude for thirty-six hours.

To this the officials, after examining the apartment, and removing from it every implement of mischief, consented. He also demanded that no judicial steps should be taken against the prisoners, till a document which he was preparing was ready to be submitted to the principal justiciary of Naples. With regard to this, he was informed that of a case so mysterious and extraordinary, no cognizance would probably be taken till a much more remote period, as the process of inquiry and examination which would be instituted could not be too minute or deliberate. In consequence, however, of the intimations of the prisoner

Schemoli, on the third night after his arrival at the castle of St. Elmo the grand justiciaries of Naples, with some of its most distinguished public characters, at midnight assembled in a subterranean apartment of the castle. A double guard was planted on every avenue of the building, and the secretary advancing to the foot of a table which was covered with black, while an assistant on each side held a torch, produced and read before the assembly a manuscript given him a few hours before by the monk Schemoli, which he had written in his prison.

XXIII

L et those who blame the extravagance of my passions, think I was a lover; let those who mock my abused credulity, reflect I was a jealous lover; let those who execrate the horrors of my revenge, remember I was an Italian.

"I am Orazio, Count of Montorio, so long believed dead, and who rises from imaginary death only to bewail that *it is* not real. I am Orazio, Count of Montorio; this is no device of imposture; I have living witnesses and incontestible proofs. I have witnesses that *can* prove my identity, and a tale that *must*—I desire not to anticipate my narrative by a display of my character, it will be sufficiently unfolded by its progress, nor would I conceal its most dark and inward foldings from the eye. I have other purpose than my own vindication in this narrative.

"Of a large family, my brother, the late Count, and I, alone arrived at the age of manhood.

"My heart had originally a capacity of affection beyond most human hearts. I loved him with a love 'passing that of women;' I was alternately to him a father and a child, an almoner and a monitor. My purse he might have exhausted, my name he might have disgraced; but my *heart*—.

"He was weak and vicious; I knew it well. It was the curse of my character to love, not for the perception or sake of worth in the object, but to gratify the wild exuberance of my own feelings. My heart was like a mine, that poured out its irrepressible pregnancy of wealth at the feet of surrounding *peasants*, which enriched the worthless and exalted the base, whose unhappy fertility was without discrimination and without gratitude.

"I had procured my brother a military commission of high rank, which his irregularities soon compelled him to resign: still I defended and upheld him, and gave to his retreat an air of angry dignity instead of disgrace. I was revolving some other plan for his advancement, and in order to pursue it had removed to Naples, where I saw her whose name I cannot, on the verge of death, write with a firm hand, Erminia di Amaldi. I loved, as few men had ever loved, without knowledge of the passion, without knowledge of the sex. Of love or of marriage I had never even thought before; and now, as usual, my first thought was resolution. I addressed her without any gentleness of approach, any arts of insinuation. I persecuted her without any gradation of advance, any intervals of deliberation. If she had even loved me, I left her no time for its avowal, almost for its consciousness. I poured out my passion before her with a violence that affrighted her, and when she was terrified into silence, I mistook it for assent. Her gentle reluctance, her timid distress, her silent dismay, nay, her tears and anguish, I heeded as much as the hunter pursuing his prey would heed the lily that he crushes in his speed.

"My impetuosity, my rank, my wealth, my munificence bore down all obstruction. I led, I dragged Erminia to the altar, where amid the solemnity, she fainted in my arms. After some time I brought her to my castle, surrounded her with every thing that woman could desire, or man procure, and courted her to be happy with magnificence and affection.

"At this period my brother married, married without my consent, without my knowledge, a woman whose family had been the long-tried and inveterate enemy of mine; married without the means of procuring his wife another meal, except from the compassion of that family, by whom before I would be assisted, I would famish a thousand times. With sore constraint I assumed severity, and refused for some time to see or admit him.

"During this period I found other employment than thinking of *him*. I discovered, or imagined I had discovered, my wife did not love me. I feel *now* that I must have thought the same of any other woman. I had imagined that passion was a something which human performance could never realize. With the purity of a matron, and the delicacy of a woman, I yet expected the blandishments of a harlot, and the ardours of a man.

"To be what I demanded would probably have disgusted me, to be less, distracted me; I loved too well to be, happy. Yet Erminia might have had more compassion, or might have dissembled more. Hours have I knelt at her feet, and have only been suffered to rise with a sigh. Hours have I held her to my heart, and felt only her cold tears trickling on my bosom. Hours have I supplicated for a smile, and been dismissed with one whose gleam played over her pale face, like moonshine upon a plain of snow, cold and uncherishing. While she was pregnant, I tried to believe that indisposition might suspend her fondness, and when she became a mother, that her children might divide it. With the vigilance of jealousy, which dreads itself, though in her presence I heaped her with tender reproach and expostulation, yet when absent, I studied, I invented devices to prevent my belief warping that way, while I tried to convince her what I dared not to think myself. Yes, Erminia might have had more compassion, or might have dissembled better.

During this interval, having made my brother for some time experience the privation of his customary indulgences, I procured for him a distinguished situation, of which he concealed from me that he had anticipated the profits by debt, even before he had expected the possession of it. I had long been personally reconciled to him, and in the third year of my marriage he came to pass some time at the Castle of Muralto.

(Here I dropt my pen, and my taper seemed to go out—it must be resumed—Erminia! Erminia! Are these tears? Often have I poured out blood to thy memory, never till this hour a tear!)

"My brother easily discovered the state of my mind; a fool might have discovered it; concealment never was one of my habits. My mind was as open as the ocean, and as soon agitated by storms. I know not how his approaches were first made, with what poison his first invisible arrow was tinged, or rather with what depth of poison, for from the first it was the green, livid venom of jealousy he infused, from that shade which scarce produces an infected spot in the mind's eye, to that deep dye which darkens the sun, and overshadows the soul with glooms unlit and impassable. I think we were sitting one day after Erminia had quitted us; I observed her dejection in terms as cold as I could, merely to find if others thought of it as I did. 'When dejection,' said he, 'arises from a local cause, it is easily removed.'—'True,' said I, without applying the remark. 'There was a report,' he continued, 'that Almoni's regiment is ordered to embark for Spain, perhaps that occasions her dejection.'—'I never heard she had any relations in Almoni's regiment.'—'I never heard she had.'—'Why then should its removal effect her?'—'What! have you never heard of—?'—'What is it you mean?'—'Nothing, nothing in the world; a mistake, it must be all a mistake; let us send for the children; they are remarkably like you.'—'I think the elder is like me.'—'They are both like you,' said he vehemently, 'by my soul they are, let people talk as they will.'

"The children came; I walked about, busied in a strife of thought; he observed it. 'Why do you not speak to the children,' said he. 'I had rather at this moment speak with you.' He came to the window against which I leaned my back that he might not observe the changes I felt my features undergoing. 'Why should the Countess be disconcerted at the removal of the regiment of that—I know not his name?'—'I, I, do not know.'—'You *do* know.'—'I only know what every one knows; why should *I* be interrogated?'—'What every one knows?'—'Yes; every one knows that the Chevalier Verdoni has a company in that regiment.'—'And of what consequence is that to *me*, to the Countess I mean?'—'What! have you never heard of Verdoni?'—'Never.'—'That is strange; never seen him at the Amaldi palace?'—'Never, I say. Oh! that there were no such things as questions and interjections upon this earth.'—'I would there were no such things as questions at this moment. But now I recollect, it is *not* strange you never saw him at the Amaldi palace; he must have been dismissed.'—'Dismissed at my approach?'—'Certainly, a rejected suitor; and every one commended the Countess's prudence. Women have a privilege of change in their *latest* period of courtship, and a woman of so much prudence must make a better wife. To keep such reports from you so long, she must have a great store indeed, and kindness too, for it is kind to prevent superfluous pain.'—'If you think so, why do you not finish your tale?'—'*I* finish it! I know nothing more. Would you have me repeat all the ribald talk of Naples, of my brother's wife too? If you have curiosity, or if you have patience, my servant, Ascanio, who lived lately with Verdoni, can tell you what he heard. But let me intreat if you have not patience, do not call him.'

He named a red-haired, ill-looking man, who attended him. I had a deep, untold aversion to that man; I started at his name. I said involuntarily, 'I shall not like to listen to what Ascanio will tell me.'—'Very possibly you will not,' observed my brother, inwardly. 'Come, shall we go to the Countess's apartment, I think I hear her harp?'—'Yes,' said I, almost unconsciously, 'let us go to—to my—to the Countess.'—'I never heard you,' said he, carelessly, 'call her the Countess so often as this evening; you used to say Erminia.'—'*And she is Erminia*,' said I, distracted by this hint, '*she is*, she *must* be *my Erminia*.' I quitted the room; I thought I heard my brother laugh as we quitted it.

"Erminia was sitting at her harp, her children were at her feet, peeping at each other through the strings, as she sung to them. I tried to listen, but every tone of voice or harp murmured 'Verdoni.' I beckoned to my brother and we quitted the apartment.

'Send for your servant,' said I, when we were alone. 'For what?' 'I shall tell *him* when he comes.' 'You must tell me before he is sent for.'—'Must?'—'Yes; and moreover, you must promise when he comes, to listen to him calmly.'—'By mentioning that condition, it is plain you know for what purpose I would send for him.'—'And by seeming to decline that condition it is plain you expect he will disclose something it is not safe for you to hear'—'I shall begin to expect it, if you do not call him immediately.'—'That apprehension alone makes me submit.'—(Precious devil!)—'I trust he will disclose nothing so bad as you expect.'—'Oh! go for him, go for him,' said I, writhing with impatience, 'while you talk I am mad.' He went; Ascanio was not to be found. This was a master-stroke. I was left a whole night to *think*; both of them pouring their suggestions into every avenue of my heart, for the same number of hours, could not have effected so much as solitude and the workings of my own thought effected. In the morning Ascanio was again summoned. I locked the apartment on him, my brother, and myself. I will not detail his serpent-windings, or his worse than serpentsting. He affected that perplexity which endeavours to conceal a secret, whenever I questioned him, and that terror which is conscious of guilt; when I grew impatient, he affected a concern for the disclosures he reluctantly made; he affected to be a character, of all others the most imposing—the honest, indignant, involuntary confident of vice. The sum of his tale was, that Verdoni had long been attached to the Countess; that in consequence of his attachment, he was indulged with an intimacy, which he had abused; that it was known they had a child, though how it was disposed of was not known; that he had been banished from the family, whose indiscretion had published their misfortune; that their lawless passion still continued, and was still gratified; and the Countess's dejection arose more from the interruption, than the disappointment of her guilty love.

I listened to this, all told with the wildest breaks of fear and remorse; I listened with that distraction which does not lose a syllable. Expletive, and letter, and look, and nod, was written on my heart with a pen of iron. The characters are uneffaced, I could read them to this hour; but to this hour its own evil is sufficient. Ascanio was dismissed, and my brother sat silent, with the aspect of one who has reluctantly betrayed a secret; at length he murmured something about inquiry and deliberation. 'I *am* deliberating,' said I, scarce hearing myself. 'Ogni Santi!' said he, 'What are you doing?'—'I believe—am I not mending a pen?—mending a pen!—mangling your flesh; it is your finger you are cutting,' said he, snatching the knife from me. I saw my fingers flowing with blood, I looked on them and laughed.

"I CANNOT, I WILL NOT follow the gradations of my ruin, I will not throw aside the covering under which my mental wounds have festered so long, to count their number, or probe their depth, or thaw by frequent touch the poison that has almost congealed in them, the blood that has ceased to flow. I was desired to observe my wife more closely; for I was told, that at night, when she believed I slept, she indulged a luxury of sorrow and passion, in which she was even heard to call on the name of her paramour. I needed no suggestions to bid me *wake*. But on the night after I received the intimation, I counterfeited sleep as soon as I lay down.

"In a short time she began to sigh heavily; it was a sultry summer-night, and she was far advanced in her pregnancy, I ascribed her depression to an obvious cause, and with the natural inconsistency of him who watches to discover what he would die to prove false, I wished that some heavy spell would steep me in drowsiness, before I discovered her sighs had another source. In a short time she arose, and wrapping a loose robe around her, took one of the tapers that burned in a veiled nich, and walked to a cabinet, of which I had often observed her care to be excessive. Through my half-closed lids I watched her every motion. She placed the taper on a marble desk, which sometimes she used as an oratory, and on which stood a crucifix. She opened the cabinet, and after examining some papers, she took out a parcel which she laid before her, and began to read. My heart throbbed audibly; as she bent over the paper, I thought a tear fell on it. 'Would she,' said I, mentally, 'weep over the guilty passion of her paramour, under the very crucifix to which I have seen her prostrate herself an hour ago?'

She put up the papers, and turning from the desk, leaned on the cabinet. The moon shone bright, and the lattice, woven with jessamine and tuberose, was open, she turned towards it; Mother of God! how lovely she looked! The taper tinged the summits of her feathery and burnished hair, with a radiance resembling that which hovers round the head of a saint. The moonlight fell on her pale face, disclosing just in the centre of her cheek a flushing spot, such as no adoration from me had ever kindled; her loose robe half disclosed a shape, of all others, the most interesting to a husband. She murmured a few broken notes of an air I had often heard her lull her infants to rest with. Every sense might have been feasted by the picture before me; but along with the odour of the jasmine, came the perfume of those fatal letters.

　　　　　CHARLES MATURIN

I noted this well. I remembered that lovers, in voluptuous gallantry, often perfumed their letters. As I gazed on her, a tear glittered in the moonshine, it was followed by another, and another, and the last was accompanied by the murmured name of 'Verdoni.' I groaned audibly; she started; she replaced the the letters and the taper, and approached the bed. 'Are you awake, my Lord?'—'I fear I am *almost awake!*'—'You fear!'—'Oh! yes, it was so sweet to dream *as I have done!*'—'Were your dreams so pleasant? I thought I heard you groan.'—'I groaned when I found you had *left* me.'—'Left you!'—'Yes, even in sleep I felt it; sleeping or waking I think only of you; (she was standing beside the bed; I knelt up in it; I grasped both her hands;) my senses, my soul, are full of you! Erminia, I adore you so, with such nice and exquisite fondness, as you can never imagine! You can never love as I do! But, though you must ever be comparatively deficient, beware, I adjure you, of being positively so; a dereliction of thought, an imagined desertion would drive me mad.' I was pouring out my whole heart with all its habitual impetuosity, at the very moment I had proposed to myself vigilance and caution.

I was still holding her hands, she sunk into a chair, beside the bed, but without withdrawing them, I sprung from the bed, and knelt at her feet. Her head was declined with the pale, pensive lily bending, that always melted me to sorrow and love. I continued to gaze on her without speaking, my voice was lost. Hear me, my Lord.'—'Hear *me*, my Lady, and my love, and life! I throw myself on your mercy, I implore your compassion for you and for myself. Do you remember the antique gem I gave you the other day? You admired the *workmanship* much, too much, more than the *gift* I fear. But I am wandering:—You remember the device, Cupid drawn by a lion, who paces quietly in his silken harness; think of me thus, dear, blessed love! Use me thus. While I am led by love, its caged emblems will not be so tender or so tame, but set free from that, I am a lion indeed, a lion who will—oh! Erminia, save me from imagining what.'

I dashed myself at her feet; I wept, I raved; my violence produced its usual effects, she was terrified and fainted. Her attendants were summoned. As I bent over her, extended in the likeness of death, I breathed an inward vow to banish for ever from my mind the subject of our conference, of which I already felt the misery insupportable, though the truth was not yet ascertained. I determined to sit down with the sufferings I could not now recal, and content with what happiness I might yet believe within my reach.

When they demanded of me the next morning what had been the event of my observations, I started as if I heard a serpent hiss. I prohibited all future mention of the subject; they quitted the apartment in silence; but Ascanio, as he was going out dropt a small key. I did not dare to think what this might mean. My first impulse was to seize it and try it where I suspected it was to be applied. I collected myself, and again called Ascanio. 'You have dropt a key.' He sprung forward to seize it with the aspect of one who curses his own carelessness.

Here I might have rested, and suffered him to depart with the shame of defeated villainy, but my curiosity, my—the devil within me wasroused—'Does that key guard a treasure, that you snatch it with such eagerness?'—'I do not know, my Lord.'—'You do not know what your own key secures?'—'My Lord, the key is not mine.'—'Not yours, whose is it then?'—'It belonged to my late master, the *Chevalier Verdoni*. He made no use of it himself, he kept it as a relic, he said, it was a key belonging to a cabinet he had presented to a lady he loved.'

"I drove him from the room. In the confusion of his fear, he again dropt the key! I seized it; I flew to Erminia's room; she was in the gardens of the castle with her children and attendants. I locked the door; to have seen my feverish tremblings, any one would have believed I was hastening to some feast of solitary delight, and at that moment, I would have changed situations with him that was writhing on the rack. One hope remained; that the key was not designed for that cabinet; I tried it. Alas, it was only the trembling of my hands that made it seem to resist; it opened. A mist overspread my sight, a gentle knock at the door aroused me; it was my eldest boy.—'You cannot come in, my darling.'—'Why, father?'—'Because I am busy.'—'I know from the sound of your voice you are not praying, father, and why may I not come in.'—I could not answer.—'Tell me what are you doing.'—'I do not know what I am doing,' said I in agony. 'Whatever it be, throw it away, if it prevents you from coming to the garden, and playing with us.' He tripped lightly away. I heard every word; the responses of an oracle had not sunk so deep into my soul—'throw it away!' The fatal papers were yet unopened. As I turned them with a shaking hand they fell, I stooped to replace them, and when my eye glanced on the first line, I could not withdraw it till I had read to the last.

"When I had done, sense and memory forsook me. I know not where my spirit went for some time, but though it seemed the very haunt of final woe, it was paradise to its return to consciousness. All was mist and cloud for some time, such as the soul struggles through, breathless and fancy-bound, in some hagridden dream. I saw the walls of the apartment, but I knew not where I was; I heard bells, and steps, and voices, but I knew not where I was; I heard the voice of the Countess in the gallery, and then I knew where and what I was.

"My despair was not easily concealed, even my domestics, I believe, observed it. In a short time, however, I became invisible to all but my brother and his servant: them only I admitted, yet them. I could not bear to behold.

"I am convinced I felt at the sight of that devil Ascanio, what a sorcerer feels in the presence of an imp whose ministry he employs, but by whom he knows he will be finally plunged in woe: his intelligence and his observation seemed necessary to existence, while they consumed it. I lived on poison. I was like the criminal travelling in the livid shade of the Upas, who must feed to live, and if he feeds must die. I had no feelings for this man but hatred and malevolence. I never saw him but my throat swelled, and my eyes seemed scalding in their sockets; yet I fastened on him for my morbid food, and devoured it with the greediness with which one would swallow the promises of hope and fortune.

"I mentioned to my brother the confessions of the guilty letters. I was astonished to perceive that he listened to the disclosure like one whose feelings were preoccupied by some darker discovery. I remarked it with that quickness which met half way all the devices employed against me. He shook his head; I urged my suspicions with vehemence. 'If,' said he, 'I could have any security that you would be patient, though after what I have seen of you I have no reason to accuse your want of patience.' I urged him franticly to proceed. 'What I have formerly disclosed,' said he, 'was accidentally and reluctantly; but I now speak from conscience and a sense of duty. Whatever errors a woman is guilty of before marriage, it is to be hoped the generous affection of a husband will lead her to shame and repentance of; but when she persists in her deviations after, she ceases to be an object of compassion or pardon.' He stopped; I waved my hand to him to proceed, I had no voice. 'I have alreaady said every thing,' said he. Again I motioned to him to go on, though I could no longer distinguish sounds. 'I have no more to say,' said he after a long pause. 'And I have no more to think,' said I. 'Have you then resolved on any thing?'—'Yes, I have, if I could tell it; but I have no words, they have all left me.'—'I know your purposes.'—'No, by my soul you do not; you are thinking of blood and horror, I take no thought of them. For *him*, for *him*, were I the master of the sulphurous lake, I would give up all minor tasks to minor imps, to watch him tossing and weltering on its waves for ever and ever. For her, who has no name, let her live in what peace she may, *my* blood and that of her paramour shall be on her head; but I could not shed a drop of *hers*, not if I might be lapped in a dream of love again for it.'—'And will you then suffer her to escape?'—'When she is delivered of the child, which I believe is mine, she shall be removed to a convent, and may the saints visit her retreat with penitence! for then will be done things that shall be a tale for ages—no, not one of those who have wrought me to this destruction shall escape!!!' As I uttered the last words, I thought I saw him grow pale. My mind was full of dark thoughts; I seized his arm, I looked eagerly in his face: 'Swear,' said I, 'that what you have told me is true.' He kissed a missal that lay on the table. I saw, I heard him.

"'Now swear that you have perjured yourself.'—'Are you mad?'—'I am, I will be in a moment unless you do; I cannot bear it.' I know not what followed; I was for some hours in a state from which alone I have since derived pauses of relief. When I recovered, I felt I had a human heart no longer; the images of affection, and wife, and child, seemed to strike on my heart with palpable impulse, and find no entrance there; there was no longer admission or inmate there, the lamp was gone out, and the door shut for ever. The first sensation I was conscious of was an unquenchable thirst. I swallowed draught after draught, and thirsted still; it was mental and inward; nothing could slake it but a thought which, while it relieved for a moment, made it more fierce and stinging: it was the blood of Verdoni in a vase before me. My brother, sometimes deprecating my violence, and sometimes bewailing his task, at length informed me that the guilty intercourse of Erminia and Verdoni still continued, unchecked by fear, or by the suspicions which my altered demeanour might have suggested to them.

"I know not how I answered him. I permitted him to arrange every thing for their detection and punishment. I was in his hands as passive as a tool, but I never relaxed my demand of being suffered to dispatch Verdoni alone.

"My brother announced that I was about making a tour to the Grecian islands. I was accompanied by some attendants as far as the shore, there I dismissed them, and hiring under an assumed name a small villa in the neighbourhood of Baiæ, awaited the intelligence my brother engaged to send me. *That* came too soon. Ascanio brought me volumes of intercepted letters, referring to interviews and indulgences stolen in my absence. Their frequent meetings, their visits to their child, their remarks on its increasing growth and beauty, every doubtful term in the letters of the cabinet repeated and confirmed, occurred in these intercepted scrolls. When perused, their effect on me was usually a paroxysm so dreadful, that the people of the house were scarcely pacified by the assurances they received of my periodical insanity: these paroxysms were followed by hours of solitude and abstraction, during which I could tolerate the presence of no one, and none dared to approach me. It was during these moments that strange thoughts were with me. My spirits fell like a subsiding tide, and like a falling tide carried away with them the dregs and wreck of its spent fury. I had relinquished every circumstance and pretension of rank and eminence. I had become a private man in habit and exterior; all the vanity of the earth was become tasteless and loathsome to me, I sickened at their hollowness, I spurned their incapacity to suspend or alleviate calamity. I execrated the celebrity that made their possessor's fall only more conspicuous, his misfortunes a more popular theme of vulgar curiosity, his degradation a more ample feast for the vultures of envy. I felt that to return to what I had been was impossible; that my outward man must partake of the change of my inward man; that I could no longer support the Count Montorio's name, when I no longer possessed the Count Montorio's mind. I cannot describe the process or the effect of this change so great and effectual, though I experience its consequences to this hour.

I was a bold, ambitious, vain man, proud of my rank, and fond of its pompous appendages: what I became suddenly and finally, my narrative will tell. I have compared my progress to that of a magnificent caravan, overwhelmed and blasted in the majesty of its march by the burning deluge of the desert, and fixed a monument of desolation where it had moved a monument of pride. The result of my meditations was anticipated by a letter from Muralto, where my brother still resided as a spy on the culprits. He told me that their passion raged with such shameless violence, that Verdoni was frequently introduced at the castle, and that he had even fixed on a night to spend there, which the Countess had confessed, and implored *him* to conceal, believing from the frequency of her lover's visits that it was no longer possible to dissemble their object. When I read this—

I need not go on, nor will I enumerate every link of the chain that they wound round me with the art of demons, every one of burning iron, that scorned without consuming. I *will* mention, however, one circumstance, which is but too strongly indicative of my character, of that part of it which is derived from hereditary propensity. I think I can recollect the impressions they intended to produce were unsettled till they introduced a wretch, a mendicant, an astrologer, who talked something about prediction, and horoscopes, and ascendants, and a trinal aspect on some hour on the appointed evening. He was a meagre, illiterate wretch; I would have spurned my lacquey for listening to him; *yet I* listened to him. I was like a sufferer bit by the tarantula, though my veins were filled with poison, they bounded and vibrated to his muttering jargon.

"The night arrived. If any being could be supposed enveloped in lightning without being consumed, and then dismissed without losing the faculties and functions of life, such I believe would he describe the moment of his existence in the fiery fluid to be, as I remember the events of that night, thus sudden, thus hot, thus blasting; gone almost when felt, without a possibility of defining or forgetting; the time of its agency a moment, of its effects, for ever.

At the close of that evening I quitted my habitation, and met my brother in a forest that skirted the Campagna, about two miles from Muralto, whose towers I could yet see through the dusk. He did not speak, and I believed all he had told me was true. We rode into a thicket, where we alighted and secured our horses. In a few moments I heard the trampling of hoofs. A cavalier passed alone, his deportment was melancholy and his pace slow. He passed us, my brother made a signal that we should again mount our horses; we did so. At some distance I saw him enter a cottage in the forest, I saw him at the door caressing a child, whom he placed before him, and disappeared in the windings of the wood. 'Adulterous villain!' said my brother. *I did not speak,* all was mist and darkness with me. I followed my brother's motions mechanically. We entered the cottage, there was only a woman within. I leaned against the door, I could not breathe the air he had poisoned. My brother passed before me to prevent her being alarmed at my appearance, it was probably most terrific. 'Who is the cavalier that has just quitted your cottage?'—'May I ask who inquires, Signor?'—'We are friends, and have important business with him; if we are right in our conjectures of his name—' 'Why, Signor, he calls himself Orsanio,' said the woman, proud of her sagacity; 'but I myself have heard his attendants address him by the name of Verdoni.'—'He visits your cottage frequently?'—'Oh, frequently, Signor! He has a beautiful babe here, whom he cannot live a day without seeing.'—'And is he always unaccompanied?'—'Oh, no, Signor! he is often met here by a lady in a veil, and they converse and weep over the child till they make me weep too, though I know not for what.'—'Do you know from whence the lady comes?'—'She leaves her carriage at the skirts of the wood, Signor; but I have heard it said that she is seen to return to the castle of Muralto, whose towers you can just see through the twilight. There are strange things told of the possessors of that great castle. Hark, Signor! could that groan have been uttered by the cavalier who leans there?'—'No, no; proceed, proceed.'

All this I heard, but after the last sentence I heard nothing. We quitted the cottage, we mounted our horses. 'What do you purpose to do?' said my brother. I could make no answer, but showing my drawn stiletto, and pointing towards the castle. We rushed into the wood; I did not see we were joined by Ascanio, till he pointed out Verdoni at a little distance before us. I sprung forward, he attempted to defend himself; and believing us from our masks and arms to be assassins, implored us to save his child. I dashed the bastard to the ground. He drew, but by this time the others had come up, and Ascanio with a blow lopped off the hand that held the sword. Possibly he saved my life, for I was so blind and impotent with fury he might have overcome me with a reed. But I had no wish to mangle or butcher, I would not touch a hair of his head. I seized the reins of his horse, and we galloped towards the castle. They asked what I purported, but I could only utter 'my wife.'

There are many private avenues which, winding beneath the ramparts, open on the wood; they were unknown except to me, for none but an enthusiast in antiquity would explore them. They followed me, therefore, as they would a magician, who discloses a path among subterranean rocks. I remembered their windings well, and remembered that one of them terminated in a dark and secret stair that communicated with the apartments of my wife. We traversed those caverns with no light but what broke through chasm or crevice above, with no sound but the inarticulate moans of the devoted Verdoni.

I will not interrupt this narrative with attempts to describe what men call their feelings; for such as mine there can be but little sympathy, for there is no knowledge. Few have been in my circumstances, none that ever I knew have had my mind. It is easy to tell of the fall of ambition and the loss of felicity; but who has dared to describe the state of Lucifer, the 'son of the morning,' when he fell from the sphere of a seraph and the harmonies of heaven into darkness and woe, into beds of fire and fetters of adamant. Such was mine, total, remediless, final: worse, none but a mortal can know the *hell of* love.

"I left our victim at the foot of the staircase with my brother; I ascended to the Countess's apartment. I traversed one in which the children were sleeping: I could not look at them. Their mother was in her bedchamber; her nurse was her only attendant. She screamed when she saw me; I attempted some insulting words, but my voice was choked. I believe in a moment she comprehended the whole of her danger: she must, for my visage was the visage of a demon, and though I had not the power of language, my voice was like the roar of ocean. 'Oh, I am betrayed and undone!' said she, staggering back and falling on the bed. Then I found words. Words! Firebrands, and arrows, and death, I hurled at her in my rage of malediction. The woman interposed, affrighted interposed. I spurned her away. Darkly I menaced something that seemed to sting her to apprehension. She sprung from the bed, she clung to my feet, she wept, she grovelled, she adjured me but to hear her—to hear her—'*let* me but be heard!' I saw, I felt, I feasted on the anguish of her soul; every arrow she had sent into my heart was returned to hers barbed with poison. 'I am innocent, by this light!'—'Adulteress!'—'By this blessed cross I kiss—' 'Adulteress! adulteress!' I roared. 'Hear me but for a moment, but for one moment; confront me with your brother. Oh, Verdoni! we are destroyed by treachery.'

I tried to force myself from her, she clung to me still. I dragged her along the ground; her shrieks were wild, her grasp was like the grasp of death. 'Oh, but for a moment hear me! Is that so much? As you expect to be heard yourself when you are stretched on the bed of death!' Suddenly I stopt. I fixed my dry and bursting eyes on her; I felt the unnatural and hushed stillness of my voice. 'I will not be heard myself in the hour of death; I have no hope, you have 'reft me of it, you have undone me for ever. The horrors and burden of this night are on my soul through you, and of you they shall be required. Ho, Ascanio! drag that adulterous villain here, his mistress is ready for her paramour.' She started from her knees, she fixed her eyes on the door by which I entered; she saw—

"I *MUST* GO ON. THEY talk of the vengeance of Italian husbands; mine outgoes example. I caused him to be deliberately stabbed before her sight!!!"

"I paused between every blow. I bid her listen to every groan! Poor distracted wretch! she thought the ravings of her love would disarm, instead of nerving my blows. When she found her shrieking supplications for 'mercy! mercy! mercy!' were vain, she became wilder than myself. With the frenzy of a lover, she reeled up and down, blind and breathless, echoing the faint cries of Verdoni, and cursing his murderers, whom she had a moment before knelt to. 'Devils! devils!' she shrieked, 'I do not pray, I do not kneel now; stab on! Oh, that my eyes would burst!' Verdoni's last blood-stifled groan came to her ear. 'Ah, that groan was ease!' she screamed. 'He is dead! Ha! ha! ha! I laugh at ye now; he is dead, he is dead!'"

"Staggering she sunk upon the body. Her *heart burst!* When I touched her, she was cold as a stone; her eyes fixed but lifeless, her limbs relaxed, her pulses extinct. When I found she was dead, gone without recall for ever, that *Erminia was dead!*—But I have no power to speak of that hour. I sprung forward with the speed of one who flies from destruction; destruction did indeed surround me on every side; and it was owing to this unexpected direction my passions took, and the inconceivable velocity with which I pursued it, that I escaped, for that night at least. I must have flown with the speed of a cloud chased by the storm, for I was many miles along the western shores of Naples by midnight. My horse, whom I had found in the wood, then sunk under me. I flew on foot, traversing the windings of the shore like a wave. My reason was not suspended, it was totally *changed*. I had become a kind of intellectual savage; a being, that with the malignity and depravation of inferior natures, still retains the reason of a man, and retains it only for his curse. Oh! that midnight darkness of the soul, in which it seeks for something whose loss has carried away every sense but one of utter and desolate privation; in which it traverses leagues in motion and worlds in thought, without consciousness of relief, yet with a dread of pausing. I had nothing to seek, nothing to recover; the whole world could not restore me an atom, could not shew me again a glimpse of what I had been or lost; yet I rushed on as if the next step would reach shelter and peace. My flight was so wild and rapid, that it was equally impossible to calculate its direction or overtake its speed. I had disappeared while they were removing the corses and the traces of blood. Other causes might have contributed to my escape: there was a storm, they said, a commotion both of air and earth. I recollect nothing of it but the report; but it probably deterred those who were not desperate like me.

"Towards morning I sprung into a small bark, it was going to Sicily; but Sicily I soon quitted, and crossed into the Grecian isles. I had an inveterate loathing, not of the human form, but of the human form under an Italian garb; aye, of the houses and trees, the language and the very air: whatever I had formerly resembled, or been conversant with, was an abomination to me. I looked on them as a condemned spirit may be supposed to look on the body in which he had sinned, now dark, deserted, and loathsome; at once the remembrancer of pleasure, and the incendiary of pain. It is remarkable, that during this term I adopted in desperation the very course that the most active and suspicious caution would have deliberately pursued. My frequent changes of residence, my private haunts, my solitude, and my disguise, preserved from discovery as effectually as if they had been intentional or even conscious.

"I rambled from isle to isle, from sand to rock, without notice and without interruption. The people were poor and simple, they had no leisure for curiosity; my appearance terrified them, and they were glad when it was removed. My miserable food was easily procured, my clothes were now ragged, and my bed the bare earth. *This was a brother's doing!* Still I wandered on, for there was something I wanted: that something was utter solitude, a total amputation from life. I had heard of a little barr islet, which was dreaded as the haunt of a spirit of wrecks and storms: I rowed myself thither in a boat one still night. Whether it was the residence of such a being, I cared not; it was enough for me no human being ventured there. Here I found all I needed, a cave, water, wild fruits, and during the winter more provisions than I could consume left on the shore by the superstitious people to propitiate the turbid spirit of the place.

"Here I sunk into a strange kind of animal life; I became quite a creature of the elements; my propensities and habits ceased to be those of humanity, of social humanity at least. I lost the use of language; I forgot my own name; yet my time was sufficiently diversified by the changes of the season and the sky. When it was tempestuous I rushed abroad, I howled and shrieked with the voices of the storm. I bared my pelted head and breast to the rain, and when cold and drenched retired to my cave and slept. When it was calm I sat on a crag of my cave and listened to the winds, whose wild and changeful moanings were wrought by the diversities of the shore into a quaint mimicry of human sounds, to the tide, whose lambent ripplings I *felt*, as well as heard, breathing tranquillity. I never thought of my former self, or of those with whom I had been; I was conscious of something like a dark recess in my thoughts, from which I seemed to have emerged lately, and into which I did not wish to venture again. Sometimes I dreamt; but my faculties were so confused that I only remembered my dream as something obscurely painful, something that interrupted that quiet exile from consciousness and thought, that seemed to be the *menstruum* of my present existence. I believe I might have lingered out many years in this state, on the principle of the longevity of ideots.

"One evening as I sat on the sea shore, I saw a boat at a small distance, which floated along its winding, as if rather to observe than to land. I lifted my heavy and stagnated eyes; but when I saw the Italian habits in the boat, I flew to hide myself in my cave, shaking with horror. I did not venture out again till it was dark; there were stars, but no moon: it was owing to this, and to the silent tread of my naked feet, that I approached unseen where two men were seated on a point of rock conferring. The Italian language came to my ear; I listened with a blind and mechanical delight at first. I loved the sound (so wild are the inconsistencies of the human mind), though at first the words were unintelligible. I was quickly awakened to their full meaning. 'You are a bold and daring devil, *Ascanio*,' said one. 'Yes, I *was once*, but I am almost spoiled for these feats now. Could I think I might hope for absolution I would turn penitent, aye, monk, and pray for the remainder of my days. The murder of the unfortunate cavalier and lady, who were as innocent as those blessed lights above, and the persecution of the wretched mad Count to this desolate and savage life; nor even to let him rest in his den, to shed his blood on these wild sands, by all the saints I wonder this rock supports us!'—'Away, fool! half the convents in Italy might be bribed with a *moiety* of the ducats we shall get for it.'

There was much more; I listened for an hour; they talked as without witness, as two murderers, solitary and undisguised. Erminia, the *unfortunate* lady, and the cavalier, *innocent!* and the *wretched mad Count*, persecuted to desperation and murder by his brother, and then by his brother traced to solitude, and slaughtered in his den!

"Oh!—but I cannot, cannot; if I should but write her name, I shall write on for unnoted days and nights volumes filled only with her name. Late and impotent repentance, and cries of posthumous despair!

"I *will* pursue my narrative. I retreated to my cave, with an instinctive provision for safety; yet when I came there I could neither devise nor employ a weapon if I had it. I fell on my bed of leaves, and awaited death. I saw a shadow darkening the entrance of my hut; one of them crept in as he would into the den of a savage, whom he feared to rouse by noise or light. I had no power of motion; by a strange but lucky infatuation I felt as if I was compelled to await the approach of my murderer. He drew near; in the darkness of my cave I could no longer see his steps, but I *felt* them; so dark was the nook in which I lay, that I felt his breath on my face, but could not see him. With an impulse, whose quickness prevented escape or resistance, I sprung up; the part I fastened on darkling was his throat. I threw him to the ground; my strength, naturally great, was rendered gigantic by my habits of hardihood and difficulty.

"I felt him gasp and quiver with the motions of death; I felt his vest for his stiletto, it was stuck in his belt unsheathed. I drew it out, and with steps that did not rouse the bat from its cleft, stole to the entrance of the cave. The other was bending over a crag that fenced it; I sprung on him when he expected his associate: he started, and beheld a form scarce human holding a dagger to his throat.

"He flew with the swiftness of fear, and I with the swiftness of revenge; delighted I perceived him toiling up a rock, which, isolated and bare, beetled over the sea, cutting off all retreat. He looked, and leaped; I bent over the ridge, and beheld him struggling in the waters. I returned to my cave; the body that lay there was black, and swoln, and stark. I did not lie in my cave that night; I vented my rage and anguish along the shores, in sounds as wild as the winds that swept them, sounds that I sometimes thought were echoed by wailing cries from the rock where I had compelled Ascanio to plunge into the dark and pitiless waters. Towards morning I searched the corse in the cave; I found letters, principally from my brother and his wife to the bearer, who was a public assassin, and his brother Ascanio.

I was at first about to describe the effects of their perusal; but I feel I *must* not. I have a task to do, for which all that remains to me of intellect is necessary. Why should I waste it in sallies of voluntary frenzy? It is enough for me to detail the contents of these letters. I *will do it most calmly and unshrinkingly.*

CHARLES MATURIN

"IT APPEARED THAT MY BROTHER had been the former lover of my wife; that his own marriage had been a match of angry disappointment, which, fermented by his wife's ambition, had suggested to him the idea of working on my credulous and vindictive disposition; and—I will go on calmly and unshrinkingly. He had planted spies about the family of Amaldi, and he had suborned a depraved servant whom Verdoni had dismissed. The secret sorrows that so visibly clouded the House of Amaldi were quickly known. Erminia had in her earliest youth been attached to Verdoni; her father, with common worldliness of character, hesitated, in the hope of a splendid suitor. But his cold policy was spurned by the lovers; they were united privately in the church of St. Antonio, in the night of the 4th December, 1667, and the following winter Erminia was delivered of an infant daughter at the house of a relative not far from Naples. About this time Verdoni's regiment was stationed in the neighbourhood of Palermo, where a powerful banditti terrified and oppressed the country. The inhabitants requested the aid of military force, Verdoni's company marched against the banditti, but misled in the windings of a forest, were assailed by an ambuscade, and cut off to a man. The names of the officers who had perished were sent to Naples, and the first among them was that of Verdoni. Erminia's marriage had not been at this time avowed, and there was now no necessity for its avowal. She wept over her fatherless babe in solitude. At this moment my disastrous proposals were urged. Wounded and shocked, Erminia appealed to her father; she told him her tale. She was answered by a command to marry the Count Montorio on pain of paternal malediction. She was told of the folly of sacrificing her youth and hopes to the cherishing of a widowed name, and of the wickedness of preferring duty to a dead husband to a living father. She wept, she trembled, and she obeyed. Oh! she was all gentleness, all *melting, pliant, weeping woman!* She impure! She was formed of thrice-fanned snow, tempered with dew from the cup of the lily of the vale, and animated by some spirit who had bathed in the cold blood of spheral light; she that should have been nested in my bosom, and fed with kisses like the suckling of my heart; she—I have vowed to write her name no more.

Shortly after our fatal marriage, her husband, who had been taken prisoner by the banditti, and confined in a subterranean cavern, after a perilous and strange emersion into light, returned to Italy. He returned in disguise, for he dreaded the pursuit of those from whom he had escaped. He returned, and found his wife the wife of another man, and the mother of other children! No one dared to tell of his return to her, still less was it probable her family would disclose their shame to me, a shame their own selfish haste had incurred. She was wandering one evening in the woods, with her own attendant; a voice called on her, she was retreating in affright; again it called, a well known voice of reproach and love. The next moments the lovers wept in agony on each other. To meet him often, to weep with him over the child of their sorrows, who could envy her this last sad consolation? It was at this moment that my brother, prompted by his Tullia of a wife (for mere man was incapable of it), determined to possess himself of rank and wealth without the doubtful and suspected means of poinard or poison. He knew neither of them could go more swiftly or silently to the seat of life than the infamy of the wife I adored, or the diminution of the honour I was an enthusiast in. He was safe, besides, for no one would venture to tell me that my wife was the wife of another, nor even if they suspected I knew it would they presume to comment on it. I was therefore shut up to the mercy of these two men, who had not kindness enough to stab me to the heart. The letters I had found in the cabinet had been written during the period of their *wedded separation* at Naples. Every expression of luscious and intimate tenderness occurred in them; but from a necessary caution, all allusions to their real situation (which would have undeceived me) were suppressed, lest they should be discovered by her father. During my absence, my abused wife had intrusted her honour and her sufferings to my brother. She had informed him that Verdoni was about to quit Italy for ever; and that she proposed, after her confinement, to retire into a convent, and assume the veil. My murdered love! amid the anguish of passion her thoughts were holy as vestal dreams! She acknowledged my affection, she avowed her gratitude to me, she implored him to sooth my disappointments in pride and in passion—*mine*, who was planning her murder!

In the dark hour of solitary woe thus she leant on him, and thus he betrayed her! Oh! why did her fatal, fatal wish to spare my feelings prevent her making the disclosure herself? My suffering would have been indeed great, but my triumph would have been great also. I would have resigned her to her first love, to the husband of her youth; resigned her without a groan, though my last had followed the sacrifice when they had left me alone. I would—But I am to tell not what I would have been, but what *I am*. In other parts of the letters I found they had resolved on a total massacre that night, that we were to have fallen by each other. Two victims had indeed fallen; but I, as I have related, had escaped by an unexpected impulse of flight, to which I yielded in the madness of the moment, without thought of safety or of danger, and which the confusion of murder had prevented them from noticing till I was many miles from Muralto.

"Since that period, which was about three years, Ascanio and his brother had pursued me through Italy; they had pursued every track and shadow of intelligence with the hot and breathless diligence of a chace of blood, while my brother, trembling in his castle, spread a report of my death, and celebrated my funeral rites in the chapel of the family. They had at length discovered me, and their charge was death, without noise and without delay. Such was the intelligence of these letters, scattered up and down, conveyed in hint and reference, confident and familiar.

"When I was perusing them, there was but one nerve in my heart whose motion was restless and inquiring, all the rest seemed seared and rivetted. I read on with an agitation which was the last alarm of nature—my *children!* I read on—they *were dead!*

"When I had read all, a fire seemed to spring up within me; a dark, solid, unconsuming fire, that preyed without destroying. I know not how to describe my sufferings (for I always suffered in solitude, there was no voice of inquiry near me, no *shadow* of a friend to fling refreshment on my cold bed of leaves); but surely never were spirit and body so strangely acted on by each other. The fire I speak of seemed to me corporal and visible. I remember sitting on a point of rock, and wondering it did not smoke and crumble beneath me; I seemed to live in fire. My muscles and nerves, swoln and rigid with agony, were like rods of red hot metal; my hairs hissed and sparkled with the flickering of flame when the wind moved them; and my eyes, their sockets seemed glowing iron, and when I closed them, long tresses of dancing fire floated from them, and they seemed to turn on an inward world of flames, on which they gazed with the anguish, but not the short duration, that the rage of the elements permits.

"I know not how long I was in this state; I had no mark of time but day and night, and to them I had been often insensible, except that I think I was conscious of greater pain from the glare of the day. When I recovered, Erminia and Verdoni were beside me: never for a moment since have I been insensible of their presence. They have been at different times my punishment and my consolation, my taskers and my companions. Four years in my rocky solitude I conferred with them alone, sometimes tranced by their whispers, and sometimes harrowed by their shrieks. I speak with the earnestness and simplicity of one who, convinced of what he speaks, is careless of being believed by others. The dreams of the night are easily dissolved, and strange shapes are sometimes seen to skimmer through the twilight of a cavern; but I have met them at noon, on the bare sunny shore. I have seen them on the distant wave, when its bed was smooth and bright as jasper; the curtained mist that hung on mole and breaker, and mingled with the sheeted spanglings of the surf, floated back from them, did not throw a fringe of its shadowy mantling on their forms. I could not be deceived. Sometimes the light was glorious beyond imagination. Towards sunset I would sometimes see a small white cloud, and watch its approach; it would fix on a point of the rock that rose beside my cave; as twilight thickened it would unfold, its centre disclosing a floating throne of pearl, and its skirts expanding into wings of iris and aurelia that upbore it. By moonlight the pomp grew richer, and the vision became exceeding glorious. Myriads of lucent shapes were visible in that unclouded shower of light which fell from the moon on the summit of the rock; myriads swam on its opal waves, wafted in a fine web of filmy radiancy, canopied with a lily's cup, and inebriate with liquid light. Among them sat the shadows of the lovers, sparkling with spheral light, and throned in the majesty of vision, but pale with the traces of mortality. There sat the lovers in sad and shadowy state together; so greatly unfortunate, so fatal, passing, fond. Sometimes, when stretched on my cold, lone bed, I have heard *her* voice warbling on the wind, touches of sweet, sad music, such as I have heard her sing when she thought herself alone and unheard. I have risen, and followed it, and heard it floating on the waters; I listened, and would have given *worlds to weep*. On a sudden the sounds would change to the most mournful and wailing cries, and Erminia, pale and convulsed as I saw her last, would pass before me, pointing to a gory shape that the waves would throw at my feet. Then they would plunge together into the waters, and where far off the moon shed a wan and cloudy light on the mid wave, I would see their visages rise dim and sad, and hear their cry die along the waste of waters.

"Often when in autumn the sun set among clouds and vapours, I sat at the mouth of my cave to watch the scenery that followed. The clouds, dark, and rapid, and broken with strong stains of red, would assume wild resemblances to things I scarcely recalled; ships, and towers, and forests on fire, and moving shapes of things that never lived. Sometimes they formed a castle, a black mountain mass of structure, its turrets were fringed with flame, and the gleamy spots below seemed like fires peeping through casement and loop hole, and the sanguine waters that reflected its shade seemed to moat it with blood; and hosts of embattled vapours, flushed with the hues of the stormy sky, seemed to march in mid air to attack it. Then, while I gazed, Erminia, in the first flash of the sieging lightnings, would burst on my sight with a face of wrath and menace, and behind her another form, dark with the rage of tempests. Oh! worse than the rage of tempests to me was his sight. I have fled to my cave, I have buried my face in my bed of leaves. But what shapes have I seen as the keen and subtle lightning's, glancing through cleft and crevice, filled the cavern with sheets of paly blue?

"It was on one of those nights that, wild and resistless as the tempest, a thought rushed on my mind; it was the only thought that for years had warmed my heart with a natural impulse, or convinced me I yet held alliance with the world of human beings. Do ye who read my story ask what was that thought? I pray ye to pause a moment, and think on my state.

"I was a nobleman, a representative of a noble house, whose honours I bore untarnished, and of whose honours I was proud. My wealth was great, my power greater; the sphere and shadow of my influence included thousands, who were cherished and sustained by it. I was loved by some, honoured by many, feared by many; and to the fear, such as remote and unbending dignity inspires, I was not averse. This was only a part of my character. I was, and I may now speak of myself as one who lives no more, a munificent patron, an invincible friend, an adoring lover. I was a husband, a father; my soul was wrapt up in my wife and children. In spite of my high thoughts and demeanour, I slept on the bosom of domestic love with a fondness of clasp and a softness of rest, such as the mildest spirit might seek in the humblest shed of privacy: such I was. I might have run my race in peace and honour: such I was. And what had I been made? by a *brother* I had cherished and saved, a *murderer*, a savage, an outcast of both worlds, a denizen of the wilds in habit, a demon in soul!

There is no describing that depravation of humanity, both physical and moral, to which he had reduced me. Nebuchadnezzar, who was driven from among men, and abode among the beasts, had probably no throbbings of remembered worth or dignity, no anguish of moral debasement to haunt his dark sleep. My sufferings comprehended the extremes of all a being could be human and suffer. I was the lover of an object no power could obtain or restore; I was the idolator of a fame which was extinguished and lost; I was a villain with unimpaired conscience; I was a madman with perfect consciousness. Is there one fool enough to ask what remained to me?

Revenge!!!

Yes, from the bare breast of an island rock, from its starved, and naked, and raving inhabitant, from a wretch who might have been shewn for a spectacle through the streets of Naples, came a burst of vindictive energy that laid one of its proudest houses in the dust.

"This event, of which I have hitherto sketched the motives, is the proper subject of this narrative. Almost the moment I conceived it, I conceived its progress, its means, and the very point of the criminal's character and situation on which it was to be made to bear. To shew him the hollowness, the worthlessness, the nothingness of that for which he had sold himself under sin, was no longer an object with revenge or with conscience; its own attainment had convinced him forcibly and awfully of it. In his letters I discovered he was a miserable man. It is usual to talk of the dreams of a murderer's night; but he was substantially wretched, wretched from suspicion, wretched from fear, wretched from the conviction that he had destroyed himself—for nothing. With him, therefore, appeal had been anticipated by conviction, and punishment superseded by remorse. But he was now surrounded by a numerous family, for whose welfare perhaps he endeavoured to reconcile himself to guilt, and to believe that the offences that had benefited his children could scarce fail of pardon. *His* children were to shine out on the world in unsuspected magnificence and unmixed acclamations; while *mine*, the native heirs of Muralto, mouldered in their mother's bloody grave, unwept but by their exiled father, the father who had lain them there! Whoever is acquainted with its direful event, may have now anticipated my purpose,—to make the children the punishers of the father, and to combine the eternal spoliation of the name and honours wrested from me with the fall of their usurper.

"I am aware that so horrible an idea never entered the human mind before. Let him that is disposed to execrate me only cast his eye on the

CHARLES MATURIN

preceding pages. I do not say I will be justified; but it will at least be confessed that he who was injured as never man was injured, should be revenged as man was never avenged. It is remarkable, that from the moment I conceived this idea, my reason was not only restored, with scarce a subsequent interval of insanity, but my powers were confirmed, condensed, invigorated to a degree of invincible iron-like force and stability, to which alone such an undertaking could be possible. I had no failing weakness of head or of heart, no suspension of my purpose from the frailties of humanity or intellect from that hour for ever.

"A total desertion of my savage habits was my first resolution. I inured myself, after many distortions of reluctance, to bear the sight of the human face and the sound of the human voice. After some time I crossed to the next inhabited islet. I endeavoured to reconcile myself to human life; to sit for an hour without start or exclamation; to eat without walking about at my food; and (most difficult of all) to pass the night in a bed, where at first I found rest impracticable. It was here, when the first vehemence of my purpose had expended itself, I began to scan the difficulties that surrounded it, and to find them numberless and perilous. I am persuaded no being whose character was not partially tinged by madness could have been adequate to its execution. I have no desire now to spend my time in magnifying the wonders of it, and gratifying a miserable ambition with the shuddering praise of the strength of a demon's wing in his flight to mischief. I have no intention of rehearsing my mental debates and toils, I merely purpose to tell their result.

"My first step was to pass into Turkey in Asia. I traversed most of the countries of Asia Minor; I visited Syria, I travelled into Persia, I crossed the Persian Gulf into Arabia. I traversed the *continent* of Arabia, and winding along the shores of the Red Sea, passed into Egypt. I visited its upper and lower regions, and returning to Cairo, embarked for Europe. An accident brought me to Candia, where assuming the habit of a Greek monk, I went on board a veffel then bound to Rhodes, but which finishing her voyage, left me in Sicily; there outwardly reconciling myself to the Catholic Communion, I procured a recommendation to the Superior of a convent in Naples, and returned to my native city.

"I do not mean to give a detail of the sufferings of a solitary stranger in a progress of fifteen years, through countries, fierce, lawless, and sanguinary. I acknowledge myself to have been almost constantly in a state of sufferance and danger, often in one of extremity. If it were asked by what means I escaped with life from such persecution, I solemnly declare I know of none, except total poverty, a hardened constitution, and a mind of desperation. A resolution, the strongest that ever occupied a strong mind, was sustained by gigantic strength and hardihood of body, the fruit of my exile and my savagery. My object in this long progress, was what no calamities could suspend, the study of the human character in its fiercer and gloomier features. Even a dungeon could shew me wardours, and torturers, and criminals. It will be asked why did I seek a knowledge of the human character, where it subsists in a state so rude and unvaried, where ignorance and oppression combine to forbid the expansion of elementary, or the acquisition of fictitious features, and to confine life to a weary, unimproving monotony?

"I answer, my search was after that part of the human character, which is equally visible through all the modifications of society, and the caprices of the individual, which is equally discernible in the savage and in the sage, but which is generally marked by more strong and prominent lines in the ruder parts of life. My search was for the existence of superstition, in every form it assumes, and for every mode of influence that could be exercised on it, for the means by which that influence might be acquired, and the possible extremes to which the passion might be urged by art and terror. Had this search been pursued in Europe, the consequence might have been what I dreaded more than the sufferings I encountered in Asia and Africa, detention, examination, discovery; perhaps an immersion into the Bastile in France, or an eternal consignment to the dungeons of the Inquisition in Spain or Italy. In Asia, if my existence was destroyed, my name and purpose would perish along with it. I should not be remembered as the man who only achieved a vast *thought*, and died from the debility of its execution. From the first moment, I was convinced that *superstition was my only engine*, the only instrument that could accomplish so great a purpose; the only one that could be applied to its most minute, and its most operose parts alike; that could dissect the most subtle and capillary fibres of the human heart, and penetrate the iron fortresses of power; that could wrench the frame of nature, and sport with the varieties of the human character; that could make the virtuous consider a crime as a duty, and the vicious make a deity of a dream. This was the only foundation that could support the structure that I purported to raise on it. I remembered my own struggles and reluctance, till something like a shadowing of fate stole over my mind, I remembered the wretched impostor that they brought to me at Baiæ.

"The execution of my purpose, perhaps, was some protection to me, in countries whose wild inhabitants are yet deeply susceptible of the delights and the terrors of superstition. In Turkey, therefore, I was a Grecian conjuror. Through Asia Minor and Syria I was one of those dervises whose supposed knowledge in secret studies is no obstruction to the sanctity of his person and profession. In Persia I was a Magian worshipper of fire, the most ancient superstition in the world. In Egypt I was all these successively, for in Egypt are mingled all the superstitions of the East. Among the vulgar I was a conjuror, but among the adepts only a novice; nor in truth could I well be more, had I been versed in all the dark wisdom of Europe, Rosicrucian, or Sully's, or Nostradamus, or Albertus Magnus's; had I been a student in the wizard walls of Salamanca, I must have bowed to the wands of the Oriental and African sages. There are among these men, however ignorant both in physics and literary antiquity, some powers still existing of the most extraordinary kind. I am perfectly willing to ascribe the wonders they produce to causes merely natural, but still the effects are such as prove an acquaintance with the depths of nature, which the most erudite and studious European has not yet obtained.

"I mention as an instance, that power of disarming serpents and noxious reptiles, possessed by some of the most ignorant and grovelling wretches I have ever met with in Egypt, a power which they pretend to exercise with spell and charm, but which when *I acquired*, I found to be attainable by means merely physical. I mention these things merely to intimate the line of operations I sought, and the powers I acquired, amid the luxuries of nature, and the labours of art, the wonders of antiquity, or the magnificence of recent dominion; in the mosque or in the cavern, the desert, or the Bazar, I pursued but one object; my labour was never remitted, nor my tenacity ever relaxed.

"It was in the spring of the year 1689 I returned to Naples, my first object to inquire into the situation and characters of the family, my next to be introduced among them. I easily learnt the former, the Count was gloomy and solitary; the family lived in retired grandeur; the sons had many splendid qualities, but their minds were of the dark, superstitious complection of their house. The latter also was easy, for the Count had become a devotee. It will perhaps be a matter of astonishment, that having arrived in my native city, and having means sufficient to prove my identity and my injuries, I did not prefer the substantial compensation of my restored honours and enjoyments to a visionary and bloody revenge.

"It will cease to astonish, when my story is read with more attention. It will be discovered that with me, ambition was only the ornament of life, happiness and love, (however hostile to their softness my character may appear) were its substance, its soul. My name, my dignity, were only the cupola that though raised to the summit, constituted the least necessary part of the pile of my happiness. For whom should I seek to be great? Was there another Erminia in the world? Were my children's graves to be opened by the trumpet of a herald? They might be avenged, but never recalled. No; I saw, without a groan, the palace and castle built by my ancestors. I saw their jewels, their treasures, their magnificence sparkling round the forms of those who had undone me, I saw without a thought of resumption, but with a determination of revenge. Ambition had not left a shadow on my mind, of love only the soul subsisted still; but of revenge, both body and soul lived within me, in a state of vigour and vitality, still capable of the most powerful functions, still imperiously demanding their sacrifice. From my own experience, I am convinced that revenge is the most long-lived of passions. Could my brother have poured at my feet his palaces, his treasures, his honours, could he have poured along with them, what was beyond the reach of human power to restore, my name, my peace, my *inward dignities* unclouded and undebased; could he have done all this, I would have spurned it all. I had but one faculty, one passion, one appetite. My body was but a corporal vehicle for revenge, its spirit seemed to actuate me instead of a soul.

"Let those who wonder at the temerity of my undertaking, think on the requisites I possessed for its success, and the train of preparation those requisites had long been in. My body was as a body of adamant; my mind was capable of filling and directing the energies of such a frame; I was invincible to the fatigues of famine, of sleeplessness, or of toil; no difficulties could exhaust, no dangers could repel; the world, its temptations, and its terrors were like dust beneath my feet. I possessed a knowledge of the human temper, deep and accurate, together with a patience of caprices and anomalies, which only experience can teach. No sallies of violence could intimidate, no rigour of obduracy could weary me. With regard to the immediate means of effecting my purpose, my mind or rather my memory was a perfect *Thesaurus terrorum*. I had powers to confound the deliberate, and to scare the bold. My body as well as my mind conspired with my purpose. My figure was gigantic, my countenance scarce bore resemblance to humanity, the intonations of my voice were like the roar of the storm and the cataract, it had been my delight in the rage of insanity to imitate; and above all, I possessed from memory a perfect knowledge of secret passages, and subterranean recesses, both at Muralto and the palace at Naples; these I had loved to explore when I was their inmate, from an enthusiastic passion for gloom and for antiquity. Such was the preparation. That I may not be thought to lay a chimerical stress on the influence of superstition, I shall mention some circumstances that occurred beyond the immediate range of my purpose. Amadeo, Duke di Monte Ceruli, was a libertine whom I had known in the earlier part of my life, about ten years previous to my marriage, when I was a gay Nobleman at Naples. I was with him and other Cavaliers at an assembly, upwards of thirty years ago; the conversation happened, strangely enough, to turn on the existence of spirits; the subject was more congenial to my mind than the babble of levity, and I spoke on it with my accustomed solemn energy. Monte Ceruli ridiculed the subject and the emphasis with which I spoke on it. I did not choose to altercate with such a trifler, and giving the conversation a ludicrous turn, proposed that we should enter into an engagement, that whoever died first, should appear to the survivor, as a punishment for scepticism, or a confirmation of orthodoxy. He accepted it, laughing; but it was not with laughter he received the proof. When in the prosecution of my plan, I appeared to Ippolito at Naples, while surrounded by a party of cavaliers, I observed Monte Ceruli among the number. When I had produced the effect of my visit, I retreated behind the tapestry, where a concealed door communicated with a secret passage, through which I escaped while they were searching for me. This was a contrivance indeed easily detected, but I had chosen my time well, it was easy to disappear amid the confusion of terror and drunkenness. The party dispersed in every direction in pursuit of me; as I was evading them, I met Monte Ceruli, who, of all the party was alone. He detained me; I heard others approaching; I dreaded discovery; I dreaded at least the dissolution of my spiritual character. I unmasked, and addressed him in my own voice, which I had carefully concealed since my return to Naples. In its hollow and peculiar tones I told him I was the spirit of his departed companion. He fell to the ground insensible, and I am told continued so till his death. On the Duke di

Pallerini, who was sent by the king (in consequence of a confession made by a dying domestic to a monk at Naples, but which involved nothing but general suspicions) to inquire into the mysterious disappearance of the late possessor of the title, on him no such influence was attempted. I knew the inquiry would terminate in my brother's detection, and consequent punishment, for I knew his own terrors would betray him, but though I had devoted him to punishment, I determined by no one but me should it be inflicted. Calling the Duke therefore to another apartment, after adjuring him to secrecy, I discovered myself, and proved the futility of a charge for the murder of one whom he beheld alive. It was owing to this resolution of reserving to myself the powers and mode of retribution, that a circumstance occurred, whose mystery is most dark and voluminous, and whose mystery can be disclosed only by me. I was (while yet a brother in the Franciscan convent,) returning from a pilgrimage to Rome, when a report which was diffused every where, met my ear, that a discovery had been made by some dying man, to a monk in Apulia, relative to the family of Montorio, whose honours, whose very existence, it was said, was involved in its substance.

By whom such a discovery could be made, (of which *I* believed myself the solitary possessor on the face of the earth,) was of less moment to inquire, than how to obstruct its disclosure. I was resolved that neither the Inquisition nor the Vatican, no power, secular or spiritual, should wrest my victim from me. The monk, it was reported, was on his journey to Rome, to procure an audience of the Pope. He travelled with all the inconsistency of fear in his preparations; he was escorted by a strong guard, yet affected to conceal his name and the motives of his progress. I had arrived on the close of my pilgrimage, at a town called Bellano, I understood there were a number of travellers at the inn, and I hastened there to receive some intelligence on the subject. I found them engaged in discussing it; a solitary, silent pilgrim, did not interrupt them. I was suffered to listen, and that was all I desired. I found that the monk was expected to pass the night at Bellano, on his journey. Many, whose business lay in other directions, had quitted them for a chance of meeting this man, about whom curiosity was thus vividly employed, and all had agreed to sit together in the great hall till he arrived, if his arrival was delayed till morning. About midnight the monk came. He looked pale, weary, and terrified with his undertaking. He looked around suspiciously and dejectedly. I was the only person who wore the sacred habit in the company, this accident determined his addressing himself to me, and to this I owe the obstruction of his progress. He spoke confidentially, as one weary of the restraints of silence and secrecy, and glad to unburthen a weak mind of a disproportioned load. He acknowledged he was terrified by the importance and danger of the commission imposed on him,—the ruin and probably the revenge of a powerful family. "I would," said he, "I were in my cell again, at the foot of the little wooden crucifix, beside my pallet; I am, however, safe tonight. I remember visiting this house before I took the vows; there is a chamber of peculiar construction in it. I have no dread of assassin, or spy, or emissary of the Montorio family, while sleeping in that chamber. I know not why, but my mind is wonderous heavy and fearful tonight." I endeavoured to encourage him, and inquired the construction of the chamber he described. "This house," said he, "was formerly the haunt of robbers, who contrived in many of the apartments, devices for escape or concealment. In one of the chambers there is a trap-door, acted on by a spring, which is continued through the wall to the adjacent apartment; beneath it is a flight of spiral steps, hollowed in the wall, and communicating with subterranean vaults, of which the extent is unknown. Should I be disturbed by any apprehensions, I can immerge myself beneath the trap-door, and remain there unsuspected, till all search or hope of my recovery had ceased." Childish as this expedient was, I appeared to approve of it, and by affecting to doubt the principle of the construction, led him to explain it sufficiently for my purpose. To *that* there was but one thing wanting,—how to fix him in that part of the room where the construction of the trap-door might operate. To effect this, I stole to his chamber, and placed a small table, on which was a crucifix, on the very spot where the boards were disjoined. Weary and timid, the monk retired to his apartment, mine (to which the spring extended, and which he had intreated me to occupy for *his security*) was the adjacent one. I watched him through a crevice of the wainscote, I saw him approach the fatal spot, and prostrate myself on it. At that moment I applied my hand to the spring, (which was only a sliding rope with a weight, and which made part of the furniture of the hangings) the trap-door opened beneath him, and I heard him plunge into the chasm with a suddenness that prevented his last scream, if he uttered one, from being heard. Never was a project so critically completed.

He was swallowed up as by the earth opening her mouth; not a vestige of him remained, when the trap-door was replaced. He was precipitated through the circular hollow down which the stairs wound, to a vault of depth incalculable. Of the confession, which he always *carried in his bosom*, he assured me there was not another copy extant. Its subject, therefore, had perished with him. The secret of the trap-door, he also informed me, was unknown to the proprietors, and confined to me and himself. This information proved to be sufficiently true, for among the inquiry and commotion this strange event occasioned, no one suspected or examined the construction of the flooring. I was satisfied to remain ignorant of the means and agent in this extraordinary confession. I was satisfied to let it moulder with the corse of him who bore it, since I had now extinguished the last gleam of light that the hands of *strangers* had presumed to throw on the gloomy secrets of our house. Am I asked whether I felt no compunctious hauntings for the murder of an innocent man? I answer, as much as a giant, who scales a mountain, feels for the insects he crushes in his progress.

"Shortly after this event, I entered into the Count's family as his confessor, and learned the characters of his sons. That was not indeed my first object, my first was to find out the grave of Erminia and her children, and there—But I will not violate the sacredness of my sufferings; I will not, for they would not, if disclosed, be believed. No one would ascribe human feelings to *me;* no one could believe *me* capable of sorrow. I would not have mentioned the subject but that the circumstances of my nightly penance there are connected with the events of my story.

"The brothers I discovered were of different characters. The elder, who resided at Naples, was volatile and impetuous; the younger, dark and deliberate. Perhaps those who think they have satiated wonder with my depravity, will still wonder that I should determine to sacrifice *both.* I understood, that united in the strictest friendship, they were inaccessible to the rest of the family. Had I assailed either separately, as their confidence was unbounded, the interference of the other would have frustrated my purpose; but as they held no communication with the rest of the family, their mutual confidence could only increase their mutual fear.

"Worlds should not bribe me to a detail of the devices by which I subdued the intellects and integrity of these youths to my purpose. Worlds did I say!—What in the reach of imagination could prevail with me to retrace those images of wickedness and horror, but the vindication of my *victims?* Yes, their vindication; their vindication which I now pursue with ten thousand-fold the devotion I once did their ruin. What but that could make me proclaim these mysteries of iniquity? What but

CHARLES MATURIN

that could *make me live* to proclaim them? I will prove it as plain, as palpable as day light; it was impossible for mere human nature to evade or to resist the snares the subtlety of my vengeance had wound around them. Around *them!*—Whom?—But soft if possible—not many hours remain to me.

"As soon as I understood their different characters, I commenced my assaults. Their distance from each other was an advantage to me; their different situations suggested different modes of temptation to me. Ippolito, who was in the concourse of a populous city, I determined to subdue by the force of spectacle and sensible representation, mixed with something of astrological jargon, to which I knew he was addicted. Annibal I devoted to the influence of solitary terror, and the supposed incumbency of a task assigned him by a spiritual agent: strong means to prevail with the inmate of an ancient castle, whose mind was gloomy, and whose sense of duty was rigid and inflexible.

Over Annibal, my influence was in a great measure anticipated by his own restless ness and solicitude, the uneasy effervescence of a vigorous mind, wasting itself in gloom and solitude. I heard him questioning an old domestic named Michelo, whom I remembered to have seen in other days, but the remembrance woke no kindliness in me now. I found Annibal so intent on his inquiries, and the old man so contrary to all my expectations, so well prepared to satisfy them, that dreading the anticipation of my purpose, from the increasing importunities of one and the feeble reserve of the other, I interfered, and privately forbad Michelo to communicate with the Signor any further. Whether my earnestness betrayed a resemblance to sounds and features, Michelo must have remembered; or whether it was the weakness of a mind broken with age and superstition, I know not; but it is certain, that from the hour Michelo received this intimation, he ceased to believe me a human being; his terrors, though they secured his confidence, preyed on his health, and I have to number this unhappy among my involuntary victims. If indeed he suspected me to be my former self, his penetration, or his memory, were beyond those of my own brother, or all who had ever known or remembered me; yet I do not think my travels, my hardships, my sufferings, any thing, had altered me effectually, till my heart and disposition underwent that change that surpassed the impressions of all.

Meanwhile my toils closed rapidly round Annibal: the tomb of Erminia, which I visited every night; her coffin, which, in pursuance of a rigid penance-vow, I tingedevery night with my blood; witnessed strange encounters:—Sometimes they watched me as I wandered thither with my lonely lamp, which they believed to be borne by no earthly hand; and sometimes they pursued me into the vault, whence they retired, shuddering with visionary horrors, and often besmeared with my blood.

I was in the habit of visiting the apartments of Erminia, they had been deserted since her death, and I visited through avenues known only to myself, in undisturbed solitude and security.—One evening while I was gazing on the bloody traces that marked the floor where Verdoni fell, I heard steps approaching. I had scarce time to conceal myself behind the tapestry, when Annibal and Michelo entered; I was at first impelled to start forth, and scare them into flight; but reflecting, that whatever increased the influence of superstition, established mine, I contrived, by looking through a rent in the tapestry, which represented a figure in the act of pointing, and by communicating to *its* arm, the motion of mine, to impel them to a search which discovered the body of Verdoni. It had been interred in a recess of the wall by Ascanio.

On another occasion, on entering the ruined chapel, which nightly witnessed my terrible orisons; I found Annibal and Michelo already there. I extinguished my lamp, and attempted to escape into the vault; Michelo confused and in the dark, obstructed me; with a nervous grasp, I seized, dragged him in with me, and closed the iron grate. Annibal hastened to the castle for assistance. During this interval, I addressed my prisoner in the hollow tones of death; I reproved his presumption, and darkly intimated those disasters which I was preparing for the house of Montorio. The old man listened to me in terror, and died the next day of the fears of superstition, and the dread of being involved in the punishment of crimes, he suspected too justly.

About this period, the monk to whom Michelo had made his dying confession thought the suspicions it contained too momentous to be suppressed, he therefore communicated them to his superior, who laid them before the king, by whom the Duke di Pallerini was dispatched, to inquire into the disappearance of the late Count of Montorio, his wife Erminia di Amaldi, and their children.—How this terminated with regard to the inquiry, is already well known; with regard to my victim Annibal, its conclusion was momentous indeed. I did not think him falling into my snares with sufficient facility; I required to have him more in my own power, that he should look more to me as the proper agent of the wonders he had witnessed or imagined.—I effected my purpose unsuspected. On the Duke di Pallerini's approach to the castle, I was commissioned by my brother, (from whom I had never concealed my knowledge of his guilt, and who also viewed me with a kind of shadowy fear) to remove the mouldering corse of Verdoni, lest the Duke, the extent of whose information they could not conjecture, should direct his search thither. I entered the apartments, removed the corse, and retiring left *the passages open.* I bore the remains of Verdoni to my closet, where I believe *they were seen by Annibal's servant,* Filippo, whose curiosity was at least sufficiently punished by meeting me in the close of evening, with the skeleton in my arms which I was about to convey to a vault at the extremity of the passage I was traversing. I perceived this fellow, who was bold and curious, followed me, I raised the carrion head above my cowl, and he fled in terror.

On that night, Annibal repaired again to the forbidden apartments; I informed the Count of his son's dangerous spirit of discovery, and led him to the spot. The criminals were confined; this was what I wished. On a mind weakened by loneliness and fear, I believed my influence would be resistless. Not easily convinced or subdued, Annibal long resisted the array of terrors I spread before him; I mingled opiates with his food that I might enter his prison unperceived, I screamed in boding and unearthly tones in the passages of the tower. I told him a tale, that while it strongly referred to the strange objects he had recently witnessed, terminated in the terrible event to which it was my purpose to lead him. Still he resisted, though he resisted more feebly. I conceived another plan. I appeared to accede to a plan proposed by the Count, to remove him by poison. I prepared an opiate of an extraordinary power, for among the secrets of which I had acquired the knowledge in the East, those of pharmacy and philtre had not been forgotten. The operation of this I knew would be sufficiently strong to deceive his father with the expected resemblance of death; and while it continued, I purposed to convey him to the vaults of the castle; where, remote from all influence but mine, I believed he would cease to resist that influence longer.

His prison was not sufficiently gloomy, nor were his spirits properly subdued for my purpose.

The plan was defeated by the dexterity of Filippo, who contrived to administer to me the opiate I had prepared for his master, and during its effect, drew from my vest the keys of the passage through which I had intended to convey him. They escaped from the castle, nor when I recovered was I sorry for their escape, I knew I should overtake them, and when I did, the terror which the appearance of one they must believe *invulnerable by poison*, would excite, I knew would be more than a balance for the suspension of my influence during the interval of their flight. But the Count was not so easily reconciled to the escape of the fugitives. Spies were employed, and immense rewards circulated for their discovery clandestinely; these were at length successful about the time that Annibal on his progress to Puzzoli, paused at a village where circumstances beyond the reach of conjecture detained him.

The influence I had obtained over the mind of the Count, was mixed and extraordinary.—My austerities, my superhuman abstinence and contempt of fatigue, and pain, and watching, had raised me to the highest pitch of his estimation as a devotee. For my interference between his danger and the requisitions of Pallerini, he felt a kind of visionary gratitude, and there were other facts of my character, that mingled awe and wonder with the controul I held over him. He perceived that I was perfectly possessed not only of those dark events whose secrecy he had believed inaccessible, but of almost every other part of his life; these subjects were therefore *spared* in our conversations by a kind of silent compromise. They were referred to, but not spoken of; he heard me hint my knowledge of them without starting, but he could not bear to speak of them himself. He certainly regarded me as a being not of this world, his mind, weakened by the perpetual harassings of guilt and danger, reposed on the idea of a visionary protector; and timid and jealous of its security, pleased itself with the thought of employing a secret and resistless minister of death. Hence he would at one time employ me as an assassin without remorse; and at another, consult me as a saint, without superstition; for where the human character is not supposed to exist, human guilt vanishes also. Believing me one to whom all things were known, he ceased to have any compunctious reserve; and believing me one to whom almost all things were possible, he called on me without hesitation, for that assistance which he believed could be conferred by *me* without a crime.

Such was the influence I had acquired over a man agitated by the fears of unsteady guilt, and the anguish of imperfect penitence, sanguinary from the dread of discovery, and superstitious from the experienced erosions of conscience, anxious to retain what had been acquired by blood, yet desirous to combine the pardon of guilt with its security. Such was the influence I was solicitous to acquire, the utmost extent of

CHARLES MATURIN

my vengeance was to the limits of *this* world. Men may smile at these illusions of romantic revenge, but it is certain that while I devoted him to death, I led him a pilgrimage of saintly preparation to it, while no power could wrest my victim from me, or buy from me one of his dying groans. I prayed, I watched, I wept with him I sentenced the sinner, but I tried to save the penitent.

"I will now rehearse the more dark and complicated means resorted to with Ippolito. I discovered, what in Naples is easily discoverable, a number of those wretches who, under various denominations, profess to hold converse with another world. To these I told a tale sufficiently plausible, and what was more plausible, I told them out handfuls of gold. The liberality or the superstition of the Count had supplied me abundantly. My plan required the aid of numbers, and it required a diversity and costliness of preparation, and of all most difficult, it required that my victim should not be *undeceived* by the vulgar rapacity of my associates, which I satisfied clandestinely myself. My first application to Ippolito was in the jargon of his favourite study. On this and many other occasions, the darkness of my habit, and the inconceivable swiftness of my motions, befriended the obscurity I affected. Afterwards I concealed myself in the confessional of a church, whither I had led him, and which I knew had a private recess, and left him with the belief that I had melted into the elements. Another time I led him to a vault, where lay a body from whose mortal fate I wished to suggest to him his own.

"At all times, by my knowledge of the passages of the palace, I had opportunities of leaving letters in his apartment, and once of entering it while he was there, where my shewing a family ring, and telling a mysterious story of its last possessor, contributed not a little to his wonder and perplexity. At length when I believed him sufficiently impressed with fantastic notions of my character and agency, I led him to a subterranean vault, where the disguises of my associates, the quaint solemnity of our language, the blue and vaporous light that played on objects not to be described, displayed every device whose influence could abuse or witch the senses or the mind.

But I discovered in both my victims that whatever facility they betrayed to the admission of gloomy and fantastic impressions, they both revolted with equal abhorrence of insulted integrity from the *end* those impressions were designed to lead to. Ippolito, impetuous and eccentric as he was pure and noble, would never have been intangled but in a web of wickedness so fine and intricate, that *human* strength could not bear its powers unhurt from its witching hold. By the skill of one of our associates, an exact model of the faces of Ippolito and the Count was procured in wax; they were moulded into masks, and the former was assumed by another, who was in figure strikingly like Ippolito. This man, placing himself in a recess of the vault where I led my victim, represented by his gestures reflected in a shaded mirror, the anguish of a mind impelled to an involuntary crime; at the moment that Ippolito, touched by a gloomy sympathy, bent over the mirror, the man uncovered his mask, and Ippolito beheld his living likeness.

"The solicitude thus excited was augmented by delay and dramatic illusions, till no longer master of his intellects, and scarce retaining his turbid and confused perceptions, he was led into another vault, and told that to obtain the knowledge he required, he must propitiate the spirit of the night by shedding the blood of a naked and unresisting victim, who was bound on an altar, dimly seen in the darkness of the vault. I remember his resistance too well. At length by the temptation of that fatal thirst of invisible knowledge which constituted the whole wonder of my influence (the engine by which I could wrest the whole moral world), he was induced to plunge his poinard into the breast of a *waxen image,* which spouted out blood upon his hands, and from which withdrawing the covering, I disclosed the face of *his father.*

"From that moment he was sealed and set apart as mine. He never could expel from his conscience the stain of imaginary blood; he never could expel that nameless dread that whispered if the object he had mangled was not the living and corporal frame of his father, it must be an inmate of that world which is peopled with shadowy resemblances of *this.* This conjecture confirmed the visionary power of those who could summon such appearances, that power verified its own predictions, and its predictions announced that he should perish as the assassin of his father. From that time I pursued him into crowds as well as society, perpetually reminded him of the midnight hour, perpetually held up to him the gory weapon; and found, from his failing resolution, that even the influence of superstition may be darkened and deepened by the consciousness of guilt.

"In a short time he fled from my persecutions; he quitted Naples. This event I had expected from his impetuosity, and made sufficient provision for it. I had diffused every where what his imprudence had assisted me in diffusing, reports of his nightly wanderings, and of his being mated in some horrible league with unblessed souls. The report spread around him an atmosphere of moral pestilence; every one shrunk from his presence, while the terrors that attended the suspicion of his presence gave to his progress a notoriety that marked every step he took, even to the distance of Muralto. At this period, by the wayward flight of my victims, they were both conducted, though unconsciously, to spots so near each other, that my double agency was easily united.

The Count's confidence in powers which he believed were not those of a mortal minister, now compelled me to leave the castle. He had received from the abbess of a convent, whose name I now forget, but which was destroyed in the late commotions of the earth, a letter acquainting him that the novice Ildefonsa Mauzoli, who had always shewed the utmost reluctance to assume the veil, had in consequence of an accident been seen by a young cavalier, who she understood was his son, and by whose sudden and impetuous passions not only her *profession* was delayed, but even her release insisted on. She added, that Ildefonsa's resolution had been confirmed by the presumption of her lover, who, it was easy to discover, had made his professions of love and liberation but too acceptable to her.

The Count, on receiving this intelligence, evinced a distraction that amazed me; I could scarce pacify him by my promises to hasten to the spot, and mar the dreams of the lovers. This I had at all events intended, as this was the period I intended to convince my victims no distance of space could shelter them from me.

"In the interval of my hurried departure, the Count had but time to acquaint me, that Ildefonsa Mauzoli was the *unowned child of Erminia and Verdoni,* who had been brought up in the solitude of a convent, and whom he had devoted to the veil, though in vain. He adjured me to hasten and prevent by *the most decisive measures* the event of this disastrous passion, of which it was easy to see he dreaded more than he disclosed of mischief and horror.

I left Muralto, and when I saw Ildefonsa, was convinced nothing but her final separation from Annibal could again place him in my power. She was the picture of her mother; I dreaded her beauty. I dreaded her excellencies, I dreaded those bland and balmy influences which innocence and love must produce on the most corroded mind. I felt that Annibal, in her arms, would wake from my persecutions as from a horrid vision. I determined she should die. Such was the Count's determination, and the abbess, wearied and provoked by her opposition, acceded readily.

In my journey to the convent, I heard that Bellano, the place where the unfortunate monk had perished with his confession, was not a mile from the convent; it was now deserted and destroyed, rendered almost a waste by indigence and superstition. This intelligence suggested to me a new and singular resolution. I determined to visit it, to explore the vault into which the monk had been precipitated, and possess myself of the papers that mouldered there with his corse. In the event of a public developement awaiting my purpose and character, I knew these papers might render me essential service. The approach to a place shunned by all was probably safe and easy, and as the abbess informed me there were vaults beneath the convent in the direction of Bellano, with the extent of which no inmate of either was acquainted, I suspected a communication between them, and the immense and unexplored windings into which the subterranean passages at Bellano spread.

I set out from the convent in the evening, and, lost in musing, wandered from my way, till looking round me, I beheld a range of mountain and rock I had never seen before. I was about to retrace my path, when near me extended at the foot of a tree, I beheld Ippolito. I determined to improve this accident. I approached, addressed him, and then bounded away into a woody dell, so tangled and intricate, that it defied all his attempts to penetrate. On emerging into the open country, I perceived him still pursuing me, and was compelled again to change the direction I had adopted to avoid him; for it was the policy of my influence to render it rare and solemn. I stopped at a town where I guessed he would follow me, and where, after dropping some mysterious hints of the character of my pursuer, I desired he should be told I had proceeded to Bellano. Thither he followed me; and there, though impeded by the interruptions of him and his servant, I descended into the cavity, and found amid the decayed garments of my victim, who had been dashed in pieces by his fall, the important papers I sought.

Ippolito followed me into the vault, as I expected; my purpose in leading him to Bellano had been to amaze with a wild and magic display of powers that seemed to mock the bounds of space and matter, sometimes to skim the air, and sometimes to dive into the entrails of earth. When I had effected this, I glided away, and through passages which I had explored previous to his descent, I regained the cemetery of the convent of St. Ursula. I entered the chapel, time enough to discover that my plan had succeeded. Ildefonsa, to whom a strong opiate had been administered, was extended on a bier, and after a tumult of unavailing opposition, she was borne yet insensible to the cemetery, where I left her with a villain of firmer hand than myself. Where extinguished humanity had never awoke a throb, the resemblance of Erminia made me—I will not say what; I will not *pollute this page with a human tear.*

"During the interval previous to Ildefonsa's imaginary death, Annibal's resort to the convent had given me opportunities almost undisturbed of renewing my persecutions. Agitated by unhappy love, and terrified by the unaverted hauntings of a being whom (supposed) poison could not destroy, Annibal's virtue or his patience hesitated almost to yielding. But my business was now with Ippolito.

"In the commotions of that night he had been wafted down the river, and the next day he entered Pozzoli, I know not with what purpose. I followed him unperceived, and the accidental mention of an absurd tradition suggested a plan, in the event of which Ippolito was utterly subdued.

"While I was revolving this plan, I perused the papers which I had found in the vaults of Bellano; they explained the mystery of the confession. Ascanio, whom I had pursued from the rock, and seen plunging in the waters, bruised and mangled had crawled to a cavern on the shore. Fishermen, coasting along the isle, found him the next morning; and half through compassion, half through curiosity, brought him to their habitation, and tended him till his recovery, if it could be called so. While he lay in anguish on his bed of straw, he was visited, like many others, with that compunction which suffering produces. He determined to disburthen his conscience of crimes that had only brought him misery, and still weak and suffering, contrived to return to Italy. Here his wounds exasperated by fatigue, and his mental anguish increased by the terrors of immediate death, his reason failed him, and escaping from his companions, he wandered a maniac in the forests of Apulia till nature was exhausted, and he expired in the cottage of a peasant, having made his confession in the short interval of recovered reason. This document I enclose; it will serve with others to identify my narrative. I hasten on.

"I have now but little to disclose, except the device which subdued Ippolito finally to my power. I assumed a lay disguise, and told a plausible tale to the principal inquisitor at Pozzoli. I informed him that a most direful suspicion brooded over the character of a cavalier of the Montorio family, who was at that time in Pozzoli, and of whom it became the holy office to take immediate cognizance. I informed him, that betrayed by accident into his subterranean haunts, I had observed there an inscription, of which a copy was extant in the cathedral church at Pozzoli (this was sufficiently true, for I had myself copied it as one of the decorations of our infernal scenery). I proposed, therefore, that he should be led by some unsuspected contrivance to the spot, where persons stationed for the purpose might note his emotions at the sight. To render it more striking, the characters were illuminated with vivid traces resembling blood. A number of gazers crowded to the spot, and his unequivocal tokens of amaze and consciousness were witnessed by many who were uninterested in observing and reporting them. The success of this expedient was decisive; he was immured in the Inquisition, where under the character of a person whose influence might lead him to confession, I had uninterrupted access to him. To render him stationary was the great object, another was to exhaust his resistance by the weariness of solitude and perpetual persecution.

"In the mean while my agents were busily employed in the discovery of Annibal, whom at length they traced, by means of his servant, to a wild hut in the windings of the wood. I communicated my information to the Count, who, in the rage of fear, commanded me immediately to seize and send them to the castle, where it was likely they would not be suffered to disturb him long. Of the fate of Ippolito he was perfectly careless. His injunctions, so far as they coincided with my own purposes, I resolved to adhere to, yet the discovery of Annibal's movements was not easy. The ruffians I employed, though hardened in horrors, recoiled from visiting a haunt which was said to be the abode of a departed spirit, and I was myself compelled to perform the parts of spy and tempter at once; in the former I believe I was detected by the loss of my cowl.

"Meantime my persecution of Ippolito was suspended by a commotion of the earth, which demolishing the tower in which he was confined, liberated him. He made his escape on board a vessel which was crowded with fugitives for Sicily. The rage of the elements again threw him on the shore, where I stood anticipating the wreck of the vessel. I need not tell of his frenzied and convulsive submission to a power which he believed had controuled the elements. I led him to a retreat I had prepared, where he was soon joined by his brother, whose

CHARLES MATURIN

flight from the forest had been intercepted by ruffians I had provided, and a guide I had corrupted. I lamented his *escape* to the *Count;* the lady was carried to the castle.

"Amid these horrors can it be believed that I feel compassion for the fate of this gentle, illfated woman? The Count, on beholding her, felt a long extinguished passion for her mother revive. To gratify a romantic illusion of posthumous passion, she was arrayed in fantastic splendour by the Count, and to appease fear and jealousy, was poisoned by his wife.

I hasten on; I seem to myself to cleave billows of blood, and push away, as I proceed, the red and weltering tides with either hand. I introduced my victims into the castle at night. The hour approached. The persecution that had depraved their reason, and blasted their existence, was no longer to be resisted. The hour, which nothing could retard or avert, approached rapidly. The Count, restless under the burden of added guilt, and augmented fear, (the blood of Ildefonsa, and the supposed flight of Annibal) had sent for me repeatedly in the course of that awful term; to facilitate my purpose, and prepare him for its event, I enjoined him an hour of *solitary* penance. I was again sent for by the miserable man. Agitated by the suspension of my purpose, I was about to break from him when he called me back.

"'You are acquainted with my guilt,' said he, 'but not with its palliations; I have a secret reserve of expiation, a hold of hope and refuge for some years. Amid the mass of murders that stained our souls, we hesitated to shed the innocent blood of infancy. The children of my brother were discovered in the cottage where they had been conveyed by their faithful attendant from the massacre of their parents. They were discovered, but they were spared; we purposed to rear them in obscurity and safety. All the *first children of my marriage* perished. Terrified at a calamity, which our smitten consciences interpreted as a judgment, and willing to purchase the security of our bloody honours by an act which was pleasant to the vacancy of natural love, we determined to rear the children of my brother, and to restore to them indirectly their lineal dignities. With the natural diffidence of villainy, I concealed this from Ascanio. I even in my letters acquainted him they were dead, but *Ippolito and Annibal are not my children, they are the orphans of my brother.*'

"I heard him; I heard all; they *were my own children*—my own children, whom I had persecuted, corrupted, destroyed, tempted to murder, plunged in infamy, hurried to death; *they were my own children!*

The deed was yet undone; I flew to my children's feet to suspend it; I could not speak; I could not say—'Hold! ye are my children.' I gasped, I writhed, I howled in speechless agony, but I had not power to utter a sound of human language. They broke from me; I fell senseless at their feet; they rushed to the chamber of imaginary parricide. When I recovered my faculties, when I dragged my spent limbs after them, my *children were murderers!*

"What their father had impelled them to, could now be neither prevented nor concealed. Worlds could not buy again the moment in which the blow was struck; but worlds shall consume away before he who impelled, shall finish its expiation. I have now no words, no voice of supplications; I cannot for my soul, whine, or beg, or bend like others; all my powers are collected into one cry, deep and piercing, and exceeding bitter, 'spare my children!'

"I do not adjure compassion, I appeal to justice. They *are not criminals*, frenzy is not criminal. Their intellects were extinguished; fatigue and sleeplessness, and visionary horrors, and all the train of devilish enginery that I had brought against them, had impaired the noblest frame of faculties that ever was abused by the wit or malice of devils. They are *not criminals;* they were impelled beyond all power of human resistance; the wisest and most upright of you that sit there to judge them, so wrought on and beset, would have been a maniac or a murderer. How often have I, with the passions of a demon, beheld them with astonishment! How often have I admired the glorious struggles of their indignation, the convulsions of their virtue! And *they were my children!* And all good angels slept! No monitory whisper, no inward shivering told me to pause! Their innocence, their friendship, exclusive and strong, their distance and dissimilarity from all the children of my brother, struck me with no start of doubt, no thrill of conjecture!—No! no!

"TO BE RESTORED TO MY wife, my children, *myself* again, could not have bribed me to outlive this discovery; but for *them*, and their vindication, I have done it. I intended to have gone off in the dark cloud of my purpose, mocking the wonder of mankind, and shrouding my retreat in the eternal train of shadowy fear and gloomy remembrance. But I am compelled to cast it off, and to stand bare and shrinking in the eye of mankind, I am compelled to say, I am the *miserable* Count of Montorio, the miserable husband, the most miserable of fathers. I am compelled to say this, but I will at least not say it like other men. No, I provoke, I solicit punishment. Bury me under manacles, macerate me with your tortures, let every hour bring more than the pangs of deaths, yet let me be many hours dying.

"I feel my crimes deserve it; I am a monster, beneath whom the earth groans. To one demon passion I have sacrificed the whole of existence; in revenge I butchered Verdoni, in revenge I murdered my wife, in revenge I—Oh! let me not say—I have destroyed my innocent sons. I have been sated with revenge, and let revenge be now sated on me.

"Oh! my sweet, noble boys! Can it be nature that springs up in a heart so blasted as mine? The thoughts of ye flow over its avenues so parched and flinty, like the first fall of Heaven's dew on the desert, long waste and waterless! Thoughts so new and dear, impulses so fresh, hopes like the first hours of vernal life, all must be extinguished;—though my children are spared, they are not spared to their father! Their miserable father must not see them live! Yet live, my children, though not for me.—I dare not, I *will not* think.—Oh! let me not be sent from the world as I have lived in it, cursing and despairing!"

THIS PAPER ENCLOSED THE CONFESSION of Ascanio and other, and equally valid documents of consequence. It was read with astonishment, but could neither be disputed nor distrusted. The Court sat late, but as almost every point of inquiry had been anticipated by the Count's memorial, they sat rather to indulge their amazement in copious debate. It was resolved, however, immediately to secure the person of the Countess, to take possession of the estates and castle of the family in the name of the King, and to summon from the Abruzzo, a woman named Teresa Zanetti, sister to the attendant of the Countess Erminia; but she had anticipated the summons of the Court. She had heard, though imperfectly, of the direful events in the Montorio family, and ascribing them with the prompt application of guilt, to the secret she had so iniquitously preserved, she hasted to Naples, to make a confession while yet she had the power of making it *voluntarily*. Her testimony was full and clear; she related that on the night of the Countess Erminia's death, her sister, Hesperia Zanetti, pale and distracted, had rushed into her cottage, in a forest, a few miles from Muralto; that she had scarce breath to hint that her lady had perished by violence, and to implore shelter and safety for the two children she bore in her arms, when exhausted by fatigue and strong emotion she expired. Teresa amazed and terrified, yet forbore to take any measure for the preservation of the children, till Ascanio tracing the flight of the too faithful Hesperia, discovered them in Teresa's cottage. Whether his employers were weary of carnage, or averse from the murder of infants, his instructions were to spare the children, but to secure the secrecy of the woman. This was too easily effected; the woman dreaded their vengeance and coveted their gold; and when, some years afterwards, the children were substituted for two sons of the Count who had lately died, she conceived the restoration to their paternal honours was an abundant compensation for the concealment of their real parentage.

This awful history of human passions was now fully unfolded; had a witness of higher dignity been required, the Duke di Pallerini, (whose unsuccessful charge had been owing to the strictness of his honour, and had drawn on him the displeasure of his sovereign,) was now discharged from his obligation to secrecy, and was ready to attest that he had recognized Orazio Count of Montorio in the Confessor Schamoli.

XXIV

————*The same*
That from your first of difference and decay
Hath followed your sad steps————
'Twas no one else, all's cheerless, dark and deadly.

—LEAR

Te teneam moriens deficiente manu.

—TIBULLUS

And thy dear hand with dying ardour press.

—GRAINGER

Over a train of events so momentous, so complicated, so mysterious, the judicial Court paused in total perplexity of judgment, in wonder which excluded decision. There was no precedent to direct them, no prescribed rule to apply to such an emergency, indignation was distracted by a diversity of depravity, and justice suspended by unresisted compassion.

At first, the guilt was so obvious and enormous, that a sentence of unqualified severity was pronounced against all the criminals. At this dreadful intelligence the families of Amaldi and Alberotti, accompanied by the most distinguished of the nobility, hastened to the palace, and throwing themselves at the feet of the King, implored him not to bury in ruin and disgrace, a family whose high and extensive connections would diffuse mourning and consternation through Italy. Even the family of Verdoni generously pleaded for its enemy, and the Court was required to revise its sentence.

Ippolito and Annibal waked from their horrible dream, and found themselves murderers without the vindication of resistless necessity, or the authority of divine commission. They were soon acquainted with the real agent and cause of their crime, and the diminished burthen of *parricide* was the first impulse that gave motion or relief to their stupid and stagnated dejection.

They sunk on their knees in gratitude. Before this period they had neither spoken nor moved, since their entrance within the walls of St. Elmo, except when the officers searching Annibal, found and attempted to take from him the picture of Ildefonsa, then he shrieked fearfully, and his convulsive resistance became so furious, that they were compelled to release it; from that moment he sat in the same posture, grasping it firmly with one hand, but apparently unconscious of what he held.

Ippolito emerged into reason first; the officers of the prison, to whom the general impulse of strong compassion extended, permitted the brothers to meet without witnesses, or any of the vexatious restraints of confinements. On their first meeting, Ippolito's tears dropped on a vacant and insensible countenance; but in a short time Annibal appeared sensible of some pleasure from his brother's presence, and held out the hand of silent kindness on his departure; and at length, though slowly, recovered his faculties uninjured.

They were constantly together; fraternal fondness brightened even the gloom of a prison and the terrors of guilt; but they had many dark hours. Annibal, ruined in love as well as in hope and existence, was the more dejected of the two, and the soothing remembrances of passion were darkened by the imminent horrors of *incest*. He had stronger motives, *moral* motives for his depression than Ippolito; the latter had consented to guilt in a convulsion of passion, the former from a conviction of reason, of reason, though perverted, strongly exerted. Ippolito, therefore, for the perpetration of the crime felt only ordinary compunction, while Annibal's was mingled with a kind of gloomy disappointment, that the supposed agent of heaven was only the victim of a monstrous illusion.

"It was in one of those dreary conferences that melancholy seeks her solace and her food from, that the door of the apartment was thrown open, and a form glided in, so faint, so fragile, so hardly visible, that while Ippolito clasped it in his arms, he almost doubted the evidence of his touch. It was the face of Cyprian, but the form of a woman. "I am no longer Cyprian," it murmured; "Cyprian was the guardian of your innocence, but for him there is no longer any employment: let me assume my original name and form, they are disastrous, and therefore are better suited to this hour. I am *Rosolia di Valozzi*, who loved you, who lived for you, whose last proof of most unhappy love is to die with you!"

CHARLES MATURIN

Ippolito wondered and believed. He held to his heart that rare and wonderous woman, who disguising her sex and hazarding her life, had quitted the convent where, in the anguish of love contending with religion, she had assumed the veil, and entering into the family of Montorio, in the page had sustained the sufferings, without the hope, of love; had devoted herself to the amelioration of Ippolito's mind and character, without the solace of being even known to him; and now that all effort was fruitless, and all hope extinct, came, amid the horrors of a prison and the certainty of her own direful punishment, to obey the last impulse of love that was "strong as death." In penitence for her apostacy, she had resolved to pursue her arduous task, uncheered by the gratitude, unrepaid by the affection of him for whom she toiled, and watched, and wept. She resolved never to disclose her sex or her name, or violate the purity of a vestal passion, by subsisting it on the grosser food of earthly love. She lived unknown, she wept unpitied, she loved unrequited.

"The only indulgence I allowed myself," said she, "was sometimes to read to you fragments that described the life and passion of a votarist of unhappy love. They *were my own;* she whom I described as thus loving, and thus suffering, was myself. I could not refuse myself the compassion you sometimes gave to sufferings, of which the victim was so near and yet unknown; I loved to feed sick fancy with sounds that could no longer excite guilty hope, or flatter desire; I loved to hear myself bewailed as dead, and triumph in the sad resolution that sought only the solace of vain and posthumous pity."

Annibal now recognizing Rosolia, asked an explanation of that mysterious night when she wept over the picture of Ildefonsa, but could not disclose the fate of the original? "Ildefonsa and I," said Rosolia, "were educated in the same convent; melancholy and enthusiasm endeared us to each other; she was the confidant of my fatal love, she was the assistant of my escape. When I saw *you* worshiping her picture, I endeavoured to dissuade you from searching for her, for I believed by that time she had assumed the veil, and that your search was hopeless."—"Would it had been so!" said Annibal retiring, but grasping the picture still. "But WE, my love," said Rosolia, "we must have done with softer thoughts; that time is gone by; we are for the dark hour, for the valley of the shadow of death! Oh! if beyond that misty vacancy that spreads before us, some bright and peculiar world, some unearthly tract should be disclosed, where no obstructions cold and dark shall mar the passion of immortals, where it will be no crime to love!"—"Alas, my love!" said Ippolito, "are these dreams of bliss for a murderer?"—"Or for an apostate!" shrieked Rosolia. "Oh! I have gone too far." They wept in each other's arms. "I thought my last moment of weakness was past," said Rosolia; "Oh! I feel they will never cease while I gaze on you. Might I dare to say it; surely I would say I have loved thee with an immortal love; anguish, and fear, and disappointment, the death of love, it bore them all, it mocked at calamity, and it survives in death. Ippolito! Oh, Ippolito!" she cried, drowned in the luxury of sorrowful passion, "Oh, how I love you at this moment!"—"But shall we indeed meet again, Rosolia?" said the sad Ippolito, "shall we see each other with these eyes? shall I behold you in that form again, and know it, Rosolia, or rather Cyprian, my better angel, my little benignant guardian, shall I know you in those bright worlds where all are so like what you would have been to me?"—"Oh! those words recal me," said Rosolia, "these hours demand other thoughts, high, and solemn, and unearthly. Kneel with me, my beloved, we are for the dark and awful conflict of the soul, for the depths of prostration and the strife of prayer! Kneel with me, my beloved! I feel my strength will just support me till your pardon is assured by penitence, and your spirit is free as those that have never erred."

They were about to kneel, and Annibal knelt too in his solitary recess, still holding to his wasted heart the picture of Ildefonsa, when Ippolito starting, caught Rosolia to his heart, and held her long and fervently.

"Let me," said he, "give this moment, this one moment to human thought, this one tear to human remembrance! Oh, Cyprian! Cyprian! think of those times when happy and innocent"—(his voice was lost.) "Oh! think of something unutterably fond and soft for this one moment, think of all that is rising in my heart this moment, think *human* thoughts, and melt with me in human sorrow, my love! my faithful love! my fond, dying love!" he repeated, mingling the tears and kisses of rapture and anguish, too sweet and bitter for words. The vestal struggled in vain with the madness of the moment. They remained locked in wild and speechless fondness. Annibal, lost in prayer, dared not to look on them: he could not look on the picture.

At this moment the doors of the apartment unfolded, and the officer who presided over that tower of the prison where the brothers were confined, entered with the air of a man who is rejoiced to communicate joy, and announced the altered sentence of the court. Ippolito and Annibal were pardoned, but required to leave Italy for ever. Orazio,

Count of Montorio, was doomed to death; the estates, the castles, and the palaces of the family were confiscated, the title extinguished and erased from the list of nobility, and the name forbidden to be revived or borne within the territories of Naples.

"But *his* life is spared!" cried Rosolia, sinking at Ippolito's feet. She was raised but to linger for a few days of resigned misery; the shock of sudden joy had been finally fatal to a frame worn to a shadow with strong emotion, and trembling with precarious existence. During this interval, she mentioned the harmless advantage she had taken of Ippolito's visionary temper in her introduction to him; it was her face that he beheld in the glass, when drawing off her mask, she looked over his shoulder. It was she, too, who alarmed by his language at Naples, had sent the officers of justice to Muralto, not to apprehend, but to protect him from a danger she could not define. But these, and all other subjects of temporal consideration, vanished as her dying hour drew nigh; it drew nigh with darkness and doubt, her religious impressions awoke, and she dreaded that her mortal love had carried her too far. Yet still she clung to the sight and image of Ippolito, and when she could no longer see, she extended her cold hand to him, even when she was no longer sensible of the pressure; her lips still endeavoured to murmur his name, till sense, and thought, and life were extinguished, and the victim of love was no more!

THERE WAS A DIFFERENT DEATH-BED scene exhibited at the castle of Muralto. The officers of justice, with decent reluctance, proceeded to announce the demolition of the honours, the name, and the wealth of the house of Montorio to its surviving representaive. Thay were ushered into the sumptuous chamber, where, amid her family who wept, her physicians who consulted, and priests who prayed, the Countess lay extended on her bed, with death in her face, and a stern tranquillity on her brow.

The officers, with many pauses, pronounced the sentence of the law. The Countess was silent. "Madonna," said her confessor, "do you hear what the officers of justice have pronounced?"—"Who is it that addresses me?" said the Countess. "It is your confessor," said the priest. "Has he forgotten that the Countess of Montorio will be addressed by no other title?" said she with a haughtiness of tone that contended with death. "That title, Lady, is no longer yours," said one of the officers. "What does he say?" said the Countess faintly. "He tells you the truth," said the confessor with energy. "Lady, it is a solemn hour; I adjure you to recal your thoughts, and meditate rather your peace with heaven."—"Your wealth and estates are confiscated," said a harsh and ignorant priest; "your palaces and your pomp are levelled with the dust; your—" "And our *name*, our *title*," said the Countess. There was a deep silence. "The name, the title of Montorio," she repeated, suddenly rising from her pillow, her eyes darting fire, and her voice thrilling with the energy of passion. "They are extinguished for ever," said one of the attendants. The Countess fell back on the bed; her face was concealed, but a convulsed and broken sound murmuring through the stillness of the chamber, announced the awful dissolution of guilty ambition.

SINCE THE HOUR OF HIS confinement, the Count Montorio had been allowed no remission, no indulgence. He had required none; when the attendants entered his apartment, they found him engaged in writing so deeply that he never raised his head, or seemed sensible of their presence. From the time it was finished, he appeared restless and agitated, but still silent. The sentinel who watched at his door heard him pace his chamber all night; but from the time that the final sentence of the court was known, he became profoundly still.

His only request was to see his sons, and this was urged with such earnest and unceasing vehemence, that at length it was accorded. The night previous to that appointed for his death, his sons were conducted to his apartment. The scene was solemn. The dark habits, the clank of chains, the heavy tread of the armed sentinels, the cheerless and funereal light of the torches, the rush of sudden motion breaking on the silence of night and a prison, and *that* hushed again, hushed by the pause of breathless passion that followed, were impressed for ever on the minds of the witnesses.

The children knelt to ask a blessing of their father, the wretched father knelt to ask forgiveness of his children. Some of the attendants wept aloud, and the sternest turned aside and veiled their faces.

During an interval of two hours not a coherent sentence was uttered, all were cries of mingled anguish, and sentences broken by bursts; the sorrow of late and unavailing recognition lost in the deeper distress of inevitable separation. Orazio lacerated the feelings of his children by perpetual prostrations, and the harrowing spectacle of paternal humiliation; these, when they could not prevent, they partook, and sunk together with him on the ground, from which he could not be raised.

As the hour of separation, prolonged by cruel indulgence, arrived, the distress grew more terrible; he would not be torn from his boys, on whom he called as he alternately embraced them in every sound in the compass of distress, from the smothered, tremulous murmur that is lost in sobs, to the ceaseless, shapeless, maniac yell of misery, that stuns the ear, and hears nothing but its own despair. The attendants faultering approached. With the shriek and grasp of a mother, he held his children to his breast, folding his mantle, and bending over them with the unconscious provision of fear.

The sons, as they yet clung to the embraces of death, felt themselves bathed in their father's blood! They recoiled; his agony had burst one of the larger vessels, and the blood gushed from his mouth in torrents. The prisoners were removed, the medical attendants of the prison were summoned, and the monks who assist and exhort the criminals hastened to the chamber of the dying man. Ippolito and Annibal knelt at the door; his broken and blood-stifled groans were fearful. They stopt their ears, and turned their asking faces to the attendants, who, horror-smote and dumb, quitted the apartment every moment. At length a priest who crossed himself came forth to order the bells of St. Elmo to toll, while he proceeded to the chapel to read the prayers for those who are in the agonies of death. The brothers grasped his habit, but they could not speak. "Release me," said the monk, "I would pray; I have beheld a sight which has left me no power but of prayer." They held him still. "When all is over," said he, moving from them, "you will hear the toll of a bell that announces the sufferer for whom we pray is no more." They listened; all was still for a moment.

A LOW AND GENERAL MURMUR broke from the chamber of death. The bell tolled; the brothers prostrated themselves, and prayed for the departing soul. The attendants passed out. "Did you hear the last words he uttered?" said the governor of St. Elmo to the principal confessor. "I could not hear his confession," said the priest. "It was no confession," said the governor; "the words were, 'The last of the Montorios has not perished on a scaffold.'"

"SUCH," SAID THE NARRATOR, "WAS the fall of the Montorio family, in whose fall the dispensation of a higher hand is visible to the most weak and limited eye. He who sought his own elevation, and the aggrandizement of his children, was defeated and destroyed by him whom he had sacrificed to his ambitious wickedness. He who sought vengeance as atrocious as the crime that provoked it, found it poured out on his own children; and they who desired the knowledge of things concealed from man, found their pursuit accompanied by guilt, and terminated by misery and punishment.

"Of the rest of the family there is little to be known; the daughters entered into convents, and the sons into foreign service under assumed names; but the unhappy men whose story I have related, were every where distinguished by their silent bravery, their solemn melancholy, their lovely affection for each other, and their reluctance to the society of women."

A Note About the Author

Charles Maturin (1780–1824) was an Irish writer and clergyman. Born and raised in Dublin, Maturin was raised in a prominent Huguenot family. Educated at Trinity College, he became ordained as curate of Loughrea, County Galway, before returning to Dublin in 1903. Due to his position in the Church of Ireland, he was forced to publish his writing under a pseudonym, achieving some acclaim for his early novels. In 1816, his play *Bertram* was staged at the Drury Lane theatre in London. Although he was encouraged by Sir Water Scott and Lord Byron, he received a devastating review from Samuel Taylor Coleridge, who deemed the play "melancholy proof of the depravation of the public mind." Forced to reveal his identity in order to claim his profits, Maturin was barred from advancement by the Church of Ireland and turned his attention to novel writing. In 1820, his Gothic novel *Melmoth the Wanderer* was published to critical acclaim, earning Maturin a reputation as a leading Romantic, influencing such writers as Charles Baudelaire and Honoré de Balzac. Controversial in his lifetime, viewed as an eccentric in his native country, Maturin would serve as inspiration to his grandnephew Oscar Wilde, as well as countless writers, artists, and aesthetes.

A Note from the Publisher

Spanning many genres, from non-fiction essays to literature classics to children's books and lyric poetry, Mint Edition books showcase the master works of our time in a modern new package. The text is freshly typeset, is clean and easy to read, and features a new note about the author in each volume. Many books also include exclusive new introductory material. Every book boasts a striking new cover, which makes it as appropriate for collecting as it is for gift giving. Mint Edition books are only printed when a reader orders them, so natural resources are not wasted. We're proud that our books are never manufactured in excess and exist only in the exact quantity they need to be read and enjoyed.

bookfinity™

Discover more of your favorite classics with Bookfinity™.

- Track your reading with custom book lists.
- Get great book recommendations for your personalized Reader Type.
- Add reviews for your favorite books.
- AND MUCH MORE!

Visit **bookfinity.com** and take the fun Reader Type quiz to get started.

Enjoy our classic and modern companion pairings!

Classic & Modern